GOING FOR
INFINITY

By Poul Anderson
from Tom Doherty Associates

Alight in the Void
All One Universe
The Armies of Elfland
The Boat of a Million Years
Conan the Rebel
The Dancer from Atlantis
The Day of Their Return
Explorations
The Fleet of Stars
Genesis
Going for Infinity
Harvest of Stars
Harvest of Fire
Hoka! (*with Gordon R. Dickson*)
Kinship with the Stars
A Knight of Ghosts and Shadows
The Long Night
The Longest Voyage
Maurai and Kith
A Midsummer Tempest
Mother of Kings
No Truce with Kings
Operation Chaos
Operation Luna
Past Times
The Saturn Game
The Shield of Time
Starfarers
The Stars Are Also Fire
Tales of the Flying Mountains
The Time Patrol
There Will Be Time
War of the Gods

GOING FOR
INFINITY

A LITERARY JOURNEY

Poul Anderson

A TOM DOHERTY ASSOCIATES BOOK
NEW YORK

GOING FOR INFINITY

Book design by Heidi Eriksen

A Tor Book
Published by Tom Doherty Associates, LLC
175 Fifth Avenue
New York, NY 10010

www.tor.com

Tor® is a registered trademark of Tom Doherty Associates, LLC.

Library of Congress Cataloging-in-Publication Data

Anderson, Poul, 1926–2001.
    Going for infinity : a literary journey / Poul Anderson.
        p. cm.
    ISBN 0-765-30359-0
    1. Anderson, Poul, 1926–2001.   2. Authors, American—20th century—
Biography.   3. Science fiction—Authorship.   4. Fantasy fiction—
Authorship.   5. Science fiction, American.   6. Fantasy fiction, American.
I. Title.

    PS3551.N378 Z465 2002
    813'.54—dc21
    [B]
                                                                                                    2001058351

First Edition: June 2002

Printed in the United States of America

0   9   8   7   6   5   4   3   2   1

To
Erik and Alexandra,
wishing you a joyous future.

CONTENTS

INTRODUCTION

You hold this book thanks largely to Robert Gleason. Having been my editor for a long time, he felt that there ought to be something covering a still longer span, my writing through the half century since it first appeared. What he had in mind was not simply another collection, but a retrospective—besides stories, something about their origins, backgrounds, contexts, a historical overview of the science fiction and fantasy field throughout those decades.

Of course, this isn't really possible. I have been only one writer among many, and how wonderfully diverse a lot they were and are! Simply naming the giants, from Asimov to Zelazny, with brief remarks about what each accomplished, would require a volume. Besides, who would be unfairly left out? No few who were less prolific or less widely acclaimed gave us classic works, pervasively and lastingly influential. All I can safely say is that the best of it offers us mind-opening ideas, narrative vitality, and a high literary standard.

Lest this look too pompous, let me just say that good science fiction and fantasy are entertaining. They engage our attention in ways agreeable and often challenging. Good art of every kind does, of course, including the most solemn or tragic. In that sense, Mozart's *Requiem* and Shakespeare's *Hamlet* are entertaining, as are, in their different ways, a Duke Ellington jazz concert or a P. G. Wodehouse story. You could even call them *fun*.

I don't claim that the finest achievements in our field belong on the same heights as the acknowledged great literature of the world. I merely think they are well worth reading. Beyond that, let posterity be the judge.

Nor will I attempt a history of the field. Several already exist. What I offer here is one man's experience of it—not from its origins, which lie very far back, but through some sixty years—as reader, writer, and acquaintance, often friend, of a number of people who had much to do with its evolution.

Even so limited an undertaking must necessarily be incomplete, a sketch, leaving out vastly more than it touches on. I can only hope that it will give a little perspective. More importantly, I hope you'll find the stories and factual anecdotes . . . entertaining.

This is no autobiography. My entry in the Gale Research *Contemporary Authors* series tells as much about my life as I would ever want anybody to publish. However, chances are you haven't seen that. Since this book deals with my personal experience, probably a little background is in order. Every writer, like every other human being, is unique, partly because of the accidents of heredity, partly because of the events of his or her life, perhaps especially early life. In relating what I think has most influenced the course that my particular career took, I hope to suggest the infinite variety that has done it for others.

My ancestors were mostly Danish, with a few dashes of other nationalities and, on my father's side, one branch that became American soon after the Civil War, although maintaining contact with the old country. His surname was originally spelled "Andersen"—no relation to Hans Christian. As small boys, my brother and I were excited on getting the impression that one of our forebears had been a pirate, then disappointed to learn that he was actually a perfectly legitimate privateer in the Napoleonic Wars, who afterward settled down as a merchant in Copenhagen. The seafaring tradition persisted; my paternal grandfather was the captain of a ship on the Greenland run. He met and married a lady on the American side, and my father was born in Philadelphia. However, the home was in Denmark and he was educated there together with his brother.

The skipper took his young sons along on two or three voyages, high points in my father's life. He wanted to be a mariner himself, but dutifully heeded the old man's dying wish and gave up the dream. Instead, he studied engineering. When the United States entered the first World War he patriotically came back to enlist in the army. There he grew tired of explaining how his name was spelled, and Anglicized it to Anderson. After discharge, he remained in the States.

My maternal grandfather was Poul Hertz. He stemmed from the poet and playwright Henrik Hertz, his wife from the poet Carsten Hauch, but he himself was a physician in Copenhagen. Among their children was my mother Astrid.

Always adventurous, she worked for a year as a medical secretary in a hospital, then with the Danish diplomatic mission to Switzerland at the end of the war, and then crossed over to Washington, D.C., to take a similar post at the Danish Legation (now Embassy). She and my father had been schoolmates for a while in Denmark, but lost touch with one another. By sheer chance, they met again. Soon they were dating, and in January 1926 they were married. I joined them on 25 November of the same year. My mother named me after her own father, Poul, thereby throwing me right back into the same difficulty; but I've been too stubborn to change, and it has of course become a trademark. The pronunciation is not an Anglo-Saxon noise, so I'll answer to any.

This was in Bristol, Pennsylvania. I have no memory of that town, because I was an infant when my father got a new job and we moved to Port Arthur, Texas. He did well in those Depression years, becoming chief estimator at the Texaco offices. My brother John, born in 1930, and I enjoyed a happy boyhood—except for school—in a pleasant suburb that still had plenty of vacant lots for kids to play in. Yet our father's heart was always with the sea. He had a fair-sized collection of books about it, he did a beautiful model of the *Flying*

Cloud, and he built two large motor sailers in succession, both named *Hobo*, for family and friends to spend many delightful hours on the waters reaching into Louisiana.

Insisting, quite rightly, that we boys learn proper English and everything else appropriate to being American, our parents nevertheless also made a point of speaking Danish at home, so that John and I grew up bilingual. We have always been grateful for that. Though he couldn't get enough vacation time to go along, our father twice sent his wife and us on extended visits with her family overseas, not exactly usual when travel was by rail and ship. Thus I got acquainted early on with that charming country.

I hope all this detail hasn't been too boring. The aim has simply been to look at some important influences on me as a writer. You can see where certain recurring themes in my stories come from—the sea, Scandinavian history and culture, a solid and loving home life.

That last suffered a shattering blow in late 1937, when John's and my father was killed in an automobile accident. He was our mother's one and only man. In spite of several offers over the years, she never remarried. We two boys were all that really mattered. Not that she ever wanted to dominate us, emotionally or in any other way. Throughout, she did her best to raise us into independent manhood.

In 1938 she took us back to Denmark. She had plenty of influential connections there to help us. But after some months she left again. Another war was too clearly coming. Besides, we were Americans, and her sons ought to grow up in their own country. Port Arthur, though, was too haunted. She got her old job back with the Danish diplomatic corps in Washington. Here the Smithsonian Institution and a scientifically minded classmate, Neil Waldrop, had their effects on me.

Otherwise this was not a very fortunate period, and Mother quit next year. Her brother Jakob—Jack—had settled in Minnesota, where his wife had kinfolk. He proposed that they two siblings buy small farms there and work them together. "It seemed like a good idea at the time." Mother had been left enough money for her share of the venture, and she thought it would provide us boys with a wholesome environment. After a cross-country trip, which introduced me to the wonders of the West and the Pacific Coast, we lodged at the college town Northfield while our farmland and buildings were being readied, and took possession in the summer of 1940.

In nearly every way it was a dreadful mistake. Uncle Jack soon went into war work and made a lot of money, but was of no help to us. We had no man on our premises except for a series of expensive, often incompetent hirelings. Neighbors joined each other for such jobs as threshing, but could do little else for us. John and I were on hand for chores morning and evening, as well as having more time on weekends and in the summers—and in winter when we'd get snowed in for several days—but otherwise, besides school in Northfield, there was a long bus ride to and fro. In any event, already then forty acres weren't enough to make pay. In about four years Mother had gone broke.

She never felt it was an utter loss. At least the necessities of farm life imposed a discipline on her fatherless boys which probably did stand us in good stead afterward. And you can find such themes in my writing as countryside, cold, storm, animals, and men and women who make their livings with their hands.

Distance joined with wartime gasoline rationing to keep us isolated from most activities in town. That troubled me less than it did my outgoing brother. By nature I was bookish and not very social. A childhood ear infection that left me hard of hearing reinforced this. I turned to our bookshelves, which included a number of Scandinavian works. And, to be sure, there was science fiction.

After I'd left the Washington area, Neil Waldrop and I kept up a correspondence. When he sent me a package of science fiction magazines, I was promptly and thoroughly hooked. We'd write stories in longhand, swapping them back and forth for comment, which strengthened that habit in me. Not that I intended to become a writer. But maybe, just maybe I could moonlight at it, and someday see my work in print alongside the creations of Robert Heinlein, L. Sprague de Camp, and the other gods.

Through a friend, Mother got a position in the library at Carleton College in Northfield, where she worked until retirement, widely beloved, sparkling good company right up to the end many years later—but it was from her that I learned what indomitability means. She managed to sell the farm, which helped finance my further education. Rejected for military service because of my scarred eardrums, I entered the University of Minnesota in 1944, with a major in physics, minors in mathematics and chemistry. Though I did not become a scientist, this training has clearly been basic to much of what I do and how I go about it.

In those years I finally got up the courage to submit my stories, and sold two or three while still an undergraduate. I did not go on to graduate studies; the money was exhausted. Instead, I supported myself precariously by writing while I searched for a job. The search grew more and more half-hearted, until presently I realized that a writer was what nature had cut me out for. John won honest employment, becoming a geologist and full professor.

College also brought me out of my shell. When I discovered and joined

the Minneapolis Fantasy Society, it led to enduring friendships, some love affairs, and a network of fellow enthusiasts around the world. That's where this
book properly begins.

—POUL ANDERSON

I

There are times when somehow the spirit opens up to the awe and mystery of the universe. Afterward dailiness returns; but those minutes or hours live on, not only as memories. They become a part of life itself, giving it much of its meaning and even its direction.

They have come to me when I have been camped out under skies wholly clear and dark, more full of stars than of night. Once it happened when I held a primitive hand ax, a piece of flint chipped into shape in the Middle Acheulean period, perhaps a hundred thousand years ago, by a hunter—Homo erectus, not yet Neandertal—and saw a tiny fossil embedded in it, left by a mollusc in a sea that drained and dried away perhaps a hundred million years ago. And others—but surely you too have had your moments.

My earliest that I recall goes back to childhood, age six or seven or thereabouts. We lived in a new suburb, with plenty of vacant lots for boys to romp in and no street lights. Nor did anybody anywhere have air conditioning. One evening after a hot summer day we went outside to enjoy the cool. Twilight gathered, purple and quiet. Stars began to blink forth. "That red one," said my mother. "Is that Mars?"

"I believe so," answered my father. He had made a few voyages with his own father, a sea captain, when navigation was mainly celestial.

"Do you think there's life on it?"

"Who knows?"

Wonder struck through me like lightning. I'd learned a little about the planets, of course. Now suddenly it came fully home to me, that I was looking at a whole other *world,* as real as the ground beneath my feet but millions of miles remote and altogether strange.

Thereafter I could not read enough astronomy books. We had a fourteenth-edition *Encyclopaedia Britannica.* Again and again I went back to its articles on the planets, and I can still see the blurry telescopic photographs, as if they lay here before me, and none of their glamour has faded. Mars was foremost—were those markings regions of growth amidst ruddy deserts and canals that watered them?—but what had made the craters and rays on the Moon, what did the clouds of Venus hide, what were the belts and zones and Great Red Spot of Jupiter?

Saturn of the jewelwork rings had a magic all its own. To this day, the sight of it through a telescope brings the same enchantment as did the very first such viewing; beauty never grows wearisome.

The years passed, until late in 1980 my wife Karen and I found ourselves at the Jet Propulsion Laboratory in Pasadena to witness Voyager One's flyby of this very planet. We'd been there for earlier events of the series, and would return for later ones, with press credentials to admit us. A number of science fiction writers did likewise; their kind of work had made its slow way from pulpish disrepute to respectability, many working scientists were openly among their readers, and they themselves were often interviewed. Those were great reunions of the old gang. But the purpose was always to experience the achievement and discoveries at first hand—to share, in however small a way, in yet another fulfillment of a lifelong dream, and find that the reality was more wondrous than any of our imaginings.

Now, as revelation after revelation unfolded, I couldn't help feeling a little extra excitement, even tension. I'd lately written a story set on Iapetus. It would see magazine publication in a couple of months. Voyager was going to scan that enigmatic Saturnian moon. Would my speculations prove completely mistaken? It's a risk that science fiction always takes, a risk that in the long run becomes an inevitability. But would this piece of mine have any run of might-be-so at all?

Not worth worrying about. I gave myself back to the wonders before me.

THE SATURN GAME

1

If we would understand what happened, which is vital if we would avoid repeated and worse tragedies in the future, we must begin by dismissing all accusations. Nobody was negligent; no action was foolish. For who could have predicted the eventuality, or recognized its nature, until too late? Rather should we appreciate the spirit with which those people struggled against disaster, inward and outward, after they knew. The fact is that thresholds exist throughout reality, and that things on their far sides are altogether different from things on their hither sides. The *Chronos* crossed more than an abyss, it crossed a threshold of human experience.

—Francis L. Minamoto,
Death Under Saturn: A Dissenting View
(Apollo University Communications, Leyburg, Luna, 2057)

"The City of Ice is now on my horizon," *Kendrick says. Its towers gleam blue.* "My griffin spreads his wings to glide." *Wind whistles among those great, rainbow-shimmering pinions. His cloak blows back from his shoulders; the air strikes through his ring mail and sheathes him in cold.* "I lean over and peer after you." *The spear in his left hand counterbalances him. Its head flickers palely with the moonlight that Wayland Smith hammered into the steel.*

"Yes, I see the griffin," *Ricia tells him*, "high and far, like a comet above the courtyard walls. I run out from under the portico for a better look. A guard tries to stop me, grabs my sleeve, but I tear the spider-silk apart and dash forth into the open." *The elven castle wavers as if its sculptured ice were turning to smoke. Passionately, she cries,* "Is it in truth you, my darling?"

"Hold, there!" *warns Alvarlan from his cave of arcana ten thousand leagues away.* "I send your mind the message that if the King suspects this is Sir Kendrick of the Isles, he will raise a dragon against him, or spirit you off beyond any chance of rescue. Go back, Princess of Maranoa. Pretend you decide that it is only an eagle. I will cast a belief-spell on your words."

"I stay far aloft," *Kendrick says.* "Save he use a scrying stone, the Elf King will not be aware this beast has a rider. From here I'll spy out city and castle." *And then—? He knows not. He knows simply that he must set her free or die in the quest. How long will it take him, how many more nights will she lie in the King's embrace?*

"I thought you were supposed to spy out Iapetus," Mark Danzig interrupted.

His dry tone startled the three others into alertness. Jean Broberg flushed with embarrassment, Colin Scobie with irritation; Luis Garcilaso shrugged, grinned, and turned his gaze to the pilot console before which he sat harnessed. For a moment silence filled the cabin, and shadows, and radiance from the universe.

To help observation, all lights were out except a few dim glows at instruments. The sunward ports were lidded. Elsewhere thronged stars, so many and so brilliant that they well-nigh drowned the blackness which held them. The Milky Way was a torrent of silver. One port framed Saturn at half phase, dayside pale gold and rich bands amidst the jewelry of its rings, nightside wanly ashimmer with starlight and moonlight upon clouds, as big to the sight as Earth over Luna.

Forward was Iapetus. The spacecraft rotated while orbiting the moon, to maintain a steady optical field. It had crossed the dawn line, presently at the middle of the inward-facing hemisphere. Thus it had left bare, crater-pocked land behind it in the dark, and was passing above sunlit glacier country. Whiteness dazzled, glittered in sparks and shards of color, reached fantastic shapes heavenward; cirques, crevasses, caverns brimmed with blue.

"I'm sorry," Jean Broberg whispered. "It's too beautiful, unbelievably beautiful, and . . . almost like the place where our game had brought us—Took us by surprise—"

"Huh!" Mark Danzig said. "You had a pretty good idea of what to expect, therefore you made your play go in the direction of something that resembled it. Don't tell me any different. I've watched these acts for eight years."

Colin Scobie made a savage gesture. Spin and gravity were too slight to give noticeable weight. His movement sent him through the air, across the crowded cabin, until he checked himself by a handhold just short of the chemist. "Are you calling Jean a liar?" he growled.

Most times he was cheerful, in a bluff fashion. Perhaps because of that, he suddenly appeared menacing. He was a big, sandy-haired man in his mid-thirties; a coverall did not disguise the muscles beneath, and the scowl on his face brought forth its ruggedness.

"Please!" Broberg exclaimed. "Not a quarrel, Colin."

The geologist glanced back at her. She was slender and fine-featured. At her age of forty-two, despite longevity treatment, the reddish-brown hair that fell to her shoulders was becoming streaked with white, and lines were engraved around large gray eyes. "Mark is right," she sighed. "We're here to do science, not daydream." She reached forth to touch Scobie's arm, smiled shyly. "You're still full of your Kendrick persona, aren't you? Gallant, protective—" She stopped. Her voice had quickened with more than a hint of Ricia. She covered her lips and flushed again. A tear broke free and sparkled off on air currents. She forced a laugh. "But I'm just physicist Broberg, wife of astronomer Tom, mother of Johnnie and Billy."

Her glance went Saturnward, as if seeking the ship where her family waited. She might have spied it, too, as a star that moved among stars, by the solar sail. However, that was now furled, and naked vision could not find even such huge hulls as *Chronos* possessed, across millions of kilometers.

Luis Garcilaso asked from his pilot's chair: "What harm if we carry on our little *commedia dell' arte*?" His Arizona drawl soothed the ear. "We won't be landin' for a while yet, and everything's on automatic till then." He was small, swart, deft, still in his twenties.

Danzig twisted the leather of his countenance into a frown. At sixty, thanks to his habits as well as to longevity, he kept springiness in a lank frame; he could joke about wrinkles and encroaching baldness. In this hour, he set humor aside.

"Do you mean you don't know what's the matter?" His beak of a nose pecked at a scanner screen which magnified the moonscape. "Almighty God! That's a new world we're about to touch down on—tiny, but a world, and strange in ways we can't guess. Nothing's been here before us except one unmanned flyby and one unmanned lander that soon quit sending. We can't rely on meters and cameras alone. We've got to use our eyes and brains." He addressed Scobie. "You should realize that in your bones, Colin, if nobody else aboard does. You've worked on Luna as well as Earth. In spite of all the settlements, in spite of all the study that's been done, did you never hit any nasty surprises?"

The burly man had recovered his temper. Into his own voice came a softness that recalled the serenity of the Idaho mountains whence he hailed. "True," he admitted. "There's no such thing as having too much information when you're off Earth, or enough information, for that matter." He paused. "Nevertheless, timidity can be as dangerous as rashness—not that you're timid, Mark," he added in haste. "Why, you and Rachel could've been in a nice O'Neill on a nice pension—"

Danzig relaxed and smiled. "This was a challenge, if I may sound pompous. Just the same, we want to get home when we're finished here. We should be in time for the Bar Mitzvah of a great-grandson or two. Which requires staying alive."

"My point is, if you let yourself get buffaloed, you may end up in a worse bind than—Oh, never mind. You're probably right, and we should not have begun fantasizing. The spectacle sort of grabbed us. It won't happen again."

Yet when Scobie's eyes looked anew on the glacier, they had not quite the dispassion of a scientist in them. Nor did Broberg's or Garcilaso's. Danzig slammed fist into palm. "The game, the damned childish game," he muttered, too low for his companions to hear. "Was nothing saner possible for them?"

2

Was nothing saner possible for them? Perhaps not.

If we are to answer the question, we should first review some history. When early industrial operations in space offered the hope of rescuing civilization, and Earth, from ruin, then greater knowledge of sister planets, prior to their development, became a clear necessity. The effort must start with Mars, the least hostile. No natural law forbade sending small manned spacecraft yonder. What did was the absurdity of as much fuel, time, and effort as were required, in order that three or four persons might spend a few days in a single locality.

Construction of the *J. Peter Vajk* took longer and cost more, but paid off when it, virtually a colony, spread its immense solar sail and took a thousand people to their goal in half a year and in comparative comfort. The payoff grew overwhelming when they, from orbit, launched Earthward the beneficiated minerals of Phobos that they did not need for their own purposes. Those purposes, of course, turned on the truly thorough, long-term study of Mars, and included landings of auxiliary craft, for ever lengthier stays, all over the surface.

Sufficient to remind you of this much; no need to detail the triumphs of the same basic concept throughout the inner Solar System, as far as Jupiter. The tragedy of the *Vladimir* became a reason to try again for Mercury . . . and, in a left-handed, political way, pushed the Britannic-American consortium into its *Chronos* project.

They named the ship better than they knew. Sailing time to Saturn was eight years.

Not only the scientists must be healthy, lively-minded people. Crewfolk, technicians, medics, constables, teachers, clergy, entertainers, every element of an entire community must be. Each must command more than a single skill, for emergency backup, and keep those skills alive by regular, tedious rehearsal. The environment was limited and austere; communication with home was soon a matter of beamcasts; cosmopolitans found themselves in what amounted to an isolated village. What were they to *do*?

Assigned tasks. Civic projects, especially work on improving the interior of the vessel. Research, or writing a book, or the study of a subject, or sports, or hobby clubs, or service and handicraft enterprises, or more private interactions, or—There was a wide choice of television tapes, but Central Control made sets usable for only three hours in twenty-four. You dared not get into the habit of passivity.

Individuals grumbled, squabbled, formed and dissolved cliques, formed and dissolved marriages or less explicit relationships, begot and raised occasional children, worshipped, mocked, learned, yearned, and for the most part found reasonable satisfaction in life. But for some, including a large proportion of the gifted, what made the difference between this and misery was their psychodramas.

—Minamoto

Dawn crept past the ice, out onto the rock. It was a light both dim and harsh, yet sufficient to give Garcilaso the last data he wanted for descent.

The hiss of the motor died away, a thump shivered through the hull, landing jacks leveled it, stillness fell. The crew did not speak for a while. They were staring out at Iapetus.

Immediately around them was desolation like that which reigns in much of the Solar System. A darkling plain curved visibly away to a horizon that, at man-height, was a bare three kilometers distant; higher up in the cabin, you saw farther, but that only sharpened the sense of being on a minute ball awhirl among the stars. The ground was thinly covered with cosmic dust and gravel; here and there a minor crater or an upthrust mass lifted out of the regolith to cast long, knife-edged, utterly black shadows. Light reflections lessened the number of visible stars, turning heaven into a bowlful of night. Halfway between the zenith and the south, half-Saturn and its rings made the vista beautiful.

Likewise did the glacier—or the glaciers? Nobody was sure. The sole knowledge was that, seen from afar, Iapetus gleamed bright at the western end of its orbit and grew dull at the eastern end, because one side was covered with whitish material while the other side was not; the dividing line passed nearly beneath the planet which it eternally faced. The probes from *Chronos* had reported the layer was thick, with puzzling spectra that varied from place to place, and little more about it.

In this hour, four humans gazed across pitted emptiness and saw wonder rear over the world-rim. From north to south went ramparts, battlements, spires, depths, peaks, cliffs, their shapes and shadings an infinity of fantasies. On the right Saturn cast soft amber, but that was nearly lost in the glare from the east, where a sun dwarfed almost to stellar size nonetheless blazed too fierce to look at, just above the summit. There the silvery sheen exploded in brilliance, diamond-glitter of shattered light, chill blues and greens; dazzled to tears, eyes saw the vision glimmer and waver, as if it bordered on dreamland, or on Faerie. But despite all delicate intricacies, underneath was a sense of chill and of brutal mass; here dwelt also the Frost Giants.

Broberg was the first to breathe forth a word. "The City of Ice."

"Magic," said Garcilaso as low. "My spirit could lose itself forever, wanderin' yonder. I'm not sure I'd mind. My cave is nothin' like this, nothin'—"

"Wait a minute!" snapped Danzig in alarm.

"Oh, yes. Curb the imagination, please." Though Scobie was quick to utter sobrieties, they sounded drier than needful. "We know from probe transmissions the scarp is, well, Grand Canyon–like. Sure, it's more spectacular than we realized, which I suppose makes it still more of a mystery." He turned to Broberg. "I've never seen ice or snow as sculptured as this. Have you, Jean? You've mentioned visiting a lot of mountain and winter scenery when you were a girl in Canada."

The physicist shook her head. "No. Never. It doesn't seem possible. What could have done it? There's no weather here . . . is there?"

"Perhaps the same phenomenon is responsible that laid a hemisphere bare," Danzig suggested.

"Or that covered a hemisphere," Scobie said. "An object seventeen hundred kilometers across shouldn't have gases, frozen or otherwise. Unless it's a ball of such stuff clear through, like a comet. Which we know it's not." As if to demonstrate, he unclipped a pair of pliers from a nearby tool rack, tossed it, and caught it on its slow way down. His own ninety kilos of mass weighed about seven. For that, the satellite must be essentially rocky.

Garcilaso registered impatience. "Let's stop tradin' facts and theories we already know about, and start findin' answers."

Rapture welled in Broberg. "Yes, let's get out. Over *there*."

"Hold on," protested Danzig as Garcilaso and Scobie nodded eagerly. "You can't be serious. Caution, step-by-step advance—"

"No, it's too wonderful for that." Broberg's tone shivered.

"Yeah, to hell with fiddlin' around," Garcilaso said. "We need at least a preliminary scout right away."

The furrows deepened in Danzig's visage. "You mean you too, Luis? But you're our pilot!"

"On the ground I'm general assistant, chief cook, and bottle washer to you scientists. Do you imagine I want to sit idle, with somethin' like that to explore?" Garcilaso calmed his voice. "Besides, if I should come to grief, any of you can fly back, given a bit of radio talk from *Chronos* and a final approach under remote control."

"It's quite reasonable, Mark," Scobie argued. "Contrary to doctrine, true; but doctrine was made for us, not vice versa. A short distance, low gravity, and we'll be on the lookout for hazards. The point is, until we have some notion of what that ice is like, we don't know what the devil to pay attention to in this vicinity, either. No, we'll take a quick jaunt. When we return, then we'll plan."

Danzig stiffened. "May I remind you, if anything goes wrong, help is at least a hundred hours away? An auxiliary like this can't boost any higher if it's to get back, and it'd take longer than that to disengage the big boats from Saturn and Titan."

Scobie reddened at the implied insult. "And may I remind you, on the ground I am the captain? I say an immediate reconnaissance is safe and desirable. Stay behind if you want—In fact, yes, you must. Doctrine is right in saying the vessel mustn't be deserted."

Danzig studied him for several seconds before murmuring, "Luis goes, however, is that it?"

"Yes!" cried Garcilaso so that the cabin rang.

Broberg patted Danzig's limp hand. "It's okay, Mark," she said gently. "We'll bring back samples for you to study. After that, I wouldn't be surprised but what the best ideas about procedure will be yours."

He shook his head. Suddenly he looked very tired. "No," he replied in a monotone, "that won't happen. You see, I'm only a hardnosed industrial chemist who saw this expedition as a chance to do interesting research. The whole way through space, I kept myself busy with ordinary affairs, including, you remember, a couple of inventions I'd wanted leisure to develop. You three, you're younger, you're romantics—"

"Aw, come off it, Mark." Scobie tried to laugh. "Maybe Jean and Luis are, a little, but me, I'm about as other-worldly as a plate of haggis."

"You played the game, year after year, until at last the game started playing you. That's what's going on this minute, no matter how you rationalize your motives." Danzig's gaze on the geologist, who was his friend, lost the defiance that had been in it and turned wistful. "You might try recalling Delia Ames."

Scobie bristled. "What about her? The business was hers and mine, nobody else's."

"Except afterward she cried on Rachel's shoulder, and Rachel doesn't keep secrets from me. Don't worry, I'm not about to blab. Anyhow, Delia got over it. But if you'd recollect objectively, you'd see what had happened to you, already three years ago."

Scobie set his jaw. Danzig smiled in the left corner of his mouth. "No, I suppose you can't," he went on. "I admit I'd no idea either, till now, how far the process had gone. At least keep your fantasies in the background while you're outside, will you? Can you?"

In half a decade of travel, Scobie's apartment had become idiosyncratically his—perhaps more so than was usual, since he remained a bachelor who seldom had women visitors for longer than a few nightwatches at a time. Much of the furniture he had made himself; the agrosections of *Chronos* produced wood, hide, and fiber as well as food and fresh air. His handiwork ran to massiveness and archaic carved decorations. Most of what he wanted to read he screened from the data banks, of course, but a shelf held a few old books, Childe's border ballads, an eighteenth-century family Bible (despite his agnosticism), a copy of *The Machinery of Freedom* which had nearly disintegrated but displayed the signature of the author, and other valued miscellany. Above them stood a model of a sailboat in which he had cruised Northern European waters, and a trophy he had won in handball aboard this ship. On the bulkheads hung his fencing sabers and numerous pictures—of parents and siblings, of wilderness areas he had tramped on Earth, of castles and mountains and heaths in Scotland where he had often been too, of his geological team on Luna, of Thomas Jefferson and, imagined, Robert the Bruce.

On a certain evenwatch he had, though, been seated before his telescreen. Lights were turned low in order that he might fully savor the image. Auxiliary craft were out in a joint exercise, and a couple of their personnel used the opportunity to beam back views of what they saw.

That was splendor. Starful space made a chalice for *Chronos*. The two huge, majestically counter-rotating cylinders, the entire complex of linkages, ports, locks, shields, collectors, transmitters, docks, all became Japanesely exquisite at a distance of several hundred kilometers. It was the solar sail which filled most of the screen, like a turning golden sun-wheel; yet remote vision could also appreciate its spiderweb intricacy, soaring and subtle curvatures, even the less-than-gossamer thinness. A mightier work than the Pyramids, a finer work than a refashioned chromosome, the ship moved on toward a Saturn which had become the second brightest beacon in the firmament.

The door chime hauled Scobie out of his exaltation. As he started across the deck, he stubbed his toe on a table leg. Coriolis force caused that. It was slight, when a hull this size spun to give a full gee of weight, and a thing to which he had long since adapted; but now and then he got so interested in something that terrestrial habits returned. He swore at his absent-mindedness, good-naturedly, since he anticipated a pleasurable time.

When he opened the door, Delia Ames entered in a single stride. At once she closed it behind her and stood braced against it. She was a tall blonde woman who did electronics maintenance and kept up a number of outside activities. "Hey!" Scobie said. "What's wrong? You look like—" he tried for levity "—something my cat wouldn't've dragged in, if we had any mice or beached fish aboard."

She drew a ragged breath. Her Australian accent thickened till he had trouble understanding: "I . . . today . . . I happened to be at the same cafeteria table as George Harding—"

Unease tingled through Scobie. Harding worked in Ames' department but had much more in common with him. In the same group to which they both belonged, Harding likewise took a vaguely ancestral role, N'Kuma the Lionslayer.

"What happened?" Scobie asked.

Woe stared back at him. "He mentioned . . . you and he and the rest . . . you'd be taking your next holiday together . . . to carry on your, your bloody act uninterrupted."

"Well, yes. Work at the new park over in Starboard Hull will be suspended till enough metal's been recycled for the water pipes. The area will be vacant, and my gang has arranged to spend a week's worth of days—"

"But you and I were going to Lake Armstrong!"

"Uh, wait, that was just a notion we talked about, no definite plan yet, and this is such an unusual chance—Later, sweetheart. I'm sorry." He took her hands. They felt cold. He essayed a smile. "Now, c'mon, we were going to cook a festive dinner together and afterward spend a, shall we say, quiet evening at home. But for a start, this absolutely gorgeous presentation on the screen—"

She jerked free of him. The gesture seemed to calm her. "No, thanks," she said, flat-voiced. "Not when you'd rather be with that Broberg woman. I only came by to tell you in person I'm getting out of the way of you two."

"Huh?" He stepped back. "What the flaming hell do you mean?"

"You know jolly well."

"I don't! She, I, she's happily married, got two kids, she's older than me, we're friends, sure, but there's never been a thing between us that wasn't in the open and on the level—" Scobie swallowed. "You suppose maybe I'm in love with her?"

Ames looked away. Her fingers writhed together. "I'm not about to go on being a mere convenience to you, Colin. You have plenty of those. Myself, I'd hoped—But I was wrong, and I'm going to cut my losses before they get worse."

"But . . . Dee, I swear I haven't fallen for anybody else, and I, I swear you're more than a body to me, you're a fine person—" She stood mute and withdrawn. Scobie gnawed his lip before he could tell her: "Okay, I admit it, a main reason I volunteered for this trip was I'd lost out in a love affair on Earth. Not that the project doesn't interest me, but I've come to realize what a big chunk out of my life it is. You, more than any other woman, Dee, you've gotten me to feel better about the situation."

She grimaced. "But not as much as your psychodrama has, right?"

"Hey, you must think I'm obsessed with the game. I'm not. It's fun and—oh, maybe 'fun' is too weak a word—but anyhow, it's just little bunches of people getting together fairly regularly to play. Like my fencing, or a chess club, or, or anything."

She squared her shoulders. "Well, then," she asked, "will you cancel the date you've made and spend your holiday with me?"

"I, uh, I can't do that. Not at this stage. Kendrick isn't off on the periphery of current events, he's closely involved with everybody else. If I didn't show, it'd spoil things for the rest."

Her glance steadied upon them. "Very well. A promise is a promise, or so I imagined. But afterward—Don't be afraid. I'm not trying to trap you. That would be no good, would it? However, if I maintain this liaison of ours, will you phase out of your game?"

"I can't—" Anger seized him. "No, God damn it!" he roared.

"Then goodbye, Colin," she said, and departed. He stared for minutes at the door she had shut behind her.

———

27

Unlike the large Titan and Saturn-vicinity explorers, landers on the airless moons were simply modified Luna-to-space shuttles, reliable but with limited capabilities. When the blocky shape had dropped below the horizon, Garcilaso said into his radio: "We've lost sight of the boat, Mark. I must say it improves the view." One of the relay microsatellites which had been sown in orbit passed his words on.

"Better start blazing your trail, then," Danzig reminded.

"My, my, you *are* a fussbudget, aren't you?" Nevertheless Garcilaso unholstered the squirt gun at his hip and splashed a vividly fluorescent circle of paint on the ground. He would do it at eyeball intervals until his party reached the glacier. Except where dust lay thick over the regolith, footprints were faint, under the feeble gravity, and absent when a walker crossed continuous rock.

Walker? No, leaper. The three bounded exultant, little hindered by spacesuits, life support units, tool and ration packs. The naked land fled from their haste, and even higher, ever more clear and glorious to see, loomed the ice ahead of them.

There was no describing it, not really. You could speak of lower slopes and palisades above, to a mean height of perhaps a hundred meters, with spires towering farther still. You could speak of gracefully curved tiers going up those braes, of lacy parapets and fluted crags and arched openings to caves filled with wonders, of mysterious blues in the depths and greens where light streamed through translucencies, of gem-sparkle across whiteness where radiance and shadow wove mandalas—and none of it would convey anything more than Scobie's earlier, altogether inadequate comparison to the Grand Canyon.

"Stop," he said for the dozenth time. "I want to take a few pictures."

"Will anybody understand them who hasn't been here?" whispered Broberg.

"Probably not," said Garcilaso in the same hushed tone. "Maybe no one but us ever will."

"What do you mean by that?" demanded Danzig's voice.

"Never mind," snapped Scobie.

"I . . . think . . . I . . . know," the chemist said. "Yes, it is a great piece of scenery, but you're letting it hypnotize you."

"If you don't cut out that drivel," Scobie warned, "we'll cut you out of the circuit. Damn it, we've got work to do. Get off our backs."

Danzig gusted a sigh. "Sorry. Uh, are you finding any clues to the nature of that—that thing?"

Scobie focused his camera. "Well," he said, partly mollified, "the different shades and textures, and no doubt the different shapes, seem to confirm what the reflection spectra from the flyby suggested. The composition is a mixture, or a jumble, or both, of several materials, and varies from place to place. Water ice is obvious, but I feel sure of carbon dioxide too, and I'd bet on ammonia, methane, and presumably lesser amounts of other stuff."

"Methane? Could they stay solid at ambient temperature, in a vacuum?"

"We'll have to find out for sure. However, I'd guess that most of the time it's cold enough, at least for methane strata that occur down inside where there's pressure on them."

Within the vitryl globe of her helmet, Broberg's features showed delight. "Wait!" she cried. "I have an idea—about what happened to the probe that landed." She drew breath. "It came down almost at the foot of the glacier, you recall. Our view of the site from space seemed to indicate that an avalanche buried it, but we couldn't understand how that might have been triggered. Well, suppose a methane layer at exactly the wrong location melted. Heat radiation from the jets may have warmed it, and later the radar beam used to map contours added the last few degrees necessary. The stratum flowed, and down came everything that had rested on top of it."

"Plausible," Scobie said. "Congratulations, Jean."

"Nobody thought of the possibility in advance?" Garcilaso scoffed. "What kind of scientists have we got along?"

"The kind who were being overwhelmed by work after we reached Saturn, and still more by data input," Scobie answered. "The universe is bigger than you or anybody can realize, hotshot."

"Oh. Sure. No offense." Garcilaso's glance returned to the ice. "Yes, we'll never run out of mysteries, will we?"

"Never." Broberg's eyes glowed enormous. "At the heart of things will always be magic. The Elf King rules—"

Scobie returned his camera to its pouch. "Stow the gab and move on," he ordered curtly.

His gaze locked for an instant with Broberg's. In the weird, mingled light, it could be seen that she went pale, then red, before she sprang off beside him.

Ricia had gone alone into Moonwood on Midsummer Eve. The King found her there and took her unto him as she had hoped. Ecstasy became terror when he afterward bore her off; yet her captivity in the City of Ice brought her many more such hours, and beauties and marvels unknown among mortals. Alvarlan, her mentor, sent his spirit in quest of her, and was himself beguiled by what he found. It was an effort of will for him to tell Sir Kendrick of the Isles where she was, albeit he pledged his help in freeing her.

N'Kuma the Lionslayer, Béla of Eastmarch, Karina of the Far West, Lady Aurelia, Olav Harpmaster had none of them been present when this happened.

The glacier (a wrong name for something that might have no counterpart in the Solar System) lifted off the plain abruptly as a wall. Standing there, the three could no longer see the heights. They could, though, see that the slope which curved steeply upward to a filigree-topped edge was not smooth. Shadows lay blue in countless small craters. The sun had climbed just sufficiently high to beget them; a Iapetan day is more than seventy-nine of Earth's.

Danzig's question crackled in earphones: "Now are you satisfied? Will you come back before a fresh landslide catches you?"

"It won't," Scobie replied. "We aren't a vehicle, and the local configuration has clearly been stable for centuries or better. Besides, what's the point of a manned expedition if nobody investigates anything?"

"I'll see if I can climb," Garcilaso offered.

"No, wait," Scobie commanded. "I've had experience with mountains and snowpacks, for whatever that may be worth. Let me study out a route for us first."

"You're going onto that stuff, the whole gaggle of you?" exploded Danzig. "Have you completely lost your minds?"

Scobie's brow and lips tightened. "Mark, I warn you again, if you don't get your emotions under control we'll cut you off. We'll hike on a ways if I decide it's safe."

He paced, in floating low-weight fashion, back and forth while he surveyed the jökull. Layers and blocks of distinct substances were plain to see, like separate ashlars laid by an elvish mason . . . where they were not so huge that a giant must have been at work. . . . The craterlets might be sentry posts on this lowest embankment of the City's defenses. . . .

Garcilaso, most vivacious of men, stood motionless and let his vision lose itself in the sight. Broberg knelt down to examine the ground, but her own gaze kept wandering aloft.

Finally she beckoned. "Colin, come over here, please," she said. "I believe I've made a discovery."

Scobie joined her. As she rose, she scooped a handful of fine black particles off the shards on which she stood and let it trickle from her glove. "I suspect this is the reason the boundary of the ice is sharp," she told him.

"What is?" Danzig inquired from afar. He got no answer.

"I noticed more and more dust as we went along," Broberg continued. "If it fell on patches and lumps of frozen stuff, isolated from the main mass, and covered them, it would absorb solar heat till they melted or, likelier, sublimed. Even water molecules would escape to space, in this weak gravity. The main mass was too big for that; square-cube law. Dust grains there would simply melt their way down a short distance, then be covered as surrounding material collapsed on them, and the process would stop."

"H'm." Scobie raised a hand to stroke his chin, encountered his helmet, and sketched a grin at himself. "Sounds reasonable. But where did so much dust come from—and the ice, for that matter?"

"I think—" Her voice dropped until he could barely hear, and her look went the way of Garcilaso's. His remained upon her face, profiled against stars. "I think this bears out your comet hypothesis, Colin. A comet struck Iapetus. It came from the direction it did because of getting so near Saturn that it was forced to swing in a hairpin bend around the planet. It was enormous; the ice of it covered almost a hemisphere, in spite of much more being vaporized and lost. The dust is partly from it, partly generated by the impact."

He clasped her armored shoulder. "*Your* theory, Jean. I was not the first to propose a comet, but you're the first to corroborate with details."

She didn't appear to notice, except that she murmured further: "Dust can account for the erosion that made those lovely formations, too. It caused differential melting and sublimation on the surface, according to the patterns it happened to fall in and the mixes of ices it clung to, until it was washed away or encysted. The craters, these small ones and the major ones we've observed from above, they have a separate but similar origin. Meteorites—"

"Whoa, there," he objected. "Any sizeable meteorite would release enough energy to steam off most of the entire field."

"I know. Which shows the comet collision was recent, less than a thousand years ago, or we wouldn't be seeing this miracle today. Nothing big has since happened to strike, yet. I'm thinking of little stones, cosmic sand, in prograde orbits around Saturn so that they hit with low relative speed. Most simply make dimples in the ice. Lying there, however, they collect solar heat because of being dark, and re-radiate it to melt away their surroundings, till they sink beneath. The concavities they leave reflect incident radiation from side to side, and thus continue to grow. The pothole effect. And again, because the different ices have different properties, you don't get perfectly smooth craters, but those fantastic bowls we saw before we landed."

"By God!" Scobie hugged her. "You're a genius."

Helmet against helmet, she smiled and said, "No. It's obvious, once you've seen for yourself." She was quiet for a bit while still they held each other. "Scientific intuition is a funny thing, I admit," she went on at last. "Considering the problem, I was hardly aware of my logical mind. What I thought was—the City of Ice, made with starstones out of that which a god called down from heaven—"

"Jesus Maria!" Garcilaso spun about to stare at them.

Scobie released the woman. "We'll go after confirmation," he said unsteadily. "To the large crater you'll remember we spotted a few klicks inward. The surface appears quite safe to walk on."

"I called that crater the Elf King's Dance Hall," Broberg mused, as if a dream were coming back to her.

"Have a care." Garcilaso's laugh rattled. "Heap big medicine yonder. The King is only an inheritor; it was giants who built these walls, for the gods."

"Well, I've got to find a way in, don't I?" Scobie responded.

"Indeed," *Alvarlan says.* "I cannot guide you from this point. My spirit can only see through mortal eyes. I can but lend you my counsel, until we have neared the gates."

"Are you sleepwalking in that fairytale of yours?" Danzig yelled. "Come back before you get yourselves killed!"

"Will you dry up?" Scobie snarled. "It's nothing but a style of talk we've got between us. If you can't understand that, you've got less use of your brain than we do."

"Listen, won't you? I didn't say you're crazy. You don't have delusions or anything like that. I do say you've steered your fantasies toward this kind of place, and now the reality has reinforced them till you're under a compulsion you don't recognize. Would you go ahead so recklessly anywhere else in the universe? Think!"

"That does it. We'll resume contact after you've had time to improve your manners." Scobie snapped off his main radio switch. The circuits that stayed active served for close-by communication but had no power to reach an orbital relay. His companions did likewise.

The three faced the awesomeness before them. "You can help me find the Princess when we are inside, Alvarlan," *Kendrick says.*

"That I can and will," *the sorcerer vows.*

"I wait for you, most steadfast of my lovers," *Ricia croons.*

Alone in the spacecraft, Danzig well-nigh sobbed, "Oh, damn that game forever!" The sound fell away into emptiness.

3

To condemn psychodrama, even in its enhanced form, would be to condemn human nature.

It begins in childhood. Play is necessary to an immature mammal, a means of learning to handle the body, the perceptions, and the outside world. The young human plays, must play, with its brain too. The more intelligent the child, the more its imagination needs exercise. There are degrees of activity, from the passive watching of a show on a screen, onward through reading, daydreaming, storytelling, and psychodrama . . . for which the child has no such fancy name.

We cannot give this behavior any single description, for the shape and course it takes depend on endlessly many variables. Sex, age, culture, and companions are only the most obvious. For example, in pre-electronic North America little girls would often play "house" while little boys played "cowboys and Indians" or "cops and robbers," whereas nowadays a mixed group of their descendants might play "dolphins" or "astronauts and aliens." In essence, a small band forms; each individual makes up a character to portray, or borrows one from fiction; simple props may be employed, such as toy weapons, or any chance object such as a stick may be declared something else such as a metal detector, or a thing may be quite imaginary, as the scenery almost always is. The children then act out a drama which they compose as they go along. When they cannot physically perform a certain action, they describe it. ("I jump real high, like you can do on Mars, an' come out over the edge o' that ol' Valles Marineris, an' take that bandit by surprise.") A large cast of characters, especially villains, frequently comes into existence by fiat.

The most imaginative member of the troupe dominates the game and the evolution of the story line, though in a rather subtle fashion, through offering the most vivid possibilities. The rest, however, are brighter than average; psychodrama in this highly developed form does not appeal to everybody.

For those to whom it does, the effects are beneficial and lifelong. Besides increasing their creativity through use, it lets them try out a play version of different adult roles and experiences. Thereby they begin to acquire insight into adulthood.

Such playacting ends when adolescence commences, if not earlier—but only in that form, and not necessarily forever in it. Grown-ups have many dream-games. This is plain to see in lodges, for example, with their titles, costumes, and ceremonies; but does it not likewise animate all pageantry, every ritual? To what extent are our heroisms, sacrifices, and self-aggrandizements the acting out of personae that we maintain? Some thinkers have attempted to trace this element through every aspect of society.

Here, though, we are concerned with overt psychodrama among adults. In Western civilization it first appeared on a noticeable scale during the middle twentieth century. Psychiatrists found it a powerful diagnostic and therapeutic technique. Among ordinary folk, war and fantasy games, many of which involved identification with imaginary or historical characters, became increasingly popular. In part this was doubtless a retreat from the restrictions and menaces of that unhappy period, but likely in larger part it was a revolt of the mind against the inactive entertainment, notably television, which had come to dominate recreation.

The Chaos ended those activities. Everybody knows about their revival in recent times—for healthier reasons, one hopes. By projecting three-dimensional scenes and appropriate sounds from a data bank—or, better yet, by having a computer produce them to order—players gained a sense of reality that intensified their mental and emotional commitment. Yet in those games that went on for episode after episode, year after real-time year, whenever two or more members of a group could get together to play, they found themselves less and less dependent on such appurtenances. It seemed that, through practice, they had regained the vivid imaginations of their childhoods, and could make anything, or airy nothing itself, into the objects and the worlds they desired.

I have deemed it necessary thus to repeat the obvious in order that we may see it in perspective. The news beamed from Saturn has brought widespread revulsion. (Why? What buried fears have been touched? This is subject matter for potentially important research.) Overnight, adult psychodrama has become unpopular; it may become extinct. That would, in many ways, be a worse tragedy than what has occurred yonder. There is no reason to suppose that the game ever harmed any mentally sound person on Earth; on the contrary. Beyond doubt, it has helped astronauts stay sane and alert on long, difficult missions. If it has no more medical use, that is because psychotherapy has become a branch of applied biochemistry.

And this last fact, the modern world's dearth of experience with madness, is at the root of what happened. Although he could not have foreseen the exact outcome, a twentieth-century psychiatrist might have warned against spending eight years, an unprecedented stretch of time, in as strange an environment as the *Chronos*. Strange it certainly has been, despite all efforts—limited, totally man-controlled, devoid of countless cues for which our evolution on Earth has fashioned us. Extra-terrestrial colonists have, thus far, had available to them any number of simulations and compensations, of which close, full contact with home and frequent opportunities to visit there are probably the most significant. Sailing time to Jupiter was long, but half of that to Saturn. Moreover, because they were earlier, scientists in the *Zeus* had much research to occupy them en route, which it would be pointless for later travelers to duplicate; by then, the interplanetary medium between the two giants held few surprises.

Contemporary psychologists were aware of this. They understood that the persons most adversely affected would be the most intelligent, imaginative, and dynamic—those who were supposed to make the very discoveries at Saturn which were the purpose of the undertaking. Being less familiar than their predecessors with the labyrinth that lies, Minotaur-haunted, beneath every human consciousness, the psychologists expected purely benign consequences of whatever psychodramas the crew engendered.

—Minamoto

Assignments to teams had not been made in advance of departure. It was sensible to let professional capabilities reveal themselves and grow on the voyage, while personal relationships did the same. Eventually such factors would help in deciding what individuals should train for what tasks. Long-term participation in a group of players normally forged bonds of friendship that were desirable, if the members were otherwise qualified.

In real life, Scobie always observed strict propriety toward Broberg. She was attractive, but she was monogamous, and he had no wish to alienate her. Besides, he liked her husband. (Tom did not partake of the game. As an astronomer, he had plenty to keep his attention happily engaged.) They had played for a couple of years, their bunch had acquired as many as it could accommodate in a narrative whose milieu and people were becoming complex, before Scobie and Broberg spoke of anything intimate.

By then, the story they enacted was doing so, and maybe it was not altogether by chance that they met when both had several idle hours. This was in the weightless recreation area at the spin axis. They tumbled through aerobatics, shouting and laughing, until they were pleasantly tired, went to the clubhouse, turned in their wingsuits, and showered. They had not seen each other nude before; neither commented, but he did not hide his enjoyment of the sight, while she colored and averted her glance as tactfully as she was able. Afterward, their clothes resumed, they decided on a drink before they went home, and sought the lounge.

Since evenwatch was approaching nightwatch, they had the place to themselves. At the bar, he thumbed a chit for Scotch, she for pinot chardonnay. The machine obliged them and they carried their refreshments out onto the balcony. Seated at a table, they looked across immensity. The clubhouse was built into the support frame on a Lunar gravity level. Above them they saw the sky wherein they had been as birds; its reach did not seem any more hemmed in by far-spaced, spidery girders than it was by a few drifting clouds. Beyond, and straight ahead, decks opposite were a commingling of masses and shapes which the scant illumination at this hour turned into mystery. Among those shadows the humans made out woods, brooks, pools, turned hoar or agleam by the light of stars which filled the skyview strips. Right and left, the hull stretched off beyond sight, a dark in which such lamps as there were appeared lost.

Air was cool, slightly jasmine-scented, drenched with silence. Underneath and throughout, subliminal, throbbed the myriad pulses of the ship.

"Magnificent," Broberg said low, gazing outward. "What a surprise."

"Eh?" asked Scobie.

"I've only been here before in daywatch. I didn't anticipate a simple rotation of the reflectors would make it wonderful."

"Oh, I wouldn't sneer at the daytime view. Mighty impressive."

"Yes, but—but then you see too plainly that everything is manmade, nothing is wild or unknown or free. The sun blots out the stars; it's as though no universe existed beyond this shell we're in. Tonight is like being in Maranoa," *the kingdom of which Ricia is Princess, a kingdom of ancient things and ways, wildernesses, enchantments.*

"H'm, yeah, sometimes I feel trapped myself," Scobie admitted. "I believed I had a journey's worth of geological data to study, but my project isn't going anywhere very interesting."

"Same for me." Broberg straightened where she sat, turned to him, and smiled a trifle. The dusk softened her features, made them look young. "Not that we're entitled to self-pity. Here we are, safe and comfortable till we reach Saturn. After that we should never lack for excitement, or for material to work with on the way home."

"True." Scobie raised his glass. "Well, skoal. Hope I'm not mispronouncing that."

"How should I know?" she laughed. "My maiden name was Almyer."

"That's right, you've adopted Tom's surname. I wasn't thinking. Though that is rather unusual these days, hey?"

She spread her hands. "My family was well-to-do, but they were—are—Jerusalem Catholics. Strict about certain things; archaistic, you might say." She lifted her wine and sipped. "Oh, yes, I've left the Church, but in several ways the Church will never leave me."

"I see. Not to pry, but, uh, this does account for some traits of yours I couldn't help wondering about."

She regarded him over the rim of her glass. "Like what?"

"Well, you've got a lot of life in you, vigor, sense of fun, but you're also—what's the word?—uncommonly domestic. You've told me you were a quiet faculty member of Yukon University till you married Tom." Scobie grinned. "Since you two kindly invited me to your last anniversary party, and I know your present age, I deduced that you were thirty then." Unmentioned was the likelihood that she had still been a virgin. "Nevertheless—oh, forget it. I said I don't want to pry."

"Go ahead, Colin," she urged. "That line from Burns sticks in my mind, since you introduced me to his poetry. 'To see oursels as others see us!' Since it looks as if we may visit the same moon—"

Scobie took a hefty dollop of Scotch. "Aw, nothing much," he said, unwontedly diffident. "If you must know, well, I have the impression that being in love wasn't the single good reason you had for marrying Tom. He'd already been accepted for this expedition, and given your personal qualifications, that would get you in too. In short, you'd grown tired of routine respectability and here was how you could kick over the traces. Am I right?"

"Yes." Her gaze dwelt on him. "You're more perceptive than I supposed."

"No, not really. A roughneck rockhound. But Ricia's made it plain to see, you're more than a demure wife, mother, and scientist—" She parted her lips. He raised a palm. "No, please, let me finish. I know it's bad manners to claim somebody's persona is a wish fulfillment, and I'm not doing that. Of course you don't want to be a free-roving, free-loving female scamp, any more than I want to ride around cutting down assorted enemies. Still, if you'd been born and raised in the world of our game, I feel sure you'd be a lot like Ricia. And that potential is part of you, Jean." He tossed off his drink. "If I've said too much, please excuse me. Want a refill?"

"I'd better not, but don't let me stop you."

"You won't." He rose and bounded off.

When he returned, he saw that she had been observing him through the vitryl door. As he sat down, she smiled, leaned a bit across the table, and told him softly: "I'm glad you said what you did. Now I can declare what a complicated man Kendrick reveals you to be."

"What?" Scobie asked in honest surprise. "Come on! He's a sword-and-shield tramp, a fellow who likes to travel, same as me; and in my teens I was a brawler, same as him."

"He may lack polish, but he's a chivalrous knight, a compassionate overlord, a knower of sagas and traditions, an appreciator of poetry and music, a bit of a bard . . . Ricia misses him. When will he get back from his latest quest?"

"I'm bound home this minute. N'Kuma and I gave those pirates the slip and landed at Haverness two days ago. After we buried the swag, he wanted to visit Béla and Karina and join them in whatever they've been up to, so we bade goodbye for the time being." Scobie and Harding had lately taken a few hours to conclude that adventure of theirs. The rest of the group had been mundanely occupied for some while.

Broberg's eyes widened. "From Haverness to the Isles? But I'm in Castle Devaranda, right in between."

"I hoped you'd be."

"I can't wait to hear your story."

"I'm pushing on after dark. The moon is bright and I've got a pair of remounts I bought with a few gold pieces from the loot." *The dust rolls white beneath drumming hoofs. Where a horseshoe strikes a flint pebble, sparks fly ardent.* Kendrick scowls. "You aren't with . . . what's his name? . . . Joran the Red? I don't like him."

"I sent him packing a month ago. He got the idea that sharing my bed gave him authority over me. It was never anything but a romp. I stand alone on the Gerfalcon Tower, looking south over moonlit fields, and wonder how you fare. The road flows toward me like a gray river. Do I see a rider come at a gallop, far and far away?"

After many months of play, no image on a screen was necessary. *Pennons on the night wind stream athwart the stars.* "I arrive. I sound my horn to rouse the gatekeepers."

"How I do remember those merry notes—"

That same night, Kendrick and Ricia become lovers. Experienced in the game and careful of its etiquette, Scobie and Broberg uttered no details about the union; they did not touch each other and maintained only fleeting eye contact; the ultimate goodnights were very decorous. After all, this was a story they composed about two fictitious characters in a world that never was.

The lower slopes of the jökull rose in tiers which were themselves deeply concave; the humans walked around their rims and admired the extravagant formations beneath. Names sprang onto lips; the Frost Garden, the Ghost Bridge, the Snow Queen's Throne, *while Kendrick advances into the City, and Ricia awaits him at the Dance Hall, and the spirit of Alvarlan carries word between them so that it is as if already she too travels beside her knight.* Nevertheless they proceeded warily, vigilant for signs of danger, especially whenever a change of texture or hue or anything else in the surface underfoot betokened a change in its nature.

Above the highest ledge reared a cliff too sheer to scale, Iapetan gravity or no, *the fortress wall.* However, from orbit the crew had spied a gouge in the vicinity, forming a pass, doubtless plowed by a small meteorite *in the war between the gods and the magicians, when stones chanted down from the sky wrought havoc so accursed that none dared afterward rebuild.* That was an eerie climb, hemmed in by heights which glimmered in the blue twilight they cast, heaven narrowed to a belt between them where stars seemed to blaze doubly brilliant.

"There must be guards at the opening," *Kendrick says.*

"A single guard," *answers the mind-whisper of Alvarlan,* "but he is a dragon. If you did battle with him, the noise and flame would bring every warrior here upon you. Fear not. I'll slip into his burnin' brain and weave him such a dream that he'll never see you."

"The King might sense the spell," *says Ricia through him.* "Since you'll be parted from us anyway while you ride the soul of that beast, Alvarlan, I'll seek him out and distract him."

Kendrick grimaces, knowing full well what means are hers to do that. She has told him how she longs for freedom and her knight; she has also hinted that elven lovemaking transcends the human. Does she wish for a final time before her rescue? . . . Well, Ricia and Kendrick have neither plighted nor practiced single troth. Assuredly Colin Scobie had not. He jerked forth a grin and continued through the silence that had fallen on all three.

They came out on top of the glacial mass and looked around them. Scobie whistled. Garcilaso stammered, "J-J-Jesus Christ!" Broberg smote her hands together.

Below them the precipice fell to the ledges, whose sculpturing took on a wholly new, eldritch aspect, gleam and shadow, until it ended at the plain. Seen from here aloft, the curvature of the moon made toes strain downward in boots, as if to cling fast and not be spun off among the stars which surrounded, rather than shone above, its ball. The spacecraft stood minute on dark, pocked stone, like a cenotaph raised to loneliness.

Eastward the ice reached beyond an edge of sight which was much closer. ("Yonder could be the rim of the world," Garcilaso said, *and Ricia replies,* "Yes, the City is nigh to there.") Bowls of different sizes, hillocks, crags, no two of them eroded the same way, turned its otherwise level stretch into a surreal maze. An arabesque openwork ridge which stood at the explorers' goal overtopped the horizon. Everything that was illuminated lay gently aglow. Radiant though the sun was, it cast the light of only, perhaps, five thousand full Lunas upon Earth. Southward, Saturn's great semidisc gave about one-half more Lunar shining; but in that direction, the wilderness sheened pale amber.

Scobie shook himself. "Well, shall we go?" His prosaic question jarred the others; Garcilaso frowned and Broberg winced.

She recovered. "Yes, hasten," *Ricia says.* "I am by myself once more. Are you out of the dragon, Alvarlan?"

"Aye," *the wizard informs her.* "Kendrick is safely behind a ruined palace. Tell us how best to reach you."

"You are at the time-gnawed Crown House. Before you lies the Street of the Shieldsmiths—"

Scobie's brows knitted. "It is noonday, when elves do not fare abroad," *Kendrick says* remindingly, commandingly. "I do not wish to encounter any of them. No fights, no complications. We are going to fetch you and escape, without further trouble."

Broberg and Garcilaso showed disappointment, but understood him. A game broke down when a person refused to accept something that a fellow player tried to put in. Often the narrative threads were not mended and picked up for many days. Broberg sighed.

"Follow the street to its end at a forum where a snow fountain springs," *Ricia directs.* "Cross, and continue on Aleph Zain Boulevard. You will know it by a gateway in the form of a skull with open jaws. If anywhere you see a rainbow flicker in the air, stand motionless until it has gone by, for it will be an auroral wolf. . . ."

At a low-gravity lope, the distance took some thirty minutes to cover. In the later part, the three were forced to detour by great banks of an ice so fine-grained that it slid about under their bootsoles and tried to swallow them. Several of these lay at irregular intervals around their destination.

There the travelers stood again for a time in the grip of awe.

The bowl at their feet must reach down almost to bedrock, a hundred meters, and was twice as wide. On this rim lifted the wall they had seen from the cliff, an arc fifty meters long and high, nowhere thicker than five meters, pierced by intricate scrollwork, greenly agleam where it was not translucent. It was the uppermost edge of a stratum which made serrations down the crater. Other outcrops and ravines were more dreamlike yet . . . was that a unicorn's head, was that a colonnade of caryatids, was that an icicle bower . . . ? The depths were a lake of cold blue shadow.

"You have come, Kendrick, beloved!" *cries Ricia, and casts herself into his arms.*

"Quiet," *warns the sending of Alvarlan the wise.* "Rouse not our immortal enemies."

"Yes, we must get back." Scobie blinked. "Judas priest, what possessed us? Fun is fun, but we sure have come a lot farther and faster than was smart, haven't we?"

"Let us stay for a little while," Broberg pleaded. "This is such a miracle—the Elf King's Dance Hall, which the Lord of the Dance built for him—"

"Remember, if we stay we'll be caught, and your captivity may be forever." Scobie thumbed his main radio switch. "Hello, Mark? Do you read me?"

Neither Broberg nor Garcilaso made that move. They did not hear Danzig's voice: "Oh, yes! I've been hunkered over the set gnawing my knuckles. How are you?"

"All right. We're at the big hole and will be heading back as soon as I've gotten a few pictures."

"They haven't made words to tell how relieved I am. From a scientific standpoint, was it worth the risk?"

Scobie gasped. He stared before him.

"Colin?" Danzig called. "You still there?"

"Yes. Yes."

"I asked what observations of any importance you made."

"I don't know," Scobie mumbled. "I can't remember. None of it after we started climbing seems real."

"Better you return right away," Danzig said grimly. "Forget about photographs."

"Correct." Scobie addressed his companions: "Forward march."

"I can't," *Alvarlan answers.* "A wanderin' spell has caught my spirit in tendrils of smoke."

"I know where a fire dagger is kept," *Ricia says.* "I'll try to steal it."

Broberg moved ahead, as though to descend into the crater. Tiny ice grains trickled over the verge from beneath her boots. She could easily lose her footing and slide down.

"No, wait," *Kendrick shouts to her.* "No need. My spearhead is of moon alloy. It can cut—"

The glacier shuddered. The ridge cracked asunder and fell in shards. The area on which the humans stood split free and toppled into the bowl. An avalanche poured after. High-flung crystals caught sunlight, glittered prismatic in challenge to the stars, descended slowly and lay quiet.

Except for shock waves through solids, everything had happened in the absolute silence of space.

Heartbeat by heartbeat, Scobie crawled back to his senses. He found himself held down, immobilized, in darkness and pain. His armor had saved, was still saving his life; he had been stunned but escaped a real concussion. Yet every breath hurt abominably. A rib or two on the left side seemed broken; a monstrous impact must have dented metal. And he was buried under more weight than he could move.

"Hello," he coughed. "Does anybody read me?" The single reply was the throb of his blood. If his radio still worked—which it should, being built into the suit—the mass around him screened him off.

It also sucked heat at an unknown but appalling rate. He felt no cold because the electrical system drew energy from his fuel cell as fast as needed to keep him warm and to recycle his air chemically. As a normal thing, when he lost heat through the slow process of radiation—and, a trifle, through

kerofoam-lined bootsoles—the latter demand was much the greater. Now conduction was at work on every square centimeter. He had a spare unit in the
equipment on his back, but no means of getting at it.

Unless—He barked forth a chuckle. Straining he felt the stuff that en-
tombed him yield the least bit under the pressure of arms and legs. And his
helmet rang slightly with noise, a rustle, a gurgle. This wasn't water ice that
imprisoned him, but stuff with a much lower freezing point. He was melting
it, subliming it, making room for himself.

If he lay passive, he would sink, while frozenness above slid down to keep
him in his grave. He might evoke superb new formations, but he would not
see them. Instead, he must use the small capability given him to work his way
upward, scrabble, get a purchase on matter that was not yet aflow, burrow to
the stars.

He began.

Agony soon racked him, breath rasped in and out of lungs aflame, strength
drained away and trembling took its place, he could not tell whether he ascended or slipped back. Blind, half suffocated, Scobie made mole-claws of his
hands and dug.

It was too much to endure. He fled from it—

*His strong enchantments failing, the Elf King brought down his towers of
fear in wreck. If the spirit of Alvarlan returned to its body, the wizard would
brood upon things he had seen, and understand what they meant, and such
knowledge would give mortals a terrible power against Faerie. Waking from
sleep, the King scryed Kendrick about to release that fetch. There was no time
to do more than break the spell which upheld the Dance Hall. It was largely
built of mist and starshine, but enough blocks quarried from the cold side of
Ginnungagap were in it that when they crashed they should kill the knight.
Ricia would perish too, and in his quicksilver intellect the King regretted that.
Nevertheless he spoke the necessary word.*

*He did not comprehend how much abuse flesh and bone can bear. Sir
Kendrick fights his way clear of the ruins, to seek and save his lady. While he
does, he heartens himself with thoughts of adventures past and future—*

—and suddenly the blindness broke apart and Saturn stood lambent within
rings.

Scobie belly-flopped onto the surface and lay shuddering.

He must rise, no matter how his injuries screamed, lest he melt himself a
new burial place. He lurched to his feet and glared around.

Little but outcroppings and scars was left of the sculpture. For the most
part, the crater had become a smooth-sided whiteness under heaven. Scarcity

of shadows made distances hard to gauge, but Scobie guessed the new depth as about seventy-five meters. And empty, empty.

"Mark, do you hear?" he cried.

"That you, Colin?" rang in his earpieces. "Name of mercy, what's happened? I heard you call out, and saw a cloud rise and sink . . . then nothing for more than an hour. Are you okay?"

"I am, sort of. I don't see Jean or Luis. A landslide took us by surprise and buried us. Hold on while I search."

When he stood upright, Scobie's ribs hurt less. He could move about rather handily if he took care. The two types of standard analgesic in his kit were alike useless, one too weak to give noticeable relief, one so strong that it would turn him sluggish. Casting to and fro, he soon found what he expected, a concavity in the tumbled snowlike material, slightly aboil.

Also a standard part of his gear was a trenching tool. Scobie set pain aside and dug. A helmet appeared. Broberg's head was within it. She too had been tunneling out.

"Jean!"—"Kendrick!" She crept free and they embraced, suit to suit. "Oh, Colin."

"How are you?" rattled from him.

"Alive," she answered. "No serious harm done, I think. A lot to be said for low gravity. . . . You? Luis?" Blood was clotted in a streak beneath her nose, and a bruise on her forehead was turning purple, but she stood firmly and spoke clearly.

"I'm functional. Haven't found Luis yet. Help me look. First, though, we'd better check out our equipment."

She hugged arms around chest, as if that would do any good here. "I'm chilled," she admitted.

Scobie pointed at a telltale. "No wonder. Your fuel cell's down to its last couple of ergs. Mine isn't in a lot better shape. Let's change."

They didn't waste time removing their backpacks, but reached into each other's. Tossing the spent units to the ground, where vapors and holes immediately appeared and then froze, they plugged the fresh ones into their suits. "Turn your thermostat down," Scobie advised. "We won't find shelter soon. Physical activity will help us keep warm."

"And require faster air recycling," Broberg reminded.

"Yeah. But for the moment, at least, we can conserve the energy in the cells. Okay, next let's check for strains, potential leaks, any kind of damage or loss. Hurry. Luis is still down underneath."

Inspection was a routine made automatic by years of drill. While her fingers searched across the man's spacesuit, Broberg let her eyes wander. "The Dance Hall is gone," *Ricia murmurs.* "I think the King smashed it to prevent our escape."

"Me too. If he finds out we're alive, and seeking for Alvarlan's soul—Hey, wait! None of that!"

Danzig's voice quavered. "How're you doing?"

"We're in fair shape, seems like," Scobie replied. "My corselet took a beating but didn't split or anything. Now to find Luis . . . Jean, suppose you spiral right, I left, across the crater floor."

It took a while, for the seething which marked Garcilaso's burial was min- uscule. Scobie started to dig. Broberg watched how he moved, heard how he breathed, and said, "Give me that tool. Just where are you bunged up, anyway?"

He admitted his condition and stepped back. Crusty chunks flew from her toil. She progressed fast, since whatever kind of ice lay at this point was, luckily, friable, and under Iapetan gravity she could cut a hole with almost vertical sides.

"I'll make myself useful," Scobie said, "namely, find us a way out."

When he started up the nearest slope, it shivered. All at once he was borne back in a tide that made rustly noises through his armor, while a fog of dry white motes blinded him. Painfully, he scratched himself free at the bottom and tried elsewhere. In the end he could report to Danzig: "I'm afraid there is no easy route. When the rim collapsed where we stood, it did more than produce a shock which wrecked the delicate formations throughout the crater. It let tons of stuff pour down from the surface—a particular sort of ice that, under local conditions, is like fine sand. The walls are covered by it. Most places, it lies meters deep over more stable material. We'd slide faster than we could climb, where the layer is thin; where it's thick, we'd sink."

Danzig sighed. "I guess I get to take a nice, healthy hike."

"I assume you've called for help."

"Of course. They'll have two boats here in about a hundred hours. The best they can manage. You knew that already."

"Uh-huh. And our fuel cells are good for perhaps fifty hours."

"Oh, well, not to worry about that. I'll bring extras and toss them to you, if you're stuck till the rescue party arrives. M-m-m . . . maybe I'd better rig a slingshot or something first."

"You might have a problem locating us. This isn't a true crater, it's a glorified pothole, the lip of it flush with the top of the glacier. The landmark we guided ourselves by, that fancy ridge, is gone."

"No big deal. I've got a bearing on you from the directional antenna, remember. A magnetic compass may be no use here, but I can keep myself oriented by the heavens. Saturn scarcely moves in this sky, and the sun and the stars don't move fast."

"Damn! You're right. I wasn't thinking. Got Luis on my mind, if nothing else." Scobie looked across bleakness toward Broberg. Perforce she was taking a short rest, stoop-shouldered above her excavation. His earpieces brought him the harsh sound in her windpipe.

He must maintain what strength was left him, against later need. He sipped from his water nipple, pushed a bite of food through his chowlock, pretended an appetite. "I may as well try reconstructing what happened," he said. "Okay, Mark, you were right, we got crazy reckless. The game—Eight years was too long to play the game, in an environment that gave us too few reminders of reality. But who could have foreseen it? My God, warn *Chronos*! I happen to know that one of the Titan teams started playing an expedition to the merfolk under the Crimson Ocean—on account of the red mists—deliberately, like us, before they set off. . . ."

Scobie gulped. "Well," he slogged on, "I don't suppose we'll ever know exactly what went wrong here. But plain to see, the configuration was only metastable. On Earth, too, avalanches can be fatally easy to touch off. I'd guess at a methane layer underneath the surface. It turned a little slushy when temperatures rose after dawn, but that didn't matter in low gravity and vacuum . . . till we came along. Heat, vibration—Anyhow, the stratum slid out from under us, which triggered a general collapse. Does that guess seem reasonable?"

"Yes, to an amateur like me," Danzig said. "I admire how you can stay academic under these circumstances."

"I'm being practical," Scobie retorted. "Luis may need medical attention earlier than those boats can come for him. If so, how do we get him to ours?"

Danzig's voice turned stark. "Any ideas?"

"I'm fumbling my way toward that. Look, the bowl still has the same basic form. The whole shebang didn't cave in. That implies hard material, water ice and actual rock. In fact, I see a few remaining promontories, jutting out above the sandlike stuff. As for what *it* is—maybe an ammonia-carbon dioxide combination, maybe more exotic—that'll be for you to discover later. Right now . . . my geological instruments should help me trace where the solid masses are least deeply covered. We all carry trenching tools, of course. We can try to shovel a path clear, along a zigzag of least effort. Sure, that may well often bring more garbage slipping down on us from above, but that in turn may expedite our progress. Where the uncovered shelves are too steep or slippery to climb, we can chip footholds. Slow and tough work; and we may run into a bluff higher than we can jump, or something like that."

"I can help," Danzig proposed. "While I waited to hear from you, I inventoried our stock of spare cable, cord, equipment I can cannibalize for wire, clothes and bedding I can cut into strips, whatever might be knotted together to make a rope. We won't need much tensile strength. Well, I estimate I can get about forty meters. According to your description, that's about half the slope length of that trap you're in. If you can climb halfway up while I trek there, I can haul you the rest of the way."

"Thanks," Scobie said, "although—"

"Luis!" shrieked in his helmet. "Colin, come fast, help me, this is dreadful!"

Regardless of pain, except for a curse or two, Scobie sped to Broberg's aid.

Garcilaso was not quite unconscious. In that lay much of the horror. They heard him mumble, "—Hell, the King threw my soul into Hell, I can't find my way out, I'm lost, if only Hell weren't so cold—" They could not see his face; the inside of his helmet was crusted with frost. Deeper and longer buried than the others, badly hurt in addition, he would have died shortly after his fuel cell was exhausted. Broberg had uncovered him barely in time, if that.

Crouched in the shaft she had dug, she rolled him over onto his belly. His limbs flopped about and he babbled, "A demon attacks me, I'm blind here but I feel the wind of its wings," in a blurred monotone. She unplugged the energy unit and tossed it aloft, saying, "We should return this to the ship if we can." Not uncommonly do trivial details serve as crutches.

Above, Scobie gave the object a morbid stare. It didn't even retain the warmth to make a little vapor, like his and hers, but lay quite inert. Its case was a metal box, thirty centimeters by fifteen by six, featureless except for two plug-in prongs on one of the broad sides. Controls built into the spacesuit circuits allowed you to start and stop the chemical reactions within and regulate their rate manually; but as a rule you left that chore to your thermostat and aerostat. Now those reactions had run their course. Until it was recharged, the cell was merely a lump.

Scobie leaned over to watch Broberg, some ten meters below him. She had extracted the reserve unit from Garcilaso's gear, inserted it properly at the small of his back, and secured it by clips on the bottom of his packframe. "Let's have your contribution, Colin," she said. Scobie dropped the meter of heavy-gauge insulated wire which was standard issue on extravehicular missions, in case you needed to make a special electrical connection or a repair. She joined it by Western Union splices to the two she already had, made a loop at the end and, awkwardly reaching over her left shoulder, secured the opposite end by a hitch to the top of her packframe. The triple strand bobbled above her like an antenna.

Stooping, she gathered Garcilaso in her arms. The Iapetan weight of him and his apparatus was under ten kilos, of her and hers about the same. Theoretically she could jump straight out of the hole with her burden. In practice, her spacesuit was too hampering; constant-volume joints allowed considerable freedom of movement, but not as much as bare skin, especially when circum-Saturnian temperatures required extra insulation. Besides, if she could have reached the top, she could not have stayed. Soft ice would have crumbled beneath her fingers and she would have tumbled back down.

"Here goes," she said. "This had better be right the first time, Colin. I don't think Luis can take much jouncing."

"Kendrick, Ricia, where are you?" Garcilaso moaned. "Are you in Hell too?"

Scobie dug heels into the ground near the edge and crouched ready. The loop in the wire rose to view. His right hand grabbed hold. He threw himself backward, lest he slide forward, and felt the mass he had captured slam to a halt. Anguish exploded in his rib cage. Somehow he dragged his burden to safety before he fainted.

He came out of that in a minute. "I'm okay," he rasped at the anxious voices of Broberg and Danzig. "Only lemme rest a while."

The physicist nodded and knelt to minister to the pilot. She stripped his packframe in order that he might lie flat on it, head and legs supported by the packs themselves. That would prevent significant heat loss by convection and cut loss by conduction. Still, his fuel cell would be drained faster than if he were on his feet, and first it had a terrible energy deficit to make up.

"The ice is clearing away inside his helmet," she reported. "Merciful Mary, the blood! Seems to be from the scalp, though; it isn't running any more. His occiput must have been slammed against the vitryl. We ought to wear padded caps in these rigs. Yes, I know accidents like this haven't happened before, but—" She unclipped the flashlight at her waist, stooped, and shone it downward. "His eyes are open. The pupils—yes, a severe concussion, and likely a skull fracture, which may be hemorrhaging into the brain. I'm surprised he isn't vomiting. Did the cold prevent that? Will he start soon? He could choke on his own vomit, in there where nobody can lay a hand on him."

Scobie's pain had subsided to a bearable intensity. He rose, went over to look, whistled, and said, "I judge he's doomed unless we get him to the boat and give him proper care almighty soon. Which isn't possible."

"Oh, Luis." Tears ran silently down Broberg's cheeks.

"You think he can't last till I bring my rope and we carry him back?" Danzig asked.

" 'Fraid not," Scobie replied. "I've taken paramedical courses, and in fact I've seen a case like this before. How come you know the symptoms, Jean?"

"I read a lot," she said dully.

"They weep, the dead children weep," Garcilaso muttered.

Danzig sighed. "Okay, then. I'll fly over to you."

"Huh?" burst from Scobie, and from Broberg: "Have you also gone insane?"

"No, listen," Danzig said fast. "I'm no skilled pilot, but I have the same basic training in this type of craft that everybody does who might ride in one. It's expendable; the rescue vessels can bring us back. There'd be no significant gain if I landed close to the glacier—I'd still have to make that rope and so forth—and we know from what happened to the probe that there would be a real hazard. Better I make straight for your crater."

"Coming down on a surface that the jets will vaporize out from under you?" Scobie snorted. "I bet Luis would consider that a hairy stunt. You, my friend, would crack up."

"Nu?" They could almost see the shrug. "A crash from low altitude, in this gravity, shouldn't do more than rattle my teeth. The blast will cut a hole clear to bedrock. True, then surrounding ice will collapse in around the hull and trap it. You may need to dig to reach the airlock, though I suspect thermal radiation from the cabin will keep the upper parts of the structure free. Even if the craft topples and strikes sidewise—in which case, it'll sink down into a deflating cushion—even if it did that on bare rock, it shouldn't be seriously damaged. It's designed to withstand heavier impacts." Danzig hesitated. "Of course, could be this would endanger you. I'm confident I won't fry you with the jets, assuming I descend near the middle and you're as far offside as you can get. Maybe, though, maybe I'd cause a . . . an ice quake that'll kill you. No sense in losing two more lives."

"Or three, Mark," Broberg said low. "In spite of your brave words, you could come to grief yourself."

"Oh, well, I'm an oldish man. I'm fond of living, yes, but you guys have a whole lot more years due you. Look, suppose the worst, suppose I don't just make a messy landing but wreck the boat utterly. Then Luis dies, but he would anyway. You two, however, you should have access to the stores aboard, including those extra fuel cells. I'm willing to run what I consider to be a small risk of my own neck, for the sake of giving Luis a chance at survival."

"Um-m-m," went Scobie, deep in his throat. A hand strayed in search of his chin, while his gaze roved around the glimmer of the bowl.

"I repeat," Danzig proceeded, "if you think this might jeopardize you in any way, we scrub it. No heroics, please. Luis would surely agree; better three people safe and one dead than four stuck with a high probability of death."

"Let me think." Scobie was mute for minutes before he said: "No, I don't believe we'd get in too much trouble here. As I remarked earlier, the vicinity has had its avalanche and must be in a reasonably stable configuration. True, ice will volatilize. In the case of deposits with low boiling points, that could happen explosively and cause tremors. But the vapor will carry heat away so fast that only material in your immediate area should change state. I daresay that the fine-grained stuff will get shaken down the slopes, but it's got too low a density to do serious harm; for the most part, it should simply act like a brief snowstorm. The floor will make adjustments, of course, which may be rather violent. However, we can be above it—do you see that shelf of rock over yonder, Jean, at jumping height? It has to be part of a buried hill; solid. That's our place to wait. . . . Okay, Mark, it's go as far as we're concerned. I can't be absolutely certain, but whoever is about anything? It seems like a good bet."

"What are we overlooking?" Broberg wondered. She glanced down to him who lay at her feet. "While we considered all the possibilities, Luis would die. Yes, fly if you want to, Mark, and God bless you."

—But when she and Scobie had brought Garcilaso to the ledge, she gestured from Saturn to Polaris and: "I will sing a spell, I will cast what small magic is mine, in aid of the Dragon Lord, that he may deliver Alvarlan's soul from Hell," *says Ricia*.

4

No reasonable person will blame any interplanetary explorer for miscalculations about the actual environment, especially when *some* decision has to be made, in haste and under stress. Occasional errors are inevitable. If we knew exactly what to expect throughout the Solar System, we would have no reason to explore it.
　　　　　　　　　　　　　　　　　　　　　　　　　—Minamoto

The boat lifted. Cosmic dust smoked away from its jets. A hundred and fifty meters aloft, thrust lessened and it stood still on a pillar of fire.

Within the cabin was little noise, a low hiss and a bone-deep but nearly inaudible rumble. Sweat studded Danzig's features, clung glistening to his beard stubble, soaked his coverall and made it reek. He was about to undertake a maneuver as difficult as rendezvous, and without guidance.

Gingerly, he advanced a vernier. A side jet woke. The boat lurched toward a nosedive. Danzig's hands jerked across the console. He must adjust the forces that held his vessel on high and those that pushed it horizontally, to get a resultant that would carry him eastward at a slow, steady pace. The vectors would change instant by instant, as they do when a human walks. The control computer, linked to the sensors, handled much of the balancing act, but not the crucial part. He must tell it what he wanted it to do.

His handling was inexpert. He had realized it would be. More altitude would have given him more margin for error, but deprived him of cues that his eyes found on the terrain beneath and the horizon ahead. Besides, when he reached the glacier he would perforce fly low, to find his goal. He would be too busy for the precise celestial navigation he could have practiced afoot.

Seeking to correct his error, he overcompensated, and the boat pitched in a different direction. He punched for "hold steady" and the computer took over. Motionless again, he took a minute to catch his breath, regain his nerve, rehearse in his mind. Biting his lip, he tried afresh. This time he did not quite approach disaster. Jets aflicker, the boat staggered drunkenly over the moonscape.

The ice cliff loomed nearer and nearer. He saw its fragile loveliness and regretted that he must cut a swathe of ruin. Yet what did any natural wonder mean unless a conscious mind was there to know it? He passed the lowest slope. It vanished in billows of steam.

Onward. Beyond the boiling, right and left and ahead, the Faerie architecture crumbled. He crossed the palisade. Now he was a bare fifty meters above surface, and the clouds reached vengefully close before they disappeared into vacuum. He squinted through the port and made the scanner sweep a magnified overview across its screen, a search for his destination.

A white volcano erupted. The outburst engulfed him. Suddenly he was flying blind. Shocks belled through the hull when upflung stones hit. Frost sheathed the craft; the scanner screen went as blank as the ports. Danzig should have ordered ascent, but he was inexperienced. A human in danger has less of an instinct to jump than to run. He tried to scuttle sideways. Without exterior vision to aid him, he sent the vessel tumbling end over end. By the time he saw his mistake, less than a second, it was too late. He was out of control. The computer might have retrieved the situation after a while, but the glacier was too close. The boat crashed.

"Hello, Mark?" Scobie cried. "Mark, do you read me? Where are you, for Christ's sake?"

Silence replied. He gave Broberg a look which lingered. "Everything seemed to be in order," he said, "till we heard a shout, and a lot of racket, and nothing. He should've reached us by now. Instead, he's run into trouble. I hope it wasn't lethal."

"What can we do?" she asked as redundantly. They needed talk, any talk, for Garcilaso lay beside them and his delirious voice was dwindling fast.

"If we don't get fresh fuel cells within the next forty or fifty hours, we'll be at the end of our particular trail. The boat should be someplace near. We'll have to get out of this hole under our own power, seems like. Wait here with Luis and I'll scratch around for a possible route."

Scobie started downward. Broberg crouched by the pilot.

"—alone forever in the dark—" she heard.

"No, Alvarlan." She embraced him. Most likely he could not feel that, but she could. "Alvarlan, hearken to me. This is Ricia. I hear in my mind how your spirit calls. Let me help, let me lead you back to the light."

"Have a care," advised Scobie. "We're too damn close to rehypnotizing ourselves as is."

"But I might, I just might get through to Luis and . . . comfort him . . . Alvarlan, Kendrick and I escaped. He's seeking a way home for us. I'm seeking you. Alvarlan, here is my hand, come take it."

On the crater floor, Scobie shook his head, clicked his tongue, and unlimbered his equipment. Binoculars would help him locate the most promising areas. Devices that ranged from a metal rod to a portable geosonar would give him a more exact idea of what sort of footing lay buried under what depth of unclimbable sand-ice. Admittedly the scope of such probes was very limited. He did not have time to shovel tons of material aside in order that he could mount higher and test further. He would simply have to get some preliminary results, make an educated guess at which path up the side of the bowl would prove negotiable, and trust he was right.

He shut Broberg and Garcilaso out of his consciousness as much as he was able, and commenced work.

An hour later, he was ignoring pain while clearing a strip across a layer of rock. He thought a berg of good, hard frozen water lay ahead, but wanted to make sure.

"Jean! Colin! Do you read?"

Scobie straightened and stood rigid. Dimly he heard Broberg: "If I can't do anything else, Alvarlan, let me pray for your soul's repose."

"Mark!" ripped from Scobie. "You okay? What the hell happened?"

"Yeah, I wasn't too badly knocked around," Danzig said, "and the boat's habitable, though I'm afraid it'll never fly again. How are you? Luis?"

"Sinking fast. All right, let's hear the news."

Danzig described his misfortune. "I wobbled off in an unknown direction for an unknown distance. It can't have been extremely far, since the time was short before I hit. Evidently I plowed into a large, um, snowbank, which softened the impact but blocked radio transmission. It's evaporated from the cabin area now. I see tumbled whiteness around, and formations in the offing. . . . I'm not sure what damage the jacks and the stern jets suffered. The boat's on its side at about a forty-five degree angle, presumably with rock beneath. But the after part is still buried in less whiffable stuff—water and CO_2 ices, I think— that's reached temperature equilibrium. The jets must be clogged with it. If I tried to blast, I'd destroy the whole works."

Scobie nodded. "You would, for sure."

Danzig's voice broke. "Oh, God, Colin! What have I done? I wanted to help Luis, but I may have killed you and Jean."

Scobie's lips tightened. "Let's not start crying before we're hurt. True, this has been quite a run of bad luck. But neither you nor I nor anybody could have known that you'd touch off a bomb underneath yourself."

"What was it? Have you any notion? Nothing of the sort ever occurred at rendezvous with a comet. And you believe the glacier is a wrecked comet, don't you?"

"Uh-huh, except that conditions have obviously modified it. The impact produced heat, shock, turbulence. Molecules got scrambled. Plasmas must have been momentarily present. Mixtures, compounds, clathrates, alloys—stuff formed that never existed in free space. We can learn a lot of chemistry here."

"That's why I came along. . . . Well, then, I crossed a deposit of some substance or substances that the jets caused to sublime with tremendous force. A certain kind of vapor refroze when it encountered the hull. I had to defrost the ports from inside after the snow had cooked off them."

"Where are you in relation to us?"

"I told you, I don't know. And I'm not sure I can determine it. The crash crumpled the direction-finding antenna. Let me go outside for a better look."

"Do that," Scobie said. "I'll keep busy meanwhile."

He did, until a ghastly rattling noise and Broberg's wail brought him at full speed back to the rock.

Scobie switched off Garcilaso's fuel cell. "This may make the difference that carries us through," he said low. "Think of it as a gift. Thanks, Luis."

Broberg let go of the pilot and rose from her knees. She straightened the limbs that had threshed about in the death struggle and crossed his hands on his breast. There was nothing she could do about the fallen jaw or the eyes that glared at heaven. Taking him out of his suit, here, would have worsened his appearance. Nor could she wipe tears off her own face. She could merely try to stop their flow. "Goodbye, Luis," she whispered.

Turning to Scobie, she asked, "Can you give me a new job? Please."

"Come along," he directed. "I'll explain what I have in mind about making our way to the surface."

They were midway across the bowl when Danzig called. He had not let his comrade's dying slow his efforts, nor said much while it happened. Once, most softly, he had offered Kaddish.

"No luck," he reported like a machine. "I've traversed the largest circle I could while keeping the boat in sight, and found only weird, frozen shapes. I can't be a huge distance from you, or I'd see an identifiably different sky, on this miserable little ball. You're probably within a twenty or thirty kilometer radius of me. But that covers a bunch of territory."

"Right," Scobie said. "Chances are you can't find us in the time we've got. Return to the boat."

"Hey, wait," Danzig protested. "I can spiral onward, marking my trail. I might come across you."

"It'll be more useful if you return," Scobie told him. "Assuming we climb out, we should be able to hike to you, but we'll need a beacon. What occurs to me is the ice itself. A small energy release, if it's concentrated, should release a large plume of methane or something similarly volatile. The gas will cool as it expands, recondense around dust particles that have been carried along—it'll steam—and the cloud ought to get high enough, before it evaporates again, to be visible from here."

"Gotcha!" A tinge of excitement livened Danzig's words. "I'll go straight to it. Make tests, find a spot where I can get the showiest result, and . . . how about I rig a thermite bomb? . . . No, that might be too hot. Well, I'll develop a gadget."

"Keep us posted."

"But I, I don't think we'll care to chatter idly," Broberg ventured.

"No, we'll be working our tails off, you and I," Scobie agreed.

"Uh, wait," said Danzig. "What if you find you can't get clear to the top? You implied that's a distinct possibility."

"Well, then it'll be time for more radical procedures, whatever they turn out to be," Scobie responded. "Frankly, at this moment my head is too full of . . . of Luis, and of choosing an optimum escape route . . . for much thought about anything else."

"M-m, yeah, I guess we've got an ample supply of trouble without borrowing more. Tell you what, though. After my beacon's ready to fire off, I'll make that rope we talked of. You might find you prefer having it to clean clothes and sheets when you arrive." Danzig was silent for seconds before he ended: "God damn it, you *will* arrive."

Scobie chose a point on the north side for his and Broberg's attempt. Two rock shelves jutted forth, near the floor and several meters higher, indicating that stone reached at least that far. Beyond, in a staggered pattern, were similar outcrops of hard ices. Between them, and onward from the uppermost, which was scarcely more than halfway to the rim, was nothing but the featureless, footingless slope of powder crystals. Its angle of repose gave a steepness that made the surface doubly treacherous. The question, unanswerable save by experience, was how deeply it covered layers on which humans could climb, and whether such layers extended the entire distance aloft.

At the spot, Scobie signalled a halt. "Take it easy, Jean," he said. "I'll go ahead and commence digging."

"Why don't we together? I have my own tool, you know."

"Because I can't tell how so large a bank of that pseudo-quicksand will behave. It might react to the disturbance by a gigantic slide."

She bridled. Her haggard countenance registered mutiny. "Why not me first, then? Do you suppose I always wait passive for Kendrick to save me?"

"As a matter of fact," he rapped, "I'll bargain because my rib is giving me billy hell, which is eating away what strength I've got left. If we run into trouble, you can better come to my help than I to yours."

Broberg bent her neck. "Oh. I'm sorry. I must be in a fairly bad state myself, if I let false pride interfere with our business." Her look went toward Saturn, around which *Chronos* orbited, bearing her husband and children.

"You're forgiven." Scobie bunched his legs and sprang the five meters to the lower ledge. The next one was slightly too far for such a jump, when he had no room for a running start.

Stooping, he scraped his trenching tool against the bottom of the declivity that sparkled before him, and shoveled. Grains poured from above, a billionfold, to cover what he cleared. He worked like a robot possessed. Each spadeful was nearly weightless, but the number of spadefuls was nearly endless. He did not bring the entire bowlside down on himself as he had half feared, half hoped. (If that didn't kill him, it would save a lot of toil.) A dry torrent went right and left over his ankles. Yet at last somewhat more of the underlying rock began to show.

From beneath, Broberg listened to him breathe. It sounded rough, often broken by a gasp or a curse. In his spacesuit, in the raw, wan sunshine, he resembled a knight who, in despite of wounds, did battle against a monster.

"All right," he called at last. "I think I've learned what to expect and how we should operate. It'll take the two of us."

"Yes . . . oh, yes, my Kendrick."

The hours passed. Ever so slowly, the sun climbed and the stars wheeled and Saturn waned.

Most places, the humans labored side by side. They did not require more than the narrowest of lanes—but unless they cut it wide to begin with, the banks to right and left would promptly slip down and bury it. Sometimes the conformation underneath allowed a single person at a time to work. Then the other could rest. Soon it was Scobie who must oftenest take advantage of that. Sometimes they both stopped briefly, for food and drink and reclining on their packs.

Rock yielded to water ice. Where this rose very sharply, the couple knew it, because the sand-ice that they undercut would come down in a mass. After the first such incident, when they were nearly swept away, Scobie always drove his geologist's hammer into each new stratum. At any sign of danger, he would seize its handle and Broberg would cast an arm around his waist. Their other hands clutched their trenching tools. Anchored, but forced to strain every muscle, they would stand while the flood poured around them, knee-high, once even chest-high, seeking to bury them irretrievably deep in its quasi-fluid substance. Afterward they would confront a bare stretch. It was generally too steep to climb unaided, and they chipped footholds.

Weariness was another tide to which they dared not yield. At best, their progress was dismayingly slow. They needed little heat input to keep warm, except when they took a rest, but their lungs put a furious demand on air recyclers. Garcilaso's fuel cell, which they had brought along, could give a single person extra hours of life, though depleted as it was after coping with his hypothermia, the time would be insufficient for rescue by the teams from *Chronos*. Unspoken was the idea of taking turns with it. That would put them in wretched shape, chilled and stifling, but at least they would leave the universe together.

Thus it was hardly a surprise that their minds fled from pain, soreness, exhaustion, stench, despair. Without that respite, they could not have gone on as long as they did.

At ease for a few minutes, their backs against a blue-shimmering parapet which they must scale, they gazed across the bowl, where Garcilaso's suited body gleamed like a remote pyre, and up the curve opposite to Saturn. The planet shone lambent amber, softly banded, the rings a coronet which a shadow band across their arc seemed to make all the brighter. That radiance overcame sight of most nearby stars, but elsewhere they arrayed themselves multitudinous, in splendor, around the silver road which the galaxy clove between them.

"How right a tomb for Alvarlan," *Ricia says in a dreamer's murmur.*

"Has he died, then?" *Kendrick asks.*

"You do not know?"

"I have been too busied. After we won free of the ruins and I left you to recover while I went scouting, I encountered a troop of warriors. I escaped, but must needs return to you by devious, hidden ways." *Kendrick strokes Ricia's sunny hair.* "Besides, dearest dear, it has ever been you, not I, who had the gift of hearing spirits."

"Brave darling. . . . Yes, it is a glory to me that I was able to call his soul out of Hell. It sought his body, but that was old and frail and could not survive the knowledge it now had. Yet Alvarlan passed peacefully, and before he did, for his last magic he made himself a tomb from whose ceiling starlight will eternally shine."

"May he sleep well. But for us there is no sleep. Not yet. We have far to travel."

"Aye. But already we have left the wreckage behind. Look! Everywhere around in this meadow, anemones peep through the grass. A lark sings above."

"These lands are not always calm. We may well have more adventures ahead of us. But we shall meet them with high hearts."

Kendrick and Ricia rise to continue their journey.

Cramped on a meager ledge, Scobie and Broberg shoveled for an hour without broadening it much. The sand-ice slid from above as fast as they could cast it down. "We'd better quit this as a bad job," the man finally decided. "The best we've done is flatten the slope ahead of us a tiny bit. No telling how far inward the shelf goes before there's a solid layer on top. Maybe there isn't any."

"What shall we do instead?" Broberg asked in the same worn tone.

He jerked a thumb. "Scramble back to the level beneath and try a different direction. But first we absolutely require a break."

They spread kerofoam pads and sat. After a while during which they merely stared, stunned by fatigue, Broberg spoke.

"I go to the brook," *Ricia relates.* "It chimes under arches of green boughs. Light falls between them to sparkle on it. I kneel and drink. The water is cold, pure, sweet. When I raise my eyes, I see the figure of a young woman, naked, her tresses the color of leaves. A wood nymph. She smiles."

"Yes, I see her too," *Kendrick joins in.* "I approach carefully, not to frighten

56

her off. She asks our names and errands. We explain that we are lost. She tells us how to find an oracle which may give us counsel."

They depart to find it.

Flesh could no longer stave off sleep. "Give us a yell in an hour, will you, Mark?" Scobie requested.

"Sure," Danzig said, "but will that be enough?"

"It's the most we can afford, after the setbacks we've had. We've come less than a third of the way."

"If I haven't talked to you," Danzig said slowly, "it's not because I've been hard at work, though I have been. It's that I figured you two were having a plenty bad time without me nagging you. However—Do you think it's wise to fantasize the way you have been?"

A flush crept across Broberg's cheeks and down toward her bosom. "You listened, Mark?"

"Well, yes, of course. You might have an urgent word for me at any minute—"

"Why? What could you do? A game is a personal affair."

"Uh, yes, yes—"

Ricia and Kendrick have made love whenever they can. The accounts were never explicit, but the words were often passionate.

"We'll keep you tuned in when we need you, like for an alarm clock," Broberg clipped. "Otherwise we'll cut the circuit."

"But—Look, I never meant to—"

"I know," Scobie sighed. "You're a nice guy and I daresay we're over-reacting. Still, that's the way it's got to be. Call us when I told you."

Deep within the grotto, the Pythoness sways on her throne, in the ebb and flow of her oracular dream. As nearly as Ricia and Kendrick can understand what she chants, she tells them to fare westward on the Stag Path until they met a one-eyed graybeard who will give them further guidance; but they must be wary in his presence, for he is easily angered. They make obeisance and depart. On their way out, they pass the offering they brought. Since they have little with them other than garments and his weapons, the Princess gave the shrine her golden hair. The knight insists that, close-cropped, she remains beautiful.

"Hey, whoops, we've cleared us an easy twenty meters," Scobie said, albeit in a voice which weariness had hammered flat. *At first the journey, through the land of Narce, is a delight.*

His oath afterward had no more life in it. "Another blind alley, seems like." *The old man in the blue cloak and wide-brimmed hat was indeed wrathful when Ricia refused him her favors and Kendrick's spear struck his own aside. Cunningly, he has pretended to make peace and told them what road they should take next. But at the end of it are trolls. The wayfarers elude them and double back.*

"My brain's stumbling around in a swamp, a fog," Scobie groaned. "My busted rib isn't exactly helping, either. If I don't get another nap I'll keep on making misjudgments till we run out of time."

"By all means, Colin," Broberg said. "I'll stand watch and rouse you in an hour."

"What?" he asked in dim surprise. "Why not join me and have Mark call us as he did before?"

She grimaced. "No need to bother him. I'm tired, yes, but not sleepy."

He lacked wit or strength to argue. "Okay," he said, stretched his insulating pad on the ice, and toppled out of awareness.

Broberg settled herself next to him. They were halfway to the heights, but they had been struggling, with occasional breaks, for worse than twenty hours, and progress grew more hard and tricky even as they themselves grew more weak and stupefied. If ever they reached the top and spied Danzig's signal, they would have something like a couple of hours' stiff travel to shelter.

Saturn, sun, stars shone through vitryl. Broberg smiled down at Scobie's face. He was no Greek god, and sweat, grime, unshavenness, the manifold marks of exhaustion were upon him, but—For that matter, she was scarcely an image of glamour herself.

Princess Ricia sits by her knight, where he slumbers in the dwarf's cottage, and strums a harp the dwarf lent her before he went off to his mine, and sings a lullaby to sweeten the dreams of Kendrick. When it is done, she passes her lips lightly across his, and drifts into the same gentle sleep.

Scobie woke a piece at a time. "Ricia, beloved," *Kendrick whispers, and feels after her. He will summon her up with kisses—*

He scrambled to his feet. "Judas priest!" She lay unmoving. He heard her breath in his earplugs, before the roaring of his pulse drowned it. The sun glared farther aloft, he could see it had moved, and Saturn's crescent had thinned more, forming sharp horns at its ends. He forced his eyes toward the watch on his left wrist.

"Ten hours," he choked.

He knelt and shook his companion. "Come, for Christ's sake!" Her lashes fluttered. When she saw the horror on his visage, drowsiness fled from her.

"Oh, no," she said, "Please, no."

Scobie climbed stiffly erect and flicked his main radio switch. "Mark, do you receive?"

"Colin!" Danzig chattered. "Thank God! I was going out of my head from worry."

"You're not off that hook, my friend. We just finished a ten-hour snooze."

"What? How far did you get first?"

"To about forty meters' elevation. The going looks tougher ahead than in back. I'm afraid we won't make it."

"Don't *say* that, Colin," Danzig begged.

"My fault," Broberg declared. She stood rigid, fists doubled, features a mask. Her tone was steady. "He was worn out, had to have a nap. I offered to wake him, but fell asleep myself."

"Not your fault, Jean," Scobie began.

She interrupted: "Yes. Mine. Perhaps I can make it good. Take my fuel cell. I'll still have deprived you of my help, of course, but you might survive and reach the boat anyway."

He seized her hands. They did not unclench. "If you imagine I, I could do that—"

"If you don't, we're both finished," she said unbendingly. "I'd rather go out with a clear conscience."

"And what about my conscience?" he shouted. Checking himself, he wet his lips and said fast: "Besides, you're not to blame. Sleep slugged you. If I'd been thinking, I'd have realized it was bound to do so, and contacted Mark. The fact that you didn't either shows how far gone you were yourself. And . . . you've got Tom and the kids waiting for you. Take my cell." He paused. "And my blessing."

"Shall Ricia forsake her true knight?"

"Wait, hold on, listen," Danzig called. "Look, this is terrible, but—oh, hell, excuse me, but I've got to remind you that dramatics only clutter the action. From what descriptions you've sent, I don't see how either of you can possibly proceed solo. Together, you might yet. At least you're rested—sore in the muscles, no doubt, but clearer in the head. The climb before you may prove easier than you think. Try!"

Scobie and Broberg regarded each other for a whole minute. A thawing went through her, and warmed him. Finally they smiled and embraced. "Yeah, right," he growled. "We're off. But first a bite to eat. I'm plain, old-fashioned hungry. Aren't you?" She nodded.

"That's the spirit," Danzig encouraged them. "Uh, may I make another suggestion? I am just a spectator, which is pretty hellish but does give me an overall view. Drop that game of yours."

Scobie and Broberg tautened.

"It's the real culprit," Danzig pleaded. "Weariness alone wouldn't have clouded your judgment. You'd never have cut me off, and—But weariness and shock and grief did lower your defenses to the point where the damned game took you over. You weren't yourselves when you fell asleep. You were those dream-world characters. They had no reason not to cork off!"

Broberg shook her head violently. "Mark," said Scobie, "you are correct about being a spectator. That means there are some things you don't understand. Why subject you to the torture of listening in, hour after hour? We'll call you back from time to time, naturally. Take care." He broke the circuit.

"He's wrong," Broberg insisted.

Scobie shrugged. "Right or wrong, what difference? We won't pass out again in the time we have left. The game didn't handicap us as we traveled. In fact, it helped, by making the situation feel less gruesome."

"Aye. Let us break our fast and set forth anew on our pilgrimage."

The struggle grew stiffer. "Belike the White Witch has cast a spell on this road," *says Ricia*.

"She shall not daunt us," *vows Kendrick*.

"No, never while we fare side by side, you and I, noblest of men."

A slide overcame them and swept them back a dozen meters. They lodged against a crag. After the flow had passed by, they lifted their bruised bodies and limped in search of a different approach. The place where the geologist's hammer remained was no longer accessible.

"What shattered the bridge?" *asks Ricia*.

"A giant," *answers Kendrick*. "I saw him as I fell into the river. He lunged at me, and we fought in the shallows until he fled. He bore away my sword in his thigh."

"You have your spear that Wayland forged," *Ricia says,* "and always you have my heart."

They stopped on the last small outcrop they uncovered. It proved to be not a shelf but a pinnacle of water ice. Around it glittered sand-ice, again quiescent.

Ahead was a slope thirty meters in length, and then the rim, and stars. The distance might as well have been thirty light-years. Whoever tried to cross would immediately sink to an unknown depth.

There was no point in crawling back down the bared side of the pinnacle. Broberg had clung to it for an hour while she chipped niches to climb by with her knife. Scobie's condition had not allowed him to help. If they sought to return, they could easily slip, fall, and be engulfed. If they avoided that, they would never find a new path. Less than two hours' worth of energy abode in their fuel cells. Attempting to push onward while swapping Garcilaso's back and forth would be an exercise in futility.

They settled themselves, legs dangling over the abyss, and held hands and looked at Saturn and at one another.

"I do not think the orcs can burst the iron door of this tower," *Kendrick says,* "but they will besiege us until we starve to death."

"You never yielded up your hope erenow, my knight," *replies Ricia, and kisses his temple.* "Shall we search about? These walls are unutterably ancient. Who knows what relics of wizardry lie forgotten within? A pair of phoenix-feather cloaks, that will bear us laughing through the sky to our home—?"

"I fear not, my darling. Our weird is upon us." *Kendrick touches the spear that leans agleam against the battlement.* "Sad and gray will the world be without you. We can but meet our doom bravely."

"Happily, since we are together." *Ricia's gamin smile breaks forth.* "I did notice that a certain room holds a bed. Shall we try it?"

Kendrick frowns. "Rather should we seek to set our minds and souls in order."

She tugs his elbow. "Later, yes. Besides—who knows?—when we dust off the blanket, we may find it is a Tarnkappe that will take us invisible through the enemy."

"You dream."

Fear stirs behind her eyes. "What if I do?" *Her words tremble.* "I can dream us free if you will help."

Scobie's fist smote the ice. "No!" he croaked. "I'll die in the world that is."

Ricia shrinks from him. He sees terror invade her. "You, you rave, beloved," *she stammers.*

He twisted about and caught her by the arms. "Don't you want to remember Tom and your boys?"

"Who—?"

Kendrick slumps. "I don't know. I have forgotten too."

She leans against him, there on the windy height. A hawk circles above.

"The residuum of an evil enchantment, surely. Oh, my heart, my life, cast it from you! Help me find the means to save us." *Yet her entreaty is uneven, and through it speaks dread.*

Kendrick straightens. He lays hand on Wayland's spear, and it is though strength flows thence, into him. "A spell in truth," *he says. His tone gathers force.* "I will not abide in its darkness, nor suffer it to blind and deafen you, my lady in domnei." *His gaze takes hold of hers, which cannot break away.* "There is but a single road to our freedom. It goes through the gates of death."

She waits, mute and shuddering.

"Whatever we do, we must die, Ricia. Let us fare hence as our own folk."

"I—no—I won't—I will—"

"You see before you the means of your deliverance. It is sharp, I am strong; you will feel no pain."

She bares her bosom. "Then quickly, Kendrick, before I am lost!"

He drives the weapon home. "I love you," *he says. She sinks at his feet.* "I follow you, my darling," *he says, withdraws the steel, braces shaft against stone, lunges forward, falls beside her.* "Now we are free."

"That was . . . a nightmare." Broberg sounded barely awake.

Scobie's voice shook. "Necessary, I think, for both of us." He gazed straight before him, letting Saturn fill his eyes with dazzle. "Else we'd have stayed . . . insane? Maybe not, by definition. But we'd not have been in reality either."

"It would have been easier," she mumbled.

"We'd never have known we were dying."

"Would you have preferred that?"

Broberg shivered. The slackness in her countenance gave place to the same tension that was in his. "Oh, no," she said, quite softly but in the manner of full consciousness. "No, you were right, of course. Thank you for your courage."

"You've always had as much guts as anybody, Jean. You just have more imagination than me." Scobie's hand chopped empty space, a gesture of dismissal. "Okay, we should call poor Mark and let him know. But first—" His words lost the cadence he had laid on them. "First—"

Her glove clasped his. "What, Colin?"

"Let's decide about that third unit, Luis's," he said with difficulty, still confronting the great ringed planet. "Your decision, actually, though we can discuss the matter if you want. I will not hog it for the sake of a few more hours. Nor will I share it; that would be a nasty way for us both to go out. However, I suggest you use it."

"To sit beside your frozen corpse?" she replied. "No. I wouldn't even feel the warmth, not in my bones—"

She turned toward him so fast that she nearly fell off the pinnacle. He caught her. *"Warmth!"* she screamed, shrill as the cry of a hawk on the wing. "Colin, we'll take our bones home!"

"In point of fact," said Danzig, "I've climbed onto the hull. That's high enough for me to see over those ridges and needles. I've got a view of the entire horizon."

"Good," grunted Scobie. "Be prepared to survey a complete circle quick. This depends on a lot of factors we can't predict. The beacon will certainly not be anything like as big as what you had arranged. It may be thin and short-lived. And, of course, it may rise too low for sighting at your distance." He cleared his throat. "In that case, we two have bought the farm. But we'll have made a hell of a try, which feels great by itself."

He hefted the fuel cell, Garcilaso's gift. A piece of heavy wire, insulation stripped off, joined the prongs. Without a regulator, the unit poured its maximum power through the short circuit. Already the strand glowed.

"Are you sure you don't want me to do it, Colin?" Broberg asked. "Your rib—"

He made a lopsided grin. "I'm nonetheless better designed by nature for throwing things," he said. "Allow me that much male arrogance. The bright idea was yours."

"It should have been obvious from the first," she said. "I think it would have been, if we weren't bewildered in our dream."

"M-m, often the simple answers are the hardest to find. Besides, we had to get this far or it wouldn't have worked, and the game helped mightily. . . . Are you set, Mark? Heave ho!"

Scobie cast the cell as if it were a baseball, hard and far through the Iapetan gravity field. Spinning, its incandescent wire wove a sorcerous web across vision. It landed somewhere beyond the rim, on the glacier's back.

Frozen gases vaporized, whirled aloft, briefly recondensed before they were lost. A geyser stood white against the stars.

"I see you!" Danzig yelped. "I see your beacon, I've got my bearing, I'll be on my way! With rope and extra energy units and everything!"

Scobie sagged to the ground and clutched at his left side. Broberg knelt and held him, as if either of them could lay hand on his pain. No large matter. He would not hurt much longer.

"How high would you guess the plume goes?" Danzig inquired, calmer.

"About a hundred meters," Broberg replied after study.

"Uh, damn, these gloves do make it awkward punching the calculator. . . . Well, to judge by what I observe of it, I'm between ten and fifteen klicks off. Give me an hour or a tadge more to get there and find your exact location. Okay?"

Broberg checked gauges. "Yes, by a hair. We'll turn our thermostats down and sit very quiet to reduce oxygen demand. We'll get cold, but we'll survive."

"I may be quicker," Danzig said. "That was a worst case estimate. All right, I'm off. No more conversation till we meet. I won't take any foolish chances, but I will need my wind for making speed."

Faintly, those who waited heard him breathe, heard his hastening footfalls. The geyser died.

They sat, arms around waists, and regarded the glory which encompassed them. After a silence, the man said: "Well, I suppose this means the end of the game. For everybody."

"It must certainly be brought under strict control," the woman answered. "I wonder, though, if they will abandon it altogether—out here."

"If they must, they can."

"Yes. We did, you and I, didn't we?"

They turned face to face, beneath that star-beswarmed, Saturn-ruled sky. Nothing tempered the sunlight that revealed them to each other, she a middle-aged wife, he a man ordinary except for his aloneness. They would never play again. They could not.

A puzzled compassion was in her smile. "Dear Friend—" she began.

His uplifted palm warded her from further speech. "Best we don't talk unless it's essential," he said. "That'll save a little oxygen, and we can stay a little warmer. Shall we try if we can sleep?"

Her eyes widened and darkened. "I dare not," she confessed. "Not till enough time has gone past. Now, I might dream."

II

In the event, Voyager One found nothing entirely incompatible with my ideas. The story was published and well received, winning awards. Meanwhile Voyager Two also spared it. Granted, the scientific evidence points toward Iapetus being an icy body, the dark half only a thin layer left by an impact or produced by the fierce photochemistry of space. However, this isn't yet certain, and in any case doesn't seem to rule out the landscape I imagined. We'll have to wait till Cassini reaches Saturn and gives us a closer look. I'm as eager to know for sure as you are.

The origins of the story offer an example of how complex such things can be. From time to time in those years Jerry Pournelle would organize and lead a meeting of what he called the Citizens' Advisory Committee on National Space Policy. It was avowedly an advocacy group for a strong, ongoing effort, but each gathering considered a specific aspect, from economic incentives to missile defense. Persons in attendance included scientists, astronauts, engineers, businessmen, high-ranking officers of the defense forces, occasional civilians in government or academe, and whoever else Jerry thought could contribute something. I sat in mostly to listen and help draft the final reports. These went to certain pretty high places, at least one (or a summary of it) as far as the White House, and may have done some good.

Lord, but we science fictioneers had become respectable! And, although everybody worked hard at the meetings, they were fascinating and actually enjoyable, being held in Larry and Marilyn Niven's mansion. I met some great people.

One was the physicist J. Peter Vajk, who presented in well-thought-out detail his concept of missions with live, human crews using solar sails. When he read "The Saturn Game" and remarked on it, I told him, "I only steal from the best sources." The least I could do was name the spaceship for him.

Before then, Karen and I had read an article or two about paradoxical Iapetus, and conversationally speculated. And we had long experience with such activities as science fiction fandom and the medievalistic Society for Creative Anachronism. Later we saw role-playing games become popular. Now, there's nothing wrong with any of these. On the contrary, for most participants they're excellent, even mind-expanding recreation. But a few get wrapped up in one of them to an unhealthy extent, where nothing really matters except the dream world. (Of course, these aren't unique in that regard. When the obsession is ideological, it can bring disaster on many an innocent.) All of this came together, and out of it grew the story.

No two happen the same way. Let me now go back in time almost thirty years from the Voyagers flying past Saturn, which itself occurred more than twenty years ago, when I'd come a long way from those early days. I hope I'm still moving onward. This book is a kind of log of the journey.

Science fiction writers tend to start out young. I began making professional sales while in college. My aim was to become a scientist, but after graduating, with no money left to continue, I supported myself by writing while I looked for honest employment. Jobs were scarce just then; the search grew more and more half-hearted; gradually I realized that what I was doing was what nature had cut me out for. Meanwhile I was learning the craft the hard way, at least as much through the rejections as the acceptances.

"Gypsy" is the earliest that seems worth including here. I could do it better nowadays. Perhaps I wouldn't do it at all, because the "science" in it is mostly what engineers and my son-in-law Greg Bear call arm waving. Still, probably more stories than not require such postulates. For a major instance, we have travel faster than light. Authors assume that present-day physics doesn't explain everything—which, as a matter of fact, it doesn't—and new discoveries may revolutionize our understanding as much as relativity and quantum mechanics did. Indeed, superluminal motion, and even time travel, no longer look as completely absurd as they used to.

I also find the writing style awkward. Nevertheless, this little tale is a landmark for me, my first attempt to celebrate the wonders of our universe.

GYPSY

From afar, I caught a glimpse of the *Traveler* as my boat swung toward the planet. The great spaceship looked like a toy at that distance, a frail bubble of metal and air and energy against the enormous background of space. I thought of the machines within her, humming and whirring and clicking very faintly as they pursued their unending round of services, making that long hull into a living world—the hull that was now empty of life—and I had a sudden odd feeling of sympathy. As if she were alive, I felt that the *Traveler* was lonely.

The planet swelled before me, a shining blue shield blazoned with clouds and continents, rolling against a limitless dark and the bitterly burning stars. Harbor, we had named that world, the harbor at the end of our long journey, and there were few lovelier names. Harbor, haven, rest and peace and a sky overhead as roof against the naked blaze of space. It was good to get home.

I searched the heavens for another glimpse of the *Traveler,* but I couldn't find her tiny form in that thronging wilderness of stars. No matter, she was still on her orbit about Harbor, moored to the planet, perhaps forever. I concentrated on bringing the spaceboat down.

Atmosphere whistled about the hull. After a month in the gloom and poisonous cold of the fifth planet, alone among utterly unhuman natives, I was usually on fire to get home and brought my craft down with a recklessness that overloaded the gravity beams. But this time I went a little more carefully, telling myself that I'd rather be late for supper than not arrive at all. Or perhaps it was that brief chance vision of the *Traveler* which made me suddenly thoughtful. After all, we had had some good times aboard her.

I sent the boat slanting toward the peninsula in the north temperate zone on which most of us were settled. The outraged air screamed behind me as I slammed down on the hard-packed earth that served us for a landing field. There were a few warehouses and service shops around it, long low buildings of the heavy timbers used by most of the colonists, and a couple of private homes a kilometer or so away. But otherwise only long grass rustled in the wind, gardens and wild groves, sunlight streaming out of a high blue sky. When I stepped from the boat, the fresh vivid scent of the land fairly leaped to meet me. I could hear the sea growling beyond the horizon.

Tokogama was on duty at the field. He was sitting on the porch of the office, smoking his pipe and watching the clouds sail by overhead, but he greeted me with the undemonstrative cordiality of old friends who know each other too well to need many words.

"So that's the portmaster," I said. "Soft touch. All you have to do is puff that vile-smelling thing and say hello to me."

"That's all," he admitted cheerfully. "I am retained only for my uncommonly high ornamental value."

It was, approximately, true. Our aircraft used the field with no formality, and we only kept this one space vessel in operation. The portmaster was on hand simply to oversee servicing and in the unlikely case of some emergency or dispute. But none of the colony's few public posts—captain, communications officer, and the rest—required much effort in as simple a society as ours, and they were filled as spare-time occupations by anyone who wanted them. There was no compensation except getting first turn at using the machinery for farming or heavy construction which we owned in common.

"How was the trip?" asked Tokogama.

"Pretty good," I said. "I gave them our machines and they filled my holds with their ores and alloys. And I managed to take a few more notes on their habits, and establish a few more code symbols for communication."

"Which is a very notable brick added to the walls of science, but in view of the fact that you're the only one who ever goes there it really makes no odds." Tokogama's dark eyes regarded me curiously. "Why do you keep on making those trips out there, Erling? Quite a few of the other boys wouldn't mind visiting Five once in a while. Will and Ivan both mentioned it to me last week."

"I'm no hog," I said. "If either of them, or anyone else, wants a turn at the trading job, let 'em learn space piloting and they can go. But meanwhile—I like the work. You know that I was one of those who voted to continue the search for Earth."

Tokogama nodded. "So you were. But that was three years ago. Even you must have grown some roots here."

"Oh, I have," I laughed. "Which reminds me I'm hungry, and judging by the sun it's the local dinner time. So I'll get on home, if Alanna knows I'm back."

"She can't help it," he smiled. "The whole continent knows when you're back, the way you rip the atmosphere coming in. That home cooking must have a powerful magnetic attraction."

"A steak aroma of about fifty thousand gauss—" I turned to go, calling over my shoulder: "Why don't you come to dinner tomorrow evening? I'll invite the other boys and we'll have an old-fashioned hot air session."

"I was sort of hinting in that direction," said Tokogama.

I got my carplane out of the hangar and took off with a whisper of air and a hum of grav-beam generators. But I flew low over the woods and meadows, dawdling along at fifty kilometers an hour and looking across the landscape. It lay quietly in the evening, almost empty of man, a green fair breadth of land veined with bright rivers. The westering sun touched each leaf and grass blade with molten gold, an aureate glow which seemed to fill the cool air like a tangible presence, and I could hear the chirp and chatter of the great bird flocks as they settled down in the trees. Yes—it was good to get home.

My own house stood at the very edge of the sea, on a sandy bluff sloping down to the water. The windy trees which grew about it almost hid the little stone and timber structure, but its lawns and gardens reached far, and beyond them were the fields from which we got our food. Down by the beach stood the boathouse and the little dock I had made, and I knew our sailboat lay waiting there for me to take her out. I felt an almost physical hunger for the sea again, the mighty surge of waves out to the wild horizon, the keen salt wind and the crying white birds. After a month in the sterile tanked air of the spaceboat, it was like being born again.

I set the plane down before the house and got out. Two small bodies fairly exploded against me—Einar and Mike. I walked into the house with my sons riding my shoulders.

Alanna stood in the doorway waiting for me. She was tall, almost as tall as I, and slim and red-haired and the most beautiful woman in the universe. We didn't say much—it was unnecessary, and we were otherwise occupied for the next few minutes.

And afterward I sat before a leaping fire where the little flames danced and chuckled and cast a wavering ruddy glow over the room, and the wind whistled outside and rattled the door, and the sea roared on the nighted beach, and I told them of my fabulous space voyage, which had been hard and monotonous and lonely but was a glamorous adventure at home. The boys' eyes never stirred from my face as I talked, I could feel the eagerness that blazed from them. The gaunt sun-seared crags of One, the misty jungles of Two, the mountains and deserts of Four, the great civilization of Five, the bitter desolation of the outer worlds—and beyond those the stars. But we were home now, we sat in a warm dry house and heard the wind singing outside.

I was happy, in a quiet way that had somehow lost the exuberance of my earlier returns. Content, maybe.

Oh, well, I thought. These trips to the fifth world were becoming routine, just as life on Harbor, now that our colony was established and our automatic and semiautomatic machines running smoothly, had quieted down from the first great riot of work and danger and work again. That was progress, that was what we had striven for, to remove want and woe and the knife-edged uncertainty which had haunted our days. We had arrived, we had graduated into a solid assurance and a comfort which still held enough unsureness and challenge to keep us from getting sluggish. Grown men don't risk their necks climbing the uppermost branches of trees, the way children do; they walk on the ground, and when they have to rise they do so safely and comfortably, in a carplane.

"What's the matter, Erling?" asked Alanna.

"Why—nothing." I started out of my reverie, suddenly aware that the children were in bed and the night near its middle. "Nothing at all. I was just sitting thinking. A little tired, I guess. Let's turn in."

"You're a poor liar, Erling," she said softly. "What were you really thinking about?"

"Nothing," I insisted. "That is, well, I saw the old *Traveler* as I was coming down today. It just put me in mind of old times."

"It would," she said. And suddenly she sighed. I looked at her in some alarm, but she was smiling again. "You're right, it is late, and we'd better go to bed."

I took the boys out in the sailboat the next day. Alanna stayed home on the excuse that she had to prepare dinner, though I knew of her theory that the proper psychodevelopment of children required a balance of paternal and maternal influence. Since I was away so much of the time, out in space or with one of the exploring parties which were slowly mapping our planet, she made me occupy the center of the screen whenever I was home.

Einar, who was nine years old and getting interested in the microbooks we had from the *Traveler*—and so, ultimately, from Earth—looked at her and said: "Back at Sol you wouldn't have to make food, Mother. You'd just set the au . . . autochef, and come out with us."

"I like to cook," she smiled. "I suppose we could make autochefs, now that the more important semirobot machinery has been produced, but it'd take a lot of fun out of life for me."

Her eyes went past the house, down to the beach and out over the restless sun-sparked water. The sea breeze ruffled her red hair, it was like a flame in the cool shade of the trees. "I think they must miss a lot in the Solar System," she said. "They have so much there that, somehow, they can't have what we've got—room to move about, lands that never saw a man before, the fun of making something ourselves."

"You might like it if you went there," I said. "After all, sweetheart, however wisely we may talk about Sol we know it only by hearsay."

"I know I like what we have here," she answered. I thought there was a faint note of defiance in her voice. "If Sol is just a legend, I can't be sure I'd like the reality. Certainly it could be no better than Harbor."

"All redheads are chauvinists," I laughed, turning down toward the beach.

"All Swedes make unfounded generalizations," she replied cheerfully. "I should'a known better than to marry a Thorkild."

"Fortunately, Mrs. Thorkild, you didn't." I bowed.

The boys and I got out the sailboat. There was a spanking breeze, and in minutes we were scudding northward, along the woods and fields and tumbling surf of the coast.

"We should put a motor on the *Naughty Nancy*, Dad," said Einar. "Suppose this wind don't hold."

"I like to sail," I said. "The chance of having to man the sweeps is part of the fun."

"Me too," said Mike, a little ambiguously.

"Do they have sailboats on Earth?" asked Einar.

"They must," I said, "since I designed the *Nancy* after a book about them. But I don't think it'd ever be quite the same, Einar. The sea must always be full of boats, most of them powered, and there'd be aircraft overhead and some sort of building wherever you made landfall. You wouldn't have the sea to yourself."

"Then why'd you want to keep looking for Earth when ever'body else wanted to stay here?" he challenged.

A nine-year-old can ask some remarkably disconcerting questions. I said slowly: "I wasn't the only one who voted to keep on searching. And—well, I admitted it at the time, it wasn't Earth but the search itself that I wanted. I liked to find new planets. But we've got a good home now, Einar, here on Harbor."

"I still don't understand how they ever lost Earth," he said.

"Nobody does," I said. "The *Traveler* was carrying a load of colonists to Alpha Centauri—that was a star close to Sol—and men had found the hyperdrive only a few years before and reached the nearer stars. Anyway, *something* happened. There was a great explosion in the engines, and we found ourselves somewhere else in the galaxy, thousands of light-years from home. We don't know how far from home, since we've never been able to find Sol again. But after repairing the ship, we spent more than twenty years looking. We never found home." I added quickly, "Until we decided to settle on Harbor. That was our home."

"I mean, how'd the ship get thrown so far off?"

I shrugged. The principles of the hyperdrive are difficult enough, involving as they do the concept of multiple dimensions and of discontinuous psi functions. No one on the ship—and everyone with a knowledge of physics had twisted his brains over the problem—had been able to figure out what catastrophe it was that had annihilated space-time for her. Speculation had involved space warps—whatever that term means, points of infinite discontinuity, undimensional fields, and Cosmos knows what else. Could we find what had happened, and purposefully control the phenomenon which had seized us by some blind accident, the galaxy would be ours. Meanwhile, we were limited to pseudovelocities of a couple of hundred lights, and interstellar space mocked us with vastness.

But how explain that to a nine-year-old? I said only: "If I knew that, I'd be wiser than anyone else, Einar. Which I'm not."

———

"I wanna go swimming," said Mike.

"Sure," I said. "That was our idea, wasn't it? We'll drop anchor in the next bay—"

"I wanna go swimming in Spacecamp Cove."

I tried to hedge, but Einar was all over me, too. It was only a few kilometers farther up the coast, and its broad sheltered expanse, its wide sandy beach, and the forest immediately behind, made it ideal for such an expedition. And after all, I had nothing against it.

Nothing—except the lure of the place.

I sighed and surrendered. Spacecamp Cove it was.

We had a good time there, swimming and picnicking, playing ball and loafing in the sand and swimming some more. It was good to lie in the sun again, with a cool wet wind blowing in from the sea and talking in the trees. And to the boys, the glamour of it was a sort of crown on the day.

But I had to fight the romance. I wasn't a child any more, playing at spacemen and aliens, I was the grown man with some responsibilities. The community of the *Traveler* had voted by an overwhelming majority to settle on Harbor, and that was that.

And here, half hidden by long grass, half buried in the blowing sand, were the unmistakable signs of what we had left.

There wasn't much. A few plasticontainers for food, a couple of broken tools of curious shape, some scattered engine parts. Just enough to indicate that a while ago—ten years ago, perhaps—a party of spacemen had landed here, camped for a while, made some repairs, and resumed their journey.

They weren't from the fifth planet. Those natives had never left their world, and even with the technological impetus we were giving them in exchange for their metals they weren't ever likely to, the pressures they needed to live were too great. They weren't from Sol, or even some colony world—not only were the remains totally unlike our equipment, but the news of a planet like Harbor, almost a duplicate of Earth but without a native intelligent race, would have brought settlers here in swarms. So—somewhere in the galaxy, someone else had mastered the hyperdrive and was exploring space.

As we had been doing—

I did my best to be cheerful all the way home, and think I succeeded on the surface. And that in spite of Einar's wildly romantic gabble about the unknown campers. But I couldn't help remembering—

In twenty years of spacing, you can see a lot of worlds, and you can have a lot of experience. We had been gods of a sort, flitting from star to star, exploring, trading, learning, now and again mixing into the destinies of the natives. We had fought and striven, suffered and laughed and stood silent in wonder. For most of us, the dreadful hunger for home, the weariness of the hopeless quest, had shadowed that panorama of worlds which reeled through my mind. But—before Cosmos, I had loved every minute of it!

I fell into unrelieved moodiness as soon as we had stowed the *Naughty Nancy* in our boathouse. The boys ran ahead of me toward the house, but I followed slowly. Alanna met me at the door.

"Better wash up right away," she said. "The company will be here any minute."

"Uh-huh."

She looked at me, for a very long moment, and laid her hand on my arm. In the long dazzling rays of the westering sun, her eyes were brighter than I had seen them before. I wondered if tears were not wavering just behind them.

"You were at Spacecamp Cove," she said quietly.

"The boys wanted to go there," I answered. "It's a good place."

"Erling—" She paused. I stood looking at her, thinking how beautiful she was. I remembered the way she had looked on Hralfar, the first time I kissed her. We had wandered a ways from the camp of the detail exploring that frosty little world and negotiating with its natives for supplies. The sky had been dark overhead, with a shrunken sun casting its thin pale light on the blue-shadowed snow. It was quiet, breathlessly quiet, the air was like sharp fire in our nostrils and her hair, the only color in that white horizon, seemed to crackle with frost. That was quite a long time ago, but nothing had changed between us since.

"Yes?" I prompted her. "Yes, what is it?"

Her voice came quickly, very low so the boys wouldn't hear: "Erling, are you really happy here?"

"Why"—I felt an almost physical shock of surprise—"of course I am, dear. That's a silly question."

"Or a silly answer?" She smiled, with closed lips. "We did have some good times on the *Traveler*. Even those who grumbled loudest at the time admit that, now when they've got a little perspective on the voyage and have forgotten something of the overcrowding and danger and weariness. But you—I sometimes think the *Traveler* was your life, Erling."

"I liked the ship, of course." I had a somewhat desperate sense of defending myself. "After all, I was born and raised on her. I never really knew anything else. Our planetary visits were so short, and most of the worlds so unterrestrial. You liked it too."

"Oh, sure, it was fun to go batting around the galaxy, never knowing what might wait at the next sun. But a woman wants a home. And—Erling, plenty of others your age, who also had never known anything else, hated it."

"I was lucky. As an officer, I had better quarters, more privacy. And, well, that 'something hid behind the ranges' maybe meant more to me than to most others. But—good Cosmos, Alanna! you don't think that now—"

"I don't think anything, Erling. But on the ship you weren't so absent-minded, so apt to fall into daydreams. You didn't sit around the place all day, you were always working on something. . . ." She bit her lip. "Don't misunderstand, Erling. I have no doubt you keep telling yourself how happy you are. You could go to your cremation, here on Harbor, thinking you'd had a rather good life. But—I sometimes wonder!"

"Now look—" I began.

"No, no, nothing more out of you. Get inside and wash up, the company'll be coming in half a minute."

I went, with my head in a whirl. Mechanically, I scrubbed myself and changed into evening blouse and slacks. When I came out of the bedroom, the first of the guests were already waiting.

MacTeague Angus was there, the old first mate of the *Traveler* and captain in the short time between Kane's death and our settling on Harbor. So was my brother Thorkild Gustav, with whom I had little in common except a mutual liking. Tokogama Hideyoshi, Petroff Ivan, Ortega Manuel, and a couple of others showed up a few minutes later. Alanna took charge of their wives and children, and I mixed drinks all around.

For a while the talk was of local matters. We were scattered over quite a wide area, and had as yet not produced enough telescreens for every house, so that communication was limited to direct personal travel by plane. A hailstorm on Gustav's farm, a minor breakdown in the vehicle factory superintended by Ortega, Petroff's project of a fleet of semirobot fishing boats—small gossip. Presently dinner was served.

Gustav was rapturous over the steak. "What is it?" he asked.

"Some local animal I shot the other day," I said. "Ungulate, reddish-brown, broad flat horns."

"Oh, yes. Hm-m-m—I'll have to try domesticating some. I've had pretty good luck with those glug-gugs."

"Huh?" Petroff stared at him.

"Another local species," laughed Gustav. "I had to call them something, and they make that kind of noise."

"The *Traveler* was never like this," said Ortega, helping himself to another piece of meat.

"I never thought the food was bad," I said.

"No, we had the hydroponic vegetables and fruits, and the synthetic meats, as well as what we picked up on different planets," admitted Ortega. But it wasn't this good, ever. Hydroponics somehow don't have the flavor of Earth-grown stuff."

"That's your imagination," said Petroff. "I can prove—"

"I don't care what you can prove, the facts remain." Ortega glanced at me. "But there were compensations."

"Not enough," muttered Gustav. "I've got room to move, here on Harbor."

"You're being unjust to the *Traveler*," I said. "She was only meant to carry about fifty people for a short voyage at that. When she lost her way for twenty years, and a whole new generation got jammed in with their parents, it's no wonder she grew crowded. Actually, her minimum crew is ten or so. Thirty people—fifteen couples, say, plus their kids—could travel in her in ease and comfort, with private apartments for all."

"And still . . . still, for over twenty years, we fought and suffered and stood the monotony and the hopelessness—to find Earth." Tokogama's voice was musing, a little awed. "When all the time, on any of a hundred uninhabited terrestroid planets, we could have had—this."

"For at least half that time," pointed out MacTeague, "we were simply looking for the right part of the galaxy. We knew Sol wasn't anywhere near, so we had no hopes to be crushed, but we thought as soon as the constellations began to look fairly familiar we'd be quickly able to find home." He shrugged. "But space is simply too big, and our astrogational tables have so little information. Star travel was still in its infancy when we left Sol.

"An error of, say, one percent could throw us light-years off in the course of several hundred parsecs. And the galaxy is lousy with GO-type suns, which are statistically almost certain to have neighbors sufficiently like Sol's to fool an unsure observer. If our tables had given positions relative to, say, S Doradus, we could have found home easily enough. But they used Sirius for their bright-star point—and we couldn't find Sirius in that swarm of stars! We just had to hop from star to star which *might* be Sol—and find it wasn't, and go on, with the sickening fear that maybe we were getting farther away all the time, maybe Sol lay just off the bows, obscured by a dark nebula. In the end—we gave it up as a bad job."

"There's more to it than that," said Tokogama. "We realized all that, you know. But there was Captain Kane and his tremendous personality, his driving will to success, and we'd all come to rely more or less blindly on him. As long as he lived, nobody quite believed in the possibility of failure. When he died, everything seemed to collapse at once."

I nodded grimly, remembering those terrible days that followed—Seymour's mutinous attempt to seize power, bringing home to us just how sick and weary we all were; the arrival at this star which might have solved it all, might have given us a happy ending, if it had been Sol; the rest on Harbor, a rest which became a permanent stay—

"Something else kept us going all those years, too," said Ortega quietly. "There was an element among the younger generation which liked to wander. The vote to stay here wasn't unanimous."

"I know," said MacTeague. His level gaze rested thoughtfully on me. "I often wonder, Erling, why some of you don't borrow the ship and visit the nearer stars, just to see what's there."

"Wouldn't do any good," I said tonelessly. "It'd just make our feet itch worse than ever—and there'd always be stars beyond those."

"But why—" Gustav fumbled for words. "Why would anyone *want* to go—stargazing that way? I . . . well, I've got my feet on ground now, my own ground, my own home . . . it's growing, I'm building and planting and seeing it come to reality before my own eyes, and it'll be there for my children and their children. There's air and wind and rain, sunlight, the sea, the woods and mountains—Cosmos! Who wants more? Who wants to trade it for sitting in a sterile metal tank, riding from star to star, homeless, hopeless?"

"Nobody," I said hastily. "I was just trying—"

"The most pointless existence—simply to be a . . . a spectator in the universe!"

"Not exactly," said Tokogama. "There was plenty we did, if you insist that somebody must do something. We brought some benefits of human civilization to quite a number of places. We did some extensive star-mapping, if we ever see Earthmen again they'll find our tables useful, and our observations within different systems. We . . . well, we were wanderers, but so what? Do you blame a bird for not having hoofs?"

"The birds have hoofs now," I said. "They're walking on the ground. And"—I flashed a glance at Alanna—"they like it."

The conversation was getting a little too hot. I steered it into safer channels until we adjourned to the living room. Over coffee and tobacco it came back.

We began reminiscing about the old days, planets we had seen, deeds we had done. Worlds and suns and moons, whirling through a raw dark emptiness afire with stars, were in our talk—strange races, foreign cities, lonely magnificence of mountains and plains and seas, the giant universe opening before us. Oh, by all the gods, we had fared far!

We had seen the blue hell-flames leaping over the naked peaks of a planet whose great sun almost filled its sky. We had sailed with a gang of happy pirates over a sea red as new-spilled blood toward the grotesque towers of a fortress older than their history. We had seen the rich color and flashing metal of a tournament on Drangor and the steely immensity of the continental cities on Alkan. We had talked philosophy with a gross wallowing cephalopod on one world and been shot at by the inhumanly beautiful natives of another. We had come as gods to a planet to lift its barbaric natives from the grip of a plague that scythed them down and we had come as humble students to the ancient laboratories and libraries of the next. We had come near perishing in a methane storm on a planet far from its sun and felt then how dear life is. We had lain on the beaches of the paradise world Luanha and let the sea sing us to sleep. We had ridden centauroids who conversed with us as they went to the aerial city of their winged enemies—

More than the wildly romantic adventures—which, after all, had been pretty dirty and bloody affairs at the time—we loved to remember the worlds themselves: a fiery sunset on the snowfields of Hralfar; a great brown river flowing through the rain forest which covered Atlang; a painted desert on Thyvari; the mighty disk of New Jupiter swelling before our bows; the cold and vastness and cruelty and emptiness and awe and wonder of open space itself. And, in our small clique of frank tramps, there had been the comradeship of the road, the calm unspoken knowledge of having friends who would stand firm—a feeling of *belonging,* such as men like Gustav had achieved only since coming here, and which we seemed to have lost.

Lost—yes, why not admit it? We didn't see each other very often any more, we were too scattered, too busy. And the talk of the others was just a little bit boring.

Well, it couldn't be helped—

It was late that night when the party broke up. Alanna and I saw the guests out to their planes. When the last vehicle had whispered into the sky, we stood for a while looking around us. The night was very still and cool, with a high starry sky in which the moon of Harbor was rising. Its light glittered on the dew under our feet, danced restlessly on the sea, threw a dim silver veil on the dreaming land—our land.

I looked down at Alanna. She was staring over the darkened view, staring as if she had never seen it before—or never would again. The moonlight was tangled like frost in her hair. *What if I never see open space again? What if I sit here till I die? This is worth it.*

She spoke at last, very slowly, as if she had to shape each word separately: "I'm beginning to realize it. Yes, I'm quite sure."

"Sure of what?" I asked.

"Don't play dumb. You know what I mean. You and Manuel and Ivan and Hideyoshi and the others who were here—except Angus and Gus, of course. And quite a few more. You don't belong here. None of you."

"How—so?"

"Look, a man who had been born and raised in a city, and had a successful life in it, couldn't be expected to take to the country all of a sudden. Maybe never. Put him among peasants, and he'd go around all the rest of his life wondering vaguely why he wasn't honestly happy."

"We—Now don't start that again, sweetheart," I begged.

"Why not? Somebody's got to. After all, Erling, this is a peasantry we've got, growing up on Harbor. More or less mechanized, to be sure, but still rooted to the soil, close to it, with the peasant strength and solidity and the peasant's provincial outlook. Why, if a ship from Earth landed tomorrow, I don't think twenty people would leave with it.

"But you, Erling, you and your friends—you grew up in the ship, and you made a successful adaptation to it. You spent your formative years wandering. By now—you're cosmopolites. For you, a mountain range will always be more than it really is, because of what's behind it. One horizon isn't enough, you've got to have many, as many as there are in the universe.

"Find Earth? Why, you yourself admitted you don't care whether Earth is ever found. You only want the search.

"You're a gypsy, Erling. And no gypsy could ever be tied to one place."

I stood for a long while, alone with her in the cold calm moonlight, and said nothing. When I looked down at her, finally, she was trying not to cry, but her lip was trembling and the tears were bright in her eyes. Every word was wrenched out of me:

"You may be right, Alanna. I'm beginning to be horribly afraid you are. But what's to be done about it?"

"Done?" She laughed, a strangely desolate laugh. "Why, it's a very simple problem. The answer is circling right there up in the sky. Get a crew who feel the way you do, and take the *Traveler*. Go roaming—forever!"

"But . . . you? You, the kids, the place here . . . you—"

"Don't you see?" Her laughter rang louder now, echoing faintly in the light night. "Don't you see? I want to go, too!" She almost fell into my arms. "I want to go, too!"

There is no reason to record the long arguments, grudging acceptances, slow preparations. In the end we won. Sixteen men and their wives, with half a dozen children, were wild to leave.

That summer blazed up into fall, winter came, spring, and summer again, while we made ready. Our last year on Harbor. And I had never realized how much I loved the planet. Almost, I gave up.

But space, free space, the open universe and the ship come alive again—!

We left the colony a complete set of plans, in the unlikely event that they should ever want to build a starship of their own, and a couple of spaceboats and duplicates of all the important automatic machinery carried by the *Traveler*. We would make astrogating tables, as our official purpose, and theoretically we might some day come back.

But we knew we never would. We would go traveling, and our children would carry the journey on after us, and their children after them, a whole new civilization growing up between the stars, rootless but tremendously alive. Those who wearied of it could always colonize a planet; we would be spreading mankind over the galaxy. When our descendants were many, they would build other ships until there was a fleet, a mobile city hurtling from sun to sun. It would be a culture to itself, drawing on the best which all races had to offer and spreading it over the worlds. It would be the bloodstream of the interstellar civilization which was slowly gestating in the universe.

As the days and months went by, my boys grew even more impatient to be off. I smiled a little. Right now, they only thought of the adventure of it, romantic planets and great deeds to be done. Well, there were such, they would have eventful lives, but they would soon learn that patience and steadfastness were needed, that there was toil and suffering and danger—and life!

Alanna—I was a little puzzled. She was very gay when I was around, merrier than I had ever seen her before. But she often went out for long walks, alone on the beach or in the sun-dappled woods, and she started a garden which she would never harvest. Well—so it went, and I was too busy with preparations to think much about it.

The end came, and we embarked on the long voyage, the voyage which has not ceased yet and, I hope, will never end. The night before, we had Angus and Gustav in for a farewell party, and it was a strange feeling to be saying good-bye knowing that we would never see them again, or hear from them. It was like dying.

But we were alone in the morning. We went out to our carplane, to fly to the landing field where the gypsies would meet. From there, a boat would take us to the *Traveler*. I still could not fully realize that I was captain—I, captain of the great ship which had been my world, it didn't seem real. I walked slowly, my head full of the sudden universe of responsibility.

Alanna touched my arm. "Look around, Erling," she whispered. "Look around at our land. You'll never see it again."

I shook myself out of my reverie and let my eyes sweep the horizon. It was early, the grass was still wet, flashing in the new sun. The sea danced and glittered beyond the rustling trees, crying its old song to the fair green land, and the wind that blew from it was keen and cold and pungent with life. The fields were stirring in the wind, a long ripple of grass, and high overhead a bird was singing.

"It's—very beautiful," I said.

"Yes." I could hardly hear her voice. "Yes, it is. Let's go, Erling."

We got into the carplane and slanted skyward. The boys crowded forward with me, staring ahead for the first glimpse of the landing field, not seeing the forests and meadows and shining rivers that slipped away beneath us.

Alanna sat behind me, looking down over the land. Her bright head was bent away so I couldn't see her face. I wondered what she was thinking, but somehow I didn't want to ask her.

III

The late great Clifford D. Simak was an inspiration to us all. He still is. I am more directly in his debt for the foregoing story. Very new in the business, as yet without an agent, I had sent it to every science fiction magazine and gotten it back with the comment that it was too long for its content. When I told him, he said in his quiet fashion, "The way to shorten a story is to write the ending." I did, and immediately placed it in *Astounding,* now *Analog,* the top market.

He gave me the advice at the Minneapolis Fantasy Society, a fan group that I had joined in 1947 when it reconstituted itself after a wartime hiatus. Meetings took place regularly, every two weeks if memory serves. Afterward several of us would go out to drink beer and talk till the bars closed, then often elsewhere to drink coffee and talk till the sun came up. Soon we began getting together in between these times. The activities of the club as such faded away until we were just a group of friends—interested in science fiction, yes, but also in everything else—with "MFS" for an informal name tag. Those friendships will endure until the last one of us who remembers is gone.

We didn't see Cliff often anymore. When we did, he was as warmly amiable as ever. But he didn't care for carousing, and he was a family man, with a responsible job on a newspaper and a home in the suburbs. Others of us, and some new people, grew ever more close-knit. Besides putting down huge quantities of beer, singing, squiring women around (the bachelors, when they could), throwing parties, playing softball in summer and touch football in fall, we talked. How we talked! Our conversations wouldn't have met the standards of an eighteenth-century *salon,* but I think they must have ranged more widely, from jests through all matters personal and public—many a slam-bam argument about history or politics—on to science and philosophy and back to cheerful nonsense, or story ideas.

Those last bounced especially between Gordon Dickson and me. While a few others in the MFS had sold a few pieces here and there, after Cliff withdrew Gordy and I were the only real writers. Mostly each of us did his own work, sometimes helped along by a suggestion, but occasionally we collaborated. The Hokas were born one day when we sat in my one-room apartment over a brew or two, a race of beings like big, energetic teddy bears with a limitless enthusiasm for human cultures. Gordy, having the more imaginative sense of humor, whipped out a first draft, then I did a rewrite, tying up loose ends and adding whatever bits of business occurred to me. We went on like that for a good many years, by telephone and mail after I moved away, and the series remains popular enough that I used to wonder aloud if the Hokas weren't what Gordy and I would be remembered for.

Now he too is gone. Everybody still alive who knew him misses him.

Of course, mainly our separate efforts weren't supposed to be funny. That includes the next story of mine in this collection. Again a bit of introduction is called for.

By 1950 I was no longer living hand to mouth but had enough reserves for travel. That year a friend and I took a cross-country drive to a conference in New York. Along the way we visited MIT to see the Bush differential analyzer, the world's most powerful computer. It was an awesome sight, tall stacks of blinking vacuum tubes reaching back through a cavernous chamber and a row of typewriters in front clicking away with no fingers on the keys. I didn't foresee how development would go, or how rapidly, until desktop sets rather than mainframes do almost all the work and I daily hold more mathematical capability in my hand than that giant had. But I'd read Norbert Wiener, and it wasn't hard to visualize a future pervaded by computers.

In 1951 I spent several months bicycling and youth hosteling abroad. Those were magnificent months, but unavoidably had their few small annoyances. One was the requirement to fill out a silly little form everywhere I stayed, with such information as my passport number, where I had last stopped, and where I was going next—a form that would only molder in local police archives. No one ever actually looked at the passport. We've since been afflicted with similar things over here, but America was more innocent then. Occasionally, somewhat childishly, I let off steam by registering as Sam Hall, the subject of a rowdy old ballad we often sang in the MFS.

Returning home, I found Senator Joseph McCarthy embarked on his infamous career as a self-styled hunter of subversives. The time that followed was not in fact the reign of terror of intellectual folklore. Nevertheless this demagogue did do great harm to a number of individuals and careers, both directly and by the atmosphere he generated. (And, by thus giving anti-Communism a bad name, he so effectively helped screen the truth about our mortal enemies and damp the will to resist them that some people have seriously wondered if he wasn't on their side.)

Once more, a number of elements came together and I found myself with a story I very much wanted to tell. Many things in it are now long since obsolete, most conspicuously the computer system itself, but there seems to be scant point in revision. I think it still has something important to say. At the very least, it forecast computer crime!

As said, just about all the self-respecting media and writers were in bitter and open opposition to McCarthy. That included us in science fiction. John

Campbell, editor of *Analog,* was himself a political conservative of the social Darwinist kind. Yet he bought "Sam Hall" and gave it the cover and the lead position when it appeared in 1953. The only thing he bowdlerized was the ballad, and that only because his publisher was prudish. I've restored the rough-hewn lyrics we used to sing above our beer.

SAM HALL

CLICK. BZZZ. WHRRR.

Citizen Blank Blank, Anytown, Somewhere, U.S.A., approaches the hotel desk. "Single with bath."

"Sorry, sir, our fuel ration doesn't permit individual baths. We can draw one for you; that will be twenty-five dollars extra."

"Oh, is that all? Okay."

Citizen Blank takes out his wallet, extracts his card, gives it to the registry machine, an automatic set of gestures. Aluminum jaws close on it, copper teeth feel for the magnetic encodings, electronic tongue tastes the life of Citizen Blank.

Place and date of birth. Parents. Race. Religion. Educational, military, and civilian service records. Marital status. Children. Occupations, from the beginning to the present. Affiliations. Physical measurements, fingerprints, retinals, blood type. Basic psychotype. Loyalty rating. Loyalty index as a function of time to moment of last test given. Click, click. Bzzz.

"Why are you here, sir?"

"Salesman. I expect to be in Cincinnati tomorrow night."

The clerk (32 yrs., married, two children; NB, confidential: Jewish. To be kept out of key occupations) punches buttons.

Click, click. The machine returns the card. Citizen Blank puts it back in his wallet.

"Front!"

The bellboy (19 yrs., unmarried; NB confidential: Catholic. To be kept out of key occupations) takes the guest's suitcase. The elevator creaks upstairs. The clerk resumes his reading. The article is entitled "Has Britain Betrayed Us?" Companion articles in the magazine include "New Indoctrination Program for the Armed Forces," "Labor Hunting on Mars," "I Was a Union Man for the Security Police," "More Plans for YOUR Future."

The machine talks to itself. Click, click. A bulb winks at its neighbor as if they shared a private joke. The total signal goes out over the wires.

Accompanied by a thousand others, it shoots down the last cable and into the sorter unit of Central Records. Click, click. Bzzz. Whrrr. Wink and glow. The distorted molecules in a particular spool show the pattern of Citizen Blank, and this is sent back. It enters the comparison unit, to which the incoming signal corresponding to him has also been shunted. The two are perfectly in phase; nothing wrong. Citizen Blank is staying in the town where, last night, he said he would, so he has not had to file a correction.

The new information is added to the record of Citizen Blank. The whole of his life returns to the memory bank. It is wiped from the scanner and comparison units, that these may be free for the next arrival.

The machine has swallowed and digested another day. It is content.

Thornberg entered his office at the usual time. His secretary glanced up to say "Good morning," and looked closer. She had been with him for enough years to read the nuances in his carefully controlled face. "Anything wrong, chief?"

"No." He spoke harshly, which was also peculiar. "No, nothing wrong. I feel a bit under the weather, maybe."

"Oh." The secretary nodded. You learned discretion in the government. "Well, I hope you get better soon."

"Thanks. It's nothing." Thornberg limped over to his desk, sat down, and took out a pack of cigarettes. He held one for a moment in nicotine-yellowed fingers before lighting it, and there was an emptiness in his eyes. Then he puffed ferociously and turned to his mail. As chief technician of Central Records, he received a generous tobacco ration and used it all.

The office was a windowless cubicle, furnished in gaunt orderliness, its only decorations pictures of his son and his late wife. Thornberg seemed too big for the space. He was tall and lean, with thin straight features and neatly brushed graying hair. He wore a plain version of the Security uniform, insignia of Technical Division and major's rank but none of the ribbons to which he was entitled. The priesthood of Matilda the Machine were a pretty informal lot.

He chain-smoked his way through the mail. Most was related to the change-over. "Come on, June," he said. Recording and later transcription sufficed for routine stuff, but best that his secretary take notes as well while he dictated anything unusual. "Let's get this out of the way fast. I've got work to do."

He held a letter before him. "To Senator E. W. Harmison, S.O.B., New Washington. Dear Sir: In re your communication of the 14th inst., requesting my personal opinion of the new ID system, may I say that it is not a technician's business to express opinions. The directive that every citizen shall have a single number for his records—birth certificate, education, rations, taxes, wages, transactions, public service, family, travel, etc.—has obvious long-range advantages, but naturally entails a good deal of work both in reconversion and interim data control. The president having decided that the gain justifies our present difficulties, the duty of citizens is to conform, not complain. Yours, and so forth." He let a cold smile flicker. "There, that'll fix him! I don't know what use Congress is anyway, except to plague honest bureaucrats."

Privately, June decided to modify the letter. Maybe a senator was only a rubber stamp, but you couldn't brush him off that curtly. Part of a secretary's job is to keep the boss out of trouble.

"Okay, let's get to the next," said Thornberg. "To Colonel M. R. Hubert, Director of Liaison Division, Central Records Agency, Security Police, etc. Dear Sir: In re your memorandum of the 14th inst., requiring a definite date for completion of the ID conversion, may I respectfully state that it is impossible for me honestly to set one. You realize we must develop a memory-modification unit which will make the changeover in our records without our having to take out and alter each of three hundred million spools. You realize too that we cannot predict the exact time needed to complete such a project. However, research is progressing satisfactorily (refer him to my last report, will you?), and I can confidently say that conversion will be finished and all citizens notified of their numbers within three months at the latest. Respectfully, and so on. Put that in a nice form, June."

She nodded. Thornberg continued through his mail, throwing most into a basket for her to answer alone. When he was done he yawned and lit a fresh cigarette. "Praise Allah that's over. Now I can get down to the lab."

"You have afternoon appointments," she reminded him.

"I'll be back after lunch. See you." He got up and went out of the office.

Down the escalator to a still lower sublevel, walking along a corridor, he returned the salutes of passing subordinates automatically. His expression did not bespeak anything; perhaps the stiff swinging of his arms did.

Jimmy, he thought. *Jimmy, boy.*

At the guard chamber, he presented hand and eye to the scanners. Finger and retinal patterns were his pass. No alarm sounded. The door opened for him and he walked into the temple of Matilda.

She squatted huge, tier upon tier of control panels, meters, indicator lights to the lofty ceiling. The spectacle always suggested to Thornberg an Aztec pyramid, whose gods winked red eyes at the acolytes and suppliants creeping about base and flanks. But they got their sacrifices elsewhere.

For a moment Thornberg stood and watched. He smiled again, a tired smile that creased his face on the left side only. A recollection touched him, book-legged stuff from the forties and fifties of the last century which he had read: French, German, British, Italian. The intellectuals had been fretful about the Americanization of Europe, the crumbling of old culture before the mechanized barbarism of soft drinks, hard sells, enormous chrome-plated automobiles (dollar grins, the Danes had called them), chewing gum, plastics. . . . None of them had protested the simultaneous Europeanization of America: bloated government, unlimited armament, official nosiness, censors, secret police, chauvinism. . . . Well, for a while there had been objectors, but first their own excesses and sillinesses discredited them, then later. . . .

Oh, well.

But Jimmy, lad, where are you now, what are they doing to you?

Thornberg sought a bench where his top engineer, Rodney, was testing a unit. "How're you coming along?" he asked.

"Pretty good, chief." Rodney didn't bother to salute. Thornberg had, in fact, forbidden it in the labs as a waste of time. "A few bugs yet, but we're chasing them out."

The project was, essentially, to develop a gimmick that would change numbers without altering anything else—not too easy a task, since the memory banks depended on individual magnetic domains. "Okay," said Thornberg. "Look, I want to run a few checks myself, out of the main coordinator. The program they've written for Section Thirteen during the conversion doesn't quite satisfy me."

"Want an assistant?"

"No, thanks. I just want not to be bothered."

Thornberg resumed his way across the floor. Hardness resounded dully under his shoes. The main coordinator was in a special armored booth nestled against the great pyramid. He must go through a second scan before the door admitted him. Not many were allowed in here. The complete archives of the nation were too valuable to risk.

Thornberg's loyalty rating was AAB-2—not absolutely perfect, but the best available among men and women of his professional caliber. His last drugged checkup had revealed certain doubts and reservations about government policy, but there was no question of disobedience. *Prima facie,* he was certainly bound to be loyal. He had served with distinction in the war against Brazil, losing a leg in action; his wife had been killed in the abortive Chinese rocket raids ten years ago; his son was a rising young Space Guard officer on Venus. He had read and listened to illegal stuff, blacklisted books, underground and foreign propaganda—but then, every intellectual dabbled with that; it was not a serious offense if your record was otherwise good and if you laughed off what the things said.

He sat for a moment regarding the board inside the booth. Its complexity would have baffled most engineers, but he had been with Matilda so long that he didn't even need the reference tables.

Well . . .

It took nerve, this. A hypnoquiz was sure to reveal what he was about to do. But such raids were, necessarily, in a random pattern. He wouldn't likely be called up again for years, especially given his rating. By the time he was found out, Jack should have risen far enough in the guard ranks to be safe.

In the privacy of the booth Thornberg permitted himself a harsh grin. "This," he murmured to the machine, "will hurt me worse than it does you."

He began punching buttons.

Here were circuits which could alter the records, take out an entire spool and write whatever was desired in the molecules. Thornberg had done the job a few times for high officials. Now he was doing it for himself.

Jimmy Obrenowicz, son of his second cousin, had been hustled off at night by Security Police on suspicion of treason. The file showed what no private citizen was supposed to know: the prisoner was in Camp Fieldstone. Those who returned from there, not a big percentage, were very quiet, and said absolutely nothing about their experiences. Sometimes they were incapable of speech.

The chief of the Technical Division, Central Records, had damn well better not have a relative in Fieldstone. Thornberg toiled at the screens and buttons for an hour, erasing, changing. The job was tough; he had to go back several generations, altering lines of descent. But when he was through, James Obrenowicz had no kinship whatsoever to the Thornbergs.

And I thought the world of that boy. Well, I'm not doing this for me, Jimmy. It's for Jack. When the cops pull your file, later today no doubt, I can't let them find you're related to Captain Thornberg on Venus and a friend of his father.

He slapped the switch that returned the spool to the memory banks. *With this act do I disown thee.*

After that he sat for a while, relishing the quiet of the booth and the clean impersonality of the instruments. He didn't even want to smoke. Presently, though, he began to think.

So now they were going to give every citizen a number, one number for everything. Already they discussed tattooing it on. Thornberg foresaw popular slang referring to the numbers as "brands" and Security cracking down on those who used the term. Disloyal language.

Well, the underground was dangerous. It was supported by foreign countries who didn't like an American-dominated world—at least, not one dominated by today's kind of America, though once "U.S.A." had meant "hope."

The rebels were said to have their own base out in space somewhere and to have honeycombed the country with their agents. That could well be. Their propaganda was subtle: we don't want to overthrow the nation; we simply want to restore the Bill of Rights. It could attract a lot of unstable souls. But Security's spy hunt was bound to drag in any number of citizens who had never meditated treason. Like Jimmy—or had Jimmy been an undergrounder after all? You never knew. Nobody ever told you.

There was a sour taste in Thornberg's mouth. He grimaced. A line of a song came back to him. *"I hate you one and all."* How had it gone? They used to sing it in his college days. Something about a very bitter character who'd committed a murder.

Oh, yes. "Sam Hall." How did it go, now? You needed a gravelly bass to sing it properly.

> Oh, my name it is Sam Hall, it is Sam Hall.
> Yes, my name is Sam Hall, it is Sam Hall.
> Oh, my name it is Sam Hall,
> And I hate you one and all,
> Yes, I hate you one and all, God damn your eyes.

That was it. And Sam Hall was about to swing for murder. Thornberg remembered now. He felt like Sam Hall himself. He looked at the machine and wondered how many Sam Halls were in it.

Idly, postponing his return to work, he punched for the data-name, Samuel Hall, no further specifications. The machine mumbled. Presently it spewed out a stack of papers, microprinted on the spot from the memory banks. Complete dossier on every Sam Hall, living and dead, from the time the records began to be kept. To hell with it. Thornberg chucked the sheets down the incinerator slot.

"Oh, I killed a man, they say, so they say—"

The impulse was blinding in its savagery. They were dealing with Jimmy at this moment, probably pounding him over the kidneys, and he, Thornberg, sat here waiting for the cops to requisition Jimmy's file, and there was nothing he could do. His hands were empty.

By God, he thought, *I'll give them Sam Hall!*

His fingers began to race; he lost his nausea in the intricate technical problem. Slipping a fake spool into Matilda wasn't easy. You couldn't duplicate numbers, and every citizen had a lot of them. You had to account for each day of his life.

Well, some of that could be simplified. The machine had only existed for twenty-five years; before then, records had been kept in a dozen different offices. Let's make Sam Hall a resident of New York, his dossier there lost in the bombing thirty years ago. Such of his papers as were in New Washington had also been lost, in the Chinese attack. That meant he simply reported as much detail as he could remember, which needn't be a lot.

Let's see. "Sam Hall" was an English song, so Sam Hall should be British himself. Came over with his parents, oh, thirty-eight years ago, when he was three, and got naturalized with them; that was before the total ban on immigration. Grew up on New York's Lower East Side, a tough kid, a slum kid. School records lost in the bombing, but he claimed to have gone through the tenth grade. No living relatives. No family. No definite occupation, just a series of unskilled jobs. Loyalty rating BBA-O, which meant that purely routine questions showed him to have no political opinions that mattered.

Too colorless. Give him some violence in his background. Thornberg punched for information on New York police stations and civilian-police officers destroyed in the last raids. He used them as the source of records that Sam Hall had been continually in trouble—drunkenness, disorderly conduct, brawls, a suspicion of holdups and burglary, but not strong enough to warrant calling in Security's hypnotechnicians for quizzing him.

Hmm. Better make him 4-F, no military service. Reason? Well, a slight drug addiction; men weren't so badly needed nowadays that hopheads had to be cured. Neo-coke didn't impair the faculties too much. Indeed, the addict was abnormally fast and strong under the influence, though he suffered a tough reaction afterwards.

Then he would have had to put in an additional term of civilian service. Let's see. He spent his four years as a common laborer on the Colorado Dam project. In such a mess of men, who would remember him? At any rate, it would be hard finding somebody who did.

Now to fill in. Thornberg called on a number of automatic devices to help him. He must account for every day in twenty-five years; but of course the majority would show no change of circumstances. Thornberg punched for cheap hotels, the kind which didn't bother keeping records of their own after the data went to Matilda. Who could remember a shabby individual patron? For Sam Hall's current address he chose the Triton, a glorified flophouse on the East Side not far from the craters. At present his man was unemployed, putatively living off savings, likelier off odd jobs and petty crime. Oh, blast! Income tax returns. Thornberg could be sketchy in creating those, however. The poor weren't expected to be meticulous, nor were they audited annually like the middle class and the rich.

Hmm . . . physical ID. Make him of average height, stocky, black-haired and black-eyed, a bent nose, a scar on his forehead—tough-looking, though not enough to be unusually memorable. Thornberg entered the precise measurements. Fingerprints and retinals being encoded, they were easy to fake; he wrote a censor into his ongoing program, lest he duplicate somebody else's by chance.

Finally he leaned back and sighed. The record was still shot full of holes, but he could plug those at his leisure. The main job was done—a couple of hours' hard work, utterly pointless, except that he had blown off steam. He felt a lot better.

He glanced at his watch. *Time to get back on the job, son.* For a rebellious moment he wished no one had ever invented clocks. They had made possible the science he loved, but they had then proceeded to mechanize man. Oh, well, too late now. He left the booth. The door closed itself behind him.

About a month later, Sam Hall committed his first murder.

The night before, Thornberg had been at home. His rank entitled him to good housing in spite of his living alone: two rooms and bath on the ninety-eighth floor of a unit in town not far from the camouflaged entrance to Matilda's underground domain. The fact that he was in Security, even if he didn't belong to the man-hunting branch, got him so much deference that he often felt lonely. The superintendent had offered him his daughter once—"Only twenty-three, sir, just released by a gentleman of marshal's rank, and looking for a nice patron, sir." Thornberg had refused, trying not to be prissy about it. *Autres temps, autres moeurs*—but still, she wouldn't have had any choice about getting client status, the first time anyway. And Thornberg's marriage had been a long and happy one.

He had been looking through his bookshelves for something to read. The Literary Bureau was trumpeting Whitman as an early example of Americanism, but though Thornberg had always liked the poet, his hands strayed perversely to a dog-eared volume of Marlowe. Was that escapism? The L.B. was very down on escapism. These were tough times. It wasn't easy to belong to the nation which was enforcing peace on a sullen world. You must be realistic and energetic and all the rest, no doubt.

The phone buzzed. He clicked on the receiver. Martha Obrenowicz's plain plump face showed in the screen; her gray hair was wild and her voice a harsh croak.

"Uh—hello," he said uneasily. He hadn't called her since the news of her son's arrest. "How are you?"

"Jimmy is dead," she told him.

He stood for a long while. His skull felt hollow.

"I got word today that he died in camp," said Martha. "I thought you'd want to know."

Thornberg shook his head, back and forth, quite slowly. "That isn't news I ever wanted, Martha," he said.

"It isn't *right!*" she shrieked. "Jimmy wasn't a traitor. I knew my son. Who ought to know him better? He had some friends I was kind of doubtful of, but Jimmy, he wouldn't ever—"

Something cold formed in Thornberg's breast. You never knew when calls were being tapped.

"I'm sorry, Martha," he said without tone. "But the police are careful about these things. They wouldn't act till they were sure. Justice is in our traditions."

She regarded him for a long time. Her eyes held a hard glitter. "You too," she said at last.

"Be careful, Martha," he warned her. "I know this is a blow to you, but don't say anything you might regret later. After all, Jimmy may have died accidentally. Those things happen."

"I—forgot," she said jerkily. "You . . . are in Security . . . yourself."

"Be calm," he said. "Think of it as a sacrifice for the national interest."

She switched off on him. He knew she wouldn't call him again. And he couldn't safely see her.

"Good-bye, Martha," he said aloud. It was like a stranger speaking.

He turned back to the bookshelf. *Not for me,* he told himself. *For Jack.* He touched the binding of *Leaves of Grass. Oh, Whitman, old rebel,* he thought, a curious dry laughter in him, *are they calling you Whirling Walt now?*

That night he took an extra sleeping pill. His head still felt fuzzy when he reported for work, and after a while he gave up trying to answer the mail and went down to the lab.

While he was engaged with Rodney, and making a poor job of understanding the technical problem under discussion, his eyes strayed to Matilda. Suddenly he realized what he needed for a cathartic. He broke off as soon as possible and went into the coordinator booth.

For a moment he paused at the keyboard. The day-by-day creation of Sam Hall had been an odd experience. He, quiet and introverted, had shaped a rowdy life and painted a rugged personality. Sam Hall was more real to him than many of his associates. *Well, I'm a schizoid type myself. Maybe I should have been a writer.* No, that would have meant too many restrictions, too much fear of offending the censor. He had done exactly as he pleased with Sam Hall.

He drew a breath and punched for unsolved murders of Security officers, New York City area, during the past month. They were surprisingly common.

Could dissatisfaction be more general than the government admitted? But when the bulk of a nation harbors thoughts labeled treasonous, does the label still apply?

He found what he wanted. Sergeant Brady had incautiously entered the Crater district after dark on the twenty-seventh on a routine checkup mission; he had worn the black uniform, presumably to give himself the full weight of authority. The next morning he had been found in an alley, his skull shattered.

> Oh, I killed a man, they say, so they say.
> Yes, I killed a man, they say, so they say.
> I beat him on the head,
> And I left him there for dead,
> Yes, I left him there for dead, God damn his eyes.

Newspapers had no doubt deplored this brutality perpetrated by the treacherous agent of enemy powers. (*"Oh, the parson, he did come, he did come."*) A number of suspects had been rounded up and given a stiff quizzing. (*"And the sheriff, he came too, he came too."*) Nothing was proven as yet, though a Joe Nikolsky (fifth generation American, mechanic, married, four children, underground pamphlets found in his room) had been arrested yesterday on suspicion.

Thornberg sighed. He knew enough of Security methods to be sure they would get somebody for such a killing. They couldn't allow their reputation for infallibility to be smirched by a lack of conclusive evidence. Maybe Nikolsky had done the crime—he couldn't *prove* he had simply been out for a walk that evening—and maybe he hadn't. But, hell's fire, why not give him a break? He had four kids. With such a black mark, their mother would find work only in a recreation house.

Thornberg scratched his head. This had to be done carefully. Let's see. Brady's body would have been cremated by now, but of course there had been a thorough study first. Thornberg withdrew the dead man's file from the machine and microprinted a replica of the evidence—zero. Erasing that, he entered the statement that a blurred thumbprint had been found on the victim's collar and referred to ID labs for reconstruction. In the ID file he inserted the report of such a job, finished only yesterday due to a great press of work. (Plausible. They were busy lately on material sent from Mars, seized in a raid on a rebel meeting place.) The probable pattern of the whorls was—and here he inserted Sam Hall's right thumb.

He returned the spools and leaned back in his chair. It was risky; if anyone thought to query the ID lab, he was in trouble. But that was unlikely. The chances were that New York would accept the findings with a routine acknowledgement which some clerk at the lab would file without studying. The more obvious dangers were not too great either: a busy police force would not stop to ask if any of their fingerprint men had actually developed that smudge; and as for hypnoquizzing showing Nikolsky really was the murderer, well, then the print would be assumed that of a passerby who had found the body and not reported it.

So now Sam Hall had killed a Security officer—grabbed him by the neck and smashed his brainpan with a weighted club. Thornberg felt considerably happier.

New York Security shot a request to Central Records for any new material on the Brady case. An automaton compared the codes and saw that fresh information had been added. The message flashed back, plus the dossier on Sam Hall and two others—for the reconstruction could not be absolutely accurate.

The two were safe, as it turned out. Both had alibis. The squad that stormed into the Triton Hotel and demanded Sam Hall met blank stares. No such person was registered. No one of that description was known there. A thorough quizzing corroborated this. Then Sam Hall had managed to fake an address. He could have done that easily by punching the buttons on the hotel register when nobody was looking. Sam Hall could be anywhere!

Joe Nikolsky, having been hypnoed and found harmless, was released. The fine for possessing subversive literature would put him in debt for the next few years—he had no influential friends to get it suspended—but he'd be all right if he watched his step. Security sent out an alarm for Sam Hall.

Thornberg derived a sardonic amusement from watching the progress of the hunt as it came to Matilda. No man with that ID card had bought tickets on any public transportation. That proved nothing. Of the hundreds who vanished every year, some at least must have been murdered for their cards, and their bodies disposed of. Matilda was set to give the alarm when the ID of a disappeared person showed up somewhere. Thornberg faked a few such reports, just to give the police something to do.

He slept more poorly each night, and his work suffered. Once he met Martha Obrenowicz on the street—passed by hastily without greeting her—and couldn't sleep at all, even after maximum permissible drugging.

The new ID system was completed. Machines sent notices to every citizen, with orders to have their numbers tatooed on the right shoulder blade within six weeks. As each center reported that such-and-such a person had had the job done, Matilda changed the record appropriately. Sam Hall, AX-428-399-

075, did not report for his tattoo. Thornberg chuckled at the AX symbol.

Then the telecasts flashed a story that made the nation exclaim. Bandits had held up the First National Bank in Americatown, Idaho (formerly Moscow), collecting a good five million dollars in assorted bills. From their discipline and equipment it was assumed that they were rebel agents, possibly having come in a spaceship from their unknown interplanetary base, and that the raid was intended to help finance their nefarious activities. Security was cooperating with the armed forces to track down the evildoers, and arrests were expected hourly, etc., etc.

Thornberg went to Matilda for a complete account. It had been a bold job. The robbers had apparently worn plastic face masks and light body armor under ordinary clothes. In the scuffle of the getaway one man's mask had slipped aside—only for a moment, but a clerk who saw had, under hypnosis, given a fairly good description. A brown-haired, heavyset fellow, Roman nose, thin lips, toothbrush mustache.

Thornberg hesitated. A joke was a joke; and helping poor Nikolsky was perhaps morally defensible; but aiding and abetting a felony which was in all likelihood an act of treason—

He grinned to himself, with scant humor. It was too much fun playing God. Swiftly he changed the record. The crook had been of medium height, dark, scar-faced, broken-nosed. . . . He sat for a while wondering how sane he was. How sane anybody was.

Security Central requisitioned complete data on the incident and any correlations the logic units could make. The description they got could have fitted many men, but geography left just a single possibility. *Sam Hall.*

The hounds bayed forth. That night Thornberg slept well.

Dear Dad,

Sorry I haven't written before. We've been too busy here. I myself was on patrol duty in the Austin Highlands. The idea was, if we can take advantage of reduced atmospheric pressure at that altitude to construct a military spaceport, a foreign country might sneak in and do the same, probably for the benefit of our domestic insurrectionists. I'm glad to say we found nothing. But it was grim going for us. Frankly, everything here is. Sometimes I wonder if I'll ever see the sun again. And lakes and forests—life; who wrote that line about the green hills of Earth? My mind feels rusty as well. We don't get much to read, and I don't care for the taped shows. Not that I'm complaining, of course. This is a necessary job.

We'd hardly gotten back when we were bundled into bathyplanes and ferried to the lowlands. I'd never been there before—thought Venus was awful, but you have to get down in that red-black ocean of hell-hot air, way down, before you know what "awful" means. Then we transferred straight to mobile sealtanks and went into action. The convicts in the new thorium mine were refusing to work on account of conditions and casualties. We needed guns to bring them to reason. Dad, I hated that. I actually felt sorry for the poor devils, I don't mind admitting it. Rocks and hammers and sluice hoses against machine guns! And conditions are *rugged. They* DELETED BY CENSOR *someone has to do that job too, and if no one will volunteer, for any kind of pay, they have to assign convicts. It's for the state.*

Otherwise nothing new. Life is pretty monotonous. Don't believe the adventure stories. Adventure is weeks of boredom punctuated by moments of being scared gutless. Sorry to be so brief, but I want to get this on the outbound rocket. Won't be another for a couple of months. Everything well, really. I hope the same for you and live for the day we'll meet again. Thanks a million for the cookies—you know you can't afford to pay the freight, you old spendthrift! Martha baked them, didn't she? I recognized the Obrenowicz touch. Say hello to her and Jim for me. And most of all, my kindest thoughts go to you.

As ever,

Jack

The telecasts carried "Wanted" messages for Sam Hall. No photographs of him were available, but an artist could draw an accurate likeness from Matilda's description, and his truculent face began to adorn public places. Not long thereafter, the Security offices in Denver were wrecked by a grenade tossed from a speeding car that vanished into traffic. A witness said he had glimpsed the thrower, and the fragmentary picture given under hypnosis was not unlike Sam Hall's. Thornberg doctored the record a bit to make it still more similar. The tampering was risky; if Security ever became suspicious, they could easily check back with their witnesses. But the chance was not too big to take, for a scientifically quizzed man told everything germane to the subject which his memory, conscious, subconscious, and cellular, held. There was never any reason to repeat such an interrogation.

Thornberg often tried to analyze his motives. Plainly, he disliked the government. He must have contained that hate all his life, carefully suppressed from awareness, and recently it had been forced into his conscious mind. Not even his subconscious could have formulated it earlier, or he would have been caught by the loyalty probes. The hate derived from a lifetime of doubts (Had there been any real reason to fight Brazil, other than to obtain those bases and mineral concessions? Had the Chinese attack perhaps been provoked—or even faked, for their government denied it?) and the million petty frustrations of the garrison state. Still—the strength of his feelings! The violence!

By creating Sam Hall he had struck back. But that was an ineffectual blow, a timid gesture. Most likely his basic motive was simply to find a halfway safe release. In Sam Hall he lived vicariously the things that the beast within him wanted to do. Several times he had intended to discontinue his sabotage, but it was like a drug: Sam Hall was becoming necessary to his own stability.

The thought was alarming. He ought to see a psychiatrist—but no, the doctor would be bound to report his tale, he would go to camp, and Jack, if not exactly ruined, would be under a cloud for the rest of his life. Thornberg had no desire to go to camp, anyway. His existence had compensations, interesting work, a few good friends, art and music and literature, decent wine, sunsets and mountains, memories. He had started this game on impulse, and now he was simply too late to stop it.

For Sam Hall had been promoted to Public Enemy Number One.

Winter came, and the slopes of the Rockies under which Matilda lay were white beneath a cold greenish sky. Air traffic around the nearby town was lost in that hugeness: brief hurtling meteors against infinity, ground traffic that could not be seen from the Records entrance. Thornberg took the special tubeway to work every morning, but he often walked the ten kilometers back, and his Sundays were usually spent in long hikes over slippery trails. That was a foolish thing to do alone in winter, except that he felt reckless.

He was in his office shortly before Christmas when the intercom said: "Major Sorensen to see you, sir. From Investigation."

Thornberg felt his stomach tie itself into a cold knot. "All right," he answered in a voice whose levelness surprised him. "Cancel any other appointments." Security Investigation took AAA priority.

Sorensen strode in with a clack of bootheels. He was a big blond man, heavy-shouldered, face expressionless, eyes pale and remote as the winter sky. His black uniform fitted him like a skin; against it, the lightning badge of his service glittered frosty. He halted before the desk. Thornberg rose to give him an awkward salute.

"Please sit down, Major Sorensen. What can I do for you?"

"Thanks." The agent's tone crackled. He lowered his bulk into a chair and let his gaze drill Thornberg. "I've come about the Sam Hall case."

"Oh, the rebel?" Thornberg's flesh prickled. He could barely meet those eyes.

"How do you know he's a rebel?" Sorensen demanded. "That's never been stated officially."

"Why—I assumed—bank raid—attacks on personnel in your service—"

Sorensen slightly inclined his cropped head. When he spoke again, he sounded relaxed, almost casual. "Tell me, Major Thornberg, have you followed the Hall developments in detail?"

Thornberg hesitated. He was not supposed to do so unless ordered; he only kept the machine running. He remembered a principle from reading and, yes, furtively cynical conversation. "When suspected of a major sin, admit minor ones frankly. That may satisfy them."

"As a matter of fact, I have," he said. "I know it's against regs, but I was interested and—well, I couldn't see any harm in it. I've not discussed it with anybody, of course."

"No matter." Sorensen waved a muscular hand. "If you hadn't, I'd have ordered you to. I want your opinion on this."

"Why—I'm not a detective—"

"You know more about Records, though, than any other person. I'll be frank with you—under the rose, naturally." Sorensen seemed almost friendly now. *Was it a trick to put his prey off guard?* "You see, there are some puzzling features about this case."

Thornberg kept silent. He wondered if Sorensen could hear the thudding of his heart.

"Sam Hall is a shadow," said the agent. "The most careful checkups eliminate any chance of his being identical with anyone else of that name. In fact, we've learned that the name occurs in a violent old drinking song. Is this coincidence, or did the song suggest crime to Sam Hall, or did he by some incredible process get that alias into his record instead of his real name? Whatever the answer there, we know that he's ostensibly without military training, yet he's pulled off some beautiful pieces of precision attack. His IQ is only 110, but he evades our traps. He has no politics, yet he turns on Security without warning. We have not been able to find a single individual who remembers him—not one, and believe me, we have been thorough. Oh, there are a few subconscious memories which might be of him, but probably aren't; and so aggressive a personality should be remembered consciously. No undergrounder or foreign operative we've caught had any knowledge of him, which defies probability. The whole business seems impossible."

Thornberg licked his lips. Sorensen, the hunter of men, must know he was frightened; but would he assume that to be the normal nervousness of a man in the presence of a Security officer?

Sorensen's face broke into a hard smile. "As Sherlock Holmes remarked," he said, "when you have eliminated every other hypothesis, then the one which remains, however improbable, must be right."

Despite himself, Thornberg was jolted. Sorensen hadn't struck him as a reader.

"Well," he asked slowly, "what is your remaining hypothesis?"

His visitor watched him for a long time, it seemed forever, before replying. "The underground is more powerful and widespread than people realize. They've had seventy years to prepare, and many good brains in their ranks. They carry on scientific research of their own. It's top secret, but we know they have perfected a type of weapon we cannot duplicate yet. It seems to be a hand gun throwing bolts of energy—a blaster, you might call it—of immense power. Sooner or later they're going to wage open war against the government.

"Now, could they have done something comparable in psychology? Could they have found a way to erase or cover up memories selectively, even on the cellular level? Could they know how to fool a personality tester, how to disguise the mind itself? If so, we may have any number of Sam Halls in our midst, undetectable until the moment comes for them to strike."

Thornberg felt almost boneless. He couldn't help gasping his relief, and hoped Sorensen would take it for a sign of alarm.

"The possibility is frightening, no?" The blond man laughed metallically. "You can imagine what is being felt in high official circles. We've put all the psychological researchers we could get to work on the problem—bah! Fools! They go by the book; they're afraid to be original even when the state tells them to.

"This may just be a wild fancy, of course. I hope it is. But we have to *know*. That's why I approached you personally, instead of sending the usual requisition. I want you to make a search of the records—everything pertaining to the subject, every man, every discovery, every hypothesis. You have a broad technical background and, from your psychorecord, an unusual amount of creative imagination. I want you to do what you can to correlate your data. Co-opt whoever you need. Submit to my office a report on the possibility—or should I say probability—of this notion; and if you find any likelihood of its being true, sketch out a research program which will enable us to duplicate the results and counteract them."

Thornberg fumbled for words. "I'll try," he said lamely. "I'll do my best."

"Good. It's for the state."

Sorensen had finished his official business, but he didn't go at once. "Rebel propaganda is subtle stuff," he said quietly, after a pause. "It's dangerous because it uses our own slogans, with a twisted meaning. Liberty, equality, justice, peace. Too many people can't appreciate that times have changed and the meanings of words have necessarily changed likewise."

"I suppose not," said Thornberg. He added the lie: "I never thought much about that kind of question."

"You should," said Sorensen. "Study your history. When we lost World War III we had to militarize to win World War IV, and after that mount guard on the whole human race. The people demanded it at the time."

The people, thought Thornberg, *never appreciated freedom till they'd lost it. They were always willing to sell their birthright. Or was it merely that, being untrained in thinking, they couldn't see through demagoguery, couldn't visualize the ultimate consequences of their wishes?* He was vaguely shocked at the thought; wasn't he able to control his mind any longer?

"The rebels," said Sorensen, "claim that conditions have changed, that militarization is no longer necessary—if it ever was—and that America would be safe in a union of free countries. Devilishly clever propaganda, Major Thornberg. Watch out for it."

He got up and took his leave. Thornberg sat for a long time staring at the door. Sorensen's last words had been odd, to say the least. Were they a hint—or a bait?

The next day Matilda received a news item which was carefully edited for the public channels. An insurrectionist force had landed aircraft in the stockade of Camp Forbes, in Utah, gunned down the guards, and taken away the prisoners. The institution's doctor had been spared, and related that the leader of the raid, a stocky man in a mask, had said to him: "Tell your friends I'll call again. My name is Sam Hall."

Space Guard ship blown up on Mesa Verde Field. On a fragment of metal someone has scrawled: "Compliments of Sam Hall."

Squad of Security Police, raiding a suspected underground hideout in Philadelphia, cut down by tommy-gun fire. Voice from a hidden bullhorn cries: "My name, it is Sam Hall!"

Matthew Williamson, chemist in Seattle, suspected of subversive connections, is gone when the arresting officers break into his home. A note left on his desk says: "Off to visit Sam Hall. Back for liberation. M.W."

Defense plant producing important robomb components near Miami is sabotaged by a planted bomb, after a phone warning gives the workers time to evacuate. The caller, who leaves the visio circuit off, styles himself Sam Hall.

Various similar places get similar warnings. These are fakes, but each costs a day's valuable work in the alarm and the search.

Scribbled on walls from New York to San Diego, from Duluth to El Paso: Sam Hall, Sam Hall, Sam Hall.

Obviously, thought Thornberg, the underground had seized on the invisible and invincible man of legend and turned him to their own purposes. Reports of him poured in from all over the country, hundreds every day—Sam Hall seen here, Sam Hall seen there. Ninety-nine percent could be dismissed as hoaxes, hallucinations, mistakes; it was another national craze, fruit of a jittery time, like the sixteenth- and seventeenth-century witch-hunts or the twentieth-century flying saucers. But Security and civilian police had to check on every one.

Thornberg planted a number of them himself.

Mostly, though, he was busy on his assignment. He could understand what it meant to the government. Life in the garrison state was inevitably founded on fear and mistrust, every man's eye on his neighbor; but at least psychotyping and hypnoquizzing had given a degree of surety. Now, that staff knocked out from under them—

His preliminary studies indicated that an invention such as Sorensen had hypothesized, while not impossible, was too far beyond the scope of contemporary science for the rebels to have perfected. Such research carried on nowadays would, from the standpoint of practicality if not of knowledge, be a waste of time and trained men.

He spent a good many sleepless hours and a month's cigarette ration before he could decide what to do. All right, he'd aided insurrection in a small way, and he shouldn't boggle at the next step. Still—nevertheless—did he want to?

Jack—his son had a career lined out for himself. He loved the big deeps beyond the sky as he would love a woman. If things changed, what then of Jack's career?

Well, what was it now? Stuck on a dreary planet as guardsman and executioner of homesick starvelings poisoned by radioactivity; never even seeing the sun. Come the day, Jack could surely wrangle a berth on a real spacer. They'd need bold men to explore beyond Saturn. Jack was too honest to make a good rebel, but Thornberg felt that after the initial shock he would welcome a new government.

But treason! Oaths!

When in the course of human events . . .

It was a small thing that decided Thornberg. He passed a shop downtown and noticed a group of the Youth Guard smashing the windows and spattering yellow paint over the goods, O Moses, Jesus, Mendelssohn, Hertz, and Einstein! Once he had chosen his path, a curious serenity possessed him. He stole a vial of prussic acid from a chemist friend and carried it in his pocket; and as for Jack, the boy would have to take his chances too.

The work was demanding and dangerous. He had to alter recorded facts which were available elsewhere, in books and journals and the minds of men. Nothing could be done about basic theory. But quantitative results could be juggled a little to set the overall picture subtly askew. He would co-opt carefully chosen experts, men whose psychotypes indicated they would take the easy course of relying on Matilda instead of checking original sources. And the correlation and integration of innumerable data, the empirical equations and extrapolations thereof, could be tampered with.

He turned his regular job over to Rodney and devoted himself entirely to the new one. He grew thin and testy; when Sorensen called, trying to hurry him, he snapped back: "Do you want speed or quality?" and wasn't too surprised at himself afterward. He got little sleep, but his mind seemed unnaturally clear.

Winter faded into spring while Thornberg and his experts labored and while the nation shook, psychically and physically, under the growing violence of Sam Hall. The report Thornberg submitted in May was so voluminous and detailed that he didn't think the government researchers would bother referring to any other source. Its conclusion: Yes, given a brilliant man applying Belloni matrices to cybernetic formulas and using some unknown kind of colloidal probe, a psychological masking technique was plausible.

The government yanked every man it could find into research. Thornberg knew it was only a matter of time before they realized they had been had. How much time, he couldn't say. But when they were sure . . .

> Now up the rope I go, up I go.
> Now up the rope I go, up I go.
> And the bastards down below,
> They say, "Sam, we told you so."
> They say, "Sam, we told you so," God damn their eyes.

REBELS ATTACK
SPACESHIPS LAND UNDER COVER OF RAINSTORM,
SEIZE POINTS NEAR N. DETROIT
FLAME WEAPONS USED AGAINST ARMY BY REBELS

"The infamous legions of the traitors have taken ground throughout the nation, but already our gallant forces have hurled them back. They have come out in early summer like toadstools, and will wither as fast—WHEEEEEE-OOOOOO!" Silence.

"All citizens will keep calm, remain loyal to their country, and stay at their usual tasks, until otherwise ordered. Civilians will report to their local defense officers. Military reservists will report immediately for active duty."

"Hello, Hawaii! Are you there? Come in, Hawaii! Calling Hawaii!"

"CQ, Mars GHQ calling . . . bzzz, wheeee . . . seized Syrtis Major Colony and . . . whoooo . . . help needed . . ."

The lunar rocket bases are assaulted and carried. The commander blows them up rather than surrender. A pinpoint flash on the moon's face, a new crater; what will they name it?

"So they've got Seattle, have they? Send a robomb flight. Scrub the place off the map. . . . Citizens? To hell with citizens! This is war!"

". . . in New York. Secretly drilled rebels emerged from the notorious Crater district and stormed . . ."

". . . assassins were shot down. The new president has already been sworn in and . . ."

BRITAIN, CANADA, AUSTRALIA REFUSE
ASSISTANCE TO GOV'T

". . . no, sir. The bombs reached Seattle all right. But they were stopped before they hit—some kind of energy gun. . . ."

"COMECO to army commanders in Florida and Georgia: Enemy action has made Florida and the keys temporarily untenable. Your units will withdraw as follows . . ."

"Today a rebel force engaging a military convoy in Donner Pass was annihilated by a well-placed tactical atomic bomb. Though our own men suffered losses on this account . . ."

"COMWECO to army commanders in California: the mutiny of units stationed around San Francisco poses a grave problem. . . ."

SP RAID REBEL HIDEOUT,
BAG FIVE OFFICERS

"Okay, so the enemy is about to capture Boston. We *can't* issue weapons to the citizens. They might turn them on us!"

SPACE GUARD UNITS EXPECTED
FROM VENUS

Jack, Jack, Jack!

It was strange, living in the midst of a war. Thornberg had never thought it would be like this. Drawn faces, furtive looks, chaos in the telecast news and the irregularly arriving papers, blackouts, civil defense drills, shortages, occasional panic when a rebel jet whistled overhead—but nothing else. No gunfire, no bombs, no more than the unreal combats you heard about. The only local casualty list were due to Security; people kept disappearing, and nobody spoke about them.

But then, why should the enemy bother with this unimportant mountain town? The self-styled Libertarian Army was grabbing key points of manufacture, transportation, communication, was engaging in pitched battles, sabotaging buildings and machines, assassinating officials. By its very purpose, it couldn't wage total war, couldn't annihilate the folk it wanted to free—an attitude historically rare among revolutionaries, Thornberg knew. Rumor said the defenders were less finicky.

Most citizens were passive. They always are. Probably no more than one-fourth of the population was ever in earshot of an engagement. City dwellers might see fire in the sky, hear crump and whistle and crash of artillery, scramble aside from soldiers and armored vehicles, cower in shelters when rockets arced overhead; but the action was outside of town. If matters came to street fighting, the rebels never pushed far in. They would either lay siege or they would rely on agents inside the town. Then a citizen might hear the crack of rifles and grenades, rattle of machine guns, sizzle of lasers, and see corpses. But the end was either a return of military government or the rebels marching in and setting up their own provisional councils. (They rarely met cheers and flowers. Nobody knew how the war would end. But they heard words whispered, and usually got good service.) As nearly as possible, the average American continued his average life.

Thornberg stayed on his personal rails. Matilda, the information nexus, was in such demand that users queued for their shared time. If the rebels ever learned where she was—

Or did they know?

He got few opportunities to conduct his private sabotages, but on that account planned each of them extra carefully. The Sam Hall reports were almost standardized in his mind—Sam Hall here, Sam Hall there, pulling off this or that incredible stunt. But what did one superman count for in these gigantic days? He needed something more.

Television and newspapers jubilantly announced that Venus had finally been contacted. Luna and Mars had fallen, but the Guard units on Venus had quickly smashed a few feeble uprisings. Mere survival there demanded quantities of powerful, sophisticated equipment, readily adaptable to military purposes. The troops would be returning at once, fully armed. Given present planetary configurations, the highest boost could not deliver them on Earth for a good six weeks. But then they might prove a decisive reinforcement.

"Looks like you may see your boy soon, chief," Rodney remarked.

"Yes," said Thornberg, "I may."

"Tough fighting." Rodney shook his head. "I'd sure as hell hate to be in it."

If Jack is killed by a rebel gun, when I have aided the rebels' cause . . .

Sam Hall, reflected Thornberg, had lived a hard life, all violence and enmity and suspicion. Even his wife hadn't trusted him.

> . . . And my Nellie dressed in blue,
> Says, "Your trifling days are through.
> Now I know that you'll be true, God damn your eyes."

Poor Sam Hall. No wonder he had killed a man.

Suspicion!

Thornberg stood for a moment while a tingle went through him. The police state was founded on suspicion. Nobody could trust anybody else. And with the new fear of psychomasking, and research on that project suspended during the crisis—

Steady, boy, steady. Can't rush into action. Have to plan very carefully.

Thornberg punched for the dossiers of key men in the administration, in the military, in Security. He did this in the presence of two assistants, for he thought that his own frequent sessions alone in the coordination booth were beginning to look funny.

"Top secret," he warned them, pleased with his cool manner. He was becoming a regular Machiavelli. "You'll be skinned alive if you mention it to anyone."

Rodney gave him a shrewd glance. "So they're not even sure of their top men now, are they?" he murmured.

"I've been told to make some checks," snapped Thornberg. "That's all you need to know."

He studied the files for many hours before coming to a decision. Secret observations were, of course, made of everyone from time to time. A cross check with Matilda showed that the cop who filed the last report on Lindahl had been killed the next day in a spontaneous and abortive uprising. The report was innocuous: Lindahl had stayed at home, studying various papers; he had been alone in the house except for a bodyguard in another room who had not seen him. And Lindahl was Undersecretary of Defense.

Thornberg changed the record. A masked man—stocky, black-haired—had come in and talked for three hours with Lindahl. They had spoken low, so that the cop's ears, outside the window, couldn't catch what was said. After the visitor left, Lindahl had retired. The cop went back in great excitement, made out his report, and gave it to the signalman, who had sent it on to Matilda.

Tough on the signalman, thought Thornberg. *They'll want to know why he didn't tell this to his chief in New Washington, if the observer was killed before doing so. He'll deny every such report, and they'll hypnoquiz him—but they don't trust that method anymore!*

His sympathy quickly faded. What counted was having the war over before Jack got home. He refiled the altered spool and did a little backtracking, shifting the last report of Sam Hall from Salt Lake City to Atlanta. More plausible. Then, as opportunity permitted, he worked on real men's records.

He must wait two haggard days before the next order came from Security for a check on Sam Hall. The scanners trod out their intricate measure, transistors awoke, in due course a cog turned. LINDAHL unrolled before the microprinter. Cross references ramified in all directions. Thornberg attached a query to the preliminary report: this looked interesting; did his superiors want more information?

They did!

Next day the telecast announced a shake-up in the Department of Defense. Nobody heard more about Lindahl.

And I, Thornberg reflected, *have grabbed a very large tiger by the tail. Now they'll have to check everybody. How does a solitary man keep ahead of the Security Police?*

Lindahl is a traitor. How did his chief ever let him get such a sensitive position? Secretary Hoheimer was a personal friend of Lindahl, too. Have Records check Hoheimer.

What's this? Hoheimer himself! Five years ago, yes, but even so—the dossier shows he lived in an apartment unit where *Sam Hall* was janitor! Grab Hoheimer! Who'll take his place? General Halliburton? That stupid old bastard? Well, at least his nose is clean. Can't trust those slick characters.

Hoheimer has a brother in Security, general's rank, good detection record.

A blind? Who knows? Slap the brother in jail, at least for the duration. Better check his staff. . . . Central Records shows that his chief field agent, Jones, has five days unaccounted for a year ago; he claimed Security secrecy at the time, but a double cross check shows it wasn't true. Shoot Jones! He has a nephew in the army, a captain. Pull that unit out of the firing line till we can study it man by man! We've had too many mutinies already.

Lindahl was also a close friend of Benson, in charge of the Tennessee Atomic Ordnance Works. Haul Benson in! Check every man connected with him! No trusting those scientists; they're always blabbing secrets.

The first Hoheimer's son is an industrialist, owns a petroleum-synthesis plant in Texas. Nab him! His wife is a sister of Leslie, head of the War Production Coordination Board. Get Leslie too. Sure, he's doing a good job, but he may be sending information to the enemy. Or he may just be waiting for the signal to sabotage the whole works. We can't trust *anybody,* I tell you!

What's this? Records relays an Intelligence report that the mayor of Tampa was in cahoots with the rebels. It's marked "Unreliable, Rumor"—but Tampa did surrender without a fight. The mayor's business partner is Gale, who has a cousin in the army, commanding a robomb base in New Mexico. Check both the Gales, Records. . . . So the cousin was absent four days without filing his whereabouts, was he? Military privilege or not, arrest him and find out where he was!

•Attention, Records, attention, Records, urgent. Brigadier John Harmsworth Gale, etc., etc., refused to divulge information required by Security Officers, claiming to have been at his base all the time. Can this be an error on your part?
•Records to Security Central, ref: etc., etc. No possibility of error exists except in information received.
•To Records, ref: etc., etc. Gale's story corroborated by three of his officers.
Put that whole damned base under arrest! Recheck those reports! Who sent them in, anyway?
•To Records, ref: etc., etc. On attempt to arrest entire personnel, Robomb Base 37-J fired on Security detachment and repulsed it. At last reports Gale was calling for rebel forces fifty miles off to assist him. Details will follow for the files as soon as possible.

So Gale was a traitor. Or was he driven by fear? Have Records find out who filed that information about him in the first place.
We can't trust anybody!

Thornberg was not much surprised when his door was kicked open and the Security squad entered. He had been expecting it for days, maybe weeks. A solitary man can't keep ahead of the game forever. No doubt accumulated inconsistencies had finally drawn suspicion his way; or, ironically, the chains of accusation he forged had by chance led to him; perhaps somebody here, like Rodney, had decided something was amiss and lodged a tip.

Were that last the case, he laid no blame. The tragedy of civil war was that it turned brother against brother. Millions of decent people were with the government because they had pledged themselves to be, or simply because they didn't believe in the alternative. Mostly, Thornberg felt tired.

He looked down the barrel of a revolver and up to the eyes of the blackcoat behind. They were equally empty of feeling. "I assume I'm under arrest?" he said tonelessly.

"On your feet," the leader snapped.

June could not hold back a whimper of pain. The man who held her was twisting her arm behind her back, obviously enjoying himself. "Don't do that," Thornberg said. "She's innocent. Had no idea what I was carrying out."

"On your feet, I told you." The leader thrust his gun closer.

"I suggest you leave me alone, too." Thornberg lifted his right hand, to show a ball he had taken from his desk when the squad arrived. "Do you see this? A thing I made against contingencies. Not a bomb *per se*—but a radio trigger. If my fingers relax, the rubber will expand and close a circuit. I believe such a device is called a dead-man switch."

The squad stiffened. Thornberg heard an oath. "Release the lady," he said.

"You surrender first!" said June's captor. He wrenched. She screamed.

"No," Thornberg said. "June, dear, I'm sorry. But have no fears. You see, I expected this visit, and made my preparations. The radio signaller won't touch off anything as melodramatic as a bomb. No, instead it will close a relay which will activate a certain program in Matilda—the Records computer, you know, the data machine. Every spool will be wiped. The government will have not a record left. Myself, I am prepared to die. But if you men let me complete that circuit, I imagine you'll wish there had been a bomb. Now do let go of the lady."

The blackcoat did, as if she had suddenly turned incandescent. She slumped sobbing to the floor.

"A bluff!" the leader shouted. Sweat made his face shiny.

"Do you wish to call it?" Thornberg made a smile. "By all means."

"You traitor—"

"I prefer 'patriot,' if you please. But be the semantics as they may, you must admit I was effective. The government has been turned end for end and upside down. The army is breaking apart, officers deserting right and left for fear they'll be arrested next, or defecting, or leading mutinies. Security is chasing its own tail around half a continent. Far more administrators are being murdered by their colleagues than the underground could possibly assassinate. The Libertarians take city after city without resistance. My guess is that they will occupy New Washington inside another week."

"Your doing!" Finger quivered on trigger.

"Oh, no. Spare my blushes. But I did make a contribution of some significance, yes. Unless you say Sam Hall did, which is fine by me."

"What . . . will . . . you do now?"

"That depends on you, my friend. Whether I am killed or only rendered unconscious, Matilda dies. You could have the technicians check out whether I'm telling the truth, and if I am, you could have them yank that program. However, at the first sign of any such move on your part, I will naturally let the ball go. Look in my mouth." He opened it briefly. "Yes, the conventional glass vial of prussic acid. I apologize for the cliché, but you will understand that I have no wish to share the fate that you people bring on yourselves."

Bafflement wrestled rage in the countenances before Thornberg. They weren't used to thinking, those men.

"Of course," he went on, "you have an alternative. At last reports, a Liberation unit was established less than two hundred kilometers from here. We could call and ask them to send a force, explaining the importance of this place. That would be to your advantage too. There is going to be a day of reckoning with you blackcoats. My influence could help you personally, however little you deserve to get off the hook."

The stared at each other. After a very long while, wherein the only sounds were June's diminishing sobs, unevenly drawn breaths among the police, and Thornberg's pulse rapid in his ears, the leader spat, "No! You lie!" He aimed his gun.

The man behind him drew and shot him in the head.

The result was ugly to see. As soon as he knew he was fully in charge, Thornberg did his best to comfort June.

"As a matter of fact," he told Sorensen, "I *was* bluffing. That was just a ball; the poison alone was real. Not that it made much difference at that stage, except to me."

"We'll need Matilda for a while yet," said Sorensen. "Want to stay on?"

"Sure, provided I can take a vacation when my son comes home."

"That shouldn't be long now. You'll be glad to hear we've finally contacted the Venus units of the Space Guard, on their way back. The commander agreed to stay out of fighting, on the grounds that his service's obligation is to the legitimate government and we'll need an election to determine what that is. Your boy will be safe."

Thornberg could find no words of response. Instead he remarked with hard-held casualness, "You know, I'm surprised to learn you were an undergrounder."

"We got a few into Security, who wrangled things so they gave each other clearances and loyalty checks." Sorensen grimaced. "That was the only part of it I enjoyed, though, till quite lately."

He leaned back in his chair, which creaked under his weight. In civilian clothes which nothing but an armband made into the uniform of a Libertarian officer, he did seem an altogether different man. Where his bulk had formerly crowded Thornberg's office, today his vitality irradiated it.

"Then Sam Hall came along," he said. "They had their suspicions at first in Security. My bosses were evil but not stupid. Well, I got myself assigned to the job of checking you out. Right away I guessed you harbored disruptive thoughts; so I gave you a clean bill of health. Afterward I cooked up that fantasy of the psychological mask and got several high-ranking men worried. When you followed my lead, I was sure you were on our side. Consequently, though the Libertarian command knew all along where Matilda was, of course they left her alone!"

"You must have joined them in person very recently."

"Yeah, the witch-hunt you started inside of Security was getting too close to me. Well worth a risk, though, to see those cockroaches busily stepping on each other."

Thornberg sat quiet awhile, then leaned over his desk. "I haven't enlisted under your banner yet," he said gravely. "I had to assume the Libertarian words about freedom were not mere rhetoric. But . . . you mentioned Matilda. You want me to continue in my work here. What are your plans for her?"

Sorensen turned equally serious. "I was waiting for you to ask that, Thorny. Look. Besides needing her to help us find some people we want rather badly, we are responsible for the sheer physical survival of the country. I'd feel easier too if we could take her apart this minute. But—"

"Yes?"

"But we've got to transcribe a lot of information first, strictly practical facts. *Then* we wipe everything else and ceremoniously dynamite this building. You're invited, no, urgently asked to sit on the board that decides the details—

in other words, we want you to help work yourself out of a job."

"Thank you," Thornberg whispered.

After a moment, in a sudden tide of happiness, he chuckled. "And that will be the end of Sam Hall," he said. "He'll go to whatever Valhalla there is for the great characters of fiction. I can see him squabbling with Sherlock Holmes and shocking the hell out of King Arthur and striking up a beautiful friendship with Long John Silver. Do you know how the ballad ends?" He sang softly: "Now up in heaven I dwell, in heaven I dwell. . . ."

Unfortunately, the conclusion is rugged. Sam Hall never was satisfied.

IV

In 1952 I attended the world science fiction convention in Chicago and there encountered a young lady named Karen Kruse. We quickly became inseparable, right through the last party in the hotel penthouse, where Stuart Byrne sang Gilbert and Sullivan till, side by side with Anthony Boucher, we saw daybreak over Lake Michigan. Afterward we kept in touch—only by mail, she being a Kentucky girl now living in the Washington, D.C. area, but the letters grew more and more frequent. Committed to go back to Europe next summer, on the way I visited her for some days, and we realized we were in love. We both wanted a change of scene and decided to try the San Francisco Bay area. I'd already seen it and liked it. Besides, through science fiction we'd become friends with a number of people there. She moved out to Berkeley and got a job. After I returned in the fall I joined her. She soon lost the job, but that was a liberation. We were married late that year. Our daughter Astrid was born in 1954. In 1960 we bought a house in suburban Orinda where, except for travels, we've lived ever since.

Anthony Boucher, co-founder and at the time co-editor of *The Magazine of Fantasy and Science Fiction* (later sole editor until he resigned), become one of the dearest of those friends. He was also a mystery writer, a book reviewer, an expert on Sherlock Holmes, a linguist, an opera buff with a radio program on which he played items from his large collection of rare recordings, a gourmet who could cook to meet his own standards, a limerickologist, a fluent and witty public speaker, a tolerant but devout Roman Catholic who knew more about his faith than most priests do, a fiendish poker player, and an all-around delightful human being. So was his wife in her quieter way.

He never let friendship affect his editorial or critical judgment, but he did buy quite a lot from me. This was where the Time Patrol stories got started and most of them appeared. They have been collected in two volumes, *The Time Patrol* and *The Shield of Time*. Then, just a few years ago, Katherine Kurtz invited me to contribute to a book she was getting together, *Tales of the Knights Templar,* and it seemed a good place for another. Since that paperback is probably less readily available by now, I'm letting this item represent the series; but I hope Tony would have liked it.

Ms. Kurtz moved its exposition of the background assumption from the body of it to the front. She was right, and I'll put those few words here.

" 'What is truth?' said jesting Pilate, and would not stay for an answer."
What is real, what is might-be or might-have-been? The quantum universe

flickers to and fro on the edge of the knowable. There is no way to foretell the destiny of a single particle; and in a chaotic world, larger destinies may turn on it. St. Thomas Aquinas declared that God Himself cannot change the past, because to hold otherwise would be a contradiction in terms; but St. Thomas was limited to the logic of Aristotle. Go into that past, and you are as free as ever you have been in your own day, free to create or destroy, guide or misguide, stride or stumble. If thereby you change the course of events that was in the history you learned, you will abide untouched, but the future that brought you into being will have gone, will never have been; it will be a reality different from what you remember. Perhaps the difference will be slight, even insignificant. Perhaps it will be monstrous. Those humans who first mastered the means of traveling through time brought about this danger. Therefore the superhumans who dwell in the ages beyond them returned to their era to ordain and establish the Time Patrol.

DEATH AND THE KNIGHT

PARIS, TUESDAY, 10 OCTOBER 1307

Clouds raced low, the hue of iron, on a wind that boomed through the streets and whined in the galleries overhanging them. Dust whirled aloft. Though the chill lessened stenches—offal, horse droppings, privies, graves, smoke ripped ragged out of flues—the city din seemed louder than erstwhile: footfalls, hoofbeats, wheels creaking, hammers thudding, voices raised in chatter, anger, plea, pitch, song, sometimes prayer. Folk surged on their manifold ways, a housewife bound for market, an artisan bound for a task, a priest bound for a deathbed, a mountebank in his shabby finery, a blind beggar, a merchant escorted by two apprentices, a drunken man-at-arms, a begowned student from the university, a wondering visitor from foreign parts, a carter driving his load through the crowd with whip and oaths, others and others and others in their hundreds. Church bells had lately rung tierce and the work of the day was fully acourse.

All made way for Hugues's Marot. That was less because of his height, towering over most men, than his garb. Tunic, hose, and shoes were of good stuff, severe cut, subdued color, and the mantle over them was plain brown; but upon it stood the red cross that signed him a Templar. Likewise did the short black hair and rough beard. Whether or no the rumors were true that the Order was in disfavor with the king, one did not wish to offend such a power.

The grimness on his lean features gave urgency to deference. At his heels trotted the boy who had brought his summons to him.

They kept close to the housefronts, avoiding as much as possible the muck in the middle of the street. Presently they came to a building somewhat bigger than its similar and substantial neighbors. Beyond its stableyard, now vacant and with the gate shut, was an oaken door set in half-timbered walls that rose three stories. This had been the home and business place of a well-to-do draper. He fell in debt to the Templars, who seized the property. It was some distance from the Paris Temple, but upon occasion could accommodate a high-born visitor or a confidential meeting.

Hugues stopped at the front door and struck it with his knuckles. A panel slid back from an opening. Someone peered through, then slowly the door swung aside. Two men gave him salutation as befitted his rank. Their faces and stances were taut, and halberds lifted in their fists—not ceremonial, but working weapons. Hugues stared.

"Do you await attack already, brothers, that you go armed indoors?" he asked.

"It is by command of the Knight Companion Fulk," replied the larger. His tone rasped.

Hugues glanced from side to side. As if to forestall any retreat, the second man added, "We are to bring you to him straightway, brother. Pray come." To the messenger: "Back to your quarters, you." The lad sped off.

Flanked by the warrior monks, Hugues entered a vestibule from which a stairway ascended. A door on his right, to the stableyard, was barred. A door on his left stood open on a flagged space filling most of the ground floor. Formerly used for work, sales, and storage, this echoed empty around wooden pillars supporting the ceiling beams. The stair went up over an equally deserted strongroom. The men climbed to the second story, where were the rooms meant for family and guests; underlings slept in the attic. Hugues was ushered to the parlor. It was still darkly wainscoted and richly furnished. A charcoal brazier made the air warm and close.

Fulk de Buchy stood waiting. He was tall, only two inches less than Hugues, hooknosed, grizzled, but as yet lithe and possessing most of his teeth. His mantle was white, as befitted a celibate knight bound by lifelong vows. At his hip hung a sword.

Hugues stopped. "In God's name . . . greeting," he faltered.

Fulk signed to his men, who took positions outside in the corridor, and beckoned. Hugues trod closer.

"In what may I serve you, Master?" he asked. Formality could be a fragile armor. The word conveyed by the boy had been just that he come at once and discreetly.

Fulk sighed. After their years together, Hugues knew that seldom-heard sound. An inward sadness had whispered past the stern mask.

"We may speak freely," Fulk said. "These are trusty men, who will keep silence. I have dismissed everyone else."

"Could we not always speak our minds, you and I?" Hugues blurted.

"Of late, I wonder," Fulk answered. "But we shall see." After a moment: "At last, we shall see."

Hugues clenched his fists, forced them open again, and said as levelly as he was able, "Never did I lie to you. I looked on you as not only my superior, not only my brother in the Order, but my—" His voice broke. "My friend," he finished.

The knight bit his lip. Blood trickled forth into the beard.

"Why else would I warn you of danger afoot?" Hugues pleaded. "I could have departed and saved myself. But I warn you anew, Fulk, and beg you to escape while time remains. In less than three days now, the ax falls."

"You were not so exact before," the other man said without tone.

"The hour was not so nigh. And I hoped—"

Fulk's hand chopped the protest short. "Have done!" he cried.

Hugues stiffened. Fulk began pacing, back and forth, like one in a cage. He bit off his words, each by each.

"Yes, you claimed a certain foresight, and what you said came to pass. Minor though those things were, they impressed me enough that when you hinted at a terrible morrow, I passed it on in a letter to my kinsman—after all, we know charges are being raised against us. But you were never clear about how you got your power. Only in these past few days, thinking, have I seen how obscure was your talk of Moorish astrologic lore and prophetic dreams." He halted, confronting his suspect, and flung, "The Devil can say truth when it fits his purposes. Whence comes your knowledge, you who call yourself Hugues Marot?"

The younger man made the sign of the cross. "Lawful, Christian—"

"Then why did you not tell me more, tell me fully what to await, that I might go to the Grand Master and all our brothers have time to make ready?"

Hugues lifted his hands to his face. "I could not. Oh, Fulk, dear friend, I cannot, even now. My tongue is locked. What I—I could utter—that little was forbidden—But you *know* me!"

Starkness responded. "I know you would have me flee, saying naught to anyone. At what peril to my soul, that I break every pledge I ever swore and abandon my brethren in Christ?" Fulk drew breath. "No, brother, if brother you be, no. I have arranged that you are under my command for the next several days. You shall remain here, sequestered, secret from all but myself and these your warders. Then, if indeed the king strikes at us, I can perhaps give you over to the Inquisition—a sorcerer, a fountainhead of evil, whom the Knights of the Temple have discovered among themselves and cast from them—"

The breath sobbed. Pain stretched the face out of shape. "But meanwhile, Hugues, I will hourly pray, with great vows, pray that you prove innocent—merely mistaken, and innocent of all save love. And can you then forgive me?"

He stood for a moment. When he spoke again, the words tolled. "It is for the Order, which we have plighted our loyalty under God. Raoul, Jehan, take him away."

Tears glistened on Hugues's cheekbones. The guards entered. He had no weapon but a knife. With a convulsive movement, he drew it and offered it hilt foremost to Fulk. The knight kept his hands back and it dropped on the floor. Mute, Hugues went off between the men. As he walked, he gripped a small crucifix that hung about his neck, symbol and source of help from beyond this world.

SAN FRANCISCO, THURSDAY, 8 MARCH 1990

Manse Everard returned to Wanda Tamberly near sunset. Light streamed through the Golden Gate. From their suite they saw cable cars go clanging down toward the waterfront, islands and the farther shore rising steep from a silver-blue bay, sails like wings of some wandering flock. They had hoped to be out there themselves.

When he came in, she read his battered face and said quietly, "You're on a new mission, aren't you?"

He nodded. "It was pretty clear that was what HQ had in mind when Nick phoned."

She could not keep all resentment out of her voice. Their time together had been less than two months. "They never leave you alone, do they? How many other Unattached agents has the Patrol got, anyway?"

"Nowhere near enough. I didn't have to accept, you know. But after studying the report, I did have to agree I'm probably the best man available for this job." That was what had kept him since morning. The report was the equivalent of a library, most of it not text or audiovisual but direct brain input—history, language, law, customs, dangers.

"Ol' noblesse oblige." Wanda sighed. She met him, laid her cheek on his breast, pressed close against the big body. "Well, it was bound to happen sooner or later. Get it done and pop back to the same hour you tell me good-bye, you hear?"

He grinned. "My idea exactly." He stroked the blond hair. "But look, I don't have to leave right away. I would like to get it behind me"—on his intricately looping world line—"but let's first make whoopee from now through tomorrow night."

"Best offer I've had all day." She raised her lips toward his and for a while the only sound in the room was murmurs.

Stepping back at last, she said, "Hey, that was fine, but before we get down to serious business, suppose you explain what the hell your assignment is." Her voice did not sound altogether steady.

"Sure," he answered. "Over beer?" When she nodded, he fetched two Sierra Nevada Pale. She settled down on the couch with hers. Restless, he kept his feet and loaded his pipe.

"Paris, early fourteenth century," he began. "A field scientist, Hugh Marlow by name, has gotten himself in deep yogurt and we need to haul him out." Speaking English rather than Temporal, he perforce used tenses and moods ill-suited to chronokinetics. "I've had medieval European experience." She shivered slightly. They had shared a part of it. "Also, he's my contemporary by birth—not American: British, but a twentieth-century Western man who must think pretty much like me. That might help a bit." A few generations can make aliens of ancestor and descendant.

"What kind of trouble?" she asked.

"He was studying the Templars, there in France where they were centered at the time, though they had chapters all over. You remember who they were?"

"Just vaguely, I'm afraid."

Everard struck fire to tobacco, drank smoke, and followed it with ale. "One of the military religious orders founded during the Crusades. After those failed, the Templars continued to be a power, almost sovereign, in fact. Besides war, they went in for banking, and ended up mainly doing that. The outfit got hog-rich. Apparently, though, most of its members stayed pretty austere, and many remained soldiers or sailors. They made themselves unpopular, being a hard and overbearing lot even by the standards of that era, but they seem to have been essentially innocent of the charges that were finally brought against them. You see, among other things King Philip the Fair wanted their treasury. He'd wrung all the gold he could out of the Jews and Lombards, and his ambitions were huge. The Pope, Clement V, was his creature and would back him up. On October thirteenth, 1307, every Templar in France who didn't manage a get-away was arrested in a set of very well-organized surprise raids. The accusations included idolatry, blasphemy, sodomy, you name it. Torture produced the confessions the king wanted. What followed is a long and complicated story. The upshot was that the Templar organization was destroyed and a number of its members, including Grand Master Jacques de Molay, were burned at the stake."

Wanda grimaced. "Poor bastards. Why'd anybody want to research them?"

"Well, they were important." Everard left unspoken that the Time Patrol required full and accurate information on the ages it guarded. She knew. Oh, but she knew! "They did keep certain of their rites and gatherings secret, for more than a century—quite a feat, huh? Of course, in the end that proved helpful to getting them railroaded.

"But what really went on? The chronicles don't say anything reliable. It'd be interesting to know, and the data might be significant. For instance, could surviving Templars, scattered across Europe, North Africa, and the Near East, have influenced, underground, the development of Christian heresies and Muslim sects? Quite a few of them joined the Moors."

Everard puffed for a minute and admired Wanda's head, bright against the deepening sky, before he proceeded.

"Marlow established an identity and enlisted in the Order. He spent a dozen years working his way up in it, till he became a close companion of a ranking knight and was let into the secrets. Then, on the eve of Philip's hit, that knight seized him and confined him incommunicado in a house. Marlow'd talked too much."

"What?" she wondered, puzzled. "He was—is—conditioned, isn't he?"

"Sure. Incapable of telling any unauthorized person he's from the future. But you have to give operatives plenty of leeway, let 'em use their own judgment as situations arise, and—" Everard shrugged. "Marlow's a scientist, an academic type, not a cop. Softhearted, maybe."

"Still, he'd have to be tough and smart to survive in that filthy period, wouldn't he?" she said.

"Uh-huh. I'll be downright eager to quiz him and learn what beans he did spill, and how." Everard paused. "To be quite fair, he did have to show a bit of occult power—forecasting events now and then, that kind of thing, if he was to advance within the Templars in anything like a reasonable time. Similar claims were common throughout the Middle Ages, and winked at if a blueblood thought they were genuine and useful to him. Marlow had permission to do it. Probably he overdid it.

"Anyhow, he got this knight, one Fulk de Buchy, believing that disaster with the king and the Inquisition was imminent. The conditioning wouldn't let him go into detail, and my guess is that Fulk realized it'd take impossibly long to get the ear of the Grand Master and convince him, if it could be done at all.

However that is, what happened was that Fulk nabbed Marlow, with the idea of turning him over to the authorities as a sorcerer if the dire prediction came true. He could hope it'd count in the Templars' favor, show they actually were good Christians and so on."

"Hmm." Wanda frowned. "How does the Patrol know this?"

"Why, naturally, Marlow has a miniature radiophone in a crucifix he always carries. Nobody would take that away from him. Once he was locked up alone, he called the milieu base and told them his problem."

"Sorry. I'm being stupid."

"Nonsense." Everard strode across to lay a hand on her shoulder. She smiled at him. "You're simply not accustomed to the devious ways of the Patrol, even after the experiences you've had."

Her smile vanished. "I hope this operation of yours will be . . . devious, not dangerous," she said slowly.

"Aw, now, don't worry. You don't get paid for it. All I have to do is snatch Marlow out of his room."

"Then why do they want *you* to do it?" she challenged. "Any officer could hop a timecycle into there, take him aboard, and hop back out."

"Um-m, the situation is a bit delicate."

"How?"

Everard sought his drink again and paced as he talked. "That's a critical point in a critical timespan. Philip isn't simply wrecking the Templars, he's undermining his feudal lords, drawing more and more power to himself. The Church, too. I said he has Pope Clement in his pocket. The Babylonian Captivity of the Popes in Avignon begins during Philip's reign. They'll return to Rome eventually, but they'll never be the same. In other words, what's in embryo there is the modern, almighty state, Louis XIV, Napoleon, Stalin, IRS." Everard considered. "I don't say that aborting it might not be a nice idea in principle, but it's part of our history, the one the Patrol is here to preserve."

"I see," Wanda replied low. "This calls for a top-notch operator. All kinds of hysteria about the Templars, fanned by the king's party. Any incident that looked like sorcery in action—or divine intervention, for that matter, I suppose—it could make the whole scene explode. With unforeseeable consequences to later events. We can't afford to blunder."

"Yeah. You are a smart girl. At the same time, you understand, we've got to rescue Marlow. He's one of ours. Besides, if he gets questioned under torture . . . he can't admit to the fact of time travel, but what the Inquisition can wring out of him could lead it to our other agents. They'd skip, sure, but that would be the end of our presence in Philip's France. And it is, I repeat, a milieu we need to keep a close eye on."

"We did remain there, though. Didn't we?"

"Yes. In our history. That doesn't mean we inevitably did. I have to make certain."

Wanda shuddered. Then she rose, went to him, took his pipe from him and laid it in an ashtray, caught both his hands in hers, and said almost calmly, "You'll come home safe and successful, Manse. I know you."

She did not know that he would. The hazards of paradox and the wounds to the soul would be overmuch, did Time Patrol people go back to visit their beloved dead or forward to see what was to become of their beloved living.

HARFLEUR, WEDNESDAY, 11 OCTOBER 1307

The chief seaport of northwestern France was a logical site for operations headquarters. Where men and cargoes arrived from many different lands and internationally ranging bargains were struck, occasional strange features, manners, or doings drew relatively scant attention. Inland, all except criminals lived in a tightly pulled net of regulations, duties, social standing, tax collection, expectations of how to act and speak and think—"sort of like late twentieth-century USA," Everard grumbled to himself. It made discretion difficult, often precarious.

Not that it was ever easy, even in Harfleur. Since first Boniface Reynaud came here from his birthtime nine hundred years futureward, he had spent two decades creating the career of Reinault Bodel, who worked his way from youthful obscurity to the status of a respectable dealer in wool. He did it so well that nobody wondered much about a dockside shed that he kept locked. Suffice it that he had freely shown the proper officials it was empty; if it stood idle, that was his affair, and indeed he talked about someday expanding his business. Nor did anybody grow unduly suspicious of the outsiders who came and went, conferring alone with him. He had chosen his servants, laborers, apprentices, and wife most carefully. To his children he was a kindly father, as medieval fathers went.

Everard's timecycle appeared in the secret space about 9 A.M. He let himself out with a Patrol key and walked to the merchant's place. Big in his own era, gigantic in this, he left a wake of stares. However, his rough garb suggested he was a mariner, likeliest English, not one to mess with. He had sent a dispatch capsule ahead and was admitted immediately to Maistre Bodel's upstairs parlor. Its door closed behind him.

In one corner were a high stool and a table cluttered with things pertaining to business and religion or personal items—ledgers, quills, an inkwell, assorted knives, a fanciful map, a small image of the Virgin, on and on. Otherwise the chamber was rather stately. A single window admitted sufficient light but no real view of the outside, for the glass in the cames, although reasonably clear, was blurringly wavy. It was noise that seeped through, Asianlike clamor of the street below, mumble and bustle of work within, once bell-thunder from the cathedral nearby. Smells were of wool, smoke, bodies, and clothes not washed very often. Yet, beneath everything, Everard had a sense of crackling energy. Harfleur—Hareflot, they still called it, as had its Norman founders—was a rookery of merchant adventurers. From harbors like this, a few lifetimes hence, men would set sail for the New World.

He took a chair across the table from Reynaud's. They had backs, armrests, and cushions, an unusual luxury. After a few hasty courtesies, he snapped in Temporal, "What can you tell me about Marlow and his situation?"

"When last he called, the situation appeared unchanged," replied the portly man in the fur-trimmed robe. "He is confined to the strongroom. It has a pallet for him to sleep on. His guards bring him food and water twice a day, and at such times a boy empties his chamber pot for him. They speak to him no more than is barely necessary. I think my message described the neighbors as being wary of the Templars and therefore leaving them strictly alone."

"M-hm. But what about Marlow? Has he told you how much information he let slip, and in what style he did it?"

"That is our main concern, of course. Correct?" Reynaud rubbed his chin. Everard heard the bristles scratching; contemporary razors didn't shave smooth. "He dares not speak to us at length or often. A listener at the door could too easily realize that he isn't actually at prayer, and so may be talking to a familiar spirit or casting a spell or the like. From what he has said, and what he earlier entered in his periodic reports—until recently, he was careful. You know he had leave to make a few predictions, describe a few events in distant places, et cetera. He explained this to the Templars partly as dreams and visions, partly as astrology. Both are everywhere taken seriously; and the Templars are especially disposed to occultism."

Everard raised his brows. "You mean they are, in fact, doing forbidden things?"

Reynaud shook his head. "No. At least, not to any great degree. Everybody nowadays is superstitious. Heresy is widespread, if mostly covert; likewise witchcraft and other pagan survivals. Heterodoxy in a thousand different forms is almost universal among the illiterate majority, ignorant of orthodox theology. The Templars have long been exposed to Islam, not always in a hostile fashion, and the Muslim world is full of magicians. It is no surprise that their leaders, their intellectuals, developed certain ideas and practices that they feel are legitimate but had better not be made public. Marlow's accounts of these are fascinating."

Everard couldn't resist. "Okay"—American word—"what *is* this idol Baphomet they'll be accused of worshiping?"

" 'Baphomet' is merely a corruption of 'Mahomet,' a smear by their enemies. It's true that the object has the shape of a head, but it is a reliquary. The relic, acquired long ago in the Holy Land, is believed to be the jawbone of Abraham."

Everard whistled. "Heterodox for sure. Dangerous. Inquisitors might recall that the ancient Greeks kept the jawbones of heroes for oracles. But still, yes, inner-circle Templars could well imagine they can venerate this while staying Christian. . . .

He sat straight. "Let's stick to our work." Wincing, he muttered out of an irrational need, "Sure, it's unpleasant. A lot of men, mostly simple, harmless rank-and-file, are going to be jailed, terrorized, tortured, some burned, the rest left with their lives wrecked, just to glut that son-of-a-bitch Philip. But he *is* the government, and governments are like that, and this is the history that produced us"—and everybody and everything they cared for. Their task was to safeguard it. Louder, harshly: "What did Marlow tell his knightly friend, and why?"

"More than a friend," Reynaud said. "They became lovers. He admits now, he could no longer endure the thought of what would happen to Fulk de Buchy."

"Hmm! So the allegations of homosexuality aren't false?"

"Not entirely." Reynaud shrugged. "What do you expect in an organization supposed to be celibate? I don't imagine more goes on than does in the average monastery. And how many kings and nobles keep favorites?"

"Oh, I'm not passing moral judgments. On the contrary." Everard thought of the lengths to which he might go were Wanda so threatened. "People's bedrooms are none of my business. But hereabouts, the state makes them its business, and may put you to the stake because you loved the wrong person." He scowled. "I'm just trying to understand what we're up against. How much did Marlow let out, and how convinced is Fulk?"

"Marlow told him in general terms that the king plans an attack on the Templars and it will be soon. He begged Fulk to make an excuse to leave France. Kings elsewhere won't follow suit at once, and in such countries as Scotland and Portugal the Templars never will be persecuted. The warning was plausible. As you doubtless know, accusations have been circulating for several years, and an investigation, officially impartial, is in progress. Fulk took Marlow seriously enough to send a letter to a cousin of his, who commands the

Templar fleet, urging him to keep his crews alert for trouble."

"Hey!" Everard exclaimed. "I remember—but my briefing only said it's a historical mystery what became of the fleet. It was never seized, nor heard of again, as far as the chronicles go. . . . What will happen?"

Reynaud was, naturally, kept informed about future developments, as the Patrol's field scientists traced them out. "When the arrests begin, the ships will put to sea," he answered. "Most will go to the Moors, like many individual Templars ashore, the men feeling betrayed and disgusted. The Moors will, quite wisely, disperse them among the naval forces of various emirs."

"So already Marlow has had a real impact," said Everard bleakly. "What else might Fulk do, even at this late hour? Once we've rescued Marlow, we'll have to deal with that gentleman . . . somehow."

"What is your plan for Marlow?" Reynaud asked.

"That's what I'm here to discuss and arrange," Everard replied. "We'll have to work out fail-safe tactics. Nothing that'll smack of the supernatural or anything else extraordinary. God knows what that could lead to."

"I expect you have ideas," Reynaud said. An unattached agent was bound to.

Everard nodded. "Can you find me a few bully boys who know their way around? My notion is that, tonight, we break into the house in Paris. Evidently nobody's staying there but the prisoner, two guards, and a scullion—a novice, I suppose. A robber gang could hear about that and decide to take advantage of it. We'll steal whatever portable goods we find and carry Marlow off with us, presumably to hold him for ransom. What with everything that's about to take place, who'll give him further thought? The robbers figured they couldn't get a ransom after all, cut his throat, and dumped him in the Seine." He paused. "I hope we won't hurt any innocent bystanders too badly."

Sometimes the Patrol must be as ruthless as history itself.

PARIS, WEDNESDAY, 11 OCTOBER 1307

After curfew, when the city gates had closed, none went abroad without necessity, save for the watch and the underworld. The timecycle appeared in a street wholly deserted. An outsize machine bearing saddles for eight, it settled onto the cobblestones with a squelp of mire that seemed loud in the silence.

Everard and his men sprang off. Narrow between high walls and elevated galleries, the street lay blacker than any open field, its air foul and cold. Glow from two small windows well up in one housefront merely deepened the dark. The raiders saw clearly. Their light-amplifying goggles ought to be taken for grotesque masks. Otherwise they wore the patched and dirty garments of the poor. All bore knives; two carried hatchets, one a cudgel, one a quarterstaff; Everard's belt upheld a falchion, short, its blade broad and curved—plausible weapons for bandits.

He squinted at the dim windows. "Damn!" he growled in English. "Somebody awake in there? Maybe just a night lamp. Well, in we go." He switched to Temporal. His team had birthdays scattered through several future centuries and around the globe. "All right, Yan, shoot."

Marlow had described the front door as massive. It would be barred on the inside. Speed was vital. When the racket began, neighbors probably wouldn't dare come to help, but they might send someone looking for a squad of the watch, or by itself it might attract that primitive constabulary. Everard's men must be gone before then, leaving no trace that lacked an ordinary explanation.

Yan, who would stand by at the transporter, saluted and swiveled around a mortar mounted on the frame. Everard had suggested the design, after which its forging and testing had taken many man-hours. It boomed. A balk of hardwood sprang out. A crash resounded. The front door sagged, splinterful, half torn from its hinges, the bar snapped. The timber could be left behind, evidence that the marauders had used a battering ram. That they must have been uncommonly strong men would be cause for alarm, but the Templar sensation ought to take minds off it.

Everard was already running. Tabarin, Rosny, Hyman, and Uhl came after. Over the threshold, through the gap and the vestibule—its own inner door open—into the workroom! There they deployed in a line, their leader at the middle, and peered about them.

Pillared and stone-floored, the chamber reached hollow. The kitchen entrance at the far end was shut for the night. The furniture remaining here was an iron coffer, three stools, and the big sales counter, on which four tallow candles in sticks made a wavery dusk to see by. They stank. In the right wall was the door to a separate room below the stairs from the vestibule, formerly for storing valuables, now secured by an ornate built-in lock. A tough-looking man in the brown habit of the Order crouched before it, gripping a halberd and yelling.

"Hold!" Everard cried in the Parisian gutter dialect he had acquired. "Lay down your pole and we'll spare you."

"God's bones, no!" the Templar clamored. Had he been a common soldier before he took his vows? "Jehan! My lord! Help!"

Everard signaled his followers. They dashed for either side of the guard.

They didn't want to kill. Sonic stun guns were nested inside their weapons. Let them close in, distract him, give him a jolt. He'd wake up supposing he'd been whacked from behind—yes, it'd be needful to bang his head with the club, but cautiously.

Two more men sprang out of the vestibule. They were naked, as folk wontedly slept, but armed. The shorter, grubby one likewise carried a halberd. The tall one lifted a long, straight sword. Its blade caught the wan light in a ripple as of fire. Its wielder—

Everard knew that aquiline face. Marlow had often surreptitiously recorded it with a microscanner, to put in his reports along with other views. Did he mean to look at it, over and over, when his mission was done and he must return home?

Fulk de Buchy, Knight of the Temple.

"Ho!" he bayed. "Go for the watch, someone!" Laughter gibed at Everard. "They'll cart away your corpses, swine."

Others clustered in the entry, half a dozen men and boys, unarmed, dismayed, imploring the saints, but witnesses.

Goddamn it, Everard groaned inwardly, *Fulk's spending the night, and he's recalled the household staff.*

"Careful with the stunners!" he barked in Temporal. Don't strike the opposition down with an invisible, sorcerous blow. Maybe he needn't have warned. These were Patrolmen he commanded. They weren't cops like him, though, they were simply the most promising he'd found among personnel familiar with this milieu, hastily briefed and drilled.

They mixed it up with the halberdiers. Fulk was plunging at him.

Too flinking much visibility here. I can't stun him unless we get so close I can fake something—or I can maneuver him in back of a pillar—and his sword's got the reach of mine, and chances are he's better. I know fencing techniques that haven't been invented yet, but they aren't a lot of use when blades like these play. Not for the first time, Everard saw that he might get killed.

As always, he was too busy to feel scared. It was as if his inner self stood aside, watching, interested in a detached fashion, now and then offering advice. The rest of him was in action.

The longsword flashed at his skull. He blocked with his falchion. Metal rang. Everard shoved. His was the advantage in mass and muscle. He forced Fulk's weapon up. His free fist doubled. No knight would expect an uppercut. Fulk disengaged with feline smoothness and flowed out of range.

For an instant they glared across two yards of stone. Everard realized how the posts hemmed him in. It could prove fatal. Almost, he reversed his sword to use the gun in the pommel. He could then move quickly enough that none would notice his enemy had fallen before being struck. But while others rioted around this chamber, Fulk stepped forward. His glaive leaped.

Everard was in karate stance. Reflex eased the tension he kept on one knee and swung him aside from the slash. It passed within an inch. Everard struck for the wrist.

Again Fulk was too swift. Rising, his blade nearly tore the Patrolman's hilt loose from the hand. He kept his left side half toward the foe, arm slanted over breast. It was as if he bore a phantom crusader shield, cross-emblazoned. Above, he grinned with battle glee. His steel snaked forth.

Everard had already cast himself downward. The sword whined barely above his head. He hit the floor in full control. Such martial arts were unknown here. Fulk would have slain a man who flopped while he tried to scramble erect. Everard was coiled, his torso up. He had perhaps half a second until the knight hewed. His falchion smote the thigh.

It bit to the bone. Blood spouted. Fulk howled. He went to his sound knee. Once more he raised his sword. Once more Everard had time only to strike. Now the metal caught the belly. Momentum drove it deep and across. A loop of gut slipped out through a red torrent.

Fulk crumpled. Everard jumped back to his feet. Both swords lay unheeded. He bent over the sprawled man. Blood had splashed him. It dripped down into what was pumping forth and spreading wide. Even as he stood, the spurt lessened, the strong heart failed.

Teeth gleamed in Fulk's beard. A last snarl at his slayer? His right hand lifted. Shakily, he drew the Christian sign. But the words he gasped were *"Hugues, O Hugues—"*

The hand fell. Eyes rolled back, mouth gaped, torn bowels went slack. Everard caught the reek of death.

"I'm sorry," he croaked. "I didn't want that."

But he had work to do. He looked around him. Both pikemen were down, unconscious but apparently not seriously hurt. It must have happened seconds ago, or his squad would have come to his aid. *Those Templars put up a good fight, they did.* Seeing him hale, the Patrolmen turned their attention to the help huddled in the entry.

"Be off or we'll kill you, too!" they bawled.

The attendants weren't schooled in battle. They bolted in abrupt, trampling panic, with a backwash of moans and screams, out the vestibule and the broken door beyond.

Stumbling through the night, they might nonetheless find city guards. "Get busy," Everard ordered. "Collect an armful of loot apiece and we'll clear out. That's as much as a gang who'd raised this kind of ruckus would stop to take." His mind couldn't keep from adding in English, *If they hung around, they'd assuredly hang.* A thought more real nudged him. "Try for well-made things, and handle with care if you can. They're going to museums uptime, you know."

And so a few bits of loveliness would be saved from oblivion, for the enjoyment of a world that, possibly, this operation had also saved. He couldn't be sure. The Patrol might have managed some different corrective action. Or events might have shaped themselves to restore their long-term course; the continuum has considerable resilience. He had merely done what seemed best.

He glanced downward at the dead man. "We had our duty," he whispered. "I think you'd've understood."

While his team hastened upstairs, he sought the strongroom. The clumsy lock would have yielded to almost any burglar tools, but those in his pouch were special and it clicked directly over. He swung the door aside.

Hugh Marlow lurched out of lightlessness. "Who're you?" he choked in English. "I heard—Oh, the Patrol." His gaze found the knight. He forced back a shriek. Then he went to the body and knelt beside it, heedless of the blood, shuddering with the effort not to weep. Everard came after and loomed above him. Marlow looked up.

"Did—did you have to do this?" he stammered.

Everard nodded. "Things happened too fast. We didn't expect we'd find him here."

"No. He . . . returned. To me. He said he could not leave me alone to face . . . whatever was on the way. I hoped . . . against hope . . . I could talk him into fleeing . . . but he wouldn't desert his brothers, either—"

"He was a man," Everard said. "At least he—I'm not cheerful about this, no, but at least he's been spared torture." Bones crushed in the boot or hauled apart on the rack or the wheel. Flesh pulled off them by red-hot pincers. Clamps on the testicles. Needles—Never mind. Governments are ingenious. If, afterward, Fulk had recanted the confession twisted out of him and denied the dishonor in it, they would have burned him alive.

Marlow nodded. "That's some consolation, isn't it?" He leaned over his friend. "Adieu, Fulk de Buchy, Knight of the Temple." Reaching out, he closed the eyes and held the jaw shut while he kissed the lips.

Everard helped him rise, for the floor had gone slippery.

"I'll cooperate fully and freely," Marlow said, flat-voiced, "and I won't ask for clemency."

"You did get reckless," Everard answered, "and it'll lead to the fleet escaping. But that was 'always' in history. It just turns out that this was how it came about. Otherwise, no harm done." Aside from a death. But all men die. "I don't think the Patrol court will be too hard on you. No more field assignments, obviously. However, you can still do useful work in compilation and analysis, and that way redeem yourself."

How smug it sounded.

Well, love doesn't excuse everything by a long shot. But is love in itself ever a sin?

The men were descending with their plunder. "Let's go," Everard said, and led them away.

V

Tony himself accepted and published the following little piece. This was rather early on and I could do it better today, but will let it stand as an example of the diversity in his magazine. He told me what a struggle he had with copy editors and proofs to keep an apostrophe out of the title, which goes to show what kind of line editor he was.

Like John Campbell, he usually either rejected a story outright or ran it as written; but, also like Campbell, he was nearly always right when he asked for revisions. The Hokas moved over to him after their original home folded. In the first of these stories he got, they were playing baseball, and he went to considerable trouble to set the details of that game right. (Have I mentioned that he was a sports fan?) At one point in it, the bedeviled human protagonist mixed some consoling martinis. He used a shaker. Tony told me, "Those martinis should be stirred in a pitcher. I'm sure that on sober reflection you will agree."

Yes, diversity. The story here is not at all funny. If some of the thinking and feeling in it seems a bit strange, please remember that it's from the 1950's. That was another country.

JOURNEYS END

—doctor bill & twinges in chest but must be all right maybe indigestion & dinner last night & wasn't audrey giving me the glad eye & how the hell is a guy to know & maybe i can try and find out & what a fool i can look if she doesn't—

—goddam idiot & they shouldn't let some people drive & oh all right so the examiner was pretty lenient with me i haven't had a bad accident yet & christ blood all over my blood let's face it i'm scared to drive but the buses are no damn good & straight up three paces & man in a green hat & judas i ran that red light—

In fifteen years a man got used to it, more or less. He could walk down the street and hold his own thoughts to himself while the surf of unvoiced voices was a nearly ignored mumble in his brain. Now and then, of course, you got something very bad, it stood up in your skull and shrieked at you.

Norman Kane, who had come here because he was in love with a girl he had never seen, got to the corner of University and Shattuck just when the light turned against him. He paused, fetching out a cigarette with nicotine-yellowed fingers while traffic slithered in front of his eyes.

It was an unfavorable time, four-thirty in the afternoon, homeward rush of nervous systems jangled with weariness and hating everything else on feet or wheels. Maybe he should have stayed in the bar down on San Pablo. It had been pleasantly cool and dim, the bartender's mind an amiable cud-chewing somnolence, and he could have suppressed awareness of the woman.

No, maybe not. When the city had scraped your nerves raw, they didn't have much resistance to the slime in some heads.

Odd, he reflected, how often the outwardly polite ones were the foully twisted inside. They wouldn't dream of misbehaving in public, but just below the surface of consciousness . . . Better not think of it, better not remember. Berkeley was at least preferable to San Francisco or Oakland. The bigger the town, the more evil it seemed to hold, three centimeters under the frontal bone. New York was almost literally uninhabitable.

There was a young fellow waiting beside Kane. A girl came down the sidewalk, pretty, long yellow hair and a well-filled blouse. Kane focused idly on her: yes, she had an apartment of her own, which she had carefully picked for a tolerant superintendent. Lechery jumped in the young man's nerves. His eyes followed the girl, Cobean-style, and she walked on . . . simple harmonic motion.

Too bad. They could have enjoyed each other. Kane chuckled to himself. He had nothing against honest lust, anyhow not in his liberated conscious mind; he couldn't do much about a degree of subconscious puritanism. Lord, you can't be a telepath and remain any kind of prude. People's lives were their own business, if they didn't hurt anyone else too badly.

—the trouble is, he thought, *they hurt me. but i can't tell them that. they'd rip me apart and dance on the pieces. the government / the military / wouldn't like a man to be alive who could read secrets but their fear-inspired anger would be like a baby's tantrum beside the red blind amok of the common man (thoughtful husband considerate father good honest worker earnest patriot) whose inward sins were known. you can talk to a priest or a psychiatrist because it is only talk & he does not live your failings with you—*

The light changed and Kane started across. It was clear fall weather, not that this area had marked seasons, a cool sunny day with a small wind blowing up the street from the water. A few blocks ahead of him, the university campus was a splash of manicured green under brown hills.

—flayed & burningburningburning moldering rotted flesh & the bones the white hard clean bones coming out gwtjklfmx—

129

Kane stopped dead. Through the vertigo he felt how sweat was drenching into his shirt.

And it was such an ordinary-looking man!

"Hey, there, buster, wake up! Ya wanna get killed?"

Kane took a sharp hold on himself and finished the walk across the street. There was a bench at the bus stop and he sat down till the trembling was over.

Some thoughts were unendurable.

He had a trick of recovery. He went back to Father Schliemann. The priest's mind had been like a well, a deep well under sun-speckled trees, its surface brightened with a few gold-colored autumn leaves . . . but there was nothing bland about the water, it had a sharp mineral tang, a smell of the living earth. He had often fled to Father Schliemann, in those days of puberty when the telepathic power had first wakened in him. He had found good minds since then, happy minds, but never one so serene, none with so much strength under the gentleness.

"I don't want you hanging around that papist, boy, do you understand?" It was his father, the lean implacable man who always wore a black tie. "Next thing you know, you'll be worshiping graven images just like him."

"But they *aren't*—"

His ears could still ring with the cuff. "Go up to your room! I don't want to see you till tomorrow morning. And you'll have two more chapters of Deuteronomy memorized by then. Maybe that'll teach you the true Christian faith."

Kane grinned wryly and lit another cigarette from the end of the previous one. He knew he smoked too much. And drank—but not heavily. Drunk, he was defenseless before the horrible tides of thinking.

He had had to run away from home at the age of fourteen. The only other possibility was conflict ending with reform school. It had meant running away from Father Schliemann too, but how in hell's red fire could a sensitive adolescent dwell in the same house as his father's brain? Were the psychologists now admitting the possibility of a sadistic masochist? Kane *knew* the type existed.

Give thanks for this much mercy, that the extreme telepathic range was only a few hundred yards. And a mind-reading boy was not altogether helpless; he could evade officialdom and the worst horrors of the underworld. He could find a decent elderly couple at the far end of the continent and talk himself into adoption.

Kane shook himself and got up again. He threw the cigarette to the ground and stubbed it out with his heel. A thousand examples told him what obscure sexual symbolism was involved in the act, but what the deuce . . . it was also a practical thing. Guns are phallic too, but at times you need a gun.

Weapons: he could not help wincing as he recalled dodging the draft in 1949. He'd traveled enough to know this country was worth defending. But it hadn't been any trick at all to hoodwink a psychiatrist and get himself marked hopelessly psychoneurotic—which he would be after two years penned with frustrated men. There had been no choice, but he could not escape a sense of dishonor.

—haven't we all sinned / every one of us / is there a single human creature on earth without his burden of shame?—

A man was coming out of the drugstore beside him. Idly, Kane probed his mind. You could go quite deeply into anyone's self if you cared to, in fact you couldn't help doing so. It was impossible merely to scan verbalized thinking: the organism is too closely integrated. Memory is not a passive filing cabinet, but a continuous process beneath the level of consciousness; in a way, you are always reliving your entire past. And the more emotionally charged the recol lection is, the more powerfully it radiates.

The stranger's name was—no matter. His personality was as much an un-changeable signature as his fingerprints. Kane had gotten into the habit of thinking of people as such-and-such a multidimensional symbolic topography; the name was an arbitrary gabble.

The man was an assistant professor of English at the university. Age forty-two, married, three children, making payments on a house in Albany. Steady sober type, but convivial, popular with his colleagues, ready to help out most friends. He was thinking about tomorrow's lectures, with overtones of a movie he wanted to see and an undercurrent of fear that he might have cancer after all, in spite of what the doctor said.

Below, the list of his hidden crimes. As a boy: tormenting a cat, well-buried Oedipean hungers, masturbation, petty theft . . . the usual. Later: cheating on a few exams, that ludicrous fumbling attempt with a girl which came to nothing because he was too nervous, the time he crashed a cafeteria line and had been shoved away with a cold remark (and praises be, Jim who had seen that was now living in Chicago) . . . still later: wincing memories of a stomach uncontrollably rumbling at a formal dinner, that woman in his hotel room the night he got drunk at the convention, standing by and letting old Carver be fired because he didn't have the courage to protest to the dean . . . now: youngest child a nasty whining little snotnose, but you can't show anyone what you really think, reading Rosamond Marshall when alone in his office, disturbing young breasts in tight sweaters, the petty spite of academic politics, giving Simonson an undeserved good grade because the boy was so beautiful, disgraceful sweating panic when at night he considered how death would annihilate his ego—

And what of it? This assistant professor was a good man, a kindly and honest man, his inwardness ought to be between him and the Recording Angel. Few of his thoughts had ever become deeds, or ever would. Let him bury them himself, let him be alone with them. Kane ceased focusing on him.

The telepath had grown tolerant. He expected little of anyone; nobody matched the mask, except possibly Father Schliemann and a few others . . . and those were human too, with human failings; the difference was that they knew peace. It was the emotional overtones of guilt which made Kane wince. God knew he himself was no better. Worse, maybe, but then his life had thrust him to it. If you had an ordinary human sex drive, for instance, but could not endure to cohabit with the thoughts of a woman, your life became one of fleeting encounters; there was no help for it, even if your austere boyhood training still protested.

"Pardon me, got a match?"

—lynn is dead / i still can't understand it that i will never see her again & eventually you learn how to go on in a chopped-off fashion but what do you do in the meantime how do you get through the nights alone—

"Sure."*—maybe that is the worst: sharing sorrow and unable to help & only able to give him a light for his cigarette—*

Kane put the matches back in his pocket and went on up University, pausing again at Oxford. A pair of large campus buildings jutted up to the left; others were visible ahead and to the right, through a screen of eucalyptus trees. Sunlight and shadow damascened the grass. From a passing student's mind he discovered where the library was. A good big library—perhaps it held a clue, buried somewhere in the periodical files. He had already arranged for permission to use the facilities: prominent young author doing research for his next novel.

Crossing wistfully named Oxford Street, Kane smiled to himself. Writing was really the only possible occupation: he could live in the country and be remote from the jammed urgency of his fellow men. And with such an understanding of the soul as was his, with any five minutes on a corner giving him a dozen stories, he made good money at it. The only drawback was the trouble of avoiding publicity, editorial summonses to New York, autographing parties, literary teas . . . he didn't like those. But you could remain faceless if you insisted.

They said nobody but his agent knew who B. Traven was. It had occurred, wildly, to Kane that Traven might be another like himself. He had gone on a long journey to find out. . . . No. He was alone on earth, a singular and solitary mutant, except for—

It shivered in him, again he sat on the train. It had been three years ago, he was in the club car having a nightcap while the streamliner ran eastward through the Wyoming darkness. They passed a westbound train, not so elegant a one. His drink leaped from his hand to the floor and he sat for a moment in stinging blindness. That flicker of thought, brushing his mind and coming aflame with recognition and then borne away again . . . Damn it, damn it, he should have pulled the emergency cord and so should *she*. They should have halted both trains and stumbled through cinders and sagebrush and found each other's arms.

Too late. Three years yielded only a further emptiness. Somewhere in the land there was, or there had been, a young woman, and she was a telepath and the startled touch of her mind had been gentle. There had not been time to learn anything else. Since then he had given up on private detectives. (How could you tell them: "I'm looking for a girl who was on such-and-such a train the night of—"?) Personal ads in all the major papers had brought him nothing but a few crank letters. Probably she didn't read the personals; he'd never done so till his search began, there was too much unhappiness to be found in them if you understood humankind as well as he did.

Maybe this library here, some unnoticed item . . . but if there are two points in a finite space and one moves about so as to pass through every infinitesimal volume dV, it will encounter the other one in finite time *provided* that the other point is not moving too.

Kane shrugged and went along the curving way to the gatehouse. It was slightly uphill. There was a bored cop in the shelter, to make sure that only authorized cars were parked on campus. The progress paradox: a ton or so of steel, burning irreplaceable petroleum to shift one or two human bodies around, and doing the job so well that it becomes universal and chokes the cities which spawned it. A telepathic society would be more rational. When every little wound in the child's soul could be felt and healed . . . when the thick burden of guilt was laid down, because everyone knew that everyone else had done the same . . . when men could not kill, because soldier and murderer felt the victim die . . .

—adam & eve? you can't breed a healthy race out of two people. but if we had telepathic children / & we would be bound to do so i think because the mutation is obviously recessive / then we could study the heredity of it & the gift would be passed on to other bloodlines in logical distribution & every generation there would be more of our kind until we could come out openly & even the mindmutes could be helped by our psychiatrists & priests & each would be fair and clean and sane—

Students were sitting on the grass, walking under the Portland Cement Romanesque of the buildings, calling and laughing and talking. The day was near an end. Now there would be dinner, a date, a show, maybe some beer at Robbie's or a drive up into the hills to neck and watch the lights below like trapped stars and the mighty constellation of the Bay Bridge . . . or perhaps, with a face-saving grumble about midterms, an evening of books, a world suddenly opened. It must be good to be young and mindmute. A dog trotted down the walk and Kane relaxed into the simple wordless pleasure of being a healthy and admired collie.

—so perhaps it is better to be a dog than a man? no / surely not / for if a man knows more grief he also knows more joy & so it is to be a telepath: more easily hurt yes but / god / think of the mindmutes always locked away in aloneness and think of sharing not only a kiss but a soul with your beloved—

The uphill trend grew steeper as he approached the library, but Kane was in fair shape and rather enjoyed the extra effort. At the foot of the stairs he paused for a quick cigarette before entering. A passing woman flicked eyes across him and he learned that he could also smoke in the lobby. Mind reading had its everyday uses. But it was good to stand here in the sunlight. He stretched, reaching out physically and mentally.

—let's see now the integral of log x dx *will make a substitution suppose we call* y *equal to log* x *then this is interesting i wonder who wrote that line about euclid has looked on beauty bare—*

Kane's cigarette fell from his mouth.

It seemed that the wild hammering of his heart must drown out the double thought that rivered in his brain, the thought of a physics student, a very ordinary young man save that he was quite wrapped up in the primitive satisfaction of hounding down a problem, and the other thought, the one that was listening in.

—she—

He stood with closed eyes, asway on his feet, breathing as if he ran up a mountain.*—are You there? are You there?—*

—not daring to believe: what do i feel?—

—i was the man on the train—

—& i was the woman—

A shuddering togetherness.

"Hey! Hey, mister, is anything wrong?"

Almost, Kane snarled. Her thought was so remote, on the very rim of indetectability, he could get nothing but sub-vocalized words, nothing of the self, and this busybody—"No, thanks, I'm O.K., just a, a little winded."—*where are You, where can i find You o my darling?—*

—image of a large white building / right over here & they call it dwinelle

hall & i am sitting on the bench outside & please come quickly please be here i never thought this could become real—

Kane broke into a run. For the first time in fifteen years, he was unaware of his human surroundings. There were startled looks, he didn't see them, he was running to her and she was running too.

—my name is norman kane & i was not born to that name but took it from people who adopted me because i fled my father (horrible how mother died in darkness & he would not let her have drugs though it was cancer & he said drugs were sinful and pain was good for the soul & he really honestly believed that) & when the power first appeared i made slips and he beat me and said it was witchcraft & i have searched all my life since & i am a writer but only because i must live but it was not aliveness until this moment—

—o my poor kicked beloved / i had it better / in me the power grew more slowly and i learned to cover it & i am twenty years old & came here to study but what are books at this moment—

He could see her now. She was not conventionally beautiful, but neither was she ugly, and there was kindness in her eyes and on her mouth.

—what shall i call you? to me you will always be You but there must be a name for the mindmutes & i have a place in the country among old trees & such few people as live nearby are good folk / as good as life will allow them to be—

—then let me come there with you & never leave again—

They reached each other and stood a foot apart. There was no need for a kiss or even a handclasp . . . not yet. It was the minds which leaped out and enfolded and became one.

—I REMEMBER THAT AT THE AGE OF THREE I DRANK OUT OF THE TOILET BOWL / THERE WAS A PECULIAR FASCINATION TO IT & I USED TO STEAL LOOSE CHANGE FROM MY MOTHER THOUGH SHE HAD LITTLE ENOUGH TO CALL HER OWN SO I COULD SNEAK DOWN TO THE DRUGSTORE FOR ICE CREAM & I SQUIRMED OUT OF THE DRAFT & THESE ARE THE DIRTY EPISODES INVOLVING WOMEN—

—AS A CHILD I WAS NOT FOND OF MY GRANDMOTHER THOUGH SHE LOVED ME AND ONCE I PLAYED THE FOLLOWING FIENDISH TRICK ON HER & AT THE AGE OF SIXTEEN I MADE AN UTTER FOOL OF MYSELF IN THE FOLLOWING MAN-NER & I HAVE BEEN PHYSICALLY CHASTE CHIEFLY BECAUSE OF FEAR BUT MY VICARIOUS EXPERIENCES ARE NUMBERED IN THE THOUSANDS—

Eyes watched eyes with horror.

—it is not that you have sinned for i know everyone has done the same or similar things or would if they had our gift & i know too that it is nothing

serious or abnormal & of course you have decent instincts & are ashamed—
    —just so / it is that you know what i have done & you know every last little wish & thought & buried uncleanness & in the top of my head i know it doesn't mean anything but down underneath is all which was drilled into me when i was just a baby & i will not admit to ANYONE *else that such things exist in* ME—

A car whispered by, homeward bound. The trees talked in the light sunny wind.

A boy and girl went hand in hand.

The thought hung cold under the sky, a single thought in two minds.

—get out i hate your bloody guts.—

VI

Science fiction people are an argumentative lot. Way back when, not so often these days, many a story came from taking someone else's idea and either carrying it further or trying to prove that, given the premise, things would work out altogether differently. This was entirely legitimate and indeed helped make the literature lively. For a single example, in "If This Goes On—" Robert Heinlein depicted an American dictatorship in the guise of a religion, which used technology to pass phony miracles and so keep the populace subservient. In the story, it was overthrown. A while later, Fritz Leiber's novel *Gather, Darkness!* supposed that the thing lasted for centuries, became worldwide, and established a neo-medieval society. An underground in rebellion against this church perforce called itself Satanistic and its own "miracles" witchcraft. Airplanes built to look like angels against airplanes built to look like devils. . . .

My story "Ghetto," which Tony published in 1954, tried to rebut what I felt was a pretty poor novel by another writer. Both drew on the phenomenon of time dilation. Travel faster than light is impossible in relativistic physics, but matter can come indefinitely close to that velocity. The closer it does, the slower time goes for it compared to time for matter at rest—very loosely speaking, of course. This is a reality, demonstrated over and over by particle accelerators and other instrumentalities. The enormous energies involved make it purely theoretical for large objects such as, say, a spaceship and its crew. However, suppose someday we can somehow get around that obstacle. Then an expedition might fare many light-years in a short span, but would find on return that as many years had passed at home.

My thought was that if this kind of traffic became common, the traffickers would grow ever more isolated culturally from dwellers on planets. They'd evolve their own society, whose members seldom married outside it; and there could be periods of history in which they were the objects of cruel discrimination or even persecution. Yes, I had medieval Jews in mind, but tried to give the Kith a character of its own.

Years afterward, I did another story about it for another magazine. And years after that, I made "Ghetto," much revised, a part of my novel *Starfarers*. I was going to incorporate "The Horn of Time the Hunter" as well, but Karen convinced me that it was too dark. Here it is, then, a far-future incident, perhaps important only to the people involved, but to them overwhelming. History knows of many such.

THE HORN OF TIME THE HUNTER

Now and then, on that planet, Jong Errifrans thought he heard the distant blowing of a horn. It would begin low, with a pulse that quickened as the notes waxed, until the snarl broke in a brazen scream and sank sobbing away. The first time he started and asked the others if they heard. But the sound was on the bare edge of audibility for him, whose ears were young and sharp, and the men said no. "Some trick of the wind, off in the cliffs yonder," Mons Rainart suggested. He shivered. "The damned wind is always hunting here." Jong did not mention it again, but when he heard the noise thereafter a jag of cold went through him.

There was no reason for that. Nothing laired in the city but seabirds, whose wings made a white storm over the tower tops and whose flutings mingled with wind skirl and drum roll of surf; nothing more sinister had appeared than a great tiger-striped fish, which patrolled near the outer reefs. And perhaps that was why Jong feared the horn: it gave the emptiness a voice.

At night, rather than set up their glower, the four would gather wood and give themselves the primitive comfort of a fire. Their camping place was in what might once have been a forum. Blocks of polished stone thrust out of the sand and wiry grass that had occupied all streets; toppled colonnades demarked a square. More shelter was offered by the towers clustered in the city's heart, still piercing the sky, the glasit windows still unbroken. But no, those windows were too much like a dead man's eyes, the rooms within were too hushed, now that the machines that had been the city's life lay corroded beneath the dunes. It was better to raise a tent under the stars. Those, at least, were much the same, after twenty thousand years.

The men would eat, and then Regor Lannis, the leader, would lift his communicator bracelet near his mouth and report their day's ransacking. The spaceboat's radio caught the message and relayed it to the *Golden Flyer,* which orbited with the same period as the planet's twenty-one-hour rotation, so that she was always above this island. "Very little news," Regor typically said. "Remnants of tools and so on. We haven't found any bones yet for a radio-activity dating. I don't think we will, either. They probably cremated their dead, to the very end. Mons has estimated that engine block we found began rusting some ten thousand years ago. He's only guessing, though. It wouldn't have lasted at all if the sand hadn't buried it, and we don't know when that happened."

"But you say the furnishings inside the towers are mostly intact, age-proof alloys and synthetics," answered Captain Ilmaray's voice. "Can't you deduce anything from their, well, their arrangement or disarrangement? If the city was plundered—"

"No, sir, the signs are too hard to read. A lot of rooms have obviously been stripped. But we don't know whether that was done in one day or over a period maybe of centuries, as the last colonists mined their homes for stuff they could no longer make. We can only be sure, from the dust, that no one's been inside for longer than I like to think about."

When Regor had signed off, Jong would usually take out his guitar and chord the songs they sang, the immemorial songs of the Kith, many translated from languages spoken before ever men left Earth. It helped drown out the wind and the surf, booming down on the beach where once a harbor had stood. The fire flared high, picking their faces out of night, tinging plain work clothes with unrestful red, and then guttering down so that shadows swallowed the bodies. They looked much alike, those four men, small, lithe, with sharp, dark features; for the Kith were a folk apart, marrying between their own ships, which carried nearly all traffic among the stars. Since a vessel might be gone from Earth for a century or more, the planetbound civilizations, flaring and dying and reborn like the flames that warmed them now, could not be theirs. The men differed chiefly in age, from the sixty years that furrowed Regor Lannis's skin to the twenty that Jong Errifrans had marked not long ago.

Ship's years, mostly, Jong remembered, and looked up to the Milky Way with a shudder. When you fled at almost the speed of light, time shrank for you, and in his own life he had seen the flower and the fall of an empire. He had not thought much about it then—it was the way of things, that the Kith should be quasi-immortal and the planetarians alien, transitory, not quite real. But a voyage of ten thousand light-years toward galactic center, and back, was more than anyone had ventured before; more than anyone would ever have done, save to expiate the crime of crimes. Did the Kith still exist? Did Earth?

After some days, Regor decided: "We'd better take a look at the hinterland. We may improve our luck."

"Nothing in the interior but forest and savannah," Neri Avelair objected. "We saw that from above."

"On foot, though, you see items you miss from a boat," Regor said. "The colonists can't have lived exclusively in places like this. They'd need farms, mines, extractor plants, outlying settlements. If we could examine one of those, we might find clearer indications than in this damned huge warren."

"How much chance would we have, hacking our way through the brush?" Neri argued. "I say let's investigate some of those other towns we spotted."

"They're more ruined yet," Mons Rainart reminded him. "Largely submerged." He need not have spoken; how could they forget? Land does not sink fast. The fact that the sea was eating the cities gave some idea of how long they had been abandoned.

"Just so." Regor nodded. "I don't propose plunging into the woods, either. That'd need more men and more time than we can spare. But there's an outsize beach about a hundred kilometers north of here, fronting on a narrow-mouthed bay, with fertile hills right behind—hills that look as if they ought to contain ores. I'd be surprised if the colonists did not exploit the area."

Neri's mouth twitched downward. His voice was not quite steady. "How long do we have to stay on this ghost planet before we admit we'll never know what happened?"

"Not too much longer," Regor said. "But we've got to try our best before we do leave."

He jerked a thumb at the city. Its towers soared above fallen walls and marching dunes into a sky full of birds. The bright yellow sun had bleached out their pastel colors, leaving them bone-white. And yet the view on their far side was beautiful, forest that stretched inland a hundred shades of shadow-rippled green, while in the opposite direction the land sloped down to a sea that glittered like emerald strewn with diamond dust, moving and shouting and hurling itself in foam against the reefs. The first generations here must have been very happy, Jong thought.

"Something destroyed them, and it wasn't simply a war," Regor said. "We need to know what. It may not have affected any other world. But maybe it did."

Maybe Earth lay as empty, Jong thought, not for the first time.

The *Golden Flyer* had paused here to refit before venturing back into man's old domain. Captain Ilmaray had chosen an F9 star arbitrarily, three hundred light-years from Sol's calculated present position. They detected no whisper of the energies used by civilized races, who might have posed a threat. The third planet seemed a paradise, Earth-mass but with its land scattered in islands around a global ocean, warm from pole to pole. Mons Rainart was surprised that the carbon dioxide equilibrium was maintained with so little exposed rock. Then he observed weed mats everywhere on the waters, many of them hundreds of square kilometers in area, and decided that their photosynthesis was active enough to produce a Terrestrial-type atmosphere.

The shock had been to observe from orbit the ruined cities. Not that colonization could not have reached this far, and beyond, during twenty thousand years. But the venture had been terminated; why?

That evening it was Jong's turn to hold a personal conversation with those in the mother ship. He got his parents, via intercom, to tell them how he fared. The heart jumped in his breast when Sorya Rainart's voice joined theirs. "Oh yes," the girl said, with an uneven little laugh, "I'm right here in the apartment. Dropped in for a visit, by chance."

Her brother chuckled at Jong's back. The young man flushed and wished hotly for privacy. But of course Sorya would have known he'd call tonight. . . . If the Kith still lived, there could be nothing between him and her. You brought your wife home from another ship. It was spaceman's law, exogamy aiding a survival that was precarious at best. If, though, the last Kith ship but theirs drifted dead among the stars; or the few hundred aboard the *Golden Flyer* and the four on this world whose name was lost were the final remnants of the human race—she was bright and gentle and swayed sweetly when she walked.

"I—" He untangled his tongue. "I'm glad you did. How are you?"

"Lonely and frightened," she confided. Cosmic interference seethed around her words. The fire spat sparks loudly into the darkness overhead. "If you don't learn what went wrong here . . . I don't know if I can stand wondering the rest of my life."

"Cut that!" he said sharply. The rusting of morale had destroyed more than one ship in the past. Although—"No, I'm sorry." He knew she did not lack courage. The fear was alive in him too that he would be haunted forever by what he had seen here. Death in itself was an old familiar of the Kith. But this time they were returning from a past more ancient than the glaciers and the mammoths had been on Earth when they left. They needed knowledge as much as they needed air, to make sense of the universe. And their first stop in that spiral arm of the galaxy which had once been home had confronted them with a riddle that looked unanswerable. So deep in history were the roots of the Kith that Jong could recall the symbol of the Sphinx; and suddenly he saw how gruesome it was.

"We'll find out," he promised Sorya. "If not here, then when we arrive at Earth." Inwardly he was unsure. He made small talk and even achieved a joke or two. But afterward, laid out in his sleeping bag, he thought he heard the horn winding in the north.

The expedition rose at dawn, bolted breakfast, and stowed their gear in the spaceboat. It purred from the city on aerodynamic drive, leveled off, flew at low speed not far above ground. The sea tumbled and flashed on the right, the land climbed steeply on the left. No herds of large animals could be seen there. Probably none existed, with such scant room to develop in. But the ocean swarmed. From above Jong could look down into transparent waters, see shadows that were schools of fish numbering in the hundreds of thousands. Further off he observed a herd of grazers, piscine but big as whales, plowing slowly through a weed mat. The colonists must have gotten most of their living from the sea.

Regor set the boat down on a cliff overlooking the bay he had described. The escarpment ringed a curved beach of enormous length and breadth, its sands strewn with rocks and boulders. Kilometers away, the arc closed in on itself, leaving only a strait passage to the ocean. The bay was placid, clear bluish-green beneath the early sun, but not stagnant. The tides of the one big moon must raise and lower it two or three meters in a day, and a river ran in from the southern highlands. Afar Jong could see how shells littered the sand below high-water mark, proof of abundant life. It seemed bitterly unfair to him that the colonists had had to trade so much beauty for darkness.

Regor's lean face turned from one man to the next. "Equipment check," he said, and went down the list: fulgurator, communication bracelet, energy compass, medikit—"My God," said Neri, "you'd think we were off on a year's trek, and separately at that."

"We'll disperse, looking for traces," Regor said, "and those rocks will often hide us from each other." He left the rest unspoken: that that which had been the death of the colony might still exist.

They emerged into cool, flowing air with the salt and iodine and clean decay smell of coasts on every Earthlike world, and made their way down the scarp. "Let's radiate from this point," Regor said, "and if nobody has found anything, we'll meet back here in four hours for lunch."

Jong's path slanted farthest north. He walked briskly at first, enjoying the motion of his muscles, the scrunch of sand and rattle of pebbles beneath his boots, the whistle of the many birds overhead. But presently he must pick his way across drifts of stone and among dark boulders, some as big as houses, which cut him off from the wind and his fellows; and he remembered Sorya's aloneness.

Oh no, not that. Haven't we paid enough? he thought. And, for a moment's defiance: *We didn't do the thing. We condemned the traitors ourselves, and threw them into space, as soon as we learned. Why should* we *be punished?*

But the Kith had been too long isolated, themselves against the universe, not to hold that the sin and sorrow of one belonged to all. And Tomakan and his coconspirators had done what they did unselfishly, to save the ship. In those last vicious years of the Star Empire, when Earthmen made the Kithfolk scapegoats for their wretchedness until every crew fled to await better times, the *Golden Flyer*'s captured people would have died horribly—had Tomakan not bought their freedom by betraying to the persecutors that asteroid where two other Kith vessels lay, readying to leave the Solar System. How could they afterward meet the eyes of their kindred, in the council that met at Tau Ceti?

The sentence was just: to go exploring to the fringes of the galactic nucleus. Perhaps they would find the Elder Races that must dwell somewhere; perhaps they would bring back the knowledge and wisdom that could heal man's inborn lunacies. Well, they hadn't; but the voyage was something in itself, sufficient to give the *Golden Flyer* back her honor. No doubt everyone who had sat in council was now dust. Still, their descendants—

Jong stopped in midstride. His shout went ringing among the rocks.

"What is it? Who called? Anything wrong?" The questions flew from his bracelet like anxious bees.

He stooped over a little heap and touched it with fingers that wouldn't hold steady. "Worked flints," he breathed. "Flakes, broken spearheads . . . shaped wood . . . something—" He scrabbled in the sand. Sunlight struck off a piece of metal, rudely hammered into a dagger. It had been, it must have been fashioned from some of the ageless alloy in the city—long ago, for the blade was worn so thin that it had snapped across. He crouched over the shards and babbled.

And shortly Mons's deep tones cut through: "Here's another site! An animal skull, could only have been split with a sharp stone, a thong—Wait, wait, I see something carved in this block, maybe a symbol—"

Then suddenly he roared, and made a queer choked gurgle, and his voice came to an end.

Jong leaped erect. The communicator jabbered with calls from Neri and Regor. He ignored them. There was no time for dismay. He tuned his energy compass. Each bracelet emitted a characteristic frequency besides its carrier wave, for location purposes, and— The needle swung about. His free hand unholstered his fulgurator, and he went bounding over the rocks.

As he broke out onto the open stretch of sand the wind hit him full in the face. Momentarily through its shrillness he heard the horn, louder than before, off beyond the cliffs. A part of him remembered fleetingly how one day on a frontier world he had seen a band of huntsmen gallop in pursuit of a wounded animal that wept as it ran, and how the chief had raised a crooked bugle to his lips and blown just such a call.

The note died away. Jong's glance swept the beach. Far down its length he saw several figures emerge from a huddle of boulders. Two of them carried a human shape. He yelled and sprinted to intercept them. The compass dropped from his grasp.

They saw him and paused. When he neared, Jong made out that the form they bore was Mons Rainart's. He swung ghastly limp between his carriers. Blood dripped from his back and over his breast.

Jong's stare went to the six murderers. They were chillingly manlike, half a meter taller than him, magnificently thewed beneath the naked white skin, but altogether hairless, with long webbed feet and fingers, a high dorsal fin, and smaller fins at heels and elbows and on the domed heads. The features were bony, with great sunken eyes and no external ears. A flap of skin drooped from pinched nose to wide mouth. Two carried flint-tipped wooden spears, two had tridents forged from metal—the tines of one were red and wet—and those who bore the body had knives slung at their waists.

"Stop!" Jong shrieked. "Let him go!"

He plowed to a halt not far off, and menaced them with his gun. The biggest uttered a gruff bark and advanced, trident poised. Jong retreated a step. Whatever they had done, he hated to—

An energy beam winked, followed by its thunderclap. The one who carried Mons's shoulders crumpled, first at the knees, then down into the sand. The blood from the hole burned through him mingled with the spaceman's, equally crimson.

They whirled. Neri Avelair pounded down the beach from the opposite side. His fulgurator spoke again. The shimmering wet sand reflected the blast. It missed, but quartz fused where it struck near the feet of the creatures, and hot droplets spattered them.

The leader waved his trident and shouted. They lumbered toward the water. The one who had Mons's ankles did not let go. The body flapped arms and head as it dragged. Neri shot a third time. Jolted by his own speed, he missed anew. Jong's finger remained frozen on the trigger.

The five giants entered the bay. Its floor shelved rapidly. In a minute they were able to dive below the surface. Neri reached Jong's side and fired, bolt after bolt, till a steam cloud rose into the wind. Tears whipped down his cheeks. "Why didn't you kill them, you bastard?" he screamed. "You could have gunned them down where you were!"

"I don't know." Jong stared at his weapon. It felt oddly heavy.

"They drowned Mons!"

"No . . . he was dead already. I could see. Must have been pierced through the heart. I suppose they ambushed him in those rocks—"

"M-m-maybe. But his body, God damn you, we could'a saved that at least!" Senselessly, Neri put a blast through the finned corpse.

"Stop that," commanded Regor. He threw himself down, gasping for breath. Dimly, Jong noticed gray streaks in the leader's hair. It seemed a matter of pity and terror that Regor Lannis the unbendable should be whittled away by the years.

What am I thinking? Mons is killed. Sorya's brother.

Neri holstered his fulgurator, covered his face with both hands, and sobbed.

After a long while Regor shook himself, rose, knelt again to examine the dead swimmer. "So there were natives here," he muttered. "The colonists must not have known. Or maybe they underestimated what savages could do."

His hands ran over the glabrous hide. "Still warm," he said, almost to himself. "Air-breathing; a true mammal, no doubt, though this male lacks vestigial nipples; real nails on the digits, even if they have grown as thick and sharp as claws." He peeled back the lips and examined the teeth. "Omnivore evolving toward carnivore, I'd guess. The molars are still pretty flat, but the rest are bigger than ours, and rather pointed." He peered into the dimmed eyes. "Human-type vision, probably less acute. You can't see so far underwater. We'll need extensive study to determine the color-sensitivity curve, if any. Not to mention the other adaptations. I daresay they can stay below for many minutes at a stretch. Doubtless not as long as cetaceans, however. They haven't evolved that far from their land ancestors. You can tell by the fins. Of some use in swimming, but not really an efficient size or shape as yet."

"You can speculate about that while Mons is being carried away?" Neri choked.

Regor got up and tried in a bemused fashion to brush the sand off his clothes. "Oh no," he said. His face worked, and he blinked several times. "We've got to do something about him, of course." He looked skyward. The air was full of wings, as the sea birds sensed meat and wheeled insolently close. Their piping overrode the wind. "Let's get back to the boat. We'll take this carcass along for the scientists."

Neri cursed at the delay, but took one end of the object. Jong had the other. The weight felt monstrous, and seemed to grow while they stumbled toward the cliffs. Breath rasped in their throats. Their shirts clung to the sweat on them, which they could smell through every sea odor.

Jong looked down at the ugly countenance beneath his hands. In spite of everything, in spite of Mons being dead—oh, never to hear his big laugh again, never to move a chessman or hoist a glass or stand on the thrumming decks with him!—he wondered if a female dwelt somewhere out in the ocean who had thought this face was beautiful.

"We weren't doing them any harm," said Neri between wheezes.

"You can't . . . blame a poison snake . . . or a carnivore . . . if you come too near," Jong said.

"But these aren't dumb animals! Look at that braincase. At that knife." Neri needed a little time before he had the lungful to continue his fury: "We've dealt with nonhumans often enough. Fought them once in a while. But they had a reason to fight . . . mistaken or not, they did. I never saw or heard of anyone striking down utter strangers at first sight."

"We may not have been strangers," Regor said.

"What?" Neri's head twisted around to stare at the older man.

Regor shrugged. "A human colony was planted here. The natives seem to have wiped it out. I imagine they had reasons then. And the tradition may have survived."

For ten thousand years or more? Jong thought, shocked. *What horror did our race visit on theirs, that they haven't been able to forget in so many millennia?*

He tried to picture what might have happened, but found no reality in it, only a dry and somehow thin logic. Presumably this colony was established by a successor civilization to the Star Empire. Presumably that civilization had crumbled in its turn. The settlers had most likely possessed no spaceships of their own; outpost worlds found it easiest to rely on the Kith for what few trade goods they wanted. Often their libraries did not even include the technical data for building a ship, and they lacked the economic surplus necessary to do that research over again.

So—the colony was orphaned. Later, if a period of especially virulent anti-Kithism had occurred here, the traders might have stopped coming; might actually have lost any record of this world's existence. *Or the Kith might have become extinct, but that is not a possibility we will admit.* The planet was left isolated.

Without much land surface it couldn't support a very big population, even if most of the food and industrial resources had been drawn from the sea. However, the people should have been able to maintain a machine culture. No doubt their society would ossify, but static civilizations can last indefinitely.

Unless they are confronted by vigorous barbarians, organized into million-man hordes under the lash of outrage. . . . But was that the answer? Given atomic energy, how could a single city be overrun by any number of neolithic hunters?

Attack from within? A simultaneous revolt of every autochthonous slave? Jong looked back to the dead face. The teeth glinted at him. *Maybe I'm soft-headed. Maybe these beings simply take a weasel's pleasure in killing.*

They struggled up the scarp and into the boat. Jong was relieved to get the thing hidden in a cold-storage locker. But then came the moment when they called the *Golden Flyer* to report.

"I'll tell his family," said Captain Ilmaray, most quietly.

But I'll still have to tell Sorya how he looked, Jong thought. The resolution stiffened in him: *We're going to recover the body. Mons is going to have a Kithman's funeral; hands that loved him will start him on his orbit into the sun.*

He had no reason to voice it, even to himself. The oneness of the Kith reached beyond death. Ilmaray asked only if Regor believed there was a chance.

"Yes, provided we start soon," the leader replied. "The bottom slopes quickly here, but gets no deeper than about thirty meters. Then it's almost flat to some distance beyond the gate, farther than our sonoprobes reached when we flew over. I doubt the swimmers go so fast they can evade us till they reach a depth too great for a nucleoscope to detect Mons' electronic gear."

"Good. Don't take risks, though." Grimly: "We're too short on future heredity as is." After a pause, Ilmaray added, "I'll order a boat with a high-powered magnascreen to the stratosphere, to keep your general area under observation. Luck ride with you."

"And with every ship of ours," Regor finished the formula.

As his fingers moved across the pilot board, raising the vessel, he said over his shoulder, "One of you two get into a spacesuit and be prepared to go down. The other watch the 'scope, and lower him when we find what we're after."

"I'll go," said Jong and Neri into each other's mouths. They exchanged a look. Neri's glared.

"Please," Jong begged. "Maybe I ought to have shot them down, when I saw what they'd done to Mons. I don't know. But anyhow, I didn't. So let me bring him back, will you?"

Neri regarded him for nearly a minute more before he nodded.

The boat cruised in slow zigzags out across the bay while Jong climbed into his spacesuit. It would serve as well underwater as in the void. He knotted a line about his waist and adjusted the other end to the little winch by the personnel lock. The metallic strand woven into its plastic would conduct phone messages. He draped a sack over one arm for the, well, the search object, and hoped he would not need the slugthrower at his hip.

"There!"

Jong jerked at Neri's shout. Regor brought the craft to hoverhalt, a couple of meters above the surface and three kilometers from shore. "You certain?" he asked.

"Absolutely. Not moving, either. I suppose they abandoned him so as to make a faster escape when they saw us coming through the air."

Jong clamped his helmet shut. External noises ceased. The stillness made him aware of his own breath and pulse and—some inner sound, a stray nerve current or mere imagination—the hunter's horn, remote and triumphant.

The lock opened, filling with sky. Jong walked to the rim and was nearly blinded by the sunlight off the wavelets. Radiance ran to the horizon. He eased himself over the lip. The rope payed out and the surface shut above him. He sank.

A cool green roofed with sunblaze enclosed him. Even through the armor he felt multitudinous vibrations; the sea lived and moved, everywhere around. A pair of fish streaked by, unbelievably graceful. For a heretical instant he wondered if Mons would not rather stay here, lulled to the end of the world.

Cut that! he told himself, and peered downward. Darkness lurked below. He switched on the powerful flash at his belt.

Particles in the water scattered the light, so that he fell as if through an illuminated cave. More fish passed near. Their scales reflected like jewels. He thought he could make out the bottom now, white sand and uplifted ranges of rock on which clustered many-colored coraloids, growing toward the sun. And the swimmer appeared.

He moved slowly to the fringe of light and poised. In his left hand he bore a trident, perhaps the one which had killed Mons. At first he squinted against the dazzle, then looked steadily at the radiant metal man. As Jong continued to descend he followed, propelling himself with easy gestures of feet and free hand, a motion as lovely as a snake's.

Jong gasped and yanked out his slugthrower.

"What's the matter?" Neri's voice rattled in his earplugs.

He gulped. "Nothing," he said, without knowing why. "Lower away."

The swimmer came a little closer. His muscles were tense, mouth open as if to bite; but the deep-set eyes remained unwavering. Jong returned the gaze. They went down together.

He's not afraid of me, Jong thought, *or else he's mastered his fear, though he saw on the beach what we can do.*

Impact jarred through his soles. "I'm here," he called mechanically. "Give me some slack and—Oh!"

The blood drained from his head as if an ax had split it. He swayed, supported only by the water. Thunders and winds went through him, and the roar of the horn.

"Jong!" Neri called, infinitely distant. "Something's wrong, I know it is, gimme an answer, for the love of Kith!"

The swimmer touched bottom too. He stood across from what had belonged to Mons Rainart, the trident upright in his hand.

Jong lifted the gun. "I can fill you with metal," he heard himself groan. "I can cut you to pieces, the way you—you—"

The swimmer shuddered (was the voice conducted to him?) but stayed where he was. Slowly, he raised the trident toward the unseen sun. With a single gesture, he reversed it, thrust it into the sand, let go, and turned his back. A shove of the great legs sent him arrowing off.

The knowledge exploded in Jong. For a century of seconds he stood alone with it.

Regor's words pierced through: "Get my suit. I'm going after him."

"I'm all right," he managed to say. "I found Mons."

He gathered what he could. There wasn't much. "Bring me up," he said.

When he was lifted from the bay and climbed through the air lock, he felt how heavy was the weight upon him. He let fall the sack and trident and crouched beside them. Water ran off his armor.

The doors closed. The boat climbed. A kilometer high, Regor locked the controls and came aft to join the others. Jong removed his helmet just as Neri opened the sack.

Mons' head rolled out and bounced dreadfully across the deck. Neri strangled a yell.

Regor lurched back. "They ate him," he croaked. "They cut him to pieces for food. Didn't they?"

He gathered his will, strode to the port, and squinted out. "I saw one of them break the surface, a short while before you came up," he said between his teeth. Sweat—or was it tears?—coursed down the gullies in his cheeks. "We can catch him. The boat has a gun turret."

"No—" Jong tried to rise, but hadn't the strength.

The radio buzzed. Regor ran to the pilot's chair forward, threw himself into it, and slapped the receiver switch. Neri set lips together, picked up the head, and laid it on the sack. "Mons, Mons, but they'll pay," he said.

Captain Ilmaray's tones filled the hull: "We just got word from the observer boat. It isn't on station yet, but the magnascreen's already spotted a horde of swimmers . . . no, several different flocks, huge, must total thousands . . . converging on the island where you are. At the rate they're going, they should arrive in a couple of days."

Regor shook his head in a stunned fashion. "How did they know?"

"They didn't," Jong mumbled.

Neri leaped to his feet, a tiger movement. "That's exactly the chance we want. A couple of bombs dropped in the middle of 'em."

"You mustn't!" Jong cried. He became able to rise too. The trident was gripped in his hand. "He gave me this."

"What?" Regor swiveled around. Neri stiffened where he stood. Silence poured through the boat.

"Down below," Jong told them. "He saw me and followed me to the bottom. Realized what I was doing. Gave me this. His weapon."

"Whatever *for*?"

"A peace offering. What else?"

Neri spat on the deck. "Peace, with those filthy cannibals?"

Jong squared his shoulders. The armor enclosing him no longer seemed an insupportable burden. "You wouldn't be a cannibal if you ate a monkey, would you?"

Neri said an obscene word, but Regor suppressed him with a gesture. "Well, different species," the pilot admitted coldly. "By the dictionary you're right. But these killers are sentient. You don't eat another thinking being."

"It's been done," Jong said. "By humans too. More often than not as an act of respect or love, taking some of the person's mana into yourself. Anyway, how could they know what we were? When he saw I'd come to gather our dead, he gave me his weapon. How else could he say he was sorry, and that we're brothers? Maybe he even realized that's literally true, after he'd had a little while to think the matter over. But I don't imagine their traditions are that old. It's enough, it's better, actually, that he confessed we were his kin simply because we also care for our dead."

"What are you getting at?" Neri snapped.

"Yes, what the destruction's going on down there?" Ilmaray demanded through the radio.

"Wait." Regor gripped the arms of his chair. His voice fell low. "You don't mean they're—"

"Yes, I do," Jong said. "What else could they be? How could a mammal that big, with hands and brain, evolve on these few islands? How could any natives have wiped out a colony that had nuclear arms? I thought about a slave revolt, but that doesn't make sense either. Who'd bother with so many slaves when they had cybernetic machines? No, the swimmers are the colonists. They can't be anything else."

"Huh?" grunted Neri.

Ilmaray said across hollow space: "It could be. If I remember rightly, Homo Sapiens is supposed to have developed from the, uh, Neandertaloid type, in something like ten or twenty thousand years. Given a small population, genetic drift, yes, a group might need less time than that to degenerate."

"Who says they're degenerate?" Jong retorted.

Neri pointed to the staring-eyed head on the deck. "That does."

"Was an accident, I tell you, a misunderstanding," Jong said. "We had it coming, blundering in blind the way we did. They aren't degenerate, they're just adapted. As the colony got more and more dependent on the sea, and mutations occurred, those who could best take this sort of environment had the most children. A static civilization wouldn't notice what was happening till too late, and wouldn't be able to do anything about it if they did. Because the new people had the freedom of the whole planet. The future was theirs."

"Yeah, a future of being savages."

"They couldn't use our kind of civilization. It's wrong for this world. If you're going to spend most of your life in salt water you can't very well keep your electric machines; and flint you can gather almost anywhere is an improvement over metal that has to be mined and smelted.

"Oh, maybe they have lost some intelligence. I doubt that, but if they have, what of it? We never did find the Elder Races. Maybe intelligence really isn't the goal of the universe. I believe, myself, these people are coming back up the ladder in their own way. But that's none of our business." Jong knelt and closed Mons's eyes. "We were allowed to atone for our crime," he said softly. "The least we can do is forgive them in our turn. Isn't it? And . . . we don't know if any other humans are left, anywhere in all the worlds, except us and these. No, we can't kill them."

"Then why did they kill Mons?"

"They're air breathers," Jong said, "and doubtless they have to learn swimming, like pinnipeds, instead of having an instinct. So they need breeding grounds. That beach, yes, that must be where the tribes are headed. A party of males went in advance to make sure the place was in order. They saw something strange and terrible walking on the ground where their children were to be born, and they had the courage to attack it. I'm sorry, Mons," he finished in a whisper.

Neri slumped down on a bench. The silence came back.

Until Ilmaray said: "I think you have the answer. We can't stay here. Return immediately, and we'll get under weigh."

Regor nodded and touched the controls. The engine hummed into life. Jong got up, walked to a port, and watched the sea, molten silver beneath him, dwindle as the sky darkened and the stars trod forth.

I wonder what that sound was, he thought vaguely. *A wind noise, no doubt, as Mons said. But I'll never be sure.* For a moment it seemed to him that he heard it again, in the thrum of energy and metal, in the beat of his own blood, the horn of a hunter pursuing a quarry that wept as it ran.

VII

Those were the years in which I hit my stride as a writer. Besides Tony Boucher, I placed a lot of work with the other great editor in the field, John Campbell of *Astounding* (whose name he eventually got changed to *Analog*). He was the man who, by his policies and the unstinting help he gave his writers, had pulled science fiction out of the pulp mire into which it had fallen and given it the form and nature we still know. He'd done the same for modern fantasy in his *Unknown,* but that brilliant magazine fell victim to wartime paper shortages and I never had the honor of appearing in it.

Elsewhere I have written at some length about him—the tribute is in *All One Universe*—and shan't repeat much here. Geography prevented my becoming as close to him as to Tony, but I was among those privileged to have a fireworks correspondence with him, and when we met in person it was always more than cordially. Our long hammer-and-tongs arguments about countless different things only added savor. From father figure he evolved to dear friend.

It was with him that Nicholas van Rijn exploded forth. While some readers couldn't stand this burly, beery, uninhibited merchant prince, on the whole he was probably the most popular character I ever hit upon, and the stories about him enjoyed a long and lusty run. I like to believe that was partly because they were more than space operas. They were where I began in earnest doing hard science fiction, the kind in which real science and its possibilities are the underlying motif. That needn't mean a dearth of more traditional literary qualities, as the work of Greg Bear, Gregory Benford, and David Brin—to name just three—amply shows.

Hal Clement, the master of worldbuilding, set the standard. My first go at it was the novel *The Man Who Counts,* featuring the oddball planet Diomedes and the beings and cultures that such a world might breed. Van Rijn was the hero, or antihero if you prefer.

Granted, Clement himself has often had to make a few counterscientific assumptions—notably faster-than-light travel, so people can get to the scene of action in a reasonable time. I did too, as of course I'd done before; and it seemed not illogical that the yet-to-be-discovered laws of nature (in my case, an extension of quantum mechanics) that allowed this would also allow a few other things, such as local control of gravity and field drives that don't require reaction mass. Otherwise, however wildly speculative, my hard stories shouldn't contain anything that wasn't at least theoretically possible in terms of present-day scientific knowledge.

This book would be incomplete without a van Rijn yarn. He isn't at the center of the one I've chosen, but he is very much there.

THE MASTER KEY

Once upon a time there was a king who set himself above the foreign merchants. What he did is of no account now; it was long ago and on another planet, and besides, the wench is dead. Harry Stenvik and I hung him by the seat of his trousers from his tallest minaret, in sight of all the people, and the name of the Polesotechnic League was great in the land. Then we made inroads on the stock-in-trade of the Solar Spice & Liquors Company factor and swore undying brotherhood.

Now there are those who maintain that Nicholas van Rijn has a cryogenic computer in that space used by the ordinary Terran for storing his heart. This may be so. But he does not forget a good workman. And I know no reason why he should have invited me to dinner except that Harry would be there, and—this being the briefest of business trips to Earth for me—we would probably have no other chance of meeting.

The flitter set me off atop the Winged Cross, where van Rijn keeps what he honestly believes is a modest little penthouse apartment. A summer's dusk softened the mass of lesser buildings that stretched to the horizon and beyond; Venus had wakened in the west and Chicago Integrate was opening multitudinous lights. This high up, only a low machine throb reached my ears. I walked among roses and jasmine to the door. When it scanned me and dilated, Harry was waiting. We fell into each other's arms and praised God with many loud violations of His third commandment.

Afterward we stood apart and looked. "You haven't changed much," he lied. "Mean and ugly as ever. Methane in the air must agree with you."

"Ammonia, where I've been of late," I corrected him. "S.O.P.: occasional bullets and endless dickering. *You're* disgustingly sleek and contented. How's Sigrid?" As it must to all men, domesticity had come to him. In his case it lasted, and he had built a house on the cliffs above Hardanger Fjord and raised mastiffs and sons. Myself—but that also is irrelevant.

"Fine. She sends her love and a box of her own cookies. Next time you must wangle a longer stay and come see us."

"The boys?"

"Same." The soft Norse accent roughened the least bit. "Per's had his troubles, but they are mending. He's here tonight."

"Well, great." The last I'd heard of Harry's oldest son, he was an apprentice aboard one of van Rijn's ships, somewhere in the Hercules region. But that was several years ago, and you can rise fast in the League if you survive. "I imagine he has master's rank by now."

"Yes, quite newly. Plus an artificial femur and a story to tell. Come, let's join them."

Hm, I thought, so Old Nick was economizing on his bird-killing stones again. He had enough anecdotes of his own that he didn't need to collect them, unless they had some special use to him. A gesture of kindness might as well be thrown into the interview.

We passed through the foyer and crossed a few light-years of trollcat rug to the far end of the living room. Three men sat by the viewer wall, at the moment transparent to sky and city. Only one of them rose. He had been seated a little to one side, in a tigery kind of relaxed alertness—a stranger to me, dark and lean, with a blaster that had seen considerable service at his hip.

Nicholas van Rijn wallowed his bulk deeper into his lounger, hoisted a beer stein and roared, "Ha! Welcome to you, Captain, and you will maybe have a small drink like me before dinner?" After which he tugged his goatee and muttered, "Gabriel will tootle before I get your bepestered Anglic through this poor old noggin. I think I have just called myself a small drink."

I bowed to him as is fitting to a merchant prince, turned, and gave Per Stenvik my hand. "Excuse my staying put," he said. His face was still pale and gaunt; health was coming back, but youth never would. "I got a trifle clobbered."

"So I heard," I answered. "Don't worry, it'll heal up. I hate to think how much of me is replacement by now, but as long as the important parts are left . . ."

"Oh, yes, I'll be okay. Thanks to Manuel. Uh, Manuel Felipe Gómez y Palomares of Nuevo México. My ensign."

I introduced myself with great formality, according to what I knew of the customs of those poor and haughty colonists from the far side of Arcturus. His courtesy was equal, before he turned to make sure the blanket was secure around Per's legs. Nor did he go back to his seat and his glass of claret before Harry and I lowered ourselves. A human servant—male, in this one van Rijn establishment—brought us our orders, *akvavit* for Harry and a martini for me. Per fiddled with a glass of Ansan vermouth.

"How long will you be home?" I asked him after the small talk had gone by.

"As long as needful," Harry said quickly.

"No more, though," van Rijn said with equal speed. "Not one millimoment more can he loaf than nature must have; and he is young and strong."

"Pardon, *señor*," Manuel said—how softly and deferentially, and with what a clang of colliding stares. "I would not gainsay my superiors. But my duty is to know how it is with my captain, and the doctors are fools. He shall rest not less than till the Day of the Dead; and then surely, with the Nativity so near, the *señor* will not deny him the holidays at home?"

Van Rijn threw up his hands. "Everyone, they call me apocalyptic beast," he wailed, "and I am only a poor lonely old man in a sea of grievances, trying so hard to keep awash. One good boy with promises I find, I watch him from before his pants dry out for I know his breed. I give him costly schooling in hopes he does not turn out another curdlebrain, and no sooner does he not but he is in the locker and my fine new planet gets thrown to the wolves!"

"Lord help the wolves," Per grinned. "Don't worry, sir, I'm as anxious to get back as you are."

"Hoy, hoy, I am not going. I am too old and fat. Ah, you think you have troubles now, but wait till time has gnawed you down to a poor old wheezer like me who has not even any pleasures left. Abdul! Abdul, you jellylegs, bring drink, you want we should dry up and puff away? . . . What, only me ready for a refill?"

"Do you really want to see that Helheim again?" Harry asked, with a stiff glance at van Rijn.

"Judas, yes," Per said. "It's just waiting for the right man. A whole *world,* Dad! Don't you remember?"

Harry looked through the wall and nodded. I made haste to intrude on his silence. "What were you there after, Per?"

"Everything," the young man said. "I told you it's an entire planet. Not one percent of the land surface has been mapped."

"Huh? Not even from orbit?"

Manuel's expression showed me what they thought of orbital maps.

"But for a starter, what attracted us in the first place, furs and herbs," Per said. Wordlessly, Manuel took a little box from his pocket, opened it, and handed it to me. A bluish-green powder of leaves lay within. I tasted. There was a sweet-sour flavor with wild overtones, and the odor went to the oldest, deepest part of my brain and roused memories I had not known were lost.

"The chemicals we have not yet understood and synthesized," van Rijn rumbled around the cigar he was lighting. "Bah! What do my chemists do all day but play happy fun games in the lab alcohol? And the furs, *ja,* I have Lupescu of the Peltery volcanomaking that he must buy them from me. He is even stooping to spies, him, he has the ethics of a paranoid weasel. Fifteen thousand he spent last month alone, trying to find where that planet is."

"How do you know how much he spent?" Harry asked blandly.

van Rijn managed to look smug and hurt at the same time.

Per said with care, "I'd better not mention the coordinates myself. It's out Pegasus way. A G-nine dwarf star, about half as luminous as Sol. Eight planets, one of them terrestroid. Brander came upon it in the course of a survey, thought it looked interesting, and settled down to learn more. He'd really only time to tape the language of the locality where he was camped, and do the basic-basic planetography and bionics. But he did find out about the furs and herbs. So I was sent to establish a trading post."

"His first command," Harry said, unnecessarily on anyone's account but his own.

"Trouble with the natives, eh?" I asked.

"Trouble is not the word," van Rijn said. "The word is not for polite ears." He dove into his beer stein and came up snorting. "After all I have done for them, the saints keep on booting me in the soul like this."

"But we seem to have it licked," Per said.

"Ah. You think so?" Van Rijn waggled a hairy forefinger at him. "That is what we should like to be more sure of, boy, before we send out and maybe lose some expensive ships."

"*Y algunos hombres buenos,*" Manuel muttered, so low he could scarcely be heard. One hand dropped to the butt of his gun.

"I have been reading the reports from Brander's people," van Rijn said. "Also your own. I think maybe I see a pattern. When you have been swindling on so many planets like me, new captain, you will have analogues at your digits for much that is new. . . . Ah, pox and pity it is to get jaded!" He puffed a smoke ring that settled around Per's bright locks. "Still, you are never sure. I think sometimes God likes a little practical joke on us poor mortals, when we get too cockish. So I jump on no conclusions before I have heard from your own teeth how it was. Reports, even on visitape, they have no more flavor than what my competition sells. In you I live again the fighting and merrylarks, everything that is now so far behind me in my doting."

This from the single-handed conqueror of Borthu, Diomedes, and t'Kela!

"Well—" Per blushed and fumbled with his glass. "There really isn't a lot to tell, you know. I mean, each of you freemen has been through so much more than—uh—one silly episode . . ."

Harry gestured at the blanketed legs. "Nothing silly there," he said.

Per's lips tightened. "I'm sorry. You're right. Men died."

Chiefly because it is not good to dwell overly long on those lost from a command of one's own, I said, "What's the planet like? 'Terrestroid' is a joke. They sit in an Earthside office and call it that if you can breathe the air."

"And not fall flat in an oof from the gravity for at least half an hour, and not hope the *whole* year round you have no brass-monkey ancestors." Van Rijn's nod sent the black ringlets swirling around his shoulders.

"I generally got assigned to places where the brass monkeys melted," Harry complained.

"Well, Cain isn't too bad in the low latitudes," Per said. His face relaxed, and his hands came alive in quick gestures that reminded me of his mother. "It's about Earth-size, average orbital radius a little over one A.U. Denser atmosphere, though, by around fifteen percent, which makes for more greenhouse effect. Twenty-hour rotation period; no moons. Thirty-two degrees of axial tilt, which does rather complicate the seasons. But we were at fifteen-forty north, in fairly low hills, and it was summer. A nearby pool was frozen every morning, and snowbanks remained on the slopes—but really, not bad for the planet of a G-nine star."

"Did Brander name it Cain?" I asked.

"Yes. I don't know why. But it turned out appropriate. Too damned appropriate." Again the bleakness. Manuel took his captain's empty glass and glided off, to return in a moment with it filled. Per drank hurriedly.

"Always there is trouble," van Rijn said. "You will learn."

"But the mission was going so well!" Per protested. "Even the language and the data seemed to . . . to flow into my head on the voyage out. In fact, the whole crew learned easily." He turned to me. "There were twenty of us, on the *Miriam Knight*. She's a real beauty, Cheland-class transport, built for speed rather than capacity, you know. More wasn't needed, when we were only supposed to erect the first post and get the idea of regular trade across to the autochthones. We had the usual line of goods, fabrics, tools, weapons, household stuff like scissors and meat grinders. Not much ornament, because Brander's xenologists hadn't been able to work out any consistent pattern for it. Individual Cainites seemed to dress and decorate themselves any way they pleased. In the Ulash area, at least, which of course was the only one we had any details on."

"And damn few there," Harry murmured. "Also as usual."

"Agriculture?" I inquired.

"Some primitive cultivation," Per said. "Small plots scratched out of the forest, tended by the Lugals. In Ulash a little metallurgy has begun, copper, gold, silver, but even they are essentially neolithic. And essentially hunters—the Yildivans, that is—along with such Lugals as they employ to help. The food supply is mainly game. In fact, the better part of what farming is done is to supply fabric."

"What do they look like, these people?"

"I've a picture here." Per reached in his tunic and handed me a photograph. "That's old Shivaru. Early in our acquaintance. He was probably scared of the camera but damned if he'd admit it. You'll notice the Lugal he has with him is frankly in a blue funk."

I studied the image with an interest that grew. The background was harsh plutonic hillside, where grass of a pale yellowish turquoise grew between dark boulders. But on the right I glimpsed a densely wooded valley. The sky overhead was wan, and the orange sunlight distorted colors.

Shivaru stood very straight and stiff, glaring into the lens. He was about two meters tall, Per said, his body build much like that of a long-legged, deep-chested man. Tawny, spotted fur covered him to the end of an elegant tail. The head was less anthropoid: a black ruff on top, slit-pupiled green eyes, round mobile ears, flat nose that looked feline even to the cilia around it, full-lipped mouth with protruding tushes at the corners, and jaw that tapered down to a V. He wore a sort of loincloth, gaudily dyed, and a necklace of raw semiprecious stones. His left hand clutched an obsidian-bladed battle-ax and there was a steel trade-knife in his belt.

"They're mammals, more or less," Per said, "though with any number of differences in anatomy and chemistry, as you'd expect. They don't sweat, however. There's a complicated system of exo- and endothermic reactions in the blood to regulate temperature."

"Sweating is not so common on cold terrestroids," van Rijn remarked. "Always you find analogs to something you met before, if you look long enough. Evolution makes parallels."

"And skew lines," I added. "Uh—Brander got some corpses to dissect, then?"

"Well, not any Yildivans," Per said. "But they sold him as many dead Lugals as he asked for, who're obviously of the same genus." He winced. "I hope to hell they didn't kill the Lugals especially for that purpose."

My attention had gone to the creature that cowered behind Shivaru. It was a squat, short-shanked, brown-furred version of the other Cainite. Forehead and chin were poorly developed and the muzzle had not yet become a nose. The being was nude except for a heavy pack, a quiver of arrows, a bow, and two spears piled on its muscular back. I could see that the skin there was rubbed naked and calloused by such burdens. "This is a Lugal?" I pointed.

"Yes. You see, there are two related species on the planet, one farther along in evolution than the other. As if Australopithecus had survived till today on Earth. The Yildivans have made slaves of the Lugals—certainly in Ulash, and as far as we could find out by spot checks, everywhere on Cain."

"Pretty roughly treated, aren't they, the poor devils?" Harry said. "*I* wouldn't trust a slave with weapons."

"But Lugals are completely trustworthy," Per said. "Like dogs. They do the hard, monotonous work. The Yildivans—male and female—are the hunters, artists, magicians, everything that matters. That is, what culture exists is Yildivan." He scowled into his drink. "Though I'm not sure how meaningful 'culture' is in this connection."

"How so?" Van Rijn lifted brows far above his small black eyes.

"Well . . . they, the Yildivans, haven't anything like a nation, a tribe, any sort of community. Family groups split up when the cubs are old enough to fend for themselves. A young male establishes himself somewhere, chases off all comers, and eventually one or more young females come join him. Their Lugals tag along, naturally—like dogs again. As near as I could learn, such families have only the most casual contact. Occasional barter, occasional temporary gangs formed to hunt extra-large animals, occasional clashes between individuals, and that's about it."

"But hold on," I objected. "Intelligent races need more. Something to be the carrier of tradition, something to stimulate the evolution of brain, a way for individuals to communicate ideas to each other. Else intelligence hasn't got any biological function."

"I fretted over that too," Per said. "Had long talks with Shivaru, Fereghir, and others who drifted into camp whenever they felt like it. We really tried hard to understand each other. They were as curious about us as we about them, and as quick to see the mutual advantage in trade relations. But what a job! A whole different planet—two or three billion years of separate evolution—and we had only pidgin Ulash to start with, the limited vocabulary Brander's people had gotten. We couldn't go far into the subtleties. Especially when they, of course, took everything about their own way of life for granted.

"Toward the end, though, I began to get a glimmering. It turns out that in spite of their oafish appearance, the Lugals are not stupid. Maybe even as bright as their masters, in a different fashion; at any rate, not too far behind them. And—in each of these family groups, these patriarchal settlements in a cave or hut, way off in the forest, there are several times as many Lugals as Yildivans. Every member of the family, even the kids, has a number of slaves. Thus you may not get Yildivan clans or tribes, but you do get the numerical equivalent among the Lugals.

"Then the Lugals are sent on errands to other Yildivan preserves, with messages or barter goods or whatever, and bring back news. And they get traded around; the Yildivans breed them deliberately, with a shrewd practical grasp of genetics. Apparently, too, the Lugals are often allowed to wander off by themselves when there's no work for them to do—much as we let our dogs run loose—and hold powwows of their own.

"You mustn't think of them as being mistreated. They are, by our standards, but Cain is a brutal place and Yildivans don't exactly have an easy life either. An intelligent Lugal is valued. He's made straw boss over the others, teaches the Yildivan young special skills and songs and such, is sometimes even asked by his owner what he thinks ought to be done in a given situation. Some families let him eat and sleep in their own dwelling, I'm told. And remember, his loyalty is strictly to the masters. What they may do to other Lugals is nothing to him. He'll gladly help cull the weaklings, punish the lazy, anything.

"So, to get to the point, I think that's your answer. The Yildivans do have a community life, a larger society—but indirectly, through their Lugals. The Yildivans are the creators and innovators, the Lugals the communicators and preservers. I daresay the relationship has existed for so long a time that the biological evolution of both species has been conditioned by it."

"You speak rather well of them," said Harry grimly, "considering what they did to you."

"But they were very decent people at first." I could hear in Per's voice how hurt he was by that which had happened. "Proud as Satan, callous, but not cruel. Honest and generous. They brought gifts whenever they arrived, with no thought of payment. Two or three offered to assign us Lugal laborers. That wasn't necessary or feasible when we had machinery along, but they didn't realize it then. When they did, they were quick to grasp the idea, and mightily impressed. I think. Hard to tell, because they couldn't or wouldn't admit anyone else might be superior to them. That is, each individual thought of himself as being as good as anyone else anywhere in the world. But they seemed to regard us as their equals. I didn't try to explain where we were really from. 'Another country' looked sufficient for practical purposes.

"Shivaru was especially interested in us. He was middle-aged, most of his children grown and moved away. Wealthy in local terms, progressive—he was experimenting with ranching as a supplement to hunting—and his advice was much sought after by the others. I took him for a ride in a flitter and he was happy and excited as any child; brought his three mates along next time so they could enjoy it too. We went hunting together occasionally. Lord, you should have seen him run down those great horned beasts, leap on their backs, and brain them with one blow of that tremendous ax! Then his Lugals would butcher the game and carry it home to camp. The meat tasted damn good, believe me. Cainite biochemistry lacks some of our vitamins, but otherwise a human can get along all right there.

"Mainly, though, I remember how we'd talk. I suppose it's old hat to you freemen, but I had never before spent hour after hour with another being, both of us at work trying to build up a vocabulary and an understanding, both getting such a charge out of it that we'd forget even to eat until Manuel or Cherkez—that was his chief Lugal, a gnarly, droll old fellow, made me think of the friendly gnomes in my fairy tale books when I was a youngster—until one of them would tell us. Sometimes my mind wandered off and I'd come back to earth realizing that I'd just sat there admiring his beauty. Yildivans are as graceful as cats, as pleasing in shape as a good gun. And as deadly, when they want to be. I found that out!

"We had a favorite spot, in the lee of a cottage-sized boulder on the hillside above camp. The rock was warm against our backs; seemed even more so when I looked at that pale shrunken sun and my breath smoking out white across the purplish sky. Far, far overhead a bird of prey would wheel, then suddenly stoop—in the thick air I could hear the whistle through its wing feathers—and vanish into the treetops down in the valley. Those leaves had a million different shades of color, like an endless autumn.

"Shivaru squatted with his tail curled around his knees, ax on the ground beside him. Cherkez and one or two other Lugals hunkered at a respectful distance. Their eyes never left their Yildivan. Sometimes Manuel joined us, when he wasn't busy bossing some phase of construction. Remember, Manuel? You really shouldn't have kept so quiet."

"Silence was fitting, Captain," said the Nuevo Méxican.

"Well," Per said, "Shivaru's deep voice would go on and on. He was full of plans for the future. No question of a trade treaty—no organization for us to make a treaty with—but he foresaw his people bringing us what we wanted in exchange for what we offered. And he was bright enough to see how the existence of a central mart like this, a common meeting ground, would affect them. More joint undertakings would be started. The idea of close cooperation would take root. He looked forward to that, within the rather narrow limits he could conceive. For instance, many Yildivans working together could take real advantage of the annual spawning run up the Mukushyat River. Big canoes could venture across a strait he knew of, to open fresh hunting grounds. That sort of thing.

"But then in a watchtick his ears would perk, his whiskers vibrate, he'd lean forward and start to ask about my own people. What sort of country did we come from? How was the game there? What were our mating and child-rearing practices? How did we ever produce such beautiful things? Oh, he had the whole cosmos to explore! Bit by bit, as my vocabulary grew, his questions got less practical and more abstract. So did mine, naturally. We were getting at each other's psychological foundations now, and were equally fascinated.

"I was not too surprised to learn that his culture had no religion. In fact, he was hard put to understand my questions about it. They practiced magic, but looked on it simply as a kind of technology. There was no animism, no equivalent of anthropomorphism. A Yildivan knew too damn well he was superior to any plant or animal. I think, but I'm not sure, that they had some vague concept of reincarnation. But it didn't interest them much, apparently, and the problem of origins hadn't occurred. Life was what you had, here and now. The world was a set of phenomena, to live with or master or be defeated by as the case might be.

"Shivaru asked me why I'd asked him about such a self-evident thing."

Per shook his head. His glance went down to the blanket around his lap and quickly back again. "That may have been my first mistake."

"No, Captain," said Manuel most gently. "How could you know they lacked souls?"

"Do they?" Per mumbled.

"We leave that to the theologians," van Rijn said. "They get paid to decide. Go on, boy."

I could see Per brace himself. "I tried to explain the idea of God," he said tonelessly. "I'm pretty sure I failed. Shivaru acted puzzled and . . . troubled. He left soon after. The Yildivans of Ulash use drums for long-range communication, have I mentioned? All that night I heard the drums mutter in the valley and echo from the cliffs. We had no visitors for a week. But Manuel, scouting around in the area, said he'd found tracks and traces. We were being watched.

"I was relieved, at first, when Shivaru returned. He had a couple of others with him, Fereghir and Tulitur, important males like himself. They came straight across the hill toward me. I was supervising the final touches on our timber-cutting system. We were to use local lumber for most of our construction, you see. Cut and trim in the woods with power beams, load the logs on a gravsled for the sawmill, then snake them directly through the induration vats to the site, where the foundations had now been laid. The air was full of whine and crash, boom and chug, in a wind that cut like a laser. I could hardly see our ship or our sealtents through dust, tinged bloody in the sun.

"They came to me, those three tall hunters, with a dozen armed Lugals hovering behind. Shivaru beckoned. 'Come,' he said. 'This is no place for a Yildivan.' I looked him in the eyes and they were filmed over, as if he'd put a glass mask between me and himself. Frankly, my skin prickled. I was unarmed—everybody was except Manuel, you know what Nuevo Méxicans are—and I was afraid I'd precipitate something by going for a weapon. In fact, I even made a point of speaking Ulash as I ordered Tom Bullis to take over for me and told Manuel to come along uphill. If the autochthones had taken some notion into their heads that we were planning harm, it wouldn't do for them to hear us use a language they didn't know.

"Not another word was spoken till we were out of the dust and racket, at the old place by the boulder. It didn't feel warm today. Nothing did. 'I welcome you,' I said to the Yildivans, 'and bid you dine and sleep with us.' That's the polite formula when a visitor arrives. I didn't get the regular answer.

"Tulitur hefted the spear he carried and asked—not rudely, understand, but with a kind of shiver in the tone—'Why have you come to Ulash?'

" 'Why?' I stuttered. 'You know. To trade.'

" 'No, wait, Tulitur,' Shivaru interrupted. 'Your question is blind.' He turned to me. 'Were you sent?' he asked. And what I would like to ask you sometime, freemen, is whether it makes sense to call a voice black.

"I couldn't think of any way to hedge. Something had gone awry, but I'd no feeblest notion what. A lie or a stall was as likely, *a priori*, to make matters worse as the truth. I saw the sunlight glisten along that dark ax head and felt most infernally glad to have Manuel beside me. Even so, the noise from the camp sounded faint and distant. Or was it only that the wind was whittering louder?

"I made myself stare back at him. 'You know we are here on behalf of others like us at home,' I said. The muscles tightened still more under his fur. Also . . . I can't read nonhuman expressions especially well. But Fereghir's lips were drawn off his teeth as if he confronted an enemy. Tulitur had grounded his spear, point down. Brander's reports observed that a Yildivan never did that in the presence of a friend. Shivaru, though, was hardest to understand. I could have sworn he was grieved.

" 'Did God send you?' he asked.

"That put the dunce's cap on the whole lunatic business. I actually laughed, though I didn't feel at all funny. Inside my head it went click-click-click. I recognized a semantic point. Ulash draws some fine distinctions between various kinds of imperative. A father's command to his small child is entirely different—in word and concept both—from a command to another Yildivan beaten in a fight, which is different in turn from a command to a Lugal, and so on through a wider range than our psycholinguists have yet measured.

"Shivaru wanted to know if I was God's slave.

"Well, this was no time to explain the history of religion, which I'm none too clear about anyway. I just said no, I wasn't; God was a being in Whose existence some of us believed, but not everyone, and He had certainly not issued me any direct orders.

"That rocked them back! The breath hissed between Shivaru's fangs, his ruff bristled aloft and his tail whipped his legs. 'Then who did send you?' he nearly screamed. I could translate as well by: 'So who *is* your owner?'

"I heard a slither alongside me as Manuel loosened his gun in the holster. Behind the three Yildivans, the Lugals gripped their own axes and spears at the ready. You can imagine how carefully I picked my words. 'We are here freely,' I said, 'as part of an association.' Or maybe the word I had to use means 'fellowship'—I wasn't about to explain economics either. 'In our home country,' I said, 'none of us is a Lugal. You have seen our devices that work for us. We have no need of Lugalhood.'

" 'Ah-h-h,' Fereghir sighed, and poised his spear. Manuel's gun clanked free. 'I think best you go,' he said to them, 'before there is a fight. We do not wish to kill.'

"Brander had made a point of demonstrating guns, and so had we. No one stirred for a time that went on eternally, in that Fimbul wind. The hair stood straight on the Lugals. They were ready to rush us and die at a word. But it wasn't forthcoming. Finally the three Yildivans exchanged glances. Shivaru said in a dead voice, 'Let us consider this thing.' They turned on their heels and walked off through the long, whispering grass, their pack close around them.

"The drums beat for days and nights.

"We considered the thing ourselves at great length. What was the matter, anyhow? The Yildivans were primitive and unsophisticated by Commonwealth standards, but not stupid. Shivaru had not been surprised at the ways we differed from his people. For instance, the fact that we lived in communities instead of isolated families had only been one more oddity about us, intriguing rather than shocking. And, as I've told you, while large-scale cooperation among Yildivans wasn't common, it did happen once in a while; so what was wrong with our doing likewise?

"Igor Yuschenkoff, the captain of the *Miriam,* had a reasonable suggestion. 'If they have gotten the idea that we are slaves,' he said, 'then our masters must be still more powerful. Can they think we are preparing a base for invasion?'

" 'But I told them plainly we are not slaves,' I said.

" 'No doubt.' He laid a finger alongside his nose. 'Do they believe you?'

"You can imagine how I tossed awake in my sealtent. Should we haul gravs altogether, find a different area and start afresh? That would mean scrapping nearly everything we'd done. A whole new language to learn was the least of the problems. Nor would a move necessarily help. Scouting trips by flitter had indicated pretty strongly that the same basic pattern of life prevailed everywhere on Cain, as it did on Earth in the paleolithic era. If we'd run afoul, not of some local taboo, but of some fundamental . . . I just didn't know. I doubt if Manuel spent more than two hours a night in bed. He was too busy tightening our system of guards, drilling the men, prowling around to inspect and keep them alert.

"But our next contact was peaceful enough on the surface. One dawn a sentry roused me to say that a bunch of natives were here. Fog had arisen overnight, turned the world into wet gray smoke where you couldn't see three meters. As I came outside I heard the drip off a trac parked close by, the only clear sound in the muffledness. Tulitur and another Yildivan stood at the edge of camp, with about fifty male Lugals behind. Their fur sheened with water, and their weapons were rime-coated. 'They must have traveled by night, Captain,' Manuel said, 'for the sake of cover. Surely others wait beyond view.' He led a squad with me.

"I made the Yildivans welcome, ritually, as if nothing had happened. I didn't get any ritual back. Tulitur said only, 'We are here to trade. For your goods we will return those furs and plants you desire.'

"That was rather jumping the gun, with our post still less than half built. But I couldn't refuse what might be an olive branch. 'That is well,' I said. 'Come, let us eat while we talk about it.' Clever move, I thought. Accepting someone's food puts you under the same sort of obligation in Ulash that it used to on Earth.

"Tulitur and his companion—Bokzahan, I remember the name now—didn't offer thanks, but they did come into the ship and sit at the mess table. I figured this would be more ceremonious and impressive than a tent; also, it was out of that damned raw cold. I ordered stuff like bacon and eggs that the Cainites were known to like. They got right to business. 'How much will you trade to us?'

" 'That depends on what you want, and on what you have to give in exchange,' I said, to match their curtness.

" 'We have brought nothing with us,' Bokzahan said, 'for we knew not if you would be willing to bargain.'

" 'Why should I not be?' I answered. 'That is what I came for. There is no strife between us.' And I shot at him: 'Is there?'

"None of those ice-green eyes wavered. 'No,' Tulitur said, 'there is not. Accordingly, we wish to buy guns.'

" 'Such things we may not sell,' I answered. Best not to add that policy allowed us to as soon as we felt reasonably sure no harm would result. 'However, we have knives to exchange, as well as many useful tools.'

"They sulked a bit, but didn't argue. Instead, they went right to work, haggling over terms. They wanted as much of everything as we'd part with, and really didn't try to bargain the price down far. Only they wanted the stuff on credit. They needed it now, they said, and it'd take time to gather the goods for payment.

"That put me in an obvious pickle. On the one hand, the Yildivans had always acted honorably and, as far as I could check, always spoken truth. Nor did I want to antagonize them. On the other hand—but you can fill that in for yourself. I flatter myself I gave them a diplomatic answer. We did not for an instant doubt their good intentions, I said. We knew the Yildivans were fine chaps. But accidents could happen, and if so, we'd be out of pocket by a galactic sum.

"Tulitur slapped the table and snorted, 'Such fears might have been expected. Very well, we shall leave our Lugals here until payment is complete. Their value is great. But then you must carry the goods where we want them.'

"I decided that on those terms they could have half the agreed amount right away."

Per fell silent and gnawed his lip. Harry leaned over to pat his hand. Van Rijn growled, "*Ja,* by damn, no one can foretell everything that goes wrong, only be sure that some bloody-be-plastered thing will. You did hokay, boy. . . . Abdul, more drink, you suppose maybe this is Mars?"

Per sighed. "We loaded the stuff on a gravsled," he went on. "Manuel accompanied in an armed flitter, as a precaution. But nothing happened. Fifty kilometers or so from camp, the Yildivans told our men to land near a river. They had canoes drawn onto the bank there, with a few other Yildivans standing by. Clearly they intended to float the goods further by themselves, and Manuel called me to see if I had any objections. 'No,' I said. 'What difference does it make? They must want to keep the destination secret. They don't trust us any longer.' Behind him, in the screen, I saw Bokzahan watching. Our communicators had fascinated visitors before now. But this time, was there some equivalent of a sneer on his face?

"I was busy arranging quarters and rations for the Lugals, though. And a guard or two, nothing obtrusive. Not that I really expected trouble. I'd heard their masters say, 'Remain here and do as the *Erziran* direct until we come for you.' But nevertheless it felt queasy, having that pack of dog-beings in camp.

"They settled down in their animal fashion. When the drums began again that night they got restless, shifted around in the pavilion we'd turned over to them and mewled in a language Brander hadn't recorded. But they were quite meek next morning. One of them even asked if they couldn't help in our work. I had to laugh at the thought of a Lugal behind the controls of a five hundred kilowatt trac, and told him no, thanks, they need only loaf and watch us. They were good at loafing.

"A few times, in the next three days, I tried to get them into conversation. But nothing came of that. They'd answer me, not in the deferential style they used to a Yildivan but not insolently either. However, the answers were meaningless. 'Where do you live?' I would say. 'In the forest yonder,' the slave replied, staring at his toes. 'What sort of tasks do you have to do at home?' 'That which my Yildivan sets for me.' I gave up.

"Yet they weren't stupid. They had some sort of game they played, involving figures drawn in the dirt, that I never did unravel. Each sundown they formed ranks and crooned, an eerie minor-key chant, with improvisations that sometimes sent a chill along my nerves. Mostly they slept, or sat and stared at nothing, but once in a while several would squat in a circle, arms around their neighbors' shoulders, and whisper together.

"Well . . . I'm making the story too long. We were attacked shortly before dawn of the fourth day.

"Afterward I learned that something like a hundred male Yildivans were in that party, and heaven knows how many Lugals. They'd rendezvoused from everywhere in that tremendous territory called Ulash, called by the drums and, probably, by messengers who'd run day and night through the woods. Our pickets were known to their scouts, and they laid a hurricane of arrows over those spots, while the bulk of them rushed in between. Otherwise I can't tell you much. I was a casualty." Per grimaced. "What a damn fool thing to happen. On my first command!"

"Go on," Harry urged. "You haven't told me any details."

"There aren't many," Per shrugged. "The first screams and roars slammed me awake. I threw on a jacket and stuffed feet into boots while my free hand buckled on a gun belt. By then the sirens were in full cry. Even so, I heard a blaster beam sizzle past my tent.

"I stumbled out into the compound. Everything was one black, boiling hell-kettle. Blasters flashed and flashed, sirens howled and voices cried battle. The cold stabbed at me. Starlight sheened on snowbanks and hoarfrost over the hills. I had an instant to think how bright and many the stars were, out there and not giving a curse.

"Then Yuschenkoff switched on the floodlamps in the *Miriam*'s turret. Suddenly an artificial sun stood overhead, too bright for us to look at. What must it have been to the Cainites? Blue-white incandescence, I suppose. They swarmed among our tents and machines, tall leopard-furred hunters, squat brown gnomes, axes, clubs, spears, bows, slings, our own daggers in their hands. I saw only one man—sprawled on the earth, gun still between his fingers, head a broken horror.

"I put the command mike to my mouth—always wore it on my wrist as per doctrine—and bawled out orders as I pelted toward the ship. We had the atom itself to fight for us, but we were twenty, no, nineteen or less, against Ulash.

"Now our dispositions were planned for defense. Two men slept in the ship, the others in sealtents ringed around her. The half dozen on guard duty had been cut off, but the rest had the ship for an impregnable retreat. What we must do, though, was rally to the rescue of those guards, and quick. If it wasn't too late.

"I saw the boys emerge from their strong point under the landing jacks. Even now I remember how Zerkowsky hadn't fastened his parka, and what a low-comedy way it flapped around his bottom. He didn't use pajamas. You notice the damnedest small things at such times, don't you? The Cainites had begun to mill about, dazzled by the light. They hadn't expected that, nor the siren, which is a terrifying thing to hear at close range. Quite a few of them were already strewn dead or dying.

"Then—but all I knew personally was a tide that bellowed and yelped and clawed. It rolled over me from behind. I went down under their legs. They pounded across me and left me in the grip of a Lugal. He lay on my chest and went for my throat with teeth and hands. Judas, but that creature was strong! Centimeter by centimeter he closed in against my pushing and gouging. Suddenly another one got into the act. Must have snatched a club from some fallen Cainite and attacked whatever part of me was handiest, which happened to be my left shin. It's nothing but pain and rage after that, till the blessed darkness came.

"The fact was, of course, that our Lugal hostages had overrun their guards and broken free. I might have expected as much. Even without specific orders, they wouldn't have stood idle while their masters fought. But doubtless they'd been given advance commands. Tulitur and Bokzahan diddled us very nicely. First they got a big consignment of our trade goods, free, and then they planted reinforcements for themselves right in our compound.

"Even so, the scheme didn't work. The Yildivans hadn't really comprehended our power. How could they have? Manuel himself dropped the two Lugals who were killing me. He needed exactly two shots for that. Our boys swept a ring of fire, and the enemy melted away.

"But they'd hurt us badly. When I came to, I was in the *Miriam*'s sick bay. Manuel hovered over me like an anxious raven. 'How'd we do?' I think I said.

" 'You should rest, *señor,*' he said, 'and God forgive me that I made the doctor rouse you with drugs. But we must have your decision quickly. Several men are wounded. Two are dead. Three are missing. The enemy is back in the wilderness, I believe with prisoners.'

"He lifted me into a carrier and took me outside. I felt no physical pain, but was lightheaded and half crazy. You know how it is when you're filled to the cap with stimulol. Manuel told me straight out that my legbone was pretty well pulverized, but that didn't seem to matter at the time. . . . What do I mean, 'seem'? Of course it didn't! Gower and Muramoto were dead. Bullis, Cheng, and Zerkowsky were gone.

"The camp was unnaturally quiet under the orange sun. My men had policed the grounds while I was unconscious. Enemy corpses were laid out in a row. Twenty-three Yildivans—that number's going to haunt me for the rest of my life—and I'm not sure how many Lugals, a hundred perhaps. I had Manuel push me along while I peered into face after still, bloody face. But I didn't recognize any.

"Our own prisoners were packed together in our main basement excavation. A couple of hundred Lugals, but only two wounded Yildivans. The rest who were hurt had been carried off by their friends. With so much construction and big machines standing around for cover, that hadn't been too hard to do. Manuel explained that he'd stopped the attack of the hostages with stunbeams. Much the best weapon. You can't prevent a Lugal fighting for his master with a mere threat to kill him.

"In a corner of the pit, glaring up at the armed men above, were the Yildivans. One I didn't know. He had a nasty blaster burn, and our medics had given him sedation after patching it, so he was pretty much out of the picture anyway. But I recognized the other, who was intact. A stunbeam had taken him. It was Kochihir, an adult son of Shivaru, who'd visited us like his father a time or two.

"We stared at each other for a space, he and I. Finally, 'Why?' I asked him. 'Why have you done this?' Each word puffed white out of my mouth and the wind shredded it.

" 'Because they are traitors, murderers, and thieves by nature, that's why,' Yuschenkoff said, also in Ulash. Brander's team had naturally been careful to find out whether there were words corresponding to concepts of honor and the reverse. I don't imagine the League will ever forget the Darborian Semantics!

"Yuschenkoff spat at Kochihir. 'Now we shall hunt down your breed like the animals they are,' he said. Gower had been his brother-in-law.

" 'No,' I said at once, in Ulash, because such a growl had risen from the Lugals that any insane thing might have happened next. 'Speak thus no more.' Yuschenkoff shut his mouth, and a kind of ripple went among those packed, hairy bodies, like wind dying out on an ocean. 'But Kochihir,' I said, 'your father was my good friend. Or so I believed. In what wise have we offended him and his people?'

"He raised his ruff, the tail lashed his ankles, and he snarled, 'You must go and never come back. Else we shall harry you in the forests, roll the hillsides down on you, stampede horned beasts through your camps, poison the wells, and burn the grass about your feet. Go, and do not dare return!'

"My own temper flared—which made my head spin and throb, as if with fever—and I said, 'We shall certainly not go unless our captive friends are returned to us. There are drums in camp that your father gave me before he betrayed us. Call your folk on those, Kochihir, and tell them to bring back our folk. After that, perhaps we can talk. Never before.'

"He fleered at me without replying.

"I beckoned to Manuel. 'No sense in stalling unnecessarily,' I said. 'We'll organize a tight defense here. Won't get taken by surprise twice. But we've got to rescue those men. Send flitters aloft to search for them. The war party can't have gone far.'

"You can best tell how you argued with me, Manuel. You said an airflit was an utter waste of energy which was badly needed elsewhere. Didn't you?"

The Nuevo Méxican looked embarrassed. "I did not wish to contradict my captain," he said. His oddly delicate fingers twisted together in his lap as he stared out into the night that had fallen. "But, indeed, I thought that aerial scouts would never find anyone in so many, many hectares of hill and ravine, water and woods. They could have dispersed, those devils. Surely, even if they traveled away in company, they would not be in such a clump that infrared detectors could see them through the forest roof. Yet I did not like to contradict my captain."

"Oh, you did, you," Per said. A corner of his mouth bent upward. "I was quite daft by then. Shouted and stormed at you, eh? Told you to jolly well obey orders and get those flitters in motion. You saluted and started off, and I called you back. You mustn't go in person. Too damned valuable here. Yes, that meant I was keeping back the one man with enough wilderness experience that he might have stood a chance of identifying spoor, even from above. But my brain was spinning down and down the sides of a maelstrom. 'See what you can do to make this furry bastard cooperate,' I said."

"It pained me a little that my captain should appoint me his torturer," Manuel confessed mildly. "Although from time to time, on various planets, when there was great need—No matter."

"I'd some notion of breaking down morale among our prisoners," Per said. "In retrospect, I see that it wouldn't have made any difference if they had cooperated, at least to the extent of drumming for us. The Cainites don't have our kind of group solidarity. If Kochihir and his buddy came to grief at our hands, that was their hard luck. But Shivaru and some of the others had read our psychology shrewdly enough to know what a hold on us their three prisoners gave.

"I looked down at Kochihir. His teeth gleamed back. He hadn't missed a syllable or a gesture, and even if he didn't know any Anglic, he must have understood almost exactly what was going on. By now I was slurring my words as if drunk. So, also like a drunk, I picked them with uncommon care. 'Kochihir,' I said, 'I have commanded our fliers out to hunt down your people and fetch our own whom they have captured. Can a Yildivan outrun a flying machine? Can he fight when its guns flame at him from above? Can he hide from its eyes that see from end to end of the horizon? Your kinfolk will dearly pay if they do not return our men of their own accord. Take the drums, Kochihir, and tell them so. If you do not, it will cost *you* dearly. I have commanded my man here to do whatever may be needful to break your will.'

"Oh, that was a vicious speech. But Gower and Muramoto had been my friends. Bullis, Cheng, and Zerkowsky still were, if they lived. And I was on the point of passing out. I did, actually, on the way back to the ship. I heard Doc Leblanc mutter something about how could he be expected to treat a patient whose system was abused with enough drugs to bloat a camel, and then the words kind of trailed off in a long gibber that went on and on, rising and falling until I thought I'd been turned into an electron and was trapped in an oscilloscope . . . and the darkness turned green and . . . and they tell me I was unconscious for fifty hours.

"From there on it's Manuel's story."

At this stage, Per was croaking. As he sank back in his lounger, I saw how white he had become. One hand picked at his blanket, and the vermouth slopped when he raised his glass. Harry watched him, with a helpless anger that smoldered at van Rijn. The merchant said, "There, there, so soon after his operation and I make him lecture us, ha? But shortly comes dinner, no better medicine than a real *rijstaffel,* and so soon after that he can walk about, he comes to my place in Djakarta for a nice old-fashioned orgy."

"Oh, hellfire!" Per exploded in a whisper. "Why're you trying to make me feel good? I ruined the whole show!"

"Whoa, son," I ventured to suggest. "You were in good spirits half an hour ago, and half an hour from now you'll be the same. It's only that reliving the bad moments is more punishment than Jehovah would inflict. I've been there too." Blindly, the blue gaze sought mine. "Look, Per," I said, "if Freeman van Rijn thought you'd botched a mission through your own fault, you wouldn't be lapping his booze tonight. You'd be selling meat to the cannibals."

A ghost of a grin rewarded me.

"Well, Don Manuel," van Rijn said, "now we hear from you, *nie?*"

"By your favor, *señor,* I am no Don," the Nuevo Méxican said, courteously, academically, and not the least humbly. "My father was a huntsman in the Sierra de los Bosques Secos, and I traveled in space as a mercenary with Rogers' Rovers, becoming sergeant before I left them for your service. No more." He hesitated. "Nor is there much I can relate of the happenings on Cain."

"Don't make foolishness," van Rijn said, finished his third or fourth liter of beer since I arrived, and signaled for more. My own glass had been kept filled too, so much so that the stars and the city lights had begun to dance in the dark outside. I stuffed my pipe to help me ease off. "I have read the official reports from your expeditioning," van Rijn continued. "They are scum-dreary. I need details—the little things nobody thinks to record, like Per has used up his lawrence in telling—I need to make a planet real for me before this cracked old pot of mine can maybe find a pattern. For it is my experience of many other planets, where I, even I, Nicholas van Rijn, got my nose rubbed in the dirt—which, ho, ho! takes a lot of dirt—it is on that I draw. Evolutions have parallels, but also skews, like somebody said tonight. Which lines is Cain's evolution parallel to? Talk, Ensign Gómez y Palomares. Brag. Pop jokes, sing songs, balance a chair on your head if you want—but talk!"

The brown man sat still a minute. His eyes were steady on us, save when they moved to Per and back.

"As the *señor* wishes," he began. Throughout, his tone was level, but the accent could not help singing.

"When they bore my captain away I stood in thought, until Igor Yuschen-koff said, 'Well, who is to take the flitters?'

" 'None,' I said.

" 'But we have orders,' he said.

" 'The captain was hurt and shaken. We should not have roused him,' I answered, and asked of the men who stood near, 'Is this not so?'

"They agreed, after small argument. I leaned over the edge of the pit and asked Kochihir if he would beat the drums for us. 'No,' he said, 'whatever you do.'

" 'I shall do nothing, yet,' I said. 'We will bring you food presently.' And that was done. For the rest of the short day I wandered about among the snows that lay in patches on the grass. Ay, this was a stark land, where it swooped down into the valley and then rose again at the end of sight in saw-toothed purple ranges. I thought of home and of one Dolores whom I had known, a long time ago. The men did no work; they huddled over their weapons, saying little, and toward evening the breath began to freeze on their parka hoods.

"One by one I spoke to them and chose them for those tasks I had in mind. They were all good men of their hands, but few had been hunters save in sport. I myself could not trail the Cainites far, because they had crossed a broad reach of naked rock on their way downward and once in the forest had covered their tracks. But Hamud ibn Rashid and Jacques Ngolo had been woodsmen in their day. We prepared what we needed. Then I entered the ship and looked on my captain—how still he lay!

"I ate lightly and slept briefly. Darkness had fallen when I returned to the pit. The four men we had on guard stood like deeper shadows against the stars which crowd that sky. 'Go now,' I said, and took out my own blaster. Their footfalls crunched away.

"The shapes that clotted the blackness of the pit stirred and mumbled. A voice hissed upward, 'Ohé, you are back. To torment me?' Those Cainites have eyes that see in the night like owls. I had thought, before, that they snickered within themselves when they watched us blunder about after sunset.

" 'No,' I said, 'I am only taking my turn to guard you.'

" 'You alone?' he scoffed.

" 'And this.' I slapped the blaster against my thigh.

"He fell silent. The cold gnawed deeper into me. I do not think the Cainites felt it much. As the stars wheeled slowly overhead, I began to despair of my plan. Whispers went among the captives, but otherwise I stood in a world where sound was frozen dead.

"When the thing happened, it went with devil's haste. The Lugals had been shifting about a while, as if restless. Suddenly they were upon me. One had stood on another's shoulders and leaped. To death, as they thought—but my shot missed, a quick flare and an amazed gasp from him that he was still alive. Had I not missed, several would have died to bring me down.

"As it was, two fell upon me. I went under, breaking hands loose from my throat with a judo release but held writhing by their mass. Hard fists beat me on head and belly. A palm over my mouth muffled my yells. Meanwhile the prisoners helped themselves out and fled.

"Finally I worked a leg free and gave one of them my knee. He rolled off with pain rattling in his throat. I twisted about on top of the other and struck him below the skull with the blade of my hand. When he went limp, I sprang up and shouted.

"Siren and floodlights came to life. The men swarmed from ship and tents. 'Back!' I cried. 'Not into the dark!' Many Lugals had not yet escaped, and those retreated snarling to the far side of the pit as our troop arrived. With their bodies they covered the wounded Yildivan from the guns. But we only fired, futilely, after those who were gone from sight.

"Guards posted themselves around the cellar. I scrabbled over the earth, seeking my blaster. It was gone. Someone had snatched it up: if not Kochihir, then a Lugal who would soon give it to him. Jacques Ngolo came to me and saw. 'This is bad,' he said.

" 'An evil turn of luck,' I admitted, 'but we must proceed anyhow.' I rose and stripped off my parka. Below were the helmet and spacesuit torso which had protected me in the fight. I threw them down, for they would only hinder me now, and put the parka back on. Hamud ibn Rashid joined us. He had my pack and gear and another blaster for me. I took them, and we three started our pursuit.

"By the mercy of God, we had never found occasion to demonstrate night-seeing goggles here. They made the world clear, though with a sheen over it like dreams. Ngolo's infrared tracker was our compass, the needle trembling toward the mass of Cainites that loped ahead of us. We saw them for a while, too, as they crossed the bare hillside, in and out among tumbled boulders; but we kept ourselves low lest they see us against the sky. The grass was rough in my face when I went all-fours, and the earth sucked heat out through boots and gloves. Somewhere a hunter beast screamed.

"We were panting by the time we reached the edge of trees. Yet in under their shadows we must go, before the Cainites fled farther than the compass would reach. Already it flickered, with so many dark trunks and so much brake to screen off radiation. But thus far the enemy had not stopped to hide his trail. I moved through the underbrush more carefully than him—legs brought forward to part the stems that my hands then guided to either side of my body— reading the book of trampled bush and snapped branch.

"After an hour we were well down in the valley. Tall trees gloomed everywhere about; the sky was hidden, and I must tune up the photomultiplier unit in my goggles. Now the book began to close. The Cainites were moving at a natural pace, confident of their escape, and even without special effort they left little spoor. And since they were now less frantic and more alert, we must follow so far behind that infrared detection was of no further use.

"At last we came to a meadow, whose beaten grass showed that they had paused here a while. And that was seen which I feared. The party had broken into three or four, each bound a different way. 'Which do we choose?' Ngolo asked.

" 'Three of us can follow three of them,' I said.

" 'Bismillah!' Hamud grunted. 'Blaster or no, I would not care to face such a band alone. But what must be, must be.'

"We took so much time to ponder what clues the forest gave that the east was gray before we parted. Plainly, the Lugals had gone toward their masters' homes, while Kochihir's own slaves had accompanied him. And Kochihir was the one we desired. I could only guess that the largest party was his, because most likely the first break had been made under his orders by his own Lugals, whose capabilities he knew. That path I chose for myself. Hamud and Ngolo wanted it too, but I used my rank to seize the honor, that folk on Nuevo México might never say a Gomez lacked courage.

"So great a distance was now between that there was no reason not to use our radios to talk with each other and with the men in camp. That was often consoling, in the long time which was upon me. For it was slow, slow, tracing those woods-wily hunters through their own land. I do not believe I could have done it, had they been only Yildivans and such Lugals as are regularly used in the chase. But plain to see, the attack had been strengthened by calling other Lugals from fields and mines and household tasks, and those were less adept.

"Late in the morning, Ngolo called. 'My gang just reached a cave and a set of lean-tos,' he said. 'I sit in a tree and watch them met by some female and half-grown Yildivans. They shuffle off to their own shed. This is where they belong, I suppose, and they are not going farther. Shall I return to the meadow and pick up another trail?'

" 'No,' I said, 'it would be too cold by now. Backtrack to a spot out of view and have a flitter fetch you.'

"Some hours later, the heart leaped in my breast. For I came upon a tree charred by unmistakable blaster shots. Kochihir had been practicing.

"I called Hamud and asked where he was. 'On the bank of a river,' he said, 'casting about for the place where they crossed. That was a bitter stream to wade!'

" 'Go no farther,' I said. 'My path is the right one. Have yourself taken back to camp.'

" 'What?' he asked. 'Shall we not join you now?'

" 'No,' I said. 'It is uncertain how near I am to the end. Perhaps so near that a flitter would be seen by them as it came down and alarm them. Stand by.' I confess it was a lonely order to give.

"A few times I stopped to eat and rest. But stimulants kept me going in a way that would have surprised my quarry who despised me. By evening his trail was again so fresh that I slacked my pace and went on with a snake's caution. Down here, after sunset, the air was not so cold as on the heights; yet every leaf glistened hoar in what starlight pierced through.

"Not much into the night, my own infrared detector began to register a source, stronger than living bodies could account for. I whispered the news into my radio and then ordered no more communication until further notice, lest we be overheard. Onward I slipped. The forest rustled and creaked about me, somewhere far off a heavy animal broke brush in panic flight, wings whirred overhead, yet *Santa María,* how silent and alone it was!

"Until I came to the edge of a small clearing.

"A fire burned there, throwing unrestful shadows on the wall of a big, windowless log cabin which nestled under the trees beyond. Two Yildivans leaned on their spears. And light glimmered from the smoke hole in the roof.

"Most softly, I drew my stun gun. The bolt snicked twice, and they fell in heaps. At once I sped across the open ground, crouched in the shadow under that rough wall, and waited.

"But no one had heard. I glided to the doorway. Only a leather curtain blocked my view. I twitched it aside barely enough that I might peer within.

"The view was dimmed by smoke, but I could see that there was just one long room. It did not seem plain, so beautiful were the furs hung and draped everywhere about. A score or so of Yildivans, mostly grown males, squatted in a circle around the fire, which burned in a pit and picked their fierce flat countenances out of the dark. Also there were several Lugals hunched in a corner. I recognized old Cherkez among them, and was glad he had outlived the battle. The Lugals in Kochihir's party must have been sent to barracks. He himself was telling his father Shivaru of his escape.

"As yet the time was unripe for happiness, but I vowed to light many candles for the saints. Because this was as I had hoped: Kochihir had not gone to his own home, but sought an agreed rendezvous. Zerkowsky, Cheng, and Bullis were here. They sat in another corner at the far end of the room, coughing from the smoke, skins drawn around them to ward off the cold.

"Kochihir finished his account and looked at his father for approval. Shivaru's tail switched back and forth. 'Strange that they were so careless about you,' he said.

" 'They are like blind cubs,' Kochihir scoffed.

" 'I am not so sure,' the old Yildivan murmured. 'Great are their powers. And . . . we know what they did in the past.' Then suddenly he grew stiff, and his whisper struck out like a knife. 'Or did they do it? Tell me again, Kochihir, how the master ordered one thing and the rest did another.'

" 'No, now, that means nothing,' said a different Yildivan, scarred and grizzled. 'What we must devise is a use for these captives. You have thought they might trade our Lugals and Gumush, whom Kochihir says they still hold, for three of their own. But I say, Why should they? Let us instead place the bodies where the *Erziran* can find them, in such condition that they will be warned away.'

" 'Just so,' said Bokzahan, whom I now spied in the gloom. 'Tulitur and I proved they are weak and foolish.'

" 'First we should try to bargain,' said Shivaru. 'If that fails . . .' His fangs gleamed in the firelight.

" 'Make an example of one, then, before we talk,' Kochihir said angrily. 'They threatened the same for me.'

"A rumble went among them, as from a beast's cage in the zoo. I thought with terror of what might be done. For my captain has told you how no Yildivan is in authority over any other. Whatever his wishes, Shivaru could not stop them from doing what they would.

"I must decide my own course immediately. Blaster bolts could not destroy them all fast enough to keep them from hurling the weapons that lay to hand upon me—not unless I set the beam so wide that our men must also be killed. The stun gun was better, yet it would not overpower them either before I went down under axes and clubs. By standing to one side I could pen them within, for they had only the single door. But Bullis, Cheng, and Zerkowsky would remain hostages.

"What I did was doubtless stupid, for I am not my captain. I sneaked back to the edge of the woods and called the men in camp. 'Come as fast as may be,' I said, and left the radio going for them to home on. Then I circled about and found a tree overhanging the cabin. Up I went, and down again from a branch to the sod roof, and so to the smoke hole. Goggles protected my eyes, but nostrils withered in the fumes that poured forth. I filled my lungs with clean air and leaned forward to see.

"Best would have been if they had gone to bed. Then I could have stunned them one by one as they slept, without risk. But they continued to sit about and quarrel over what to do with their captives. How hard those poor men tried to be brave, as that dreadful snarling broke around them, as slit eyes turned their way and hands went stroking across knives!

"The time felt long, but I had not completed the Rosary in my mind when thunder awoke. Our flitters came down the sky like hawks. The Yildivans roared. Two or three of them dashed out the door to see what was afoot. I dropped them with my stunner, but not before one had screamed, 'The *Erziran* are here!'

"My face went back to the smoke hole. It was turmoil below. Kochihir screeched and pulled out his blaster. I fired but missed. Too many bodies in between, *señores*. There is no other excuse for me.

"I took the gun in my teeth, seized the edge of the smoke hole, and swung myself as best I could before letting go. Thus I struck the dirt floor barely outside the firepit, rolled over and bounced erect. Cherkez leaped for my throat. I sent him reeling with a kick to the belly, took my gun, and fired around me.

"Kochihir could not be seen in the mob which struggled from wall to wall. I fought my way toward the prisoners. Shivaru's ax whistled down. By the grace of God, I dodged it, twisted about and stunned him point-blank. I squirmed between two others. A third got on my back. I snapped my head against his mouth and felt flesh give way. He let go. With my gun arm and my free hand I tossed a Lugal aside and saw Kochihir. He had reached the men. They shrank from him, too stupefied to fight. Hate was on his face, in his whole body, as he took unpracticed aim.

"He saw me at his sight's edge and spun. The blaster crashed, blinding in that murk. But I had dropped to one knee as I pulled trigger. The beam scorched my parka hood. He toppled. I pounced, got the blaster, and whirled to stand before our people.

"Bokzahan raised his ax and threw it. I blasted it in mid air and then killed him. Otherwise I used the stunner. And in a minute or two more, the matter was finished. A grenade brought down the front wall of the cabin. The Cainites fell before a barrage of knockout beams. We left them to awaken and returned to camp."

Again silence grew upon us. Manuel asked if he might smoke, politely declined van Rijn's cigars, and took a vicious-looking brown cigarette from his own case. That was a lovely, grotesque thing, wrought in silver on some planet I could not identify.

"Whoof!" van Rijn gusted. "But this is not the whole story, from what you have written. They came to see you before you left."

Per nodded. "Yes, sir," he said. A measure of strength had rearisen in him. "We'd about finished our preparations when Shivaru himself arrived, with ten other Yildivans and their Lugals. They walked slowly into the compound, ruffs erect and tails held stiff, looking neither to right nor left. I guess they wouldn't have been surprised to be shot down. I ordered such of the boys as were covering them to holster guns and went out on my carrier to say hello with due formality.

"Shivaru responded just as gravely. Then he got almost tongue-tied. He couldn't really apologize. Ulash doesn't have the phrases for it. He beckoned to Cherkez. 'You were good to release our people whom you held,' he said." Per chuckled. "Huh! What else were we supposed to do, keep feeding them? Cherkez gave him a leather bag. 'I bring a gift,' he told me, and pulled out

Tulitur's head. 'We shall return as much of the goods he got from you as we can find,' he promised, 'and if you will give us time, we shall bring double payment for everything else.'

"I'm afraid that after so much blood had gone over the dam, I didn't find the present as gruesome as I ought. I only sputtered that we didn't require such tokens.

" 'But we do,' he said, 'to cleanse our honor.'

"I invited them to eat, but they declined. Shivaru made haste to explain that they didn't feel right about accepting our hospitality until their debt was paid off. I told them we were pulling out. Though that was obvious from the state of the camp, they still looked rather dismayed. So I told them we, or others like us, would be back, but first it was necessary to get our injured people home.

"Another mistake of mine. Because being reminded of what they'd done to us upset them so badly that they only mumbled when I tried to find out why they'd done it. I decided best not press that issue—the situation being delicate yet—and they left with relief branded on them.

"We should have stuck around a while, maybe, because we've got to know what the trouble was before committing more men and equipment to Cain. Else it's all too likely to flare up afresh. But between our being shorthanded, and having a couple of chaps who needed first-class medical treatment, I didn't think we could linger. All the way home we wondered and argued. What had gone wrong? And what, later, had gone right? We still don't know."

Van Rijn's eyes glittered at him. "What is your theory?" he demanded.

"Oh—" Per spread his hands. "Yuschenkoff's, more or less. They were afraid we were the spearhead of an invasion. When we acted reasonably decently—refraining from mistreatment of prisoners, thanks to Manuel, and using stunners rather than blasters in the rescue operation—they decided they were mistaken."

Manuel had not shifted a muscle in face or body, as far as I could see. But van Rijn's battleship prow of a nose swung toward him and the merchant laughed, "You have maybe a little different notion, ha? Come, spew it out."

"My place is not to contradict my captain," said the Nuevo Méxican.

"So why you make fumblydiddles against orders, that day on Cain? When you know better, then you got a duty, by damn, to tell us where to stuff our heads."

"If the *señor* commands. But I am no learned man. I have no book knowledge of studies made on the psychonomy. It is only that . . . that I think I know those Yildivans. They seem not so unlike men of the barranca country on my home world, and again among the Rovers."

"How so?"

"They live very near death, their whole lives. Courage and skill in fighting, those are what they most need to survive, and so are what they most treasure. They thought, seeing us use machines and weapons that kill from afar, seeing us blinded by night and most of us clumsy in the woods, hearing us talk about what our life is like at home—they thought we lacked *cojones*. So they scorned us. They owed us nothing, since we were spiritless and could never understand their own spirit. We were only fit to be the prey, first of their wits and then of their weapons." Manuel's shoulders drew straight. His voice belled out so that I jumped in my seat. "When they found how terrible men are, that they themselves are the weak ones, we changed in their eyes from peasants to kings!"

Van Rijn sucked noisily on his cigar. "Any other shipboard notions?" he asked.

"No, sir, those were our two schools of thought," Per said.

Van Rijn guffawed. "So! Take comfort, freemen. No need for angelometrics on pinheads. Relax and drink. You are both wrong."

"I *beg* your pardon," Harry rapped. "You were not there, may I say."

"No, not in the flesh." Van Rijn slapped his paunch. "Too much flesh for that. But tonight I have been on Cain up here, in this old brain, and it is rusty and afloat in alcohol but it has stored away more information about the universe than maybe the universe gets credit for holding. I see now what the parallels are. Xanadu, Dunbar, Tametha, Disaster Landing . . . oh, the analogue is never exact and on Cain the thing I am thinking of has gone far and far . . . but still I see the pattern, and what happened makes sense.

"Not that we have got to have an analogue. You gave us so many clues here that I could solve the puzzle by logic alone. But analogues help, and also they show my conclusion is not only correct but possible."

Van Rijn paused. He was so blatantly waiting to be coaxed that Harry and I made a long performance out of refreshing our drinks. Van Rijn turned purple, wheezed a while, decided to keep his temper for a better occasion, and chortled.

"Hokay, you win," he said. "I tell you short and fast, because very soon we eat if the cook has not fallen in the curry. Later you can study the formal psychologics.

"The key to this problem is the Lugals. You have been calling them slaves, and there is your mistake. They are not. They are domestic animals."

Per sat bolt upright. "Can't be!" he exclaimed. "Sir. I mean, they have language and—"

"*Ja, ja, ja,* for all I care they do mattress algebra in their heads. They are still tame animals. What is a slave, anyhows? A man who has got to do what another man says, willy-billy. Right? Harry said he would not trust a slave with weapons, and I would not either, because history is too pocked up with slave revolts and slaves running away and slaves dragging their feet and every such foolishness. But your big fierce expensive dogs, Harry, you trust them with their teeth, *nie?* When your kids was little and wet, you left them alone in rooms with a dog to keep watches. There is the difference. A slave may or may not obey. But a domestic animal has got to obey. His genes won't let him do anything different.

"Well, you yourselves figured the Yildivans had kept Lugals so long, breeding them for what traits they wanted, that this had changed the Lugal nature. Must be so. Otherwise the Lugals would be slaves, not animals, and could not always be trusted the way you saw they were. You also guessed the Yildivans themselves must have been affected, and this is very sleek thinking only you did not carry it so far you ought. Because everything you tell about the Yildivans goes to prove by nature they are *wild* animals.

"I mean wild, like tigers and buffalos. They have no genes for obediences, except to their parents when they are little. So long have they kept Lugals to do the dirty work—before they really became intelligent, I bet, like ants keeping aphids; for remember, you found no Lugals that was not kept—any gregarious-making genes in the Yildivans, any inborn will to be led, has gone foof. This must be so. Otherwise, from normal variation in ability, some form of Yildivan ranks would come to exist, *nie?*

"This pops your fear-of-invasion theory, Per Stenvik. With no concept of a tribe or army, they can't have any notions about conquest. And wild animals don't turn humble when they are beat, Manuel Gómez y Palomares, the way you imagine. A man with a superiority complexion may lick your boots when you prove you are his better; but an untamed carnivore hasn't got any such pride in the first place. He is plain and simple independent of you.

"Well, then, what did actual go on in their heads?"

"Recapitalize. Humans land and settle down to deal. Yildivans have no experience of races outside their own planet. They natural assume you think like them. In puncture of fact, I believe they could not possible imagine anything else, even if they was told. Your findings about their culture structure shows their half-symbiosis with the Lugals is psychological too; they are specialized in the brains, not near so complicated as man.

"But as they get better acquaintanced, what do they see? People taking orders. How can this be? No Yildivan ever took orders, unless to save his life when an enemy stood over him with a sharp thing. Ah, ha! So some of the strangers is Lugal type. Pretty soon, I bet, old Shivaru decides all of you is Lugal except young Stenvik, because in the end all orders come from him. Some others, like Manuel, is straw bosses maybe, but no more. Tame animals.

"And then Per mentions the idea of God."

Van Rijn crossed himself with a somewhat irritating piety. "I make no blasfuming," he said. "But everybody knows our picture of God comes in part from our kings. If you want to know how Oriental kings in ancient days was spoken to, look in your prayer book. Even now, we admit He is the Lord, and we is supposed to do His will, hoping He will not take too serious a few things that happen to anybody like anger, pride, envy, gluttony, lust, sloth, greed, and the rest what makes life fun.

"Per said this. So Per admitted he had a master. But then he must also be a Lugal—an animal. No Yildivan could possible confess to having even a mythical master, as shown by the fact they have no religion themselves though their Lugals seem to.

"Give old boy Shivaru his credits, he came again with some friends to ask further. What did he learn? He already knew everybody else was a Lugal, because of obeying. Now Per said he was no better than the rest. This confirmed Per was also a Lugal. And what blew the cork out of the bottle was when Per said he nor none of them had any owners at home!

"Whup, whup, slow down, youngster. You could not have known. Always we make discoveries the hard way. Like those poor Yildivans.

"They was real worried, you can imagine. Even dogs turn on people now and then, and surely some Lugals go bad once in a while on Cain and make big trouble before they can get killed. The Yildivans had seen some of your powers, knew you was dangerous . . . and your breed of Lugal must have gone mad and killed off its own Yildivans. How else could you be Lugals and yet have no masters?

"So. What would you and I do, friends, if we lived in lonely country houses and a pack of wild dogs what had killed people set up shop in our neighborhood?"

Van Rijn gurgled beer down his throat. We pondered for a while. "Seems pretty farfetched," Harry said.

"No." Per's cheeks burned with excitement. "It fits. Freeman van Rijn put into words what I always felt as I got to know Shivaru. A—a single-mindedness about him. As if he was incapable of seeing certain things, grasping certain ideas, though his reasoning faculties were intrinsically as good as mine. Yes . . ."

I nodded at my pipe, which had been with me when I clashed against stranger beings than that.

"So two of them first took advantage of you," van Rijn said, "to swindle away what they could before the attack because they wasn't sure the attack would work. No shame there. You was outside the honor concept, being animals. Animals whose ancestors must have murdered a whole race of true humans, in their views. Then the alarmed males tried to scrub you out. They failed, but hoped maybe to use their prisoners for a lever to pry you off their country. Only Manuel fooled them."

"But why'd they change their minds about us?" Per asked.

Van Rijn wagged his finger. "Ha, there you was lucky. You gave a very clear and important order. Your men disobeyed every bit of it. Now Lugals might go crazy and kill off Yildivans, but they are so bred to being bossed that they can't stand long against a leader. Or if they do, it's because they is too crazy to think straight. Manuel, though, was thinking straight like a plumber line. His strategy worked five-four-three-two-one-zero. Also, your people did not kill more Yildivans than was needful, which crazy Lugals would do.

"So you could not be domestic animals after all, gone bad or not. Therefore you had to be wild animals. The Cainite mind—a narrow mind like you said—can't imagine any third horn on that special bull. If you had proved you was not Lugal type, you must be Yildivan type. Indications to the contrariwise, the way you seemed to take orders or acknowledge a Lord, those must have been misunderstandings on the Cainites' part.

"Once he had time to reason this out, Shivaru saw his people had done yours dirty. Partway he felt bad about it in his soul, if he has one stowed somewhere; Yildivans do have some notion about upright behavior to other Yildivans. And besides, he did not want to lose a chance at your fine trade goods. He convinced his friends. They did what best they could think about to make amendments."

Van Rijn rubbed his palms together in glee. "Oh, ho, ho, what customers they will be for us!" he roared.

We sat still for another time, digesting the idea, until the butler announced dinner. Manuel helped Per rise. "We'll have to instruct everybody who goes to Cain," the young man said. "I mean, not to let on that we aren't wild animals, we humans."

"But, Captain," Manuel said, and his head lifted high, "we are."

Van Rijn stopped and looked at us a while. Then he shook his own head violently and shambled bearlike to the viewer wall. "No," he growled. "Some of us are."

"How's that?" Harry wondered.

"We here in this room are wild," van Rijn said. "We do what we do because we want to or because it is right. No other motivations, *nie?* If you made slaves of us, you would for sure not be wise to let us near a weapon.

"But how many slaves has there been, in Earth's long history, that their masters could trust? Quite some! There was even armies of slaves, like the

Janissaries. And how many people today is domestic animals at heart? Wanting somebody else should tell them what to do, and take care of their needfuls, and protect them not just against their fellow men but against themselves? Why has every free human society been so short-lived? Is this not because the wild-animal men are born so heartbreaking seldom?"

He glared out across the city, where it winked and glittered beneath the stars, around the curve of the planet. "Do you think they yonder is free?" he shouted. His hand chopped downward in scorn.

VIII

The last time we met, at his office in New York, John Campbell was in such pain from gout that when we went out to lunch I had to help him on with his topcoat. He told me this matter-of-factly and said nothing more about it. Rather, his conversation flashed with all the wonted intellectual pyrotechnics. When I wondered aloud, "If reptiles are post-amphibian, and mammals are post-reptilian, what might a post-mammalian animal be like?" he at once, almost casually, tossed off a dazzling idea. His thought was that the anatomy he suggested would confer unprecedented cursorial ability, but I saw that it would allow something still more spectacular—a creature on a planet similar to Earth, big enough to carry around a brain sufficient for intelligence, yet able to fly. How glad I am that he lived to buy, though not publish, a short story about humans discovering these Ythrians.

Meanwhile, elsewhere I'd been spinning yarns about Dominic Flandry, intelligence agent for a decadent Terran Empire. It had occurred to me that van Rijn could well have lived centuries earlier and now be remembered in folklore. How the exuberant libertarianism of the early interstellar period devolved through the Hansa-like Polesotechnic League and its collapse to the Empire, and what came after, gave rise to a number of stories, each self-explanatory but all parts of a "future history."

In it, humans and Ythrians jointly colonize a world and gradually develop a hybrid society like none ever seen before. The details are in a novel, *The People of the Wind*, but several briefer tales take place here at various stages of the development. This one harks back to the period of exploration before settlement, when the name Avalon had not yet been bestowed.

THE PROBLEM OF PAIN

Maybe only a Christian can understand this story. In that case I don't qualify. But I do take an interest in religion, as part of being an amateur psychologist, and—for the grandeur of its language if nothing else—a Bible is among the reels that accompany me wherever I go. This was one reason Peter Berg told me what had happened in his past. He desperately needed to make sense of it, and no priest he'd talked to had quite laid his questions to rest. There was an outside chance that an outside viewpoint like mine would see what a man within the faith couldn't.

His other reason was simple loneliness. We were on Lucifer, as part of a study corporation. That world is well named. It will never be a real colony for any beings whose ancestors evolved amidst clean greenery. But it might be marginally habitable, and if so, its mineral wealth would be worth exploiting. Our job was to determine whether that was true. The gentlest-looking environment holds a thousand death traps until you have learned what the difficulties are and how to grip them. (Earth is no exception.) Sometimes you find problems which can't be solved economically, or can't be solved at all. Then you write off the area or the entire planet, and look for another.

We'd contracted to work three standard years on Lucifer. The pay was munificent, but presently we realized that no bank account could buy back one day we might have spent beneath a kindlier sun. It was a knowledge we carefully avoided discussing with teammates.

About midway through, Peter Berg and I were assigned to do an in-depth investigation of a unique cycle in the ecology of the northern middle latitudes. This meant that we settled down for weeks—which ran into months—in a sample region, well away from everybody else to minimize human disturbances. An occasional supply flitter gave us our only real contact; electronics were no proper substitute, especially when that hell-violent star was forever disrupting them.

Under such circumstances, you come to know your partner maybe better than you know yourself. Pete and I got along well. He's a big, sandy-haired, freckle-faced young man, altogether dependable, with enough kindliness, courtesy, and dignity that he need not make a show of them. Soft-spoken, he's a bit short in the humor department. Otherwise I recommend him as a companion. He has a lot to tell from his own wanderings, yet he'll listen with genuine interest to your memories and brags; he's well-read too, and a good cook when his turn comes; he plays chess at just about my level of skill.

I already knew he wasn't from Earth, had in fact never been there, but from Aeneas, nearly 200 light-years distant, more than 300 from Lucifer. And, while he'd gotten an education at the new little university in Nova Roma, he was raised in the outback. Besides, that town is only a far-off colonial capital. It helped explain his utter commitment to belief in a God who became flesh and died for love of man. Not that I scoff. When he said his prayers, night and morning in our one-room shelterdome, trustingly as a child, I didn't rag him nor he reproach me. Of course, over the weeks, we came more and more to talk about such matters.

At last he told me of that which haunted him.

We'd been out through the whole of one of Lucifer's long, long days; we'd toiled, we'd sweated, we'd itched and stunk and gotten grimy and staggered from weariness, we'd come near death once: and we'd found the uranium-concentrating root which was the key to the whole weirdness around us. We came back to base as day's fury was dying in the usual twilight gale; we washed, ate something, went to sleep with the hiss of storm-blown dust for a lullaby. Ten or twelve hours later we awoke and saw, through the vitryl panels, stars cold and crystalline beyond this thin air, auroras aflame, landscape hoar, and the twisted things we called trees all sheathed in glittering ice.

"Nothing we can do now till dawn," I said, "and we've earned a celebration." So we prepared a large meal, elaborate as possible—breakfast or supper, what relevance had that here? We drank wine in the course of it, and afterward much brandy while we sat, side by side in our loungers, watching the march of constellations which Earth or Aeneas never saw. And we talked. Finally we talked of God.

"—maybe you can give me an idea," Pete said. In the dim light, his face bore a struggle. He stared before him and knotted his fingers.

"M-m, I dunno," I said carefully. "To be honest, no offense meant, theological conundrums strike me as silly."

He gave me a direct blue look. His tone was soft: "That is, you feel the paradoxes don't arise if we don't insist on believing?"

"Yes. I respect your faith, Pete, but it's not mine. And if I did suppose a, well, a spiritual principle or something is behind the universe—" I gestured at the high and terrible sky "—in the name of reason, can we confine, can we understand whatever made *that*, in the bounds of one little dogma?"

"No. Agreed. How could finite minds grasp the infinite? We can see parts of it, though, that've been revealed to us." He drew breath. "Way back before space travel, the Church decided Jesus had come only to Earth, to man. If other intelligent races need salvation—and obviously a lot of them do!—God will have made His suitable arrangements for them. Sure. However, this does not mean Christianity is not true, or that certain different beliefs are not false."

"Like, say, polytheism, wherever you find it?"

"I think so. Besides, religions evolve. The primitive faiths see God, or the gods, as power; the higher ones see Him as justice; the highest see Him as love." Abruptly he fell silent. I saw his fist clench, until he grabbed up his glass and drained it and refilled it in nearly a single savage motion.

"I must believe that," he whispered.

I waited a few seconds, in Lucifer's crackling night stillness, before saying: "An experience made you wonder?"

"Made me . . . disturbed. Mind if I tell you?"

"Certainly not." I saw he was about to open himself; and I may be an unbeliever, but I know what is sacred.

"Happened about five years ago. I was on my first real job. So was the—" his voice stumbled the least bit—"the wife I had then. We were fresh out of school and apprenticeship, fresh into marriage." In an effort at detachment: "Our employers weren't human. They were Ythrians. Ever heard of them?"

I sought through my head. The worlds, races, beings are unknowably many, in this tiny corner of this one dust-mote galaxy which we have begun to explore a little. "Ythrians, Ythrians . . . wait. Do they fly?"

"Yes. Surely one of the most glorious sights in creation. Your Ythrian isn't as heavy as a man, of course; adults mass around twenty-five or thirty kilos— but his wingspan goes up to six meters, and when he soars with those feathers shining gold-brown in the light, or stoops in a crack of thunder and whistle of wind—"

"Hold on," I said. "I take it Ythri's a terrestroid planet?"

"Pretty much. Somewhat smaller and drier than Earth, somewhat thinner atmosphere—about like Aeneas, in fact, which it's not too far from as interstellar spaces go. You can live there without special protection. The biochemistry's quite similar to ours."

"Then how the devil can those creatures be that size? The wing loading's impossible, when you have only cell tissue to oxidize for power. They'd never get off the ground."

"Ah, but they have antlibranchs as well." Pete smiled, though it didn't go deep. "Those look like three gills, sort of, on either side, below the wings. They're actually more like bellows, pumped by the wing muscles. Extra oxygen is forced directly into the bloodstream during flight. A biological supercharger system."

"Well, I'll be a . . . never mind what." I considered, in delight, this new facet of nature's inventiveness. "Um-m-m . . . if they spend energy at that rate, they've got to have appetites to match."

"Right. They're carnivores. A number of them are still hunters. The advanced societies are based on ranching. In either case, obviously, it takes a lot of meat animals, a lot of square kilometers, to support one Ythrian. So they're fiercely territorial. They live in small groups—single families or extended households—which attack, with intent to kill, any uninvited outsider who doesn't obey an order to leave."

"And still they're civilized enough to hire humans for space exploration?"

"Uh-huh. Remember, being flyers, they've never needed to huddle in cities in order to have ready communication. They do keep a few towns, mining or manufacturing centers, but those are inhabited mostly by wing-clipped slaves.

I'm glad to say that institution's dying out as they get modern machinery."

"By trade?" I guessed.

"Yes," Pete replied. "When the first Grand Survey discovered them, their most advanced culture was at an Iron Age level of technology; no industrial revolution, but plenty of sophisticated minds around, and subtle philosophies." He paused. "That's important to my question—that the Ythrians, at least of the Planha-speaking *choths*, are not barbarians and have not been for many centuries. They've had their equivalents of Socrates, Aristotle, Confucius, Galileo, yes, and their prophets and seers."

After another mute moment: "They realized early what the visitors from Earth implied, and set about attracting traders and teachers. Once they had some funds, they sent their promising young folk off-planet to study. I met several at my own university, which is why I got my job offer. By now they have a few spacecraft and native crews. But you'll understand, their technical people are spread thin, and in several branches of knowledge they have no experts. So they employ humans."

He went on to describe the typical Ythrian: warm-blooded, feathered like a golden eagle (though more intricately) save for a crest on the head, and yet not a bird. Instead of a beak, a blunt muzzle full of fangs juts before two great eyes. The female bears her young alive. While she does not nurse them, they have lips to suck the juices of meat and fruits, wherefore their speech is not hopelessly unlike man's. What were formerly the legs have evolved into arms bearing three taloned fingers, flanked by two thumbs, on each hand. Aground, the huge wings fold downward and, with the help of claws at the angles, give locomotion. That is slow and awkward—but aloft, ah!

"They become more alive, flying, than we ever do," Pete murmured. His gaze had lost itself in the shuddering auroras overhead. "They must: the metabolic rate they have then, and the space around them, speed, sky, a hundred winds to ride on and be kissed by. . . . That's what made me think Enherrian, in particular, believed more keenly than I could hope to. I saw him and others dancing, high, high in the air, swoops, glides, hoverings, sunshine molten on their plumes; I asked what they did, and was told they were honoring God."

He sighed. "Or that's how I translated the Planha phrase, rightly or wrongly," he went on. "Olga and I had taken a cram course, and our Ythrian teammates all knew Anglic; but nobody's command of the foreign tongue was perfect. It couldn't be. Multiple billion years of separate existence, evolution, history—what a miracle that we could think as alike as we did!

"However, you could call Enherrian religious, same as you could call me that, and not be too grotesquely off the mark. The rest varied, just like humans. Some were also devout, some less, some agnostics or atheists; two were pagans, following the bloody rites of what was called the Old Faith. For that matter, my Olga—" the knuckles stood forth where he grasped his tumbler of brandy— "had tried, for my sake, to believe as I did, and couldn't.

"Well. The New Faith interested me more. It was new only by compari-son—at least half as ancient as mine. I hoped for a chance to study it, to ask questions and compare ideas. I really knew nothing except that it was mono-theistic, had sacraments and a theology though no official priesthood, upheld a high ethical and moral standard—for Ythrians, I mean. You can't expect a race which can only live by killing animals, and has an oestrous cycle, and is in-capable by instinct of maintaining what we'd recognize as a true nation or government, and on and on—you can't expect them to resemble Christians much. God has given them a different message. I wished to know what. Surely we could learn from it." Again he paused. "After all . . . being a faith with a long tradition . . . and not static but seeking, a history of prophets and saints and believers . . . I thought it must know God is love. Now what form would God's love take to an Ythrian?"

He drank. I did too, before asking cautiously: "Uh, where was this expe-dition?"

Pete stirred in his lounger. "To a system about eighty light-years from Ythri's," he answered. "The original Survey crew had discovered a terrestroid planet there. They didn't bother to name it. Prospective colonists would choose their own name anyway. Those could be human or Ythrian, conceivably both— if the environment proved out.

"Offhand, the world—our group called it, unofficially, Gray, after that old captain—the world looked brilliantly promising. It's intermediate in size be-tween Earth and Ythri, surface gravity 0.8 terrestrial; slightly more irradiation, from a somewhat yellower sun, than Earth gets, which simply makes it a little warmer; axial tilt, therefore seasonal variations, a bit less than terrestrial; length of year about three-quarters of ours, length of day a bit under half; one small, close-in, bright moon; biochemistry similar to ours—we could eat most native things, though we'd require imported crops and livestock to supplement the diet. All in all, seemingly well-nigh perfect."

"Rather remote to attract Earthlings at this early date," I remarked. "And from your description, the Ythrians won't be able to settle it for quite a while either."

"They think ahead," Pete responded. "Besides, they have scientific curiosity and, yes, in them perhaps even more than in the humans who went along, a spirit of adventure. Oh, it was a wonderful thing to be young in that band!"

He had not yet reached thirty, but somehow his cry was not funny.

He shook himself. "Well, we had to make sure," he said. "Besides planetology, ecology, chemistry, oceanography, meteorology, a million and a million mysteries to unravel for their own sakes—we must scout out the death traps, whatever those might be.

"At first everything went like Mary's smile on Christmas morning. The spaceship set us off—it couldn't be spared to linger in orbit—and we established base on the largest continent. Soon our hundred-odd dispersed across the globe, investigating this or that. Olga and I made part of a group on the southern shore, where a great gulf swarmed with life. A strong current ran eastward from there, eventually striking an archipelago which deflected it north. Flying over those waters, we spied immense, I mean immense, patches—no, floating islands—of vegetation, densely interwoven, grazed on by monstrous marine creatures, no doubt supporting any number of lesser plant and animal species.

"We wanted a close look. Our camp's sole aircraft wasn't good for that. Anyhow, it was already in demand for a dozen jobs. We had boats, though, and launched one. Our crew was Enherrian, his wife Whell, their grown children Rusa and Arrach, my beautiful new bride Olga, and me. We'd take three or four Gray days to reach the nearest atlantis weed, as Olga dubbed it. Then we'd be at least a week exploring before we turned back—a vacation, a lark, a joy."

He tossed off his drink and reached for the bottle. "You ran into grief," I prompted.

"No." He bent his lips upward, stiffly. "It ran into us. A hurricane. Unpredicted; we knew very little about that planet. Given the higher solar energy input and, especially, the rapid rotation, the storm was more violent than would've been possible on Earth. We could only run before it and pray

"At least, I prayed, and imagined that Enherrian did."

Wind shrieked, hooted, yammered, hit flesh with fists and cold knives. Waves rumbled in that driven air, black and green and fang-white, fading from view as the sun sank behind the cloud-roil which hid it. Often a monster among them loomed castlelike over the gunwale. The boat slipped by, spilled into the troughs, rocked onto the crests and down again. Spindrift, icy, stinging, bitter on lips and tongue, made a fog across her length.

"We'll live if we can keep sea room," Enherrian had said when the fury first broke. "She's well-found. The engine capacitors have ample kilowatt-hours in them. Keep her bow on and we'll live."

But the currents had them now, where the mighty gulfstream met the outermost islands and its waters churned, recoiled, spun about and fought. Minute by minute, the riptides grew wilder. They made her yaw till she was broadside on and surges roared over her deck; they shocked her onto her beam ends, and the hull became a toning bell.

Pete, Olga, and Whell were in the cabin, trying to rest before their next watch. That was no longer possible. The Ythrian female locked hands and wing-claws around the net-covered framework wherein she had slept, hung on, and uttered nothing. In the wan glow of a single overhead fluoro, among thick restless shadows, her eyes gleamed topaz. They did not seem to look at the crampedness around—at what, then?

The humans had secured themselves by a line onto a lower bunk. They embraced, helping each other fight the leaps and swings which tried to smash them against the sides. Her fair hair on his shoulder was the last brightness in his cosmos. "I love you," she said, over and over, through hammerblows and groans. "Whatever happens, I love you, Pete, I thank you for what you've given me."

"And you," he would answer. *And You,* he would think. *Though You won't take her, not yet, will You? Me, yes, if that's Your will. But not Olga. It'd leave Your creation too dark.*

A wing smote the cabin door. Barely to be heard through the storm, an Ythrian voice—high, whistly, but reasonant out of full lungs—shouted: "Come topside!"

Whell obeyed at once, the Bergs as fast as they could slip on life jackets. Having taken no personal grav units along, they couldn't fly free if they went overboard. Dusk raved around them. Pete could just see Rusa and Arrach in the stern, fighting the tiller. Enherrian stood before him and pointed forward. "Look," the captain said. Pete, who had no nictitating membranes, must shield eyes with fingers to peer athwart the hurricane. He saw a deeper darkness hump up from a wall of white; he heard surf crash.

"We can't pull free," Enherrian told him. "Between wind and current—too little power. We'll likely be wrecked. Make ready."

Olga's hand went briefly to her mouth. She huddled against Pete and might have whispered, "Oh, no." Then she straightened, swung back down into the cabin, braced herself as best she could and started assembling the most vital things stored there. He saw that he loved her still more than he had known.

The same calm descended on him. Nobody had time to be afraid. He got busy too. The Ythrians could carry a limited weight of equipment and supplies, but sharply limited under these conditions. The humans, buoyed by their jackets, must carry most. They strapped it to their bodies.

When they re-emerged, the boat was in the shoals. Enherrian ordered them to take the rudder. His wife, son, and daughter stood around—on hands which clutched the rails with prey-snatching strength—and spread their wings to give a bit of shelter. The captain clung to the cabin top as lookout. His yelled commands reached the Bergs dim, tattered.

"Hard right!" Upward cataracts burst on a skerry to port. It glided past, was lost in murk. "Two points starboard—steady!" The hull slipped between a pair of rocks. Ahead was a narrow opening in the island's sheer black face. To a lagoon, to safety? Surf raged on either side of that gate, and everywhere else.

The passage was impossible. The boat struck, threw Olga off her feet and Arrach off her perch. Full reverse engine could not break loose. The deck canted. A billow and a billow smashed across.

Pete was in the water. It grabbed him, pulled him under, dragged him over a sharp bottom. He thought: *Into Your hands, God. Spare Olga, please, please—* and the sea spewed him back up for one gulp of air.

Wallowing in blindness, he tried to gauge how the breakers were acting, what he should do. If he could somehow belly-surf in, he might make it, he barely might. . . . He was on the neck of a rushing giant, it climbed and climbed, it shoved him forward at what he knew was lunatic speed. He saw the reef on which it was about to smash him and knew he was dead.

Talons closed on his jacket. Air brawled beneath wings. The Ythrian could not raise him, but could draw him aside . . . the bare distance needed, and Pete went past the rock whereon his bones were to have been crushed, down into the smother and chaos beyond. The Ythrian didn't get free in time. He glimpsed the plumes go under, as he himself did. They never rose.

He beat on, and on, without end.

He floated in water merely choppy, swart palisades to right and left, a slope of beach ahead. He peered into the clamorous dark and found nothing. "Olga," he croaked. "Olga. Olga."

Wings shadowed him among the shadows. "Get ashore before an undertow eats you!" Enherrian whooped, and beat his way off in search.

Pete crawled to gritty sand, fell, and let annihilation have him. He wasn't unconscious long. When he revived, Rusa and Whell were beside him. Enherrian was further inland. The captain hauled on a line he had snubbed around a tree. Olga floated at the other end. She had no strength left, but he had passed a bight beneath her arms and she was alive.

At wolf-gray dawn the wind had fallen to gale force or maybe less, and the cliffs shielded lagoon and strand from it. Overhead it shrilled, and outside the breakers cannonaded, their rage aquiver through the island. Pete and Olga huddled together, a shared cloak across their shoulders. Enherrian busied himself checking the salvaged material. Whell sat on the hindbones of her wings and stared seaward. Moisture gleamed on her grizzled feathers like tears.

Rusa flew in from the reefs and landed. "No trace," he said. His voice was emptied by exhaustion. "Neither the boat nor Arrach." Through the rust in his own brain, Pete noticed the order of those words.

Nevertheless—he leaned toward the parents and brother of Arrach, who had been beautiful and merry and had sung to them by moonlight. "How can we say—?" he began, realized he didn't have Planha words, and tried in Anglic: "How can we say how sorry we both are?"

"No necessity," Rusa answered.

"She died saving me!"

"And what you were carrying, which we needed badly." Some energy returned to Rusa. He lifted his head and its crest. "She had deathpride, our lass."

Afterward Pete, in his search for meaning, would learn about that Ythrian concept. "Courage" is too simple and weak a translation. Certain Old Japanese words come closer, though they don't really bear the same value either.

Whell turned her hawk gaze full upon him. "Did you see anything of what happened in the water?" she asked. He was too unfamiliar with her folk to interpret the tone: today he thinks it was loving. He did know that, being creatures of seasonal rut, Ythrians are less sexually motivated than man is, but probably treasure their young even more. The strongest bond between male and female is children, who are what life is all about.

"No, I . . . I fear not," he stammered.

Enherrian reached out to lay claws, very gently and briefly, on his wife's back. "Be sure she fought well," he said. "She gave God honor." (Glory? Praise? Adoration? His due?)

Does he mean she prayed, made her confession, while she drowned? The question dragged itself through Pete's weariness and caused him to murmur: "She's in heaven now." Again he was forced to use Anglic words.

Enherrian gave him a look which he could have sworn was startled. "What do you say? Arrach is dead."

"Why, her . . . her spirit—"

"Will be remembered in pride." Enherrian resumed his work.

Olga said it for Pete: "So you don't believe the spirit outlives the body?"

"How could it?" Enherrian snapped. "Why should it?" His motions, his posture, the set of his plumage added: Leave me alone.

Pete thought: *Well, many faiths, including high ones, including some sects which call themselves Christian, deny immortality. How sorry I feel for these my friends, who don't know they will meet their beloved afresh!*

They will, regardless. It makes no sense that God, Who created what is because in His goodness he wished to share existence, would shape a soul only to break it and throw it away.

Never mind. The job on hand is to keep Olga alive, in her dear body. "Can I help?"

"Yes, check our medical kit," Enherrian said.

It had come through undamaged in its box. The items for human use—stimulants, sedatives, anesthetics, antitoxins, antibiotics, coagulants, healing promoters, et standard cetera—naturally outnumbered those for Ythrians. There hasn't been time to develop a large scientific pharmacopoeia for the latter species. True, certain materials work on both, as does the surgical and monitoring equipment. Pete distributed pills which took the pain out of bruises and scrapes, the heaviness out of muscles. Meanwhile Rusa collected wood, Whell started and tended a fire, Olga made breakfast. They had considerable food, mostly freeze-dried, gear to cook it, tools like knives and a hatchet, cord, cloth, flash-beams, two blasters and abundant recharges: what they required for survival.

"It may be insufficient," Enherrian said. "The portable radio transceiver went down with Arrach. The boat's transmitter couldn't punch a call through that storm, and now the boat's on the bottom—nothing to see from the air, scant metal to register on a detector."

"Oh, they'll check on us when the weather slacks off," Olga said. She caught Pete's hand in hers. He felt the warmth.

"If their flitter survived the hurricane, which I doubt," Enherrian stated. "I'm convinced the camp was also struck. We had built no shelter for the flitter, our people will have been too busy saving themselves to secure it, and I think that thin shell was tumbled about and broken. If I'm right, they'll have to call for an aircraft from elsewhere, which may not be available at once. In either case, we could be anywhere in a huge territory; and the expedition has no time or personnel for an indefinite search. They will seek us, aye; however, if we are not found before an arbitrary date—" A ripple passed over the feathers of face and neck; a human would have shrugged.

"What . . . can we do?" the girl asked.

"Clear a sizeable area in a plainly artificial pattern, or heap fuel for beacon fires should a flitter pass within sight—whichever is practicable. If nothing comes of that, we should consider building a raft or the like."

"Or modify a life jacket for me," Rusa suggested, "and I can try to fly to the mainland."

Enherrian nodded. "We must investigate the possibilities. First let's get a real rest."

The Ythrians were quickly asleep, squatted on their locked wing joints like idols of a forgotten people. Pete and Olga felt more excited and wandered a distance off, hand in hand.

Above the crag-enclosed beach, the island rose toward a crest which he estimated as three kilometers away. If it was in the middle, this was no large piece of real estate. Nor did he see adequate shelter. A mat of mossy, intensely green plants squeezed out any possibility of forest. A few trees stood isolated. Their branches tossed in the wind. He noticed particularly one atop a great outcrop nearby, gaunt brown trunk and thin leaf-fringed boughs that whipped insanely about. Blossoms, torn from vines, blew past, and they were gorgeous; but there would be naught to live on here, and he wasn't hopeful about learning, in time, how to catch Gray's equivalent of fish.

"Strange about them, isn't it?" Olga murmured.

"Eh?" He came, startled, out of his preoccupations.

She gestured at the Ythrians. "Them. The way they took poor Arrach's death."

"Well, you can't judge them by our standards. Maybe they feel grief less than we would, or maybe their culture demands stoicism." He looked at her and did not look away again. "To be frank, darling, I can't really mourn either. I'm too happy to have you back."

"And I you—oh, Pete, Pete, my only—"

They found a secret spot and made love. He saw nothing wrong in that. Do you ever in this life come closer to the wonder which is God?

Afterward they returned to their companions. Thus the clash of wings awoke them, hours later. They scrambled from their bedrolls and saw the Ythrians swing aloft.

The wind was strong and loud as yet, though easing off in fickleness, flaws, downdrafts, whirls, and eddies. Clouds were mostly gone. Those which remained raced gold and hot orange before a sun low in the west, across blue serenity. The lagoon glittered purple, the greensward lay aglow. It had warmed up till rich odors of growth, of flowers, blent with the sea salt.

And splendid in the sky danced Enherrian, Whell, and Rusa. They wheeled, soared, pounced, and rushed back into light which ran molten off their pinions. They chanted, and fragments blew down to the humans: *"High flew your spirit on many winds. . . . be always remembered. . . ."*

"What *is* that?" Olga breathed.

"Why, they—they—" The knowledge broke upon Pete. "They're holding a service for Arrach."

He knelt and said a prayer for her soul's repose. But he wondered if she, who had belonged to the air, would truly want rest. And his eyes could not leave her kindred.

Enherrian screamed a hunter's challenge and rushed down at the earth. He flung himself meteoric past the stone outcrop Pete had seen; for an instant the man gasped, believing he would be shattered; then he rose, triumphant.

He passed by the lean tree of thin branches. Gusts flailed them about. A nearly razor edge took off his left wing. Blood spurted; Ythrian blood is royal purple. Somehow Enherrian slewed around and made a crash landing on the bluff top, just beyond range of what has since been named the surgeon tree.

Pete yanked the medikit to him and ran. Olga wailed, briefly, and followed. When they reached the scene, they found that Whell and Rusa had pulled feathers from their breasts to try staunching the wound.

Evening, night, day, evening, night.

Enherrian sat before a campfire. Its light wavered, picked him red out of shadow and let him half-vanish again, save for the unblinking yellow eyes. His wife and son supported him. Stim, cell-freeze, and plasma surrogate had done their work, and he could speak in a weak roughness. The bandages on his stump were a nearly glaring white.

Around crowded shrubs which, by day, showed low and russet-leaved. They filled a hollow on the far side of the island, to which Enherrian had been carried on an improvised litter. Their odor was rank, in an atmosphere once more subtropically hot, and they clutched at feet with raking twigs. But this was the most sheltered spot his companions could find, and he might die in a new storm on the open beach.

He looked through smoke, at the Bergs, who sat as close together as they were able. He said—the surf growled faintly beneath his words, while never a leaf rustled in the breathless dark—"I have read that your people can make a lost part grow forth afresh."

Pete couldn't answer. He tried but couldn't. It was Olga who had the courage to say, "We can do it for ourselves. None except ourselves." She laid her head on her man's breast and wept.

Well, you need a lot of research to unravel a genetic code, a lot of development to make the molecules of heredity repeat what they did in the womb. Science hasn't had time yet for other races. It never will for all. They are too many.

"As I thought," Enherrian said. "Nor can a proper prosthesis be engineered in my lifetime. I have few years left; an Ythrian who cannot fly soon becomes sickly."

"Grav units—" Pete faltered.

The scorn in those eyes was like a blow. *Dead metal to raise you, who have had wings?*

Fierce and haughty though the Ythrian is, his quill-clipped slaves have never rebelled: for they are only half-alive. Imagine yourself, human male, castrated. Enherrian might flap his remaining wing and the stump to fill his blood with air; but he would have nothing he could do with that extra energy, it would turn inward and corrode his body, perhaps at last his mind.

For a second, Whell laid an arm around him.

"You will devise a signal tomorrow," Enherrian said, "and start work on it. Too much time has already been wasted."

Before they slept, Pete managed to draw Whell aside. "He needs constant care, you know," he whispered to her in the acrid booming gloom. "The drugs got him over the shock, but he can't tolerate more and he'll be very weak."

True, she said with feathers rather than voice. Aloud: "Olga shall nurse him. She cannot get around as easily as Rusa or me, and lacks your physical strength. Besides, she can prepare meals and the like for us."

Pete nodded absently. He had a dread to explain. "Uh . . . uh . . . do you think—well, I mean in your ethic, in the New Faith—might Enherrian put an end to himself?" And he wondered if God would really blame the captain.

Her wings and tail spread, her crest erected, she glared, "You say that of *him?*" she shrilled. Seeing his concern, she eased, even made a *krrr* noise which might answer to a chuckle. "No, no, he has his deathpride. He would never rob God of honor."

After survey and experiment, the decision was to hack a giant cross in the island turf. That growth couldn't be ignited, and what wood was burnable—deadfall—was too scant and stingy of smoke for a beacon.

The party had no spades; the vegetable mat was thick and tough; the toil became brutal. Pete, like Whell and Rusa, would return to camp and topple into sleep. He wouldn't rouse till morning, to gulp his food and plod off to labor. He grew gaunt, bearded, filthy, numb-brained, sore in every cell.

Thus he did not notice how Olga was waning. Enherrian was mending, somewhat, under her care. She did her jobs, which were comparatively light, and would have been ashamed to complain of headaches, giddiness, diarrhea, and nausea. Doubtless she imagined she suffered merely from reaction to disaster, plus a sketchy and ill-balanced diet, plus heat and brilliant sun and—she'd cope.

The days were too short for work, the nights too short for sleep. Pete's terror was that he would see a flitter pass and vanish over the horizon before the Ythrians could hail it. Then they might try sending Rusa for help. But that was a long, tricky flight; and the gulf coast camp was due to be struck rather soon anyway.

Sometimes he wondered dimly how he and Olga might do if marooned on Gray. He kept enough wits to dismiss his fantasy for what it was. Take the simple fact that native life appeared to lack certain vitamins—

Then one darkness, perhaps a terrestrial week after the shipwreck, he was roused by her crying his name. He struggled to wakefulness. She lay beside him. Gray's moon was up, nearly full, swifter and brighter than Luna. Its glow drowned most of the stars, frosted the encroaching bushes, fell without pity to show him her fallen cheeks and rolling eyes. She shuddered in his arms; he heard her teeth clapping. "I'm cold, darling, I'm cold," she said in the subtropical summer night. She vomited over him, and presently she was delirious.

The Ythrians gave what help they could, he what medicines he could. By sunrise (an outrageousness of rose and gold and silver-blue, crossed by the jubilant wings of waterfowl) he knew she was dying.

He examined his own physical state, using a robot he discovered he had in his skull: yes, his wretchedness was due to more than overwork, he saw that now; he too had had the upset stomach and the occasional shivers, nothing like the disintegration which possessed Olga, nevertheless the same kind of thing. Yet the Ythrians stayed healthy. Did a local germ attack humans while finding the other race undevourable?

The rescuers, who came on the island two Gray days later, already had the answer. That genus of bushes is widespread on the planet. A party elsewhere, after getting sick and getting into safety suits, analyzed its vapors. They are a cumulative poison to man; they scarcely harm an Ythrian. The analysts named it the hell shrub.

Unfortunately, their report wasn't broadcast until after the boat left. Meanwhile Pete had been out in the field every day, while Olga spent her whole time in the hollow, over which the sun regularly created an inversion layer.

Whell and Rusa went grimly back to work. Pete had to get away. He wasn't sure of the reason, but he had to be alone when he screamed at heaven, "Why did You do this to her, why did You do it?" Enherrian could look after Olga, who had brought him back to a life he no longer wanted. Pete had stopped her babblings, writhings, and saw-toothed sounds of pain with a shot. She ought to sleep peacefully into that death which the monitor instruments said was, in the absence of hospital facilities, ineluctable.

He stumbled off to the heights. The sea reached calm, in a thousand hues of azure and green, around the living island, beneath the gentle sky. He knelt in all that emptiness and put his question.

After an hour he could say, "Your will be done" and return to camp.

Olga lay awake. "Pete, Pete!" she cried. Anguish distorted her voice till he couldn't recognize it; nor could he really see her in the yellowed sweating skin and lank hair drawn over a skeleton, or find her in the stench and the nails which flayed him as they clutched. "Where were you, hold me close, it hurts, how it hurts—"

He gave her a second injection, to small effect.

He knelt again, beside her. He has not told me what he said, or how. At last she grew quiet, gripped him hard and waited for the pain to end.

When she died, he says, it was like seeing a light blown out.

He laid her down, closed eyes and jaw, folded her hands. On mechanical feet he went to the pup tent which had been rigged for Enherrian. The cripple calmly awaited him. "She is fallen?" he asked.

Pete nodded.

"That is well," Enherrian said.

"It is not," Pete heard himself reply, harsh and remote. "She shouldn't have aroused. The drug should've—did you give her a stim shot? Did you bring her back to suffer?"

"What else?" said Enherrian, though he was unarmed and a blaster lay nearby for Pete to seize. *Not that I'll ease* him *out of his fate!* went through the man in a spasm. "I saw that you, distraught, had misgauged. You were gone and I unable to follow you. She might well die before your return."

Out of his void, Pete gaped into those eyes. "You mean," rattled from him, "you mean . . . she . . . mustn't?"

Enherrian crawled forth—he could only crawl, on his single wing—to take Pete's hands. "My friend," he said, his tone immeasurably compassionate, "I honored you both too much to deny her her deathpride."

Pete's chief awareness was of the cool sharp talons.

"Have I misunderstood?" asked Enherrian anxiously. "Did you not wish her to give God a battle?"

Even on Lucifer, the nights finally end. Dawn blazed on the tors when Pete finished his story.

I emptied the last few ccs into our glasses. We'd get no work done today. "Yeh," I said. "Cross-cultural semantics. Given the best will in the universe, two beings from different planets—or just different countries, often—take for granted they think alike; and the outcome can be tragic."

"I assumed that at first," Pete said. "I didn't need to forgive Enherrian—how could he know? For his part, he was puzzled when I buried my darling. On Ythri they cast them from a great height into wilderness. But neither race wants to watch the rotting of what was loved, so he did his lame best to help me."

He drank, looked as near the cruel bluish sun as he was able, and mumbled: "What I couldn't do was forgive God."

"The problem of evil," I said.

"Oh, no. I've studied these matters, these past years: read theology, argued with priests, the whole route. Why does God, if He is a loving and personal God, allow evil? Well, there's a perfectly good Christian answer to that. Man—intelligence everywhere—must have free will. Otherwise we're puppets and have no reason to exist. Free will necessarily includes the capability of doing wrong. We're here, in this cosmos during our lives, to learn how to be good of our unforced choice."

"I spoke illiterately," I apologized. "All that brandy. No, sure, your logic is right, regardless of whether I accept your premises or not. What I meant was: the problem of pain. Why does a merciful God permit undeserved agony? If He's omnipotent, He isn't compelled to.

"I'm not talking about the sensation which warns you to take your hand from the fire, anything useful like that. No, the random accident which wipes out a life . . . or a mind—" I drank. "What happened to Arrach, yes, and to Enherrian, and Olga, and you, and Whell. What happens when a disease hits, or those catastrophes we label acts of God. Or the slow decay of us if we grow very old. Every such horror. Never mind if science has licked some of them; we have enough left, and then there were our ancestors who endured them all.

"Why? What possible end is served? It's not adequate to declare we'll receive an unbounded reward after we die and therefore it makes no difference whether a life was gusty or grisly. That's no explanation."

"Is this the problem you're grappling with, Pete?"

"In a way." He nodded, cautiously, as if he were already his father's age. "At least, it's the start of the problem.

"You see, there I was, isolated among Ythrians. My fellow humans sympathized, but they had nothing to say that I didn't know already. The New Faith, however. . . . Mind you, I wasn't about to convert. What I did hope for was an insight, a freshness, that'd help me make Christian sense of our losses. Enherrian was so sure, so learned, in his beliefs—

"We talked, and talked, and talked, while I was regaining my strength. He was as caught as me. Not that he couldn't fit our troubles into his scheme of things. That was easy. But it turned out that the New Faith has no satisfactory answer to the problem of *evil*. It says God allows wickedness so we may win honor by fighting for the right. Really, when you stop to think, that's weak, especially in carnivore Ythrian terms. Don't you agree?"

"You know them, I don't," I sighed. "You imply they have a better answer to the riddle of pain than your own religion does."

"It seems better." Desperation edged his slightly blurred tone:

"They're hunters, or were until lately. They see God like that, as the Hunter. Not the Torturer—you absolutely must understand this point—no, He rejoices in our happiness the way we might rejoice to see a game animal gamboling. Yet at last He comes after us. Our noblest moment is when we, knowing He is irresistible, give Him a good chase, a good fight.

"Then He wins honor. And some infinite end is furthered. (The same one as when my God is given praise? How can I tell?) We're dead, struck down, lingering at most a few years in the memories of those who escaped this time. And that's what we're here for. That's why God created the universe."

"And this belief is old," I said. "It doesn't belong just to a few cranks. No, it's been held for centuries by millions of sensitive, intelligent, educated beings. You can live by it, you can die by it. If it doesn't solve every paradox, it solves some that your faith won't, quite. This is your dilemma, true?"

He nodded again. "The priests have told me to deny a false creed and to acknowledge a mystery. Neither instruction feels right. Or am I asking too much?"

"I'm sorry, Pete," I said, altogether honestly. It hurt. "But how should I know? I looked into the abyss once, and saw nothing, and haven't looked since. You keep looking. Which of us is the braver?"

"Maybe you can find a text in Job. I don't know, I tell you, I don't know."

The sun lifted higher above the burning horizon.

IX

Again we jump back through time, now to 1960. That was the year when *Astounding* serialized *The High Crusade*. This romp remains one of the most popular things I've ever done, going through many book editions in several languages. George Pal had thoughts of filming it, but then he died. Eventually a German studio did. I've avoided seeing the result after being told on good authority that it's a piece of botchwork, and suggest that you might enjoy the novel more.

Briefly put, in the story the evil Wersgor empire has been expanding through space in leapfrog fashion, as its scouts find those widely scattered planets that are suitable for colonization—which happens to mean similar to ours. One lands on Earth. The site is an English village, the year is 1345, and the local baron, Sir Roger de Tourneville, is making ready to depart with the troop of free companions he has been gathering to join King Edward III in France. As usual when they come upon intelligent natives, the Wersgorix immediately set about terrorizing them, dropping a gangway to the ground, stepping forth, and opening fire with their energy handguns. It is a rude shock to them that the air is suddenly full of crossbow bolts and clothyard arrows, whereafter cavalrymen gallop up the gangway, followed by foot soldiers, into the ship. Only one Wersgor survives.

The English wonder if these malformed, blue-skinned creatures are demons. However, they can be killed, and when the prisoner is sprinkled with holy water he does not go up in a puff of smoke but merely waxes indignant. Besides, there are clergymen on hand, and no powers of Hell can prevail over good Christians. A monk, Brother Parvus, who will at last chronicle all the events, establishes basic communication with Branithar, the last Wersgor. He must be desperate, babbling such fantasies as the stars being suns. But so much the better. He can be quelled into piloting the ship for his captors and teaching them how. Obviously they need to know, against a day when more may arrive.

The vessel is so huge that it can accommodate not only the troops but everybody in the village: yeomen, artisans, women, children, even livestock. Why not take them along? They should actually be safer in an invincible, overawing craft than if left behind. Sir Roger expects he can end the French war, free the Holy Land, and be back in time for hay harvest.

The ship lifts off. Branithar sets the autopilot to bring it to the heart of the empire, locks the command in, and defies the humans to do their worst. They refrain, but manage to learn something about operating the guns. At the end of the voyage, they promptly attack a fortress. Return fire wrecks the ship. They crash land, themselves unharmed, and take the place by storm. The Wersgorix are totally unprepared for that kind of warfare.

To their dismay, the English find that battle damage includes the ship's records. Branithar doesn't have the navigational data in his head. He knows merely that his expedition traveled far into a wilderness of stars. Earth is lost.

From then on, they must improvise. At first they exploit surprise. It can only help for a while, but gets them to a point where Sir Roger can open negotiations with other local starfaring races, who also dislike the Wersgorix but haven't had the strength to do much. All these civilizations have lost the knack for intrigue and double-dealing that he takes for granted—and he admits he's no expert, no Italian. As John Campbell observed in a blurb for one installment, our ancestors were ignorant of many things, but they weren't stupid.

The humans have their own failings. Troubles among them come near bringing them to catastrophe. However, things work out, and at last Brother Parvus can write of good King Roger reigning over the mightiest nation known among the stars.

Maybe this is an unnecessarily long synopsis. It's meant to give the background for a short story I wrote years afterward and reprint here as a representative of the novel.

QUEST

A chapter from *The Annals of Chivalry* by Sir Thomas Hameward. Writing in his old age, this knight baron intended to continue Friar Parvus' artless chronicle of the High Crusade, in a style more elevated. Deriving as it does from medieval romances, the style is better described as more florid, while the account is autobiographical rather than historical. Nevertheless, if nothing else, the book is of some interest as depicting later stages of interaction between long-established starfaring societies and those humans who, carried out into the galaxy against their will, overcame their would-be enslavers and founded the English Empire.

As nearly as the astrologers could calculate it from what scanty data were in the records, lost Terra had celebrated thirty Easters, and the year of Our Lord was 1375, when King Roger summoned a Grand Council to his seat of Troynovaunt. His purpose therein was threefold. Imprimis, he would have all of us join him in offering solemn thanks to Almighty God for His many mercies and blessings. Secundus, he would renew old acquaintances and strengthen bonds of fellowship through worldly festivities, as well as get to know the grown children of his followers in desperate adventure, these three decades agone. Tertius, he would discuss present challenges and future endeavors with his lords, his knights, and such of his ladies as nowadays held fiefs of their own among the worlds.

From star after star they came, across as much as a hundred light-years, in spaceships emblazoned with their arms and achievements, themselves in splendor of embroideries, velvets, silklikes, and furs. Banners flew, trumpets and drums resounded, horses and steeds of unearthly stocks pranced proud, as they debarked at the Port Royal and rode in, beneath high walls and gleaming battlements, to the palace. Yet ever borne in a place of honor were the weapons they had first brought from England. These were less often sword or lance than yeoman's bow, sergeant's ax, or serf's billhook. Remember, O reader, the original company had not been large, even reckoning in the civilians—men, women, children, clerics—who joined Sir Roger de Tourneville's free companions. Perforce, nearly everyone who survived the Crusade was eventually ennobled and put in charge of some portion of their conquests. At that, more than half the great folk now arriving were nonhumans of one sort or another, who had accepted the True Faith and paid homage to our puissant sovereign.

Besides this reminder of our origins, the necessity of caution was wholesomely chastening. We had broken the cruel imperium of the Wersgorix, made them subject to us, and thereby earned the gratitude of those other races whom they had decimated and oppressed. Certain of our former enemies had become our friends and, indeed, risen high among us because of their quick intelligence and technical erudition. However, more of them remained sullenly hostile. Some had attempted revolt. Many had fled beyond our ken, to skulk in a wilderness of uncharted suns. They still commanded terrible powers. A single nuclear warhead would demolish this city and abolish both monarchy and Papacy. We English were as yet thinly spread. Without the leadership and resources at Troynovaunt, our hegemony would be all too vulnerable to attack from without and within. Were it overthrown, that would spell the doom of Christendom, and belike of Adam's seed, among the stars. Therefore warcraft patrolled the Angevin System and virtually englobed Planet Winchester. No vessel might come near before it had been boarded and thoroughly inspected.

Natheless, the mood was joyous, the behavior often riotous, as English met English again, here at the heart of their triumphs. I own to downing more Jair liquor than was wise.

The carpenters at work in my head next morning may perhaps excuse my feelings at Mass. This I attended with my master, Sir Eric de Tourneville, youngest son of the King, whose squire I had lately become. Churches were so crowded that he sought a palace chapel; and the priest, Father Marcus of Uralura, preached a sermon that bade fair to last until Judgment. As I write, his words arise from the past and once more drone on within me.

"Praise God in sooth, and wonder at His foresightful care for us. The very fact that we are sundered from Terra exemplifies this. Only consider. A Wersgor scout vessel, seeking fresh territory for its people to overrun, landed at Ansby village with terror and slaughter. Hardy men counterattacked and seized it. Thereupon they sought to use it to end the French war and liberate the Holy Land; but they were tricked into a long voyage hither, where they must fight for survival. By divine grace, as well as valor and cunning, they prevailed. In the original turmoil, navigational notes were lost. The stars are so many, each planet of theirs so vast and preoccupying, that no explorer has found a way back to the mother world. But do not join those who lament the failure. Reflect, instead, that thereby Rome and Jerusalem have been spared possible destruction in space warfare. Meanwhile, the exiles were *forced* to bring Christian teaching and English rule to the benighted heathen. Enormous have been the rewards, secular as well as spiritual, albeit the latter are, of course, all that have any real importance—"

I have written down this part of the homily as a belated penance for having, about then, fallen asleep. Otherwise I was aflame with eagerness. My master had confided to me something of the endeavor which he would propose.

Being a son of John the Red, Count of New Lincolnshire and Baron of P'thng'gung, and being the squire of Sir Eric, a prince of the blood though not destined for the throne, I was present when the Grand Council met. Like my counterparts, I was kept so busy dashing to and fro with refreshments that I had little chance to observe. Recollection blurs into a brightness of sunlight striking through stained glass at tapestries, mounted weapons and trophies, rich garments, jewelry of gold and precious stones; a rumble of voices, now and then a shout or guffaw, while an orchestra tweedles unheard in a balcony; odors of meat, wine, ale, incense, humanity thickening the air; hounds and daggercats getting underfoot as they snatch at bones thrown down to them; gray hair, heavy bodies, faces scarred and furrowed, with youth here and there along the tables to relieve this dignity; in the Griffin Seat, King Roger, his own olden blade naked on his lap, emblem of power and of the fidelity that he has pledged to his people.

But I remember Sir Eric's words, when the microphone came to him in order of precedence; for they struck that assembly mute with wonder. Those words are on record, as is the debate that followed. I will only set down the gist of them. He stood, hawk-featured, bronze-locked, his frame lean and medium-tall—a young man, quite newly knighted, though he had wandered and fought widely—and cried forth:

"Your Highness, my lords and ladies, I've an undertaking for us, and what an undertaking! Not another punitive expedition against Wersgor holdouts, not another random search for Terra, but the quest for a treasure great and sacred— the object of chivalry since Arthur or before, the outward sign of salvation and vessel of power, that chalice into which at the Last Supper Our Lord and Saviour did pour the wine which became His most precious blood—the Holy Grail!"

Amazement went through the chamber like a gale wind. The King responded first, in that hard practicality which was ever his: "What are you thinking of? Is not the Sangreal back somewhere in England, whither Joseph of Arimathea brought it? I've heard my share of legends about the matter, and meaning no disrespect, some of them are pretty wild. But they agree that none save he who is without sin may ever achieve the Grail—and I know you better than that, my lad. We've more urgent business than a harebrained dash into God knows what."

Sir Eric flushed. Once the speech he had composed beforehand was exhausted, he was no orator. "Well, 'tis like this," he replied. "We, er, everybody acknowledges there's a dangerous shortage of saints' relics among us. We've merely those few that got taken along from the abbey at Ansby. And they're nothing much; not even a splinter of the True Cross among them. Superstition is causing people to venerate things that Father Marcus tells me can't possibly be genuine. I hate to imagine what bad luck—what Heavenly displeasure that could bring on us. But if we had the actual Holy Grail, now—"

Stumblingly, he explained. His farings, and a certain innate friendliness and openmindedness, had brought him together with numerous nonhumans. Of late they included a former Wersgor space captain named Insalith. He was an obstinate pagan, who attributed all events to the operations of quantum mechanics. However, otherwise he had accepted civilization. His religious blindness made his story the more plausible, in that piety could not have led him into wishful thinking.

Now retired, he had many years before been on several of his race's expeditions prospecting for new worlds to conquer and settle. They had come upon one afar that looked promising. It was untenanted except for a set of buildings that, in retrospect, resembled a Christian monastery. Landing to investigate afoot, the Wersgorix spied a monster, a veritable dragon, but it shunned them and they approached the church. There they met a few beings who, in retrospect, seemed human. Through the open doors they glimpsed something silvery and chalice-like upon an altar, and heard ineffably sweet music. Though the white-robed persons offered them no threat, such awe came upon them that they fled. Afterward, if only for fear of ridicule from their hard-souled colleagues and damage to their careers, they filed a report that tests had shown this planet to be biochemically unsuitable for colonization.

Today, having outlived the rest of that crew, having seen our kind enter his realm and erect houses of God, Insalith yearned back. Perhaps yonder was a proof of the Gospels that would satisfy his scientific mind and bring him spiritual peace. He was willing to navigate a ship there.

"If we humble mortals could make it into space," argued Sir Eric, "the Holy Grail should have no difficulties. I don't believe we dare neglect this account. It might prove false, I grant you, but then, it might truly be a sign unto us, a command from Heaven." Meanwhile his nostrils twitched. He yearned to be off on such an incredible venture. I had come to know him.

"Aye, go, go, in Jesus' name!" cried Archbishop William, who was himself of Wersgor stock.

King Roger stroked his chin, stared upward at the vaulted ceiling and the battle banners that hung from it, and said slowly: "Remember everything else we've taken counsel about. We can't dispatch a fleet. The risk of our homes getting raided would become much too great. But—well, son, you do have a ship of your own, and—and—" His voice lifted to a roar. His fist crashed down on the chair arm. "And by our Lady, how I wish I were going along!"

I forebear to describe the tumult that followed, before Sir Eric won leave to depart. Next day, in his exhilaration, he swept like fire through a tournament, unhorsing every opponent until at last he could ride to accept a wreath from the Queen of Love and Beauty. She was Matilda Mountjoy, of whom even I already had knowledge, and he was on a unicorn. However, the genetic craftsmen who supply animals of this sort have not yet succeeded in giving them the ability to make fine distinctions among ladies.

The *Bonaventura* was of modest size and armament, as nuclear missiles and energy projectors go. Half a dozen men, two nonhumans, and their horses crowded its hull. Luckily, the engine was of the best, weaving us in and out of 4-space at a quasi-velocity which brought us to our goal, far outside mapped regions, in about a month.

Just the same, that proved a wearisome journey. The fault did not lie with my fellow Englishmen. Like me, they were young and cheerful, buoyed rather than oppressed by the sanctity of their mission. Besides the knight and myself, we numbered two men-at-arms, a planetologist, and a pilot-cum-engineer-cum-gunner in case any automaton failed. To pass the time, we practiced combat techniques, gambled, drank, pursued minor arts, and bragged about our feats on various planets and women.

Nor can I accuse Insalith of creating tedium. In appearance he was a typical Wersgor, though age had stooped his squat five-foot frame, made gaunt the short tail, faded the hairless blue skin, wrinkled the snouted face and pointed ears, dulled the yellow eyes. None of these changes were overly conspicuous, and he retained a sharp mind and dry wit. We enjoyed listening to his reminiscences of voyages and deeds, aye, even as an officer in the war against our fathers.

Be it confessed, our chaplain was what often made the traveling dismal. Father Marcus was an Uraluran, converted and ordained, abrim with zeal. He preached, he reproved, he set unreasonable penances, he stared chillingly out of his three huge orbs, he waggled a flexible finger or windmilled all four arms or sent his blobby green countenance through the most hideous contortions as he quacked about what transgressors we were. (I write "he" for lack of a better word, the Uralurans being hermaphrodites who reproduce only on ceremonial occasions. To this very day, because of their modesty, that fact is not widely known off their planet. Marvelous are the works of God. Yet at the time, I could not keep from wishing that He had not chosen to create a species so devoid of human failings.) Besides his seven bony feet of height, the ecclesiastical authority bestowed upon him daunted us.

After all, we were in quest of the Holy Grail. If that truly was the thing we sought, then we could not attain to it if we were wicked. We would fail, and belike perish miserably. On the other hand, if our information had misled us, then we must be sufficiently well-informed on spiritual matters and free of pride to recognize this when we arrived. Else we might fall into some snare of Satan.

Father Marcus had therefore ordered a special program for the library of the ship's computer—every tale of the Grail that anybody could remember, with commentaries upon the accuracy of those memories, as well as a compendium of theology. And he kept shriving us and shriving us.

Sir Eric himself, while not always without merriment, had grown unwontedly pious. I often saw him on his knees in the chapel cabin. To the crucifix he uplifted his cross-hilted blade. It was a Singing Sword, whose haft he had commissioned from an electronician. Lately he had ordered me to insert therein a tape of hymns, that the weapon would chant if brought into action.

Father Marcus had opined that we would be blasphemous to carry firearms, let alone scientific instruments, into the possible Presence. But Insalith had bespoken a dragon. Quite likely, we thought, the forces of Hell had established a watcher, which could not enter the sacred precincts but would seek to deter Christians from doing so. Sir Eric did not mean to go altogether unarmed.

The planet was a white-swirled sapphire circling a golden sun, circled in its turn by two small, silvery moons. Spectroscopy showed the air to be salubrious for us, and an instrumented biochemical probe reported no poisons, but, rather, edible life upon arable soil. There was not so much of that soil, for land consisted simply of islands, a few large, most not. This, though, meant that climate almost everywhere was mild. "If ever the Holy Grail was borne from Terra," exclaimed our captain, "how perfect a new home for it!"

"Ah, but is not your intent to bring it back?" asked Insalith. Somehow, strangely, he seemed alarmed.

"We cannot remove it without permission of its guardians," replied Father Marcus, "but perhaps they will allow folk to make pilgrimage hither."

"That would be a profitable passenger route to have," murmured our pilot.

Horrified at his crassness, the priest gave him five hundred Aves and as many Paternosters to say, but Sir Eric declared that we could not afford the time just yet. He was white-hot with impatience to land.

Insalith identified the island of the shrine, a major one, and instruments did reveal a trio of buildings near a lake at its center. They also confirmed a lack of other habitation, of any trace of native intelligence. Had God reserved this world since the Creation for its present use? A chill went along my spine.

Descending on reverentially throttled gravitics, we set down in a meadow three leagues from our goal. "Piety doubtless requires we approach on foot," Sir Eric said. "Alayne and Robert"—he meant our pilot and planetologist— "shall stay inboard, ready to carry word home should we come to grief . . . if, h'm, they can't scramble to our aid."

He himself made a splendid sight as he trod forth into day. The sun turned helmet, chain mail, the shield on his left arm agleam; its radiance caressed fluttering plume and scarlet cloak and a pennon atop the antenna of a radio transceiver secured to his left shoulder. Behind him, I bore the de Tourneville gonfalon and Father Marcus a gilt crucifix. At their backs, the men-at-arms, Samkin Brown and Hobden Tyler, carried ax and pike respectively on either side of withered little Insalith.

Ah, the country was like Eden. Overhead reached a blueness full of wings. The cries and songs of those flying creatures descended through a breeze whose warmth brought odors akin to spice and perfume. Grasslike growth rippled underfoot, intensely green, starred with white flowers. As verdant and graceful were the trees, which soon grew more dense, until we were walking through a forest. There boughs met above us like a cathedral roof and sunbeams pierced rustling dimness. We had no trouble with underbrush, for we had come upon a trail leading in our direction, broad and hard-packed as if by something ponderous.

Sir Eric broke the hush: "A glorious planet. I hope to Mary we don't get our nobles at feud over whose fief it shall be."

"God have mercy!" wailed Father Marcus. "How can you think such a thing, here of all places?"

"Well, they thought it at the Holy Sepulchre back on Terra, didn't they?" the knight replied. "Yes, and fought it, too. You don't have to fret about man's fallen state. People like me do."

"Nay, that's my vocation," the cleric protested. "Why did God leave us Uralurans free of the seven deadly sins, if not to set your wayward race an example?"

Ignorant of theology, Samkin blurted, "What, d'you mean your kind are not fallen? You're, uh, *angels?*"

"No, no, no!" said Father Marcus in haste. "My poor species is all too prone to such temptations as quirling and vosheny; my own confessor has often had to set me a severe penance for golarice."

"An object of veneration in your midst would surely inspire you Christians of every sort to reform themselves," suggested Insalith. "Isn't it reasonable, in your belief, that your God has been saving the relic for this purpose?"

"I have cogitated on that question," Father Marcus answered. "In the era of the Table Round, none save Galahad the pure could reach to the Holy Grail. Yet through him it was, for a moment, revealed to that whole company; and earlier, at the first Eucharist, even Judas beheld it. For this imperilled outpost of Christendom, divine policy may conceivably have been further modified. Or it may not have been. We can but go forward, look for ourselves, then pray for illumination." He paused before adding: "One thing does strike me as curious. Salvation is not easily won. Nor should the Grail be, that is its sacrosanct emblem. Whether or not God surrounds it with obstacles, one would expect that the Devil—"

As if on cue, a hoarse bellowing interrupted him. We stopped in our tracks. Terror stabbed me. A stench as of fire and brimstone rolled through the forest air. Around a bend in the path crawled a dragon.

Fifty feet in length it was, from fanged maw to spiked tailtip. Steel-gray scales armored it. The six clawed feet that pulled it along made earth shiver beneath monstrous weight. Smoke gusted from its gullet, within which flames flickered. Straight toward us it moved, and its roars smote our ears with hammerblows.

"It left *us* alone!" I heard Insalith yammer.

"You were heathens," rapped Sir Eric.

"Quick, call the ship!"

"No. The leaf canopy—no way to aim—the beams would slay us too."

"The Beast, Satan's Beast," moaned Father Marcus. He fell to his double-jointed knees and held the crucifix aloft. It trembled like a twig in the wind. *"Apage, diabole!"*

The dragon paid no attention. Closer it came. I was aware of the men-at-arms, about to bolt in panic, and of myself ready to join them.

"God send the right!" shouted Sir Eric, and plunged to do battle. His sword blazed forth. "St. George for merry England!"

Somehow that restored my heart to me. I ran after him, howling my own defiance, the spearhead atop my standard pole slanted down. After an instant, Samkin and Hobden followed.

Sir Eric was already engaged. His blade flew, struck, slashed, drew foul black blood from the unprotected nose of the firedrake. And it sang as it hewed. I heard—

not Latin but English; not a *Te Deum* but:

> "Oh, give me a haunch of ruddy beef,
> And nut-brown ale in my pot,
> Then a lusty wench with a sturdy arse
> To bounce upon my cot—"

and realized, dismayed, that I had gotten the wrong tape.

If doomed by my folly, I could at least die like a man. I thrust my weapon down the flaming gape. The crossarm jammed tight and our banner charred. The dragon hiccoughed thunderously. Meanwhile our companions were stabbing and chopping away.

The creature hissed like a cataract. It scuttled backward. Incredulous, we saw it twist around a tree and make haste out of our sight.

For a long while, we stared at each other, not quite understanding our deliverance. Strength fled me, I sank to the ground and darkness whirled through my head. When I returned to my senses, I felt the priest shaking me and jubilating, "Rouse, my son, rouse, and give thanks to the Lord God of Hosts!"

We did, in fervor, regardless of smoke-stained garments and sweat-stinking bodies. Gratitude welled up in my bosom, and I mingled my tears with those of two hardened sergeants. How strange, how perturbing in a distant fashion, to see the frown upon Sir Eric's brow.

Well, I thought, whatever the trouble was, it did take his mind off my blunder.

I reckoned myself as brave as most fighting men, and had hunted dangerous animals erenow. Natheless, for a space I trembled, tingled, and tottered. That was less because we had been imperilled than because we had evidently encountered a thing from Hell. Samkin and Hobden were in like case. Sir Eric, though, remained withdrawn, while Father Marcus was full of exaltation and Insalith trotted eagerly onward.

Steadiness came back to me as we fared; for had we not in fact been victorious, and was that not a wondrous portent? When we arrived, my resolution turned to awe.

We had emerged from the wood into cleared acres of garden and orchard. Foreign to us were yon blossoms, hedgerows, fruits aglow in mellow afternoon light; or were they? Did they not hint at those roses, apples, hawthorns, and other English beauties whereof our parents spoke so wistfully? The lake blinked and sheened on our right, argent on azure; beyond it lifted a serenity of hills. Before us were the buildings.

They were three in number, arranged around a mosaic courtyard. Their smallness reminded me of that stable where Our Lord was born, the poor cottages that sheltered Him during His ministry, the unpretentious loft room wherein He gathered His disciples for the Last Supper. But they were exquisite, of alabaster hue and perfect workmanship. Colonnaded, one seemed to be for utility; opposite it stood another, whose glazed windows suggested a dormitory and refectory. Between them, facing us across the pavement, rose the church. I thought it must be the epitome of that English Perpendicular style which our architects strove to emulate from drawings done by some of those who remembered. Slender pillars, ogive arches and windows, saints in their niches, rose beneath twin towers. Melody wafted thence, notes surely like those from the harps of Paradise. The doors stood open in an eternal welcome.

We hastened among the flowerbeds. Gravel crunched under our feet, until the courtyard rang. In the mosaic I saw, delicately wrought, a Tree of Jesse.

We halted at a staircase flanked by sculptures of the Lamb and the Fish. Suddenly I unbuckled my helmet and tucked it beneath my arm. A man had stepped out onto the porch.

He came to a stop, there above us, handsome, solemn, hair and beard as white as his robe, right hand lifted in benediction. Upon his brow shone a golden crown. In his left hand he bore a trident, and he limped. A supernatural thrill passed over me, for I recalled the Fisher King.

Organ tones formed words of Norman French: "In the name of the father, and of the Son, and of the Holy Ghost, well met, pilgrims. Enter ye now unto the mystery ye have sought, that which shall save your peoples."

Father Marcus' response wavered. "Have we, have we indeed come . . . to the abiding place . . . of the Sangreal?"

"Enter," said the crowned man gently, "and see, and give praise."

Sir Eric too removed his helmet. He laid it down beside his shield and scabbarded sword. The men-at-arms did likewise, and I. We signed ourselves. I felt that I read anguish, indecision, behind the knight's stiff features, and wondered anew, with a touch of dread, what wrongness possessed his soul.

"Come," said the crowned man, and gestured us toward him.

Insalith hesitated. "I am not christened," he said in a near whisper.

The other smiled. "You will be, my son, you will be, as will every sentience in the universe. Come you also and worship."

Slowly, we mounted the stairs.

For a moment, splendor overwhelmed me. Windows depicting Bible scenes cast their rainbow glow over nave, aisles, choir, columns, the Stations of the Cross wrought in gold. Under a great rose window, candles burned before an image of the Virgin that seemed alive in its tenderness and majesty. Music soared amidst fragrances. At a font shaped like a lily, we dipped our fingers and again dared bless ourselves.

Our gaze went to the altar. Upon it, below a crucifix of piteous realness, sheened a silver chalice. It must have stood three feet high on a broad base, though the grace of its proportions came near cloaking that size. Attired in white habits, two women kept vigil at the sides, their heads bowed in prayer, beads streaming between their fingers.

The man of the trident urged us onward. At the rail he turned about, traced the Cross, and said gladly:

"Lo, here is the joy of chivalrous desiring, the Grail of Our Lord and Saviour Jesus Christ. Before your fathers ventured against the paynim of the stars, God transported it hither and set it in care of these pure maidens and my unworthy self, that we might guard it until men had need of it among them. Fear not, my sons. We shall take communion, and you shall abide this night, and tomorrow you shall bear the Holy Grail back to your people."

Father Marcus prostrated himself. Insalith went on all fours, the Wersgor attitude of submission. After a heartbeat, Samkin, Hobden, and I knelt. Yet— I quailed in my breast—we could not take our heed off the sisters. They were identical twins, young, fair beyond any man's dreams. Their garb did not conceal sweet curves beneath. Oh, I thought amid the racketing of my pulse, God forgive me my weakness, but it *has* been a long journey.

And Sir Eric stayed on his feet. His own eyes were aimed at the warden, like lanceheads.

Did the lame one show the least unease? "Why do you stand thus, my son?" he asked. "Kneel, confess your sins—to God Himself, Who will absolve you—while I fetch the wine and the Host."

The knight's words tramped forth: "Why is the cup so large? I expected it would be small and simple, as befitting celebrants who were not wealthy. This is the size of a soup kettle."

"It must needs hold the salvation of the world."

"Let me examine it. You understand. If it is a forgery, and I bring it home, I shall be doing the Devil's work."

"Why, no. I agree, well, true, authentication is necessary. But you are not qualified to judge. It will be no sin if you convey the vessel to those who are—your Pope, your King-Emperor. Rather, that is your duty."

"Step aside! On my head be this." And Sir Eric started past the crowned man, toward the chancel.

I gasped in horror. "Sacrilege!" hooted Father Marcus from the floor.

The warden snatched after the prince. Sir Eric shoved him off. He stumbled, his trident clattered to the flagstones. "Beatrice, Berenice, stop him!" he cried. "Sir, you'd not lay hand on the holy sisters, would you?"

The maidens moved to bar Sir Eric's way. Gently but remorselessly, he cast arms about their waists and dragged them from in front of the altar. He let them go, took the chalice, and lifted. I saw by the motion that the weight was heavy.

It was as if time died while he turned the huge cup over and over beneath his eyes. Finally he looked across it at the damsels. They had shrunk back against the rail, but the glances that responded to his were quickening away from timidity. Even in the wan light, I saw a flush spread across his cheeks, and theirs.

The crowned man picked up his trident and shook it. "You'll burn forever, unless you are mad and know not what you do!" he shouted. "Englishmen, seize him! Save the Holy Grail!"

I groaned as my heart tore asunder.

Sir Eric set the chalice down again. Luminance ran blood-red and heaven-blue over his mail. Straightening, he called to us: "We'll see who is the evildoer. If I am, how could I be a menace to the veritable Grail? And should not its guardians be perfect in the Faith? Father Marcus, arise and put these persons through the Catechism."

He thumbed his radio while he strode down to us. I heard him speak a command, not to the men aboard our ship but directly to the computer: "Activate your theological program."

Our chaplain may have been somewhat unversed in human ways, but he could scarcely miss seeing how the warden snarled or hearing the sisters shriek. I thought fleetingly that those feminine cries were not altogether agonized. The priest could be swift when he chose. He sprang to join Sir Eric in confrontation of the robed man.

"My good sir," he puffed, "you should be happy to establish your bona fides by explicating a few simple doctrinal points. From whence proceeds the Holy Ghost?"

"Are you mad too?" yelled the crowned one. "If I were iniquitous—in as grave a matter as this is—would God let me administer the sacraments? They would not be valid."

Father Marcus stiffened. "Ah, ha! That sounds very much like the Donatist heresy. Let us go into details, if you please."

Pausing only to consult his reference by radio, our chaplain set question after question. They bewildered me. I must needs admire the boldness with which the man stood his ground and flung back responses.

After minutes, Father Marcus wheezed a sigh, shook his head, and declared, "No more. You have in addition exposed yourself as an Arian, a Pelagian, a Catharist, and a Gnostic. This cup of yours must be a blasphemous fraud. Who are you, in truth?"

Sir Eric crouched, a leopard out of England's arms. His gaze lashed forth, to Insalith in the shadows. "You led us hither," he said low.

The Wersgor reached under his coat. Forth came an energy pistol. "Hold where you are," he rasped.

We froze. A single sweep of the beam from that weapon could incinerate us. He stalked toward the altar.

"Wait!" howled the crowned man, in the principal Wersgor tongue. "You'd not set it off?"

"Yes," said Insalith. "Destroy the evidence, and these monsters as well." He entered the chancel. The maidens screamed and fled from him. He reached the false Grail.

Sir Eric pounced. He snatched the trident from its owner's grasp, and hurled it. Insalith lurched. Tine-deep, the weapon shuddered in his belly. He fell, and his blood washed the floor of that house which was never a church.

Bonaventura throbbed about us. Stars crowded the viewports. We were bound home.

Sir Eric summoned us to the messroom—Father Marcus, the two crewmen, the two men-at-arms, the two maidens, and myself. Beatrice and Berenice had discarded their coifs, revealing topaz-hued locks, and belted their gowns closely, revealing marvelous shapes. Weary but triumphant, the knight laughed aloud at the head of the table and bade us be seated.

"The prisoner has confessed," he said. "I needed no violence upon him. His nerve broke when I threatened to take that alleged relic along on board."

"What is it in truth, what device of Satan?" asked Father Marcus low.

Sir Eric grinned. "Nothing so terrible," he answered, "although dangerous enough. It contains a nuclear bomb in the base, using a fissionable transuranic of small critical mass. And there are sensors worked into the ornamentation, and a recognition program keyed to detonate it when in the presence of either my royal father or the Pope. The blast would not have been of more than tactical force, but it would have sufficed to lay Troynovaunt waste, and thereby all our hopes."

"This, then, was a, a Wersgor plot from the, the beginning, my lord?" I stammered.

Sir Eric nodded. "Aye, hatched in a secret base of their outlaw remnants— whose location I now have. He who played the Fisher King is a human traitor, a criminal who fled from justice. The conspirators found him, trained him, and promised him rich reward. These damsels"—he bowed toward them—"are clones of a comely woman who never knew that a minor 'accident' was arranged to remove a few cells from her. Accelerated growth produced adult bodies within a half-dozen years." He smiled. "Yet they remain daughters of Eve, raised among falsehoods and therefore innocent in themselves. We'll bring them home baptized, I'm sure. Their story, their virginity, their consecration as true nuns will doubtless inspire many of us to live better lives."

The twins blushed rosy. However, the glance they exchanged, out of large blue eyes, seemed less than elated.

"The whole thing was cleverly done," Sir Eric went on. "We could well have been deceived, and carried yon fatal engine back. It's God's mercy that petty flaws in the plan, because the Wersgorix are not human and do not understand us in our innermost depths—those flaws betrayed it."

"What were they, my son?" wondered Father Marcus. "I am fain to think a divine revelation was vouchsafed you."

"Oh, no," denied Sir Eric, raising his palm. "Never me. I am no saint, but a sinner who stumbles more often than most. On that account, mayhap my hope of doing some holy work was higher than the conspirators foresaw, and led me to look closer when their illusions did not quite meet my expectations.

"I thought that the dragon yielded far too easily, the more so when the

Singing Sword was—well—In a matter of such importance, would Satan let his minion flee after a few cuts? Could the beast have been merely a biotechnical device, set there because it belonged in the picture but not intended to give serious resistance?

"The Fisher King bore no sign of being ordained, and legend does not make him a priest. But he offered us Holy Communion. He spoke reverently of the Grail, but did not doff his crown in its chapel. His haste to conduct the business and see us begone struck me as unseemly.

"The chalice itself was larger and massier than was reasonable.

"Er—be it confessed, and intending no discourtesy, when I embraced these two charming young ladies, what immediately stirred in my heart was lust. Would God have made a person as gross as me the bearer of His Grail?"

Sir Eric winced. "I wanted to believe," he finished. "How I longed to believe! But I decided we should put matters to a test. If I were mistaken, on my soul be the wrath. God knows I am weak and sinful, but He also knows I swore an oath of fealty to King and Church."

We men hailed him with the honor that was his due, the maidens with adoration. Those twain had not hitherto understood how wretched was their lot. Now joy blossomed in them, and a convent was the last place they wished to enter. I thought that Father Marcus had better make haste to give them Christian instruction, and my lord to find them good husbands when we came home.

X

There were other series. They were never planned beforehand, it was just that one story would suggest more, exploring the theme further. The Maurai chronicles began with a novelette, "The Sky People," and ended with a novel, *Orion Shall Rise*. The basic premise came from a book by Harrison Brown, *The Challenge of Man's Future*, published long ago but still well worth reading, very pertinent to the world around us today. (As said earlier, I steal only from the best sources.) The author pointed out that our civilization got started by exploiting a treasury of ores, coal, petroleum, timber, fertile soil, and everything else. As these have grown scarcer and more expensive, we have so far found substitutes, ways to economize and recycle, and generally keep going. Indeed, on the whole, our high-tech societies grow ever richer, and could do better yet were it not for their wars, ideologies, and other tragic, all too human foolishnesses.

But meanwhile the less fortunate majority of the race sinks ever deeper into poverty. It's not that those people aren't as intelligent as anybody else or that the well-educated among them don't have access to the same science and technology. The reasons are manifold. A major one is that population growth is pressing too hard on depleted resources. They can't make the necessary capital investment. Whether the luckier societies can help them get over the threshold remains to be seen. Let us hope.

Meanwhile, the balance on which high-tech civilization rests is more precarious than we like to think. Suppose it collapses, perhaps as the result of an all-out nuclear war, which is what my stories assume. Can it rebuild itself? The knowledge won't be lost; it's too widely distributed, in too many books and, for that matter, too many heads. But neither was the knowledge of how to build good highways, strong bridges, and municipal sewers lost when Rome fell. It was just that for the next thousand years Europe was too chaotic and too poor.

Moreover, as Harrison Brown observed, by now the great iron mines, oil fields, forests, and other sources of raw materials and energy have been worked out. Doubtless much could be salvaged from the wreckage if the rebuilders were well organized and knew precisely what needed doing. Basically, though, they'd have to work with lean resources and low power. How far might they be able to go?

How far might they *want* to go?

That would depend on who they were, what their ethos was. I imagined several different civilizations rising from the ruins in several different regions, each with its own *Weltanschauung* and ambitions. Most powerful were the Maurai of the Pacific basin. Highly sophisticated, their technology was based on renewability, because this was the all-overriding ideal of their otherwise tolerant and easygoing society, that the mistakes which had devastated life on Earth must never be repeated.

Here is an incident out of their effort to impose it everywhere.

WINDMILL

—and though it was night, when land would surely be colder than sea, we had not looked for such a wind as sought to thrust us away from Calforni. Our craft shuddered and lurched. Wickerwork creaked in the gondola, rigging thrummed, the gasbag boomed, propeller noise mounted to a buzz saw whine. From my seat I glimpsed, by panel lights whose dimness was soon lost in shadows, how taut were the faces of Taupo and Wairoa where they battled to keep control, how sweat ran down their necks and bare chests and must be drenching their sarongs even in this chill.

Yet we moved on. Through the port beside me I saw ocean glimmer yield to gray and black, beneath high stars. A deeper dark, blotted far inland, must be the ruins of Losanglis. The few fires which twinkled there gave no comfort, for the squatters are known to be robbers and said to be cannibals. No Merican lord has ever tried to pacify that concrete wilderness; all who have claimed the territory have been content to cordon its dwellers off in their misery. I wonder if we Sea People should—

But I drift, do I not, Elena Kalakaua? Perhaps I write that which you have long been aware of. Forgive me. The world is so big and mysterious, civilization so thin a web across it, bound together by a few radio links and otherwise travel which is so slow, it's hard to be sure what any one person knows of it, even a best-beloved girl whose father is in Parliament. Let me drift, then. You have never been outside the happy islands of the Maurai Federation. I want to give you something of the feel, the reality, of this my last mission.

I was glad when meganecropolis fell aft out of sight and we neared the clean Muahvay. But then Captain Bowenu came to me. His hair glowed white in the gloom, yet he balanced himself with an ease learned during a youth spent in the topmasts of ships. "I'm afraid we must let you off sooner than planned," he told me. "This head wind's making the motors gulp power, and the closest recharging station is in S'Anton."

Actually it was northward, at Sannacruce. But we couldn't risk letting the

Overboss there know of our presence—when that which I sought lay in country he said was his. The Meycan realm was safely distant and its Dons friendly.

One dare not let the accumulators of an aircraft get too low. For a mutinous moment I wished we could have come in a jet. But no, I understand well, such machines are too few, too precious, above all too prodigal of metal and energy; they must be reserved for the Air Force. I only tell you this passing mood of mine because it may help give you sympathy for my victims. Yes, my victims.

"Indeed, Rewi Bowenu," I said. "May I see the map?"

"Of course, Toma Nakamuha." Sitting down beside me, he spread a chart across our laps and pinpointed our location. "If you bear east-northeast, you should reach Hope before noon. Of course, your navigation can't be too accurate, with neither compass nor timepiece. But the terrain shouldn't throw you so far off course that you can't spy the windmills when they come over your horizon."

He left unspoken what would follow if he was wrong or I blundered. Buzzards, not gulls, would clean my bones, and they would whiten very far from our sea.

But the thought of those windmills and what they could mean nerved me with anger. Also, you know how Wiliamu Hamilitonu was my comrade from boyhood. Together we climbed after coconuts, prowled gillmasked among soft-colored corals and fanciful fish, scrambled up Mauna Loa to peer down its throat, shipped on a trimaran trader whose sails bore us around this whole glorious globe till we came back to Awaii and drank rum and made love to you and Lili beneath an Island moon. Wiliamu had gone before me, seeking to learn on behalf of us all what laired in the settlement that called itself Hope. He had not returned, and now I did not think he ever would.

That is why I volunteered, yes, pulled ropes for the task. The Service had other men available, some better qualified, maybe. But we are always so short of hands that I did not need to wrangle long. When will they see in Wellantoa how undermanned we are, in this work which matters more than any other?

I unbuckled, collected my gear, and went to hang on a strap by an exit hatch. The craft slanted sharply downward. Crosscurrents tore at us like an orca pack at a right whale. I hardly noticed, being busy in a last-minute review of myself.

Imagine me: tall for the Meycan I would claim to be, but not impossibly so, and you yourself have remarked on the accidents of genetics which have blent parts of my ancestry in a jutting Iniolike nose and coppery skin. Language and manners: In sailor days I was often in Meycan ports, and since joining the Service have had occasion to visit the hinterlands in company with natives. Besides, the deserts are a barrier between them and Calforni which is seldom crossed. My Spanyol and behavior ought to pass. Dress: shirt, trousers, uniform jacket, serape, sombrero, boots, all worn and dirty. Equipment: bedroll, canteen, thin pack of dried-out rations, knife, *spada* slung across back for possible machete work or self-defense. I hoped greatly I would not need it for that last. We learn the use of weapons, as well as advanced judo and karate arts, in training; nonetheless, the thought of opening up human flesh made a knot in my guts.

But what had been done to Wiliamu?

Maybe nothing. Maybe Hope was altogether innocent. We could not call in the armed forces unless we were certain. Even under the Law of Life, even under our covenant with the Overboss of Sannacruce, not even the mighty Maurai Federation can invade foreign territory like that without provoking a crisis. Not to speak of the hurt and slain, the resources and energy. We *must* be sure it was worth the cost—Now I do go astray, telling this to a politician's daughter who's spent as much time in N'Zealann as Awaii. I am too deeply back in my thoughts, as I clung there waiting.

"Level off!" Taupo sang from his seat forward. The ship struggled to a somewhat even keel. Evidently the altimeter said we were in rope's length of the ground.

Rewi, who had been beside me, squeezed my shoulder. "Tanaroa be with you, Toma," he murmured underneath the racket. He traced a cross. "Lesu Haristi deliver you from evil."

Wairoa laughed and called: "No need for deliverance from shark-toothed Nan! You'd never catch him in those dunes!" He must always have his joke. Yet his look at me was like a handclasp.

We opened the hatch and cast out a weighted line. When its windlass had stopped spinning, I threw a final glance around the cabin. I wouldn't see this gaiety of tapa and batik soon again, if ever. Supposing Hope proved harmless, I'd still have to make my own way, with mule train after mule train from trading post to trading post, to Sandago and our agents there. It would not do to reveal myself as a Maurai spy and ask to use Hope's transmitter to call for an airlift. That could make other people, elsewhere around the world, too suspicious of later strangers, in their midst. (You realize, Elena, this letter is for none save you.)

"Farewell, shipmate," the men said together; and as I went out and down the rope, I heard them begin the Luck-Wishing Song.

The wind tore it from me. That was a tricky passage down, when the cord threshed like an eel and I didn't want to burn the hide off my palms. But at last I felt earth underfoot. I shook a signal wave up the rope, stepped back, and watched.

For a minute the long shape hung over me, a storm cloud full of propeller thunder. Then the line was gathered in and the craft rose. It vanished astonishingly fast.

I looked around. Deserts had never much appealed to me. But this one was different: natural, not man-made. Life had not died because water was gone, topsoil exhausted, poisons soaked into the ground. Here it had had all the geological time it needed to grow into a spare environment.

The night was as clear as I've ever seen, fantastic with stars, more stars than there was crystal blackness in between them, and the Milky Way a torrent. The land reached pale under heaven-glow, speckled by silver-gray of scattered sagebrush and black weird outlines of joshua trees; I could see across its rises and arroyos to hills on the horizon, which stood blue. The wind was cold, flowing under my thin fluttering garments and around my flesh, but down here it did not shout, it murmured, and pungencies were borne upon it. From afar I heard coyotes yip. When I moved, the sandy soil crunched and gave a little beneath my feet, as alive in its own way as water.

I picked my guiding constellations out of the swarm overhead and started to walk.

Dawn was infinitely shadowed, in that vast wrinkled land. I saw a herd of wild sheep and rejoiced in the grandeur of their horns. The buzzard which took station high up in sapphire was no more terrible than my gulls, and no less beautiful. An intense green darkness against rockslopes red and tawny meant stands of piñon or juniper.

And it was April. My travels around western Meyco had taught me to know some of the wildflowers I came upon wherever shade and moisture were: bold ocotillo, honey-hued nolina plume, orchids clustered around a tiny spring. Most, shy beneath the sage and greasewood and creosote bush, I did not recognize by name. I've heard them called bellyflowers, because you have to get down on your belly to really see and love them. It amazed me how many they were, and how many kinds.

Lesser animals scuttered from me, lizards, snakes, mantises; dragonflies hovered over that mini-oasis on wings more splendid than an eagle's; I surprised a jackrabbit, which went lolloping off with a special sort of gracefulness. But a couple of antelope surprised me in turn, because I was watching a dogfight between a hawk and a raven while I strode. Suddenly I rounded a clump of chaparral and we found each other. The first antelope I'd ever met, they were delightful as dolphins and almost as fearless: because I was not wolf or grizzly or cougar; their kind had forgotten mine, which had not come slaughtering since the War of Judgment. At least, not until lately—

I discovered that I cared for the desert, not as a thing which the books said was integral to the whole regional ecology, but as a miracle.

Oh, it isn't our territory, Elena. We'll never want to live there. Risen, the sun hammered on my temples and speared my eyeballs, the air seethed me till my mouth was gummed, sand crept into my boots to chew my feet and the jumping cholla lived up to its name, fang-sharp burrs coming at me from nowhere. Give me Mother Ocean and her islands. But I think one day I'll return for a long visit. And . . . if Wiliamu had lost his way or perished in a sandstorm or otherwise come to natural grief in these reaches, as the Hope folk said he must have done . . . was that a worse death than on the reefs or down into the deeps?

—Rewi Bowenu had been optimistic. The time was midafternoon and the land become a furnace before I glimpsed the windmills. Their tall iron skeletons wavered through heat-shimmer. Nonetheless I felt a chill. Seven of them were much too many.

Hope was a thousand or so adults and their children. It was white-washed, red-tiled adobes centered on a flagged plaza where a fountain played: no extravagance in this dominion of dryness, for vision has its own thirst, which that bright leaping slaked. (Flower beds as well as vegetable gardens surrounded most houses, too.) It was irrigation ditches fanning outward to turn several square kilometers vivid with crops and orchards.

And it was the windmills.

They stood on a long hill behind the town, to catch every shift of air. Huge they were. I could but guess at the man-years of toil which had gone into shaping them, probably from ancient railway tracks or bridge girders hauled across burning emptiness, reforged by the muscles of men who themselves could not be bent. Ugly they were, and in full swing they filled my ears with harsh creakings and groanings. But beauty and quietness would come, I was told. This community had been founded a decade and a half ago. The first several years had gone for barebones survival. Only of late could people begin to take a little ease, think beyond time's immediate horizon.

Behind the hill, invisible from the town, stood a large shed-like building. From it, handmade ceramic pipes, obviously joined to the mill system, led over the ridge to a great brick tank, just below the top on this side. From that tank in turn, sluices fed the canals, the dwellings and workshops, and—via a penstock—a small structure at the foot of the hill which Danil Smit said contained a hydroelectric generator. (Some days afterward, I was shown that machine. It was pre-Judgment. The labor of dragging it here from its ancient site and re-constructing it must have broken hearts.)

He simply explained at our first encounter: "The mills raise water from the spring, you see, it bein' too low for proper irrigation. On the way down again, the flow powers that dynamo, which charges portable accumulators people bring there. This way we get a steady supply of electricity, not big, but enough for lights an' such." (Those modern Everlast fluorescents were almost shock-ingly conspicuous in homes where almost everything else was as primitive as any woods-runner's property.)

"Why do you not use solar screens?" I asked. "Your power supply would be limited only by the number of square meters you could cover with them."

My pronunciation of their dialect of Ingliss passed quite easily for a Span-yol accent. As for vocabulary, well, from the start I hadn't pretended to be an ordinary wandering worker. I was Miwel Arruba y Gonsals, of a *rico* family in Tamico, fallen on ill days when our estates were plundered during the Wa-temalan War. Trying to mend my fortunes, I enlisted with a mercenary com-pany. We soldiered back and forth across the troubled lands, Tekkas, Zona, Vada, Ba-Calforni, till the disaster at Montrey, of which the *señores* had doubt-less heard, from which I counted myself lucky to escape alive. . . .

Teeth gleamed in Smit's beard. "Ha! Usin' what for money to buy 'em? Remember, we had to start here with no more'n we could bring in oxcarts. Everything you see around you was dug, forged, sawed an' dovetailed together, fire-baked, planted, plowed, cultivated, harvested, threshed, with these."

He held out his hands, and they were like the piñon boles, strong, hard, but unmercifully gnarled. I watched his eyes more, though. In that shaggy, craggy face they smoldered with a prophet's vision.

Yet the mayor of Hope was no backwoods fanatic. Indeed, he professed indifference to rite and creed. "Oktai an' his fellow gods are a bunch of Asians, an' Calforni threw out the Mong long ago," he remarked once to me. "As for Tanaroa, Lesu Haristi, an' that lot, well, the sophisticated thing nowadays in Sannacruce is to go to their church, seein' as how the Sea People do. No disrespect to anybody's faith, understand. I know you Meycans also worship— uh—Esu Carito, is that what you call him? But me, my trust is in physics, chemistry, genetics, an' a well-trained militia." For he had been a prosperous engineer in the capital, before he led the migration hither.

I would have liked to discuss philosophy with him and, still more, applied science. It's so hard to learn how much knowledge of what kind has survived, even in the upper classes of a realm with which we have as regular intercourse as we do with Sannacruce.

Do you fully realize that? Many don't. I didn't, till the Service academy and Service experience had educated me. You can't help my sorrow unless you know its source. Let me therefore spell out what we both were taught as children, in order then to point out how oversimplified it is.

The War of Judgment wiped out a number of cities, true; but most simply died on the vine, in the famines, plagues, and worldwide political collapse which followed; and the reason for the chaos was less direct destruction than it was the inability of a resources-impoverished planet to support a gross overpopulation when the industrial machinery faltered for just a few years. (The more I see and ponder, the more I believe those thinkers are right who say that crowding, sensory deprivation, loss of all touch with a living world in which mankind evolved as one animal among millions—that that very unnaturalness brought on the mass lunacy which led to thermonuclear war. If this be true, my work is sacred. Help me never to believe, Elena, that any of the holiness has entered my own self.)

Well, most of the books, records, even technical apparatus remained, being too abundant for utter destruction. Thus, during the dark centuries, barbarians might burn whole libraries to keep alive through a winter; but elsewhere, men preserved copies of the same works, and the knowledge of how to read them. When a measure of stability returned, in a few of the least hard-hit regions, it was not ignorance which kept people from rebuilding the old high-energy culture.

It was lack of resources. The ancestors used up the rich deposits of fuel and minerals. Then they had the means to go on to exploit leaner substances. But once their industrial plant had stopped long enough to fall into decay, it was impossible to reconstruct. This was the more true because nearly all human effort must go into merely keeping half-alive, in a world whose soil, water, forests and wildlife had been squandered.

If anything, we are more scientific nowadays, we are more ingenious engineers, than ever men were before—we islands of civilization in the barbarian swamp which slowly, slowly we try to reclaim—but we must make do with what we have, which is mostly what the sun and living things can give us. The amount of that is measured by the degree to which we have nursed Earth's entire biosphere back toward health.

Thus the text we offer children. And it is true, of course. It's just not the whole truth.

You see—this is the point I strive to make, Elena, this is why I started by repeating the tricky obvious—our machinations are only one small force in a typhoon of forces. Traveling, formerly as a sailor, now as an agent of the Ecological Service, I have had borne in upon me how immense the world is, how various and mysterious. We look through Maurai eyes. How well do those see into the soul of the Calfornian, Meycan, Orgonian, Stralian . . . of folk they often meet . . . and what have they glimpsed of the depths of Sudamerca, Africa, Eurasia? We may be the only great power; but we are, perhaps, ten million among, perhaps, twenty times our number; and the rest are strangers to us, they were blown on different winds during the dark centuries, today they begin to set their own courses and these are not ours.

Maurai crewmen may carouse along the waterfront of Sannacruce. Maurai captains may be invited to dine at the homes of merchants, Maurai admirals with the Overboss himself. But what do we know of what goes on behind the inner walls, or behind the faces we confront?

Why, a bare three years ago we heard a rumor that an emigrant colony was flourishing in the Muahvay fringe. Only one year ago did we get around to verifying this from the air, and seeing too many windmills, and sending Wiliamu Hamilitonu to investigate and die.

Well. I would, as I said, have liked to talk at length with this intelligent and enigmatic man, Mayor Danil Smit. But my role as a *cab'llero* forbade. Let my tale go on.

They had received me with kindness in the settlement. Eager curiosity was there too, of course. Their communal radio could pick up broadcasts from Sannacruce city; but they had turned their backs on Sannacruce, and anyhow, it's not what we would call a thriving cultural center. Periodic trips to trading posts maintained by the Sandagoan Mercanteers, albeit the caravans brought books and journals back among the supplies, gave no real satisfaction to their news-hunger. Besides, having little to barter with and many shortages of no cessities, they could not afford much printed matter.

Yet they seemed, on the whole, a happy folk.

Briun Smit, son of Danil, and his wife Jeana gave me lodging. I shared the room of their five living children, but that was all right, those were good, bright youngsters; it was only that I was hard put to invent enough adventures of Lieutenant Arruba for them, when we lay together on rustling cornshuck pallets and they whispered and giggled in the dark before sleep or the dawn before work.

Briun was taller, leaner and blonder than his father, and seemingly less fervent. He cultivated hardly any land, preferring to serve the community as a ranger. This was many things: to ride patrol across the desert against possible bandits, to guard the caravans likewise when they traveled, to prospect for minerals, to hunt bighorn, antelope and mustang for meat. Besides crossbow and blowgun, he was deadly expert with ax, recurved hornbow, sling, lasso and bolas. The sun had leathered him still more deeply than his neighbors and carved crow's-feet around his eyes. His clothes were the general dull color—scant dyestuff was being made thus far—but flamboyant in cut and drape and in the cockade he bore on his curve-brimmed hat.

"Sure, Don Miwel, you just stay with me long's you've a mind to," he said out of the crowd which gathered when I made my dusty way into town.

"I fear I lack the skill to help you at farming, sir," I answered quite truthfully. "But perhaps I have some at carpentry, ropework and the like," which every sailor must and a landed aristocrat might.

Jeana was soon as delighted by what I could do as by what I could tell. It pleased me to please her—for instance, by making a bamboo-tube sprinkler grid for her garden, or a Hilsch arrangement out of sheet metal not immediately needed elsewhere, that really cooled the house whenever the frequent winds blew, or by telling her that Maurai scientists had developed insects and germs to prey on specific plant pests and how to order these through the Mercanteers. She was a small woman, but beautifully shaped beneath the drab gown, of elfin features and vivid manner and a fair complexion not yet bleached by the badlands.

"You have a lovely wife, *señor,* if I may say so," I remarked to Briun, the second evening at his home. We sat on the verandah, taking our ease after the day's jobs. Our feet were on the rail, we had pipes in our right hands and mugs of cider in our left, which she had fetched us. Before us stood only a couple of other houses, this one being on the edge of town; beyond gleamed the canals, palm trees swaying along their banks, the first shoots of grain an infinitely delicate green, until far, far out, the edge of sight, began the umber of untouched desert. Long light-beams cast shadows from the west and turned purple the eastern hills. It was blowing, coolness borne out of lands already nighted, and I heard the iron song of the unseen windmills.

"Thanks," the ranger said to me. He grinned. "I think the same." He took a drink and a puff before adding, slowly now and soberly: "She's a reason we're here."

"Really?" I leaned forward.

"You'd learn the story regardless. Might as well tell you right off, myself." Briun scowled. "Her father was a forester o' rank in Sannacruce. But that didn't help much when the Overboss's eye lit on her, an' she fourteen. He liked—likes 'em young, the swine. When she refused presents, he started pressurin' her parents. They held out, but everybody knew it couldn't be for long. If nothin' else, some night a gang o' bully boys would break in an' carry her off. Next mornin', done bein' done, her parents might as well accept his bribes, hopin' when he was tired of her he'd find a poor man who'd take another gift to marry her. We'd seen cases."

"Terrible," I said. And it is. Among them, it's more than an angering, perhaps frightening episode of coercion; they set such store by virginity that the victim is apt to be soul-scarred for life. My question which followed was less honest, since I already knew the answer: "Why do the citizens tolerate that kind of ruler?"

"He has the men-at-arms," Briun sighed. "An', o' course, he don't directly offend a very big percentage. Most people like bein' secure from pirates or invaders, which the bastard does give 'em. Finally, he's hand in glove with the Sea People. Long's they support him, or at least don't oppose an' boycott him, he's got the metal to hire those soldiers." He shook his head. "I can't see why they do, I really can't. The Maurai claim to be decent folk."

"I have heard," I said cautiously, "he follows their advice about things like reforestation, soil care, bio-control, wildlife management, fisheries."

"But not about human bein's!"

"Perhaps not, Mister Briun. I do not know. I do know this, however. The ancestors stripped the planet nearly to its bones. Unless and until we put flesh back, no human beings anywhere will be safe from ruin. In truth, my friend, we cannot maintain what technology we have except on a biological basis. For example, when almost everything has to be made from wood, we must keep the forests in equilibrium with the lumberers. Or, since the oil is gone, or nearly gone, we depend greatly on microbial fuel cells . . . and the fuels they consume are by-products of life, so we require abundant life. If the oil did come back—if we made some huge strike again, by some miracle—we would still not dare burn much. The ancestors found what happens when you poison the environment."

He gave me a sharp look. I realized I had stepped out of character. In haste, I laughed and said: "I have had more than one Maurai agent lecture me, in old days on our estate, you see. Now tell me, what happened in Sannacruce?"

"Well—" He relaxed, I hoped. "The discontent had been growin' for quite a while anyway, you understand. Not just Overboss Charl; the whole basic policy, which won't change while the Sea People keep their influence. We're becomin' too many to live well, when not enough fallow land or fishin' ground is bein' opened for use."

I refrained from remarks about birth control, having learned that what seems only natural to a folk who spend their lives on shipboard and on islands, comes slowly indeed to those who imagine they have a continent at their free disposal. Until they learn, they will die back again and again; we can but try to keep them from ravaging too much nature in the meantime. Thus the doctrine. But, Elena, can you picture how hard it is to apply that doctrine to living individuals, to Briun and Jeana, eager hobbledehoy Rodj and little, trusting Dorthy?

"There'd been some explorin'," he continued after another sip and another pungent blue smoke-plume trailed forth into the evening. "The good country's all taken where it isn't reserved. But old books told how desert had been made to bloom, in places like Zona. Maybe a possibility closer to home? Well, turned out true. Here, in the Muahvay, a natural wellspring, ample water if it was channeled. Dunno how the ancestors missed it. My father thinks it didn't exist back then; an earthquake split the strata, sometime durin' the dark centuries, an' opened a passage to a bigger water table than had been suspected before.

"Anyhow, Jeana's case was sort of a last straw. Her dad an' mine led a few pioneers off, on a pretext. They did the basic work of enclosin' the spring, diggin' the first short canal, erectin' the first windmill an' makin' an' layin' the first pipelines. They hired nomad Inios to help, but nevertheless I don't see how they did it, an' in fact several died o' strain.

"When the rest came back, families quietly sold out, swappin' for wagons, tools, gene-tailored seed an' such. The Overboss was took by surprise. If he'd tried to forbid the migration, he'd've had a civil war on his hands. He still claims us, but we don't pay him any tax or any mind. If ever we link up to anybody else, I reckon it'll be Sandago. But we'd rather stay independent, an' I think we can. This territory will support a big population once it's developed."

"A heroic undertaking," I said low.

"Well, a lot died in the second group, too, and a lot are half crippled from overwork in those early days, but we made it." His knuckles stood forth around the handle of his mug, as if it were a weapon. "We're self-supportin' now, an' our surplus to trade grows larger every year. We're free!"

"I admire what you have done, also as a piece of engineering," I said. "Perhaps you have ideas here we could use when at last I go home again. Or perhaps I could suggest something to you?"

"Um." He sucked on his pipe and frowned, abruptly uncomfortable.

"I would like to see your whole hydraulic system," I said; and my heart knocked within me. "Tomorrow can you introduce me to the man in charge, and I go look at the water source and the windmills?"

"No!" He sprang from his chair. For a moment he loomed over me, and I wondered if he'd drop his pipe and snatch the knife at his belt. Shadows were thickening and I couldn't make out his face too well, but eyes and teeth stood aglisten.

After a long few seconds he eased. His laugh was shaky as he sat down. "Sorry, Don Miwel." He was not a skilled liar. "But we've had that kind o' trouble before, which is why I, uh, overreacted." He sought solace in tobacco. "I'm afraid Windmill Ridge is off limits to everybody except the staff an' the mayor; likewise the springhouse. You see, uh, we've got just the one source, big though it is, an' we're afraid o' pollution or damage or—All right, in these lands water's worth more than blood. We can't risk any spy for a possible invader seein' how our defenses are arranged. No insult meant. You understand, don't you, guest-friend?"

Sick with sorrow, I did.

Still, the Service would require absolute proof. It seemed wise to bide my time, quietly study the layout for a few weeks, observe routines, gather bits and pieces of information, while the dwellers in Hope came fully to accept Miwel Arruba.

The trouble was, I in my turn came to accept them.

When Briun's boy Rodj told me about their winter visitor, his excitement glowed. "Clear from Awaii, he was, Miwel! A geologist, studyin' this country; an' the stories he could tell!" Quickly: "Not full of action like yours. But he's been clear around the world."

Wiliamu hadn't expected he would need a very thick cover.

Not wanting to prompt Briun's suspicion, I asked further of Jeana, one day when he was out and the children napping or at school. It bespoke a certain innocence that, despite the restrictive sexual customs, none looked askance at my hostess and me for the many hours we spent alone together. I confess it was hard for me to keep restraint—not only this long celibacy, but herself, sweet, spirited and bright, as kindled by my newness as her own children.

I'd finished the sprinkler layout and hooked it to the cistern on the flat roof. "See," I said proudly, and turned the wooden spigot. Water danced over the furrows she hoed alone. "No more lugging a heavy can around."

"Oh, Miwel!" She clapped small work-bitten hands. "I don't know how to—This calls for a celebration. We'll throw a party come Saddiday. But right now—" She caught my arm. "Come inside. I'm bakin'." The rich odors had already told me that. "You get the heels off the first loaf out o' the oven."

There was tea as well, rare and costly when it must be hauled from Sina, or around the Horn from Florda. We sat on opposite sides of a plank table, in the kitchen dimness and warmth, and smiled at each other. Sweat made tiny beads on her brow; the thin dress clung. "I wish I could offer you lemonade," she said. "This is lemonade weather. My mother used to make it, back home. She died in Sandstorm Year an' never—Well." A forlorn cheerfulness: "Lemonade demands ice, which we haven't yet."

"You will?"

"Father Danil says prob'ly nex' year we—Hope'll have means to buy a couple o' fridges, an' the power plant'll be expanded enough so we can afford to run them."

"Will you build more windmills for that?" A tingle went through me. I struggled to be casual. "Seems you already have plenty for more than your fluorolights."

Her glance was wholly frank and calm. "We have to pump a lot o' water. It don't gush from a mountainside, remember, it bubbles from low ground."

I hated to risk spoiling her happiness, but duty made me press in: "A Maurai geologist visited here not long before, I have heard. Could he not have given you good advice?"

"I . . . I don't know. That's man talk. Anyway, you heard how we can't let most of ourselves in there—I've never been—let alone strangers, even nice ones like you."

"He would have been curious, though. Where did he go on to? Maybe I can find him later."

"I don't know. He left sudden-like, him an' his two Inio guides. One mornin' they were gone, nary a word o' good-bye except, naturally, to the mayor. I reckon he got impatient."

Half of me wanted to shout at her: *When our "Geological Institute" radioed inquiries about its man, your precious village elders gave us the same answer, that he'd departed, that if he failed to arrive elsewhere he must have met with some misfortune on the way. But that wouldn't happen! Would it? An experienced traveler, two good natives at his side, well supplied, no rumor of bandits in this region for years past. . . . Have you thought about that, Jeana? Have you dared think about it?*

But the rest of me held my body still. "More tea?" she asked.

I am not a detective. Folk less guileless would have frozen at my questions. I did avoid putting them in the presence of fierce old Danil Smit, and others who had spent adult years in the competition and intrigues of Sannacruce city. As for the rest, however . . . they invited me to dinner, we drank and yarned, we shared songs beneath that unutterably starry sky, several times we rode forth to see a spectacular canyon or simply for the joy of riding. . . . It was no trick to niggle information out of them.

For example, I wondered aloud if they might be over-hunting the range. Under the Law of Life, it could be required that a qualified game warden be established among them, directly responsible to the International Conservation

Tribunal. Briun bristled a moment, then pointed out correctly that man always upsets nature's balance when he enters a land, and that what counts is to strike a new balance. Hope was willing to keep a trained wildlife manager around; but let him be a local person, albeit educated abroad, somebody who knew local conditions. (And would keep local secrets.)

In like manner, affable men assigned to duty on Windmill Ridge told me their schedules, one by one, as I inquired when they would be free for sociability. My work for the younger Smit household had excited a great deal of enthusiasm; in explaining it, I could slip in questions about their own admirable hydraulic system. Mere details about rate of flow, equipment ordered or built, equipment hoped for—mere jigsaw fragments.

Presently I had all but the final confirmation. My eyewitness account would be needed to call in the troops. What I had gained hitherto justified the hazard in entering the forbidden place.

A caravan was being organized for Barstu trading post. I could accompany it, and thence make my way to Sandago. And that, I trusted, I feared, would be my last sight of these unbreakable people whom I had come to love.

The important thing was that no sentry was posted after dark. The likelihood of trouble was small, the need of sleep and of strength for next day's labor was large.

I slipped from among the children. Once I stepped on a pallet in the dark, the coarseness crackled beneath my bare foot, Dorthy whimpered in her blindness and I stiffened. But she quieted. The night was altogether deserted as I padded through the memorized house, out beneath stars and a bitter-bright gibbous moon. It was cold and breezy; I heard the windmills. Afar yelped coyotes. (There were no dogs. They hadn't yet any real need for them. But soon would come the cattle and sheep, not just a few kept at home but entire herds. Then farewell, proud bighorn and soaring antelope.) The streets were gritty. I kept out of the gray-white light, stayed in the shadows of gray-white houses. Beyond the village, rocks barked my toes, sagebrush snatched at my ankles, while I trotted around to the other side of the Ridge.

There stood the low, wide adobe structure which, I was told, covered the upwelling water, to minimize loss by evaporation and downfall of alkaline dust into it. From there, I was told, it was lifted by the mills into the brick basin, from which it went to its work. Beyond the springhouse the land rolled upward, dim and empty of man. But I could make out much else, sage, joshua trees, an owl ghosting by.

My knife had electromagnetic devices built into its handle. I scarcely needed it to get in, save for not wanting to leave signs of breakage. The padlock on the door was as flimsy as the walls proved to be thin. Pioneers in a stern domain had had nothing to spare for more than the most pathetic of frauds.

I entered, closed the door behind me, flashed light from that gem-pommel on my knife, which was actually a lens. The air was cold in here, too. I saw moisture condensed on pipes which plunged into the clay floor and up through the roof, and somehow smelled it. Otherwise, in an enormous gloom, I barely glimpsed workbenches, toolracks, primitive machinery. I could not now hear the turning sails of the windmills which drove the pumps; but the noise of pistons in crudely fashioned tallow-lubricated cylinders was like bones sliding across each other.

There was no spring. I hadn't expected any.

A beam stabbed at me. I doused my own, reversed it to make a weapon, recoiled into murk. From behind the glare which sought about, a deep remembered voice said, more weary than victorious: "Never mind, Miwel or whoever you are, I know you haven't got a gun. I do. The town's firearm. Buckshot loaded."

Crouched among bulky things and my pulsebeats, I called back: "It will do you less than good to kill me, Danil Smit"—and shifted my position fast. The knife was keen in my hand, my thumb braced easily against the guard. I was young, in top shape, trained; I could probably take him in the dark. I didn't want to. Lesu Haristi knows how I didn't want to, and knows it was not merely for fear of having to flee ill prepared into the desert.

He sighed, like the night wind beyond these walls. "You're a Maurai spy, aren't you?"

"An agent of the Ecological Service," I answered, keeping moving. "We've treaty arrangements with the Overboss. I agree he's a rat in some ways, but he cooperates in saving his land for his great-grandchildren . . . and yours."

"We weren't sure, me an' my partners," Danil Smit said. "We figured we'd take turns watchin' here till you left. You might've been honest."

"Unlike you—you murderers." But somehow I could not put anger into that word, not even for Wiliamu my shipmate and his two nameless guides.

"I s'pose you've got backup?" he called.

"Yes, of course," I said. "Losing our first man was plenty to make us suspicious. Losing the second . . . imagine." Leap, leap went my crouch-bent legs. I prayed the noise of the pumping masked my foot-thuds from him. "It's clear what your aim is, to grow in obscurity till you're so large and strong you can defy everybody—the Federation itself—from behind your barrier of desert distances. But don't you see," I panted, "my superiors have already guessed this? And they don't propose to let the menace get that big!"

You know I exaggerated. Manpower and equipment is spread so thin, close to the breaking point. It might well be decided that there are more urgent matters than one rebellious little community. Wiliamu and I might be written off. Sweat stood chill upon me. So many seas unsailed, lands unwalked, girls unloved, risings of Orion and the Cross unseen!

"You haven't realized how determined we are," I told him. "The Law of Life isn't rhetoric, Danil Smit. It's survival."

"What about our survival?" he groaned.

"Listen," I said, "if I come out into view, can we talk before Tanaroa?"

"Huh? . . . Oh." He stood a while, and in that moment I knew what it is to be of a race who were once great and are no longer. Well, in their day *they* were the everywhere-thrusting aliens; and if they devoured the resources which were the very basis of their power, what could they expect but that Earth's new masters would come from the poor and forgotten who had had less chance to do likewise? Nevertheless, that was long ago, it was dead. Reality was Danil Smit, humbled into saying, "Yes," there in the dark of the shed, he who had seen no other way than murder to preserve his people's freedom.

I switched my own flash back on and set it down by his on a bench; to let light reflect off half-seen shapes and pick his beard and hands and pleading eyes out of the rattling, gurgling murk. I said to him, fast, because I did not like saying it:

"We suspected you weren't using a natural outflow. After centuries, the overnight discovery of such a thing would have been strange. No, what you found was a water table, and you're pumping it dry, in this land of little rain, and that breaks the Law of Life."

He stood before me, in the last rags of his patriarchy, and cried: "But why? All right, all right, eventually we'll've exhausted it. But that could be two-three hundred years from now! Don't you see, we could use that time for livin'!"

"And afterward?" I challenged, since I must keep reminding myself that my cause is right, and must make him believe that my government is truly fanatical on this subject. (He would not have met enough of our easy-going islanders to realize crusades are impossible to us—that, at most, a tiny minority of devotees strive to head off disaster at the outset, before the momentum of it has become too huge.) My life might hang upon it. The shotgun dangled yet in his grasp. He had a good chance of blasting me before I could do more than wound him.

I went on: "Afterward! Think. Instead of what life we have today, to enlarge human knowledge and, yes, the human spirit . . . instead of that, first a sameness of crops and cattle, then a swarm of two-legged ants, then barrenness. We must resist this wherever it appears. Otherwise, in the end—if we can't, as a whole species, redeem ourselves—will be an Earth given back to the algae, or an Earth as bare as the moon."

"Meanwhile, though," he said desperately, "we'd build aqueducts . . . desalinization plants . . . fusion power—"

I did not speak of rumors I have heard that controlled fusion has in fact been achieved, and been suppressed. Besides its being an Admiralty secret, if true, I had no heart to explain to the crumbling old man that Earth cannot live through a second age of energy outpouring and waste. One remote day, folk may come to know in their blood that the universe was not made for them alone; then they can safely be given the power to go to the stars. But not in our lifetimes.

Not in the lifetime that Wiliamu my comrade might have had.

I closed my teeth on the words: "The fact is, Danil Smit, this community was founded on the exhaustion of groundwater vital to an entire ecology. That was a flat violation of the Law and of international covenants. To maintain it, you and your coconspirators resorted to murder. I'll presume most of the dwellers in Hope are innocent—most believe there is a natural spring here—but where are the bodies of our men? Did you at least have the decency to give them back to the earth?"

The soul went out of him. Hope's founding father crept into my arms and wept.

I stroked his hair and whispered, "It could be worse, it could be worse, I'll work for you, don't give up," while my tears and his ran together.

After all, I will remind my admirals, we have islands to reclaim, stoninesses in the middle of a living ocean.

Give the pioneers topsoil and seeds, give them rainwater cisterns and solar stills, teach them palm and breadfruit culture and the proper ranching of the sea. Man does not have to be always the deathmaker. I know my proposal is a radical break with tradition. But it would be well—it would be a most hopeful precedent—if these, who are not of our kind, could be made into some of our strongest lifebringers. Remember, we have an entire worldful of people, unimaginably diverse, to educate thus, if we can. We must begin somewhere.

I swore I would strive to the utmost to have this accepted. I actually dared say I thought our government could be persuaded to pardon Danil Smit and his few associates in the plot. But if an example must be made, they are ready to hang, begging only that those they have loved be granted exile instead of a return to the tyrant.

Elena, speak to your father. Speak to your friends in Parliament. Get them to help us.

But do not tell them this one last thing that happened. Only think upon it at night, as I do, until I come home again.

We trod forth when dawn was whitening the east, Danil Smit and I. Stars held out in a westward darkness, above the dunes and eldritch trees. But those were remote, driven away by fields and canals carved from the tender desert. And a mordant wind made the mills on the ridge overhead creak and clang and roar as they sucked at the planet.

He raised a hand toward them. His smile was weary and terrible. "You've won this round, Nakamuha, you an' your damned nature worshipers," he said. "My children an' children's children 'ull fit into your schemes, because you're powerful. But you won't be forever. What then, Nakamuha? What then?"

I looked up to the whirling skeletons, and suddenly the cold struck deep into me.

XI

So far I've been recalling a career in science fiction. I've also written fantasy. The distinction between the two genres is as tenuous as the science in the first-named often becomes. Tony Boucher once told me that, judging by the mail he got, most of his readers actually preferred fantasy to science fiction but didn't know it.

After all, as I've remarked elsewhere, the evidence for, say, life after death and at least one God is, at the present state of our knowledge, probably better than the evidence for psionic powers, time travel, or travel faster than light. Which themes belong in which category seems pretty arbitrary. At most, one can argue that the underlying premise of science fiction is the scientific premise itself, that the universe makes sense and no matter what surprises we come upon, they'll fit in with what we already know. Fantasy is under no such obligation.

But we don't absolutely know that the scientific premise is true. We simply have to make it, or else give up trying to learn more with any reasonable degree of certainty. And it has in fact served us well. To me, whether a story should be hard or soft science fiction depends merely on what the story line wants, and as for fantasy, let 'er rip!

When Tony bought a short version of *Three Hearts and Three Lions* way back in 1953, he asked me to throw in some stuff about parallel universes or whatever, to satisfy the demand for "scientific explanation." I was quite willing. After all, L. Sprague de Camp and Fletcher Pratt had done likewise in their splendid Harold Shea stories, which were my main inspiration. I left this material in when I later rewrote the tale, expanding it to book length. Why not? Part of the fun, actually.

It begins in 1938, when Holger Carlsen is a young engineer working in the United States. He was a foundling, raised in Denmark and still of that nationality. World War II breaks out, and the Germans occupy his country. By 1941 he feels duty-bound to return, and crosses on a neutral ship. At home he gets a job and joins the underground resistance. Late in 1943 he is with a group that has just put a key anti-fascist aboard a boat for Sweden when a German patrol comes upon them. They stand fast, fighting a rearguard action while the boat escapes. A grazing bullet knocks Holger out.

He returns to consciousness in a great woodland unlike any Danish forest. Nearby stands a huge black stallion, friendly to him, saddled and bridled, the name Papillon on the headstall. A sword and shield hang at the side. He also finds a full set of clothes and warlike gear, including helmet and chain-mail byrnie. Though he is a big man, they fit him perfectly. The shield bears the device of three red hearts and three golden lions.

Bewildered, he can only think to take these gifts, if gifts they are, and ride off in search of information and help. At the hut of a somewhat sinister crone he finds he has become fluent in a language he guesses is Old French. She claims to be a witch, casts a spell that apparently reveals a little about him, evades his questions, but says he should seek out Duke Alfric of Faerie and explains how to find the dwarf Hugi, who can guide him.

Gnarled and grumpy, Hugi nonetheless agrees, perches on the saddlebow, and along the way gets to like him. So he first takes him to meet Alianora. She is fully human, a beautiful young woman, but a waif raised among the woods dwellers. Out of affection they have given her the brief garment of white feathers she wears, which enables her to turn herself into a swan and back again whenever she chooses. Such an ally will be valuable indeed to travelers through perilous country. High-spirited and attracted to Holger, she gladly joins them.

Piecemeal Holger learns that he is in a borderland between the Christian and Saracen realms to the west and Faerie to the east. This world is, in fact, the universe of the medieval Carolingian romances and *chansons de geste*. Uncouth though the human civilizations may be, ultimately they stand for Law. Lovely though ever-twilit Faerie be, at its heart is Chaos. Lately it has been encroaching westward, and wild forces and terrible beings are already loose in these marches. Holger's band encounters some, but wins through.

Duke Alfric and his court make the visitors lavishly welcome and promise to help Holger get home. Meanwhile he is invited to a feast in Elf Hill. Alianora learns of this barely in time to warn him. While one night passes in there, a hundred years go by outside. Thwarted, the elves resort to force. Holger and Alianora fight their way free, together with Hugi, and flee back westward.

Monstrous forms haunt their first camp. Later a dragon attacks; Holger manages to rout it. Morgan le Fay herself finds him alone and almost seduces him; again Alianora breaks it up. A cannibalistic ogre traps them; Holger tricks him to his doom. Clearly, the knight of the hearts and lions is a key figure in the struggle between Law and Chaos, and indeed rumors of a Deliverer have long been going about—but only Alfric and his allies seem to know who and what this person may be. Alianora, by now in love with Holger, suggests going to a wizard of her acquaintance. He's a very minor mage, but well-disposed. Perhaps he can give a little aid or advice. They make for his village.

The following incident occupies two chapters I added to the full-length version. Among other things, it's a mystery story, with clues to the solution of the puzzle. I wrote it that way in Tony's honor.

THREE HEARTS AND THREE LIONS

Afternoon found them still descending, but at a gentler pace and in milder air than before lunch. The woodland, oak and beech and scattered firs, revealed signs of man: stumps, second growth, underbrush grazed off, razorback shoats, at last a road of sorts twisting toward the village Alianora expected they could reach today. Exhausted by his encounter with Balamorg, Holger drowsed in the saddle. Birdsong lulled him so that hours went by before he noticed that that was the only noise.

They passed a farmstead. The thatched log house and sheepfolds bespoke a well-to-do owner. But no smoke rose; nothing stirred save a crow that hopped in the empty pens and jeered at them. Hugi pointed to the trail. "As I read the marks, he drave his flocks toonward some days agone," said the dwarf. "Why?"

The sunlight that poured through leafy arches felt less warm to Holger than it had.

At evening they emerged in cleared land. Ripening grainfields stretched ahead, doubtless cultivated by the villagers. The sun had gone down behind the forest, which stood black to the west against a few lingering red gleams. Eastward over the mountains, the first stars blinked forth. There was just enough light for Holger to see a dustcloud a mile or so down the road. He clucked at Papillon and the stallion broke into a weary trot. Alianora, who had amused herself buzzing the bats that emerged with sunset, landed behind the man and resumed her own species. "No sense in alarming yon folk," she said. "Whate'er's their trouble, 'twill ha' made them shy enough."

Hugi's big nose snuffed the air. "They're driving sheep and cattle within the walls," he said. "Eigh, how rank wi' sic smell! And yet's a whiff underneath . . . sweat smells sharper when a man's afeared . . . an' a ghost o' summat else, spooky." He huddled back on the saddlebow, against Holger's mailed breast.

The flocks were considerable. They spilled off the road and across the grain. The boys and dogs who ran about rounding up strays trampled swathes of their own. Some emergency must have forced this, Holger decided. He drew rein as several spearmen challenged him. Squinting through the dusk, he saw the peasants were a sturdy, fair-complexioned folk, bearded and long-haired, clad in rough wadmal coats and cross-gartered pants. They were too stolid to be made hysterical, but the voices which asked his name were harsh with unease.

"Sir Holger du Danemark and two friends," he said. No use explaining the long-winded truth. "We come in peace, and would like to stay the night."

" 'Olger?" A burly middle-aged man who seemed a leader let his spear down and scratched his head. "Have I not heard that name somewhere before, or its like?"

A murmur went among the men, but no one had an immediate answer and the livestock gave no time for reflection. Holger said quickly, "Whoever bears any such name is not me. I'm a stranger from afar, only passing through."

"Well, sir, welcome to Lourville," said the chief peasant. "I fear you come at an ill time, but Sir Yve will be glad to see you. . . . You, there, head off that bloody-be-damned-to-hell heifer before she ends up in the next duchy! . . . My name's Raoul, Sir 'Olger. Begging your pardon for this hurlyburly."

"What's the trouble?" asked Alianora. "I see ye're housing your beasts within the toon this nicht, which 'twas scarce meant for."

Holger overheard an older man mumble something about these foreign tourists and their scandalously unclad doxies. Someone else hushed him up: "I've heard of her, granther, a swan-may living a bit north and west of Lourville territory. They say she's a kindly one." Holger paid more attention to Raoul:

"Yes, m'lady, we've been grazing everybody's stock in one herd, these last several days, and shutting them in the town after dark. This night, even the people must crowd within the walls; none dare be alone any more, on the outlying garths, when night's fallen. A werewolf goes abroad."

"Hoy, say ye so?" barked Hugi. "A skin-turner?"

"Aye. Much has gone wrong these past years, misfortune after misfortune in every household. My own ax slipped and laid my leg open this spring, and then did the same to my oldest son. We were three weeks abed, right in sowing time. Not a family but has some such tale. They do say 'tis because of the marshalling in the Middle World beyond the mountains, sorcery grown so strong that its power reaches this far and turns everything awry. So they say." Raoul crossed himself. "I don't know, me. The *loup-garou* is the worst thing thus far. Christ guard us."

"Could it no be a natural wolf that raided your folds?" Alianora asked. "Full oft I've heard folk say someone must be shape-strong, when in fact 'twas but a beast larger and more cunning than most."

"That might have been," said Raoul dourly, "though 'twas hard to see how a natural animal could have broken so many gates or lifted so many latches. Nor do true wolves slay a dozen sheep at a time, for mere sport, like a weasel. But last night the matter was settled. Pier Bigfoot and Berte his wife were in their cottage, three miles within the forest, when the gray one burst through the window and snatched their baby from the cradle. Pier struck with his billhook, and swears the iron passed through the wolf's ribs without doing harm. Then Berte got wild and foolish, and hit the beast with an old silver spoon she had from her grandmother. He dropped the baby—not too badly hurt, by God's grace—and fled out the window. I ask you, is that a natural animal?"

"No," said Alianora, low and frightened.

Raoul spat. "So we'll sleep within the town walls while this danger lasts, and let the wolf prowl untenanted woods. Mayhap we can discover who's turning shape, and burn him." In a gentler tone: "A great pity for Sir Yve, this, just when his daughter Raimberge was readying to travel west and wed the Marchgrave's third son in Vienne. Pray God for a speedy end of our grief."

"Our lord will not be able to entertain you as well as you deserve, Sir 'Olger," added a boy. "He means to walk on the walls this whole night, lest the wolf overleap them. And his lady Blancheflor lies sick abed. But his son and daughter will do what they can."

Holger supposed he should volunteer to help on sentry-go, but he didn't think that after today he could stay awake. As she rode slowly on ahead of the flock, he asked Alianora to explain the menace.

"There be two ways that men take animal shape," she answered. "One is by magic on a common human, as my own feather garb does for me whene'er I make the wish. The other is more darksome. Certain folk be born with twin natures. They need no spell to change form, and each nicht the desire to turn bear, or wild boar, or wolf, or whate'er the animal may be for the person . . . each nicht that desire overwhelms them. And then they run mad. Kind and sensible folk they may be when walking as humans, but as animals they canna cease wreaking harm till the blood thirst is slaked, or till fear o' discovery makes them go back into our form. Whilst beasts, they're nigh impossible to kill, sith wounds knit upon the instant. Only silver pains them, and a silver weapon would slay. But from such they can run swifter nor any true flesh and blood."

"If the, uh, werewolf can't help it, then this local one must be a stranger, not so? A native would have been plaguing the district for years."

"Nay. Methinks as yon crofter said, belike the creature is one o' theirs. For a thin taint o' warg blood micht go unnoticed, unknown, through a lifetime, not being strong enough to reveal itself. 'Tis only o' late, when the witchcraft forces ha' grown so, that the sleeping demon was wakened. I make no doubt the werewolf himself is horror-struck. God help him if e'er the folk learn who he be."

"God help any un yon fear-haggard yokels may decide on for the warg," grunted Hugi.

Holger scowled as he rode on to the gate. It made sense, of the weird sort that prevailed in this universe. Werewolfery . . . what was the word? . . . oh, yes, lycanthropy was probably inherited as a set of recessive genes. If you had the entire set, you were a lycanthrope always and everywhere—and would most likely be killed the first time your father found a wolf cub in his baby's cradle. With an incomplete inheritance, the tendency to change was weaker. It must have been entirely latent and unsuspected in the poor devil of a peasant who bore the curse hereabouts: until the redoubled sorcery in the Middle World blew over the mountains and reinforced whatever body chemistry was involved.

He peered through the gloaming. The village was surrounded by a heavy stockade, with a walkway on which Sir Yve would make his rounds tonight. Inside were jammed narrow wooden houses of two or three stories. The streets that wound among them were mere lanes, stinking from the muck of the animals packed in each night. The one on which he entered was a little broader and straighter, but not much. A number of women in long dresses and wimples, shock-haired children, and aproned artisans gaped at him as he passed the gate. Most carried torches that flared and sputtered under the deep-purple sky. Their voices chattered respectfully low as they trailed him.

He stopped near a street leading to one side, a tunnel of blackness walled by the surrounding houses and roofed by their overhanging galleries. Silhouetted above the ridge poles, he could just see the top of a square tower which doubtless belonged to Sir Yve's hall. He leaned toward a husky man, who tugged his forelock and said, "Odo the blacksmith, sir, at your service."

Holger pointed down the alley. "Is this the way to your lord's house?"

"Aye, sir. You, Frodoart, is master at home yet?"

A young man in faded scarlet hose, wearing a sword, nodded. "I did but now leave him, armed cap-a-pie, having a stoup of ale ere he mounts the walls. I am his esquire, Sir Knight. I'll guide you thither. This place is indeed a maze."

Holger removed his helmet, for his hair was dank with sweat after being iron-clad the whole day and the dusk breeze was cool if smelly. He couldn't expect anything lavish at the hall, he realized. Sir Yve de Lourville was obviously not rich—a boondocks knight with a handful of retainers, guarding these environs against bandits and administering a rough justice. Raoul had been filled with civic pride at the daughter's betrothal to a younger son of a minor noble, west in the Empire.

Oh, well, he thought, *something to eat and a place to sleep is all I could make use of anyhow.*

The esquire lifted a torch ahead of him. He patted Papillon for encouragement and started down the lane.

A woman shrieked.

Holger had slapped his helmet back on and drawn his sword before her cry ended. Papillon whirled about. The people drew close to each other; voices rose. The guttering torchlight threw unrestful shadows on the houses across the main street; their upper stories were lost in blackness. Every window was shuttered and door closed, Holger saw. The woman screamed again, behind one of those walls.

A shutter, fastened with an iron bolt, splintered. The shape that sprang forth was long and shaggy, gray as steel in the thick red-shot gloom. It had butted its way out. As it dropped to the street, the muzzle lifted off the chest. Gripped between the jaws there squirmed a naked infant.

"The wolf!" choked the blacksmith. "Holy Mary, we've locked the wolf in with us!"

The child's mother appeared at the window. "It burst in from the rear," she howled witlessly. She stretched her arms toward the beast and them all. "It burst in and snatched Lusiane! There she is, there she is, God strike you down, you men, get my Lusiane back!"

Papillon sped forward. The wolf grinned around the baby. Blood was smeared on her pink skin, but she still cried thinly and struggled. Holger hewed. The wolf wasn't there. Uncannily swift, it had darted between Papillon's legs and was off along the street.

Frodoart the esquire plunged to intercept it. The wolf didn't even break stride as it sprang over him. Ahead was another alley mouth. Holger whirled Papillon around and galloped in pursuit. Too late, though, he thought, too late. Once into that warren of lightless byways, the wolf could devour its prey and turn human again long before any search could—

White wings whirred. Alianora the swan struck with her beak at the warg's eyes. It laid its ears back, twisted aside, and streaked toward the next exit. She swooped in front of it. Like a snowstorm full of buffetings, she halted the runner.

Then Holger had arrived. This far from the torches he was nearly blind, but he could see the great shadowy shape. His sword whistled. He felt the edge cleave meat. Lupine eyes flared at him, cold green and hating. He raised his sword, the blade caught what light there was and he saw it unbloodied. Iron had no power to wound.

Papillon struck with his hoofs, knocked the *loup-garou* to earth and hammered it. The hairy form rolled free, still unhurt. It vanished down the alley. But the child it had dropped lay screaming.

By the time the villagers pounded up, Alianora was human again. She held the girl-baby, smeared with blood and muck, against her. "Och, poor darling, poor lassie, there, there, there. 'Tis over wi' this now. Ye're no too mickle hurt, nobbut a wee bit slashed. Och, 'tis scared ye be. Think how ye can tell your ain children, the best knicht in the world saved ye. There, my love, croodle-doo—" A black-bearded man who must be the father snatched the infant from her, stared a moment, and fell to his knees, shaken with unpracticed weeping.

Holger applied the bulk of Papillon and the flat of his sword to drive the crowd back. "Take it easy," he shouted. "Let's have some order. The kid's all right. You, you, you, come here. I want some torchbearers. Don't stand jabbering. We've got to catch that wolf."

Several men turned green, crossed themselves, and edged away. Odo the blacksmith shook a fist at the alley mouth and said, "How? This mud holds no tracks, nor the paving elsewhere. The fiend will reach his own house unfollowed, and turn back into one of us."

Frodoart regarded the faces which bobbed in and out of moving shadows. "We know he's none of us here," said the esquire above the babble, "nor any of the herders at the gate. That's some help. Let each man remember who stands nigh him."

Hugi tugged Holger's sleeve. "We can track him if ye wish," he said. "Ma nase hairs be atwitch wi' his stink."

Holger wrinkled his own nose. "All I smell is dung and garbage."

"Ah, but ye're no a woods dwarf. Quick, lad, set me doon and let me follow the spoor. But mind ye stay close!"

Holger lifted Alianora back onto his saddle—the child's father kissed her mired feet—and followed Hugi's brown form. Frodoart and Odo walked on either side, torches aloft. Some score of men pressed behind, the boldest villagers, armed with knives and staves and spears. If they caught the lycanthrope, Holger thought, it should be possible to hold him by main strength till ropes could be tied on. Then . . . but he didn't like to think of what would follow.

Hugi wound down the lanes for several minutes. He emerged in the marketplace, which was cobbled and showed a little lighter under the stars. "Aye, clear as mustard, the scent," he called. "Naught i' the world has a stench like a werebeast in his animal shape." Holger wondered if glandular secretions were responsible. The stones rang hollow under Papillon's shoes.

The street they took off the market square was also more or less paved, and comparatively wide. Here and there were lighted houses, but Hugi ignored the people inside. Straight he ran, until a cry went up at Holger's back.

"No!" groaned Frodoart. "Not my master's hall!"

The knight's dwelling stood on a plaza of its own, opposite the church and otherwise hemmed in with houses. Kitchen and stables were separate buildings. The hall was unimpressive, a thatched wooden affair not much larger than the average bungalow in Holger's world. It was T-shaped, with the left branch of the cross-arm rising in the tower he had noticed before. The front was at the end of the T's upright, and closed. Light gleamed from shuttered windows; dogs clamored in the stables.

Hugi approached the iron-studded door. "Straight in here the warg fled," he declared.

"With my master's family alone!" Frodoart tried the latch. "Barred. Sir Yve! Can you hear me? Are you well?"

"Odo, cover the rear," snapped Holger. "Alianora, get aloft and report anything unusual." He rode up to the door and knocked with the pommel of his sword. The blacksmith gathered several men and ran around in back. Hugi followed. More people streamed into the square. By fugitive yellow torch gleams, Holger recognized some of the herders among them. Raoul the peasant pushed through the crowd to join him, spear in hand.

The knocking boomed hollow. "Are they dead in there?" sobbed Frodoart. "Burst this down! Are you men or dogs, standing idle when your lord needs you?"

"Are there any back doors?" Holger asked. The blood thudded in his temples. He had no fear of the werewolf, nor even any sense of strangeness. This was *right:* the work for which he had been born.

Hugi threaded a way among legs and rattled his stirrup for attention. "No other door, but windows eneugh, each locked tighter nor the last," the dwarf reported. "Yet the warg ha' no left this bigging. I snuffed everywhere aboot. E'en had he jumped from yon tower, I'd ha' covered the ground where he maun land. Noo all ways oot are blockaded. We ha' him trapped."

Holger glanced around. The villagers had stopped milling; they surrounded the hall, packed and very still. Torchlight fluttered across a woman's frightened pale face, a man's sweating hairiness, a startling gleam of eyeballs in shadow. Weapons bristled above, spears, axes, bills, scythes, flails. "What about servants?" he asked Frodoart.

"None in there, sir," said the esquire. "The house servants are townsfolk, who go home after dark, leaving only old Nicolas to do for the family. I see him yonder, as well as the stablehands. . . . Get us inside!"

"I'm about to, if you'll give me some room."

Frodoart and Raoul cleared a space with well-meant if brutal efficiency. Holger stroked Papillon's mane and murmured, "Okay, boy, let's see what we're good for." He reared the horse. The forefeet smashed against the panels. Once, twice, thrice, then the bolt tore loose and the door sprang open.

Holger rode into a single long room. The dirt floor was strewn with rushes. Above the built-in benches along the walls hung weapons and hunting trophies.

Dusty battle banners stirred among the rafters. Sconced candles lit the place fairly well, showing it empty down to a doorway at the end. Beyond must lie the crossbar of the T, private apartments of Sir Yve and his family. A yell rose from the men who crowded in behind Holger. For that doorway was blocked by a form shining steely in the candleglow.

"Who are you?" The man waved a sword above his shield. "What is this outrage?"

"Sir Yve!" exclaimed Frodoart. "The wolf has not harmed you?"

"What wolf? What the devil are you up to? You, sirrah, what excuse have you for forcing your way in? Are you a blood-enemy of mine? If not, by God's death, I can soon make you one!"

Holger dismounted and walked close. Sir Yve de Lourville was a tall, rather thin man with a melancholy horse face and drooping gray mustaches. He wore more elaborate armor than the Dane, a visored casque, corselet, brassards, elbowpieces, cuisses, greaves, plus chain-mail. His shield bore a wolf's head crased, sable on barry of six, gules and argent, which Holger found eerily suggestive. If some distant ancestor had been a full-fledged *loup-garou,* the fact might be hushed up by later generations, but could linger as a traditional coat of arms. . . .

"I'm called Holger du Danemark. The werewolf appeared before me as well as many other people. Only by God's mercy did we rescue the baby it had stolen. Now we've tracked it here."

"Aye," said Hugi. "The trail runs clear to yersel'."

A gasp went among the commoners, like the first sigh of wind before a storm.

"You lie, dwarf! I've sat here this eventide. No beast entered." Sir Yve jabbed his sword toward Holger. "None are present but my lady, who's ill, and my two children. If you claim aught else, you must prove it on my body."

His voice wobbled. He wasn't a very good blusterer. Raoul was the first to snarl, "If matters be as you say, Sir Yve, then one of your own must be the fiend."

"I forgive you this time," said Sir Yve frantically. "I know you're overwrought. But the next man who speaks such words will dangle from the gallows."

Frodoart stood with the tears whipping down his cheeks. "Dwarf, dwarf, how can you be sure?" he groaned.

Sir Yve seized upon the question. "Aye, who would you trust—this misshapen mannikin and this hedge-knight, or your lord who has warded you all these years?"

A boy of fourteen or so appeared behind him, slender and blond. He had put on a helmet, snatched sword and shield, in obvious haste, for otherwise he wore the colorful tunic and hose which was the local equivalent of a white tie. Of course, thought Holger faintly, in an outpost of civilization every aristocrat dressed for dinner.

"Here I am, father," panted the youth. His green eyes narrowed at Holger. "I am Gui, son of Yve de Lourville, and though not yet knighted I call you false and defy you to battle." It would have been more impressive if his voice hadn't developed an adolescent crack, but was nonetheless touching.

Sure, why not? The lycanthrope is a perfectly decent person, except when the skin-turning rage is upon him.

Holger sighed and put away his blade. "I don't want to fight," he said. "If your people don't believe me, I'll go away."

The commoners shifted about, stared at the floor, back at Holger and Yve. Frodoart aimed a furtive kick at Hugi, who dodged. Then Odo the smith came in the door and forced a path for Alianora. "The swan-may would speak," he trumpeted. "The swan-may who saved Lusiane. Be quiet, there, you mutton-heads, ere I clobber you."

A hush fell until they could hear the dogs howl outside. Holger saw Raoul's knuckles whiten about his spear. A little man in priestly robe went to his knees, crucifix in hand. Gui's beardless jaw dropped. Sir Yve crouched as if wounded. No eye left Alianora. She stood slender and straight, the candleglow shimmering in the coppery-brown hair, and said:

"Some o' ye must ken my name, I who dwell by Lake Arroy. I mislike brags, but they'll tell ye in places closer to my home, like Tarnberg and Cromdhu, how many strayed children I've fetched back from the woods and how I got Mab hersel' to take off the curse she laid on Philip the miller. I ha' kenned Hugi my whole life, and vouch for him. We've none o' us aught to gain by slander. 'Tis your fortune that the finest knicht who ever lived has come by in time to free ye from the warg ere it takes a human life. Hearken to him, I say!"

An old man tottered forth. He blinked half-blind and said into the stillness, "Mean you this is the Defender?"

"What are you talking about?" asked Holger with some dismay.

"The Defender . . . he that shall return in our greatest need . . . the legend my grandsire told me gives not his name, but are you him, Lord Knight, are you him?"

"No—" Holger's protest was drowned in a rumble like the incoming tide. Raoul sprang forward with spear poised.

"By heaven, he's no master of mine who snatches children!" the peasant yelled. Frodoart swung at him with his sword, but weakly. The blow was turned by the spearshaft. A moment later four men had pinned the esquire down.

Sir Yve leaped at Holger. The Dane got his weapon out barely in time to parry the blow. He struck back so hard he cracked the other's shield-rim. Yve staggered. Holger knocked the sword from his grasp. Two peasants caught their overlord's arms. Gui tried to attack, but a pitchfork pricked his breast and drove him back against the wall.

"Get these people under control, Odo, Raoul!" Holger gasped. "Don't let them hurt anyone. You, you, you." He pointed out several big eager-looking youths. "Guard this doorway. Don't let anybody past. Alianora, Hugi, come with me."

He sheathed his sword again and hurried through. A corridor paneled in carven wood ran transversely to the main room, a door at either end and one in the middle. Holger tried that one. It swung open on a chamber hung with skins and a moth-eaten tapestry. The light of tapers fell on a woman who lay in the canopied bed. Her graying hair was lank around a handsome flushed face; she snuffled and sneezed into a handkerchief. A bad case of influenza, Holger decided. The girl who had sat next to the bed and now rose was more interesting—only about sixteen, but with a pleasant figure, long yellow tresses, blue eyes, tip-tilted nose and attractive mouth. She wore a simple pullover dress, gathered with a golden-buckled belt.

Holger bowed. "Forgive the intrusion, madame, mademoiselle. Necessity compels."

"I know," said the girl unsteadily. "I heard."

"The Demoiselle Raimberge, are you not?"

"Yes, daughter to Sir Yve. My mother Blancheflor." The lady in question wiped her nose and looked at Holger with fear blurred by physical misery. Raimberge wrung her small hands. "I cannot believe what you think, sir. That one of us is . . . is that thing—" She bit back tears; she was a knight's daughter.

"The scent gaes hither," said Hugi.

"Could either of you have witnessed the beast's entry?" asked Holger.

Blancheflor shook her head. Raimberge explained: "We were separate in our chambers, Gui in his and I in mine, readying to sup, my lady mother sleeping here. Our doors were closed. My father was in the main hall. When I heard the tumult, I hastened to comfort my mother."

"Then Yve himself must be the warg," Alianora said.

"No, not my father!" Raimberge whispered. Blancheflor covered her face. Holger turned on his heel. "Let's look about," he said.

Gui's room was at the foot of the tower, to whose top a stair led. It was crammed with boyish souvenirs. Raimberge's was at the opposite end of the corridor, with a chestful of trousseau, a spinning wheel, and whatever else pertained to a young girl of shabby-genteel birth. All three rear rooms had

windows, and Hugi couldn't follow the scent in detail. He said it was everywhere; the wolf had haunted this part of the house night after night. Not that
anyone need see the apparition. It could use a window for exit and re-entrance,
when everybody else was asleep.

"One o' three," said Alianora. Her voice was unhappy.

"Three?" Hugi lifted his brows. "Why think ye the lady canna be the beast?
Would she no ha' her health as soon's she turned wolf?"

"Would she? I dinna know. The wargs are no so common that I e'er heard
talk o' wha' happens when one falls ill. . . . Four, then. One o' four."

Holger returned glum to the feasting chamber. Raoul and Odo had established a sort of order. The men stood around the walls, Papillon by the main
door. Yve and Gui sat in the high seat, bound hand and foot. Frodoart huddled
beneath, disarmed but otherwise unhurt. The priest told his beads.

"Well!" Raoul turned fiercely on the newcomers. "Who's the cursed one?"

"We dinna know," said Alianora.

Gui spat toward Holger. "When first I saw you helmetless, I didn't imagine
you a knight," the boy taunted. "Now when I see you bursting in on helpless
women, I know you're not."

Raimberge entered behind Hugi. She went to her father and kissed his
cheek. With a glare that swept the hall, she called: "Worse than beasts, you,
who turn on your own liege lord!"

Odo shook his head. "No, ma'm'selle," he said. "The lord who fails his
people is none. I got little ones of my own. I'll not hazard them being eaten
alive."

Raoul struck the wainscot with his spear butt. "Silence, there!" he barked.
"The wolf dies this night. Name him, Sir 'Olger. Or her. Name us the wolf."

"I—" Holger felt suddenly ill. He wet his lips.

"We canna tell," said Hugi.

"So." Raoul scowled at the grim rough-clad assembly. "I feared that. Well,
will the beast confess himself? I'll slay him mercifully, with a silver knife in
the heart."

"Iron will do, while he's human," said Odo. "Come, now. Speak up. I'd
not like to put you to torture."

Frodoart stirred. "Before you do that," he said, "you must peel my hands
off your throat." They ignored him.

"If none will confess," said Raoul, "then best they all die. We've the priest
here to shrive them."

Gui fought back a sob. Raimberge grew death-still. They heard Blancheflor
cough at the dark end of the house.

Yve seemed to shrink into himself. "Very well," he said, tonelessly. "I am the wolf."

"No!" Gui shrilled. "I am!"

Raimberge stood for a moment, until a hard smile touched her lips. "They both lie nobly," she said. "The skin-turner is myself, though, good folk. And you need not slay me, only guard me until time that I go to my wedding in Vienne. That far from the lands of Faerie, I'll be beyond range of the powers which forced me to change."

"Believe her not," said Gui. Yve shook his head violently. A hoarse call might have been Blancheflor taking the blame on herself.

"This gets us no further," said Raoul. "We can't risk letting the *loup-garou* go free. Father Valdabrun, will you ready the last rites for this family?"

Holger drew sword and sprang before the high seat. "You'll not kill the innocent while I'm alive," said a voice and a will he recognized with amazement as his own.

The blacksmith Odo clenched his fists. "I'd be loath to overfall you, Sir 'Olger," he said, "but if I must for my children, I must."

"If you are the Defender," said Raoul, "then name us our enemy."

The stillness fell again, stretched close to breaking. Holger felt the three pairs of eyes burn at his back: careworn Yve, ardent Gui, Raimberge who had been so hopeful. He heard the wheezing of the sick woman. *O Christ who cast out demons, aid me now*. Only afterward did he realize he had said his first conscious prayer since childhood.

What came to the forefront of his mind was something else, the workaday engineer's approach. He was no longer sure of his old belief that all problems in life were practical problems. But this one was. A question of rational anal ysis. He was no detective, but neither was the warg a professional criminal. There must be—

It blazed in him. "By the Cross, yes!" he shouted.

"What? What? What?" Men started to their feet. Holger waved his sword aloft. The words spilled from him. He didn't know himself what he would say next, he was thinking aloud in a roar, but they heard him with wonder:

"Look, the one we're after is shape-strong by birth. He doesn't need any magical skin, like the swan-may here. But then his clothes can't change with him, can they? So he must go forth naked. Frodoart told me, a moment before the wolf showed up, he'd just left his master full-armed in the hall. And alone. Though even with help Sir Yve couldn't have gotten out of that armor, and back into it afterward, in the few minutes he had. So he's not the warg.

"Gui tried to plead guilty too, to save whoever else was. But he'd already scuttled himself. He mentioned having seen me helmetless. I was for one minute, when I stopped to inquire my way here. I put the helmet back on when the racket started. The wolf couldn't have seen that. He—no, she—she was inside a house. She broke in through the rear door and escaped out a front window, which had been shuttered. The only way Gui could have seen me bareheaded in the torchlight was from the top of the tower above his room. I noticed it sticking over the roofs. He must have gone up to watch the flocks being driven in. So he was not anywhere near the place we saw the warg.

"Lady Blancheflor—" He stopped. How on earth, on all the Earths, could he explain the germ theory of disease? "Lady Blancheflor has been sick, with an illness that the dog tribe doesn't get. If changing into a wolf did not make her well, then she'd be too weak to dash around as I saw the animal do. If the change did make her well, the, uh, the agent causing the disease couldn't live in her animal body. She wouldn't have a fever and a runny nose at this moment, would she? In either case, she's eliminated."

Raimberge cowered back against the wall. Her father made a broken noise and twisted about, trying to reach her with his bound hands. "No, no, no," he keened. A noise like the wolf itself lifted from the commons. They began to edge close, one mass of hands and weapons.

The girl dropped on all fours. Her face writhed and altered, horrible to watch. "Raimberge!" Holger bawled. "Don't! I won't let them—" Raoul's spear stabbed for her. Holger knocked it aside and cut the shaft across with his sword.

Raimberge howled. Alianora dropped to her knees and caught the half-altered body in her arms. "Nay," she pleaded. "Nay, my sister, come back. He swears he'll save ye." The jaws snapped at her. She got her forearm crosswise into the mouth, forcing lips over fangs so the wolf couldn't bite. She wrestled the creature to a standstill. "Lassie, lassie, we mean ye well."

Holger waded into the mob. Turmoil broke loose. But after he had knocked several down, with a fist or the flat of his blade, they quieted. They snarled and grumbled, but the man in the hauberk overawed them.

He turned to Raimberge. She had resumed her human form and lay weeping in Alianora's embrace. "I didn't want to be. I didn't want to. It came on me. And, and, and I was so afraid they'd burn me—Is my soul lost, Father Valdabrun? I th-think I must be in hell already. The way those babies screamed—"

Holger exchanged a look with the priest. "Sick," said the Dane. "She's not evil of her own will. She can't help it."

Yve stared like a blind man. "I had thought it might be her," he mumbled. "When the wolf ran in, past me, and I knew where Blancheflor and Gui were—I barred the door. I hoped, if this could only pass over until she departed—"

Holger squared his shoulders. "I don't see why not," he answered. "The idea is perfectly sound, as I understand the matter. Let her get far enough away, and the Middle World influence will be too weak to affect her. Till then, of course, you'll have to keep her under restraint. She's sorry now, but I don't think that'll last."

"At dawn it will, when her human soul awakens," said the priest. "Then she will indeed need comforting."

"Well," said Holger, "nothing too serious ever happened. Her father can pay compensation to the people who suffered loss and the parents whose kids were injured. Start her off for Vienne as soon as possible. I daresay a hundred miles would be quite far enough for safety. No one in the Empire has to know."

Raoul, with a black eye, threw himself at Sir Yve's feet while Odo, with a bloody nose, fumbled to release the knight and his son. "Master, forgive us," the peasant begged.

Yve made a weary smile. "I fear 'tis I must ask your forgiveness. And yours above all, Sir 'Olger."

Raimberge lifted her wet face. "Take me off," she stammered. "I, I, I feel the darkness returning. Lock me away till dawn." She held out her arms for the ropes taken off her father. "Tomorrow, Sir Knight, I can truly thank you . . . who saved my soul from hell."

Frodoart embraced Holger's knees. "The Defender is come," he said.

"Oh, Lord!" protested the Dane. "Please, lay off that nonsense. I mean, I hate emotional scenes and I only came here to bum a meal. But could I have some wine first?"

XII

Not all straight science fiction draws directly on science, but much does and I wish that more would. The idea for the next story came from an article by John von Neumann in *Scientific American* proposing an autonomous, environmentally benign, virtually cost-free system for extracting minerals from sea water. It may even have been the first instance of the conceptually important von Neumann machine. As far as I know, nothing has yet been done toward developing it, though it seems eminently worth trying to me. Maybe this will happen yet, and in any event I could assume so and extrapolate from there.

Almost forty years have passed since then, and my text shows its age in several ways. However, the concept still seems fresh, and I've let most of the "anachronisms" stand, such as the use of English rather than metric units. Feminists who object to the heroine being referred to as a "girl" are reminded that back then the word was a perfectly polite synonym for "young woman," and invited to consider the role she plays.

After John Campbell bought the novelette he sent me one of his typically long, disputatious letters, maintaining that things couldn't work out that way. Nevertheless he ran the story exactly as written. Hal Clement has praised it, which is reason enough to include it here.

EPILOGUE

1

His name was a set of radio pulses. Converted into equivalent sound waves, it would have been an ugly squawk; so because he, like any consciousness, was the center of his own coordinate system, let him be called Zero.

He was out hunting that day. Energy reserves were low in the cave. That other who may be called One—being the most important dweller in Zero's universe—had not complained. But there was no need to. He also felt a dwindling potential. Accumulators grew abundantly in their neighborhood, but an undue amount of such cells must be processed to recharge One while she was creating. Motiles had more concentrated energy. And, of course, they were more highly organized. Entire parts could be taken from the body of a motile, needing little or no reshaping for One to use. Zero himself, though the demands on his functioning were much less, wanted a more easily assimilated charge than the accumulators provided.

In short, they both needed a change of diet.

Game did not come near the cave anymore. The past hundred years had taught that it was unsafe. Eventually, Zero knew, he would have to move. But the thought of helping One through mile upon mile, steep, overgrown, and dangerous, made him delay. Surely he could still find large motiles within a few days' radius of his present home. With One's help he fastened a carrier rack on his shoulders, took weapons in hand, and set forth.

That was near sunset. The sky was still light when he came on spoor: broken earthcrystals not yet healed, slabs cut from several boles, a trace of lubricant. Tuning his receptors to the highest sensitivity, he checked all the bands commonly made noisy by motiles. He caught a low-amplitude conversation between two persons a hundred miles distant, borne this far by some freak of atmospherics; closer by he sensed the impulses of small scuttering things, not worth chasing; a flier jetted overhead and filled his perception briefly with static. But no vibration of the big one. It must have passed this way days ago and now be out of receptor-shot.

Well, he could follow the trail, and catch up with the clumsy sawyer in time. It was undoubtedly a sawyer—he knew these signs—and therefore worth a protracted hunt. He ran a quick check on himself. Every part seemed in good order. He set into motion, a long stride which must eventually overhaul anything on treads.

Twilight ended. A nearly full moon rose over the hills like a tiny cold lens. Night vapors glowed in masses and streamers against a purple black sky where stars glittered in the optical spectrum and which hummed and sang in the radio range. The forest sheened with alloy, flashed with icy speckles of silicate. A wind blew through the radiation-absorber plates overhead, setting them to ringing against each other; a burrower whirred, a grubber crunched through lacy crystals, a river brawled chill and loud down a ravine toward the valley below.

As he proceeded, weaving among trunks and girders and jointed rods with the ease of long practice, Zero paid most attention to his radio receptors. There was something strange in the upper communication frequencies tonight, an occasional brief note . . . set of notes, voice, drone, like nothing he had heard before or heard tell of. . . . But the world was a mystery. No one had been past the ocean to the west or the mountains to the east. Finally Zero stopped listening and concentrated on tracking his prey. That was difficult, with his optical sensors largely nullified by the darkness, and he moved slowly. Once he tapped lubricant from a cylinder growth and once he thinned his acids with a drink of water. Several times he felt polarization in his energy cells and stopped for a while to let it clear away: he rested.

Dawn paled the sky over distant snowpeaks, and gradually turned red. Vapors rolled up the slopes from the valley, tasting of damp and sulfide. Zero could see the trail again, and began to move eagerly.

Then the strangeness returned—louder.

Zero slid to a crouch. His lattice swiveled upward. Yes, the pulses did come from above. They continued to strengthen. Soon he could identify them as akin to the radio noise associated with the functioning of a motile. But they did not sense like any type he knew. And there was something else, a harsh flickering overtone, as if he also caught leakage from the edge of a modulated short-wave beam—

The sound struck him.

At first it was the thinnest of whistles, high and cold above the dawn clouds. But within seconds it grew to a roar that shook the earth, reverberated from the mountains, and belled absorber plates until the whole forest rang. Zero's head became an echo chamber; the racket seemed to slam his brain from side to side. He turned dazzled, horrified sensors heavenward. And he saw the thing descending.

For a moment, crazily, he thought it was a flier. It had the long spindle-shaped body and the airfins. But no flier had ever come down on a tail of multicolored flame. No flier blocked off such a monstrous portion of sky. When the thing must be two miles away!

He felt the destruction as it landed, shattered frames, melted earthcrystals, a little burrower crushed in its den, like a wave of anguish through the forest. He hurled himself flat on the ground and hung on to sanity with all four hands. The silence which followed, when the monster had settled in place, was like a final thunderclap.

Slowly Zero raised his head. His perceptions cleared. An arc of sun peered over the sierra. It was somehow outrageous that the sun should rise as if nothing had happened. The forest remained still, hardly so much as a radio hum to be sensed. The last echoes flew fading between the hills.

A measure of resolution: this was no time to be careful of his own existence. Zero poured full current into his transmitter. *"Alarm, alarm! All persons receiving, prepare to relay. Alarm!"*

Forty miles thence, the person who may as well be called Two answered, increasing output intensity the whole time: "Is that you, Zero? I noticed something peculiar in the direction of your establishment. What is the matter?"

Zero did not reply at once. Others were coming in, a surge of voices in his head, from mountaintops and hills and lowlands, huts and tents and caves, hunters, miners, growers, searakers, quarriers, toolmakers, suddenly become a unity. But he was flashing at his own home: "Stay inside, One. Conserve energy. I am unharmed, I will be cautious, keep hidden and stand by for my return."

"Silence!" called a stridency which all recognized as coming from Hundred. He was the oldest of them, he had probably gone through a total of half a dozen bodies. Irreversible polarization had slowed his thinking a little, taken the edge off, but the wisdom of his age remained and he presided over their councils. "Zero, report what you have observed."

The hunter hesitated. "That is not easy. I am at—" He described the location. ("Ah, yes," murmured Fifty-Six, "near that large galena lick.") "The thing somewhat resembles a flier, but enormous, a hundred feet long or more. It came down about two miles north of here on an incandescent jet and is now quiet. I thought I overheard a beamed signal. If so, the cry was like nothing any motile ever made."

"In these parts," Hundred added shrewdly. "But the thing must have come from far away. Does it look dangerous?"

"Its jet is destructive," Zero said, "but nothing that size, with such relatively narrow fins, could glide about. Which makes me doubt it is a predator."

"Lure accumulators," said Eight.

"Eh? What about them?" asked Hundred.

"Well, if lure accumulators can emit signals powerful enough to take control of any small motile which comes near and make it enter their grinders, perhaps this thing has a similar ability. Then, judging from its size, its lure must have tremendous range and close up could overpower large motiles. Including even persons?"

Something like a shiver moved along the communication band.

"It is probably just a grazer," said Three. "If so—" His overt signal trailed off, but the thought continued in all their partly linked minds: *A motile that big! Megawatt-hours in its energy cells. Hundreds or thousands of usable parts. Tons of metal. Hundred, did your great-grandcreator recall any such game, fabulous millennia ago?*

No.

If it is dangerous, it must be destroyed or driven off. If not, it must be divided among us. In either case: attacked!

Hundred rapped the decision forth. "All male persons take weapons and proceed to rendezvous at Broken Glade above the Coppertaste River. Zero, stalk as close as seems feasible, observe what you can, but keep silence unless something quite unforeseeable occurs. When we are gathered, you can describe details on which we may base a specific plan. Hasten!"

The voices toned away in Zero's receptor circuits. He was alone again.

The sun cleared the peaks and slanted long rays between the forest frames. Accumulators turned the black faces of their absorber plates toward it and drank thirstily of radiation. The mists dissipated, leaving boles and girders ashine with moisture. A breeze tinkled the silicate growths underfoot. For a moment Zero was astonishingly conscious of beauty. The wish that One could be here beside him, and the thought that soon he might be fused metal under the monster's breath, sharpened the morning's brightness.

Purpose congealed in him. Further down was a turmoil of frank greed. In all the decades since his activation there had been no such feast as this quarry should provide. Swiftly, he prepared himself. First he considered his ordinary weapons. The wire noose would never hold the monster, nor did he think the iron hammer would smash delicate moving parts (it did not seem to have any), or the steel bolts from his crossbow pierce a thin plate to short out a crucial circuit. But the clawed, spearheaded pry bar might be of use. He kept it in one hand while two others unfastened the fourth and laid it with his extra armament in the carrier rack. Thereupon they deftly hooked his cutting torch in its place. No one used this artificial device except for necessary work, or to finish off a big motile whose cells could replace the tremendous energy expended by the flame, or in cases of dire need. But if the monster attacked him, that would surely constitute dire need. His only immediate intention was to spy on it.

Rising, he stalked among shadows and sun reflections, his camouflage-painted body nearly invisible. Such motiles as sensed him fled or grew very still. Not even the great slasher was as feared a predator as a hunting person. So it had been since that ancient day when some forgotten savage genius made the first crude spark gap and electricity was tamed.

Zero was about halfway to his goal, moving slower and more carefully with each step, when he perceived the newcomers.

He stopped dead. Wind clanked the branches above him, drowning out any other sound. But his electronic sensors told him of . . . two . . . three moving shapes, headed from the monster. And their emission was as alien as its own.

In a different way. Zero stood for a long time straining to sense and to understand what he sensed. The energy output of the three was small, hardly detectable even this close; a burrower or skitterer used more power to move itself. The output felt peculiar, too, not really like a motile's: too simple, as if a mere one or two circuits oscillated. Flat, cold, activityless. But the signal output, on the other hand—it *must* be signal, that radio chatter—why, that was a shout. The things made such an uproar that receptors tuned at minimum could pick them up five miles away. As if they did not know about game, predators, enemies.

Or as if they did not care.

A while more Zero paused. The eeriness of this advent sent a tingle through him. It might be said he was gathering courage. In the end he gripped his pry bar more tightly and struck off after the three.

They were soon plain to his optical and radar senses among the tall growths. He went stock-still behind a frame and watched. Amazement shocked his very mind into silence. He had assumed, from their energy level, that the things were small. But they stood more than half as big as he did! And yet each of them had only one motor, operating at a level barely sufficient to move a person's arm. That could not be their power source. But what was?

Thought returned to him. He studied their outlandishness in some detail. They were shaped not altogether unlike himself, though two-armed, hunch-backed, and featureless. Totally unlike the monster, but unquestionably associated with it. No doubt it had sent them forth as spy eyes, like those employed by a boxroller. Certain persons had been trying for the last century or so to develop, from domesticated motiles, similar assistants for hunting persons. Yes, a thing as big and awkward as the monster might well need auxiliaries.

Was the monster then indeed a predator? Or even—the idea went like a lightning flash through Zero's entire circuitry—a thinker? Like a person? He struggled to make sense of the modulated signals between the three bipeds. No, he could not. But—

Wait!

Zero's lattice swung frantically back and forth. He could not shake off the truth. That last signal had come from the monster, hidden by a mile of forest. From the monster to the bipeds. And were they answering?

The bipeds were headed south. At the rate they were going, they might easily come upon traces of habitation, and follow those traces to the cave where One was, long before Hundred's males had gathered at Broken Glade.

The monster would know about One.

Decision came. Zero opened his transmitter to full output, but broadcast rather than beamed in any degree. He would give no clue where those were whom he called. "*Attention, attention!* Tune in on me: direct sensory linkage. I am about to attempt capture of these motiles."

Hundred looked through his optics, listened with his receptors, and exclaimed, "No, wait, you must not betray our existence before we are ready to act."

"The monster will soon learn of our existence in any event," Zero answered. "The forest is full of old campsites, broken tools, traps, chipped stones, slag heaps. At present I should have the advantage of surprise. If I fail and am destroyed, that ought still to provide you with considerable data. Stand alert!"

He plunged from behind the girders.

The three had gone past. They sensed him and spun about. He heard a jagged modulation of their signal output. A reply barked back, lower in frequency. The voice of the monster? There was no time to wonder about that. Slow and clumsy though they were, the bipeds had gotten into motion. The central one snatched a tube slung across its back. Pounding toward them, through shattering crystals and clangorous branches, Zero thought, *I have not yet made any overtly hostile move, but—* The tube flashed and roared.

An impact sent Zero staggering aside. He went to one knee. Ripped circuits overwhelmed him with destruction signals. As the pain throbbed toward extinction, his head cleared enough to see that half his upper left arm was blown off.

The tube was held steady on him. He rose. The knowledge of his danger flared in him. A second biped had its arms around the third, which was tugging a smaller object from a sheath.

Zero discharged full power through his effectors. Blurred to view by speed, he flung himself to one side while his remaining left hand threw the pry bar. It went meteorlike across a shaft of sunlight and struck the tube. The tube was pulled from the biped's grasp, slammed to the ground and buckled.

Instantly Zero was upon the three of them. He had already identified their communication system, a transmitter and antenna actually outside the skin! His one right hand smashed across a biped's back, tearing the radio set loose. His torch spat with precision. Fused, the communicator of a second biped went dead.

The third one tried to escape. Zero caught it in four strides, plucked off its antenna, and carried it wildly kicking under one arm while he chased the other two. When he had caught the second, the first stood its ground and battered forlornly at him with its hands. He lashed them all together with his wire rope. As a precaution, he emptied the carrier rack of the one which had shot him. Those thin objects might be dangerous even with the tube that had launched them broken. He stuffed the bipeds into his own carrier.

For a moment, then, he lingered. The forest held little sonic noise except the wind in the accumulators. But the radio spectrum clamored. The monster howled; Zero's own broadcast rolled between sky and mountainside, from person to person and so relayed across the land.

"No more talk now," he finished his report. "I do not want the monster to track me. I have prevented these auxiliaries from communicating with it. Now I shall take them to my cave for study. I hope to present some useful data at the rendezvous."

"This may frighten the monster off," Seventy-Two said.

"So much the better," Hundred answered.

"In that case," Zero said, "I will at least have brought back something from my hunt."

He snapped off his transmission and faded into the forest shadows.

2

The boat had departed from the spaceship on a mere whisper of jets. Machinery inboard hummed, clicked, murmured, sucked in exhausted air and blew out renewed; busied itself with matters of warmth and light, computation and propulsion. But it made no more than a foundation for silence.

Hugh Darkington stared out the forward port. As the boat curved away from the mother ship's orbit, the great hull gleamed across his sky—fell astern and rapidly dwindled until lost to view. The stars which it had hidden sprang forth, icy-sharp points of glitter against an overwhelming blackness.

They didn't seem different to him. They were, of course. From Earth's surface the constellations would be wholly alien. But in space so many stars were visible that they made one chaos, at least to Darkington's eyes. Captain Thurshaw had pointed out to him, from the ship's bridge, that the Milky Way had a new shape, this bend was missing and that bay had not been there three billion years ago. To Darkington it remained words. He was a biologist and had never paid much attention to astronomy. In the first numbness of loss and isolation, he could think of nothing which mattered less than the exact form of the Milky Way.

Still the boat spiraled inward. Now the moon drifted across his view. In those eons since the *Traveler* left home, Luna had retreated from Earth: not as far as might have been predicted, because (they said) Bering Straits had vanished with every other remembered place; but nonetheless, now it was only a tarnished farthing. Through the ship's telescopes it had looked like itself. Some new mountains, craters, and maria, some thermal erosion of old features, but Thurshaw could identify much of what he once knew. It was grotesque that the moon should endure when everything else had changed.

Even the sun. Observed through a dimmer screen, the solar disc was bloated and glaring. Not so much in absolute terms, perhaps. Earth had moved a little closer, as the friction of interplanetary dust and gas took a millennial toll. The sun itself had grown a little bigger and hotter, as nuclear reactions intensified. In three billion years such things became noticeable even on the cosmic scale. To a living organism they totaled doomsday.

Darkington cursed under his breath and clenched a fist till the skin stretched taut. He was a thin man, long-faced, sharp-featured, his brown hair prematurely sprinkled with gray. His memories included beautiful spires above an Oxford quad, wonder seen through a microscope, a sailboat beating into the wind off Nantucket, which blew spray and a sound of gulls and church bells at him, comradeship bent over a chessboard or hoisting beer steins, forests hazy and ablaze with Indian summer: and all these things were dead. The shock had worn off, the hundred men and women aboard the *Traveler* could function again, but home had been amputated from their lives and the stump hurt.

Frederika Ruys laid her own hand on his and squeezed a little. Muscle by muscle he untensed himself, until he could twitch a smile in response to hers. "After all," she said, "we knew we'd be gone a long time. That we might well never come back."

"But we'd have been on a living planet," he mumbled.

"So we can still find us one," declared Sam Kuroki from his seat at the pilot console. "There're no less than six G-type stars within fifty light-years."

"It won't be the same," Darkington protested.

"No," said Frederika. "In a way, though, won't it be more? We, the last humans in the universe, starting the race over again?"

There was no coyness in her manner. She wasn't much to look at, plump, plain, with straight yellow hair and too wide a mouth. But such details had ceased to matter since the ship ended time acceleration. Frederika Ruys was a brave soul and a skilled engineer. Darkington felt incredibly lucky that she had picked him.

"Maybe we aren't the last, anyhow," Kuroki said. His flat features broke in one of his frequent grins; he faced immensity with a sparrow's cockiness. "Ought to've been other colonies than ours planted, oughtn't there? Of course, by now their descendants 'ud be bald-headed dwarfs who sit around thinking in calculus."

"I doubt that," Darkington sighed. "If humans had survived anywhere else in the galaxy, don't you think they would at least have come back and . . . and reseeded this with life? The mother planet?" He drew a shaken breath. They had threshed this out a hundred times or more while the *Traveler* orbited about unrecognizable Earth, but they could not keep from saying the obvious again and again, as a man must keep touching a wound on his body. "No, I think the war really did begin soon after we left. The world situation was all set to explode."

That was why the *Traveler* had been built, and even more why it had departed in such haste, his mind went on. Fifty couples scrambling off to settle on Tau Ceti II before the missiles were unleashed. Oh, yes, officially they were a scientific team, and one of the big foundations had paid for the enterprise. But in fact, as everyone knew, the hope was to insure that a fragment of civilization would be saved, and someday return to help rebuild. (Even Panasia admitted that a total war would throw history back a hundred years; Western governments were less optimistic.) Tension had mounted so horribly fast in the final months that no time was taken for a really careful check of the field drive. So new and little understood an engine ought to have had scores of test flights before starting out under full power. But . . . well . . . next year might be too late. And exploratory ships *had* visited the nearer stars, moving just under the speed of light, their crews experiencing only a few weeks of transit time. Why not the *Traveler*?

"The absolute war?" Frederika said, as she had done so often already. "Fought until the whole world was sterile? No. I won't believe it."

"Not in that simple and clean-cut a way," Darkington conceded. "Probably the war did end with a nominal victor: but he was more depopulated and devastated than anyone had dared expect. Too impoverished to reconstruct, or even to maintain what little physical plant survived. A downward spiral into the Dark Ages."

"M-m-m, I dunno," Kuroki argued. "There were a lot of machines around. Automation, especially. Like those self-reproducing, sun-powered, mineral-collecting sea rafts. And a lot of other self-maintaining gadgets. I don't see why industry couldn't be revived on such a base."

"Radioactivity would have been everywhere," Darkington pointed out. "Its long-range effect on ecology . . . Oh, yes, the process may have taken centuries, as first one species changed or died, and then another dependent on it, and then more. But how could the human survivors recreate technology when biology was disintegrating around them?" He shook himself and stiffened his back, ashamed of his self-pity a minute ago, looking horror flatly in the face. "That's my guess. I could be wrong, but it seems to fit the facts. We'll never know for certain, I suppose."

Earth rolled into sight. The planetary disc was still edged with blueness darkening toward black. Clouds still trailed fleecy above shining oceans; they gleamed upon the darkness near the terminator as they caught the first light before sunrise. Earth was forever fair.

But the continental shapes were new, speckled with hard points of reflection upon black and ocher where once they had been softly green and brown. There were no polar caps; sea level temperatures ranged from eighty to two hundred degrees Fahrenheit. No free oxygen remained: the atmosphere was nitrogen, its oxides, ammonia, hydrogen sulfide, sulfur dioxide, carbon dioxide, and steam. Spectroscopes had found no trace of chlorophyll or any other complex organic compound. The ground cover, dimly glimpsed through clouds, was metallic.

This was no longer Earth. There was no good reason why the *Traveler* should send a boat and three highly unexpendable humans down to look at its lifelessness. But no one had suggested leaving the Solar System without such a final visit. Darkington remembered being taken to see his grandmother when she was dead. He was twelve years old and had loved her. It was not her in the box, that strange unmeaningful mask, but where then was she?

"Well, whatever happened seems to be three billion years in the past," Kuroki said, a little too loudly. "Forget it. We got troubles of our own."

Frederika's eyes had not left the planet. "We can't ever forget, Sam," she said. "We'll always wonder and hope—they, the children at least—hope that it didn't happen to them too cruelly." Darkington started in surprise as she went on murmuring, very low, oblivious of the men:

> *"to tell you of the ending of the day.*
> *And you will see her tallness with surprise,*
> *and looking into gentle, shadowed eyes*
> *protest: it's not that late; you have to stay*
> *awake a minute more, just one, to play*
> *with yonder ball. But nonetheless you rise*
> *so they won't hear her say, 'A baby cries,*
> *but you are big. Put all your toys away.'*

> *"She lets you have a shabby bear in bed,*
> *though frankly doubting that you two can go*
> *through dream-shared living rooms or wingless flight.*
> *She tucks the blankets close beneath your head*
> *and smooths your hair and kisses you, and so*
> *goes out, turns off the light. 'Good night. Sleep tight.' "*

Kuroki glanced around at her. The plaid shirt wrinkled across his wide shoulders. "Pomes yet," he said. "Who wrote that?"

"Hugh," said Frederika. "Didn't you know he published poetry? Quite a bit. I admired his work long before I met him."

Darkington flushed. Her interest was flattering, but he regarded *Then Death Will Come* as a juvenile effort.

However, his embarrassment pulled him out of sadness. (On the surface. Down beneath, it would always be there, in every one of them. He hoped they would not pass too much of it on to their children. Let us not weep eternally for Zion.) Leaning forward, he looked at the planet with an interest that mounted as the approach curve took them around the globe. He hoped for a few answers to a hell of a lot of questions.

For one thing, why, in three billion years, had life not re-evolved? Radioactivity must have disappeared in a few centuries at most. The conditions of primordial Earth would have returned. Or would they? What had been lacking this time around?

He woke from his brown study with a jerk as Kuroki said, "Well, I reckon we can steepen our trajectory a bit." A surprising interval had passed. The pilot touched controls and the mild acceleration increased. The terrestrial disc, already enormous, swelled with terrifying velocity, as if tumbling down upon them.

Then, subtly, it was no longer to one side or above, but was beneath; and it was no longer a thing among the stars but the convex floor of bowl-shaped creation. The jets blasted more strongly. Kuroki's jaws clenched till knots of muscle stood forth. His hands danced like a pianist's.

He was less the master of the boat, Darkington knew, than its helper. So many tons, coming down through atmospheric turbulence at such a velocity, groping with radar for a safe landing spot, could not be handled by organic brain and nerves. The boat's central director—essentially a computer whose input came from the instruments and whose efferent impulses went directly to the controls—performed the basic operations. Its task was fantastically complex: very nearly as difficult as the job of guiding the muscles when a man walks. Kuroki's fingers told the boat, "Go that way," but the director could overrule him.

"I think we'll settle among those hills." The pilot had to shout now, as the jets blasted stronger. "Want to come down just east of the sunrise line, so we'll have a full day ahead of us, and yonder's the most promising spot in this region. The lowlands look too boggy."

Darkington nodded and glanced at Frederika. She smiled and made a thumbs-up sign. He leaned over, straining against his safety harness, and brushed his lips across hers. She colored with a pleasure that he found oddly moving.

Someday, on another planet—that possibly hadn't been born when they left Earth—

He had voiced his fears to her, that the engine would go awry again when they started into deep space, and once more propel them through time, uncontrollably until fuel was exhausted. A full charge in the tanks was equivalent to three billion years, plus or minus several million; or so the physicists aboard had estimated. In six billion A.D. might not the sun be so swollen as to engulf them when they emerged?

She had rapped him across the knuckles with her calculator and said no, you damned biologist, but you'll have to take my word for it because you haven't got the math. I've studied it as far as differential equations, he said.

She grinned and answered that then he'd never had a math course. It seemed, she said, that time acceleration was readily explained by the same theory which underlay the field drive. In fact, the effect had been demonstrated in laboratory experiments. Oh, yes, I know about that, he said; reactive thrust is rotated through a fourth dimension and gets applied along the temporal rather than a spatial axis. You do not know a thing about it, she said, as your own words have just proved. But never mind. What happened to us was that a faulty manifold generated the t-acceleration effect in our engine. Now we've torn everything down and rebuilt from scratch. We know it'll work right. The tanks are recharged. The ship's ecosystem is in good order. Any time we want, we can take off for a younger sun, and travel fifty light-years without growing more than a few months older. After which, seeing no one else was around, she sought his arms; and that was more comforting than her words.

A last good-bye to Grandmother Earth, he thought. *Then we can start the life over again that we got from her.*

The thrust upon him mounted. Toward the end he lay in his chair, now become a couch, and concentrated on breathing.

They reached ground.

Silence rang in their ears for a long while. Kuroki was the first to move. He unstrapped his short body and snapped his chair back upright. One hand unhooked the radio microphone, another punched buttons. "Boat calling *Traveler*," he intoned. "We're okay so far. Come in, *Traveler*. Hello, hello."

Darkington freed himself, stiffly, his flesh athrob, and helped Frederika rise. She leaned on him a minute. "Earth," she said. Gulping: "Will you look out the port first, dearest? I find I'm not brave enough."

He realized with a shock that none of them had yet glanced at the landscape. Convulsively, he made the gesture.

He stood motionless for so long that finally she raised her head and stared for herself.

3

They did not realize the full strangeness before they donned spacesuits and went outside. Then, saying very little, they wandered about looking and feeling. Their brains were slow to develop the gestalts which would allow them really to see what surrounded them. A confused mass of detail could not be held in the memory, the underlying form could not be abstracted from raw sense impressions. A tree is a tree, anywhere and anywhen, no matter how intricate its branching or how oddly shaped its leaves and blossoms. But what is a—

—thick shaft of gray metal, planted in the sand, central to a labyrinthine skeleton of straight and curved girders, between which run still more enigmatic structures embodying helices and toruses and Möbius strips and less familiar geometrical elements; the entire thing some fifty feet tall; flaunting at the top several hundred thin metal plates whose black sides are turned toward the sun?

When you have reached the point of being able to describe it even this crudely, then you *have* apprehended it.

Eventually Darkington saw that the basic structure was repeated, with infinite variation of size and shape, as far as he could see. Some specimens tall and slender, some low and broad, they dominated the hillside. The deeper reaches were made gloomy by their overhang, but sun speckles flew piercingly bright within those shadows as the wind shook the mirror faces of the plates. That same wind made a noise of clanking and clashing and far-off deep booming, mile after metal mile.

There was no soil, only sand, rusty red and yellow. But outside the circle which had been devastated by the boat's jets, Darkington found the earth carpeted with prismatic growths, a few inches high, seemingly rooted in the ground. He broke one off for closer examination and saw tiny crystals, endlessly repeated, in some transparent siliceous material: like snowflakes and spiderwebs of glass. It sparkled so brightly, making so many rainbows, that he couldn't well study the interior. He could barely make out at the center a dark clump of . . . wires, coils, transistors? *No,* he told himself, *don't be silly.* He gave it to Frederika, who exclaimed at its beauty.

He himself walked across an open stretch, hoping for a view even vaguely familiar. Where the hillside dropped too sharply to support anything but the crystals—they made it one dazzle of diamonds—he saw eroded contours, the remote white sword of a waterfall, strewn boulders and a few crags like worn-out obelisks. The land rolled away into blue distances; a snowcapped mountain range guarded the eastern horizon. The sky overhead was darker than in his day, faintly greenish blue, full of clouds. He couldn't look near the fierce big sun.

Kuroki joined him. "What d'you think, Hugh?" the pilot asked.

"I hardly dare say. You?"

"Hell, I can't think with that bloody boiler factory clattering at me." Kuroki grimaced behind his faceplate. "Turn off your sonic mike and let's talk by radio."

Darkington agreed. Without amplification, the noise reached him through his insulated helmet as a far-off tolling. "We can take it for granted," he said, "that none of this is accidental. No minerals could simply crystallize out like this."

"Don't look manufactured to me, though."

"Well," said Darkington, "you wouldn't expect them to turn out their products in anything like a human machine shop."

"Them?"

"Whoever . . . whatever . . . made this. For whatever purpose."

Kuroki whistled. "I was afraid you'd say something like that. But we didn't see a trace of—cities, roads, anything—from orbit. I know the cloudiness made seeing pretty bad, but we couldn't have missed the signs of a civilization able to produce stuff on this scale."

"Why not? If the civilization isn't remotely like anything we've ever imagined?"

Frederika approached, leaving a cartful of instruments behind. "The low and medium frequency radio spectrum is crawling," she reported. "You never heard so many assorted hoots, buzzes, whirrs, squeals, and whines in your life."

"We picked up an occasional bit of radio racket while in orbit," Kuroki nodded. "Didn't think much about it, then."

"Just noise," Frederika said hastily. "Not varied enough to be any kind of, of communication. But I wonder what's doing it?"

"Oscillators," Darkington said. "Incidental radiation from a variety of—oh, hell, I'll speak plainly—machines."

"But—" Her hand stole toward his. Glove grasped glove. She wet her lips. "No, Hugh, this is absurd. How could any one be capable of making . . . what we see . . . and not have detected us in orbit and—and done something about us?"

Darkington shrugged. The gesture was lost in his armor. "Maybe they're biding their time. Maybe they aren't here at the moment. The whole planet could be an automated factory, you know. Like those ocean mineral harvesters we had in our time"—it hurt to say that—"which Sam mentioned on the way down. Somebody may come around periodically and collect the production."

"Where do they come from?" asked Kuroki in a rough tone.

"I don't know, I tell you. Let's stop making wild guesses and start gathering data."

Silence grew between them. The skeleton towers belled. Finally Kuroki nodded. "Yeah. What say we take a little stroll? We may come on something."

Nobody mentioned fear. They dared not.

Re-entering the boat, they made the needful arrangements. The *Traveler* would be above the horizon for several hours yet. Captain Thurshaw gave his reluctant consent to an exploration on foot. The idea conflicted with his training, but what did survey doctrine mean under these conditions? The boat's director could keep a radio beam locked on the ship and thus relay communication between Earth and orbit. While Kuroki talked, Darkington and Frederika prepared supplies. Not much was needed. The capacitor pack in each suit held charge enough to power thermostat and air renewer for a hundred hours, and they only planned to be gone for three or four. They loaded two packboards with food, water, and the "buckets" used for such natural functions as eating, but that was only in case their return should be delayed. The assorted scientific instruments they took were more to the point. Darkington holstered a pistol. When he had finished talking, Kuroki put the long tube of a rocket gun and a rackful of shells on his own back. They closed their helmets anew and stepped out.

"Which way?" Frederika asked.

"Due south," Darkington said after studying the terrain. "We'll be following this long ridge, you see. Harder to get lost." There was little danger of that, with the boat emitting a continuous directional signal. Nonetheless they all had compasses on their wrists and took note of landmarks as they went.

The boat was soon lost to view. They walked among surrealistic rods and frames and spirals, under ringing sheet metal. The crystals crunched beneath their tread and broke sunlight into hot shards of color. But not many rays pushed through the tangle overhead; shadows were dense and restless. Darkington began to recognize unrelated types of structure. They included long, black, seemingly telescopic rods, fringed with thin plates; glassy spheres attached to intricate grids; cables that looped from girder to girder. Frequently a collapsed object was seen crumbling on the ground.

Frederika looked at several disintegrated specimens, examined others in good shape, and said: "I'd guess the most important material, the commonest, is an aluminum alloy. Though—see here—these fine threads embedded in the core must be copper. And this here is probably manganese steel with a protective coating of . . . um . . . something more inert."

Darkington peered at the end of a broken strut through a magnifying glass. "Porous," he said. "Good Lord, are these actually capillaries to transport water?"

"I thought a capillary was a hairy bug with lots of legs that turned into a butterfly," said Kuroki. He ducked an imaginary fist. "Okay, okay, somebody's got to keep up morale."

The boat's radio relayed a groan from the monitor aboard the ship. Frederika said patiently, "No, Sam, the legs don't turn into a butterfly—" but then she remembered there would never again be bravely colored small wings on Earth and banged a hand against her faceplate as if she had been about to knuckle her eyes.

Darkington was still absorbed in the specimen he held. "I never heard of a machine this finely constructed," he declared. "I thought nothing but a biological system could—"

"Stop! Freeze!"

Kuroki's voice rapped in their earphones. Darkington laid a hand on his pistol butt. Otherwise only his head moved, turning inside the helmet. After a moment he saw the thing too.

It stirred among shadows, behind a squat cylinder topped with the usual black-and-mirror plates. Perhaps three feet long, six or eight inches high . . . It came out into plain view. Darkington glimpsed a slim body and six short legs of articulated dull metal. A latticework swiveled at the front end like a miniature radio-radar beamcaster. Something glinted beadily beneath, twin lenses? Two thin tentacles held a metal sliver off one of the great stationary structures. They fed it into an orifice, and sparks shot back upward—

"Holy Moses," Kuroki whispered.

The thing stopped in its tracks. The front-end lattice swung toward the humans. Then the thing was off, unbelievably fast. In half a second there was nothing to see.

Nobody moved for almost a minute. Finally Frederika clutched Darkington's arm with a little cry. The rigidness left him and he babbled of experimental robot turtles in the early days of cybernetic research. Very simple gadgets. A motor drove a wheeled platform, steered by a photoelectric unit that approached light sources by which the batteries might be recharged and, when this was done, became negatively phototropic and sought darkness. An elementary feedback circuit. But the turtles had shown astonishing tenacity, had gone over obstacles or even around. . . .

"That beast there was a good deal more complicated," she interrupted.

"Certainly, certainly," Darkington said. "But—"

"I'll bet it heard Sam talk on the radio, spotted us with radar—or maybe eyes, if those socketed glass things were eyes—and took off."

"Very possibly, if you must use anthropomorphic language. However—"

"It was eating that strut." Frederika walked over to the piece of metal which the runner had dropped. She picked it up and came stiffly back with it. "See, the end has been ground away by a set of coarse emery wheels or something. You couldn't very well eat alloy with teeth like ours. You have to grind it."

"Hey!" Kuroki objected. "Let's not go completely off the deep end."

"What the hell's happened down there?" called the man aboard the *Traveler*.

They resumed walking, in a dreamlike fashion, as they recounted what they had seen. Frederika concluded: "This . . . this arrangement might conceivably be some kind of automated factory—chemosynthetic or something—if taken by itself. But not with beasts like that one running loose."

"Now wait," Darkington said. "They could be maintenance robots, you know. Clear away rubbish and wreckage."

"A science advanced enough to build what we see wouldn't use such a clumsy system of maintenance," she answered. "Get off your professional caution, Hugh, and admit what's obvious."

Before he could reply, his earphones woke with a harsh jabber. He stopped and tried to tune in—it kept fading out, he heard it only in bursts—but the bandwidth was too great. What he did hear sounded like an electronic orchestra gone berserk. Sweat prickled his skin.

When the sound had stopped: "Okay," breathed Kuroki, "you tell me."

"Could have been a language, I suppose," said Frederika, dry-throated. "It wasn't just a few simple oscillations like that stuff on the other frequencies."

Captain Thurshaw himself spoke from the orbiting ship. "You better get back to the boat and sit prepared for quick blastoff."

Darkington found his nerve. "No, sir. If you please. I mean, uh, if there are intelligences . . . if we really do want to contact them . . . now's the time. Let's at least make an effort."

"Well—"

"We'll take you back first, of course, Freddie."

"Nuts," said the girl. "I stay right here."

Somehow they found themselves pushing on. Once, crossing an open spot where only the crystals stood, they spied something in the air. Through binoculars, it turned out to be a metallic object shaped vaguely like an elongated manta. Apparently it was mostly hollow, upborne by air currents around the fins and propelled at low speed by a gas jet. "Oh, sure," Frederika muttered. "Birds."

They re-entered the area of tall structures. The sonic amplifiers in their helmets were again tuned high, and the clash of plates in the wind was deafening. Like a suit of armor, Darkington thought idiotically. Could be a poem in that. Empty armor on a wild horse, rattling and tossing as it was galloped down an inexplicably deserted city street—symbol of—

The radio impulses that might be communication barked again in their earphones. "I don't like this," Thurshaw said from the sky. "You're dealing with too many unknowns at once. Return to the boat and we'll discuss further plans."

They continued walking in the same direction, mechanically. *We don't seem out of place here ourselves, in this stiff cold forest,* Darkington thought. *My God, let's turn around. Let's assert our dignity as organic beings. We aren't mounted on rails!*

"That's an order," Thurshaw stated.

"Very well, sir," Kuroki said. "And, uh, thanks."

The sound of running halted them. They whirled. Frederika screamed.

"What's the matter?" Thurshaw shouted. "What's the matter?" The unknown language ripped across his angry helplessness.

Kuroki yanked his rocket gun loose and put the weapon to his shoulder. "Wait!" Darkington yelled. But he grabbed at his own pistol. The oncomer rushed in a shower of crystal splinters, whipping rods and loops aside. Its gigantic weight shuddered in the ground.

Time slowed for Darkington, he had minutes or hours to tug at his gun, hear Frederika call his name, see Kuroki take aim and fire. The shape was mountainous before him. Nine feet tall, he estimated in a far-off portion of his rocking brain, three yards of biped four-armed monstrosity, head horned with radio lattice, eyes that threw back sunlight in a blank glitter, grinder orifice and—The rocket exploded. The thing lurched and half fell. One arm was in ruins.

"Ha!" Kuroki slipped a fresh shell into his gun. "Stay where you are, you!"

Frederika, wildly embracing Darkington, found time to gasp, "Sam, maybe it wasn't going to do any harm," and Kuroki snapped, "Maybe it was. Too goddam big to take chances with." Then everything smashed.

Suddenly the gun was knocked spinning by a hurled iron bar they hadn't even noticed. And the giant was among them. A swat across Kuroki's back shattered his radio and dashed him to earth. Flame spat and Frederika's voice was cut short in Darkington's receivers.

He pelted off, his pistol uselessly barking. "Run, Freddie!" he bawled into his sonic microphone. "I'll try and—" The machine picked him up. The pistol fell from his grasp. A moment later, Thurshaw's horrified oaths were gone: Darkington's radio antenna had been plucked out by the roots. Frederika tried to escape, but she was snatched up just as effortlessly. Kuroki, back on his feet, stood where he was and struck with ludicrous fists. It didn't take long to secure him either. Hog-tied, stuffed into a rack on the shoulders of the giant, the three humans were borne off southward.

4

At first Zero almost ran. The monster must have known where its auxiliaries were and something of what had happened to them. Now that contact was broken, it might send forth others to look for them, better armed. Or it might even come itself, roaring and burning through the forest. Zero fled.

Only the monster's voice, raggedly calling for its lost members, pursued him. After a few miles he crouched in a rod clump and strained his receptors. Nothing was visible but thickly growing accumulators and bare sky. The monster had ceased to shout. Though it still emitted an unmodulated signal, distance had dwindled this until the surrounding soft radio noise had almost obliterated that hum.

The units Zero had captured were making considerable sound-wave radiation. If not simply the result of malfunction in their damaged mechanism, it must be produced by some auxiliary system which they had switched on through interior controls. Zero's sound receptors were not sensitive enough to tell him whether the emission was modulated. Nor did he care. Certain low forms of motile were known to have well-developed sonic parts, but anything so limited in range was useless to him except as a warning of occurrences immediately at hand. A person needed many square miles to support himself. How could there be a community of persons without the effortless ability to talk across trans-horizon distances?

Irrelevantly, for the first time in his century and a half of existence, Zero realized how few persons he had ever observed with his own direct optics. How few he had touched. Now and then, for this or that purpose, several might get together. A bride's male kin assisted her on her journey to the groom's dwelling. Individuals met to exchange the products of their labor. But still— this rally of all functional males at Broken Glade, to hunt the monster, would be the greatest assemblage in tradition. Yet not even Hundred had grasped its uniqueness.

For persons were always communicating. Not only practical questions were discussed. In fact, now that Zero thought about it, such problems were the least part of discourse. The major part was ritual, or friendly conversation, or art. Zero had seldom met Seven as a physical entity, but the decades in which they criticized each other's poetry had made them intimate. The abstract tone constructions of Ninety-six, the narratives of Eighty, the speculations about space and time of Fifty-nine—such things belonged to all.

Direct sensory linkage, when the entire output of the body was used to modulate the communication band, reduced still further the need for physical contact. Zero had never stood on the seashore himself. But he had shared consciousness with Fourteen, who lived there. He had perceived the slow inward movement of waves, their susurrus, the salt in the air; he had experienced the smearing of grease over his skin to protect it from corrosion, drawing an aquamotile from a net and feasting. For those hours, he and the searaker had been one. Afterward he had shown Fourteen the upland forest. . . .

What am I waiting for? Consciousness of his here-and-now jarred back into Zero. The monster had not pursued. The units on his back had grown quiescent. But he was still a long way from home. He rose and started off again, less rapidly but with more care to obliterate his traces.

As the hours passed, his interior sensors warned him increasingly of a need for replenishment. About midday he stopped and unloaded his three prizes. They were feebly squirming and one of them had worked an arm loose. Rather than lash them tight again, he released their limbs and secured them by passing the rope in successive loops around their middles and a tall stump, then welding everything fast with his torch.

That energy drain left him ravenous. He scouted the forest in a jittery spiral until he found some accumulators of the calathiform sort. A quick slash with his pry bar exposed their spongy interiors, rich with energy storage cells and mineral salts. They were not very satisfying eaten unprocessed, but he was too empty to care. With urgency blunted, he could search more slowly and thoroughly. Thus he found the traces of a burrow, dug into the sand, and came upon a female digger. She was heavy with a half-completed new specimen and he caught her easily. This too would have been better if treated with heat and acid, but even raw the materials tasted good in his grinder.

Now to get something for One. Though she, better than he, could slow down her functioning when nourishment was scarce, a state of coma while the monster was abroad could be dangerous. After hunting for another hour, Zero had the good luck to start a rotor. It crashed off among the rods and crystals, faster than he could run, but he put a crossbow bolt through its hub. Dismembered and packed into his carrier, it made an immensely cheering burden.

He returned to his prizes. Moving quietly in comparison to the windy clatter of the forest, he came upon them unobserved. They had quit attempting to escape—he saw the wire was shiny where they had tried to saw it on a sharp rock—and were busy with other tasks. One of them had removed a boxlike object from its back and inserted its head(?) and arms through gasketed holes. A second was just removing a similar box from its lower section. The third had plugged a flexible tube from a bottle into its face.

Zero approached. "Let me inspect those," he said, before thinking how ridiculous it was to address them. They shrank away from him. He caught the one with the bottle and unplugged the tube. Some liquid ran out. Zero extended his chemical sensor and tasted cautiously. Water. Very pure. He did not recall ever having encountered water so free of dissolved minerals.

Thoughtfully, he released the unit. It stoppered the tube. So, Zero reflected, they required water like him, and carried a supply with them. That was natural; they (or, rather, the monster they served) could not know where the local springs and streams were. But why did they suck through a tube? Did they lack a proper liquid-ingestion orifice? Evidently. The small hole in the head, into which the tube had fitted, had automatically closed as the nipple was withdrawn.

The other two had removed their boxes. Zero studied these and their contents. There were fragments of mushy material in both, vaguely similar to normal body sludge. Nourishment or waste? Why such a clumsy system? It was as if the interior mechanism must be absolutely protected from contact with the environment.

He gave the boxes back and looked more thoroughly at their users. They were not quite so awkward as they seemed at first. The humps on their backs were detachable carriers like his. Some of the objects dangling at their waists or strapped to their arms must also be tools. (Not weapons or means of escape, else they would have used them before now. Specialized artificial attachments, then, analogous to a torch or a surgical ratchet.) The basic bipedal shape was smoother than his own, nearly featureless except for limb joints. The head was somewhat more complicated, though less so than a person's. Upon the cylindrical foundation grew various parts, including the sound-wave generators which babbled as he stood there watching. The face was a glassy plate, behind which moved . . . what? Some kind of jointed, partly flexible mechanism.

There was no longer any possibility of radio communication with—or through—them. Zero made a few experimental gestures, but the units merely stirred about. Two of them embraced. The third waved its arms and made sonic yelps. All at once it squatted and drew geometrical shapes in the sand, very much like the courtship figures drawn by a male dune-runner.

So . . . they not only had mechanical autonomy, like the spy eyes of a boxroller, but were capable of some independent behavior. They were more than simple remote-control limbs and sensors of the monster. Most probably they were domesticated motiles.

But if so, then the monster race had modified their type even more profoundly than the person race had modified the type of its own tamed motiles down in the lowlands. These bipeds were comically weak in proportion to size; they lacked grinders and liquid-ingestion orifices; they used sonics to a degree that argued their radio abilities were primitive; they required ancillary apparatus; in short, they were not functional by themselves. Only the care and shelter furnished by their masters allowed them to remain long in existence.

But what are the masters? Even the monster may well be only another motile. Certainly it appeared to lack limbs. The masters may be persons like us, come from beyond the sea or the mountains with skills and powers transcending our own.

But then what do they want? Why have they not tried to communicate with us? Have they come to take our land away?

The question was jolting. Zero got hastily into motion. With his rack loaded, he had no room for his prizes. Besides, being crammed into it for hours was doubtless harmful to them; they moved a good deal more strongly now, after a rest, than when he first took them out. He simply left them tied together, cut the wire loose from the stump, and kept that end in one hand. Since he continued to exercise due caution about leaving a trail, he did not move too fast for them to keep up. From time to time they would stagger and lean on each other for support—apparently their energy cells polarized more quickly than his—but he found they could continue if he let them pause a while, lie down, use their curious artifacts.

The day passed. At this time of year, not long past the vernal equinox, the sun was up for about twenty hours. After dark, Zero's captives began stumbling and groping. He confirmed by direct sense perception that they had no radar. If they ever did, that part had been wrecked with their communicators. After some thought, he fashioned a rough seat from a toppled bole and nudged them to sit upon it. Thus he carried them in two hands. They made no attempt to escape, emitted few sounds, obviously they were exhausted. But to his surprise, they began to stir about and radiate sonics when he finally reached home and set them down. He welded the end of their rope to an iron block he kept for emergencies.

Part of him reflected that their mechanism must be very strange indeed, maybe so strange that they would not prove ingestible. Obviously their cells went to such extremes of polarization that they became comatose, which a person only did in emergencies. To them, such deactivation appeared to be normal, and they roused spontaneously.

He dismissed speculation. One's anxious voice had been rushing over him while he worked. "What has happened? You are hurt! Come closer, let me see, oh, your poor arm! Oh, my dear!"

"Nothing serious," he reassured her. "I shot a rotor. Prepare yourself a meal before troubling about me."

He lowered himself to the cave floor beside her great beautiful bulk. The glow globes, cultivated on the rough stone walls, shed luster on her skin and on the graceful tool tendrils that curled forth to embrace him. His chemical sensor brought him a hint of solvents and lubricants, an essence of femaleness. The cave mouth was black with night, save where one star gleamed bright and somehow sinister above the hills. The forest groaned and tolled. But here he had light and her touch upon his body. He was home.

She unshipped the rack from his shoulders but made no motion toward the food-processing cauldron. Most of her tools and all her attention were on his damaged arm. "We must replace everything below the elbow," she decided; and, as a modulation: "Zero, you brave clever adored fool, why did you hazard yourself like that? Do you not understand, even yet, without you my world would be rust?"

"I am sorry . . . to take so much from the new one," he apologized.

"No matter. Feed me some more nice large rotors like this and I will soon replace the loss, and finish all the rest too." Her mirth fluttered toward shyness. "I want the new one activated soon myself, you know, so we can start another."

The memory of that moment last year, when his body pattern flowed in currents and magnetic fields through hers, when the two patterns heterodyned and deep within her the first crystallization took place, glowed in him. Sensory linkage was a wan thing by comparison.

What they did together now had a kindred intimacy. When she had removed the ruined forearm and he had thrust the stump into her repair orifice, a thousand fine interior tendrils enfolded it, scanning, relaying, and controlling. Once again, more subtly than in reproduction, the electro-chemical-mechanical systems of One and Zero unified. The process was not consciously controllable; it was a female function; One was at this moment no different from the most primitive motile joined to her damaged mate in a lightless burrow.

It took time. The new person which her body was creating within itself was, of course, full size and, as it happened, not far from completion. (Had the case been otherwise, Zero would have had to wait until the new one did in fact possess a well-developed arm.) But it was not yet activated; its most delicate and critical synaptic pathways were still only half-finished, gradually crystallizing out of solution. A part could not lightly nor roughly be removed.

But in the end, One's functions performed the task. Slowly, almost reluctantly, Zero withdrew his new hand. His mind and hers remained intertwined a while longer. At last, with a shaky little overtone of humor, she exclaimed, "Well, how do your fingers wiggle? Is everything good? Then let us eat. I am famished!"

Zero helped her prepare the rotor for consumption. They threw the damaged forearm into the cauldron too. While they processed and shared the meal, he recounted his experiences. She had shown no curiosity about the three bipeds. Like most females, she lacked any great interest in the world beyond her home, and had merely assumed they were some new kind of wild motile. As he talked, the happiness died in her. "Oh, no," she said, "you are not going out to fight the lightning breather, are you?"

"Yes, we must." He knew what image terrified her, himself smashed beyond hope of reconstruction, and added in haste: "If we leave it free, no tradition or instinct knows what it may do. But surely, at the very least, so large a thing will cause extensive damage. Even if it is only a grazer, its appetite will destroy untold acres of accumulators; and it may be a predator. On the other hand, if we destroy it, what a hoard of nourishment! Your share and mine will enable us to produce a dozen new persons. The energy will let me range for hundreds of miles, thus gaining still more food and goods for us."

"If the thing can be assimilated," she said doubtfully. "It could be full of hydrofluoric acid or something, like a touch-me-not."

"Yes, yes. For that matter, the flier may be the property of intelligent beings: which does not necessarily mean we will not destroy and consume it. I intend to find out about that aspect right now. If the monster's auxiliaries are ingestible, the monster itself is almost sure to be."

"But if not—Zero, be careful!"

"I will. For your sake also." He stroked her and felt an answering vibration. It would have been pleasant to sit thus all night, but he must soon be on his way to rendezvous. And first he must dissect at least one specimen. He took up his pry bar and approached the three units.

5

Darkington awoke from a nightmare-ridden half-sleep when he was dumped on the cave floor. He reached for Frederika and she came to him. For a space there was nothing but their murmuring.

Eventually they crouched on the sand and looked about. The giant that captured them had welded the free end of the wire rope to an immovable chunk of raw iron. Darkington was attached at that side, then the girl, and Kuroki on the outer end. They had about four feet of slack from one to the next. Nothing in the kit remaining to them would cut those strands.

"Limestone cave, I guess," Kuroki croaked. Behind the faceplate he was gaunt, bristly, and sunken-eyed. Frederika didn't look much better. They might not have survived the trip here if the robot hadn't carried them the last few hours. Nonetheless an odd, dry clarity possessed Darkington's brain. He could observe and think as well as if he had been safe on shipboard. His body was one enormous ache, but he ignored that and focused on comprehending what had happened.

Here near the entrance, the cave was about twenty feet high and rather more wide. A hundred feet deeper inward, it narrowed and ended. That area was used for storage: a junk shop of mechanical and electronic parts, together with roughly fashioned metal and stone tools that looked almost homelike. The walls were overgrown with thin wires that sprouted scores of small crystalline globes. These gave off a cool white light that made the darkness outside appear the more elemental.

"Yes, a cave in a sheer hillside," said Frederika. "I saw that much. I kept more or less conscious all the way here, trying to keep track of our route. Not that that's likely to do us much good, is it?" She hugged her knees. "I've got to sleep soon—oh, but I have to sleep!"

"We got to get in touch." Kuroki's voice rose. (Thank heaven and some ages-dead engineer that sound mikes and earphones could be switched on by shoving your chin against the right button! With talk cut off, no recourse would have remained but to slip quietly into madness.) "God damn it, I tried to show that tin nightmare we're intelligent. I drew diagrams and—" He checked himself. "Well, probably its builders don't monitor it. We'll have another go when they show up."

"Let's admit the plain facts, Sam," Frederika said tonelessly. "There aren't any builders. There never were any."

"Oh, no." The pilot gave Darkington a beggar's look. "You're the biologist, Hugh. Do you believe that?"

Darkington bit his lip. "I'm afraid she's right."

Frederika's laugh barked at them. "Do you know what that big machine is, there in the middle of the cave? The one the robot is fooling around with? I'll tell you. His wife!" She broke off. Laughter echoed too horribly in their helmets.

Darkington gazed in that direction. The second object had little in common with the biped shape, being low and wide—twice the bulk—and mounted on eight short legs which must lend very little speed or agility. A radio lattice, optical lenses, and arms (two, not four) were similar to the biped's. But numerous additional limbs were long goosenecks terminating in specialized appendages. Sleek blued metal covered most of the body.

And yet, the way those two moved—

"I think you may be right about that also," Darkington said at last.

Kuroki beat the ground with his fist and swore. "Sorry, Freddie," he gulped. "But won't you, for God's sake, explain what you're getting at? This mess wouldn't be so bad if it made some sense."

"We can only guess," Darkington said.

"Well, guess, then!"

"Robot evolution," Frederika said. "After man was gone, the machines that were left began to evolve."

"No," said Kuroki, "that's nuts. Impossible!"

"I think what we've seen would be impossible any other way," Darkington said. "Metallic life couldn't arise spontaneously. Only carbon atoms make the long hookups needed for the chemical storage of biological information. But electronic storage is equally feasible. And . . . before the *Traveler* departed . . . self-reproducing machines were already in existence."

"I think the sea rafts must have been the important ones." Frederika spoke like someone in dream. Her eyes were fixed wide and unblinking on the two robots. "Remember? They were essentially motorized floating boxes, containing metallurgic processing plants and powered by solar batteries. They took dissolved minerals out of sea water, magnesium, uranium, whatever a particular raft was designed for. When it had a full cargo, it went to a point on shore where a depot received its load. Once empty, it returned to open waters for more. It had an inertial navigation device, as well as electronic sensors and various homeostatic systems, so it could cope with the normal vicissitudes of its environment.

"And it had electronic templates which bore full information on its own design. They controlled mechanisms aboard, which made any spare part that might be needed. Those same mechanisms also kept producing and assembling complete duplicate rafts. The first such outfit cost hundreds of millions of dollars to manufacture, let alone the preliminary research and development. But once made, it needed no further investment. Production and expansion didn't cost anyone a cent.

"And after man was gone from Earth . . . all life had vanished . . . the sea rafts were still there, patiently bringing their cargoes to crumbling docks on barren shores, year after year after meaningless year—"

She shook herself. The motion was violent enough to be seen in armor. "Go on, Hugh," she said, her tone turned harsh. "If you can."

"I don't know any details," he began cautiously. "You should tell me how mutation was possible to a machine. But if the templates were actually magnetic recordings on wire or tape, I expect that hard radiation would affect them, as it affects an organic gene. And for a while there was certainly plenty of hard radiation around. The rafts started making imperfect duplicates. Most were badly designed and, uh, foundered. Some, though, had advantages. For instance, they stopped going to shore and hanging about for decades waiting to be unloaded. Eventually some raft was made which had the first primitive ability to get metal from a richer source than the ocean: namely, from other rafts. Through hundreds of millions of years, an ecology developed. We might as well call it an ecology. The land was reconquered. Wholly new *types* of machine proliferated. Until today, well, what we've seen."

"But where's the energy come from?" Kuroki demanded.

"The sun, I suppose. By now, the original solar battery must be immensely refined. I'd make a guess at dielectric storage on the molecular level, in specialized units—call them cells—which may even be of microscopic size. Of course, productivity per acre must be a good deal lower than it was in our day. Alloys aren't as labile as amino acids. But that's offset to a large extent by their greater durability. And, as you can see in this cave, by interchangeability."

"Huh?"

"Sure. Look at those spare parts stacked in the rear. Some will no doubt be processed, analogously to our eating and digesting food. But others are probably being kept for use as such. Suppose you could take whole organs from animals you killed and install them in yourself to replace whatever was wearing out. I rather imagine that's common on today's Earth. The 'black box' principle was designed into most machines in our own century. It would be inherited."

"Where's the metal come from in the first place?"

"From lower types of machine. Ultimately from sessile types that break down ores, manufacture the basic alloys, and concentrate more dielectric energy than they use. Analogous to vegetation. I daresay the, uh, metabolism involves powerful reagents. Sulfuric and nitric acids in glass-lined compartments must be the least of them. I doubt if there are any equivalent of microbes, but the ecology seems to manage quite well without. It's a grosser form of existence than ours. But it works. It works."

"Even sex." Frederika giggled a little crazily.

Darkington squeezed her gauntleted hand until she grew calmer. "Well," he said, "quite probably in the more complex machines, reproduction has become the specialty of one form while the other specializes in strength and agility. I daresay there are corresponding psychological differences."

"Psychological?" Kuroki bridled. "Wait a minute! I know there is—was—a lot of loose talk about computers being electronic brains and such rot, but—"

"Call the phenomenon what you like," Darkington shrugged. "But that robot uses tools which are made, not grown. The problem is how to convince it that *we* think."

"Can't it see?" Frederika exclaimed. "We use tools too. Sam drew mathematical pictures. What more does it want?"

"I don't know enough about this world to even guess," Darkington said tiredly. "But I suppose . . . well . . . we might once have seen a trained ape doing all sorts of elaborate things, without ever assuming it was more than an ape. No matter how odd it looked."

"Or maybe the robot just doesn't give a damn," Kuroki said. "There were people who wouldn't have."

"If Hugh's guess about the 'black box' is right," Frederika added slowly, "then the robot race must have evolved as hunters, instead of hunting being invented rather late in their evolution. As if men had descended from tigers instead of simians. How much psychological difference would that make?"

No one replied. She leaned forlornly against Darkington. Kuroki turned his eyes from them, perhaps less out of tact than loneliness. His girl was several thousand miles away, straight up, with no means for him to call her and say good-bye.

Thurshaw had warned the insistent volunteers for this expedition that there would be no rescue. He had incurred sufficient guilt in letting three people— three percent of the human race—risk themselves. If anything untoward happened, the *Traveler* would linger a while in hopes the boat could somehow return. But in the end the *Traveler* would head for the stars. Kuroki's girl would have to get another father for the boy she might name Sam.

I wish to hell Freddie were up there with her, Darkington thought. *Or do I? Isn't that simply what I'm supposed to wish?*

God! Cut that out. Start planning!

His brain spun like wheels in winter mud. What to do, what to do, what to do? His pistol was gone, so were Kuroki's rockets, nothing remained but a few tools and instruments. At the back of the cave there were probably stored some weapons with which a man could put up a moment's fight. (Only a moment, against iron and lightning; but that would end the present, ultimate horror, of sitting in your own fear-stink until the monster approached or the air-renewal batteries grew exhausted and you strangled.) The noose welded around his waist, ending in a ton of iron, choked off any such dreams. They must communicate, somehow, anyhow, plead, threaten, promise, wheedle. But the monster hadn't cared about the Pythagorean theorem diagrammed in sand. What next, then? How did you say "I am alive" to something that was not alive?

Though what was aliveness? Were proteins inherently and unescapably part of any living creature? If the ancient sea rafts had been nothing except complicated machines, at what point of further complication had their descendants come to life? *Now stop that, you're a biologist, you know perfectly well that any such question is empirically empty, and anyhow it has nothing to do with preserving the continuity of certain protein chemistries which are irrationally much loved.*

"I think it talks by radio." Kuroki's slow voice sounded oddly through the thudding in Darkington's head. "It probably hasn't got any notion that sound waves might carry talk. Maybe it's even deaf. Ears wouldn't be any too useful in that rattletrap jungle. And our own radios are busted." He began to fumble in the girl's pack. "I'm not feeling you up, Freddie. Your spacesuit isn't exactly my type. But I think I could cobble together one working set from the pieces of our three, if I can borrow some small tools and instruments. Once we make systematic noises on its talk band, the robot might get interested in trying to savvy us."

"Sam," she said faintly, "for that idea you can feel me up all you want."

"I'll take a rain check." He could actually chuckle, Darkington heard. "I'm sweaty enough in this damn suit to pass for a rainstorm just by myself."

He began to lay out the job. Darkington, unable to help, ashamed that he had not thought of anything, turned attention back to the robots. They were coupled together, ignoring him.

Frederika dozed off. How slowly the night went. But Earth was old, rotating as wearily as . . . as himself. . . . He slept.

A gasp awoke him.

The monster stood above them. Tall, tall, higher than the sky, it bestrode their awareness and looked down with blank eyes upon Kuroki's pitiful, barely begun work. One hand was still a torch and another hand had been replaced, it was invulnerable and soulless as a god. For an instant Darkington's half-aroused self groveled before it.

Then the torch spat, slashed the wire rope across, and Kuroki was pulled free.

Frederika cried out. "Sam!"

"Not . . . so eager . . . pal," the pilot choked in the robot's arms. "I'm glad you like me, but . . . ugh . . . careful!"

With a free hand, the robot twisted experimentally at Kuroki's left leg. The suit joints turned, Kuroki shrieked, Darkington thought he heard the leg bones leave their sockets.

"No! You filthy machine!" He plunged forward. The rope stopped him cold. Frederika covered her faceplate and begged Kuroki to be dead.

He wasn't, yet. He wasn't even unconscious. He kept on screaming as the robot used a prying tool to drag the leg off his armor. Leakseal compound flowed from between the fabric layers and preserved the air in the rest of his suit.

The robot dropped him and sprang back, frantically fanning itself. A whiff of oxygen, Darkington realized amidst the red and black disintegration of his sanity. Oxygen was nearly as reactive as fluorine, and there had been no free oxygen on Earth since—Kuroki's agony jerked toward silence.

The robot reapproached with care, squatted above him, poked at the exposed flesh, tore loose a chunk for examination and flung it aside. The metal off a joint seemed better approved.

Darkington realized vaguely that Frederika lay on the ground close to Kuroki and wept. The biologist himself was even nearer. He could have touched the robot as well as the body. Instead, though, he retreated, mumbling and mewing.

The robot had clearly learned a lesson from the gas, but was just as clearly determined to go on with the investigation. It stood up, moved a cautious distance away, and jetted a thin, intensely blue flame from its torch hand. Kuroki's corpse was divided across the middle.

Darkington's universe roared and exploded. He lunged again. The rope between him and Frederika was pulled across the firebeam. The strands parted like smoke.

The robot pounced at him, ran into the oxygen gushing from Kuroki's armor, and lurched back. Darkington grabbed the section of rope that joined him to the block. The torch was too bright to look at. If he touched its flame, that was the end of him too. But there was no chance to think about such matters. Blindly and animally, he pulled his leash across the cutting jet.

He was free.

"Get out, Freddie!" he coughed, and ran straight toward the robot. No use trying to run from a thing that could overtake him in three strides. The torch had stopped spitting fire, but the giant moved in a wobbly, uncertain fashion, still dazed by the oxygen. By pain? Savagely, in the last spark of awareness, Darkington hoped so. *"Get out, Freddie!"*

The robot staggered in pursuit of him. He dodged around the other machine, the big one that they had called female. To the back of the cave. A weapon to fight with, gaining a moment where Frederika might escape. An extra pry bar lay on the floor. He snatched it and whirled. The huge painted shape was almost upon him.

He dodged. Hands clashed together just above his helmet. He pelted back to the middle of the cave. The female machine was edging into a corner. But slow, awkward—

Darkington scrambled on top of it.

An arm reached from below to pluck him off. He snarled and struck with the pry bar. The noise rang in the cave. The arm sagged, dented. This octopod had nothing like the biped's strength. Its tool tendrils, even more frail, curled away from him.

The male robot loomed close. Darkington smashed his weapon down on the radio lattice at his feet. It crumpled. He brandished the bar and howled senselessly, "Stand back, there! One step more and I'll give her the works! I'll kill her!"

The robot stopped. Monstrous it bulked, an engine that could tear apart a man and his armor, and raised its torch hand.

"Oh, no," Darkington rasped. He opened a bleeder valve on his suit, kneeling so the oxygen would flow across the front end of the thing on which he rode. Sensors ought to be more vulnerable than skin. He couldn't hear if the she-robot screamed as Kuroki had done. That would be on the radio band. But when he gestured the male back, it obeyed.

"Get the idea?" he panted, not as communication but as hatred. "You can split my suit open with your flame gun, but my air will pour all over this contraption here. Maybe you could knock me off her by throwing something, but at the first sign of any such move on your part, I'll open my bleeder valve again. She'll at least get a heavy dose of oxy. And meanwhile I'll punch the sharp end of this rod through one of those lenses. Understand? Well, then, stay where you are, machine!"

The robot froze.

Frederika came near. She had slipped the loop of cable joining her to Kuroki off what was left of his torso. The light shimmered on her faceplate so Darkington couldn't see through, and her voice was strained out of recognition. "Hugh, oh, Hugh!"

"Head back to the boat," he ordered. Rationality was returning to him.

"Without you? No."

"Listen, this is not the place for grandstand heroics. Your first duty is to become a mother. But what I hope for, personally, is that you can return in the boat and fetch me. You're no pilot, but they can instruct you by radio from the ship if she's above the horizon. The general director does most of the work in any event. You land here, and I can probably negotiate a retreat for myself."

"But—but—the robot needed something like twenty hours to bring us here. And it knew the way better than I do. I'll have to go by compass and guess, mostly. Of course, I won't stop as often as it did. No more than I have to. But still—say twenty hours for me—you can't hold out that long!"

"I can damn well try," he said. "You got any better ideas?"

"All right, then. Good-bye, Hugh. No, I mean so long. I love you."

He grunted some kind of answer, but didn't see her go. He had to keep watching the robot.

6

"Zero!" his female called, just once, when the unit sprang upon her back. She clawed at it. The pry bar smashed across her arm. He felt the pain-surge within her sensors, broadcast through her communicator, like a crossbow bolt in his body.

Wildly, he charged. The enemy unit crashed the bar down on One's lattice. She shrilled in anguish. Affected by the damage that crippled her radar, her communicator tone grew suddenly, hideously different. Zero slammed himself to a halt.

Her sobbing, his own name blindly repeated, overwhelmed the burning in him where the corrosive gas had flowed. He focused his torch to narrow beam and took careful aim.

The unit knelt, fumbling with its free hand. One screamed again, louder. Her tendrils flailed about. Numbly, Zero let his torch arm droop. The unit rose and poised its weapon above her lenses. A single strong thrust downward through the glass could reach her brain. The unit gestured him back. He obeyed.

"Help," One cried. Zero could not look at the wreckage of her face. There was no escaping her distorted voice. "Help, Zero. It hurts so much."

"Hold fast," he called in his uselessness. "I cannot do anything. Not now. The thing is full of poison. That is what you received." He managed to examine his own interior perceptions. "The pain will abate in a minute . . . from such a small amount. But if you got a large dose—I do not know. It might prove totally destructive. Or the biped might do ultimate mechanical damage before I could prevent it. Hold fast, One mine. Until I think of something."

"I am afraid," she rattled. "For the new one."

"Hold fast," he implored. "If that unit does you any further harm, I will destroy it slowly. I expect it realizes as much."

The other functional biped came near. It exchanged a few ululations with the first, turned and went quickly from the cave. "It must be going back to the flying monster," said One. The words dragged from her, now and then she whimpered as her perceptions of damage intensified, but she could reason again. "Will it bring the monster here?"

"I cannot give chase," said Zero unnecessarily. "But—" He gathered his energy. A shout blasted from his communicator. *"Alarm, alarm! All persons receiving, prepare to relay. Alarm!"*

Voices flashed in his head, near and far, and it was as if they poured strength into him. He and One were not alone in a night cave, a scuttling horror on her back and the taste of poison only slowly fading. Their whole community was here.

He reported the situation in a few phrases. "You have been rash," Hundred said, shaken. "May there be no further penalties for your actions."

"What else would you have had him do?" defended Seven. "We cannot deal randomly with a thing as powerful as the monster. Zero took upon himself the hazards of gathering information. Which he has succeeded in, too."

"Proving the danger is greater than we imagined," shuddered Sixteen.

"Well, that is a valuable datum."

"The problem now is, what shall we do?" Hundred interrupted. "Slow though you say it is, I expect the auxiliary that escaped can find the monster long before we can rendezvous and get up into the hills."

"Until it does, though, it cannot communicate, its radio being disabled," Zero said. "So the monster will presumably remain where it is, ignorant of events. I suggest that those persons who are anywhere near this neighborhood strike out directly toward that area. They can try to head off the biped."

"You can certainly capture it in a few minutes," Hundred said.

"I cannot leave this place."

"Yes, you can. The thing that has seized your female will not logically do anything more to her, unprovoked, lest she lose her present hostage value."

"How do you know?" Zero retorted. "In fact, I believe if I captured its companion, this unit would immediately attack One. What hope does it have except in the escape of the other, that may bring rescue?"

"Hope is a curious word to use in connection with an elaborated spy eye," Seven said.

"If it is," Zero said. "Their actions suggest to me that these bipeds are more than unthinking domesticated motiles."

"Let be!" Hundred said. "There is scant time to waste. We may not risk the entire community for the sake of a single member. Zero, go fetch back that biped."

Unmodulated radio buzzed in the night. Finally Zero said, "No." One's undamaged hand reached toward him, but she was too far away for them to touch each other. Nor could she caress him with radar.

"We will soon have you whole again," he murmured to her. She did not answer, with the community listening.

Hundred surrendered, having existed long enough to recognize unbendable negation. "Those who are sufficiently near the monster to reach it before dawn, report," he directed. When they had finished—about thirty all told—he said, "Very well, proceed there. Wherever feasible, direct your course to intercept the probable path of the escaped unit. If you capture it, inform us at once. The rest of us will rendezvous as planned."

One by one the voices died out in the night, until only Hundred, who was responsible, and Seven, who was a friend, were in contact with Zero. "How are you now, One?" Seven asked gently.

"I function somewhat," she said in a tired, uneven tone. "It is strange to be radar blind. I keep thinking that heavy objects are about to crash into me. When I turn my optics that way, there isn't anything." She paused. "The new one stirred a little bit just now. A motor impulse pathway must have been completed. Be careful, Zero," she begged. "We have already taken an arm tonight."

"I cannot understand your description of the bipeds' interior," Hundred said practically. "Soft, porous material soaked in sticky red liquid; acrid vapors— How do they *work*? Where is the mechanism?"

"They are perhaps not functional at all," Seven proposed. "They may be purely artificial devices, powered by chemical action."

"Yet they act intelligently," Zero argued. "If the monster—or the monster's masters—do not have them under direct control—and certainly there is no radio involved—"

"There may be other means than radio to monitor an auxiliary," Seven said. "We know so little, we persons."

"In that case," Zero answered, "the monster has known about this cave all the time. It is watching me at this moment, through the optics of that thing on One's back."

"We must assume otherwise," Hundred said.

"I do," Zero said. "I act in the belief that these bipeds are out of contact with the flier. But if nevertheless they perform as they have been doing, then they certainly have independent function, including at least a degree of intelligence." A thought crashed through him, so stunning that he could not declare it at once. Finally: "They may be the monster's masters! It may be the auxiliary, they the persons!"

"No, no, that is impossible," Hundred groaned. Seven's temporary acceptance was quicker; he had always been able to leap from side to side of a discussion. He flashed:

"Let us assume that in some unheard-of fashion, these small entities are indeed the domesticators, or even the builders, of that flying thing. Can we negotiate with them?"

"Not after what has happened," Zero said bleakly. He was thinking less about what he had done to them than what they had done to One.

Seven continued: "I doubt it myself, on philosophical grounds. They are too alien. Their very functioning is deadly: the destruction wrought by their flier, the poison under their skins. Eventually, a degree of mutual comprehension may be achieved. But that will be a slow and painful process. Our first responsibility is to our own form of existence. Therefore we must unmistakably get the upper hand, before we even try to talk with them." In quick excitement, he added, "And I think we can."

Zero and Hundred meshed their intellects with his. The scheme grew like precipitation in a supersaturated pond. Slow and feeble, the strangers were only formidable by virtue of highly developed artifacts (or, possibly, domesticated motiles of radically modified type): the flier, the tube which had blown off

Zero's arm, and other hypothetical weapons. But armament unused is no threat. If the flier could be immobilized—

Of course, presumably there were other dwarf bipeds inside it. Their voices had been heard yesterday. But Zero's trip here had proven that they lacked adequate nighttime senses. Well, grant them radar when in an undamaged condition. Radar can be confused, if one knows how.

Hundred's orders sprang forth across miles to the mountaineers now converging on the flier: "Cut the heaviest accumulator strands you can find in the forest. Twist them into cables. Under cover of darkness, radar window, and distraction objects, surround the monster. We believe now that it may not be sentient, only a flier. Weld your cables fast to deeply founded boles. Then, swiftly, loop them around the base of the flier. Tie it down!"

"No," said Twenty-nine, aghast. "We cannot weld the cables to its skin. It would annihilate us with one jetblast. We would have to make nooses first and—"

"So make the nooses," Zero said. "The monster is not a perfectly tapered spindle. The jets bulge out at the base. Slip the nooses around the body just above the jets. I hardly think it can rise then, without tearing its own tubes out."

"Easy for you to say, Zero, safe in your cave."

"If you knew what I would give to have matters otherwise—"

Abashed, the hunters yielded. Their mission was not really so dangerous. The nooses—two should be ample if the cable was heavy—could be laid in a broad circle around the area which the jets had flattened and devastated. They could be drawn tight from afar, and would probably slip upward by themselves, coming to rest just above the tubes, where the body of the flier was narrowest. If a cable did get stuck on something, someone would have to dash close and free it. A snort of jetfire during those few seconds would destroy him. But quite probably the flier, or its masters, could be kept from noticing him.

"And when we do have the monster leashed, what then?" asked Twenty-nine.

"We will do what seems indicated," Hundred said. "If the aliens do not seem to be reaching a satisfactory understanding with us—if we begin to entertain any doubts—we can erect trebuchets and batter the flier to pieces."

"That might be best," said Zero, with a revengeful look at One's rider.

"Proceed as ordered," said Hundred.

"But what about us?" Zero asked. "One and myself?"

"I shall come to you," Seven said. "If nothing else, we can stand watch and watch. You mentioned that the aliens polarize more easily than we do. We can wait until it drops from exhaustion."

"Good," said Zero. Hope lifted in him as if breaking through a shell. "Did you hear, One? We need only wait."

"Pain," she whispered. Then, resolutely: "I can minimize energy consumption. Comatose, I will not sense anything. . . ." He felt how she fought down terror, and guessed what frightened her: the idea that she might never be roused.

"I will be guarding you all the time," he said. "You and the new one."

"I wish I could touch you, Zero—" Her radiation dimmed, second by second. Once or twice consciousness returned, kicked upward by fear; static gasped in Zero's perception; but she slipped again into blackness.

When she was quite inert, he stood staring at the unit on her. No, the entity. Somewhere behind that glass and horrible tissue, a brain peered back at him. He ventured to move an arm. The thing jerked its weapon aloft. It seemed indeed to have guessed that the optics were her most vulnerable spot. With immense care, Zero let his arm fall again. The entity jittered about, incapable of his own repose. Good. Let it drain its energy the faster.

He settled into his own thoughts. Hours wore away. The alien paced on One's broad back, sat down, sprang up again, slapped first one hand and then another against its body, made long noises that might possibly be intended to fight off coma. Sometimes it plugged the water tube into its face. Frequently Zero saw what looked like a good chance to catch it off guard—with a sudden rush and a flailing blow, or an object snatched off the floor and thrown, or even a snap shot with his torch—but he decided not to take the hazard. Time was his ally.

Besides, now that his initial rage had abated, he began to hope he might capture the entity undamaged. Much more could be learned from a functional specimen than from the thing which lay dismembered near the iron block. Faugh, the gases it was giving off! Zero's chemical sensor retracted in disgust.

The first dawnlight grayed the cave mouth.

"We have the flier!" Twenty-nine's exuberant word made Zero leap where he stood. The alien scrambled into motion. When Zero came no closer, it sagged again. "We drew two cables around its body. No trouble whatsoever. It never stirred. Only made the same radio hum. It still has not moved."

"I thought—" someone else in his party ventured. "Not long ago . . . was there not a gibberish signal from above?"

"There might well be other fliers above the clouds," agreed Hundred from the valley. "Have a care. Disperse yourselves. Remain under cover. The rest of us will have rendezvoused by early afternoon. At that time we will confer afresh. Meanwhile, report if anything happens. And . . . good work, hunters."

Twenty-nine offered a brief sensory linkage. Thus Zero saw the place: the cindered blast area, and the upright spindle shining in the first long sunlight, and the cables that ran from its waist to a pair of old and mighty accumulator boles. Yes, the thing was captured for certain. Wind blew over the snowpeaks, set forest to chiming and scattered the little sunrise clouds. He had rarely known his land so beautiful.

The perception faded. He was in his cave again. Seven called: "I am getting close now, Zero. Shall I enter?"

"No, best not. You might alarm the alien into violence. I have watched its movements the whole night. They grow more slow and irregular each hour. It must be near collapse. Suppose you wait just outside. When I believe it to be comatose, I will have you enter. If it does not react to the sight of you, we will know it has lost consciousness."

"If it is conscious," mused Seven. "Despite our previous discussion, I cannot bring myself to believe quite seriously that these are anything but motiles or artifacts. Very ingenious and complex, to be sure . . . but *aware*, like a person?"

The unit made a long series of sonic noises. They were much weaker than hitherto. Zero allowed satisfaction to wax in him. Nevertheless, he would not have experienced this past night again for any profit.

Several hours later, a general alarm yanked his attention back outward. "The escaped auxiliary has returned! It has entered the flier!"

"What? You did not stop it?" Hundred demanded.

Twenty-nine gave the full report. "Naturally, after the change of plan, we were too busy weaving cables and otherwise preparing ourselves to beat the forest for the dwarf. After the flier was captured, we dispersed ourselves broadly as ordered. We made nothing like a tight circle around the blasted region. Moreover, our attention was directed at the flier, in case it tried to escape, and at the sky in case there should be more fliers. Various wild motiles were about, which we ignored, and the wind has gotten very loud in the accumulators. Under such circumstances, you will realize that probability actually favored the biped unit passing between us and reaching the open area unobserved.

"When it was first noticed, no person was close enough to reach the flier before it did. It slid a plate aside in one of the jacks which support the flier and pulled a switch. A portal opened in the body above and a ladder was extruded. By that time, a number of us had entered the clearing. The unit scrambled up the ladder. We hesitated, fearing a jetblast. None came. But how could we have predicted that? When at last we did approach, the ladder had been retracted and the portal was closed. I pulled the switch myself but nothing happened. I suppose the biped, once inside, deactivated that control by means of a master switch."

"Well, at least we know where it is," Hundred said. "Disperse again, if you have not already done so. The biped may try to escape, and you do not want to get caught in the jetblast. Are you certain the flier cannot break your cables?"

"Quite certain. Closely observed, the monster—the flier seems to have only a thin skin of light alloy. Nor would I expect it to be strong against the unnatural kind of stresses imposed by our tethers. If it tries to rise, it will pull itself in two."

"Unless," said Fourteen, as he hastened through valley mists toward Broken Glade, "some biped emerges with a torch and cuts the cables."

"Just let it dare!" said Twenty-nine, anxious to redeem his crew's failure.

"It may bring strong weapons," Zero warned.

"Ten crossbows are cocked and aimed at that portal. If a biped shows itself, we will fill it with whetted steel."

"I think that will suffice," Zero said. He looked at the drooping shape upon One. "They are not very powerful, these things. Ugly, cunning, but weak."

Almost as if it knew it was being talked about, the unit reeled to its feet and shook the pry bar at him. Even Zero could detect the dullness in its noises. *Another hour,* he thought, *and One will be free.*

Half that time had gone by when Seven remarked from outside, "I wonder why the builders . . . whoever the ultimate intelligences are behind these manifestations . . . why have they come?"

"Since they made no attempt to communicate with us," Zero said in renewed grimness, "we must assume their purpose is hostile."

"And?"

"Teach them to beware of us."

He felt already the pride of victory. But then the monster spoke.

Up over the mountains rolled the voice, driven by the power which hurled those hundreds of tons through the sky. Roaring and raging through the radio spectrum, louder than lightning, enormous enough to shake down moon and stars, blasted that shout. Twenty-nine and his hunters yelled as the volume smote their receptors. Their cry was lost, drowned, engulfed by the tide which seethed off the mountainsides. Here and there, where some accumulator happened to resonate, blue arcs of flame danced in the forest. Thirty miles distant, Zero and Seven still perceived the noise as a clamor in their heads. Hundred and his followers in the valley stared uneasily toward the ranges. On the seashore, females called, "What is that? What is that?" and aquamotiles dashed themselves about in the surf.

Seven forgot all caution. He ran into the cave. The enemy thing hardly moved. But neither Zero nor Seven observed that. Both returned to the entrance and gazed outward with terror.

The sky was empty. The forest rang in the breeze. Only that radio roar from beyond the horizon told of anything amiss. "I did not believe—" stammered Seven. "I did not expect—a tone that loud—"

Zero, who had One to think about, mustered decisiveness. "It is not hurting us," he said. "I am glad not to be as close as the hunters are, but even they should be able to endure it for a while. We shall see. Come, let us two go back inside. Once we have secured our prisoner—"

The monster began to talk.

No mere outrageous cry this time, but speech. Not words, except occasionally. A few images. But such occurrences were coincidental. The monster spoke in its own language, which was madness.

Seized along every radio receptor channel there was in him, total sensory and mental linkage, Zero became the monster.

DITditditditDAHdit-nulnulnulnul-ditditDAHdah & the vector sum: infinitesimals infinitelyadded from nul-to-INFINITY, dit—ditdit—DA—ditditditnul (gammacolored chaos, *bang* goes a universe scattering stars&planets& bursts-of-fire BLOCK THAT NEUTRON BLOCK THAT NEUTRON BLOCK THAT BLOCK THAT BLOCK THAT NEUTRON) oneone***nononul— DATTA—ditditchitterchitterchitter burning suns & moons, burning stars & brains, burningburningburning Burning DahditDahditDahdit give me fifty million logarithms this very microsecond or you will Burn ditditditdit— DAYADHVAM—DAMYATA

and one long wild logarithmic spiral down spacetimeenergy continuum of potentialgradient Xproduct i,j,k but multiply Time by the velocity of light in nothingness and the square root of minus one (two, three, four, five, six CHANGE for duodecimal computation   zzzzzzzzzzz)

buzzzzzzzzzzzZ

integral over sigma of del cross H d sigma equals one over c times integral over sigma partial of E with respect to t dot d sigma but correct for nonsphericalshapentropicoordinatetransformationtop&quantumelectrodynamichargelectricalephaselagradientemperature rising to burning Burning BURNING

dit-dit-chitterchitterchitter from eyrie to blind gnawer and back again O help the trunk is burningburningburning THEREFORE ANNUL in the name of the seven thunders

Everything-that-has-been, break up the roots of existence and strike flat the thick rotundity o' the world RRRIP spacetime across and throw it on the upleaping primordial energy for now all that was & will be, the very fact that it once *did* exist, is canceled and torn to pieces and Burning

Burning

Burning

Burning

As the sun fell down the bowl of sky, and the sky cracked open, and the mountains ran like rivers forming faces that gaped and jeered, and the moon rose in the west and spat the grisliness of what he had done at him, Zero ran. Seven did not; could not; lay by the cave entrance, which was the gate of all horrors and corruptions, as if turned to salt. And when God descended, still shouting in His tongue which was madness, His fiery tail melted Seven to a pool.

Fifty million years later the star called Wormwood ascended to heaven; and a great silence fell upon the land.

Eventually Zero returned home. He was not surprised to find that the biped was gone. Of course it had been reclaimed by its Master. But when he saw that One was not touched, he stood mute for a long while indeed.

After he roused her, she—who had been unawake when the world was broken and refashioned—could not understand why he led her outside to pray that they be granted mercy, now and in the hour of their dissolution.

7

Darkington did not regain full consciousness until the boat was in space. Then he pulled himself into the seat beside Frederika. "How did you do it?" he breathed.

Her attention remained focused on piloting. Even with the help of the director and radio instructions from the ship, it was no easy task for a novice. Absently, she answered, "I scared the robots away. They'd made the boat fast, you see. With cables too thick to pull apart. I had to go back out and cut them with a torch. But I'd barely gotten inside ahead of the pack. I didn't expect they would let me emerge. So I scared them off. After that, I went out, burned off the cables, and flew to get you."

"Barely in time," he shuddered. "I was about to pass out. I did keel over once I was aboard." A time went by with only the soft rushing noise of brake jets. "Okay," he said, "I give up. I admit you're beautiful, a marvel of resourcefulness, and I can't guess how you shooed away the enemy. So tell me."

The director shut off the engine. They floated free. She turned her face, haggard, sweaty, begrimed, and dear, toward him and said diffidently, "I didn't have any inspiration. Just a guess and nothing to lose. We knew for pretty sure that the robots communicated by radio. I turned the boat's 'caster on full blast, hoping the sheer volume would be too much for them. Then something else occurred to me. If you have a radio transceiver in your head, hooked directly into your nervous system, wouldn't that be sort of like telepathy? I mean, it seems more direct somehow than routing everything we say through a larynx.

Maybe I could confuse them by emitting unfamiliar signals. Not any old signals, of course. They'd be used to natural radio noise. But—well—the boat's general director includes a pretty complicated computer, carrying out millions of operations per second. Information is conveyed, not noise; but at the same time, it didn't seem to me like information that a bunch of semisavages could handle.

"Anyhow, there was no harm in trying. I hooked the broadcaster in parallel with the effector circuits, so the computer's output not only controlled the boat as usual but also modulated the radio emission. Then I assigned the computer a good tough problem in celestial navigation, put my armor back on, summoned every ounce of nerve I had, and went outside. Nothing happened. I cut the cables without seeing any trace of the robots, I kept the computer 'talking' while I jockeyed the boat over in search of the cave. It must have been working frantically to compensate for my clumsiness; I hate to imagine what its output 'sounded' like. Felt like? Well, when I'd landed, I opened the airlock and, and you came inside, and—" Her fists doubled. "Oh, God, Hugh! How can we tell Sam's girl?"

He didn't answer.

With a final soft impulse, the boat nudged against the ship. As grapnels made fast, the altered spin of the vessels put Earth back in view. Darkington looked at the planet for minutes before he said:

"Good-by. Good luck."

Frederika wiped her eyes with hands that left streaks of dirt in the tears. "Do you think we'll ever come back?" she wondered.

"No," he said. "It isn't ours any more."

XIII

Early on, Tony Boucher was pointing out that quite a few science fiction stories deal with crime or contain a mystery to be solved by reasoning from clues. On that basis he persuaded the Mystery Writers of America, in which organization he was a leading light, to admit the authors to membership. For long years afterward, Karen and I found the meetings to be rewarding experiences. Tony also encouraged science fiction writers to work directly in the field.

The result for me was three novels and several short stories. The hero of most was Trygve Yamamura, Hawaiian-born to a Japanese-American father and a Norwegian mother, eventually a private detective in Berkeley, California. Skilled in martial arts, he never used violence except when there was absolutely no choice, and then only what he absolutely must, being a gentle soul as well as an incisive thinker. I would have liked to continue with him, but was earning so much more by science fiction that it became impractical.

This tale skirts fantasy. It's set in 1962, when the great Columbus Day storm struck the Bay Area just as the Cuban missile crisis was brewing. Karen worked out the plot with me and therefore shared the byline. I wish the same to be understood here.

DEAD PHONE

That was an evil autumn, when the powers bared their teeth across an island in the Spanish Main and it seemed the world might burn. Afterward Americans looked at each other with a kind of wonder, and for a while they walked more straight. But whatever victory they had gained was soon taken away from them.

As if to warn, a fortnight earlier the weather ran amok. On the Pacific coast, gale force winds flung sea against land, day and night without end, and rainfall in northern California redressed the balance of a three-year drought in less than a week. At the climax of it, the hills around San Francisco Bay started to come down in mudslides that took houses and human bodies along, and the streets of some towns were turned into rivers.

Trygve Yamamura sat up late. His wife had taken the children to visit her cousin in the Mother Lode country over the Columbus Day weekend. His work kept him behind; so now he prowled the big hollow house on the Berkeley steeps, smoked one pipe after another, listened to the wind and the rain lashing

296

his roof and to the radio whose reports grew ever more sinister, and could not sleep.

Oh, yes, he told himself often and often, he was being foolish. They had undoubtedly arrived without trouble and were now snug at rest. In any event, he could do nothing to help, he was only exhausting himself, in violation of his entire philosophy. Tomorrow morning the phone line that had snapped, somewhere in those uplands, would be repaired, and he would hear their voices. But meanwhile his windowpanes were holes of blackness, and he started when a broken tree branch crashed against the wall.

He sought his basement gym and tried to exercise himself into calm. That didn't work either, simply added a different kind of weariness. He was worn down, he knew, badly in need of a vacation, with no immediate prospect of one. His agency had too many investigations going for him to leave the staff unsupervised.

He was also on edge because through various connections he knew more about the Cuban situation than had yet gotten into the papers. A nuclear showdown was beginning to look all too probable. Yamamura was not a pacifist, even when it came to that kind of war; but no sane man, most especially no man with wife and children, could coolly face abomination.

Toward midnight he surrendered. The Zen techniques had failed, or he had. His eyes felt hot and his brain gritty. He stripped, stood long under the shower, and at last, with a grimace, swallowed a sleeping pill.

The drug took quick hold of his unaccustomed body, but nonetheless he tossed about half awake and half in nightmare. It gibbered through his head, he stumbled among terrors and guilts, the sun had gone black while horrible stars rained down upon him. When the phone beside his bed rang he struck out with his fists and gasped.

Brring! the bell shouted across a light-year of wind and voices, *brring,* come to me, you must you must before that happens which has no name, *brring, brring,* you are damned to come and *brring* me her *brring brring brrRING!*

He struggled to wake. Night strangled him. He could not speak or see, so great was his need of air. The receiver made lips against his ear and kissed him obscenely while the dark giggled. Through whirl and seethe he heard a click, then a whistle that went on forever, and he had a moment to think that the noise was not like any in this world, it was as if he had a fever or as if nothing was at the other end of the line except the huntsman wind. His skull resounded with the querning of the planets. Yet when the voice came it was clear, steady, a little slow and very sad—but how remote, how monstrously far away.

"Come to me. It's so dark here."

Yamamura lay stiff in his own darkness.

"I don't understand," said the voice. "I thought . . . afterward I would know everything, or else nothing. But instead I don't understand. Oh, God, but it's lonely!"

For a space only the humming and the chill whistle were heard. Then: "Why did I call you, Trygve Yamamura? For help? What help is there now? You don't even know that we don't understand afterward. Were those pigs that I heard grunting in the forest, and did she come behind them in a black cloak? I'm all alone."

And presently: "Something must be left. I read somewhere once that you don't die in a piece. The last and lowest cells work on for hours. I guess that's true. Because you're still real, Trygve Yamamura." Another pause, as if for the thoughtful shaking of a weary head. "Yes, that must be why I called. What became of me, no, that's of no account any more. But the others. They won't stay real for very long. I had to call while they are, so you can help them. Come."

"Cardynge," Yamamura mumbled.

"No," said the voice. "Goodbye."

The instrument clicked off. Briefly the thin screaming continued along the wires, and then it too died, and nothing remained but the weight in Yamamura's hand.

He became conscious of the storm that dashed against the windows, fumbled around and snapped the lamp switch. The bedroom sprang into existence: warm yellow glow on the walls, mattress springy beneath him and covers tangled above, the bureau with the children's pictures on top. The clock said 1:35. He stared at the receiver before laying it back in its cradle.

"Whoof," he said aloud.

Had he dreamed that call? No, he couldn't have. As full awareness flowed into him, every nerve cried alarm. His lanky, thick-chested frame left the bed in one movement. Yanking the directory from its shelf below the stand, he searched for an address. Yes, here. He took the phone again and dialed.

"Berkeley police," said a tone he recognized.

"Joe? This is Trig Yamamura. I think I've got some trouble to report. Client of mine just rang me up. Damndest thing I ever heard, made no sense whatsoever, but he seems to be in a bad way and the whole thing suggests—" Yamamura stopped.

"Yes, what?" said the desk officer.

Yamamura pinched his lips together before he said, "I don't know. But you'd better send a car around to have a look."

"Trig, do *you* feel right? Don't you know what's happening outdoors? We may get a disaster call any minute, if a landslide starts, and we've got our hands full as is with emergencies."

"You mean this is too vague?" Yamamura noticed the tension that knotted his muscles. One by one he forced them to relax. "Okay, I see your point," he said. "But you know I don't blow the whistle for nothing, either. Dispatch a car as soon as possible, if you don't hear anything else from me. Meanwhile I'll get over there myself. The place isn't far from here."

"M-m-m . . . well, fair enough, seeing it's you. Who is the guy and where does he live?"

"Aaron Cardynge." Yamamura spelled the name and gave the address he had checked.

"Oh, yeah, I've heard of him. Medium-big importer, isn't he? I guess he wouldn't rouse you without some reason. Go ahead, then, and we'll alert the nearest car to stop by when it can."

"Thanks." Yamamura had started to skin out of his pajamas before he hung up.

He was back into his clothes, with a sweater above, very nearly as fast, and pulled on his raincoat while he kicked the garage door open. The wind screeched at him. When he backed the Volkswagen out, it trembled with that violence. Rain roared on its metal and flooded down the windshield; his headlights and the rear lamps were quickly gulped down by night. Through everything he could hear how water cascaded along the narrow, twisting hill streets and sheeted under his wheels. The brake drums must be soaked, he thought, and groped his way in second gear.

But the storm was something real to fight, that cleansed him of vague horrors. As he drove, with every animal skill at his command, he found himself thinking in a nearly detached fashion.

Why should Cardynge call me? I only met him once. And not about anything dangerous. Was it?

"I'm sorry, Mr. Cardynge," Yamamura said. "This agency doesn't handle divorce work."

The man across the desk shifted in his chair and took out a cigaret case. He was large-boned, portly, well-dressed, with gray hair brushed back above a rugged face. "I'm not here about that." He spoke not quite steadily and had some difficulty keeping his eyes on the detective's.

"Oh? I beg your pardon. But you told me—"

"Background. I . . . I'd tell a doctor as much as I could, too. So he'd have a better chance of helping me. Smoke?"

"No, thanks. I'm strictly a pipe man." More to put Cardynge at his ease than because he wanted one, Yamamura took a briar off the rack and charged it. "I don't know if we can help. Just what is the problem?"

"To find my son, I said. But you should know why he left and why it's urgent to locate him." Cardynge lit his cigaret and consumed it in quick, nervous puffs. "I don't like exposing my troubles. Believe me. Always made my own way before."

Yamamura leaned back, crossed his long legs, and regarded the other through a blue cloud. "I've heard worse than anything you're likely to have on your mind," he said. "Take your time."

Cardynge's troubled gaze sought the flat half-Oriental countenance before him. "I guess the matter isn't too dreadful at that," he said. "Maybe not even as sordid as it looks from the inside. And it's nearing an end now. But I've got to find Bayard, my boy, soon.

"He's my son by my first marriage. My wife died two years ago. I married Lisette a year later. Indecent haste? I don't know. I'd been so happy before. Hadn't realized how happy, till Maria was gone and I was rattling around alone in the house. Bayard was at the University most of the time, you see. This would be his junior year. He had an apartment of his own. We'd wanted him to, the extra cost was nothing to us and he should have that taste of freedom, don't you think? Afterward . . . he'd have come back to stay with me if I asked. He offered to. But, oh, call it kindness to him, or a desire to carry on what Maria and I had begun, or false pride—I said no, that wasn't necessary, I could get along fine. And I did, physically. Had a housekeeper by day but cooked my own dinner, for something to do. I'm not a bad amateur cook."

Cardynge brought himself up short, stubbed out his cigaret, and lit another. "Not relevant," he said roughly, "except maybe to show why I made my mistake. A person gets lonesome eating by himself.

"Bayard's a good boy. He did what he could for me. Mainly that amounted to visiting me pretty often. More and more, he'd bring friends from school along. I enjoyed having young people around. Maria and I had always hoped for several children.

"Lisette got included in one of those parties. She was older than the rest, twenty-five, taking a few graduate courses. Lovely creature, witty, well-read, captivating manners. I . . . I asked Bayard to be sure and invite her for next time. Then I started taking her out myself. Whirlwind courtship, I suppose. I'm still not sure which of us was the whirlwind, though."

Cardynge scowled. His left hand clenched. "Bayard tried to warn me," he said. "Not that he knew her any too well. But he did know she was one of the—it isn't fashionable to call them beat any more, is it? The kind who spend most of their time hanging around in the coffee shops bragging about what they're going to do someday, and meanwhile cadging their living any way they can. Though that doesn't describe Lisette either. She turned out to have a good deal more force of character than that bunch. Anyhow, when he saw I was serious, Bayard begged me not to go any further with her. We had quite a fight about it. I married her a couple of days later."

Cardynge made a jerky sort of shrug. "Never mind the details," he said. "I soon learned she was a bitch on wheels. At first, after seeing what happened to our joint checking account, I thought she was simply extravagant. But what she said, and did, when I tried to put the brakes on her—! Now I'm morally certain she didn't actually spend most of the money, but socked it away somewhere. I also know she had lovers. She taunted me with that, at the end.

"Before then she drove Bayard out. You can guess how many little ways there are to make a proud, sensitive young man unwelcome in his own father's house. Finally he exploded and told the truth about her, to both our faces. I still felt honor bound to defend her, at least to the extent of telling him to shut up or leave. 'Very well, I'll go,' he said, and that was the last I saw of him. Four months back. He simply left town."

"Have you heard anything from him since?" Yamamura asked.

"A short letter from Seattle, some while ago." Cardynge finished his cigaret and extracted a fresh one. "Obviously trying to mend his friendship with me, if not her. He only said he was okay, but the job he'd found was a poor one. He'd heard of better possibilities elsewhere, so he was going to go have a look and he'd write again when he was settled. I haven't heard yet. I tried to get his current address from his draft board, but they said they weren't allowed to release any such information. So I came to you."

"I see." Yamamura drew on his pipe. "Don't worry too much, Mr. Cardynge. He sounds like a good, steady kid, who'll land on his feet."

"Uh-huh. But I must locate him. You see, Lisette and I separated month before last. Not formally. We . . . we've even seen each other on occasion. She can still be lovely in every way, when she cares to. I've been sending her money, quite a decent sum. But she says she wants to come back."

"Do you want her yourself?"

"No. It's a fearful temptation, but I'm too well aware of what the end result would be. So she told me yesterday, if I didn't take her back, she'd file for divorce. And you know what a woman can do to a man in this state."

"Yeah."

"I'm quite prepared to make a reasonable settlement," Cardynge said. "A man ought to pay for his mistakes. But I'll be damned if I'll turn over so much to her that it ruins the business my son was going to inherit."

"Um-m-m . . . are you sure he really wants to?"

"I am. He was majoring in business administration on that account. But your question's a very natural one, though, which is also bound to occur to the courts. If Bayard isn't here at the trial, it won't seem as if he has much interest that needs protection. Also, he's the main witness to prove the, the mental cruelty wasn't mine. At least, not entirely mine—I think." Cardynge gestured savagely with his cigaret. "All right, I married a girl young enough to be my daughter. We look at life differently. But I tried to please her."

Yamamura liked him for the admission.

"I've no proof about the lovers," Cardynge said, "except what she told me herself in our last fight. And, well, indications. You know. Never mind, I won't ask anyone to poke into that. Lisette was nearly always charming in company. And I'm not given to weeping on my friends' shoulders. So, as I say, we need Bayard's testimony. If there's to be any kind of justice done. In fact, if we can get him back before the trial, I'm sure she'll pull in her horns. The whole wretched business can be settled quietly, no headlines, no—You understand?"

"I believe so." Yamamura considered him a while before asking gently, "You're still in love with her, aren't you?"

Cardynge reddened. Yamamura wondered if he was going to get up and walk out. But he slumped and said, "If so, I'll get over it. Will you take the case?"

The rest of the discussion was strictly ways and means.

Rain pursued Yamamura to the porch of the house. Right and left and behind was only blackness, the neighborhood slept. But here light spilled from the front windows, made his dripping coat shimmer and glistened on the spears that slanted past the rail. The wind howled too loudly for him to hear the doorbell.

But the man inside ought to—

Yamamura grew aware that he had stood ringing for well over a minute. Perhaps the bell was out of order. He seized the knocker and slammed it down hard, again and again. Nothing replied but the storm.

Damnation! He tried the knob. The door opened. He stepped through and closed it behind him. "Hello," he called. "Are you here, Mr. Cardynge?"

The whoop outside felt suddenly less violent than it was—distant, unreal, like that voice over the wire. The house brimmed with silence.

It was a big, old-fashioned house; the entry hall where he stood was only dully lit from the archway to the living room. Yamamura called once more and desisted. The sound was too quickly lost. *Maybe he went out. I'll wait.* He hung coat and hat on the rack and passed on in.

The room beyond, illuminated by a ceiling light and a floor lamp, was large and low, well furnished but with the comfortable slight shabbiness of a long-established home. At the far end was a couch with a coffee table in front.

Cardynge lay there.

Yamamura plunged toward him. "Hey!" he shouted, and got no response. Cardynge was sprawled full length, neck resting across the arm of the couch. Though his eyes were closed, the jaw had dropped open and the face was without color. Yamamura shook him a little. The right leg flopped off the edge; its shoe hit the carpet with a thud that had no resonance.

Judas priest! Yamamura grabbed a horribly limp wrist. The flesh did not feel cold, but it yielded too much to pressure. He couldn't find any pulse.

His watch crystal was wet. On the table stood a nearly empty fifth of bourbon, a glass with some remnants of drink, and a large pill bottle. Yamamura reached out, snatched his fingers back—possible evidence there—and brought Cardynge's left arm to the mouth. That watch didn't fog over.

His first thought was of artificial respiration. Breath and heart could not have stopped very long ago. He noticed the dryness of the tongue, the uncleanliness elsewhere. *Long enough,* he thought, and rose.

The storm hurled itself against silence and fell back. In Yamamura's mind everything was overriden by the marble clock that ticked on the mantel, the last meaningful sound in the world. He had rarely felt so alone.

What had Cardynge said, in his call?

Yamamura started across the room to the telephone, but checked himself. Could be fingerprints. The police would soon arrive anyway, and there was no use in summoning a rescue squad which might be needed another place.

He returned to the body and stood looking down. Poor Cardynge. He hadn't appeared a suicidal type; but how much does any human know of any other? The body was more carefully dressed, in suit and clean shirt and tie, than one might have expected from a man baching it. Still, the room was neat too. Little more disturbed its orderliness than a couple of butts and matches in an ashtray on the end table next to the couch. No day servant could maintain such conditions by herself.

Wait a bit. A crumpled sheet of paper, on the floor between couch and coffee table. Yamamura stopped, hesitated, and picked it up. Even dead, his client had a claim on him.

He smoothed it out with care. It had originally been folded to fit an envelope. A letter, in a woman's handwriting, dated yesterday.

My dear Aaron—

—for you were very dear to me once, and in a way you still are. Not least, I suppose, because you have asked me to return to you, after all the heartbreak and bitterness. And yes, I believe you when you swear you will try to make everything different between us this time. Will you, then, believe me when I tell you how long and agonizingly hard I have thought since we spoke of this? How it hurts me so much to refuse you that I can't talk of it, even over the phone, but have to write this instead?

But if I came back it would be the same hideous thing over again. Your temper, your inflexibility, your suspicion. Your son returning, as he will, and your inability to see how insanely he hates me for taking his mother's place, how he will work and work until he succeeds in poisoning your mind about me. And I'm no saint myself. I admit that. My habits, my outlook, my demands—am I cruel to say that you are too old for them?

No, we would only hurt each other the worse. I don't want that, for you or for myself. So I can't come back.

I'm going away for a while, I don't know where, or if I did know I wouldn't tell you, because you might not stop pleading with me and that would be too hard to bear. I don't want to see you again. Not for a long time, at least, till our wounds have scarred. I'll get an attorney to settle the business part with you. I wish you everything good. Won't you wish the same for me? Goodbye, Aaron.

Lisette

Yamamura stared into emptiness. *I wonder what she'll think when she learns what this letter drove him to do.*

She may even have counted on it.

He put the sheet back approximately as he had found it, and unconsciously wiped his fingers on his trousers. In his need to keep busy, he squatted to examine the evidence on the table. His nose was keen, he could detect a slight acridness in the smell about the glass. The bottle from the drugstore held sleeping pills prescribed for Cardynge. It was half empty. Barbiturates and alcohol can be a lethal combination.

And yet—Yamamura got to his feet. He was not unacquainted with death, he had looked through a number of its many doors and the teachings of the Buddha made it less terrible to him than to most. But something was wrong here. The sense of that crawled along his nerves.

Perhaps only the dregs of the nightmare from which Cardynge had roused him.

Yamamura wanted his pipe in the worst way. But better not smoke before the police had seen what was here . . . as a matter of form, if nothing else. Form was something to guard with great care, on this night when chaos ran loose beyond the walls and the world stood unmeasurably askew within them.

He began to prowl. A wastepaper basket was placed near the couch. Struck by a thought—his logical mind functioned swiftly and unceasingly, as if to weave a web over that which lay below—he crouched and looked in. Only two items. The housekeeper must have emptied the basket today, and Cardynge tossed these in after he got back from his office. He wouldn't have observed the holiday; few establishments did, and he would have feared leisure. Yamamura fished them out.

One was a cash register receipt from a local liquor store, dated today. The amount shown corresponded to the price of a fifth such as stood on the table. Lord, but Cardynge must have been drunk, half out of his skull, when he prepared that last draught for himself!

The other piece was an envelope, torn open by hand, addressed here and postmarked yesterday evening in Berkeley. So he'd have found it in his mail when he came home this afternoon. In the handwriting of the letter, at the upper left corner, stood *Lisette Cardynge* and the apartment address her husband had given Yamamura.

The detective dropped them back into the basket and rose with a rather forced shrug. So what? If anything, this clinched the matter. One need merely feel compassion now, an obligation to find young Bayard—no, not even that, since the authorities would undertake it—so, no more than a wish to forget the whole business. There was enough harm and sorrow in the world without brooding on the unamendable affairs of a near stranger.

Only . . . Cardynge had wakened him, helplessly crying for help. And the wrongness would not go away.

Yamamura swore at himself. What was it that looked so impossible here? Cardynge's telephoning? He'd spoken strangely, even—or especially—for a man at the point of self-murder. *Though he may have been delirious. And certainly I was half asleep, in a morbid state, myself. I could have mixed his words with my dreams, and now be remembering things he never said.*

The suicide, when Cardynge read Lisette's ultimate refusal?

Or the refusal itself? Was it in character for her? Yamamura's mind twisted away from the room, two days backward in time.

———

He was faintly relieved when she came to his office. Not that the rights or wrongs of the case had much to do with the straightforward task of tracing Bayard and explaining why he should return. But Yamamura always preferred to hear both sides of a story.

He stood up as she entered. Sunlight struck through the window, a hurried shaft between clouds, and blazed on her blond hair. She was tall and slim, with long green eyes in a singularly lovely face, and she walked like a cat. "How do you do?" he said. Her hand lingered briefly in his before they sat down, but the gesture looked natural. He offered her a cigaret from a box he kept for visitors. She declined.

"What can I do for you, Mrs. Cardynge?" he asked, with a little less than his normal coolness.

"I don't know," she said unhappily. "I've no right to bother you like this."

"You certainly do, since your husband engaged me. I suppose he is the one who told you?"

"Yes. We saw each other yesterday, and he said he'd started you looking for his son. Do you think you'll find him?"

"I have no doubts. The man I sent to Seattle called in this very morning. He'd tracked down some of Bayard's associates there, who told him the boy had gone to Chicago. No known address, but probably as simple a thing as an ad in the paper will fetch him. It's not as if he were trying to hide."

She stared out of the window before she swung those luminous eyes back and said, "How can I get you to call off the search?"

Yamamura chose his words with care. "I'm afraid you can't. I've accepted a retainer."

"I could make that up to you."

Yamamura bridled. "Ethics forbid."

One small hand rose to her lips. "Oh, I'm so sorry. Please don't think I'm offering a bribe. But—" She blinked hard, squared her shoulders, and faced him head on. "Isn't there such a thing as a higher ethic?"

"Well-ll . . . what do you mean, Mrs. Cardynge?"

"I suppose Aaron praised Bayard at great length. And quite honestly, too, from his own viewpoint. His only son, born of his first wife, who must have been a dear person. How *could* Aaron see how evil he is?"

Yamamura made a production of charging his pipe. "I hear there was friction between you and the boy," he said.

A tired little smile tugged at her mouth. "You put it mildly. And of course I'm prejudiced. After all, he wrecked my marriage. Perhaps 'evil' is too strong a word. Nasty? And that may apply to nothing but his behavior toward me.

Which in turn was partly resentment at my taking his mother's place, and partly—" Lisette stopped.

"Go on," said Yamamura, low.

Color mounted in her cheeks. "If you insist. I think he was in love with me. Not daring to admit it to himself, he did everything he could to get me out of his life. And out of his father's. He was more subtle than a young man ought to be, though. Insinuations; provocations; disagreements carefully nursed into quarrels—" She gripped the chair arms. "Our marriage, Aaron's and mine, would never have been a simple one to make work. The difference in age, outlook, everything. I'm not perfect either, not easy to live with. But I was trying. Then Bayard made the job impossible for both of us."

"He left months ago," Yamamura pointed out.

"By that time the harm was done, even if he didn't realize it himself."

"Does it matter to you any more what he does?"

"Yes. I—Aaron wants me to come back." She looked quickly up. "No doubt he's told you otherwise. He has a Victorian sense of privacy. The sort of man who maintains appearances, never comes out of his shell, until at last the pressure inside gets too great and destroys him. But he's told me several times since I left that I can come back any time I want."

"And you're thinking of doing so?"

"Yes. Though I can't really decide. It would be hard on us both, at best, and nearly unbearable if we fail again. But I do know that Bayard's presence would make the thing absolutely impossible." She clasped her purse with a desperate tightness. "And even if I decide not to try, if I get a divorce, the lies Bayard would tell—Please, Mr. Yamamura! Don't make a bad matter worse!"

The detective struck match to tobacco and did not speak until he had the pipe going. "I'm sorry," he said. "But I can't decree that a father should not get in touch with his son. Even if I did resign from the case, he can hire someone else. And whatever happens, Bayard won't stay away forever. Sooner or later you'll have to face this problem. Won't you?"

The bright head bent. "I'm sorry," Yamamura said again.

She shook herself and jumped to her feet. "That's all right," she whispered. "I see your point. Of course. Don't worry about me. I'll manage. Thanks for your trouble." He could scarcely rise before she was gone.

The doorbell jarred Yamamura to awareness. As he opened for the patrolman, the storm screamed at him. "Hi, Charlie," he said in a mutter. "You didn't have a useless trip. Wish to hell you had."

Officer Moffat hung up his slicker. "Suicide?"

"Looks that way. Though—well, come see for yourself."

Moffat spoke little before he had examined what was in the living room. Then he said, "Joe told me this was a client of yours, and he called you tonight. What'd he want?"

"I don't know." Yamamura felt free, now, to console himself with his pipe. "His words were so incoherent, and I was so fogged with sleep myself, that I can't remember very well. Frankly I'm just as glad."

"That figures for a suicide. Also the Dear John letter. What makes you so doubtful?"

Yamamura bit hard on his pipestem. The bowl became a tiny campfire over which to huddle. "I can't say. You know how it is when you're having a dream, and something is gruesomely wrong but you can't find out what, only feel that it is? That's what this is like."

He paused. "Of course," he said, seeking rationality, "Cardynge and his wife told me stories which were somewhat inconsistent. She claimed to me he wanted her back; he denied it. But you know how big a liar anyone can become when his or her most personal affairs are touched on. Even if he spoke truth at the time, he could have changed his mind yesterday. In either case, he'd have gotten drunk when she refused in this note, and if it turned out to be an unhappy drunk he could have hit the absolute bottom of depression and killed himself."

"Well," Moffat said, "I'll send for the squad." He laid a handkerchief over the phone and put it to his ear. "Damn! Line must be down somewhere. I'll have to use the car radio."

Yamamura remained behind while the policeman grumbled his way back into the rain. His eyes rested on Cardynge's face. It was so recently dead that a trace of expression lingered, but nothing he could read. As if Cardynge were trying to tell him something. . . . The thought came to Yamamura that this house was now more alive than its master, for it could still speak.

Impulsively, he went through the inner door and snapped on the light. Dining room, with a stiff, unused look; yes, the lonely man doubtless ate in the kitchen. Yamamura continued thither.

That was a fair-sized place, in cheerful colors which now added to desolation. It was as neat as everything else. One plate, silverware, and coffee apparatus stood in the drainrack. They were dry, but a dishtowel hung slightly damp. Hm . . . Cardynge must have washed his things quite shortly before he mixed that dose. Something to do with his hands, no doubt, a last effort to fend off the misery that came flooding over him. Yamamura opened the garbage pail, saw a well-gnawed T-bone and the wrappers from packages of frozen peas and French fries. Proof, if any were needed, that Cardynge had eaten here, doubtless been here the whole time. The refrigerator held a good bit of food; one ice tray was partly empty. Yamamura went on to the bathroom and bedrooms without noticing anything special.

Moffat came back in as the other man regained the living room. "They're on their way," he said. "I'll stick around here. You might as well go on home, Trig."

"I suppose so." Yamamura hesitated. "Who'll notify his wife?"

Moffat regarded him closely. "You've met her, you said, and know something about the case. Think you'd be able to break the news gently?"

"I don't know. Probably not. Anyhow, looks as if I'll have to tell his son, when we find him."

Moffat tilted back his cap and rubbed his head. "Son left town? We'll have to interview him ourselves. To tie up loose ends, make sure he really was away and so forth. Not that—Huh?"

Yamamura picked his pipe off the floor.

"What's the matter, Trig?"

"Nothing." The detective wheeled about, stared at the body on the couch and then out the window into night.

"Uh, one thing," Moffat said. "Since you do know a little about her. Think we should notify Mrs. Cardynge at once, or let her sleep till morning?"

It yelled within Yamamura.

"I mean, you know, theoretically we should send someone right off," Moffat said, "but even if she has left him, this is going to be a blow. Especially since she's indirectly respon—"

Yamamura snatched Moffat's arm. "Yes!" he cried. "Right away! Can you get a man there this instant?"

"What?"

"To arrest her!"

"Trig, are you crazy as that stiff was?"

"We may already be too late. Get back to your radio!"

Moffat wet his lips. "What do you mean?"

"The purse. Hers. The evidence will be there, if she hasn't had time to get rid of it—By God, if you don't, I'll make a citizen's arrest myself!"

Moffat looked into the dilated eyes a full second before he pulled himself loose. "Okay, Trig. What's her address again?" Yamamura told him and he ran off without stopping to put on his coat.

Yamamura waited, pipe smoldering in his hand. A dark peace rose within him. The wrongness had departed. There was nothing here worse than a dead man and a night gone wild.

Moffat re-entered, drenched and shivering. "I had to give them my word I had strong presumptive evidence," he said. "Well, I know what you've done in the past. But this better be good."

"Good enough, if we aren't too late," Yamamura said. He pointed to the ashtray. "Cardynge was pretty nervous when he talked to me," he went on. "He hated to bare his soul. So he smoked one cigaret after another. But here—two butts for an entire evening. If you look in the kitchen, you'll find that he made a hearty meal. And washed up afterward. Does any of this square with a man utterly shattered by a Dear John letter?

"The dishes are dry in the rack. But something was washed more recently. The towel is still moist, even though the saliva has dried in the corpse's mouth. What was washed? And by whom?"

Moffat grew rigid. "You mean that letter's a plant? But the envelope—"

"Something else was in that envelope. 'Dear Aaron, can I come see you tonight on a very private matter? Lisette.' She came with a pretext for discussion that could not have been particularly disturbing to him. Nor could her presence have been; his mind was made up about her. But they had a few drinks together.

"At some point she went to the bathroom, taking her glass along, and loaded it with powder poured from the capsules. Then, I'd guess, while he went, she switched glasses with him. She'd know he used sleeping pills. Convenient for her. Still, if he had not, she could have gotten some other poison without too much trouble or danger.

"Of course, she couldn't be sure the dose would prove fatal, especially since I doubt if they drank much. Maybe she patted his head, soothed him, so he drifted into unconsciousness without noticing. He'd take a while, possibly an hour or two, to die. She must have waited, meanwhile arranging things. Washed both glasses that had her prints on them, fixed the one on the table here and clasped his hand around it for prints and poured most of the whiskey down the sink.

"If he'd started coming around, she could have returned the pill bottle to the bathroom and told him he'd had a fainting spell or whatever. She could even say she'd tried to get a doctor, but none could or would come. He wouldn't be suspicious. As things turned out, though, he died and she left. The only thing she overlooked was the evidence of the food and cigarets."

Moffat tugged his chin. "The autopsy will show how much he did or did not drink," he said. "Did that occur to her?"

"Probably. But it's no solid proof. He didn't *have* to be on a tear when he decided to end his life. The missing booze could've been spilled accidentally.

But it would help plant the idea of suicide in people's minds. She's clever. Ruthless. And one hell of a fine actress."

"Motive?"

"Money. If Bayard testified against her in the divorce proceedings, she'd get nothing but the usual settlement. But as a widow, she'd inherit a mighty prosperous business. She married him in the first place for what she could get out of him, of course."

Moffat clicked his tongue. "I'd hoped for better than this from you, Trig," he said with a note of worry. "You're really reaching."

"I know. This is more hunch than anything else. There won't even be legal grounds for an indictment, if she's disposed of the proof."

"Do you suppose she was mistaken about his being dead, and after she left he roused himself long enough to call you? That sounds unlikeliest of all."

"No argument," said Yamamura grimly. "That call's the one thing I can't explain."

They fell silent, amidst the rain and wind and relentless clock-tick, until the homicide squad arrived. The first officer who came in the door looked pleased, in a bleak fashion. "We got the word on our way here," he said. "She wasn't home, so the patrolman waited. She arrived a few minutes afterward."

"Must have left this house—" Yamamura looked at his watch. 2:27. Had the whole thing taken so short a while? "About an hour ago, seeing I was phoned then. Even in this weather, that's slow driving."

"Why, no. She said twenty minutes or thereabouts."

"What? You're sure? How do you know?"

"Oh, she broke down and confessed all over the place, as soon as Hansen asked where she'd been and looked in her purse."

Yamamura let out his breath in a long, shaken sigh.

"What was there?" Moffat asked.

"The original note, which asked for this meeting and furnished an envelope to authenticate the fake one," Yamamura said. "I was hoping she'd taken it back with her, to destroy more thoroughly than she might have felt safe in doing here." More sadness than victory was in his tone: "I admit I'm surprised she spilled her guts so fast. But it must have affected her more than she'd anticipated, to sit and watch her husband die, with nothing but that clock speaking to her."

The discrepancy hit him anew. He turned to the homicide officer and protested: "She can't have left here only twenty minutes ago. That's barely before my arrival. Cardynge woke me almost half an hour before that!"

"While she was still here—?" Moffat contemplated Yamamura for a time that grew long. "Well," he said at length, "maybe she'd gone to the can." He took the phone. "We just might be able to check that call, if we hurry."

"The line's dead," Yamamura reminded him.

"No, I get a dial tone now," Moffat said. "They must've repaired it a few minutes ago. Hello, operator—"

Yamamura became occupied with explaining his presence and showing the squad around. When they came back to the living room, Moffat had cradled the phone. He stood so unmoving that their own feet halted.

"What's the matter, Charlie?" the inspector asked. "You look like the devil. Couldn't you find out anything?"

"No." Moffat shook his head, slowly, as if it weighed too much. "There wasn't any call."

"What?" Yamamura exclaimed.

"You heard me," Moffat said. "This line went down about midnight. Wasn't fixed till now." He took a step forward. "Okay, Trig. What really brought you here?"

"A phone call, I tell you." Yamamura's back ached with a tension he could not will away. "From Cardynge."

"And I tell you that's impossible."

Yamamura stood a while hearing the clock tick. Finally, flatly, he said: "All right. Maybe there never was a call. I was half asleep, half awake, my brain churning. I guess that subconsciously I was worried about Cardynge, and so I dreamed the message, even took the phone off the rack, it felt so real."

"Well . . . yes." Moffat began to relax. "That must be what happened. Funny coincidence, though."

"It better be a coincidence," Yamamura said.

The men looked simultaneously at the body, and at the phone, and away.

XIV

A personal note: The Columbus Day storm sank a houseboat that Jack Vance, Frank Herbert, and I were building. We'd worked on her for two or three years' worth of Sundays—unforgettable companionship and jollity—and were near completion. Twin hulls supported the house. Unbeknownst to us, the Fiberglas on one had been rubbed off against a piling at the little marina where she lay docked and teredos had gotten at the plywood underneath. When wind and wave battered the weakened structure, it gave way and went down, pulling the ventilator on its mate below the water and thus flooding it too. At high tide only a corner of the house stuck forlornly into the air.

In those days before *Dune* Frank had a newspaper job. So it fell on Jack and me to raise her. We worked full-time for a month, trying this and that, till we found a way. In case you ever need to know, we filled a lot of gunny sacks with scrap plastic foam, which gave them so much flotation that a swimmer couldn't submerge them by himself. We tied a rock and a hook to a rope. One man stood on the wharf, attached a bag, and threw it over the side. Then the other, in a wet suit, took it down and secured it to the bottom of a hull. We learned that barnacles gripped it hard enough that nothing else was needed, probably the first use anybody has found for barnacles since keelhauling went out of fashion. He unhooked it and swam back while the dry man pulled the apparatus up again. After scores of repetitions, she rose. Frank joined us in pumping her out, beaching her, and making repairs—which, this time, included filling the hulls with foam.

He and his wife moved to Seattle before the job was finished. A friend replaced him, not a writer but a good guy just the same. At last we could motor her up to the beautiful Sacramento-San Joaquin Delta country to be a floating summer cottage for our families. What grand times those were too.

Ever since the old pulp magazine days, science fiction people, fans and pros together, have had that unique closeness, forming what's been almost an extended family. The sheer size of the field has now much diluted this, but it's still there at the core, and many a work has originated half accidentally, because somebody happened to be with somebody else and it sparked an idea. The next story here gives an example.

When Damon Knight and his wife lived in Milford, Pennsylvania, they took to hosting an annual, invitational writers' conference. Attenders brought manuscripts for their peers to criticize, often ruthlessly, then in the evenings they partied. Karen and I were only there in 1966, but enjoyed it immensely.

Who wouldn't, in company with the likes of Gordon Dickson, Richard MacKenna, James Blish, John Brunner, Anne McCaffrey, Alan Nourse, Ted Cogswell, Phyllis Gotlieb—The list would be too long. On one of those evenings Harlan Ellison felt like doing a new story. He settled down with his typewriter in the otherwise empty dining room. From time to time he'd pop out into the smoky, boozy, noisy, cheery turmoil, shout a question at someone, get a reply, and pop back in. I remember he asked me about a point in Norse mythology and, caught off guard, I gave him a not-quite-correct answer; but no matter. Next day we all saw the story. It was "I Have No Mouth and I Must Scream"—a title which, by the way, came from a cartoon by fan artist William Rotsler.

I think it was these associations as well as its power that made it haunt me. No doubt Cocteau's film *Orpheus* had some influence too. Finally everything crystallized as "Goat Song." About the only similarity between the two science fiction tales is the concept of human personalities preserved after death as data in a giant, probably quantum-mechanical computer system, for eventual resurrection either into virtual reality or as downloads into new bodies. Harlan didn't have a patent on it, but it was pretty new at the time, and I thought it proper to request his okay, which he graciously gave. The story quickly sold to a well-paying magazine, but hadn't been published when the magazine folded. After it had languished for years, I got it back (my thanks to Barry Malzberg for advice about what to do) and placed it in *Fantasy and Science Fiction*. It was well-received, winning awards and being reprinted several times, though not recently. How I wish Tony could have seen it. But he had long since resigned his editorship, and died in 1968.

GOAT SONG

Three women: one is dead; one is alive; One is both and neither, and will never live and never die, being immortal in SUM.

On a hill above that valley through which runs the highroad, I await Her passage. Frost came early this year, and the grasses have paled. Otherwise the slope is begrown with blackberry bushes that have been harvested by men and birds, leaving only briars, and with certain apple trees. They are very old, those trees, survivors of an orchard raised by generations which none but SUM now remembers (I can see a few fragments of wall thrusting above the brambles)— scattered crazily over the hillside and as crazily gnarled. A little fruit remains on them. Chill across my skin, a gust shakes loose an apple. I hear it knock on the earth, another stroke of some eternal clock. The shrubs whisper to the wind.

Elsewhere the ridges around me are wooded, afire with scarlets and brasses and bronzes. The sky is huge, the westering sun wan-bright. The valley is filling with a deeper blue, a haze whose slight smokiness touches my nostrils. This is Indian summer, the funeral pyre of the year.

There have been other seasons. There have been other lifetimes, before mine and hers; and in those days they had words to sing with. We still allow ourselves music, though, and I have spent much time planting melodies around my rediscovered words. *"In the greenest growth of the Maytime—"* I unsling the harp on my back, and tune it afresh, and sing to her, straight into autumn and the waning day.

> "—You came, and the sun came after,
> And the green grew golden above:
> And the flag-flowers lightened with laughter,
> And the meadowsweet shook with love."

A footfall stirs the grasses, quite gently, and the woman says, trying to chuckle, "Why, thank you."

Once, so soon after my one's death that I was still dazed by it, I stood in the home that had been ours. This was on the hundred and first floor of a most desirable building. After dark the city flamed for us, blinked, glittered, flung immense sheets of radiance forth like banners. Nothing but SUM could have controlled the firefly dance of a million aircars among the towers: or, for that matter, have maintained the entire city, from nuclear powerplants through automated factories, physical and economic distribution networks, sanitation, repair, services, education, culture, order, everything as one immune immortal organism. We had gloried in belonging to this as well as to each other.

But that night I told the kitchen to throw the dinner it had made for me down the waste chute, and ground under my heel the chemical consolations which the medicine cabinet extended to me, and kicked the cleaner as it picked up the mess, and ordered the lights not to go on, anywhere in our suite. I stood by the viewall, looking out across megalopolis, and it was tawdry. In my hands I had a little clay figure she had fashioned herself. I turned it over and over and over.

But I had forgotten to forbid the door to admit visitors. It recognized this woman and opened for her. She had come with the kindly intention of teasing me out of a mood that seemed to her unnatural. I heard her enter, and looked around through the gloom. She had almost the same height as my girl did, and her hair chanced to be bound in a way that my girl often favored, and the figurine dropped from my grasp and shattered, because for an instant I thought she was my girl. Since then I have been hard put not to hate Thrakia.

This evening, even without so much sundown light, I would not make that mistake. Nothing but the silvery bracelet about her left wrist bespeaks the past we share. She is in wildcountry garb: boots, kilt of true fur and belt of true leather, knife at hip and rifle slung on shoulder. Her locks are matted and snarled, her skin brown from weeks of weather; scratches and smudges show beneath the fantastic zigzags she has painted in many colors on herself. She wears a necklace of bird skulls.

Now that one who is dead was, in her own way, more a child of trees and horizons than Thrakia's followers. She was so much at home in the open that she had no need to put off clothes or cleanliness, reason or gentleness, when we sickened of the cities and went forth beyond them. From this trait I got many of the names I bestowed on her, such as Wood's Colt or Fallow Hind or, from my prowlings among ancient books, Dryad and Elven. (She liked me to choose her names, and this pleasure had no end, because she was inexhaustible.)

I let my harpstring ring into silence. Turning about, I say to Thrakia, "I wasn't singing for you. Not for anyone. Leave me alone."

She draws a breath. The wind ruffles her hair and brings me an odor of her: not female sweetness, but fear. She clenches her fists and says, "You're crazy."

"Wherever did you find a meaningful word like that?" I gibe; for my own pain and—to be truthful—my own fear must strike out at something, and here she stands. "Aren't you content any longer with 'untranquil' or 'disequilibrated'?"

"I got it from you," she says defiantly, "you and your damned archaic songs. There's another word, 'damned.' And how it suits you! When are you going to stop this morbidity?"

"And commit myself to a clinic and have my brain laundered nice and sanitary? Not soon, darling." I use *that* last word aforethought, but she cannot know what scorn and sadness are in it for me, who know that once it could also have been a name for my girl. The official grammar and pronunciation of language is as frozen as every other aspect of our civilization, thanks to electronic recording and neuronic teaching; but meanings shift and glide about like subtle serpents. (O adder that stung my Foalfoot!)

I shrug and say in my driest, most city-technological voice, "Actually, I'm the practical, nonmorbid one. Instead of running away from my emotions—via drugs, or neuroadjustment, or playing at savagery like you, for that matter—

I'm about to implement a concrete plan for getting back the person who made me happy."

"By disturbing Her on Her way home?"

"Anyone has the right to petition the Dark Queen while She's abroad on earth."

"But this is past the proper time—"

"No law's involved, just custom. People are afraid to meet Her outside a crowd, a town, bright flat lights. They won't admit it, but they are. So I came here precisely not to be part of a queue. I don't want to speak into a recorder for subsequent computer analysis of my words. How could I be sure She was listening? I want to meet Her as myself, a unique being, and look in Her eyes while I make my prayer."

Thrakia chokes a little. "She'll be angry."

"Is She able to be angry, anymore?"

"I . . . I don't know. What you mean to ask for is so impossible, though. So absurd. That SUM should give you back your girl. You know It never makes exceptions."

"Isn't She Herself an exception?"

"That's different. You're being silly. SUM has to have a, well, a direct human liaison. Emotional and cultural feedback, as well as statistics. How else can It govern rationally? And She must have been chosen out of the whole world. Your girl, what was she? Nobody!"

"To me, she was everybody."

"You—" Thrakia catches her lip in her teeth. One hand reaches out and closes on my bare forearm, a hard hot touch, the grimy fingernails biting. When I make no response, she lets go and stares at the ground. A V of outbound geese passes overhead. Their cries come shrill through the wind, which is loudening in the forest.

"Well," she says "you are special. You always were. You went to space and came back, with the Great Captain. You're maybe the only man alive who understands about the ancients. And your singing, yes, you don't really entertain, your songs trouble people and can't be forgotten. So maybe She will listen to you. But SUM won't. It can't give special resurrections. Once that was done, a single time, wouldn't it have to be done for everybody? The dead would overrun the living."

"Not necessarily," I say. "In any event, I mean to try."

"Why can't you wait for the promised time? Surely, then, SUM will re-create you two in the same generation."

"I'd have to live out this life, at least, without her," I say, looking away also, down to the highroad which shines through shadow like death's snake, the length of the valley. "Besides, how do you know there ever will be any resurrections? We have only a promise. No, less than that. An announced policy."

She gasps, steps back, raises her hands as if to fend me off. Her soul bracelet casts light into my eyes. I recognize an embryo exorcism. She lacks ritual; every "superstition" was patiently scrubbed out of our metal-and-energy world, long ago. But if she has no word for it, no concept, nevertheless she recoils from blasphemy.

So I say, wearily, not wanting an argument, wanting only to wait here alone: "Never mind. There could be some natural catastrophe, like a giant asteroid striking, that wiped out the system before conditions had become right for resurrections to commence."

"That's impossible," she says, almost frantic. "The homeostats, the repair functions—"

"All right, call it a vanishingly unlikely theoretical contingency. Let's declare that I'm so selfish I want Swallow Wing back now, in this life of mine, and don't give a curse whether that'll be fair to the rest of you."

You won't care either, anyway, I think. None of you. You don't grieve. It is your own precious private consciousnesses that you wish to preserve; no one else is close enough to you to matter very much. Would you believe me if I told you I am quite prepared to offer SUM my own death in exchange for It releasing Blossom-in-the-Sun?

I don't speak that thought, which would be cruel, nor repeat what is crueller: my fear that SUM lies, that the dead never will be disgorged. For (I am not the All-Controller, I think not with vacuum and negative energy levels but with ordinary earth-begotten molecules; yet I can reason somewhat dispassionately, being disillusioned) consider—

The object of the game is to maintain a society stable, just, and sane. This requires satisfaction not only of somatic, but of symbolic and instinctual needs. Thus children must be allowed to come into being. The minimum number per generation is equal to the maximum: that number which will maintain a constant population.

It is also desirable to remove the fear of death from men. Hence the promise: At such time as it is socially feasible, SUM will begin to refashion us, with our complete memories but in the pride of our youth. This can be done over and over, life after life across the millennia. So death is, indeed, a sleep.

—*in that sleep of death, what dreams may come*—No. I myself dare not dwell on this. I ask merely, privately: Just when and how does SUM expect conditions (in a stabilized society, mind you) to have become so different from today's that the reborn can, in their millions, safely be welcomed back?

I see no reason why SUM should not lie to us. We, too, are objects in the world that It manipulates.

"We've quarreled about this before, Thrakia," I sigh. "Often. Why do you bother?"

"I wish I knew," she answers low. Half to herself, she goes on: "Of course I want to copulate with you. You must be good, the way that girl used to follow you about with her eyes, and smile when she touched your hand, and—But you can't be better than everyone else. That's unreasonable. There are only so many possible ways. So why do I care if you wrap yourself up in silence and go off alone? Is it that that makes you a challenge?"

"You think too much," I say. "Even here. You're a pretend primitive. You visit wildcountry to 'slake inborn atavistic impulses' . . . but you can't dismantle that computer inside yourself and simply feel, simply be."

She bristles. I touched a nerve there. Looking past her, along the ridge of fiery maple and sumac, brassy elm and great dun oak, I see others emerge from beneath the trees. Women exclusively, her followers, as unkempt as she; one has a brace of ducks lashed to her waist, and their blood has trickled down her thigh and dried black. For this movement, this unadmitted mystique has become Thrakia's by now: that not only men should forsake the easy routine and the easy pleasure of the cities, and become again, for a few weeks each year, the carnivores who begot our species; women too should seek out starkness, the better to appreciate civilization when they return.

I feel a moment's unease. We are in no park, with laid-out trails and campground services. We are in wildcountry. Not many men come here, ever, and still fewer women; for the region is, literally, beyond the law. No deed done here is punishable. We are told that this helps consolidate society, as the most violent among us may thus vent their passions. But I have spent much time in wildcountry since my Morning Star went out—myself in quest of nothing but solitude—and I have watched what happens through eyes that have also read anthropology and history. Institutions are developing; ceremonies, tribalisms, acts of blood and cruelty and acts elsewhere called unnatural are becoming more elaborate and more expected every year. Then the practitioners go home to their cities and honestly believe they have been enjoying fresh air, exercise, and good tension-releasing fun.

Let her get angry enough and Thrakia can call knives to her aid.

Wherefore I make myself lay both hands on her shoulders, and meet the tormented gaze, and say most gently, "I'm sorry. I know you mean well. You're afraid She will be annoyed and bring misfortune on your people."

Thrakia gulps. "No," she whispers. "That wouldn't be logical. But I'm afraid of what might happen to you. And then—" Suddenly she throws herself against me. I feel arms, breasts, belly press through my tunic, and smell meadows in her hair and musk in her mouth. "You'd be gone!" she wails. "Then who'd sing to us?"

"Why, the planet's crawling with entertainers," I stammer.

"You're more than that," she says. "So much more. I don't like what you sing, not really—and what you've sung since that stupid girl died, oh, meaningless, horrible!—but, I don't know why, I *want* you to trouble me."

Awkward, I pat her back. The sun now stands very little above the treetops. Its rays slant interminably through the booming, frosting air. I shiver in my tunic and buskins and wonder what to do.

A sound rescues me. It comes from one end of the valley below us, where further view is blocked off by two cliffs; it thunders deep in our ears and rolls through the earth into our bones. We have heard that sound in the cities, and been glad to have walls and lights and multitudes around us. Now we are alone with it, the noise of Her chariot.

The women shriek, I hear them faintly across wind and rumble and my own pulse, and they vanish into the woods. They will seek their camp, dress warmly, build enormous fires; presently they will eat their ecstatics, and rumors are uneasy about what they do after that.

Thrakia seizes my left wrist, above the soul bracelet, and hauls. "Harper, come with me!" she pleads. I break loose from her and stride down the hill toward the road. A scream follows me for a moment.

Light still dwells in the sky and on the ridges, but as I descend into that narrow valley I enter dusk, and it thickens. Indistinct bramblebushes whicker where I brush them, and claw back at me. I feel the occasional scratch on my legs, the tug as my garment is snagged, the chill that I breathe, but dimly. My perceived-outer-reality is overpowered by the rushing of Her chariot and my blood. My inner-universe is fear, yes, but exaltation too, a drunkenness which sharpens instead of dulling the senses, a psychedelia which opens the reasoning mind as well as the emotions; I have gone beyond myself, I am embodied purpose. Not out of need for comfort, but to voice what Is, I return to words whose speaker rests centuries dust, and lend them my own music. I sing:

> "—Gold is my heart, and the world's golden,
>   And one peak tipped with light;
> And the air lies still about the hill
>   With the first fear of night;
>
> Till mystery down the soundless valley
>   Thunders, and dark is here;

And the wind blows, and the light goes,
  And the night is full of fear.

And I know one night, on some far height,
  In the tongue I never knew,
I yet shall hear the tidings clear
  From them that were friends of you.

They'll call the news from hill to hill,
  Dark and uncomforted,
Earth and sky and the winds; and I
  Shall know that you are dead.—"

But I have reached the valley floor, and She has come in sight.

Her chariot is unlit, for radar eyes and inertial guides need no lamps, nor sun nor stars. Wheel-less, the steel tear rides on its own roar and thrust of air. The pace is not great, far less than any of our mortals' vehicles are wont to take. Men say the Dark Queen rides thus slowly in order that She may perceive with Her own senses and so be the better prepared to counsel SUM. But now Her annual round is finished; She is homeward bound; until spring She will dwell with It which is our lord. Why does She not hasten tonight?

Because Death has never a need of haste? I wonder. And as I step into the middle of the road, certain lines from the yet more ancient past rise tremendous within me, and I strike my harp and chant them louder than the approaching car:

    "I that in heill was and gladness
    Am trublit now with great sickness
    And feblit with infirmitie:—
    Timor mortis conturbat me."

The car detects me and howls a warning. I hold my ground. The car could swing around, the road is wide and in any event a smooth surface is not absolutely necessary. But I hope, I believe that She will be aware of an obstacle in Her path, and tune in Her various amplifiers, and find me abnormal enough to stop for. Who, in SUM's world—who, even among the explorers that It has sent beyond in Its unappeasable hunger for data—would stand in a cold wild-country dusk and shout while his harp snarls

    "Our pleasance here is all vain glory,
    This fals world is but transitory,

The flesh is bruckle, the Feynd is slee:—
Timor mortis conturbat me.

The state of man does change and vary,
Now sound, now sick, now blyth, now sary,
Now dansand mirry, now like to die:—
Timor mortis conturbat me.

No state in Erd here standis sicker;
As with the wynd wavis the wicker
So wannis this world's vanitie:—
Timor mortis conturbat me.—?"

The car draws alongside and sinks to the ground. I let my strings die away into the wind. The sky overhead and in the west is gray-purple; eastward it is quite dark and a few early stars peer forth. Here, down in the valley, shadows are heavy and I cannot see very well.

The canopy slides back. She stands erect in the chariot, thus looming over me. Her robe and cloak are black, fluttering like restless wings; beneath the cowl Her face is a white blur. I have seen it before, under full light, and in how many thousands of pictures; but at this hour I cannot call it back to my mind, not entirely. I list sharp-sculptured profile and pale lips, sable hair and long green eyes, but these are nothing more than words.

"What are you doing?" She has a lovely low voice; but is it, as oh, how rarely since SUM took Her to Itself, is it the least shaken? "What is that you were singing?"

My answer comes so strong that my skull resonates; for I am borne higher and higher on my tide. "Lady of Ours, I have a petition."

"Why did you not bring it before Me when I walked among men? Tonight I am homebound. You must wait till I ride forth with the new year."

"Lady of Ours, neither You nor I would wish living ears to hear what I have to say."

She regards me for a long while. Do I indeed sense fear also in Her? (Surely not of me. Her chariot is armed and armored, and would react with machine speed to protect Her should I offer violence. And should I somehow, incredibly, kill Her, or wound Her beyond chemosurgical repair, She of all beings has no need to doubt death. The ordinary bracelet cries with quite sufficient radio loudness to be heard by more than one thanatic station, when we die; and in that shielding the soul can scarcely be damaged before the Winged Heels arrive to bear it off to SUM. Surely the Dark Queen's circlet can call still further, and is still better insulated, than any mortal's. And She will most absolutely be re-created. She has been, again and again; death and rebirth every seven years keep Her eternally young in the service of SUM. I have never been able to find out when She was first born.)

Fear, perhaps, of what I have sung and what I might speak?

At last She says—I can scarcely hear through the gusts and creakings in the trees—"Give me the Ring, then."

The dwarf robot which stands by Her throne when She sits among men appears beside Her and extends the massive dull-silver circle to me. I place my left arm within, so that my soul is enclosed. The tablet on the upper surface of the Ring, which looks so much like a jewel, slants away from me; I cannot read what flashes onto the bezel. But the faint glow picks Her features out of murk as She bends to look.

Of course, I tell myself, the actual soul is not scanned. That would take too long. Probably the bracelet which contains the soul has an identification code built in. The Ring sends this to an appropriate part of SUM, Which instantly sends back what is recorded under that code. I hope there is nothing more to it. SUM has not seen fit to tell us.

"What do you call yourself at the moment?" She asks.

A current of bitterness crosses my tide. "Lady of Ours, why should You care? Is not my real name the number I got when I was allowed to be born?"

Calm descends once more upon Her. "If I am to evaluate properly what you say, I must know more about you than these few official data. Name indicates mood."

I too feel unshaken again, my tide running so strong and smooth that I might not know I was moving did I not see time recede behind me. "Lady of Ours, I cannot give You a fair answer. In this past year I have not troubled with names, or with much of anything else. But some people who knew me from earlier days call me Harper."

"What do you do besides make that sinister music?"

"These days, nothing, Lady of Ours. I've money to live out my life, if I eat sparingly and keep no home. Often I am fed and housed for the sake of my songs."

"What you sang is unlike anything I have heard since—" Anew, briefly, that robot serenity is shaken. "Since before the world was stabilized. You should not wake dead symbols, Harper. They walk through men's dreams."

"Is that bad?"

"Yes. The dreams become nightmares. Remember: Mankind, every man who ever lived, was insane before SUM brought order, reason, and peace."

"Well, then," I say, "I will cease and desist if I may have my own dead wakened for me."

She stiffens. The tablet goes out. I withdraw my arm and the Ring is stored away by Her servant. So again She is faceless, beneath flickering stars, here at the bottom of this shadowed valley. Her voice falls cold as the air: "No one can be brought back to life before Resurrection Time is ripe."

I do not say, "What about You?" for that would be vicious. What did She think, how did She weep, when SUM chose Her of all the young on earth? What does She endure in Her centuries? I dare not imagine.

Instead, I smite my harp and sing, quietly this time:

> "Strew on her roses, roses,
>   And never a spray of yew.
> In quiet she reposes:
>   Ah! would that I did too."

The Dark Queen cries, "What are you doing? Are you really insane?" I go straight to the last stanza.

> "Her cabin'd, ample Spirit
>   It flutter'd and fail'd for breath.
> To-night it doth inherit
>   The vasty hall of Death."

I know why my songs strike so hard: because they bear dreads and passions that no one is used to—that most of us hardly know could exist—in SUM's ordered universe. But I had not the courage to hope She would be as torn by them as I see. Has She not lived with more darkness and terror than the ancients themselves could conceive? She calls, "Who has died?"

"She had many names, Lady of Ours," I say. "None was beautiful enough. I can tell You her number, though."

"Your daughter? I . . . sometimes I am asked if a dead child cannot be brought back. Not often, anymore, when they go so soon to the crèche. But sometimes. I tell the mother she may have a new one; but if ever We started re-creating dead infants, at what age level could We stop?"

"No, this was my woman."

"Impossible!" Her tone seeks to be not unkindly but is, instead, well-nigh frantic. "You will have no trouble finding others. You are handsome, and your psyche is, is, is extraordinary. It burns like Lucifer."

"Do You remember the name Lucifer, Lady of Ours?" I pounce. "Then You are old indeed. So old that You must also remember how a man might

324

desire only one woman, but her above the whole world and heaven."

She tries to defend Herself with a jeer: "Was that mutual, Harper? I know more of mankind than you do, and surely I am the last chaste woman in existence."

"Now that she is gone, Lady, yes, perhaps You are. But we— Do You know how she died? We had gone to a wildcountry area. A man saw her, alone, while I was off hunting gem rocks to make her a necklace. He approached her. She refused him. He threatened force. She fled. This was desert land, viper land, and she was barefoot. One of them bit her. I did not find her till hours later. By then the poison and the unshaded sun— She died quite soon after she told me what had happened and that she loved me. I could not get her body to chemosurgery in time for normal revival procedures. I had to let them cremate her and take her soul away to SUM."

"What right have you to demand her back, when no one else can be given their own?"

"The right that I love her, and she loves me. We are more necessary to each other than sun or moon. I do not think You could find another two people of whom this is so, Lady. And is not everyone entitled to claim what is necessary to his life? How else can society be kept whole?"

"You are being fantastic," She says thinly. "Let me go."

"No, Lady, I am speaking sober truth. But poor plain words won't serve me. I sing to You because then maybe You will understand." And I strike my harp anew; but it is more to her than Her that I sing.

> "If I had thought thou couldst have died,
>   I might not weep for thee:
> But I forgot, when by thy side,
>   That thou couldst mortal be:
> It never through my mind had past
>   The time would e'er be o'er,
> And I on thee should look my last,
>   And thou shouldst smile no more!"

"I cannot—" She falters. "I did not know—any such feelings—so strong—existed any longer."

"Now You do, Lady of Ours. And is that not an important datum for SUM?"

"Yes. If true." Abruptly She leans toward me. I see Her shudder in the murk, under the flapping cloak, and hear Her jaws clatter with cold. "I cannot

GOING FOR INFINITY

linger here. But ride with Me. Sing to Me. I think I can bear it."

So much have I scarcely expected. But my destiny is upon me. I mount into the chariot. The canopy slides shut and we proceed.

The main cabin encloses us. Behind its rear door must be facilities for Her living on earth; this is a big vehicle. But here is little except curved panels. They are true wood of different comely grains: so She also needs periodic escape from our machine existence, does She? Furnishing is scant and austere. The only sound is our passage, muffled to a murmur for us; and, because their photomultipliers are not activated, the scanners show nothing outside but night. We huddle close to a glower, hands extended toward its fieriness. Our shoulders brush, our bare arms, Her skin is soft and Her hair falls loose over the thrown-back cowl, smelling of the summer which is dead. What, is She still human?

After a timeless time, She says, not yet looking at me: "The thing you sang, there on the highroad as I came near—I do not remember it. Not even from the years before I became what I am."

"It is older than SUM," I answer, "and its truth will outlive It."

"Truth?" I see Her tense Herself. "Sing Me the rest."

My fingers are no longer too numb to call forth chords.

> "—Unto the Death gois all Estatis,
> Princis, Prelattis, and Potestatis,
> Baith rich and poor of all degree:—
> *"Timor mortis conturbat me.*
>
> He takis the knichtis in to the field
> Enarmit under helm and scheild;
> Victor he is at all mellie:—
> *Timor mortis conturbat me.*
>
> That strong unmerciful tyrand
> Takis, on the motheris breast sowkand,
> The babe full of benignitie:—
> *Timor mortis conturbat me.*
>
> He takis the campion in the stour,
> The captain closit in the tour,
> The ladie in bour full of bewtie:—"

(There I must stop a moment.)

> *"Timor mortis conturbat me.*

He sparis no lord for his piscence,
Na clerk for his intelligence;
His awful straik may no man flee:—
Timor mortis conturbat me."

She breaks me off, clapping hands to ears and half shrieking, "No!"

I, grown unmerciful, pursue Her: "You understand now, do You not? You are not eternal either. SUM isn't. Not Earth, not sun, not stars. We hid from the truth. Every one of us. I too, until I lost the one thing which made everything make sense. Then I had nothing left to lose, and could look with clear eyes. And what I saw was Death."

"Get out! Let Me alone!"

"I will not let the whole world alone, Queen, until I get her back. Give me her again, and I'll believe in SUM again. I'll praise It till men dance for joy to hear Its name."

She challenges me with wildcat eyes. "Do you think such matters to It?"

"Well," I shrug, "songs could be useful. They could help achieve the great objective sooner. Whatever that is. 'Optimization of total human activity'— wasn't that the program? I don't know if it still is. SUM has been adding to Itself so long. I doubt if You Yourself understand Its purposes, Lady of Ours."

"Don't speak as if It were alive," She says harshly. "It is a computer-effector complex. Nothing more."

"Are You certain?"

"I—yes. It thinks, more widely and deeply than any human ever did or could; but It is not alive, not aware, It has no consciousness. That is one reason why It decided It needed Me."

"Be that as it may, Lady," I tell Her, "the ultimate result, whatever It finally does with us, lies far in the future. At present I care about that; I worry; I resent our loss of self-determination. But that's because only such abstractions are left to me. Give me back my Lightfoot, and she, not the distant future, will be my concern. I'll be grateful, honestly grateful, and You Two will know it from the songs I then choose to sing. Which, as I said, might be helpful to It."

"You are unbelievably insolent," She says without force.

"No, Lady, just desperate," I say.

The ghost of a smile touches Her lips. She leans back, eyes hooded, and murmurs, "Well, I'll take you there. What happens then, you realize, lies outside My power. My observations, My recommendations, are nothing but a few items to take into account, among billions. However . . . we have a long way to travel this night. Give me what data you think will help you, Harper."

I do not finish the Lament. Nor do I dwell in any other fashion on grief.

Instead, as the hours pass, I call upon those who dealt with the joy (not the fun, not the short delirium, but the joy) that man and woman might once have of each other.

Knowing where we are bound, I too need such comfort.

And the night deepens, and the leagues fall behind us, and finally we are beyond habitation, beyond wildcountry, in the land where life never comes. By crooked moon and waning starlight I see the plain of concrete and iron, the missiles and energy projectors crouched like beasts, the robot aircraft wheeling aloft: and the lines, the relay towers, the scuttling beetle-shaped carriers, that whole transcendent nerve-blood-sinew by which SUM knows and orders the world. For all the flitting about, for all the forces which seethe, here is altogether still. The wind itself seems to have frozen to death. Hoarfrost is gray on the steel shapes. Ahead of us, tiered and mountainous, begins to appear the castle of SUM.

She Who rides with me does not give sign of noticing that my songs have died in my throat. What humanness She showed is departing; Her face is cold and shut, Her voice bears a ring of metal. She looks straight ahead. But She does speak to me for a little while yet:

"Do you understand what is going to happen? For the next half year I will be linked with SUM, integral, another component of It. I suppose you will see Me, but that will merely be My flesh. What speaks to you will be SUM."

"I know." The words must be forced forth. My coming this far is more triumph than any man in creation before me has won; and I am here to do battle for my Dancer-on-Moonglades; but nonetheless my heart shakes me, and is loud in my skull, and my sweat stinks.

I manage, though, to add: "You *will* be a part of It, Lady of Ours. That gives me hope."

For an instant She turns to me, and lays Her hand across mine, and something makes Her again so young and untaken that I almost forget the girl who died; and she whispers, "If you knew how I hope!"

The instant is gone, and I am alone among machines.

We must stop before the castle gate. The wall looms sheer above, so high and high that it seems to be toppling upon me against the westward march of the stars, so black and black that it does not only drink down every light, it radiates blindness. Challenge and response quiver on electronic bands I cannot sense. The outer-guardian parts of It have perceived a mortal aboard this craft. A missile launcher swings about to aim its three serpents at me. But the Dark Queen answers—She does not trouble to be peremptory—and the castle opens its jaws for us.

We descend. Once, I think, we cross a river. I hear a rushing and hollow echoing and see droplets glitter where they are cast onto the viewports and outlined against dark. They vanish at once: liquid hydrogen, perhaps, to keep certain parts near absolute zero?

Much later we stop and the canopy slides back. I rise with Her. We are in a room, or cavern, of which I can see nothing, for there is no light except a dull bluish phosphorescence which streams from every solid object, also from Her flesh and mine. But I judge the chamber is enormous, for a sound of great machines at work comes very remotely, as if heard through dream, while our own voices are swallowed up by distance. Air is pumped through, neither warm nor cold, totally without odor, a dead wind.

We descend to the floor. She stands before me, hands crossed on breast, eyes half shut beneath the cowl and not looking at me nor away from me. "Do what you are told, Harper," She says in a voice that has never an overtone, "precisely as you are told." She turns and departs at an even pace. I watch Her go until I can no longer tell Her luminosity from the formless swirlings within my own eyeballs.

A claw plucks my tunic. I look down and am surprised to see that the dwarf robot has been waiting for me this whole time. How long a time that was, I cannot tell.

Its squat form leads me in another direction. Weariness crawls upward through me, my feet stumble, my lips tingle, lids are weighted and muscles have each their separate aches. Now and then I feel a jag of fear, but dully. When the robot indicates *Lie down here,* I am grateful.

The box fits me well. I let various wires be attached to me, various needles be injected which lead into tubes. I pay little attention to the machines which cluster and murmur around me. The robot goes away. I sink into blessed darkness.

I wake renewed in body. A kind of shell seems to have grown between my forebrain and the old animal parts. Far away I can feel the horror and hear the screaming and thrashing of my instincts; but awareness is chill, calm, logical. I have also a feeling that I slept for weeks, months, while leaves blew loose and snow fell on the upper world. But this may be wrong, and in no case does it matter. I am about to be judged by SUM.

The little faceless robot leads me off, through murmurous black corridors where the dead wind blows. I unsling my harp and clutch it to me, my sole friend and weapon. So the tranquility of the reasoning mind which has been decreed for me cannot be absolute. I decide that It simply does not want to be bothered by anguish. (No; wrong; nothing so humanlike; It has no desires; beneath that power to reason is nullity.)

At length a wall opens for us and we enter a room where She sits enthroned.

The self-radiation of metal and flesh is not apparent here, for light is provided, a featureless white radiance with no apparent source. White, too, is the muted sound of the machines which encompass Her throne. White are Her robe and face. I look away from the multitudinous unwinking scanner eyes, into Hers, but She does not appear to recognize me. Does She even see me? SUM has reached out with invisible fingers of electromagnetic induction and taken Her back into Itself. I do not tremble or sweat—I cannot—but I square my shoulders, strike one plangent chord, and wait for It to speak.

It does, from some invisible place. I recognize the voice It has chosen to use: my own. The overtones, the inflections are true, normal, what I myself would use in talking as one reasonable man to another. Why not? In computing what to do about me, and in programming Itself accordingly, SUM must have used so many billion bits of information that adequate accent is a negligible sub-problem.

No . . . there I am mistaken again . . . SUM does not do things on the basis that It might as well do them as not. This talk with myself is intended to have some effect on me. I do not know what.

"Well," It says pleasantly, "you made quite a journey, didn't you? I'm glad. Welcome."

My instincts bare teeth to hear those words of humanity used by the unfeeling unalive. My logical mind considers replying with an ironic "Thank you," decides against it, and holds me silent.

"You see," SUM continues after a moment that whirrs, "you are unique. Pardon Me if I speak a little bluntly. Your sexual monomania is just one aspect of a generally atavistic, superstition-oriented personality. And yet, unlike the ordinary misfit, you're both strong and realistic enough to cope with the world. This chance to meet you, to analyze you while you rested, has opened new insights for Me on human psychophysiology. Which may lead to improved techniques for governing it and its evolution."

"That being so," I reply, "give me my reward."

"Now look here," SUM says in a mild tone, "you if anyone should know I'm not omnipotent. I was built originally to help govern a civilization grown too complex. Gradually, as My program of self-expansion progressed, I took over more and more decision-making functions. They were *given* to Me. People were happy to be relieved of responsibility, and they could see for themselves how much better I was running things than any mortal could. But to this day, My authority depends on a substantial consensus. If I started playing favorites, as by re-creating your girl, well, I'd have troubles."

"The consensus depends more on awe than on reason," I say. "You haven't abolished the gods, You've simply absorbed them into Yourself. If You choose to pass a miracle for me, your prophet singer—and I will be Your prophet if You do this—why, that strengthens the faith of the rest."

"So you think. But your opinions aren't based on any exact data. The historical and anthropological records from the past before Me are unquantitative. I've already phased them out of the curriculum. Eventually, when the culture's ready for such a move, I'll order them destroyed. They're too misleading. Look what they've done to you."

I grin into the scanner eyes. "Instead," I say, "people will be encouraged to think that before the world was, was SUM. All right. I don't care, as long as I get my girl back. Pass me a miracle, SUM, and I'll guarantee You a good payment."

"But I have no miracles. Not in your sense. You know how the soul works. The metal bracelet encloses a pseudo-virus, a set of giant protein molecules with taps directly to the bloodstream and nervous system. They record the chromosome pattern, the synapse flash, the permanent changes, everything. At the owner's death, the bracelet is dissected out. The Winged Heels bring it here, and the information contained is transferred to one of My memory banks. I can use such a record to guide the growing of a new body in the vats: a young body, on which the former habits and recollections are imprinted. But you don't understand the complexity of the process, Harper. It takes Me weeks, every seven years, and every available biochemical facility, to re-create My human liaison. And the process isn't perfect, either. The pattern is affected by storage. You might say that this body and brain you see before you remembers each death. And those are short deaths. A longer one—man, use your sense. Imagine."

I can; and the shield between reason and feeling begins to crack. I had sung, of my darling dead,

> "No motion has she now, no force;
>   She neither hears nor sees;
> Roll'd round in earth's diurnal course,
>   With rocks, and stones, and trees."

Peace, at least. But if the memory-storage is not permanent but circulating; if, within those gloomy caverns of tubes and wire and outerspace cold, some remnant of her psyche must flit and flicker, alone, unremembering, aware of nothing but having lost life—No!

I smite the harp and shout so the room rings: "Give her back! Or I'll kill you!"

SUM finds it expedient to chuckle; and, horribly, the smile is reflected for a moment on the Dark Queen's lips, though otherwise She never stirs. "And how do you propose to do that?" It asks me.

It knows, I know, what I have in mind, so I counter: "How do You propose to stop me?"

"No need. You'll be considered a nuisance. Finally someone will decide you ought to have psychiatric treatment. They'll query My diagnostic outlet. I'll recommend certain excisions."

"On the other hand, since You've sifted my mind by now, and since You know how I've affected people with my songs—even the Lady yonder, even Her—wouldn't you rather have me working for You? With words like, *'O taste, and see, how gracious the Lord is; blessed is the man that trusteth in him. O fear the Lord, ye that are his saints: for they that fear him lack nothing.'* I can make You into God."

"In a sense, I already am God."

"And in another sense not. Not yet." I can endure no more. "Why are we arguing? You made Your decision before I woke. Tell me and let me go!"

With an odd carefulness, SUM responds: "I'm still studying you. No harm in admitting to you, My knowledge of the human psyche is as yet imperfect. Certain areas won't yield to computation. I don't know precisely what you'd do, Harper. If to that uncertainty I added a potentially dangerous precedent—"

"Kill me, then." Let my ghost wander forever with hers, down in Your cryogenic dreams.

"No, that's also inexpedient. You've made yourself too conspicuous and controversial. Too many people know by now that you went off with the Lady." Is it possible that, behind steel and energy, a nonexistent hand brushes across a shadow face in puzzlement? My heartbeat is thick in the silence.

Suddenly It shakes me with decision: "The calculated probabilities do favor your keeping your promises and making yourself useful. Therefore I shall grant your request. However—"

I am on my knees. My forehead knocks on the floor until blood runs into my eyes. I hear through storm winds:

"—testing must continue. Your faith in Me is not absolute; in fact, you're very skeptical of what you call My goodness. Without additional proof of your willingness to trust Me, I can't let you have the kind of importance which your getting your dead back from Me would give you. Do you understand?"

The question does not sound rhetorical. "Yes," I sob.

"Well, then," says my civilized, almost amiable voice, "I computed that you'd react much as you have done, and prepared for the likelihood. Your woman's body was re-created while you lay under study. The data which make personality are now being fed back into her neurones. She'll be ready to leave this place by the time you do.

"I repeat, though, there has to be a testing. The procedure is also necessary for its effect on you. If you're to be My prophet, you'll have to work pretty closely with Me; you'll have to undergo a great deal of reconditioning; this night we begin the process. Are you willing?"

"Yes, yes, yes, what must I do?"

"Only this: Follow the robot out. At some point, she, your woman, will join you. She'll be conditioned to walk so quietly you can't hear her. Don't look back. Not once, until you're in the upper world. A single glance behind you will be an act of rebellion against Me, and a datum indicating you can't really be trusted . . . and that ends everything. Do you understand?"

"Is that all?" I cry. "Nothing more?"

"It will prove more difficult than you think," SUM tells me. My voice fades, as if into illimitable distances: "Farewell, worshiper."

The robot raises me to my feet. I stretch out my arms to the Dark Queen. Half blinded with tears, I nonetheless see that She does not see me. "Good-bye," I mumble, and let the robot lead me away.

Our walking is long through those mirk miles. At first I am in too much of a turmoil, and later too stunned, to know where or how we are bound. But later still, slowly, I become aware of my flesh and clothes and the robot's alloy, glimmering blue in blackness. Sounds and smells are muffled; rarely does another machine pass by, unheeding of us. (What work does SUM have for them?) I am so careful not to look behind me that my neck grows stiff.

Though it is not prohibited, is it, to lift my harp past my shoulder, in the course of strumming a few melodies to keep up my courage, and see if perchance a following illumination is reflected in this polished wood?

Nothing. Well, her second birth must take time—O SUM, be careful of her!—and then she must be led through many tunnels, no doubt, before she makes rendezvous with my back. Be patient, Harper.

Sing. Welcome her home. No, these hollow spaces swallow all music; and she is as yet in that trance of death from which only the sun and my kiss can wake her; if, indeed, she has joined me yet. I listen for other footfalls than my own.

Surely we haven't much farther to go. I ask the robot, but of course I get no reply. Make an estimate. I know about how fast the chariot traveled coming down. . . . The trouble is, time does not exist here. I have no day, no stars, no clock but my heartbeat and I have lost the count of that. Nevertheless, we must come to the end soon. What purpose would be served by walking me through this labyrinth till I die?

Well, if I am totally exhausted at the outer gate, I won't make undue trouble when I find no Rose-in-Hand behind me.

No, now that's ridiculous. If SUM didn't want to heed my plea, It need merely say so. I have no power to inflict physical damage on Its parts.

Of course, It might have plans for me. It did speak of reconditioning. A series of shocks, culminating in that last one, could make me ready for whatever kind of gelding It intends to do.

Or It might have changed Its mind. Why not? It was quite frank about an uncertainty factor in the human psyche. It may have re-evaluated the probabilities and decided: better not to serve my desire.

Or It may have tried, and failed. It admitted the recording process is imperfect. I must not expect quite the Gladness I knew; she will always be a little haunted. At best. But suppose the tank spawned a body with no awareness behind the eyes? Or a monster? Suppose, at this instant, I am being followed by a half-rotten corpse?

No! Stop that! SUM would know, and take corrective measures.

Would It? *Can It?*

I comprehend how this passage through night, where I never look to see what follows me, how this is an act of submission and confession. I am saying, with my whole existent being, that SUM is all-powerful, all-wise, all-good. To SUM I offer the love I came to win back. Oh, It looked more deeply into me than ever I did myself.

But I shall not fail.

Will SUM, though? If there has indeed been some grisly error . . . let me not find it out under the sky. Let her, my only, not. For what then shall we do? Could I lead her here again, knock on the iron gate, and cry, "Master, You have given me a thing unfit to exist. Destroy it and start over."—? For what might the wrongness be? Something so subtle, so pervasive, that it does not show in any way save my slow, resisted discovery that I embrace a zombie? Doesn't it make better sense to look—make certain while she is yet drowsy with death— use the whole power of SUM to correct what may be awry?

No, SUM wants me to believe that It makes no mistakes. I agreed to that price. And to much else . . . I don't know how much else, I am daunted to imagine, but that word "recondition" is ugly. . . . Does not my woman have some rights in the matter too? Shall we not at least ask her if she wants to be the wife of a prophet; shall we not, hand in hand, ask SUM what the price of her life is to her?

Was that a footfall? Almost, I whirl about. I check myself and stand shaking; names of hers break from my lips. The robot urges me on.

Imagination. It wasn't her step. I am alone. I will always be alone.

The halls wind upward. Or so I think; I have grown too weary for much kinesthetic sense. We cross the sounding river and I am bitten to the bone by the cold which blows upward around the bridge, and I may not turn about to offer the naked newborn woman my garment. I lurch through endless chambers where machines do meaningless things. She hasn't seen them before. Into what nightmare has she risen; and why don't I, who wept into her dying senses that I loved her, why don't I look at her, why don't I speak?

Well, I could talk to her. I could assure the puzzled mute dead that I have come to lead her back into sunlight. Could I not? I ask the robot. It does not reply. I cannot remember if I may speak to her. If indeed I was ever told. I stumble forward.

I crash into a wall and fall bruised. The robot's claw closes on my shoulder. Another arm gestures. I see a passageway, very long and narrow, through the stone. I will have to crawl through. At the end, at the end, the door is swinging wide. The dear real dusk of Earth pours through into this darkness. I am blinded and deafened.

Do I hear her cry out? Was that the final testing; or was my own sick, shaken mind betraying me; or is there a destiny which, like SUM with us, makes tools of suns and SUM? I don't know. I know only that I turned, and there she stood. Her hair flowed long, loose, past the remembered face from which the trance was just departing, on which the knowing and the love of me had just awakened—flowed down over the body that reached forth arms, that took one step to meet me and was halted.

The great grim robot at her own back takes her to it. I think it sends lightning through her brain. She falls. It bears her away.

My guide ignores my screaming. Irresistible, it thrusts me out through the tunnel. The door clangs in my face. I stand before the wall which is like a mountain. Dry snow hisses across concrete. The sky is bloody with dawn; stars still gleam in the west, and arc lights are scattered over the twilit plain of the machines.

Presently I go dumb. I become almost calm. What is there left to have feelings about? The door is iron, the wall is stone fused into one basaltic mass. I walk some distance off into the wind, turn around, lower my head, and charge. Let my brains be smeared across Its gate; the pattern will be my hieroglyphic for hatred.

I am seized from behind. The force that stops me must needs be bruisingly great. Released, I crumple to the ground before a machine with talons and wings. My voice from it says, "Not here. I'll carry you to a safe place."

"What more can You do to me?" I croak.

"Release you. You won't be restrained or molested on any orders of Mine."

"Why not?"

"Obviously you're going to appoint yourself My enemy forever. This is an unprecedented situation, a valuable chance to collect data."

"You tell me this, You warn me, deliberately?"

"Of course. My computation is that these words will have the effect of provoking your utmost effort."

"You won't give her again? You don't want my love?"

"Not under the circumstances. Too uncontrollable. But your hatred should, as I say, be a useful experimental tool."

"I'll destroy You," I say.

It does not deign to speak further. Its machine picks me up and flies off with me. I am left on the fringes of a small town farther south. Then I go insane.

I do not much know what happens during that winter, nor care. The blizzards are too loud in my head. I walk the ways of Earth, among lordly towers, under neatly groomed trees, into careful gardens, over bland, bland campuses. I am unwashed, uncombed, unbarbered; my tatters flap about me and my bones are near thrusting through the skin; folk do not like to meet these eyes sunken so far into this skull, and perhaps for that reason they give me to eat. I sing to them.

> "From the hag and hungry goblin
> That into rags would rend ye
> And the spirit that stan' by the naked man
> In the Book of Moons defend ye!
> That of your five sound senses
> You never be forsaken
> Nor travel from yourselves with Tom
> Abroad to beg your bacon."

Such things perturb them, do not belong in their chrome-edged universe. So I am often driven away with curses, and sometimes I must flee those who would arrest me and scrub my brain smooth. An alley is a good hiding place, if I can find one in the oldest part of a city; I crouch there and yowl with the cats. A forest is also good. My pursuers dislike to enter any place where any wildness lingers.

But some feel otherwise. They have visited parklands, preserves, actual wildcountry. Their purpose was overconscious—measured, planned savagery, and a clock to tell them when they must go home—but at least they are not afraid of silences and unlighted nights. As spring returns, certain among them begin to follow me. They are merely curious, at first. But slowly, month by month, especially among the younger ones, my madness begins to call to something in them.

"With an host of furious fancies
Whereof I am commander
With a burning spear, and a horse of air,
To the wilderness I wander.
By a knight of ghosts and shadows
I summoned am to tourney
Ten leagues beyond the wide world's edge.
Me thinks it is no journey."

They sit at my feet and listen to me sing. They dance, crazily, to my harp. The girls bend close, tell me how I fascinate them, invite me to copulate. This I refuse, and when I tell them why they are puzzled, a little frightened maybe, but often they strive to understand.

For my rationality is renewed with the hawthorn blossoms. I bathe, have my hair and beard shorn, find clean raiment, and take care to eat what my body needs. Less and less do I rave before anyone who will listen; more and more do I seek solitude, quietness, under the vast wheel of the stars, and think.

What is man? Why is man? We have buried such questions; we have sworn they are dead—that they never really existed, being devoid of empirical meaning—and we have dreaded that they might raise the stones we heaped on them, rise and walk the world again of nights. Alone, I summon them to me. They cannot hurt their fellow dead, among whom I now number myself.

I sing to her who is gone. The young people hear and wonder. Sometimes they weep.

"Fear no more the heat o' the sun,
  Nor the furious winter's rages;
Thou thy worldly task hast done,
  Home art gone, and ta'en thy wages:
Golden lads and girls all must
As chimney-sweepers, come to dust."

"But this is not so!" they protest. "We will die and sleep awhile, and then we will live forever in SUM."

I answer as gently as may be: "No. Remember I went there. So I know you are wrong. And even if you were right, it would not be right that you should be right."

"What?"

"Don't you see, it is not right that a thing should be the lord of man. It is not right that we should huddle through our whole lives in fear of finally losing them. You are not parts in a machine, and you have better ends than helping the machine run smoothly."

I dismiss them and stride off, solitary again, into a canyon where a river clangs, or onto some gaunt mountain peak. No revelation is given me. I climb and creep toward the truth.

Which is that SUM must be destroyed, not in revenge, not in hate, not in fear, simply because the human spirit cannot exist in the same reality as It.

But what, then, is our proper reality? And how shall we attain to it?

I return with my songs to the lowlands. Word about me has gone widely. They are a large crowd who follow me down the highroad until it has changed into a street.

"The Dark Queen will soon come to these parts," they tell me. "Abide till She does. Let Her answer those questions you put to us, which make us sleep so badly."

"Let me retire to prepare myself," I say. I go up a long flight of steps. The people watch from below, dumb with awe, till I vanish. Such few as were in the building depart. I walk down vaulted halls, through hushed high-ceilinged rooms full of tables, among shelves made massive by books. Sunlight slants dusty through the windows.

The half memory has plagued me of late: once before, I know not when, this year of mine also took place. Perhaps in this library I can find the tale that—casually, I suppose, in my abnormal childhood—I read. For man is older than SUM: wiser, I swear; his myths hold more truth than Its mathematics. I spend three days and most of three nights in my search. There is scant sound but the rustling of leaves between my hands. Folk place offerings of food and drink at the door. They tell themselves they do so out of pity, or curiosity, or to avoid the nuisance of having me die in an unconventional fashion. But I know better.

At the end of the three days I am little further along. I have too much material; I keep going off on sidetracks of beauty and fascination. (Which SUM means to eliminate.) My education was like everyone else's, science, rationality, good sane adjustment. (SUM writes our curricula, and the teaching machines have direct connections to It.) Well, I can make some of my lopsided training work for me. My reading has given me sufficient clues to prepare a search program. I sit down before an information retrieval console and run my fingers across its keys. They make a clattery music.

Electron beams are swift hounds. Within seconds the screen lights up with words, and I read who I am.

It is fortunate that I am a fast reader. Before I can press the Clear button, the unreeling words are wiped out. For an instant the screen quivers with form-lessness, then appears

I HAD NOT CORRELATED THESE DATA WITH THE FACTS CONCERNING YOU. THIS INTRODUCES A NEW AND INDETERMINATE QUANTITY INTO THE COMPU-TATIONS.

The nirvana which has come upon me (yes, I found that word among the old books, and how portentous it is) is not passiveness, it is a tide more full and strong than that which bore me down to the Dark Queen those ages apast in wildcountry. I say, as coolly as may be, "An interesting coincidence. If it is a coincidence." Surely sonic receptors are emplaced hereabouts.

EITHER THAT, OR A CERTAIN NECESSARY CONSEQUENCE OF THE LOGIC OF EVENTS.

The vision dawning within me is so blinding bright that I cannot refrain from answering, "Or a destiny, SUM?"

MEANINGLESS. MEANINGLESS. MEANINGLESS.

"Now why did You repeat Yourself in that way? Once would have sufficed. Thrice, though, makes an incantation. Are You by any chance hoping Your words will make me stop existing?"

I DO NOT HOPE. YOU ARE AN EXPERIMENT. IF I COMPUTE A SIGNIFICANT PROBABILITY OF YOUR CAUSING SERIOUS DISTURBANCE, I WILL HAVE YOU TER-MINATED.

I smile. "SUM," I say, "I am going to terminate You." I lean over and switch off the screen. I walk out into the evening.

Not everything is clear to me yet, that I must say and do. But enough is that I can start preaching at once to those who have been waiting for me. As I talk, others come down the street, and hear, and stay to listen. Soon they number in the hundreds.

I have no immense new truth to offer them: nothing that I have not said before, although piecemeal and unsystematically; nothing they have not felt themselves, in the innermost darknesses of their beings. Today, however, know-ing who I am and therefore why I am, I can put these things in words. Speaking quietly, now and then drawing on some forgotten song to show my meaning, I tell them how sick and starved their lives are; how they have made themselves slaves; how the enslavement is not even to a conscious mind, but to an insensate inanimate thing which their own ancestors began; how that thing is not the

centrum of existence, but a few scraps of metal and bleats of energy, a few sad
stupid patterns, adrift in unbounded space-time. Put not your faith in SUM, I
tell them. SUM is doomed, even as you and I. Seek out mystery; what else is
the whole cosmos but mystery? Live bravely, die and be done, and you will
be more than any machine. You may perhaps be God.

They grow tumultuous. They shout replies, some of which are animal
howls. A few are for me, most are opposed. That doesn't matter. I have reached
into them, my music is being played on their nerve-strings, and this is my
entire purpose.

The sun goes down behind the buildings. Dusk gathers. The city remains
unilluminated. I soon realize why. She is coming, the Dark Queen Whom they
wanted me to debate with. From afar we hear Her chariot thunder. Folk wail
in terror. They are not wont to do that either. They used to disguise their
feelings from Her and themselves by receiving Her with grave sparse ceremony.
Now they would flee if they dared. I have lifted the masks.

The chariot halts in the street. She dismounts, tall and shadowy cowled.
The people make way before Her like water before a shark. She climbs the
stairs to face me. I see for the least instant that Her lips are not quite firm and
Her eyes abrim with tears. She whispers, too low for anyone else to hear, "Oh,
Harper, I'm sorry."

"Come join me," I invite. "Help me set the world free."

"No. I cannot. I have been too long with It." She straightens. Imperium
descends upon Her. Her voice rises for everyone to hear. The little television
robots flit close, bat shapes in the twilight, that the whole planet may witness
my defeat. "What is this freedom you rant about?" She demands.

"To feel," I say. "To venture. To wonder. To become men again."

"To become beasts, you mean. Would you demolish the machines that keep
us alive?"

"Yes. We must. Once they were good and useful, but we let them grow
upon us like a cancer, and now nothing but destruction and a new beginning
can save us."

"Have you considered the chaos?"

"Yes. It too is necessary. We will not be men without the freedom to know
suffering. In it is also enlightenment. Through it we travel beyond ourselves,
beyond earth and stars, space and time, to Mystery."

"So you maintain that there is some undefined ultimate vagueness behind
the measurable universe?" She smiles into the bat eyes. We have each been
taught, as children, to laugh on hearing sarcasms of this kind. "Please offer me
a little proof."

"No," I say. "Prove to me instead, beyond any doubt, that there is *not* something we cannot understand with words and equations. Prove to me likewise that I have no right to seek for it.

"The burden of proof is on You Two, so often have You lied to us. In the name of rationality, You resurrected myth. The better to control us! In the name of liberation, You chained our inner lives and castrated our souls. In the name of service, You bound and blinkered us. In the name of achievement, You held us to a narrower round than any swine in its pen. In the name of beneficence, You created pain, and horror, and darkness beyond darkness." I turn to the people. "I went there. I descended into the cellars. I know!"

"He found that SUM would not pander to his special wishes, at the expense of everyone else," cries the Dark Queen. Do I hear shrillness in Her voice? "Therefore he claims SUM is cruel."

"I saw my dead," I tell them. "She will not rise again. Nor yours, nor you. Not ever. SUM will not, cannot raise us. In Its house is death indeed. We must seek life and rebirth elsewhere, among the mysteries."

She laughs aloud and points to my soul bracelet, glimmering faintly in the gray-blue thickening twilight. Need She say anything?

"Will someone give me a knife and an ax?" I ask.

The crowd stirs and mumbles. I smell their fear. Streetlamps go on, as if they could scatter more than this corner of the night which is rolling upon us. I fold my arms and wait. The Dark Queen says something to me. I ignore Her.

The tools pass from hand to hand. He who brings them up the stairs comes like a flame. He kneels at my feet and lifts what I have desired. The tools are good ones, a broad-bladed hunting knife and a long double-bitted ax.

Before the world, I take the knife in my right hand and slash beneath the bracelet on my left wrist. The connections to my inner body are cut. Blood flows, impossibly brilliant under the lamps. It does not hurt; I am too exalted.

The Dark Queen shrieks. "You meant it! Harper, Harper!"

"There is no life in SUM," I say. I pull my hand through the circle and cast the bracelet down so it rings.

A voice of brass: *"Arrest that maniac for correction. He is deadly dangerous."*

The monitors who have stood on the fringes of the crowd try to push through. They are resisted. Those who seek to help them encounter fists and fingernails.

I take the ax and smash downward. The bracelet crumples. The organic material within, starved of my secretions, exposed to the night air, withers.

I raise the tools, ax in right hand, knife in bleeding left. "I seek eternity where it is to be found," I call. "Who goes with me?"

A score or better break loose from the riot, which is already calling forth weapons and claiming lives. They surround me with their bodies. Their eyes are the eyes of prophets. We make haste to seek a hiding place, for one military robot has appeared and others will not be long in coming. The tall engine strides to stand guard over Our Lady, and this is my last glimpse of Her.

My followers do not reproach me for having cost them all they were. They are mine. In me is the godhead which can do no wrong.

And the war is open, between me and SUM. My friends are few, my enemies many and mighty. I go about the world as a fugitive. But always I sing. And always I find someone who will listen, will join us, embracing pain and death like a lover.

With the Knife and the Ax I take their souls. Afterward we hold for them the ritual of rebirth. Some go thence to become outlaw missionaries; most put on facsimile bracelets and return home, to whisper my word. It makes little difference to me. I have no haste, who own eternity.

For my word is of what lies beyond time. My enemies say I call forth ancient bestialities and lunacies; that I would bring civilization down in ruin; that it matters not a madman's giggle to me whether war, famine, and pestilence will again scour the earth. With these accusations I am satisfied. The language of them shows me that here, too, I have reawakened anger. And that emotion belongs to us as much as any other. More than the others, maybe, in this autumn of mankind. We need a gale, to strike down SUM and everything It stands for. Afterward will come the winter of barbarism.

And after that the springtime of a new and (perhaps) more human civilization. My friends seem to believe this will come in their very lifetimes: peace, brotherhood, enlightenment, sanctity. I know otherwise. I have been in the depths. The wholeness of mankind, which I am bringing back, has its horrors.

> When one day
>   the Eater of the Gods returns
>   the Wolf breaks his chain
>   the Horsemen ride forth
>   the Age ends
>   the Beast is reborn

then SUM will be destroyed; and you, strong and fair, may go back to earth and rain.

I shall await you.

My aloneness is nearly ended, Daybright. Just one task remains. The god must die, that his followers may believe he is raised from the dead and lives forever. Then they will go on to conquer the world.

There are those who say I have spurned and offended them. They too, borne on the tide which I raised, have torn out their machine souls and seek in music and ecstasy to find a meaning for existence. But their creed is a savage one, which has taken them into wildcountry, where they ambush the monitors sent against them and practice cruel rites. They believe that the final reality is female. Nevertheless, messengers of theirs have approached me with the suggestion of a mystic marriage. This I refused; my wedding was long ago, and will be celebrated again when this cycle of the world has closed.

Therefore they hate me. But I have said I will come and talk to them.

I leave the road at the bottom of the valley and walk singing up the hill. Those few I let come this far with me have been told to abide my return. They shiver in the sunset; the vernal equinox is three days away. I feel no cold myself. I stride exultant among briars and twisted ancient apple trees. If my bare feet leave a little blood in the snow, that is good. The ridges around are dark with forest, which waits like the skeleton dead for leaves to be breathed across it again. The eastern sky is purple, where stands the evening star. Overhead, against blue, cruises an early flight of homebound geese. Their calls drift faintly down to me. Westward, above me and before me, smolders redness. Etched black against it are the women.

When science suggests a story, the result isn't always the hard kind. Although the idea of black holes had been around for a long time, it was obscure until theorists working on the frontiers of general relativity began giving it close attention. I don't recall that the name was even used when I read an article on the subject in the journal *Science* in 1967, nor will you find it in what I thereupon wrote.

Besides employing the physics as carefully as I was able to, I brought in some rather fantastical concepts, not only faster-than-light travel by way of hyperspatial jumps but a being that is mostly a plasma vortex and telepathy across cosmic distances. That's what the story wanted. It's generally best to go along.

I wrote shortly before Vatican Two set the Latin mass aside. Well, I still prefer it, and who knows but what it will make a comeback in the future. I gave the order of St. Martha of Bethany a chapter on the Moon in memory of Tony Boucher, for it appears in some of his mystery fiction.

"Kyrie" was well received and got several reprints, one from Ursula K. Le Guin. Jack Williamson did me the honor of putting it on the reading list for his college course in science fiction.

KYRIE

On a high peak in the Lunar Carpathians stands a convent of St. Martha of Bethany. The walls are native rock; they lift dark and cragged as the mountainside itself, into a sky that is always black. As you approach from Northpole, flitting low to keep the force screens along Route Plato between you and the meteoroidal rain, you see the cross which surmounts the tower, stark athwart Earth's blue disc. No bells resound from there—not in airlessness.

You may hear them inside at the canonical hours, and throughout the crypts below where machines toil to maintain a semblance of terrestrial environment. If you linger a while you will also hear them calling to requiem mass. For it has become a tradition that prayers be offered at St. Martha's for those who have perished in space; and they are more with every passing year.

This is not the work of the sisters. They minister to the sick, the needy, the crippled, the insane, all whom space has broken and cast back. Luna is full of such, exiles because they can no longer endure Earth's pull or because it is feared they may be incubating a plague from some unknown planet or because men are so busy with their frontiers that they have no time to spare for the failures. The sisters wear space suits as often as habits, are as likely to hold a medikit as a rosary.

But they are granted some time for contemplation. At night, when for half a month the sun's glare has departed, the chapel is unshuttered and stars look down through the glaze-dome to the candles. They do not wink and their light is winter cold. One of the nuns in particular is there as often as may be, praying for her own dead. And the abbess sees to it that she can be present when the yearly mass, that she endowed before she took her vows, is sung.

Requiem aeternam dona eis, Domine, et lux perpetua luceat eis.
Kyrie eleison, Christe eleison, Kyrie eleison.

The Supernova Sagittarii expedition comprised fifty human beings and a flame. It went the long way around from Earth orbit, stopping at Epsilon Lyrae to pick up its last member. Thence it approached its destination by stages.

This is the paradox: time and space are aspects of each other. The explosion was more than a hundred years past when noted by men on Lasthope. They were part of a generations-long effort to fathom the civilization of creatures altogether unlike us; but one night they looked up and saw a light so brilliant it cast shadows.

That wave front would reach Earth several centuries hence. By then it would be so tenuous that nothing but another bright point would appear in the sky. Meanwhile, though, a ship overleaping the space through which light must creep could track the great star's death across time.

Suitably far off, instruments recorded what had been before the outburst, incandescence collapsing upon itself after the last nuclear fuel was burned out. A jump, and they saw what happened a century ago, convulsion, storm of quanta and neutrinos, radiation equal to the massed hundred billion suns of this galaxy.

It faded, leaving an emptiness in heaven, and the *Raven* moved closer. Fifty light-years—fifty years—inward, she studied a shrinking fieriness in the midst of a fog which shone like lightning.

Twenty-five years later the central globe had dwindled more, the nebula had expanded and dimmed. But because the distance was now so much less, everything seemed larger and brighter. The naked eye saw a dazzle too fierce to look straight at, making the constellations pale by contrast. Telescopes showed a blue-white spark in the heart of an opalescent cloud delicately filamented at the edges.

The *Raven* made ready for her final jump, to the immediate neighborhood of the supernova.

Captain Teodor Szili went on a last-minute inspection tour. The ship murmured around him, running at one gravity of acceleration to reach the desired intrinsic velocity. Power droned, regulators whickered, ventilation systems rustled. He felt the energies quiver in his bones. But metal surrounded him, blank and comfortless. Viewports gave on a dragon's hoard of stars, the ghostly arch of the Milky Way: on vacuum, cosmic rays, cold not far above absolute zero, distance beyond imagination to the nearest human hearthfire. He was about to take his people where none had ever been before, into conditions none was sure about, and that was a heavy burden on him.

He found Eloise Waggoner at her post, a cubbyhole with intercom connections directly to the command bridge. Music drew him, a triumphant serenity he did not recognize. Stopping in the doorway, he saw her seated with a small tape machine on the desk.

"What's this?" he demanded.

"Oh!" The woman (he could not think of her as a girl, though she was barely out of her teens) started. "I . . . I was waiting for the jump."

"You were to wait at the alert."

"What have I to do?" she answered less timidly than was her wont. "I mean, I'm not a crewman or a scientist."

"You are in the crew. Special communications technician."

"With Lucifer. And he likes the music. He says we come closer to oneness with it than in anything else he knows about us."

Szili arched his brows. "Oneness?"

A blush went up Eloise's thin cheeks. She stared at the deck and her hands twisted together. "Maybe that isn't the right word. Peace, harmony, unity . . . God? . . . I sense what he means, but we haven't any word that fits."

"Hm. Well, you are supposed to keep him happy." The skipper regarded her with a return of the distaste he had tried to suppress. She was a decent enough sort, he supposed, in her gauche and inhibited way; but her looks! Scrawny, big-footed, big-nosed, pop eyes, and stringy dust-colored hair—and, to be sure, telepaths always made him uncomfortable. She said she could only read Lucifer's mind, but was that true?

No. Don't think such things. Loneliness and otherness can come near breaking you out here, without adding suspicion of your fellows.

If Eloise Waggoner was really human. She must be some kind of mutant at the very least. Whoever could communicate thought to thought with a living vortex had to be.

"What are you playing, anyhow?" Szili asked.

"Bach. The Third Brandenburg Concerto. He, Lucifer, he doesn't care for the modern stuff. I don't either."

You wouldn't, Szili decided. Aloud: "Listen, we jump in half an hour. No telling what we'll emerge in. This is the first time anyone's been close to a recent supernova. We can only be certain of so much hard radiation that we'll be dead if the screenfields give way. Otherwise we've nothing to go on except theory. And a collapsing stellar core is so unlike anything anywhere else in the universe that I'm skeptical about how good the theory is. We can't sit day-dreaming. We have to prepare."

"Yes, sir." Whispering, her voice lost its usual harshness.

He stared past her, past the ophidian eyes of meters and controls, as if he could penetrate the steel beyond and look straight into space. There, he knew, floated Lucifer.

The image grew in him: a fireball twenty meters across, shimmering white, red, gold, royal blue, flames dancing like Medusa locks, cometary tail burning for a hundred meters behind, a shiningness, a glory, a piece of hell. Not the least of what troubled him was the thought of that which paced his ship.

He hugged scientific explanations to his breast, though they were little better than guesses. In the multiple star system of Epsilon Aurigae, in the gas and energy pervading the space around, things took place which no laboratory could imitate. Ball lightning on a planet was perhaps analogous, as the for-mation of simple organic compounds in a primordial ocean is analogous to the life which finally evolves. In Epsilon Aurigae, magnetohydrodynamics had done what chemistry did on Earth. Stable plasma vortices had appeared, had grown, had added complexity, until after millions of years they became some-thing you must needs call an organism. It was a form of ions, nuclei, and force-fields. It metabolized electrons, nucleons, X rays; it maintained its configuration for a long lifetime; it reproduced; it thought.

But what did it think? The few telepaths who could communicate with the Aurigeans, who had first made humankind aware that the Aurigeans existed, never explained clearly. They were a queer lot themselves.

Wherefore Captain Szili said, "I want you to pass this on to him."

"Yes, sir." Eloise turned down the volume on her taper. Her eyes unfocused. Through her ears went words, and her brain (how efficient a transducer was it?) passed the meanings on out to him who loped alongside *Raven* on his own reaction drive.

"Listen, Lucifer. You have heard this often before, I know, but I want to be positive you understand in full. Your psychology must be very foreign to ours. Why did you agree to come with us? I don't know. Technician Waggoner said you were curious and adventurous. Is that the whole truth?

"No matter. In half an hour we jump. We'll come within five hundred million kilometers of the supernova. That's where your work begins. You can go where we dare not, observe what we can't, tell us more than our instruments would ever hint at. But first we have to verify we can stay in orbit around the star. This concerns you too. Dead men can't transport you home again.

"So. In order to enclose you within the jumpfield, without disrupting your body, we have to switch off the shield screens. We'll emerge in a lethal radiation zone. You must promptly retreat from the ship, because we'll start the screen generator up sixty seconds after transit. Then you must investigate the vicinity. The hazards to look for—" Szili listed them. "Those are only what we can foresee. Perhaps we'll hit other garbage we haven't predicted. If anything seems like a menace, return at once, warn us, and prepare for a jump back to here. Do you have that? Repeat."

Words jerked from Eloise. They were a correct recital; but how much was she leaving out?

"Very good." Szili hesitated. "Proceed with your concert if you like. But break it off at zero minus ten minutes and stand by."

"Yes, sir." She didn't look at him. She didn't appear to be looking anywhere in particular.

His footsteps clacked down the corridor and were lost.

—Why did he say the same things over? asked Lucifer.

"He is afraid," Eloise said.

—?—

"I guess you don't know about fear," she said.

—Can you show me? . . . No, do not. I sense it is hurtful. You must not be hurt.

"I can't be afraid anyway, when your mind is holding mine."

(Warmth filled her. Merriment was there, playing like little flames over the surface of Father-leading-her-by-the-hand-when-she-was-just-a-child-and-they-went-out-one-summer's-day-to-pick-wildflowers; over strength and gentleness and Bach and God.) Lucifer swept around the hull in an exuberant curve. Sparks danced in his wake.

—Think flowers again. Please.

She tried.

—They are like (image, as nearly as a human brain could grasp, of fountains blossoming with gamma-ray colors in the middle of light, everywhere light). But so tiny. So brief a sweetness.

"I don't understand how you can understand," she whispered.

—You understand for me. I did not have that kind of thing to love, before you came.

"But you have so much else. I try to share it, but I'm not made to realize what a star is."

—Nor I for planets. Yet ourselves may touch.

Her cheeks burned anew. The thought rolled on, interweaving its counterpoint to the marching music.—That is why I came, do you know? For you. I am fire and air. I had not tasted the coolness of water, the patience of earth, until you showed me. You are moonlight on an ocean.

"No, don't," she said. "Please."

Puzzlement:—Why not? Does joy hurt? Are you not used to it?

"I, I guess that's right." She flung her head back. "No! Be damned if I'll feel sorry for myself!"

—Why should you? Have we not all reality to be in, and is it not full of suns and songs?

"Yes. To you. Teach me."

—If you in turn will teach me—The thought broke off. A contact remained, unspeaking, such as she imagined must often prevail among lovers.

She glowered at Motilal Mazundar's chocolate face, where the physicist stood in the doorway. "What do you want?"

He was surprised. "Only to see if everything is well with you, Miss Waggoner."

She bit her lip. He had tried harder than most aboard to be kind to her. "I'm sorry," she said. "I didn't mean to bark at you. Nerves."

"We are everyone on edge." He smiled. "Exciting though this venture is, it will be good to come home, correct?"

Home, she thought: four walls of an apartment above a banging city street. Books and television. She might present a paper at the next scientific meeting, but no one would invite her to the parties afterward.

Am I that horrible? she wondered. I know I'm not anything to look at, but I try to be nice and interesting. Maybe I try too hard.

—You do not with me, Lucifer said.

"You're different," she told him.

Mazundar blinked. "Beg pardon?"

"Nothing," she said in haste.

"I have wondered about an item," Mazundar said in an effort at conversation. "Presumably Lucifer will go quite near the supernova. Can you still maintain contact with him? The time dilation effect, will that not change the frequency of his thoughts too much?"

"What time dilation?" She forced a chuckle. "I'm no physicist. Only a little librarian who turned out to have a wild talent."

"You were not told? Why, I assumed everybody was. An intense gravitational field affects time just as a high velocity does. Roughly speaking, processes take place more slowly than they do in clear space. That is why light from a massive star is somewhat reddened. And our supernova core retains almost three solar masses. Furthermore, it has acquired such a density that its attraction at the surface is, ah, incredibly high. Thus by our clocks it will take infinite time to shrink to the Schwarzschild radius; but an observer on the star itself would experience this whole shrinkage in a fairly short period."

"Schwarzschild radius? Be so good as to explain." Eloise realized that Lucifer had spoken through her.

"If I can without mathematics. You see, this mass we are to study is so great and so concentrated that no force exceeds the gravitational. Nothing can counterbalance. Therefore the process will continue until no energy can escape. The star will have vanished out of the universe. In fact, theoretically the contraction will proceed to zero volume. Of course, as I said, that will take forever as far as we are concerned. And the theory neglects quantum-mechanical considerations which come into play toward the end. Those are still not very well understood. I hope, from this expedition, to acquire more knowledge." Mazundar shrugged. "At any rate, Miss Waggoner, I was wondering if the frequency shift involved would not prevent our friend from communicating with us when he is near the star."

"I doubt that." Still Lucifer spoke, she was his instrument and never had she known how good it was to be used by one who cared. "Telepathy is not a wave phenomenon. Since it transmits instantaneously, it cannot be. Nor does it appear limited by distance. Rather, it is a resonance. Being attuned, we two may well be able to continue thus across the entire breadth of the cosmos; and I am not aware of any material phenomenon which could interfere."

"I see." Mazundar gave her a long look. "Thank you," he said uncomfortably. "Ah . . . I must get to my own station. Good luck." He bustled off without stopping for an answer.

Eloise didn't notice. Her mind was become a torch and a song. "Lucifer!" she cried aloud. "Is that true?"

—I believe so. My entire people are telepaths, hence we have more knowledge of such matters than yours do. Our experience leads us to think there is no limit.

"You can always be with me? You always will?"

—If you so wish, I am gladdened.

The comet body curvetted and danced, the brain of fire laughed low.—Yes, Eloise, I would like very much to remain with you. No one else has ever— Joy. Joy. Joy.

They named you better than they knew, Lucifer, she wanted to say, and perhaps she did. They thought it was a joke; they thought by calling you after the devil they could make you safely small like themselves. But Lucifer isn't the devil's real name. It means only Light Bearer. One Latin prayer even addresses Christ as Lucifer. Forgive me, God, I can't help remembering that. Do You mind? He isn't Christian, but I think he doesn't need to be, I think he must never have felt sin, Lucifer, Lucifer.

She sent the music soaring for as long as she was permitted.

The ship jumped. In one shift of world line parameters she crossed twenty-five light-years to destruction.

Each knew it in his own way, save for Eloise who also lived it with Lucifer.

She felt the shock and heard the outraged metal scream, she smelled the ozone and scorch and tumbled through the infinite falling that is weightlessness. Dazed, she fumbled at the intercom. Words crackled through: ". . . unit blown . . . back EMF surge . . . how should I know how long to fix the blasted thing? . . . stand by, stand by . . ." Over all hooted the emergency siren.

Terror rose in her, until she gripped the crucifix around her neck and the mind of Lucifer. Then she laughed in the pride of his might.

He had whipped clear of the ship immediately on arrival. Now he floated in the same orbit. Everywhere around, the nebula filled space with unrestful rainbows. To him, *Raven* was not the metal cylinder which human eyes would have seen, but a lambence, the shield screen reflecting a whole spectrum. Ahead lay the supernova core, tiny at this remove but alight, alight.

—Have no fears (he caressed her). I comprehend. Turbulence is extensive, so soon after the detonation. We emerged in a region where the plasma is especially dense. Unprotected for the moment before the guardian field was reestablished, your main generator outside the hull was short-circuited. But you are safe. You can make repairs. And I, I am in an ocean of energy. Never was I so alive. Come, swim these tides with me.

Captain Szili's voice yanked her back. "Waggoner! Tell that Aurigean to get busy. We've spotted a radiation source on an intercept orbit, and it may be too much for our screen." He specified coordinates. "What *is* it?"

For the first time, Eloise felt alarm in Lucifer. He curved about and streaked from the ship.

Presently his thought came to her, no less vivid. She lacked words for the terrible splendor she viewed with him: a million-kilometer ball of ionized gas where luminance blazed and electric discharges leaped, booming through the haze around the star's exposed heart. The thing could not have made any sound, for space here was still almost a vacuum by Earth's parochial standards; but she heard it thunder, and felt the fury that spat from it.

She said for him: "A mass of expelled material. It must have lost radial velocity to friction and static gradients, been drawn into a cometary orbit, held together for a while by internal potentials. As if this sun were trying yet to bring planets to birth—"

"It'll strike us before we're in shape to accelerate," Szili said, "and overload our shield. If you know any prayers, use them."

"Lucifer!" she called; for she did not want to die, when he must remain.

—I think I can deflect it enough, he told her with a grimness she had not hitherto met in him.—My own fields, to mesh with its; and free energy to drink; and an unstable configuration; yes, perhaps I can help you. But help me, Eloise. Fight by my side.

His brightness moved toward the juggernaut shape.

She felt how its chaotic electromagnetism clawed at his. She felt him tossed and torn. The pain was hers. He battled to keep his own cohesion, and the combat was hers. They locked together, Aurigean and gas cloud. The forces that shaped him grappled as arms might; he poured power from his core, hauling that vast tenuous mass with him down the magnetic torrent which streamed from the sun; he gulped atoms and thrust them backward until the jet splashed across heaven.

She sat in her cubicle, lending him what will to live and prevail she could, and beat her fists bloody on the desk.

The hours brawled past.

In the end, she could scarcely catch the message that flickered out of his exhaustion:—Victory.

"Yours," she wept.

—Ours.

Through instruments, men saw the luminous death pass them by. A cheer lifted.

"Come back," Eloise begged.

—I cannot. I am too spent. We are merged, the cloud and I, and are tumbling in toward the star. (Like a hurt hand reaching forth to comfort her:) Do not be afraid for me. As we get closer, I will draw fresh strength from its glow, fresh substance from the nebula. I will need a while to spiral out against that pull. But how can I fail to come back to you, Eloise? Wait for me. Rest. Sleep.

Her shipmates led her to sickbay. Lucifer sent her dreams of fire flowers and mirth and the suns that were his home.

But she woke at last, screaming. The medic had to put her under heavy sedation.

He had not really understood what it would mean to confront something so violent that space and time themselves were twisted thereby.

His speed increased appallingly. That was in his own measure; from *Raven* they saw him fall through several days. The properties of matter were changed. He could not push hard enough or fast enough to escape.

Radiation, stripped nuclei, particles born and destroyed and born again, sleeted and shouted through him. His substance was peeled away, layer by layer. The supernova core was a white delirium before him. It shrank as he approached, ever smaller, denser, so brilliant that brilliance ceased to have meaning. Finally the gravitational forces laid their full grip upon him.

—Eloise! he shrieked in the agony of his disintegration.—Oh, Eloise, help me!

The star swallowed him up. He was stretched infinitely long, compressed infinitely thin, and vanished with it from existence.

The ship prowled the farther reaches. Much might yet be learned.

Captain Szili visited Eloise in sickbay. Physically she was recovering.

"I'd call him a man," he declared through the machine mumble, "except that's not praise enough. We weren't even his kin, and he died to save us."

She regarded him from eyes more dry than seemed natural. He could just make out her answer. "He is a man. Doesn't he have an immortal soul too?"

"Well, uh, yes, if you believe in souls, yes, I'd agree."

She shook her head. "But why can't he go to his rest?"

He glanced about for the medic and found they were alone in the narrow metal room. "What do you mean?" He made himself pat her hand. "I know, he was a good friend of yours. Still, his must have been a merciful death. Quick, clean; I wouldn't mind going out like that."

"For him . . . yes, I suppose so. It has to be. But—" She could not continue. Suddenly she covered her ears. "Stop! Please!"

Szili made soothing noises and left. In the corridor he encountered Mazundar. "How is she?" the physicist asked.

The captain scowled. "Not good. I hope she doesn't crack entirely before we can get her to a psychiatrist."

"Why, what is wrong?"

"She thinks she can hear him."

Mazundar smote fist into palm. "I hoped otherwise," he breathed.

Szili braced himself and waited.

"She does," Mazundar said. "Obviously she does."

"But that's impossible! He's dead!"

"Remember the time dilation," Mazundar replied. "He fell from the sky and perished swiftly, yes. But in supernova time. Not the same as ours. To us, the final stellar collapse takes an infinite number of years. And telepathy has no distance limits." The physicist started walking fast, away from that cabin. "He will always be with her."

XVI

Here's another passage from a novel, again fantasy.

The period in which this was written, the late '60's and early '70's, saw a renaissance of the whole field. It had lain long in the doldrums, most of what appeared being dull and derivative, supernovas like Fritz Leiber's *The Big Time* doubly dazzling by comparison. Such an atmosphere deadens almost everybody. One doesn't want to be a hack, one tries one's damnedest for freshness, but without stimulation from others it's bloody hard—as vicious a circle as ever there was. Now, almost overnight, came any number of new writers—original, vivid, explosive with new ideas and new ways of storytelling. They rekindled the fire in old-timers too.

How these things happen is a mystery. I don't think it's merely a question of statistical fluctuations. But, anyway, they happen. I believe some of my own best work was done then, and like to believe that the standard has not fallen.

This was when *Tau Zero* came to be. James Blish called it the ultimate hard-science work. I didn't quite agree—having Hal Clement and others in mind—but appreciated the compliment, and in fact the novel has been used in some physics classes and a planetarium show to help get certain concepts of relativity across. People have told me it's a pretty good story too.

So maybe this is what I should have excerpted here. But it doesn't seem to lend itself to that very well. Also, the evidence has become strong that our universe is flat, not closed as was commonly thought in those days. Finally, although "A Midsummer Tempest" proved to be caviar to the general, it's a special favorite of mine, if only because it was sheer joy to write.

It's my homage to Shakespeare—not that I can hold a candle to him, but here was a chance to drop all modern conventions and let the language roll whither and however it wanted to. The setting is a world in which his plays are not fiction but reports of historical fact. This means that Hamlet really lived, Bohemia did once have a seacoast, and on and on. In fact, since almost everybody in the chronicles spoke Elizabethan English, and purely English types such as Bottom were to be found in such places as ancient Greece, the Anglo-Israelite notion must be true. They have had a slight technological edge on us—consider, for example, the eyeglasses mentioned in *King Lear* or the cannon mentioned in *King John*—so it's plausible that an Industrial Revolution would begin in the seventeenth century. Educated people commonly talk in blank verse, often ending in rhymed couplets, and sometimes members of the lower classes do too.

I'd played with the notion for years. Then at last Karen suggested that the period be the English Civil War and the hero Prince Rupert of the Rhine. Suddenly everything crystallized for me, and I was off on my romp.

Here is as good a place as any to make an all too small acknowledgment of her contributions—no, partnership is a better word—over the years. Often and often she has come up with an idea, or we have sparked one between us, from which a story has sprung. Sometimes she's shot one of mine down, pointing out what's wrong, before I wasted time trying to write it. Always she's been what she calls my resident nitpicker, with a hawk eye for errors, inconsistencies, and misuses of language. She reads more than I do and retains it better, so that she's been able to answer many a question off the top of her head. When not, it hasn't mattered, because she's an incomparable researcher. And proofreader and cook and delightful, keenly observant traveling companion and all else that a writer needs. She's published just a few things of her own, and shared just a few bylines with me, but hardly any of my work would be what it is without her.

Returning to this novel, the passage here is meant only as a sample, and there's no need for a synopsis. Briefly, Rupert has reason to think that help for his cause may be found on Prospero's island, where the magician sank his books of lore just before he went home from exile. The problem is to find the island, and Rupert goes in search. Meanwhile his sweetheart Jennifer has been taken captive into France. She manages to escape in a small boat, but it is soon becalmed and she alone, desperate, on an empty sea. Attuned to magical currents, the sprite Ariel comes flying to her, raises a wind, and brings her to the island.

A MIDSUMMER TEMPEST

THE ISLAND

Hills lifted high from wide white beaches and intimate coves. They were bedecked with forest—here pine and juniper, there tall hardwoods—or meadows star-sky full of flowers. Springs gave rise to brooks which tumbled over moss-softened cobbles and rang down cliffsides. Odors of growth, blossom, sun-warmed resin drenched the air. It was always singing, for wings were overhead in the thousands: chirrup, trill, carol, and chant.

Ariel's medicines had already brought Jennifer close to full recovery. She followed an upward trail. Cathedral coolness dwelt beneath the branches which vaulted it. Sunbeams dissolved into green and gold in those leaves, or reached the earth and minted coins among the shadows. The sprite flitted around and around her. Occasionally he zipped aside to startle a ladybird, play tag with a robin, or drain the dew lingering in an orchid cup.

"And have I died," she asked at last in a sleepwalker's voice, "to find this Paradise?"

"Nay, it is earthly, though thou well hast earned it." Ariel descended to perch on her shoulder. "Is not the whole wide world itself an Eden, and man himself its snake and fiery guardian? The first and foremost miracle thou'lt find, here too as elsewhere, is thy living flesh. That it may get its due, I'm guiding thee toward the cell that Prospero had carved from out a bluff, to house him and his girl. We'll quickly sweep and garnish it for thee, and heap sweet boughs and grasses for thy bed."

He quivered his wings as he went eagerly on: "Thou'lt find the island fare we bring not simple. Each well we tap has its own icy tang, each honeycomb's uniquely from one field, each grape's most subtly blent of sun, earth, rain, while truffles taste of treasures buried deep and mushrumps have the smack of shade and damp, to emphasize the cunning of an herb or quench the acrid ardor of a leek as apple tartness is made soft by pears. That's but to name a few of many plants. Our crabs and lobsters clack self-praise enough; the oysters rightly feel they need no boast. Soon hazelnuts and quinces will be ripe, and I could hymn what hymeneal things occur when they are introduced to trout. I think I shall—"

"A moment, pray, kind sir," Jennifer interrupted. She was coming out of her daze. "Thou speak'st of 'we.' Who else dwells hereabouts?"

Ariel arched his brows. "Who dost thou think? . . . And here he comes to meet me."

Jennifer cried aloud in shock.

The being which shambled around a bend in the path seemed twice hideous against woods, birds, and elf. He was roughly manlike, somewhat beneath her in height. That was partly due to the shortness of his bowlegs, partly to his hunched stance, for the shoulders were broad. Arms dangled past knees; like the splay feet, they ended in black-rimmed unclipped nails. A matted white shock of hair disguised, at first, how small his head was. It had no brow or chin; the eyes crouched deep in great caverns of bone, the face was mostly muzzle, flat nose and gash of a mouth. His skin, sallow and brown-spotted, was covered by nothing save a filthy loincloth.

"Be not affrighted," said Ariel: "neither one of ye."

The creature's jaw dropped, showing tushes which must once have been fearsome but were now a few yellow snags. "What is?" he asked hoarsely. "What fetch is this thou fetched—" Abruptly he bawled *"Miranda!"* and cast himself forward and down.

Jennifer braced body and spirit. The monster groveled at her ankles. Through his head and his clasping arms she was shaken by his weeping.

" 'Tis merely Caliban," Ariel told her through the ragged sobs, "these many years quite harmless, or at least in check to me. I do confess his outburst's a surprise."

"Who's Caliban?" Her nose wrinkled at the animal rankness rising about her.

"He's a foul witch's whelp, that Prospero did find when small, and taught to speak a tongue thou hear'st as English here—and raised to be a servant unto him. A nasty, surly, sneaky one he was, who at the end sought to betray his lord, but soon got tipsy, reeled through foolishness, and later ululated his regret. When Prospero released me and went home, he left this hulk behind as well. What use a Caliban in Italy, except to be such butt of japes and bait of dogs as to ignite his flimsy wits in rage, and make him pluck someone apart, and hang? So he's grown old alone upon the isle, save now and then when I, in quest of sport or in an idle kindliness, pay calls and make mirages for his entertainment."

"Miranda, oh, Miranda," grated the monster, and lifted his wet visage toward Jennifer's.

Ariel fluttered off to regard her. "Nay, thou'rt not," he deemed. "Aside from clothes, cropped hair, and all the rest, thou'rt fairer than she was, more tall— Ah, well. She was the only maid he ever saw, and in the many years between, though begged, I never thought it proper to bring back the darling semblance in a show for him." He pondered what appeared to be a new thought. "So ghosts do age and change in mortal wise?"

Shuddering still, Caliban got up. He flung arms widely and wildly, drummed his breast, broke off at every few words to give a bark of pain. "Thou art not a Miranda? But thou art! This must be a Miranda, Ariel. Thou'rt clever in the tinting of the air, but never hast thou wrought a dream like this. Behold how sweetly curved, how finely carved! Thou hast no skill to melt and mold a moonbeam and taper it to make those hands of hers. Couldst thou invent that vein within her throat, as blue as shadow on a sunlit cloud? What melody of thine could sing her walk? And—oh, I'm sorry for thee, Ariel!—thou hast no nose like mine, to drink the breeze that she perfumes; thou knowest common roses, while I could drowse a million happy years within the summer meadow of her breath. Her cheeks are soft as sleep. . . . Lie not to me! I've not forgotten what Mirandas are, and this Miranda's real—is real—is real!"

He began to hop about, chattering, slavering, baring what was left of his teeth at the sprite. "Thou shalt not take away this new Miranda!" he screamed. "Thou squirrel, raven, thievish heartless mocker, hast thou not hoarded up bright gauds enough that I may keep one realness of mine own? Come down, thou insect! See, my gape stands wide and bids thee enter—though 'twill spit thee out to make a meal for blowflies!"

"Caliban," said Ariel sternly, "thou'rt overheated as of yore." To Jennifer, who had backed off in alarm: "I'll quench him."

A whine whirled over the path. Ariel became a tiny thunderhead through which leaped needles of toy lightning. Caliban yammered, raised arms for shield, and crouched. Rain and hail flogged him, bolts jagged into his skin. It was a harmless punishment, to judge by the lack of wounds, but painful, to judge by how he jerked and wailed.

"Don't hurt him more," Jennifer pleaded after a minute. "His hair's too white for this."

Ariel resumed his usual shape. Caliban lay snuffling. "Why, it was mild," said the sprite. "I've felt much worse than it myself when riding on the rampant gales." As Caliban dared look at him: "Methinks this is the first of any time thou hast been pitied, since thou wast a pup. Thou might give thanks for that."

The creature crawled back to his feet. Jennifer saw how he winced, not at the chastisement he had taken, but at the ache of age within his bones. "I do, I do," he rumbled abjectly. "Aye, sweetness goes with being a Miranda." He tugged his forelock and attempted a bow in her direction. "Be not afraid. 'Tis I'm afraid of thee. When I was young, and with the first Miranda, I own I terrified her tenderness, but none had taught me better how to be. The thoughts do drop and trickle very slow through this thick bone that sits atop my chine. Natheless I've had a deal of years to brood on how 'tis best Mirandas be adored. I'll clean thy place each day, and bring it flowers, and chop thee plenty firewood, scrub the pots, lie watchdog at thy feet, and if thou wilt, show thee a secret berry patch I have. Or anything, Miranda. Only tell."

"Come," said Ariel. "Let us go prepare for her that cell."

XVII

In 1998 Gordon van Gelder, then the editor of *The Magazine of Fantasy and Science Fiction* (today its publisher as well), invited me to contribute to the fiftieth anniversary issue, which would appear in late 1999. How could I possibly not want to? It had been far too long since I was last in those pages.

For a good many years Karen and I have been active in Contact. This is perhaps more a series of events than an organization, although, naturally, it has a hard-working, dedicated core. It features an annual long-weekend gathering of scientists—notably anthropologists, but other kinds also—plus writers, artists, teachers, students, and anyone else who's interested, at which the central theme is some aspect of possible interaction between humans and extraterrestrial intelligent beings. Variations are endless; contact may be physical, by interstellar radio, or something else, the aliens—and often the humans—as strange as disciplined imagination can make them. For the ideal is that of hard science fiction, to stay within the terms of real science except when an extra postulate or two becomes absolutely necessary. Separate discussion groups explore details, then at the end the actual contact scenario is played out, an on-stage improvisation in which the developments almost always surprise everybody, not least the players.

Other, related activities go on simultaneously. It's fascinating, fun, and mind-opening. In fact, the project of designing a planet, the life upon it, the sentient inhabitants and their culture, from the ground up, that make sense in terms of real physics, chemistry, biology, sociology, and logic, is a great "hands-on" way to master those principles. A growing number of teachers have adopted it for their classes. NASA has gotten interested too, since it regards science education as one of its functions. Contact now regularly has NASA scientists on its programs and a day of lectures at the Ames facility.

If you'd like to know more, I suggest you see their website at <www.cabrillo.cc.ca.us/contact/new.html>, or write to CONTACT c/o Dr. James Funaro, P.O. Box 1300, Sequim WA 98382, with "ATT: Request for information" on the envelope.

A couple of Japanese guests were impressed enough to start their own organization. Karen and I were invited to its third meeting. In return, we were asked to provide a plausible world and dwellers at a real star within twenty light-years, so that radio communication wouldn't be too slow. We put in quite a lot of time and effort, and I may yet get a novel out of it. In that case, I promised, there will be at least one important Japanese character!

The event took place at a meeting center where everybody stayed in dormitory style—all by itself, a unique experience for us. Afterward we traveled around for a while on our own. It's an expensive country, but at our age this was an opportunity we couldn't afford *not* to take advantage of. I've observed earlier how close-knit the heart of the science fiction world still is. You can meet somebody in person for the first time and instantly be good friends. We found it doubly true in Japan, where everybody was overwhelmingly kind and generous.

So, returning home, what else could I do but make my story a tribute to that beautiful land and her people?

THE SHRINE FOR LOST CHILDREN

KAMAKURA

She had seen him a hundred times or more—who has not?—in travel books, on postcards, as a miniature copy in San Francisco's Japanese Tea Garden. But when he sat before her, seeming to fill half the sky with the mightiness of his peace, she knew that she had never known him.

Her days of fine weather had turned cold, with a sharp little wind. The Great Buddha loomed green-bronze against a gray overcast. Maybe that helped the feeling to well up in her that nothing else mattered, not the low buildings and autumnal trees around or the other visitors chattering and photographing or even her own life. Or rather, said a bewildered thought, everything mattered equally, everything was the same, for Amida was in all that was.

From more than six tall man-heights he looked outward and slightly downward, as he had done for more than seven centuries. The smile of compassion barely touched the serenity of his face. His robes flowed to hands lying curled on his lap, the attitude of meditation, as if so bared to the truth that they had no need to grip it, so strong that they would not ever need to wield their power.

She was not religious—had not been unless as a small girl, sometimes in the dark crying out to Jesus. She only stayed for a while that she did not measure, drawing a kind of silence around herself, gazing, half lost in the presence.

She had seen much beauty thus far, and much charm, and something of a foreign history and the soul within it. Too much too fast, really; it blurred together in her mind. A few things stood clearly forth—the Temple of the Golden Pavilion mirrored in still water; children taken in bright traditional clothes to their festival at Sumiyoshi Taisha; the Sengakuji like an island in

Tokyo's sea of cars and high-rises, forever remembering the Forty-Seven Ronin and their stark story. The image here had immediately joined the foremost.

Are you feeling what I feel, Jenny? she wondered. Have you been sharing the journey? Has it helped you a little bit?

She did not know whether she feared or hoped for an answer. There had been nothing since that last day and night before she left home.

BERKELEY

It happened without warning, as it often did. They were taking a coffee break in the office, and Alice Holt mentioned acquiring a kitten. "I think we'll call her Jennyanydots."

Here I am. What can we do?

She lurched at the suddenness of it. The Styrofoam cup almost dropped from her hand. Some of the coffee splashed down onto the floor.

No, Jenny! Not here. Later.

But you called. I heard.

That wasn't me. We can't do anything here. Wait for me.

You're always waiting for me, she thought.

But I'm lonesome.

I know. Frantically: Be good and wait. We'll do things later, I promise. I'll sing you songs, I'll tell you a wonderful story, but I can't right now where I am.

This isn't a nice place?

It is, it is. It's just different from home. We both have to wait a while. I'll call you as soon as I can. I promise. Please.

A hand closed on her arm. "Are you all right?" asked Joe Bowers.

"Yes," she whispered. "Something surprised me, that's all. I'll clean up the mess."

"No, I think you better sit down," said Alice. "We'll take care of it. Don't worry, dear."

Their looks followed her as she—"groped" was the word—to her desk, fell into the chair, and drew long, slow breaths. Vaguely, she sensed their attention still upon her. She could well imagine their thoughts. This wasn't the first time, in the few months of her employment, they'd seen her stare at what seemed to them to be nothing. Or else she'd shiver or gasp. Usually it was not when Jenny stirred, simply when memories broke in on her. But of course they didn't know.

You aren't happy.

Later, I told you! she yelled.

She felt the puzzled hurt. Blindly, fleeingly, she attacked her work.

Mr. Robertson came by. He stood for a while looking over her shoulder at the computer screen and down at the papers and printouts. Then he told her to come into his own office. After closing the door, he said, "I'm afraid we'll have to let you go." He sounded more grim than regretful. "You've messed up the accounting again."

She mumbled an apology but didn't ask for another chance. If she'd done that, the tears would probably have started, and in the past several years she'd tried hard to school herself out of crying.

"Frankly, I believe you need help," he said, relief gentling his tone. "Counseling, maybe therapy. Take care of yourself. We'll mail you your pay and severance with a little extra."

The knowledge came to her: "Thank you, but I won't be at the same address. Could you direct-deposit it in my bank, please? I'll leave the account number on my desk. Thank you. Goodbye."

She didn't tell her workmates why she left early. They doubtless guessed. Outside, the loveliness of Indian summer in the Bay Area, sycamores in the park across the street showing their first gold to a mild sun, barely touched her awareness. It was the same when a city bus set her off in the flatlands and she walked between drab walls to the apartment.

Dave sprawled on the couch amidst general messiness, scribbling one of the poems he read aloud in coffeehouses. He scowled at the interruption. When she told him she'd been fired he exclaimed, "How long have you ever kept any job?"

"How long have you?" she replied wearily.

He rose and came to her. His smile flashed as smoothly as his voice flowed. "Hey, don't get mad, lover. I know you've got problems. I wish you'd tell me what they are, but anyway, I understand." He took her by the shoulders. His hands might as well have been two beanbags. "Let's crack a beer and smoke a joint and hit the good old futon, okay? Then you won't toss around and moan tonight, will you?"

At least I fake my responses well, she thought.

"You take this pretty easily, don't you?" she said.

"Well, it's not a disaster, is it? We've got a nice cash stash to see us through."

She met his eyes. "We?"

His hands dropped. "Uh, you do. Your divorce settlement, I mean. About fifteen thousand bucks, right?"

"That's what's left. I don't intend to waste any more of it."

He took a step backward. "Huh? What do you mean, waste? We need to eat and pay the rent, don't we?"

She sighed. "Find yourself a job. Or another woman."

He gaped.

"Don't worry," she said. "You will soon enough."

Why had she ever come to California? And why did she take up with this guy? Hoping for—for what, anyway?

Oh, he was handsome, beguiling, not a dullard. She felt a brief, frozen pity for him as well as that other. "I'll pack my things and clear out," she told him.

"Just like *that*?"

No, she thought. The decision had come all at once, but it had been building up inside her. Maybe throughout her life.

."Where'll you *go*?" she heard.

To a motel, she supposed, one with a restaurant and a bar close by, though she'd better not have more than a couple of drinks after forcing down some food. Then in her room she'd do what she had promised Jenny, reach a truce of sorts with herself, and at last be able to sleep.

"Don't worry," she repeated. "And I'm not angry with you, Dave. We've squabbled, but we've also enjoyed ourselves. Be happy."

She did not think: If only I could be. Endurance was the one defense left to her.

KAMAKURA

Maybe she had him to thank for getting her interested in Japan. He talked such a lot about Zen. But no. Already before she set off, the reading she did and her conversations with people who were informed had shown how scant his knowledge was, how close to zero his understanding. Zen was a set of attitudes and practices; it had scarcely anything to do with what was in this temple.

Nor did she.

She clutched her purse as if it were the peace that was fading out of her and walked hastily around the courtyard.

A mistake. Seen from behind, Daibutsu was almost featureless, a metal mass. A booth at the side gave access, for a fee, to the interior. Obviously no worshipper considered the idea sacrilegious—it must be like an American's attitude at the Statue of Liberty—but she didn't want to enter. What she saw might well wreck her memory of the mood she had lost.

Better go. She glanced at her watch. Yes. She also meant to see the other temple, Hase-dera, before returning to her lodgings. According to the guidebook, at this time of year it closed at five, and the afternoon was wearing on.

Or should she make the visit? That shrine—

Well, she could pass by it and head straight for the famous things. Roy wasn't here to call her a neurotic coward. Nobody was.

She went from the Great Buddha, never looking back.

PHOENIX

Summer laid even an extravagantly well-watered suburb in a furnace. The window out which she stared seemed an ice-fragile barrier. It would shatter if she touched it, and her conditioned air spill forth to be devoured by the heat-shimmers on the pavement. No. Ridiculous. This moment in time was the glass that was breaking apart. Her gaze went between a pair of neighbor houses, to the desert beyond.

"I loved you. I did. Once," Roy said.

Or you loved the girl who tumbled from junior college into marriage four years ago because a man asked her, she thought. If I could have changed—

He'd said essentially the same thing earlier this afternoon, when the words had been harder. If she'd pulled herself together and overcome her moodiness, her sloppiness, yes, her frigidity. If she'd simply put on enough of a mask that they could have a decent social life. That was important for business too. The business was going to hell. He couldn't concentrate on it, the way things were. And lately he'd found another woman. Inevitably, he'd said.

"Don't be afraid," he went on. "We needn't spend a fortune on lawyers. I'll give you the best settlement I can afford."

She turned around to confront him again. Having foreseen this day and braced herself for it, she was able to reply, "Enough to put me on my feet. No more. I won't parasitize you . . . and her."

It hurt unexpectedly much to see his astonishment. "By God, you do have guts."

"I've needed them. You don't believe that, but it's true."

"To fight yourself. Why? I've pleaded with you, never mind expense, see a psychiatrist. Get rid of those demons, whatever they are." He paused. "Or—okay, we're not Catholic, but at last I wondered, I'm still wondering, maybe an exorcist—"

"No!" she cried, less at him than at the horror.

Getting rid—if it could be done at all—the final, unbearable guilt.

He slumped where he stood. "Well, we've been over this ground and over it, haven't we?" he said dully. "Too late now in any case. But I'll always wish you the best."

A civilized lie, she thought. Not that you'll wish me the worst. You'll simply be too free and happy to care one way or another. "The same to you," she said.

"Too bad things didn't work out. But—" He straightened. "Well, they didn't. We can stay friends, can't we? How about a drink? Or we could go out to dinner. Or whatever."

She shook her head. "No, thanks. You go, Roy. Please. Till tomorrow. I'd rather be alone overnight."

"You sure?"

She nodded. After a few further, embarrassed exchanges, he left. She knew where he was bound. No matter.

The westering sun began to soften a ridge on the horizon with purple and shadows.

It was a comfort, the comfort that is in surrender, when Jenny asked, *Will we go home now?* Yes, Jenny had listened, a little bewildered and scared but with unshaken faith in her.

No, she answered. Don't you remember? Mother's not there anymore.

I know. Where is she?

Poor tormented Mother. Did Jenny understand at all about death?

Resting, she answered. You and I aren't ready to. Not yet. Let's find someplace else.

KAMAKURA

Traffic went thick on the narrow street, cars, trucks, motorcycles crowding left-sidedly along, noise she didn't notice at the temple. Though lessening, the wind that searched through her thin coat kept the air fresh. On this gray day in November she might be the single foreigner in the Hase district. Certainly she saw none but Japanese. Most of them walked briskly but without hustle. They didn't look alien. Their clothes were Western style, except for one lady unself-consciously in a kimono. An occasional jacket or sweatshirt on a youngster flaunted some overseas name or slogan, generally American; mature men were often in business suits. Few were small—well-nourished, the past couple of generations had grown to European-like sizes—nor were their faces actually unfamiliar. By any standard, a number of the men were handsome, a remarkably high percentage of the women beautiful.

Emptiness asked: What can I find here? Gorgeous sights, interesting places, glimpses of customs and rituals, but for me, are they anything more than museum pieces? This is a high-tech, cutting-edge, world-power country. I might have done better on a Southwestern Indian reservation. No, there they'd have nothing whatever they could share with outsiders; everything goes by kinship. Here I can at least get around as easily and safely as I could in France or Holland. Relax. Forget any pilgrimage nonsense. Be just a tourist. I'm no more an outsider than I have always been everywhere.

Still, the snatches of conversation she overheard were incomprehensible, the signs unreadable. The walk was supposed to take about ten minutes. The guidebook contained a sketchy map. But when a longer time than that had passed, she realized she'd missed a turn. She stopped, unreasonably dismayed. How helpless you felt when you had become illiterate.

She looked around and around. Could she manage to retrace her steps? Then it might not be worthwhile starting over. Already the day was noticeably darkening.

"Excuse, prease." A middle-aged woman had halted, to address her in English with a friendly smile. "You need assistance?"

"I've lost my way. If you could tell me how to get to—" She hesitated, aware she'd mangle the pronunciation. "Hase-dera?"

"Come." The woman took her elbow. "I show you."

"No, thank you very much—ah—*arigato*. I don't want to trouble you."

"No troubre. You come, prease." The woman led her off.

"Really—I mean—weren't you headed the other way?"

"No troubre. You come from United States?"

"Yes. Near San Francisco." Her last port of call.

"Ah, Carifornia, yes? You enjoy your visit?"

The American nodded wordlessly. The Japanese accent was hard for her to follow. She'd encountered several individuals with perfect English; they got plenty of chances to practice. This lady had to make an effort, besides going in a direction that wasn't hers.

It was a short while, though, till she pointed up a lane. "Straight there. Watch out for cars. They come srow, but you go stand on side, okay?"

"Thank you—*arigato, arigato*—" She recalled that the proper expression involved another word or two, but couldn't bring them to mind. She bowed awkwardly. Her guide smiled again, wished her a pleasant evening, and disappeared into the crowd.

She stood for a minute harking back to earlier incidents after her arrival. You expected politeness from bellhops and waiters and such, and received it with never a hint of surliness. However, this wasn't the first time a stranger had freely come to her aid. She thought the Japanese must be not only the most courteous but the most considerate people on earth. She almost wished she had been born as one of them.

Born—No. No, no, no.

She snapped a cold breath. She had indeed come a long way from her beginnings. Why couldn't she leave them behind?

NORTHFIELD

Spring in Minnesota was a flirt, bright and thawing, bleak and wet, then at last all-yielding. Leaves glowed newly green, blossoms sprang forth overnight. The arboretum became an enchanted forest. It was the pride of the college, forty acres of trees and shrubs, where footpaths wound and a brook lazed glittery under a wooden bridge. Fragrances and early birdsong filled the breeze. And she walked here with Tim. Tim!

The world had wobbled yesterday when he suggested it as school was closing for the weekend. They'd passed through the same grades since she and Mother moved to this town, but hardly ever spoken, and he wasn't just lately turned sixteen, half a year older than her, he was Tim, big, outgoing, popular, active in the science club and the band, a basketball whiz and surely great on the dance floor with any girl lucky enough to be his partner. For a couple of sick heartbeats she'd thought it must be some cruel joke. But no, he'd joined her offside where nobody else could hear, and his smile was almost shy. She didn't sleep much Friday night.

That made no difference. She had never been as alive as she was today. If I cut myself somehow, she thought once, wildly, I bet the blood would sparkle.

Underneath: Please don't let anything spoil this. Oh, please.

They hadn't found a lot to say, though. He'd gotten out a few words about having lunch later on, like at Ingrid's Sandwich Shop, and she'd stammered that her mother expected her home then and had been terrified that she'd have to admit it was because she hadn't dared say anything about her date, but he made it good right away by answering, "Too bad. Some other time soon, I hope? And we could sit together in lunch hour at school if you want."

She, with him, who always sat by herself.

Otherwise they strolled under the leaves. He didn't take her hand, but once in a while his brushed hers and a tingling shot through her.

The path bent toward the stream. Near the bridge was a bench. "Care to sit down?" he asked.

They did, side by side, beneath the sky and the sun. The water clucked and murmured where it flowed around the piers.

"How nice," she managed after a while. "Extra nice right now."

He turned his head to look at her. She half looked at him. "You ought to know. You come here a lot, don't you?"

He's *noticed*? "Yes. It's, it's peaceful."

"Quiet. Like you."

She sat mute.

"You're so quiet," he said. "So alone. Why?"

"N-nobody asks me . . . to do anything."

"Don't blame them. You kind of scare them, you know? You often seem like your mind's off in another dimension or something. Or else you've got your nose buried in a book."

Was that an attack? She stiffened. "I like books."

Books don't call me idle, careless, worthless. They don't tell me, "Jenny would never have done that."

They don't cry for help.

He sensed the change in her. "Hey, wait." The words stumbled over each other. "I didn't mean any harm. Honest. I like you. You've got brains."

The fear melted out of her. She felt the heat in her cheeks. "Thank you," she whispered, staring down at the damp earth.

He regained his usual self-assurance. "It's just there's more in life," he said earnestly. "Fun, games—Not that I'm a lightweight. I have my ambitions."

Safe ground. Maybe. She found she could turn her eyes back toward his. "What do you want to do?"

"I think I'll go into electronics. Research and development. That's the future."

"Unless it's biology. Or psychology. They're doing big things in genetics and brain chemistry."

"You read science magazines too? Yeah, you're no airhead." He leaned closer. "I'd like to know you better. What's your dream?"

Confusion overwhelmed her. "To be happy, I guess."

My daydream. When I can dream it. At night—No, don't think about what happens some nights. Not now. Hang onto this sunlight, Tim here beside me, yonder cherry blossoms.

"You aren't?" he wondered.

"I'm all right," she insisted.

"You don't need to be lonesome." Amazed, she saw him blush too. "You— you're real pretty."

His arm went around her shoulder, ever so gently. His lips drew near hers. I'm in love, she knew amidst the uproar, in love, in love.

You're leaving me! Jenny screamed. *Don't leave me alone! It's dark here!*

Her throat gave back the cry. She wrenched free, leaped up, and ran. Through the sobs she heard Tim call out, but he didn't come after her.

KAMAKURA

Small open-fronted shops flanked this lane, most of them offering tourist wares, better stuff than their American counterparts. A few homes stood in fenced gardens. The buildings were old, attractive, exotic in ways she could not clearly identify. As her guide had warned, pedestrians yielded when a vehicle nosed through.

I won't have time for much, she realized. The view over the city. The Kannon Hall and its huge image. It wouldn't be right if I didn't pay my respects to the Goddess of Mercy. Not that I believe she can grant me any. But somehow, in some unreasoned way, it's something I can do for Jenny.

Or because of Jenny? I don't know. How long has it been since I last asked myself such a question? I don't even know what I came searching for, besides a few bright memories to take back with me. But why has Jenny been silent this whole while?

Never mind. Never.

I can come back tomorrow for the other sanctuaries and the garden. The book says they're exquisite. That'd mean changing my itinerary, but who's with me to care?

Only—then I'd have to pass twice, to and fro, by the shrine for the children. How would that be for you, Jenny?

She tensed herself against an answer. There was none.

Abruptly, impulsively, she turned into one of the shops and bought a few incense sticks and a book of matches. She could have fragrance in her hotel room tonight, and afterward at home, wherever that would next be.

Not pausing at the lower complex, she kept on till she saw the staircase rise long and steep. Below it she stopped, unsure whether she really should continue.

Yes. Every time she made herself do what a normal human being would, she gained more control. If Kamakura had nothing else to give her, it offered this slight strengthening. She began to climb. The effort made her feel, for a foolish moment, as if she were climbing out of her past.

MINNEAPOLIS

How softly the snow fell. You couldn't see across the street through that tumbling white stillness. She wished she were out in it, the air on her cheeks like a cool kiss, the flakes on her tongue tasting of sky. Mother kept the house awful hot in winter.

But she'd tried to pick Gumball up for a hug, and the kitten was beside the lamp and she'd knocked the lamp over. Its glass globe lay in shiny pieces across the rug.

Mother loomed above, as tall as the ceiling. She kept her voice cold. That meant she was angry. "You're a bad girl. Bad, do you hear?"

"I'm sorry."

" 'Sorry' isn't enough. You must be *careful*."

She hung her head. The tears began. She tried to sniffle them away.

"Don't blubber at me," Mother said. "You're four years old. High time you learned proper behavior."

She knuckled her eyes and sort of stopped crying.

"Go to your room," Mother said. "Stay there till dinnertime."

"Yes." It came out like a puppy barking.

"Show more respect, young lady."

She bit her lip. "Yes, Mother."

"Go and think about Jenny. She would have been a good child." When no reply came: "Wouldn't she?"

Real quick: "Yes, Mother."

The woman bent down and spoke more softly. "I'm not being mean to you. I'm trying to make you as good as Jenny." She sighed. "And I have to do it all by myself, now that your father has left us. I love you. I want you to love me too, love me as much as both of you together should have done. That way you'll make up for crowding Jenny out of the world. Do you see?"

She nodded and nodded and nodded.

Mother straightened. "I know you didn't do it on purpose," she said in the flat way she'd said this often before. "It hurt you too. Your sister would have been your friend, your playmate. You would have grown up sharing everything, in a loving home. Instead, you've never known her. But you can think about her. I do. That's why I gave her a name, so we will never forget her."

It was not my fault! She mustn't say that. She remembered too well what came of it when she did. But words escaped: "I won't. I know her. You never did."

Mother went pale and tight around the mouth. "That's enough. I've told you again and again not to act crazy. Don't say mean things, either." She pointed. "Go."

The corridor was high and hollow. Feet sounded loud on bare boards. This was a big house. Mother kept telling how she had wanted a big family. Now Mother wondered if they could afford to stay anywhere in the city.

The door clicked shut on the room. It was very quiet too. The light through the window and the snow fell shadowy-gray. The pictures on the walls, mostly of cute animals, seemed to lose their colors. But they had never been changed and she hardly saw them any longer. She had her toys, a large rubber ball, a tea set, crayons, paper, scissors, paste. She had her books. A teddy bear and a doll sat on top of the dresser. Between them lay a rattle. Mother had told her she must always keep it there, because it would have been Jenny's.

She sat down in her chair, looked out at the snow, and said into the quietness: "We're alone now."

The sad little voice grew hopeful. *Will you play with me?*

Sure I will, she answered.

Who else was there?

KAMAKURA

No, of course you couldn't leave your past behind you. It was yourself.

As she climbed, her view became wide. Trees in their fall colors spread a tapestry across the hillside, subdued by the gathering dimness. The eastern sky arched slaty, the western dull silver. Lights were beginning to shine along the streets below. Southward glimmered Sagami Bay.

She reached a turn of the ascent and found the images. They were meant to welcome, but they brought her to a halt as if they barred the way. For a moment her heart stopped.

Rank upon rank, rank above rank, hundreds upon hundreds upon hundreds, they lined this part of the stair, which otherwise turned upward to the left, and surrounded a landing. They were alike, doll-sized figures of a robed man, unpainted, earth hue. That made the articles of clothing on a number of them, mainly red caps or bibs, doubly vivid, even at this hour.

Jizo, a boddhisatva, one of those who have attained Enlightenment but deferred entering Buddhahood that they might help lead others toward salvation—Jizo, patron of travelers and the savior of children.

This was the place she had meant to pass by, and suddenly could not.

The landing was a small strip of ground that led off to a small and simple shrine. Here the caps and bibs were closer together, and she noticed tiny offerings of food at the feet of several. Mothers came here, to bind on memorial cloths, lay down their sacrifices, light incense sticks. Mothers of babies who had been aborted, naturally or deliberately, or were stillborn.

Stillborn like my twin. Though that was a strange case, an entangling umbilicus, a thing that could not have happened at all if we had not been two.

She felt with a faint astonishment that the thought did not hurt as it always had before. Her heart beat evenly and gently.

What stung her eyes was a nearby image wearing a cap with Mickey Mouse's face on it and a bib on which was printed I LOVE MY DADDY. She might have given that, if she had known her father. But this must be from a Japanese family. Did they have living children who liked American cartoons?

A sense of abiding strength touched her. The outside influence showed merely that here was faith held by real people in a real world.

How right that Kannon watches over this ground, she thought. I should go on and see the Merciful One before it's too late.

She couldn't.

Why not?

Jenny, do you want something? Tell me. Come to me.

There was no answer.

Mother would never let go of you. She would never let you rest. But she's gone. Why haven't you departed too? Why can't you?

An impulse rose and rose in her, like a tide. She glanced back and forth, upward and downward. Nobody else was in sight. Nobody would take offense if a foreign unbeliever made a clumsy gesture.

A gesture, no more. But she'd had the courage to come this far. It would be wrong to deny Jenny a token, which was also a sign to herself—a declaration not of bitterness, in spite of everything, but of love.

Was that the blind wish that had driven her? Then where had it come from?

Let her carry it through and be done.

She stepped off onto the landing and passed between the little statues. At the shrine she paused, uncertain. What to do? She bowed deeply, as best she was able. Jizo, Kannon, and Amida must know she meant reverence.

Fumbling in her purse, she got a coin—it felt like a hundred-yen piece, which wasn't much but had flowers on it—and tossed it into an offering box. The wind had died down, and the disc landed with a sound that almost pealed. Reaching in again, she took an incense stick and the matches. She struck fire and set it in a bowl of sand where others had burned out. She breathed the sweet smoke.

For you, Jenny.

Once more she bowed.

It was as if she heard a faraway chorus of children's voices. But the one that spoke to her was a woman's, calm and joyful.

Thank you, thank you, my sister.

Jenny, is that you?

Yes. At last at peace.

In unsurprised acceptance, she thought that Jenny hadn't foreseen either. How could a small child? But Jenny had come to know with a wordless wisdom that lies beyond life, that here was release.

Goodbye, my dearest. Peace be with you too, forever.

She stood alone, altogether alone, yet open to all that was. Never before now had she been happy.

I have not reached heaven, she knew. I have simply found—or been granted—enough Enlightenment that I can go home and share in the living world.

What is Enlightenment but Understanding?

It was not only Jenny who clung to me. I would not let go. Here I have freed myself from myself.

She went on upward, to Hase Kannon, to give her own thanks.

XVIII

My writing career began with John Campbell, and after his death continued at *Analog* with Ben Bova, later with Stanley Schmidt, both of them great guys as well as worthy successors. Yet, although I'm less closely identified with it, *The Magazine of Fantasy and Science Fiction* has meant equally much to me. Since a story from the first opens this retrospective, I'd like to close with a story from the second, even though it means one more leap back through time.

After Tony resigned, I had the pleasure and privilege of working with each of the men who, in turn, took the helm. While Robert Mills did a good job, he's perhaps most notable for starting a regrettably short-lived companion magazine, *Venture Science Fiction*. This went in more for action stories than the "literary" kind—and what's wrong with that?—but, like the long-defunct pulp *Planet Stories,* was free of most of the puritanical taboos that still bound popular fiction, including science fiction. As a result, it ran a few such extraordinary things as Theodore Sturgeon's "Affair with a Green Monkey" and Walter Miller Jr.'s "Vengeance for Nikolai." My *Virgin Planet* wasn't in that class, but did at least have some bawdy humor. I mention this largely to show that the "New Wave" of the late sixties and early seventies wasn't quite as new as its more excitable spokespeople have claimed.

Avram Davidson gave story ideas to both Karen and me and, like John Campbell, never took any credit for them.

I think it was under Edward Ferman that the magazine started occasionally dedicating a particular issue to a particular writer, who contributed a feature story and was portrayed on the cover, while an appreciative essay or two by colleagues and a bibliography also appeared. Certainly it was Mr. Ferman who, in 1971, did this for me—a stunning honor, seeing that it had earlier come to Fritz Leiber and Theodore Sturgeon. The painting by Kelly Freas still hangs in my study, along with my investiture in the Baker Street Irregulars and several Rembrandt etchings.

Of course I gave the story everything I had to give. It's hard science fiction in that the setting is worked out as carefully as I was able and the only perhaps questionable assumption is that certain nonhumans possess a kind of telepathic capability. It's fantasy in its atmosphere, derived partly from medieval Danish folk ballads. It reflects my interest in Jungian psychology and, yes, if you look closely, Sherlock Holmes. It was well received, winning awards and being reprinted in several different places. But that was long ago, and I trust that by now it will be new to most readers. Let me close this introduction with my introductory remarks way back then.

"The Queen of Air and Darkness" is a figure of unknown antiquity who continues to haunt the present day. T. H. White, in The Once and Future King, *identified her with Morgan le Fay. Before him, A. E. Housman had written one of his most enigmatic poems about her. But actually the title—a counterpart to the traditional attributes of Satan—is borne by the demonic female who appears over the centuries in many legends and many guises. She is Lilith of rabbinical lore, who in turn goes back to Babylon; she is the great she-jinni of the Arabs; the Japanese were particularly afraid of* kami *who had the form of women; American Indians dreaded one who went hurrying through the sky at night. In medieval Europe, one of her shapes, among others, is that of the mistress of the elf hill, against whom Scottish and Danish ballads warn the belated traveler, and who reappears in the Tannhäuser story. Her weapon here is the beauty and—in the old sense of the word—the charm by which she lures men away from her enemy God. Certain finds lead me to suspect that they knew about her in the Old Stone Age, and she will surely go on into the future.*

THE QUEEN OF AIR AND DARKNESS

The last glow of the last sunset would linger almost until midwinter. But there would be no more day, and the northlands rejoiced. Blossoms opened, flamboyance on firethorn trees, steelflowers rising blue from the brok and rainplant that cloaked all hills, shy whiteness of kiss-me-never down in the dales. Flitteries darted among them on iridescent wings; a crownbuck shook his horns and bugled through warmth and flower odors. Between horizons the sky deepened from purple to sable. Both moons were aloft, nearly full, shining frosty on leaves and molten on waters. The shadows they made were blurred by an aurora, a great blowing curtain of light across half heaven. Behind it the earliest stars had come out.

A boy and a girl sat on Wolund's Barrow just under the dolmen it upbore. Their hair, which streamed halfway down their backs, showed startlingly forth, bleached as it was by summer. Their bodies, still dark from that season, merged with earth and bush and rock; for they wore only garlands. He played on a bone flute and she sang. They had lately become lovers. Their age was about sixteen, but they did not know this, considering themselves Outlings and thus indifferent to time, remembering little or nothing of how they had once dwelt in the lands of men.

His notes piped cold around her voice:

> "Cast a spell,
> weave it well.
> of dust and dew
> and night and you."

A brook by the grave mound, carrying moonlight down to a hill-hidden river, answered with its rapids. A flock of hellbats passed black beneath the aurora.

A shape came bounding over Cloudmoor. It had two arms and two legs, but the legs were long and claw-footed and feathers covered it to the end of a tail and broad wings. The face was half-human, dominated by its eyes. Had Ayoch been able to stand wholly erect, he would have reached to the boy's shoulder.

The girl rose. "He carries a burden," she said. Her vision was not meant for twilight like that of a northland creature born, but she had learned how to use every sign her senses gave her. Besides the fact that ordinarily a pook would fly, there was a heaviness to his haste.

"And he comes from the south." Excitement jumped in the boy, sudden as a green flame that went across the constellation Lyrth. He sped down the mound. "Ohoi, Ayoch!" he called. "Me here, Mistherd!"

"And Shadow-of-a-Dream," the girl laughed, following.

The pook halted. He breathed louder than the soughing in the growth around him. A smell of bruised yerba lifted where he stood.

"Well met in winterbirth," he whistled. "You can help me bring this to Carheddin."

He held out what he bore. His eyes were yellow lanterns above. It moved and whimpered.

"Why, a child," Mistherd said.

"Even as you were, my son, even as you were. Ho, ho, what a snatch!" Ayoch boasted. "They were a score in yon camp by Fallowwood, armed, and besides watcher engines they had big ugly dogs aprowl while they slept. I came from above, however, having spied on them till I knew that a handful of daze-dust—"

"The poor thing." Shadow-of-a-Dream took the boy and held him to her small breasts. "So full of sleep yet, aren't you, littleboo?" Blindly, he sought a nipple. She smiled through the veil of her hair. "No, I am still too young, and you already too old. But come, when you wake in Carheddin under the mountain you shall feast."

"Yo-ah," said Ayoch very softly. "She is abroad and has heard and seen. She comes." He crouched down, wings folded. After a moment Mistherd knelt, and then Shadow-of-a-Dream, though she did not let go the child.

The Queen's tall form blocked off the moons. For a while she regarded the three and their booty. Hill and moor sounds withdrew from their awareness until it seemed they could hear the northlights hiss.

At last Ayoch whispered, "Have I done well, Starmother?"

"If you stole a babe from a camp full of engines," said the beautiful voice, "then they were folk out of the far south who may not endure it as meekly as yeomen."

"But what can they do, Snowmaker?" the pook asked. "How can they track us?"

Mistherd lifted his head and spoke in pride. "Also, now they too have felt the awe of us."

"And he is a cuddly dear," Shadow-of-a-Dream said. "And we need more like him, do we not, Lady Sky?"

"It had to happen in some twilight," agreed she who stood above. "Take him onward and care for him. By this sign," which she made, "is he claimed for the Dwellers."

Their joy was freed. Ayoch cartwheeled over the ground till he reached a shiverleaf. There he swarmed up the trunk and out on a limb, perched half hidden by unrestful pale foliage, and crowed. Boy and girl bore the child toward Carheddin at an easy distance-devouring lope which let him pipe and her sing:

"Wahaii, wahaii!
Wayala, laii!
Wing on the wind
high over heaven,
shrilly shrieking,
rush with the rainspears,
tumble through tumult,
drift to the moonhoar trees and the dream-heavy shadows beneath
  them,
and rock in, be one with the clinking wavelets of lakes where the
  starbeams drown."

As she entered, Barbro Cullen felt, through all grief and fury, stabbed by dismay. The room was unkempt. Journals, tapes, reels, codices, file boxes, bescribbled papers were piled on every table. Dust filmed most shelves and corners. Against one wall stood a laboratory setup, microscope and analytical equipment. She recognized it as compact and efficient, but it was not what you would expect in an office, and it gave the air a faint chemical reek. The rug was threadbare, the furniture shabby.

This was her final chance?

Then Eric Sherrinford approached. "Good day, Mrs. Cullen," he said. His tone was crisp, his handclasp firm. His faded gripsuit didn't bother her. She wasn't inclined to fuss about her own appearance except on special occasions. (And would she ever again have one, unless she got back Jimmy?) What she observed was a cat's personal neatness.

A smile radiated in crow's feet from his eyes. "Forgive my bachelor housekeeping. On Beowulf we have—we had, at any rate—machines for that, so I never acquired the habit myself, and I don't want a hireling disarranging my tools. More convenient to work out of my apartment than keep a separate office. Won't you be seated?"

"No, thanks. I couldn't," she mumbled.

"I understand. But if you'll excuse me, I function best in a relaxed position."

He jackknifed into a lounger. One long shank crossed the other knee. He drew forth a pipe and stuffed it from a pouch. Barbro wondered why he took tobacco in so ancient a way. Wasn't Beowulf supposed to have the up-to-date equipment that they still couldn't afford to build on Roland? Well, of course old customs might survive anyhow. They generally did in colonies, she remembered reading. People had moved starward in the hope of preserving such outmoded things as their mother tongues or constitutional government or rational-technological civilization . . .

Sherrinford pulled her up from the confusion of her weariness: "You must give me the details of your case, Mrs. Cullen. You've simply told me that your son was kidnapped and your local constabulary did nothing. Otherwise I know just a few obvious facts, such as your being widowed rather than divorced; and you're the daughter of outwayers in Olga Ivanoff Land who, nevertheless, kept in close telecommunication with Christmas Landing; and you're trained in one of the biological professions; and you had several years' hiatus in field work until recently you started again."

She gaped at the high-cheeked, beak-nosed, black-haired and gray-eyed countenance. His lighter made a *scrit* and a flare which seemed to fill the room. Quietness dwelt on this height above the city, and winter dusk was seeping in through the windows. "How in cosmos do you know that?" she heard herself exclaim.

He shrugged and fell into the lecturer's manner for which he was notorious. "My work depends on noticing details and fitting them together. In more than a hundred years on Roland, the people, tending to cluster according to their origins and thought-habits, have developed regional accents. You have a trace of the Olgan burr, but you nasalize your vowels in the style of this area, though you live in Portolondon. That suggests steady childhood exposure to metropolitan speech. You were part of Matsuyama's expedition, you told me, and took your boy along. They wouldn't have allowed any ordinary technician to do that; hence you had to be valuable enough to get away with it. The team was conducting ecological research; therefore you must be in the life sciences. For the same reason, you must have had previous field experience. But your skin is fair, showing none of the leatheriness one gets from prolonged exposure to this sun. Accordingly, you must have been mostly indoors for a good while before you went on your ill-fated trip. As for widowhood—you never mentioned a husband to me, but you have had a man whom you thought so highly of that you still wear both the wedding and the engagement ring he gave you."

Her sight blurred and stung. The last of those words had brought Tim back, huge, ruddy, laughterful and gentle. She must turn from this other person and stare outward. "Yes," she achieved saying, "you're right."

The apartment occupied a hilltop above Christmas Landing. Beneath it the city dropped away in walls, roofs, archaistic chimneys and lamplit streets, goblin lights of human-piloted vehicles, to the harbor, the sweep of Venture Bay, ships bound to and from the Sunward Islands and remoter regions of the Boreal Ocean, which glimmered like mercury in the afterglow of Charlemagne. Oliver was swinging rapidly higher, a mottled orange disc a full degree wide; closer to the zenith which it could never reach, it would shine the color of ice. Alde, half the seeming size, was a thin slow crescent near Sirius, which she remembered was near Sol, but you couldn't see Sol without a telescope—

"Yes," she said around the pain in her throat, "my husband is about four years dead. I was carrying our first child when he was killed by a stampeding monocerus. We'd been married three years before. Met while we were both at the University—'casts from School Central can only supply a basic education, you know—we founded our own team to do ecological studies under contract—you know, can a certain area be settled while maintaining a balance of nature, what crops will grow, what hazards, that sort of question—Well, afterward I did lab work for a fisher co-op in Portolondon. But the monotony, the . . . shut-in-ness . . . was eating me away. Professor Matsuyama offered me a position on the team he was organizing to examine Commissioner Hauch Land. I thought, God help me, I thought Jimmy—Tim wanted him named James, once the tests showed it'd be a boy, after his own father and because of 'Timmy and Jimmy' and—Oh, I thought Jimmy could safely come along. I couldn't bear to leave him behind for months, not at his age. We could make sure he'd never wander out of camp. What could hurt him inside it? *I* had never believed those stories about the Outlings stealing human children. I supposed parents were trying to hide from themselves the fact they'd been careless, they'd let a kid get lost in the woods or attacked by a pack of satans or—Well, I learned better, Mr. Sherrinford. The guard robots were evaded and the dogs were drugged and when I woke, Jimmy was gone."

He regarded her through the smoke from his pipe. Barbro Engdahl Cullen was a big woman of thirty or so (Rolandic years, he reminded himself, ninety-five percent of Terrestrial, not the same as Beowulfan years), broad-shouldered, long-legged, full-breasted, supple of stride; her face was wide, straight nose, straightforward hazel eyes, heavy but mobile mouth; her hair was reddish-brown, cropped below the ears, her voice husky, her garment a plain street robe. To still the writhing of her fingers, he asked skeptically, "Do you now believe in the Outlings?"

"No. I'm just not so sure as I was." She swung about with half a glare for him. "And we have found traces."

"Bits of fossils," he nodded. "A few artifacts of a neolithic sort. But apparently ancient, as if the makers died ages ago. Intensive search has failed to turn up any real evidence for their survival."

"How intensive can search be, in a summer-stormy, winter-gloomy wilderness around the North Pole?" she demanded. "When we are, how many, a million people on an entire planet, half of us crowded into this one city?"

"And the rest crowding this one habitable continent," he pointed out.

"Arctica covers five million square kilometers," she flung back, "The Arctic Zone proper covers a fourth of it. We haven't the industrial base to establish satellite monitor stations, build aircraft we can trust in those parts, drive roads through the damned darklands and establish permanent bases and get to know them and tame them. Good Christ, generations of lonely outwaymen told stories about Graymantle, and the beast was never seen by a proper scientist till last year!"

"Still, you continue to doubt the reality of the Outlings?"

"Well, what about a secret cult among humans, born of isolation and ignorance, lairing in the wilderness, stealing children when they can for—" She swallowed. Her head drooped. "But you're supposed to be the expert."

"From what you told me over the visiphone, the Portolondon constabulary questions the accuracy of the report your group made, thinks the lot of you were hysterical, claims you must have omitted a due precaution and the child toddled away and was lost beyond your finding."

His dry words pried the horror out of her. Flushing, she snapped: "Like any settler's kid? No. I didn't simply yell. I consulted Data Retrieval. A few too many such cases are recorded for accident to be a very plausible explanation. And shall we totally ignore the frightened stories about reappearances? But when I went back to the constabulary with my facts, they brushed me off. I suspect that was not entirely because they're undermanned. I think they're afraid too. They're recruited from country boys; and Portolondon lies near the edge of the unknown."

Her energy faded. "Roland hasn't got any central police force," she finished drably. "You're my last hope."

The man puffed smoke into twilight, with which it blent, before he said in a kindlier voice than hitherto: "Please don't make it a high hope, Mrs. Cullen. I'm the solitary private investigator on this world, having no resources beyond myself, and a newcomer to boot."

"How long have you been here?"

"Twelve years. Barely time to get a little familiarity with the relatively civilized coastlands. You settlers of a century or more—what do you, even, know about Arctica's interior?"

Sherrinford sighed. "I'll take the case, charging no more than I must, mainly for the sake of the experience," he said. "But only if you'll be my guide and assistant, however painful it will be for you."

"Of course! I dreaded waiting idle. Why me, though?"

"Hiring someone else as well qualified would be prohibitively expensive, on a pioneer planet where every hand has a thousand urgent tasks to do. Besides, you have motive. And I'll need that. I, who was born on another world altogether strange to this one, itself altogether strange to Mother Earth, I am too dauntingly aware of how handicapped we are."

Night gathered upon Christmas Landing. The air stayed mild, but glimmer-lit tendrils of fog, sneaking through the streets, had a cold look, and colder yet was the aurora where it shuddered between the moons. The woman drew closer to the man in this darkening room, surely not aware that she did, until he switched on a fluoropanel. The same knowledge of Roland's aloneness was in both of them.

One light-year is not much as galactic distances go. You could walk it in about 270 million years, beginning at the middle of the Permian Era, when dinosaurs belonged to the remote future, and continuing to the present day when spaceships cross even greater reaches. But stars in our neighborhood average some nine light-years apart; and barely one percent of them have planets which are manhabitable; and speeds are limited to less than that of radiation. Scant help is given by relativistic time contraction and suspended animation en route. These make the journeys seem short; but history meanwhile does not stop at home.

Thus voyages from sun to sun will always be few. Colonists will be those who have extremely special reasons for going. They will take along germ plasm for exogenetic cultivation of domestic plants and animals—and of human infants, in order that population can grow fast enough to escape death through genetic drift. After all, they cannot rely on further immigration. Two or three times a century, a ship may call from some other colony. (Not from Earth. Earth has long ago sunk into alien concerns.) Its place of origin will be an old settlement. The young ones are in no position to build and man interstellar vessels.

Their very survival, let alone their eventual modernization, is in doubt. The founding fathers have had to take what they could get, in a universe not especially designed for man.

Consider, for example, Roland. It is among the rare happy finds, a world where humans can live, breathe, eat the food, drink the water, walk unclad if they choose, sow their crops, pasture their beasts, dig their mines, erect their homes, raise their children and grandchildren. It is worth crossing three quarters of a light-century to preserve certain dear values and strike new roots into the soil of Roland.

But the star Charlemagne is of type F9, forty percent brighter than Sol, brighter still in the treacherous ultraviolet and wilder still in the wind of charged particles that seethes from it. The planet has an eccentric orbit. In the middle of the short but furious northern summer, which includes periastron, total insolation is more than double what Earth gets; in the depth of the long northern winter, it is barely less than Terrestrial average.

Native life is abundant everywhere. But lacking elaborate machinery, not economically possible to construct for more than a few specialists, man can only endure the high latitudes. A ten-degree axial tilt, together with the orbit, means that the northern part of the Arctican continent spends half its year in unbroken sunlessness. Around the South Pole lies an empty ocean.

Other differences from Earth might superficially seem more important. Roland has two moons, small but close, to evoke clashing tides. It rotates once in thirty-two hours, which is endlessly, subtly disturbing to organisms evolved through gigayears of a quicker rhythm. The weather patterns are altogether unterrestrial. The globe is a mere 9500 kilometers in diameter; its surface gravity is 0.42×980 cm/sec^2; the sea-level air pressure is slightly above one Earth atmosphere. (For actually Earth is the freak, and man exists because a cosmic accident blew away most of the gas that a body its size ought to have kept, as Venus has done.)

However, *Homo* can truly be called *sapiens* when he practices his specialty of being unspecialized. His repeated attempts to freeze himself into an all-answering pattern or culture or ideology, or whatever he has named it, have repeatedly brought ruin. Give him the pragmatic business of making his living and he will usually do rather well. He adapts, within broad limits.

These limits are set by such factors as his need for sunlight and his being, necessarily and forever, a part of the life that surrounds him and a creature of the spirit within.

Portolondon thrust docks, boats, machinery, warehouses into the Gulf of Polaris. Behind them huddled the dwellings of its 5000 permanent inhabitants: concrete walls, storm shutters, high-peaked tile roofs. The gaiety of their paint looked forlorn amidst lamps; this town lay past the Arctic Circle.

Nevertheless Sherrinford remarked, "Cheerful place, eh? The kind of thing I came to Roland looking for."

Barbro made no reply. The days in Christmas Landing, while he made his preparations, had drained her. Gazing out the dome of the taxi that was whirring them downtown from the hydrofoil that brought them, she supposed he meant the lushness of forest and meadows along the road, brilliant hues and phosphorescence of flowers in gardens, clamor of wings overhead. Unlike Terrestrial flora in cold climates, Arctican vegetation spends every daylit hour in frantic growth and energy storage. Not till summer's fever gives place to gentle winter does it bloom and fruit; and estivating animals rise from their dens and migratory birds come home.

The view was lovely, she had to admit: beyond the trees, a spaciousness climbing toward remote heights, silvery-gray under a moon, an aurora, the diffuse radiance from a sun just below the horizon.

Beautiful as a hunting satan, she thought, and as terrible. That wilderness had stolen Jimmy. She wondered if she would at least be given to find his little bones and take them to his father.

Abruptly she realized that she and Sherrinford were at their hotel and that he had been speaking of the town. Since it was next in size after the capital, he must have visited here often before. The streets were crowded and noisy; signs flickered, music blared from shops, taverns, restaurants, sports centers, dance halls; vehicles were jammed down to molasses speed; the several-stories-high office buildings stood aglow. Portolondon linked an enormous hinterland to the outside world. Down the Gloria River came timber rafts, ores, harvest of farms whose owners were slowly making Rolandic life serve them, meat and ivory and furs gathered by rangers in the mountains beyond Troll Scarp. In from the sea came coastwise freighters, the fishing fleet, produce of the Sunward Islands, plunder of whole continents further south where bold men adventured. It clanged in Portolondon, laughed, blustered, swaggered, connived, robbed, preached, guzzled, swilled, toiled, dreamed, lusted, built, destroyed, died, was born, was happy, angry, sorrowful, greedy, vulgar, loving, ambitious, human. Neither the sun's blaze elsewhere nor the half year's twilight here—wholly night around midwinter—was going to stay man's hand.

Or so everybody said.

Everybody except those who had settled in the darklands. Barbro used to take for granted that they were evolving curious customs, legends, and superstitions, which would die when the outway had been completely mapped and controlled. Of late, she had wondered. Perhaps Sherrinford's hints, about a change in his own attitude brought about by his preliminary research, were responsible.

Or perhaps she just needed something to think about besides how Jimmy, the day before he went, when she asked him whether he wanted rye or French bread for a sandwich, answered in great solemnity—he was becoming interested in the alphabet—"I'll have a slice of what we people call the F bread."

She scarcely noticed getting out of the taxi, registering, being conducted to a primitively furnished room. But after she unpacked she remembered Sherrinford had suggested a confidential conference. She went down the hall and knocked on his door. Her knuckles sounded less loud than her heart.

He opened the door, finger on lips, and gestured her toward a corner. Her temper bristled until she saw the image of Chief Constable Dawson in the visiphone. Sherrinford must have chimed him up and must have a reason to keep her out of scanner range. She found a chair and watched, nails digging into knees.

The detective's lean length refolded itself. "Pardon the interruption," he said. "A man mistook the number. Drunk, by the indications."

Dawson chuckled. "We get plenty of those." Barbro recalled his fondness for gabbing. He tugged the beard which he affected, as if he were an outwayer instead of a townsman. "No harm in them as a rule. They only have a lot of voltage to discharge, after weeks or months in the backlands."

"I've gathered that that environment—foreign in a million major and minor ways to the one that created man—I've gathered that it does do odd things to the personality." Sherrinford tamped his pipe. "Of course, you know my prac-

385

tice has been confined to urban and suburban areas. Isolated garths seldom need private investigators. Now that situation appears to have changed. I called to ask you for advice."

"Glad to help," Dawson said. "I've not forgotten what you did for us in the de Tahoe murder case." Cautiously: "Better explain your problem first."

Sherrinford struck fire. The smoke that followed cut through the green odors—even here, a paved pair of kilometers from the nearest woods—that drifted past traffic rumble through a crepuscular window. "This is more a scientific mission than a search for an absconding debtor or an industrial spy," he drawled. "I'm looking into two possibilities: that an organization, criminal or religious or whatever, has long been active and steals infants; or that the Outlings of folklore are real."

"Huh?" On Dawson's face Barbro read as much dismay as surprise. "You can't be serious!"

"Can't I?" Sherrinford smiled. "Several generations' worth of reports shouldn't be dismissed out of hand. Especially not when they become more frequent and consistent in the course of time, not less. Nor can we ignore the documented loss of babies and small children, amounting by now to over a hundred, and never a trace found afterward. Nor the finds which demonstrate that an intelligent species once inhabited Arctica and may still haunt the interior."

Dawson leaned forward as if to climb out of the screen. "Who engaged you?" he demanded. "That Cullen woman? We were sorry for her, naturally, but she wasn't making sense and when she got downright abusive—"

"Didn't her companions, reputable scientists, confirm her story?"

"No story to confirm. Look, they had the place ringed with detectors and alarms, and they kept mastiffs. Standard procedure in a country where a hungry sauroid or whatever might happen by. Nothing could've entered unbeknownst."

"On the ground. How about a flyer landing in the middle of camp?"

"A man in a copter rig would've roused everybody."

"A winged being might be quieter."

"A living flyer that could lift a three-year-old boy? Doesn't exist."

"Isn't in the scientific literature, you mean, Constable. Remember Graymantle; remember how little we know about Roland, a planet, an entire world. Such birds do exist on Beowulf—and on Rustum, I've read. I made a calculation from the local ratio of air density to gravity and, yes, it's marginally possible here too. The child could have been carried off for a short distance before wing muscles were exhausted and the creature must descend."

Dawson snorted. "First it landed and walked into the tent where mother and boy were asleep. Then it walked away, toting him, after it couldn't fly further. Does that sound like a bird of prey? And the victim didn't cry out, the dogs didn't bark, nothing!"

"As a matter of fact," Sherrinford said, "those inconsistencies are the most interesting and convincing feature of the whole account. You're right, it's hard to see how a human kidnapper could get in undetected, and an eagle type of creature wouldn't operate in that fashion. But none of this applies to a winged intelligent being. The boy could have been drugged. Certainly the dogs showed signs of having been."

"The dogs showed signs of having overslept. Nothing had disturbed them. The kid wandering by wouldn't do so. We don't need to assume one damn thing except, first, that he got restless and, second, that the alarms were a bit sloppily rigged—seeing as how no danger was expected from inside camp—and let him pass out. And, third, I hate to speak this way, but we must assume the poor tyke starved or was killed."

Dawson paused before adding: "If we had more staff, we could have given the affair more time. And would have, of course. We did make an aerial sweep, which risked the lives of the pilots, using instruments which would've spotted the kid anywhere in a fifty-kilometer radius, unless he was dead. You know how sensitive thermal analyzers are. We drew a complete blank. We have more important jobs than to hunt for the scattered pieces of a corpse."

He finished brusquely, "If Mrs. Cullen's hired you, my advice is you find an excuse to quit. Better for her, too. She's got to come to terms with reality."

Barbro checked a shout by biting her tongue.

"Oh, this is merely the latest disappearance of the series," Sherrinford said. She didn't understand how he could maintain his easy tone when Jimmy was lost. "More thoroughly recorded than any before, thus more suggestive. Usually an outwayer family has given a tearful but undetailed account of their child who vanished and must have been stolen by the Old Folk. Sometimes, years later, they'd tell about glimpses of what they swore must have been the grown child, not really human any longer, flitting past in murk or peering through a window or working mischief upon them. As you say, neither the authorities nor the scientists have had personnel or resources to mount a proper investigation. But as I say, the matter appears to be worth investigating. Maybe a private party like myself can contribute."

"Listen, most of us constables grew up in the outway. We don't just ride patrol and answer emergency calls, we go back there for holidays and reunions. If any gang of . . . of human sacrificers was around, we'd know."

"I realize that. I also realize that the people you came from have a widespread and deep-seated belief in nonhuman beings with supernatural powers. Many actually go through rites and make offerings to propitiate them."

"I know what you're leading up to," Dawson fleered. "I've heard it before, from a hundred sensationalists. The aborigines are the Outlings. I thought better of you. Surely you've visited a museum or three, surely you've read literature from planets which do have natives—or damn and blast, haven't you ever applied that logic of yours?"

He wagged a finger. "Think," he said. "What have we in fact discovered? A few pieces of worked stone; a few megaliths that might be artificial; scratchings on rock that seem to show plants and animals, though not the way any human culture would ever have shown them; traces of fires and broken bones; other fragments of bone that seem as if they might've belonged to thinking creatures, as if they might've been inside fingers or around big brains. If so, however, the owners looked nothing like men. Or angels, for that matter. Nothing! The most anthropoid reconstruction I've seen shows a kind of two-legged crocagator.

"Wait, let me finish. The stories about the Outlings—oh, I've heard them too, plenty of them; I believed them when I was a kid—the stories tell how there're different kinds, some winged, some not, some half-human, some completely human except maybe for being too handsome—It's fairyland from ancient Earth all over again. Isn't it? I got interested once and dug into the Heritage Library microfiles, and be damned if I didn't find almost the identical yarns, told by peasants centuries before spaceflight.

"None of it squares with the scanty relics we have, if they are relics, or with the fact that no area the size of Arctica could spawn a dozen different intelligent species, or . . . hellfire, man, with the way your common sense tells you aborigines would behave when humans arrived!"

Sherrinford nodded. "Yes, yes," he said. "I'm less sure than you that the common sense of nonhuman beings is precisely like our own. I've seen so much variation within mankind. But, granted, your arguments are strong. Roland's too few scientists have more pressing tasks than tracking down the origins of what is, as you put it, a revived medieval superstition."

He cradled his pipe bowl in both hands and peered into the tiny hearth of it. "Perhaps what interests me most," he said softly, "is why—across that gap of centuries, across a barrier of machine civilization and its utterly antagonistic worldview—no continuity of tradition whatsoever—why have hardheaded, technologically organized, reasonably well-educated colonists here brought back from its grave a belief in the Old Folk?"

"I suppose eventually, if the University ever does develop the psychology department they keep talking about, I suppose eventually somebody will get a thesis out of that question." Dawson spoke in a jagged voice, and he gulped when Sherrinford replied:

"I propose to begin now. In Commissioner Hauch Land, since that's where the latest incident occurred. Where can I rent a vehicle?"

"Uh, might be hard to do—"

"Come, come. Tenderfoot or not, I know better. In an economy of scarcity, few people own heavy equipment. But since it's needed, it can always be rented. I want a camper bus with a ground-effect drive suitable for every kind of terrain. And I want certain equipment installed which I've brought along, and the top canopy section replaced by a gun turret controllable from the driver's seat. But I'll supply the weapons. Besides rifles and pistols of my own, I've arranged to borrow some artillery from Christmas Landing's police arsenal."

"Hoy? Are you genuinely intending to make ready for . . . a war . . . against a myth?"

"Let's say I'm taking out insurance, which isn't terribly expensive, against a remote possibility. Now, besides the bus, what about a light aircraft carried piggyback for use in surveys?"

"No." Dawson sounded more positive than hitherto. "That's asking for disaster. We can have you flown to a base camp in a large plane when the weather report's exactly right. But the pilot will have to fly back at once, before the weather turns wrong again. Meteorology's underdeveloped on Roland, the air's especially treacherous this time of year, and we're not tooled up to produce aircraft that can outlive every surprise." He drew breath. "Have you no idea of how fast a whirly-whirly can hit, or what size hailstones might strike from a clear sky, or—? Once you're there, man, you stick to the ground." He hesitated. "That's an important reason our information is so scanty about the outway and its settlers are so isolated."

Sherrinford laughed ruefully. "Well, I suppose if details are what I'm after, I must creep along anyway."

"You'll waste a lot of time," Dawson said. "Not to mention your client's money. Listen, I can't forbid you to chase shadows, but—"

The discussion went on for almost an hour. When the screen finally blanked, Sherrinford rose, stretched, and walked toward Barbro. She noticed anew his peculiar gait. He had come from a planet with a fourth again Earth's gravitational drag, to one where weight was less than half Terrestrial. She wondered if he had flying dreams.

"I apologize for shuffling you off like that," he said. "I didn't expect to reach him at once. He was quite truthful about how busy he is. But having made contact, I didn't want to remind him overmuch of you. He can dismiss my project as a futile fantasy which I'll soon give up. But he might have frozen completely, might even have put up obstacles before us, if he'd realized through you how determined we are."

"Why should he care?" she asked in her bitterness.

"Fear of consequences, the worse because it is unadmitted—fear of consequences, the more terrifying because they are unguessable." Sherrinford's gaze went to the screen, and thence out the window to the aurora pulsing in glacial blue and white immensely far overhead. "I suppose you saw I was talking to a frightened man. Down underneath his conventionality and scoffing, he believes in the Outlings—oh, yes, he believes."

The feet of Mistherd flew over yerba and outpaced windblown driftweed. Beside him, black and misshapen, hulked Nagrim the nicor, whose earthquake weight left a swathe of crushed plants. Behind, luminous blossoms of a firethorn shone through the twining, trailing outlines of Morgarel the wraith.

Here Cloudmoor rose in a surf of hills and thickets. The air lay quiet, now and then carrying the distance-muted howl of a beast. It was darker than usual at winterbirth, the moons being down and aurora a wan flicker above mountains on the northern worldedge. But this made the stars keen, and their numbers crowded heaven, and Ghost Road shone among them as if it, like the leafage beneath, were paved with dew.

"Yonder!" bawled Nagrim. All four of his arms pointed. The party had topped a ridge. Far off glimmered a spark. "Hoah, hoah! 'Ull we right off stamp dem flat, or pluck dem apart slow?"

We shall do nothing of the sort, bonebrain, Morgarel's answer slid through their heads. *Not unless they attack us, and they will not unless we make them aware of us, and her command is that we spy out their purposes.*

"Gr-r-rum-m-m. I know deir aim. Cut down trees, stick plows in land, sow deir cursed seed in de clods and in deir shes. 'Less we drive dem into de bitterwater, and soon, soon, dey'll wax too strong for us."

"Not too strong for the Queen!" Mistherd protested, shocked.

Yet they do have new powers, it seems, Morgarel reminded him. *Carefully must we probe them.*

"Den carefully can we step on dem?" asked Nagrim.

The question woke a grin out of Mistherd's own uneasiness. He slapped the scaly back. "Don't talk, you," he said. "It hurts my ears. Nor think; that hurts your head. Come, run!"

Ease yourself, Morgarel scolded. *You have too much life in you, human-born.*

Mistherd made a face at the wraith, but obeyed to the extent of slowing down and picking his way through what cover the country afforded. For he traveled on behalf of the Fairest, to learn what had brought a pair of mortals questing hither.

Did they seek that boy whom Ayoch stole? (He continued to weep for his mother, though less and less often as the marvels of Carheddin entered him.) Perhaps. A birdcraft had left them and their car at the now abandoned campsite, from which they had followed an outward spiral. But when no trace of the cub had appeared inside a reasonable distance, they did not call to be flown home. And this wasn't because weather forbade the farspeaker waves to travel, as was frequently the case. No, instead the couple set off toward the mountains of Moonhorn. Their course would take them past a few outlying invader steadings and on into realms untrodden by their race.

So this was no ordinary survey. Then what was it?

Mistherd understood now why she who reigned had made her adopted mortal children learn, or retain, the clumsy language of their forebears. He had hated that drill, wholly foreign to Dweller ways. Of course, you obeyed her, and in time you saw how wise she had been. . . .

Presently he left Nagrim behind a rock—the nicor would only be useful in a fight—and crawled from bush to bush until he lay within man-lengths of the humans. A rainplant drooped over him, leaves soft on his bare skin, and clothed him in darkness. Morgarel floated to the crown of a shiverleaf, whose unrest would better conceal his flimsy shape. He'd not be much help either. And that was the most troublous, the almost appalling thing here. Wraiths were among those who could not just sense and send thoughts, but cast illusions. Morgarel had reported that this time his power seemed to rebound off an invisible cold wall around the car.

Otherwise the male and female had set up no guardian engines and kept no dogs. Belike they supposed none would be needed, since they slept in the long vehicle which bore them. But such contempt of the Queen's strength could not be tolerated, could it?

Metal sheened faintly by the light of their campfire. They sat on either side, wrapped in coats against a coolness that Mistherd, naked, found mild. The male drank smoke. The female stared past him into a dusk which her flame-dazzled eyes must see as thick gloom. The dancing glow brought her vividly forth. Yes, to judge from Ayoch's tale, she was the dam of the new cub.

Ayoch had wanted to come too, but the Wonderful One forbade. Pooks couldn't hold still long enough for such a mission.

The man sucked on his pipe. His cheeks thus pulled into shadow while the light flickered across nose and brow, he looked disquietingly like a shearbill about to stoop on prey.

"—No, I tell you again, Barbro, I have no theories," he was saying. "When facts are insufficient, theorizing is ridiculous at best, misleading at worst."

"Still, you must have some idea of what you're doing," she said. It was plain that they had threshed this out often before. No Dweller could be as persistent as her or as patient as him. "That gear you packed—that generator you keep running—"

"I have a working hypothesis or two, which suggested what equipment I ought to take."

"Why won't you tell me what the hypotheses are?"

"They themselves indicate that that might be inadvisable at the present time. I'm still feeling my way into the labyrinth. And I haven't had a chance yet to hook everything up. In fact, we're really only protected against so-called telepathic influence—"

"What?" She started. "Do you mean . . . those legends about how they can read minds too—" Her words trailed off and her gaze sought the darkness beyond his shoulders.

He leaned forward. His tone lost its clipped rapidity, grew earnest and soft. "Barbro, you're racking yourself to pieces. Which is no help to Jimmy if he's alive, the more so when you may well be badly needed later on. We've a long trek before us, and you'd better settle into it."

She nodded jerkily and caught her lip between her teeth for a moment before she answered, "I'm trying."

He smiled around his pipe. "I expect you'll succeed. You don't strike me as a quitter or a whiner or an enjoyer of misery."

She dropped a hand to the pistol at her belt. Her voice changed; it came out of her throat like knife from sheath. "When we find them, they'll know what I am. What humans are."

"Put anger aside also," the man urged. "We can't afford emotions. If the Outlings are real, as I told you I'm provisionally assuming, they're fighting for their homes." After a short stillness he added: "I like to think that if the first explorers had found live natives, men would not have colonized Roland. But too late now. We can't go back if we wanted to. It's a bitter-end struggle, against an enemy so crafty that he's even hidden from us the fact that he is waging war."

"Is be? I mean, skulking, kidnapping an occasional child—"

"That's part of my hypothesis. I suspect those aren't harassments, they're tactics employed in a chillingly subtle strategy."

The fire sputtered and sparked. The man smoked awhile, brooding, until he went on:

"I didn't want to raise your hopes or excite you unduly while you had to wait on me, first in Christmas Landing, then in Portolondon. Afterward we were busy satisfying ourselves Jimmy had been taken further from camp than he could have wandered before collapsing. So I'm only telling you now how thoroughly I studied available material on the . . . Old Folk. Besides, at first I did it on the principle of eliminating every imaginable possibility, however absurd. I expected no result other than final disproof. But I went through everything, relics, analyses, histories, journalistic accounts, monographs; I talked to outwayers who happened to be in town and to what scientists we have who've taken any interest in the matter. I'm a quick study. I flatter myself I became as expert as anyone—though God knows there's little to be expert on. Furthermore, I, a comparative stranger, maybe looked on the problem with fresh eyes. And a pattern emerged for me.

"If the aborigines became extinct, why didn't they leave more remnants? Arctica isn't enormous; and it's fertile for Rolandic life. It ought to have supported a population whose artifacts ought to have accumulated over millennia. I've read that on Earth, literally tens of thousands of paleolithic hand axes were found, more by chance than archaeology.

"Very well. Suppose the relics and fossils were deliberately removed, between the time the last survey party left and the first colonizing ships arrived. I did find some support for that idea in the diaries of the original explorers. They were too preoccupied with checking the habitability of the planet to make catalogues of primitive monuments. However, the remarks they wrote down indicate they saw much more than later arrivals did. Suppose what we have found is just what the removers overlooked or didn't get around to.

"That argues a sophisticated mentality, thinking in long-range terms, doesn't it? Which in turn argues that the Old Folk were not mere hunters or neolithic farmers."

"But nobody ever saw buildings or machines or any such thing," Barbro protested.

"No. Most likely the natives didn't go through our kind of metallurgic-industrial evolution. I can conceive of other paths to take. Their full-fledged civilization might have begun, rather than ended, in biological science and technology. It might have developed potentialities of the nervous system, which might be greater in their species than in man. We have those abilities to some degree ourselves, you realize. A dowser, for instance, actually senses variations in the local magnetic field caused by a water table. However, in us, these talents are maddeningly rare and tricky. So we took our business elsewhere. Who needs to be a telepath, say, when he has a visiphone? The Old Folk may have seen it the other way around. The artifacts of their civilization may have been, may still be, unrecognizable to men."

"They could have identified themselves to the men, though," Barbro said. "Why didn't they?"

"I can imagine any number of reasons. As, they could have had a bad experience with interstellar visitors earlier in their history. Ours is scarcely the sole race that has spaceships. However, I told you I don't theorize in advance of the facts. Let's say no more than that the Old Folk, if they exist, are alien to us."

"For a rigorous thinker, you're spinning a mighty thin thread."

"I've admitted this is entirely provisional." He squinted at her through a roil of campfire smoke. "You came to me, Barbro, insisting in the teeth of officialdom your boy had been stolen; but your own talk about cultist kidnappers was ridiculous. Why are you reluctant to admit the reality of nonhumans?"

"In spite of the fact that Jimmy's being alive probably depends on it," she sighed. "I know." A shudder: "Maybe I don't dare admit it."

"I've said nothing thus far that hasn't been speculated about in print," he told her. "A disreputable speculation, true. In a hundred years, nobody has found valid evidence for the Outlings being more than a superstition. Still, a few people have declared it's at least possible intelligent natives are at large in the wilderness."

"I know," she repeated. "I'm not sure, though, what has made you, overnight, take those arguments seriously."

"Well, once you got me started thinking, it occurred to me that Roland's outwayers are not utterly isolated medieval crofters. They have books, telecommunications, power tools, motor vehicles, above all they have a modern science-oriented education. Why *should* they turn superstitious? Something must be causing it." He stopped. "I'd better not continue. My ideas go further than this; but if they're correct, it's dangerous to speak them aloud."

Mistherd's belly muscles tensed. There was danger for fair, in that shearbill head. The Garland Bearer must be warned. For a minute he wondered about summoning Nagrim to kill these two. If the nicor jumped them fast, their firearms might avail them naught. But no. They might have left word at home, or—He came back to his ears. The talk had changed course. Barbro was murmuring, "—why you stayed on Roland."

The man smiled his gaunt smile. "Well, life on Beowulf held no challenge for me. Heorot is—or was; this was decades past, remember—Heorot was densely populated, smoothly organized, boringly uniform. That was partly due to the lowland frontier, a safety valve that bled off the dissatisfied. But I lack the carbon-dioxide tolerance necessary to live healthily down there. An expedition was being readied to make a swing around a number of colony worlds, especially those which didn't have the equipment to keep in laser contact. You'll recall its announced purpose, to seek out new ideas in science, arts, sociology, philosophy, whatever might prove valuable. I'm afraid they found little on Roland relevant to Beowulf. But I, who had wangled a berth, I saw opportunities for myself and decided to make my home here."

"Were you a detective back there, too?"

"Yes, in the official police. We had a tradition of such work in our family. Some of that may have come from the Cherokee side of it, if the name means anything to you. However, we also claimed collateral descent from one of the first private inquiry agents on record, back on Earth before spaceflight. Regardless of how true that may be, I found him a useful model. You see, an archetype—"

The man broke off. Unease crossed his features. "Best we go to sleep," he said. "We've a long distance to cover in the morning."

She looked outward. "Here is no morning."

They retired. Mistherd rose and cautiously flexed limberness back into his muscles. Before returning to the Sister of Lyrth, he risked a glance through a pane in the car. Bunks were made up, side by side, and the humans lay in them. Yet the man had not touched her, though hers was a bonny body, and nothing that had passed between them suggested he meant to do so.

Eldritch, humans. Cold and claylike. And they would overrun the beautiful wild world? Mistherd spat in disgust. It must not happen. It would not happen. She who reigned had vowed that.

The lands of William Irons were immense. But this was because a barony was required to support him, his kin and cattle, on native crops whose cultivation was still poorly understood. He raised some Terrestrial plants as well, by summerlight and in conservatories. However, these were a luxury. The true conquest of northern Arctica lay in yerba hay, in bathyrhiza wood, in pericoup and glycophyllon and eventually, when the market had expanded with population and industry, in chalcanthemum for city florists and pelts of cage-bred rover for city furriers.

That was in a tomorrow Irons did not expect he would live to see. Sherrinford wondered if the man really expected anyone ever would.

The room was warm and bright. Cheerfulness crackled in the fireplace. Light from fluoropanels gleamed off hand-carven chests and chairs and tables, off colorful draperies and shelved dishes. The outwayer sat solid in his highseat, stoutly clad, beard flowing down his chest. His wife and daughters brought coffee, whose fragrance joined the remnant odors of a hearty supper, to him, his guests, and his sons.

But outside, wind hooted, lightning flared, thunder bawled, rain crashed on roof and walls and roared down to swirl among the courtyard cobblestones. Sheds and barns crouched against hugeness beyond. Trees groaned; and did a wicked undertone of laughter run beneath the lowing of a frightened cow? A burst of hailstones hit the tiles like knocking knuckles.

You could feel how distant your neighbors were, Sherrinford thought. And nonetheless they were the people whom you saw oftenest, did daily business with by visiphone (when a solar storm didn't make gibberish of their voices and chaos of their faces) or in the flesh, partied with, gossiped and intrigued with, intermarried with; in the end, they were the people who would bury you. The lights and machinery of the coastal towns were monstrously farther away.

William Irons was a strong man. Yet when now he spoke, fear was in his tone. "You'd truly go over Troll Scarp?"

"Do you mean Hanstein Palisades?" Sherrinford responded, more challenge than question.

"No outwayer calls it anything but Troll Scarp," Barbro said.

And how had a name like that been reborn, light-years and centuries from Earth's dark ages?

"Hunters, trappers, prospectors—rangers, you call them—travel in those mountains," Sherrinford declared.

"In certain parts," Irons said. "That's allowed, by a pact once made 'tween a man and the Queen after he'd done well by a jack-o'-the-hill that a satan had hurt. Wherever the plumablanca grows, men may fare, if they leave man-goods on the altar boulders in payment for what they take out of the land. Elsewhere—" one fist clenched on a chair arm and went slack again "—'s not wise to go."

"It's been done, hasn't it?"

"Oh, yes. And some came back all right, or so they claimed, though I've heard they were never lucky afterward. And some didn't, they vanished. And some who returned babbled of wonders and horrors, and stayed witlings the rest of their lives. Not for a long time has anybody been rash enough to break the pact and overtread the bounds." Irons looked at Barbro almost entreatingly. His woman and children stared likewise, grown still. Wind hooted beyond the walls and rattled the storm shutters. "Don't you."

"I've reason to believe my son is there," she answered.

"Yes, yes, you've told and I'm sorry. Maybe something can be done. I don't know what, but I'd be glad to, oh, lay a double offering on Unvar's Barrow this midwinter, and a prayer drawn in the turf by a flint knife. Maybe they'll return him." Irons sighed. "They've not done such a thing in man's memory, though. And he could have a worse lot. I've glimpsed them myself, speeding madcap through twilight. They seem happier than we are. Might be no kindness, sending your boy home again."

"Like in the Arvid song," said his wife.

Irons nodded. "M-hm. Or others, come to think of it."

"What's this?" Sherrinford asked. More sharply than before, he felt himself a stranger. He was a child of cities and technics, above all a child of the skeptical intelligence. This family *believed*. It was disquieting to see more than a touch of their acceptance in Barbro's slow nod.

"We have the same ballad in Olga Ivanoff Land," she told him, her voice less calm than the words. "It's one of the traditional ones, nobody knows who composed them, that are sung to set the measure of a ring-dance in a meadow."

"I noticed a multilyre in your baggage, Mrs. Cullen," said the wife of Irons. She was obviously eager to get off the explosive topic of a venture in defiance of the Old Folk. A songfest could help. "Would you like to entertain us?"

Barbro shook her head, white around the nostrils. The oldest boy said quickly, rather importantly, "Well, sure, I can, if our guests would like to hear."

"I'd enjoy that, thank you." Sherrinford leaned back in his seat and stoked his pipe. If this had not happened spontaneously, he would have guided the conversation toward a similar outcome.

In the past he had had no incentive to study the folklore of the outway, and not much chance to read the scanty references on it since Barbro brought him her trouble. Yet more and more he was becoming convinced he must get an understanding—not an anthropological study; a feel from the inside out—of the relationship between Roland's frontiersmen and those beings which haunted them.

A bustling followed, rearrangement, settling down to listen, coffee cups refilled and brandy offered on the side. The boy explained, "The last line is the chorus. Everybody join in, right?" Clearly he too hoped thus to bleed off some of the tension. Catharsis through music? Sherrinford wondered, and added to himself: No; exorcism.

A girl strummed a guitar. The boy sang, to a melody which beat across the storm-noise:

> "It was the ranger Arvid
> rode homeward through the hills
> among the shadowy shiverleafs,
> along the chiming hills.
> *The dance weaves under the firethorn.*

"The night wind whispered around him
with scent of brok and rue.
Both moons rose high above him
and hills aflash with dew.
  The dance weaves under the firethorn.

"And dreaming of that woman
who waited in the sun,
he stopped, amazed by starlight,
and so he was undone.
  The dance weaves under the firethorn.

"For there beneath a barrow
that bulked athwart a moon,
the Outling folk were dancing
in glass and golden shoon.
  The dance weaves under the firethorn.

"The Outling folk were dancing
like water, wind and fire
to frosty-ringing harpstrings,
and never did they tire.
  The dance weaves under the firethorn.

"To Arvid came she striding
from where she watched the dance,
the Queen of Air and Darkness,
with starlight in her glance.
  The dance weaves under the firethorn.

"With starlight, love, and terror
in her immortal eye,
the Queen of Air and Darkness—"

"No!" Barbro leaped from her chair. Her fists were clenched and tears flogged her cheekbones. "You can't—pretend that—about the things that stole Jimmy!"

She fled from the chamber, upstairs to her guest bedroom.

But she finished the song herself. That was about seventy hours later, camped in the steeps where rangers dared not fare.

She and Sherrinford had not said much to the Irons family after refusing repeated pleas to leave the forbidden country alone. Nor had they exchanged many remarks at first as they drove north. Slowly, however, he began to draw her out about her own life. After a while she almost forgot to mourn, in her remembering of home and old neighbors. Somehow this led to discoveries— that he beneath his professorial manner was a gourmet and a lover of opera and appreciated her femaleness; that she could still laugh and find beauty in the wild land around her—and she realized, half guiltily, that life held more hopes than even the recovery of the son Tim gave her.

"I've convinced myself he's alive," the detective said. He scowled. "Frankly, it makes me regret having taken you along. I expected this would be only a fact-gathering trip, but it's turning out to be more. If we're dealing with real creatures who stole him, they can do real harm. I ought to turn back to the nearest garth and call for a plane to fetch you."

"Like bottommost hell you will, mister," she said. "You need somebody who knows outway conditions; and I'm a better shot than average."

"M-m-m . . . it would involve considerable delay too, wouldn't it? Besides the added distance, I can't put a signal through to any airport before this current burst of solar interference has calmed down."

Next "night" he broke out his remaining equipment and set it up. She recognized some of it, such as the thermal detector. Other items were strange to her, copied to his order from the advanced apparatus of his birthworld. He would tell her little about them. "I've explained my suspicion that the ones we're after have telepathic capabilities," he said in apology.

Her eyes widened. "You mean it could be true, the Queen and her people can read minds?"

"That's part of the dread which surrounds their legend, isn't it? Actually there's nothing spooky about the phenomenon. It was studied and fairly well defined centuries ago, on Earth. I daresay the facts are available in the scientific microfiles and Christmas Landing. You Rolanders have simply had no occasion to seek them out, any more than you've yet had occasion to look up how to build power beamcasters or spacecraft."

"Well, how does telepathy work, then?"

Sherrinford recognized that her query asked for comfort as much as it did for facts, and spoke with deliberate dryness: "The organism generates extremely long-wave radiation which can, in principle, be modulated by the nervous system. In practice, the feebleness of the signals and their low rate of information transmission make them elusive, hard to detect and measure. Our prehuman ancestors went in for more reliable senses, like vision and hearing. What telepathic transceiving we do is marginal at best. But explorers have found extra-terrestrial species that got an evolutionary advantage from developing the system further, in their particular environments. I imagine such species could include one which gets comparatively little direct sunlight—in fact, appears to hide from broad day. It could even become so able in this regard that, at short range, it can pick up man's weak emissions and make man's primitive sensitivities resonate to its own strong sendings."

"That would account for a lot, wouldn't it?" Barbro asked faintly.

"I've now screened our car by a jamming field," Sherrinford told her, "but it reaches only a few meters past the chassis. Beyond, a scout of theirs might get a warning from your thoughts, if you knew precisely what I'm trying to do. I have a well-trained subconscious which sees to it that I think about this in French when I'm outside. Communication has to be structured to be intelligible, you see, and that's a different enough structure from English. But English is the only human language on Roland, and surely the Old Folk have learned it."

She nodded. He had told her his general plan, which was too obvious to conceal. The problem was to make contact with the aliens, if they existed. Hitherto they had only revealed themselves, at rare intervals, to one or a few backwoodsmen at a time. An ability to generate hallucinations would help them in that. They would stay clear of any large, perhaps unmanageable expedition which might pass through their territory. But two people, braving all prohibitions, shouldn't look too formidable to approach. And . . . this would be the first human team which not only worked on the assumption that the Outlings were real but possessed the resources of modern, off-planet police technology.

Nothing happened at that camp. Sherrinford said he hadn't expected it would. The Old Folk seemed cautious this near to any settlement. In their own lands they must be bolder.

And by the following "night," the vehicle had gone well into yonder country. When Sherrinford stopped the engine in a meadow and the car settled down, silence rolled in like a wave.

They stepped out. She cooked a meal on the glower while he gathered wood, that they might later cheer themselves with a campfire. Frequently he glanced at his wrist. It bore no watch—instead, a radio-controlled dial, to tell what the instruments in the bus might register.

Who needed a watch here? Slow constellations wheeled beyond glimmering aurora. The moon Alde stood above a snowpeak, turning it argent, though this place lay at a goodly height. The rest of the mountains were hidden by the forest that crowded around. Its trees were mostly shiverleaf and feathery white plumablanca, ghostly amid their shadows. A few firethorns glowed, clustered dim lanterns, and the underbrush was heavy and smelled sweet. You could see surprisingly far through the blue dusk. Somewhere nearby a brook sang and a bird fluted.

"Lovely here," Sherrinford said. They had risen from their supper and not yet sat down or kindled their fire.

"But strange," Barbro answered as low. "I wonder if it's really meant for us. If we can really hope to possess it."

His pipestem gestured at the stars. "Man's gone to stranger places than this."

"Has he? I . . . oh, I suppose it's just something left over from my outway childhood, but do you know, when I'm under them I can't think of the stars as balls of gas, whose energies have been measured, whose planets have been walked on by prosaic feet. No, they're small and cold and magical; our lives are bound to them; after we die, they whisper to us in our graves." Barbro glanced downward. "I realize that's nonsense."

She could see in the twilight how his face grew tight. "Not at all," he said. "Emotionally, physics may be a worse nonsense. And in the end, you know, after a sufficient number of generations, thought follows feeling. Man is not at heart rational. He could stop believing the stories of science if those no longer felt right."

He paused. "That ballad which didn't get finished in the house," he said, not looking at her. "Why did it affect you so?"

"I was overwrought. I couldn't stand hearing *them*, well, praised. Or that's how it seemed. My apologies for the fuss."

"I gather the ballad is typical of a large class."

"Well, I never thought to add them up. Cultural anthropology is something we don't have time for on Roland, or more likely it hasn't occurred to us, with everything else there is to do. But—now you mention it, yes, I'm surprised at how many songs and stories have the Arvid motif in them."

"Could you bear to recite it for me?"

She mustered the will to laugh. "Why, I can do better than that if you want. Let me get my multilyre and I'll perform."

She omitted the hypnotic chorus line, though, when the notes rang out, except at the end. He watched her where she stood against moon and aurora.

"—the Queen of Air and Darkness
cried softly under sky:

" 'Light down, you ranger Arvid,
and join the Outling folk.

You need no more be human,
which is a heavy yoke.'

"He dared to give her answer:
'I may do naught but run.
A maiden waits me, dreaming
in lands beneath the sun.

" 'And likewise wait me comrades
and tasks I would not shirk,
for what is Ranger Arvid
if he lays down his work?

" 'So wreak your spells, you Outling,
and cast your wrath on me.
Though maybe you can slay me,
you'll not make me unfree.'

"The Queen of Air and Darkness
stood wrapped about with fear
and northlight-flares and beauty
he dared not look too near.

"Until she laughed like harpsong
and said to him in scorn:
'I do not need a magic
to make you always mourn.

" 'I send you home with nothing
except your memory
of moonlight, Outling music,
night breezes, dew, and me.

" 'And that will run behind you,
a shadow on the sun,
and that will lie beside you
when every day is done.

" 'In work and play and friendship
your grief will strike you dumb
for thinking what you are—and—
what you might have become.

" 'Your dull and foolish woman
treat kindly as you can.

Go home now, Ranger Arvid,
set free to be a man!'

"In flickering and laughter
the Outling folk were gone.
He stood alone by moonlight
and wept until the dawn.
The dance weaves under the firethorn."

She laid the lyre aside. A wind rustled leaves. After a long quietness Sherrinford said, "And tales of this kind are part of everyone's life in the outway?"

"Well, you could put it thus," Barbro replied. "Though they're not all full of supernatural doings. Some are about love or heroism. Traditional themes."

"I don't think your particular tradition has arisen of itself." His tone was bleak. "In fact, I think many of your songs and stories were not composed by humans."

He snapped his lips shut and would say no more on the subject. They went early to bed.

Hours later, an alarm roused them.

The buzzing was soft, but it brought them instantly alert. They slept in gripsuits, to be prepared for emergencies. Sky-glow lit them through the canopy. Sherrinford swung out of his bunk, slipped shoes on feet and clipped gun holster to belt. "Stay inside," he commanded.

"What's here?" Her pulse thudded.

He squinted at the dials of his instruments and checked them against the luminous telltale on his wrist. "Three animals," he counted. "Not wild ones happening by. A large one, homeothermic, to judge from the infrared, holding still a short ways off. Another . . . hm, low temperature, diffuse and unstable emission, as if it were more like a . . . a swarm of cells coordinated somehow . . . pheromonally? . . . hovering, also at a distance. But the third's practically next to us, moving around in the brush; and that pattern looks human."

She saw him quiver with eagerness, no longer seeming a professor. "I'm going to try to make a capture," he said. "When we have a subject for interrogation—Stand ready to let me back in again fast. But don't risk yourself, whatever happens. And keep this cocked." He handed her a loaded big-game rifle.

His tall frame poised by the door, opened it a crack. Air blew in, cool, damp, full of fragrances and murmurings. The moon Oliver was now also aloft, the radiance of both unreally brilliant, and the aurora seethed in whiteness and ice-blue.

Sherrinford peered afresh at his telltale. It must indicate the directions of the watchers, among those dappled leaves. Abruptly he sprang out. He sprinted past the ashes of the campfire and vanished under trees. Barbro's hand strained on the butt of her weapon.

Racket exploded. Two in combat burst onto the meadow. Sherrinford had clapped a grip on a smaller human figure. She could make out by streaming silver and rainbow flicker that the other was nude, male, long-haired, lithe, and young. He fought demoniacally, seeking to use teeth and feet and raking nails, and meanwhile he ululated like a satan.

The identification shot through her: A changeling, stolen in babyhood and raised by the Old Folk. This creature was what they would make Jimmy into.

"Ha!" Sherrinford forced his opponent around and drove stiffened fingers into the solar plexus. The boy gasped and sagged. Sherrinford manhandled him toward the car.

Out from the woods came a giant. It might itself have been a tree, black and rugose, bearing four great gnarly boughs; but earth quivered and boomed beneath its leg-roots, and its hoarse bellowing filled sky and skulls.

Barbro shrieked. Sherrinford whirled. He yanked out his pistol, fired and fired, flat whipcracks through the half-light. His free arm kept a lock on the youth. The troll shape lurched under those blows. It recovered and came on, more slowly, more carefully, circling around to cut him off from the bus. He couldn't move fast enough to evade unless he released his prisoner—who was his sole possible guide to Jimmy—

Barbro leaped forth. "Don't!" Sherrinford shouted. "For God's sake, stay inside!" The monster rumbled and made snatching motions at her. She pulled trigger. Recoil slammed her in the shoulder. The colossus rocked and fell. Somehow it got its feet back and lumbered toward her. She retreated. Again she shot and again. The creature snarled. Blood began to drip from it and gleam oilily amidst dewdrops. It turned and went off, breaking branches, into the darkness that laired beneath the woods.

"Get to shelter!" Sherrinford yelled. "You're out of the jammer field!"

A mistiness drifted by overhead. She barely glimpsed it before she saw the new shape at the meadow edge. "Jimmy!" tore from her.

"Mother." He held out his arms. Moonlight coursed in his tears. She dropped her weapon and ran to him.

Sherrinford plunged in pursuit. Jimmy flitted away into the brush. Barbro crashed after, through clawing twigs. Then she was seized and borne away.

———

Standing over his captive, Sherrinford strengthened the fluoro output until vision of the wilderness was blocked off from within the bus. The boy squirmed beneath that colorless glare.

"You are going to talk," the man said. Despite the haggardness in his features, he spoke quietly.

The boy glowered through tangled locks. A bruise was purpling on his jaw. He'd almost recovered ability to flee while Sherrinford chased and lost the woman. Returning, the detective had barely caught him. Time was lacking to be gentle, when Outling reinforcements might arrive at any moment. Sherrinford had knocked him out and dragged him inside. Now he sat lashed into a swivel seat.

He spat. "Talk to you, man-clod?" But sweat stood on his skin and his eyes flickered unceasingly around the metal which caged him.

"Give me a name to call you by."

"And have you work a spell on me?"

"Mine's Eric. If you don't give me another choice, I'll have to call you . . . m-m-m . . . Wuddikins."

"What?" However eldritch, the bound one remained a human adolescent. "Mistherd, then." The lilting accent of his English somehow emphasized its sullenness. "That's not the sound, only what it means. Anyway, it's my spoken name, naught else."

"Ah, you keep a secret name you consider to be real?"

"She does. I don't know myself what it is. She knows the real names of everybody."

Sherrinford raised his brows. "She?"

"Who reigns. May she forgive me, I can't make the reverent sign when my arms are tied. Some invaders call her the Queen of Air and Darkness."

"So." Sherrinford got pipe and tobacco. He let silence wax while he started the fire. At length he said:

"I'll confess the Old Folk took me by surprise. I didn't expect so formidable a member of your gang. Everything I could learn had seemed to show they work on my race—and yours, lad—by stealth, trickery, and illusion."

Mistherd jerked a truculent nod. "She created the first nicors not long ago. Don't think she has naught but dazzlements at her beck."

"I don't. However, a steel-jacketed bullet works pretty well too, doesn't it?"

Sherrinford talked on, softly, mostly to himself: "I do still believe the, ah, nicors—all your half-humanlike breeds—are intended in the main to be seen, not used. The power of projecting mirages must surely be quite limited in range and scope as well as in the number of individuals who possess it. Otherwise she wouldn't have needed to work as slowly and craftily as she has. Even outside our mind-shield, Barbro—my companion—could have resisted, could have remained aware that whatever she saw was unreal . . . if she'd been less shaken, less frantic, less driven by need."

Sherrinford wreathed his head in smoke. "Never mind what I experienced," he said. "It couldn't have been the same as for her. I think the command was simply given us, 'You will see what you most desire in the world, running away from you into the forest.' Of course, she didn't travel many meters before the nicor waylaid her. I'd no hope of trailing them; I'm no Arctican woodsman, and besides, it'd have been too easy to ambush me. I came back to you." Grimly: "You're my link to your overlady."

"You think I'll guide you to Starhaven or Carheddin? Try making me, clod-man."

"I want to bargain."

"I s'pect you intend more'n that." Mistherd's answer held surprising shrewdness. "What'll you tell after you come home?"

"Yes, that does pose a problem, doesn't it? Barbro Cullen and I are not terrified outwayers. We're of the city. We brought recording instruments. We'd be the first of our kind to report an encounter with the Old Folk, and that report would be detailed and plausible. It would produce action."

"So you see I'm not afraid to die," Mistherd declared, though his lips trembled a bit. "If I let you come in and do your man-things to my people, I'd have naught left worth living for."

"Have no immediate fears," Sherrinford said. "You're merely bait." He sat down and regarded the boy through a visor of calm. (Within, it wept in him: *Barbro, Barbro!*) "Consider. Your Queen can't very well let me go back, bringing my prisoner and telling about hers. She has to stop that somehow. I could try fighting my way through—this car is better armed than you know—but that wouldn't free anybody. Instead, I'm staying put. New forces of hers will get here as fast as they can. I assume they won't blindly throw themselves against a machine gun, a howitzer, a fulgurator. They'll parley first, whether their intentions are honest or not. Thus I make the contact I'm after."

"What d'you plan?" The mumble held anguish.

"First, this, as a sort of invitation." Sherrinford reached out to flick a switch. "There. I've lowered my shield against mind-reading and shape-casting. I daresay the leaders, at least, will be able to sense that it's gone. That should give them confidence."

"And next?"

"Why, next we wait. Would you like something to eat or drink?"

During the time which followed, Sherrinford tried to jolly Mistherd along, find out something of his life. What answers he got were curt. He dimmed the interior lights and settled down to peer outward. That was a long few hours.

They ended at a shout of gladness, half a sob, from the boy. Out of the woods came a band of the Old Folk.

Some of them stood forth more clearly than moons and stars and north-lights should have caused. He in the van rode a white crownbuck whose horns were garlanded. His form was manlike but unearthly beautiful, silver-blond hair falling from beneath the antlered helmet, around the proud cold face. The cloak fluttered off his back like living wings. His frost-colored mail rang as he fared.

Behind him, to right and left, rode two who bore swords whereon small flames gleamed and flickered. Above, a flying flock laughed and trilled and tumbled in the breezes. Near them drifted a half-transparent mistiness. Those others who passed among trees after their chieftain were harder to make out. But they moved in quicksilver grace, and as it were to a sound of harps and trumpets.

"Lord Luighaid." Glory overflowed in Mistherd's tone. "Her master Knower—himself."

Sherrinford had never done a harder thing than to sit at the main control panel, finger near the button of the shield generator, and not touch it. He rolled down a section of canopy to let voices travel. A gust of wind struck him in the face, bearing odors of the roses in his mother's garden. At his back, in the main body of the vehicle, Mistherd strained against his bonds till he could see the incoming troop.

"Call to them," Sherrinford said. "Ask if they will talk with me."

Unknown, flutingly sweet words flew back and forth. "Yes," the boy interpreted. "He will, the Lord Luighaid. But I can tell you, you'll never be let go. Don't fight them. Yield. Come away. You don't know what 'tis to be alive till you've dwelt in Carheddin under the mountain."

The Outlings drew nigh.

Jimmy glimmered and was gone. Barbro lay in strong arms against a broad breast, and felt the horse move beneath her. It had to be a horse, though only a few were kept any longer on the steadings, and they for special uses or love. She could feel the rippling beneath its hide, hear a rush of parted leafage and the thud when a hoof struck stone; warmth and living scent welled up around her through the darkness.

He who carried her said mildly, "Don't be afraid, darling. It was a vision. But he's waiting for us and we're bound for him."

She was aware in a vague way that she ought to feel terror or despair or something. But her memories lay behind her—she wasn't sure just how she had come to be here—she was borne along in a knowledge of being loved. At peace, at peace, rest in the calm expectation of joy. . . .

After a while the forest opened. They crossed a lea where boulders stood gray-white under the moons, their shadows shifting in the dim hues which the aurora threw across them. Flitteries danced, tiny comets, above the flowers between. Ahead gleamed a peak whose top was crowned in clouds.

Barbro's eyes happened to be turned forward. She saw the horse's head and thought, with quiet surprise: Why, this is Sambo, who was mine when I was a girl. She looked upward at the man. He wore a black tunic and a cowled cape, which made his face hard to see. She could not cry aloud, here. "Tim," she whispered.

"Yes, Barbro."

"I buried you—"

His smile was endlessly tender. "Did you think we're no more than what's laid back into the ground? Poor torn sweetheart. She who's called us is the All Healer. Now rest and dream."

"Dream," she said, and for a space she struggled to rouse herself. But the effort was weak. Why should she believe ashen tales about . . . atoms and energies, nothing else to fill a gape of emptiness . . . tales she could not bring to mind . . . when Tim and the horse her father gave her carried her on to Jimmy? Had the other thing not been the evil dream, and this her first drowsy awakening from it?

As if he heard her thoughts, he murmured, "They have a song in Outling lands. The Song of the Men:

> "The world sails
> to an unseen wind.
> Light swirls by the bows.
> The wake is night.
> But the Dwellers have no such sadness."

"I don't understand," she said.

He nodded. "There's much you'll have to understand, darling, and I can't see you again until you've learned those truths. But meanwhile you'll be with our son."

She tried to lift her head and kiss him. He held her down. "Not yet," he said. "You've not been received among the Queen's people. I shouldn't have come for you, except that she was too merciful to forbid. Lie back, lie back."

Time blew past. The horse galloped tireless, never stumbling, up the mountain. Once she glimpsed a troop riding down it and thought they were bound for a last weird battle in the west against . . . who? . . . one who lay cased in iron and sorrow—Later she would ask herself the name of him who had brought her into the land of the Old Truth.

Finally spires lifted splendid among the stars, which are small and magical and whose whisperings comfort us after we are dead. They rode into a courtyard where candles burned unwavering, fountains splashed and birds sang. The air bore fragrance of brok and pericoup, of rue and roses; for not everything that man brought was horrible. The Dwellers waited in beauty to welcome her. Beyond their stateliness, pooks cavorted through the gloaming; among the trees darted children; merriment caroled across music more solemn.

"We have come—" Tim's voice was suddenly, inexplicably a croak. Barbro was not sure how he dismounted, bearing her. She stood before him and saw him sway on his feet.

Fear caught her. "Are you well?" She seized both his hands. They felt cold and rough. Where had Sambo gone? Her eyes searched beneath the cowl. In this brighter illumination, she ought to have seen her man's face clearly. But it was blurred, it kept changing. "What's wrong, oh, what's happened?"

He smiled. Was that the smile she had cherished? She couldn't completely remember. "I, I must go," he stammered, so low she could scarcely hear. "Our time is not ready." He drew free of her grasp and leaned on a robed form which had appeared at his side. A haziness swirled over both their heads. "Don't watch me go . . . back into the earth," he pleaded. "That's death for you. Till our time returns—There, our son!"

She had to fling her gaze around. Kneeling, she spread wide her arms. Jimmy struck her like a warm, solid cannonball. She rumpled his hair, she kissed the hollow of his neck, she laughed and wept and babbled foolishness; and this was no ghost, no memory that had stolen off when she wasn't looking. Now and again, as she turned her attention to yet another hurt which might have come upon him—hunger, sickness, fear—and found none, she would glimpse their surroundings. The gardens were gone. It didn't matter.

"I missed you so, Mother. Stay?"

"I'll take you home, dearest."

"Stay. Here's fun. I'll show. But you stay."

A sighing went through the twilight. Barbro rose. Jimmy clung to her hand. They confronted the Queen.

Very tall she was in her robes woven of northlights, and her starry crown and her garlands of kiss-me-never. Her countenance recalled Aphrodite of Milos, whose picture Barbro had often seen in the realms of men, save that the Queen's was more fair, and more majesty dwelt upon it and in the night-blue eyes. Around her the gardens woke to new reality, the court of the Dwellers and the heaven-climbing spires.

"Be welcome," she spoke, her speaking a song, "forever."

Against the awe of her, Barbro said, "Moonmother, let us go home."

"That may not be."

"To our world, little and beloved," Barbro dreamed she begged, "which we build for ourselves and cherish for our children."

"To prison days, angry nights, works that crumble in the fingers, loves that turn to rot or stone or driftweed, loss, grief, and the only sureness that of the final nothingness. No. You too, Wanderfoot who is to be, will jubilate when the banners of the Outworld come flying into the last of the cities and man is made wholly alive. Now go with those who will teach you."

The Queen of Air and Darkness lifted an arm in summons. It halted, and none came to answer.

For over the fountains and melodies lifted a gruesome growling. Fires leaped, thunders crashed. Her hosts scattered screaming before the steel thing which boomed up the mountainside. The pooks were gone in a whirl of frightened wings. The nicors flung their bodies against the unalive invader and were consumed, until their Mother cried to them to retreat.

Barbro cast Jimmy down and herself over him. Towers wavered and smoked away. The mountain stood bare under icy moons, save for rocks, crags, and farther off a glacier in whose depths the auroral light pulsed blue. A cave mouth darkened a cliff. Thither folk streamed, seeking refuge underground. Some were human of blood, some grotesques like the pooks and nicors and wraiths; but most were lean, scaly, long-tailed, long-beaked, not remotely men or Outlings.

For an instant, even as Jimmy wailed at her breast—perhaps as much because the enchantment had been wrecked as because he was afraid—Barbro pitied the Queen who stood alone in her nakedness. Then that one also had fled, and Barbro's world shivered apart.

The guns fell silent, the vehicle whirred to a halt. From it sprang a boy who called wildly, "Shadow-of-a-Dream, where are you? It's me, Mistherd, oh, come, come!"—before he remembered that the language they had been raised in was not man's. He shouted in that until a girl crept out of a thicket where she had hidden. They stared at each other through dust, smoke, and moonglow. She ran to him.

A new voice barked from the car, "Barbro, hurry!"

Christmas Landing knew day: short at this time of year, but sunlight, blue skies, white clouds, glittering water, salt breezes in busy streets, and the sane disorder of Eric Sherrinford's living room.

He crossed and uncrossed his legs where he sat, puffed on his pipe as if to make a veil, and said, "Are you certain you're recovered? You mustn't risk overstrain."

"I'm fine," Barbro Cullen replied, though her tone was flat. "Still tired, yes, and showing it, no doubt. One doesn't go through such an experience and bounce back in a week. But I'm up and about. And to be frank, I must know what's happened, what's going on, before I can settle down to regain my full strength. Not a word of news anywhere."

"Have you spoken to others about the matter?"

"No. I've simply told visitors I was too exhausted to talk. Not much of a lie. I assumed there's a reason for censorship."

Sherrinford looked relieved. "Good girl. It's at my urging. You can imagine the sensation when this is made public. The authorities agreed they need time to study the facts, think and debate in a calm atmosphere, have a decent policy ready to offer voters who're bound to become rather hysterical at first." His mouth quirked slightly upward. "Furthermore, your nerves and Jimmy's get their chance to heal before the journalistic storm breaks over you. How is he?"

"Quite well. He continues pestering me for leave to go play with his friends in the Wonderful Place. But at his age, he'll recover—he'll forget."

"He may meet them later anyhow."

"What? We didn't—" Barbro shifted in her chair. "I've forgotten too. I hardly recall a thing from our last hours. Did you bring back any kidnapped humans?"

"No. The shock was savage, as was, without throwing them straight into an . . . an institution. Mistherd, who's basically a sensible young fellow, assured me they'd get along, at any rate as regards survival necessities, till arrangements can be made." Sherrinford hesitated. "I'm not sure what the arrangements will be. Nobody is, at our present stage. But obviously they include those people—or many of them, especially those who aren't full-grown—rejoining the human race. Though they may never feel at home in civilization. Perhaps in a way that's best, since we will need some kind of mutually acceptable liaison with the Dwellers."

His impersonality soothed them both. Barbro became able to say, "Was I too big a fool? I do remember how I yowled and beat my head on the floor."

"Why, no." He considered the big woman and her pride for a few seconds before he rose, walked over and laid a hand on her shoulder. "You'd been lured and trapped by a skillful play on your deepest instincts, at a moment of sheer nightmare. Afterward, as that wounded monster carried you off, evidently another type of being came along, one that could saturate you with close-range neuropsychic forces. On top of this, my arrival, the sudden brutal abolishment of every hallucination, must have been shattering. No wonder if you cried out in pain. Before you did, you competently got Jimmy and yourself into the bus, and you never interfered with me."

"What did you do?"

"Why, I drove off as fast as possible. After several hours, the atmospherics let up sufficiently for me to call Portolondon and insist on an emergency airlift. Not that that was vital. What chance had the enemy to stop us? They didn't even try. But quick transportation was certainly helpful."

"I figured that's what must have gone on." Barbro caught his glance. "No, what I meant was, how did you find us in the backlands?"

Sherrinford moved a little off from her. "My prisoner was my guide. I don't think I actually killed any of the Dwellers who'd come to deal with me. I hope not. The car simply broke through them, after a couple of warning shots, and afterward outpaced them. Steel and fuel against flesh wasn't really fair. At the cave entrance, I did have to shoot down a few of those troll creatures. I'm not proud of it."

He stood silent. Presently: "But you were a captive," he said. "I couldn't be sure what they might do to you, who had first claim on me." After another pause: "I don't look for any more violence."

"How did you make . . . the boy . . . cooperate?"

Sherrinford paced from her, to the window, where he stood staring out at the Boreal Ocean. "I turned off the mind shield," he said. "I let their band get close, in full splendor of illusion. Then I turned the shield back on and we both saw them in their true shapes. As we went northward I explained to Mistherd how he and his kind had been hoodwinked, used, made to live in a world that was never really there. I asked him if he wanted himself and whoever he cared about to go on till they died as domestic animals—yes, running in limited freedom on solid hills, but always called back to the dream-kennel." His pipe fumed furiously. "May I never see such bitterness again. He had been taught to believe he was free."

Quiet returned, above the hectic traffic. Charlemagne drew nearer to setting; already the east darkened.

Finally Barbro asked, "Do you know why?"

"Why children were taken and raised like that? Partly because it was in the pattern the Dwellers were creating; partly in order to study and experiment on members of our species—minds, that is, not bodies; partly because humans have special strengths which are helpful, like being able to endure full daylight."

"But what was the final purpose of it all?"

Sherrinford paced the floor. "Well," he said, "of course the ultimate motives of the aborigines are obscure. We can't do more than guess at how they think, let alone how they feel. But our ideas do seem to fit the data.

"Why did they hide from man? I suspect they, or rather their ancestors—for they aren't glittering elves, you know; they're mortal and fallible too—I suspect the natives were only being cautious at first, more cautious than human primitives, though certain of those on Earth were also slow to reveal themselves to strangers. Spying, mentally eavesdropping, Roland's Dwellers must have picked up enough language to get some idea of how different man was from them, and how powerful; and they gathered that more ships would be arriving, bringing settlers. It didn't occur to them that they might be conceded the right to keep their lands. Perhaps they're still more fiercely territorial than us. They determined to fight, in their own way. I daresay, once we begin to get insight into that mentality, our psychological science will go through its Copernican revolution."

Enthusiasm kindled in him. "That's not the sole thing we'll learn, either," he went on. "They must have science of their own, a nonhuman science born on a planet that isn't Earth. Because they did observe us as profoundly as we've ever observed ourselves; they did mount a plan against us, that would have taken another century or more to complete. Well, what else do they know? How do they support their civilization without visible agriculture or aboveground buildings or mines or anything? How can they breed whole new intelligent species to order? A million questions, ten million answers!"

"*Can* we learn from them?" Barbro asked softly. "Or can we only overrun them as you say they fear?"

Sherrinford halted, leaned elbow on mantel, hugged his pipe and replied: "I hope we'll show more charity than that to a defeated enemy. It's what they are. They tried to conquer us, and failed, and now in a sense we are bound to conquer them, since they'll have to make their peace with the civilization of the machine rather than see it rust away as they strove for. Still, they never did us any harm as atrocious as what we've inflicted on our fellow man in the past. And, I repeat, they could teach us marvelous things; and we could teach them, too, once they've learned to be less intolerant of a different way of life."

"I suppose we can give them a reservation," she said, and didn't know why he grimaced and answered so roughly:

"Let's leave them the honor they've earned! They fought to save the world they'd always known from that—" he made a chopping gesture at the city— "and just possibly we'd be better off ourselves with less of it."

He sagged a trifle and sighed, "However, I suppose if Elfland had won, man on Roland would at last—peacefully, even happily—have died away. We live with our archetypes, but can we live in them?"

Barbro shook her head. "Sorry, I don't understand."

"What?" He looked at her in a surprise that drove out melancholy. After a laugh: "Stupid of me. I've explained this to so many politicians and scientists and commissioners and Lord knows what, these past days, I forgot I'd never explained to you. It was a rather vague idea of mine, most of the time we were traveling, and I don't like to discuss ideas prematurely. Now that we've met the Outlings and watched how they work, I do feel sure."

He tamped down his tobacco. "In limited measure," he said, "I've used an archetype throughout my own working life. The rational detective. It hasn't been a conscious pose—much—it's simply been an image which fitted my personality and professional style. But it draws an appropriate response from most people, whether or not they've ever heard of the original. The phenomenon is not uncommon. We meet persons who, in varying degrees, suggest Christ or Buddha or the Earth Mother or, say, on a less exalted plane, Hamlet or d'Artagnan. Historical, fictional, and mythical, such figures crystallize basic aspects of the human psyche, and when we meet them in our real experience, our reaction goes deeper than consciousness."

He grew grave again: "Man also creates archetypes that are not individuals. The Anima, the Shadow—and, it seems, the Outworld. The world of magic, of glamour—which originally meant enchantment—of half-human beings, some like Ariel and some like Caliban, but each free of mortal frailties and sorrows—therefore, perhaps, a little carelessly cruel, more than a little tricksy; dwellers in dusk and moonlight, not truly gods but obedient to rulers who are enigmatic and powerful enough to be—Yes, our Queen of Air and Darkness knew well what sights to let lonely people see, what illusions to spin around them from time to time, what songs and legends to set going among them. I wonder how much she and her underlings gleaned from human fairy tales, how much they made up themselves, and how much men created all over again, all unwittingly, as the sense of living on the edge of the world entered them."

Shadows stole across the room. It grew cooler and the traffic noises dwindled. Barbro asked mutedly: "But what could this do?"

"In many ways," Sherrinford answered, "the outwayer *is* back in the dark ages. He has few neighbors, hears scanty news from beyond his horizon, toils to survive in a land he only partly understands, that may any night raise unforeseeable disasters against him and is bounded by enormous wildernesses. The machine civilization which brought his ancestors here is frail at best. He could lose it as the dark-age nations had lost Greece and Rome, as the whole of Earth seems to have lost it. Let him be worked on, long, strongly, cunningly, by the archetypical Outworld, until he has come to believe in his bones that the magic of the Queen of Air and Darkness is greater than the energy of engines: and first his faith, finally his deeds will follow her. Oh, it wouldn't happen fast. Ideally, it would happen too slowly to be noticed, especially by self-satisfied city people. But when in the end a hinterland gone back to the ancient way turned from them, how could they keep alive?"

Barbro breathed, "She said to me, when their banners flew in the last of our cities, we would rejoice."

"I think we would have, by then," Sherrinford admitted. "Nevertheless, I believe in choosing one's own destiny."

He shook himself, as if casting off a burden. He knocked the dottle from his pipe and stretched, muscle by muscle. "Well," he said, "it isn't going to happen."

She looked straight at him. "Thanks to you."

A flush went up his thin cheeks. "In time, I'm sure, somebody else would have—Anyhow, what matters is what we do next, and that's too big a decision for one individual or one generation to make."

She rose. "Unless the decision is personal, Eric," she suggested, feeling heat in her own face.

It was curious to see him shy. "I was hoping we might meet again."

"We will."

Ayoch sat on Wolund's Barrow. Aurora shuddered so brilliant, in such vast sheafs of light, as almost to hide the waning moons. Firethorn blooms had fallen; a few still glowed around the tree roots, amidst dry brok which crackled underfoot and smelled like woodsmoke. The air remained warm but no gleam was left on the sunset horizon.

"Farewell, fare lucky," the pook called. Mistherd and Shadow-of-a-Dream never looked back. It was as if they didn't dare. They trudged on out of sight, toward the human camp whose lights made a harsh new star in the south.

Ayoch lingered. He felt he should also offer goodbye to her who had lately joined him that slept in the dolmen. Likely none would meet here again for loving or magic. But he could only think of one old verse that might do. He stood and trilled:

"Out of her breast
a blossom ascended.
The summer burned it.
The song is ended."

Then he spread his wings for the long flight away.